FOREFATHERS

'Best known for her historical novels of her native Australia, Nancy Cato has added a new element to an already enriched literary career with *Forefathers*. Sometimes sad, often funny, exciting and vivid, it's a true and moving account of the historical development of a great country and its people.'

Cork Examiner

'A book in which to lose yourself as you experience the struggles, courtships, dangers, passions and changing life-style of an emerging civilisation. The characters are well defined and interesting and the whole concept of the book demands admiration.'

Liverpool Daily Post

*Also by Nancy Cato
and available from New English Library:*

ALL THE RIVERS RUN
NORTH-WEST BY SOUTH
BROWN SUGAR

Forefathers

Nancy Cato

NEW ENGLISH LIBRARY
Hodder and Stoughton

Copyright © 1983 by Nancy Cato

First published in Great Britain in 1983 by
New English Library

'Prayer Before Birth' from THE COLLECTED POEMS OF
LOUIS MACNEICE is reproduced by permission
of Faber and Faber Publishers.

All rights reserved. No part of this publication may be
reproduced or transmitted, in any form or by any means,
without permission of the publishers.

First NEL Paperback Edition 1983
Ninth impression 1987

British Library C.I.P.

Cato, Nancy
  Forefathers
  I. Title
  823'.[F]   PR9619.3.C394

ISBN 0 450 05651 1

---

*The characters and situations in this book are
entirely imaginary and bear no relation to any real
person or actual happening*

This book is sold subject to the condition that
it shall not, by way of trade or otherwise, be
lent, re-sold, hired out or otherwise circulated
without the publisher's prior consent in any
form of binding or cover other than that in
which this is published and without a similar
condition including this condition being
imposed on the subsequent purchaser.

Printed and bound in Great Britain for
Hodder and Stoughton Paperbacks, a
division of Hodder and Stoughton Ltd.,
Mill Road, Dunton Green, Sevenoaks,
Kent (Editorial Office: 47 Bedford
Square, London, WC1B 3DP) by
Cox & Wyman Ltd., Reading.

Our fathers came of roving stock
That could not fixed abide,
And we have followed field and flock
Since first we learnt to ride;
By miner's camp and shearing shed,
The land of heat and drought,
With fortune always on ahead
And always further out.

A. B. Paterson

Author's Note

For those who have read the author's earlier novel, *Brown Sugar*, some of the same characters will be recognised: Emily Duguid, Fiona and Joseph (Tula) Efate, Chukka Brown, George Tombua, Anna Brown and her Islander and Aboriginal cousins.

Their ancestry is traced in the stories of Andrew and Amelia Duguid, Angus Johnstone and the first Joseph, so the forefathers of Joseph Forbes King are not traced back to their first arrival in Australia in this present book.

N.C.

Contents

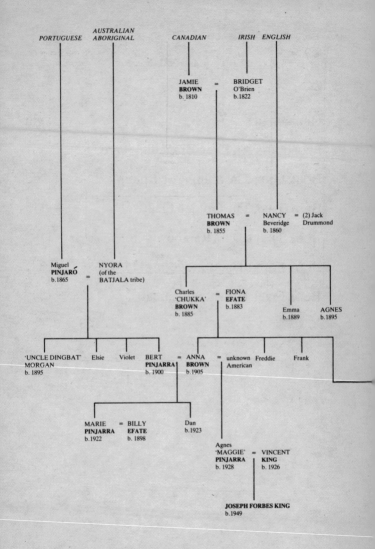

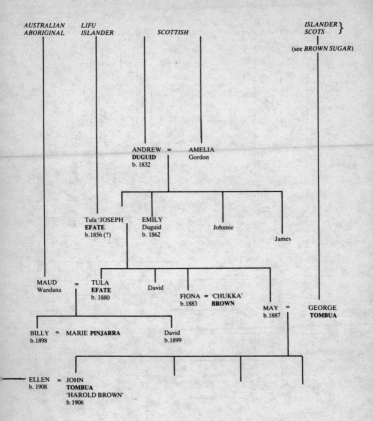

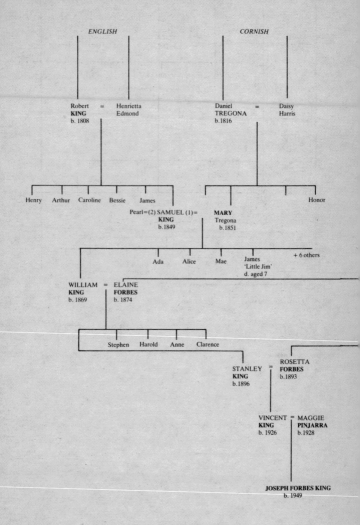

ENGLISH   CORNISH

Robert **KING** b. 1808 = Henrietta Edmond   Daniel **TREGONA** b.1816 = Daisy Harris

Henry Arthur Caroline Bessie James   Honor

Pearl=(2) **SAMUEL** (1)= **MARY**
     KING   Tregona
     b.1849   b.1851

Ada Alice Mae James 'Little Jim' d. aged 7 + 6 others

WILLIAM KING b. 1869 = **ELAINE FORBES** b. 1874

Stephen Harold Anne Clarence

STANLEY KING b.1896 = **ROSETTA FORBES** b.1893

VINCENT KING b. 1926 = **MAGGIE PINJARRA** b.1928

JOSEPH FORBES KING b. 1949

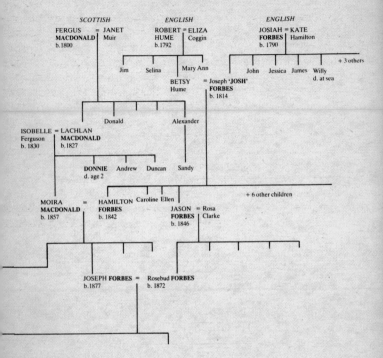

PROLOGUE

An Ever-Branching Tree

As buds give rise by growth to fresh buds, and these, if vigorous, branch out and overtop on all sides many a feebler branch, so by generation I believe it has been with the great Tree of Life, which fills with its dead and broken branches the crust of the earth, and covers the surface with its ever-branching and beautiful ramifications.

CHARLES DARWIN   *The Origin of Species*

BY ALL the laws of probability, Joseph Forbes King should not have been born at all. His father, engaged in a highly dangerous occupation, might have died before his conception. When his life was begun, contraceptive devices his mother was using should have prevented it, but failed.

His King grandfather had almost died in an Indian Hill station as an infant; his great-grandfather survived when his only brother was killed, and his great-great-grandfather, Samuel King, was one of twin babies whose twin died at birth.

And each of his ancestors had been the product of just such a random meeting as had led to the birth of Joseph King in 1949. JFK – whose initials then carried no connotations of either greatness or tragedy – was born as the result of an extraordinary series of chances over which he had no control.

For generations his forefathers had travelled, met and mated to produce this one human being. Farmers from England, miners from Cornwall, convicts from Canada, Scottish pioneers and Irish emigrants, squatters and shearers and sugar plantation workers brought from the Pacific Islands, all had a part in his heredity. And all had one thing in common: they had made a new life in a strange land, and for the most part they were rovers and nomads like the dark wandering tribes they dispossessed, and who also played a part in his destiny.

From both sides of the Pacific, from a princely State of India to the sheep stations of the Riverina, from the Western Isles of Scotland to the island of Tasmania in the southern hemisphere, from the Yukon to the Condamine, the multifarious threads could be traced down like the fine, spreading roots of some enormous tree.

All those characteristics which we term 'innate' – race, sex, colouring, features, mental ability – were already decided when Destiny picked him with a random hand from the barrel where all possibilities, all combinations for future life lay jumbled.

Two million million cells had grown and divided in a blind process which followed the moment of conception, to pro-

3

duce a complete and perfect being – a new, unique individual of the human race – when the walls of his nine-month home began to contract, to eject him. Expelled from the warm darkness of the womb where he had floated, dreaming and inviolate, he fought his way head-first into the world with as much reluctant agony as most men show in leaving it.

Life, like the starry Scorpion which presided over the heavens at his birth, gleamed with bright promise but carried a sting in its tail. The sting was death. Like every man before him, from the time he drew his first breath J F K was condemned to die. He was born in Queensland, Australia, just in time to be old enough for the next war.

BOOK ONE

The Shining Scorpion

1824–1894

Oh! when that we were landed, upon that fatal shore,
The planters they came flocking round, full twenty score or more,
They ranked us up like horses, and sold us out of hand,
And they yoked us to the plough, my boys, to plough
   Van Diemen's Land.

OLD CONVICT SONG

One

THE FIRST Joseph Forbes in the new land, JFK's great-great-great grandfather, arrived in Australia when he was ten years old, in 1824. He too had been born under the sign of Scorpio, in the month of November, but his mother always said his astrological sign must be the Water Scorpion, that long-legged insect found in the creeks and ponds of Van Diemen's Land which could breathe under water through its long tail and which had no sting. For Josh, as he was called, loved the water.

His father Josiah and his mother, the former Kate Hamilton, had emigrated from Bedfordshire with their five children. Little Willy, aged two, died on the long voyage out from England, and Kate had to watch her youngest buried at sea, in the deep blue waters of the Indian Ocean. Though she bore Josiah seven sons altogether, she never failed to mourn the one who was lost. And Josiah, calling the last one Septimus, declared that his quiver was full; he would father no more children. He said he hoped he had enough self-control not to go on subjecting his wife to confinements year after year. (He named no names, but his brother William now had ten, and his wife Sophie was to die of the eleventh.) Kate's feelings in the matter were not consulted.

She became rather over-protective towards her boys and her one daughter. She begged Josh not to go swimming in the Brushy Creek; she feared he would be bitten by a snake. But he grew tall and sturdy, brown all over from his frequent dips, and from riding his shaggy pony, Oliver, in all weathers.

Josiah Forbes believed that it was possible for a man of vigour and enterprise to make his fortune in the Antipodes with very little capital. The new colony he saw as a place of opportunity, even for the felons being transported there against their will from overcrowded England.

Labour was cheap, for assigned convicts could be employed

as farm labourers, shepherds, and house servants by anyone who would take over their keep from the Government.

'Oh that we could transport England, with all it contains, into the Southern Seas!' he wrote enthusiastically to William in Bedfordshire, urging him to migrate. 'We all enjoy excellent health, and no wonder, for the climate is really delightful . . .'

He did not add that Hobart Town was as full of rogues and thieves as London, while in the country there were bushrangers bailing up coaches and robbing farmhouses. Not to mention the hostile Aborigines, who objected to giving up their hunting grounds and were waging a determined guerilla war against the invaders.

As head of the Commissariat, Josiah helped organise the rounding up and deporting of all the Aborigines to an offshore island; and for this Governor Arthur rewarded him with a grant of 2,500 acres. He had already bought 1,500 acres cheaply in the north, where landholders were being terrorised, their sheep and shepherds speared and clubbed to death.

As soon as 'the Aboriginal question' had been solved to the satisfaction of all but the unfortunate natives (banished and pining for their homeland across the Strait), Josiah found himself wealthy. Land values rose spectacularly, and with four assigned servants and his oldest five sons to work the land, he soon had orchards established at Newtown and Lenah Valley, using seedlings propagated from some acclimatised apple trees he had picked up in Cape Town on the voyage out.

Like the human stock from all over the world now mixing and marrying there, the imported apples grew and flourished in the new land. The dry summers and crisp winters suited them. The trees set so much fruit that they had to prop up the boughs with forked sticks to save them from breaking under the weight of ripe apples.

He was relieved that he did not have to send his boys 'Home' to get an education. Josh and his brothers attended the Grammar School in Macquarie street. Riding home late one afternoon on Oliver, Josh noticed uneasily the blue-black, bruised-looking sky above 'Old Cloudmaker', Mount

Wellington, which towered over the valley and the Derwent estuary.

Overhead the sky was filled with giant fists of cloud at the end of long grey arms, seeming to threaten the earth with destruction. Lightning zagged and forked downwards. Thunder rumbled a warning, and the first drops of rain fell, heavy as lumps of quicksilver. Josh urged his horse to a fast canter.

Through the rain he could just see the iron gate between the two holly-trees which marked the entrance to their drive. Then the sky cracked open. Just as he leant to open the catch, there was a sizzling, blinding flash. He did not hear the crash of thunder that followed. He came to, lying some yards from the gate where he had been thrown. There was a black burn in the palm of his hand. The pony lay beside the gate, dead.

He lifted the limp, heavy head with its staring, glassy eyes. Then, though his legs felt turned to jelly, he pushed open the gate and ran down the drive, past the fountain set in the lawn, past the ivy-covered dairy, and in at the back door. He was sobbing with fright and shock.

'What be the commotion about, Master Josh?' asked the cook, emerging from the kitchen with floury hands.

'Mamma! I want Mamma!'

Kate came rushing out of her sewing-room, white-faced, a piece of purple brocade in her hand. She had heard the storm and was worrying about him; the others were safe home.

'Josh! Oh! Are you all right? I thought that last bolt had struck the house.'

He showed his blackened hand. 'It struck the front gate. And Oliver – Oliver is dead!'

Josh had a healthy respect for electrical storms for the rest of his life, much of which was spent in the open. Leaving the orchard management to his brothers, he went to a farm at St Paul's Plains for two years to learn how to manage a sheep property. His father's land was at the South Esk River, near Campbell Town, and though it was only 2,000 acres it could carry five sheep to the acre. When Josh took over its management he employed a stockman and six shepherds, some of them convicts on a 'ticket of leave'.

One of the duties that went with being a landowner was that, young as he was, he had to take a turn as magistrate in the local court where convict servants were sentenced to secondary punishment for such crimes as getting drunk, stealing stores, or just being impertinent to their masters.

Josh, a large, easy-going young man with a certain calm confidence in his own ability, did not like this duty. During his first months he thought up other punishments instead of the lash – short rations, loss of a week's pay for ticket-of-leave men, or even a week in solitary confinement. He had once seen a man flogged with the 'cat' till his back was a mangled piece of raw flesh and blood, and he never wanted to be responsible for such suffering.

One morning a man was brought before him who could have been in his late twenties, though his face was seamed with suffering and weatherbeaten from working on the roads and in the quarries.

'James Brown, being on ticket of leave, charged with being abroad in the streets of Campbell Town after eight o'clock p.m. without lawful excuse. What have you to say?'

The man stood up straight and looked him in the eye. He was thin, even emaciated, but well-built, with deep grooves in his brown cheeks which might have been made by smiling in an earlier, happier life. He spoke up in a strong voice, no convict's whine here:

'I'm sorry, I know it looks bad, but the fact is that I left my employer's, Mr Leake's, rather late in the day, having waited for him to give me my pay – '

'Wait a minute. Why were you so late in the day getting paid?'

'Mr Leake was, er – indisposed. In fact, he'd been out late the night before and was sleeping it off.'

Josh allowed the ghost of a smile to show in his grey eyes. Leake, a large landowner, and reputedly mean with his labourers, was known in the district for his heavy tippling.

'In fact, it was just after eight when I arrived. It was either walk all the way home again, or spend the night in the bush and come back in the morning to report myself. Instead I went to the public house, and there the Constables picked me up.'

10

'Your voice is unusual,' said Josh. 'Educated, with a slight American accent?'

'Canadian; I am one of the Canadian Exiles, unjustly transported because we loved our country and wished her to be free.'

'Oh, a rebel, eh? What was your occupation before?'

'Cabinetmaker. I can make anything in wood –'

'Well, Brown, I sentence you to five days in the Watchhouse. I happen to know the Constable's wife wants a kitchen cupboard installed, so off you go and measure it up. Oh, and Brown –'

'Yes, Mr Forbes?'

'When your year is up with Mr Leake, if you're looking for a place, I need an overseer, someone I can trust. I could offer you £10 a year, which will be better than you're getting.'

'Yes, indeed! I'll remember.'

Josh liked the look of James Brown the Canadian patriot. Reliable men were getting scarce, for free labourers and emancipists were all crossing the Strait to the Port Phillip District, where wages were much higher.

He had heard such reports of the new settlement on the mainland, and how sheep seemed to thrive so much better in the drier climate, that he was thinking of investing in land over there. He was allowed to keep the wool cheque from his father's flock and had used it last year to buy six Saxon Merino rams to improve the stock. He worked hard in the shearing season, rolling the fleeces and sorting them himself, supervising the washing pen and the shearing pens. He was beginning to be knowledgeable about wool. Though prices had been falling lately, it was said that the superfine Merino fleeces from Port Phillip were always in demand by England's woollen mills for high quality worsted. He resolved to seek his fortune across the water.

Two

EARLIER, IN April 1839, towards the end of a long, dry summer, the convict ship *Buffalo* had arrived at Hobart Town and anchored in the Derwent estuary under the shadow of Mount Wellington. On board was a cargo of new transportees from Canada: the 'Canadian Patriots'.

The former Lieutenant-Governor of Van Diemen's Land, now Sir George Arthur, had been appointed Governor of Upper Canada just in time to deal with the rebels. Led by William MacKenzie, they had been arrested in Toronto after an abortive uprising against the British Crown, believing the Province was ripe for shaking off the yoke of British rule. Many Americans, remembering their own successful rebellion, had joined them and been arrested along with them. The ringleaders were sentenced to be hung. Governor Arthur, well used to executions – he had signed the death warrant of fifteen hundred men and women in his twelve years in Van Diemen's Land – had a scaffold specially erected beside the gaol. There James Brown, of Kingston, Upper Canada, saw his fellow patriots hanged by the neck till they were dead.

By some miracle his own sentence was commuted to transportation. He was sick for much of the voyage from Canada and believed that he would die. He had scurvy and a bad eye infection, but after some fresh fruit and vegetables were taken on at Rio, he began to improve. The doctor ordered that he should be allowed to take exercise on deck every day.

He saw two of his comrades buried at sea: both older men, one of them, separated from a loved wife and six children, dying it seemed of a broken heart. For the first time he wondered if those executed were better off, with a quick end to their sufferings.

At Hobart Town they were received by Mr Gunn, the Chief Police Magistrate, in the captain's cabin, where each was taken separately to be interrogated. Two clerks took down

12

James Brown's answers to a long series of questions:

Where born? – Upper Canada, Kingston. Age? – Twenty-seven. Religion? – Presbyterian. Trade, former occupation? – Woodworker, carpenter. Married? – No. Parents alive? – Yes. Where parents born? – Scotland. Self able to read and write? – Of course. (Just answer Yes or No.) Where arrested? – Toronto. For what tried and sentenced? – Patriotism. You mean, rebellion. Any distinguishing marks or scars? – Wounded in left shoulder; white scar tissue. Mole on right cheek, dark pigmented. Colour of hair: – Dark, red-brown. Eyes, dark brown. Eyebrows, black, bushy. Teeth: good condition. Height: Five feet eleven. Weight (he had lost half a stone on the voyage): 147 pounds.

A group of constables was waiting to escort the prisoners as soon as they were ashore, but after so long at sea they could scarcely stand. The earth seemed to be rising and falling, heaving beneath their feet. A crowd which had collected to see 'the Yankee rebels' jeered at their staggering gait.

'Come, come, you lazy crawlers!' cried the blue-clad constables, threatening them with their bludgeons. 'Ah, you're not quite so sprightly as you were in Canada, shooting the loyal subjects of our good Queen; but tomorrow you'll be not only walking, but pulling a cart as well.'

Along the road a little way they passed a chain-gang, men in rough grey suits and leather caps, all tied together with heavy chains while they toiled with picks and shovels. Round a bend they met a load coming from the foothills where many prisoners worked in the stone-quarry. The cart was drawn not by horses, but by eight men in harness like dumb beasts. James Brown stared, sickened and horrified. What sort of place had they come to? He knew when they passed, on their way to the 'tench', or penitentiary, a gibbet where bodies hung in chains.

Next day their own clothes were taken away and they were forced to dress in the grey trousers and jacket of coarse grey wool of the convict garb, with an ill-fitting leather cap, a striped cotton shirt, and a pair of clumsy shoes. For James the greatest privation was not to be allowed underwear. From a child he had worn vest and drawers, and the rough fustian material chafed his skin. That and hunger were the worst.

13

Technically, their rations were a pound per day of fly-blown boiled meat, a pint of skilly with a little flour in it for breakfast, and a pound or more of sticky dark bread. They craved for vegetables; sometimes they scraped in the rubbish under the cook's window for potato parings and turnip-tops and cooked them in a stew.

The convicts dared not complain. The rations should have been enough, for the Commissariat Department was well enough run at the top with Josiah Forbes, an honest man, in charge; but as the allowance filtered down through overseers, clerks, constables, cooks, and the wardsmen who distributed it, a little was subtracted at every level. If they murmured, the convicts could be sentenced to thirty-six lashes for 'wrongful complaints'.

Jamie's hands began to blister on the third day of using a heavy, rough-handled pick and shovel on the roads, but at least he was not in chains. That was a secondary punishment for trying to escape. So he was glad when the overseer transferred him to the carts, even though his neck had to go through a humiliating collar, attached to a long handle. He had to pull a six-foot cart with the help of three other men; one was a convicted murderer, one an Army deserter, and the other was Orrin Smith, an American who had joined the rebels. He was a small man who had never done any labouring work in his life.

'Oh my God, Brown, I can never stand this!' he muttered in a kind of muted shriek.

So Jamie, of sturdy Lowland stock though born in Canada, put his shoulders into the collar so that his mate in the team did not have to pull so hard. He had heard, from a bullock-driver who towed logs to a railway siding near Kingston, that there were bullocks so cunning they could give every appearance of pulling in a team when they were actually taking no weight at all.

Though it was a relief to their hands to be placed in the cart, the labour was severe. The load was of heavy stones and dirt, and they had to draw ten loads a day for a mile full and a mile empty. When one of the men got ill and had to be taken to hospital in Hobart Town, it was almost like a holiday to draw his slight and malnourished form over the rough roads.

14

He knew that he was dying.

'Jamie!' he said. 'Jim, old chap – God bless you. And Canada – how I wish she was free from England and her bloody tyrants – and I would to God I did not have to die in their hands. I shall never see Canada again, I fear . . . Goodbye, mates.'

They left him to go to muster, and by next morning he was dead.

It was strange, thought Jamie, but all that burning desire for political freedom, that hatred of British tyranny, had been subdued by simple hunger. At first, when he was bullied by some underling official, his blood had boiled in his veins, and he had longed to get his hands on a rifle, just for five minutes, so he could shoot the tyrants down. He thought continually of escape.

But to 'take to the bush' was a desperate measure. Men rarely escaped the soldiers or the dogs, and without a ship standing by there was no way of leaving the island, which was a vast prison. The only resort then was to get hold of some firearms and become highwaymen, holding up coaches and outlying farms until eventually, inevitably, they were shot, or apprehended and hung.

The roadworkers were always hungry. The rations they received were often only half the proper allowance. They would rise in the morning tormented by hunger; they worked through the day with the gnawings of hunger unsatisfied and lay down at night, after a meal of maggoty meat and sour, half-cooked bread, still feeling hungry. For two long years, not a day passed when they were not half starved.

Three of the men, in desperation, took to the bush. They remained at large for only two weeks before they were captured. Then they were sentenced to secondary punishment at the dreaded Port Arthur, from which few men ever escaped except to death.

Now James Brown concentrated all his will upon simple survival. He had a bad cough, but he was still physically strong, toughened by hard labour in all weathers.

From the Penitentiary in Hobart Town, he was sent next with his fellow-Canadians to a penal station some thirty miles to the north. It was midwinter when they were sent off with their total belongings – a tin plate, a cup, and a day's dry rations rolled in a pair of blankets – to walk for two days on the Launceston road with the 'swag' across their shoulders. Escorted by constables in blue, they had a hard day's march of nearly eighteen miles. Walking on the well-made road was at first preferable to pulling a cart in the quarry; but the hard road, the ill-fitting shoes without socks to soften their rough inner surface, soon blistered Jamie's feet. He took off and carried the shoes, but his feet were then so swollen and tender that he could not get them on again. In the morning there was a white frost. He screamed with the pain of walking in the crisp, white grass till he got to the road; after that it was not so bad, for traffic had melted the icy surface.

Their next task was to work in a quarry near Ross, getting stone for a new bridge, and here the superintendent was a bully, an ex-convict who had been advanced to oversee other convicts. He was often drunk when he took the evening muster, and in a nasty mood. As each name was called, he insisted that the prisoner must touch his cap, make a bow, and say 'Yes sir.'

This made the more independent men squirm with rage, to have to touch their caps to a fellow-convict who had got where he was by crawling to the officers, no doubt, and informing on his fellows. The first night, when the name was called – James Brown! – there was no answer.

'Call that name again!' cried the overseer, Sandlands.

'JAMES BROWN!'

Silence. 'Which man is Brown?'

Jamie stepped forward. 'Now, Brown,' said Sandlands, 'now, do you touch your cap to me, sir! And when your name is called, do you say, Yes, Sir, or I'll have you trussed to the triangles for three dozen lashes.'

Jamie, feeling sick and faint, bowed his head. When his name was called a third time, he touched his cap and muttered, 'Yes, sir . . .', feeling that the words would choke him.

The men at last became so sullen and bitter that someone less full of his own importance than Sandlands might have feared for his life. The men talked it over, and decided, at whatever risk, to get rid of him.

Jamie, as an expert in woodworking, was asked to make

16

two stout, heavy bludgeons from wood which the men who pulled the wood-cart each day had thrown off in the long grass. Then they all drew lots, and the two men who pulled the shortest straws stole out after dark and hid behind a rock, on the path where Sandlands usually came home drunk.

They watched in vain till well past midnight, when a storm blew up and they returned to their hut. Sandlands did not come home that night. They heard later that he had fallen, drunk, down the stone steps at the front of the pub where he drank, and had a badly broken leg. He did not come again to muster them, and the men were perhaps saved from dying on the gallows.

The new overseer, White, was a milder man altogether, though of uncertain temper. He'd once had a man flogged for picking up a piece of tobacco in the road – for tobacco, with other comforts, was utterly forbidden.

A smoke was known to appease the pangs of hunger, so that even those who were not addicted would smoke in secret if they got the chance. One day a settler passing on his horse threw Jamie half a flour damper and a plug of tobacco, which he quickly picked up and secreted. Next day he was asked to make some barrow handles in the workshop, so he roughly fashioned a pipe with the tools there, and began to have a quiet smoke while he worked on the handles.

There was a window above the bench, and looking out he saw the solid form of the superintendent approaching. Frantically fanning at the smoke-laden air, he hastily hid the pipe under some shavings. White came in, asking for a dry pine board he wanted, and while looking round saw the shavings beginning to smoulder.

'Ah!' he said. 'And what might that be, pray? It looks like smoke?'

'Y-yes, it is smoke. You see – well, I had a bit of tobacco, and I thought no-one would see me if I had a quick smoke –'

'But you see I have caught you at it!'

'Yes, I'm afraid you have.' He could see the triangle looming up, the flagellator with the cat-o'-nine-tails at the ready . . .

White looked at him lazily, like a cat toying with a mouse. 'Well, Brown, I will let it pass this time. I didn't actually see you smoking, did I? But don't let me ever catch you again, or *look out*!'

Jamie could not believe his luck; but White picked up the length of wood and walked out.

Three

JAMIE WAS feeling desperate enough to take to the bush and chance the consequences, when he realised that although time had seemed to drag, two years had passed since his arrival and he was due for his ticket of leave. As soon as his name appeared in the Government Gazette, he repaired to the nearest magistrate's office and presented a certificate from the convict superintendent giving all his particulars. With his companions who had served the two years on the roads with him, he was given a three-day pass to travel to the district of his choice, which was Oatlands, on the road to Launceston, in the midlands. If their behaviour was good, at the end of their seven years' sentence or perhaps earlier they would be emancipated – full citizens, and free to travel the island, but not to leave it.

Sleeping out in the open the first night, each with only a thin blanket, they were so cold that they lit a small fire: this was against the law, only free men could light fires. At four in the morning they were hailed by a party of travelling constables: Why had they lit a fire?

'Because it's so bloody cold,' replied one of the men. 'We had to build a fire to keep warm.'

'Against regulations,' said the chief officer. 'You must put out the fire.'

They grumbled and groaned but had to do as they were told. There was nothing for it but to start walking. The air was clear and frosty; the stars were sharp as icicles in the dark sky,

18

seeming to be caught among the branches of the thin-leaved gumtrees.

On the second night, they managed to get a sort of lodging in the labourers' huts on an outlying farm, and as one of them had trapped a kangaroo the night before – and even this was against regulations – they had fresh meat and delicious kangaroo-tail soup.

There seemed to be no work available for ticket of leave men in Oatlands, so Jamie went again to the authorities and asked leave to proceed to Campbell Town, further north. He was still far from a free man; as soon as he arrived at a new place, he had to report to the police station. He called at an outlying farm on his way there, and by luck was accepted to work for a year for £8 and his keep. He would live in a hut a short distance from the house and cook his own rations, which would be more generous in quantity than on the roads.

The proprietor, Mr Leake, proved to be a thin, gaunt fellow of about fifty-five, with long sidewhiskers that made his face look longer and grimmer than it might otherwise have done. His small eyes were deep-set and almost invisible, and he had what was known as a lantern-jaw. He was a widower with four plain unmarried daughters, which perhaps explained his rather morose expression. But he was not a tyrant, and as long as his men performed their tasks fairly he did not hustle them.

His estate ran six thousand sheep, at about three or four sheep to the acre, the sheep placed under the care of shepherds who lived in huts out on the run.

'You're one of those Yankee rebels, I believe,' was Mr Leake's greeting. 'Well, Brown, we'll have no rebelling here. You look a strong fellow – '

'I am not a Yankee!' interrupted Jamie hotly. 'I am as British born as yourself, from Canada, and we did but stand up for our rights against a tyrannous government at Home. And there may come a time when you, Australians and Van Diemonians, will have to fight for the right to elect your own rulers, not be administered from twelve thousand miles away by men who know nothing of your problems – '

'That's enough, Brown,' said Leake sourly. 'Now get to your quarters, and when the bell rings, do you come up for

19

your supper to the kitchen door. You can join the other two shepherds in the morning, and learn the ropes. Ever handled sheep?'

'Never. But I'm willing to learn – sir.'

The last word came out with an effort, but it occurred to Jamie that he had better not start off on the wrong foot with his master. Leake could have him arraigned before the local magistrate, flogged on the slightest pretext. He had resolved that if they tried to flog him, he would die first. In spite of hunger and privation and indignity, his spirit was not yet broken.

It was not long before he found that his master regularly got drunk at the hotel in Campbell Town. Then he would come home full of uncustomary bonhomie and would sometimes call at one of the shepherds' stone huts for a talk, however late the hour.

One of the greatest boons to Jamie was being able to keep clean now that he had a hut of his own. He could bathe in the creek, but also bring water from the rainwater tank and heat it on the fire for a bath. One night, after he had been there about six months, he had been knocking up a small box-table out of bits of wood he'd found lying about the farm. He worked until late, and then, being chilled, built up the fire and began to heat himself a bath. He had of course not even a hip-bath, but by folding himself up small he could squat in the biggest tin dish he had, and soap himself all over. He was saving up to buy some under-drawers, when he would feel he had once more joined the human race.

He had just poured the rinsing-water over himself, splashing it all over the floor, when he heard a rap at the door. What could it be at this hour – the constables? He grabbed the length of old rag he used as a towel, and wrapped it round his middle. He opened the door a crack. Leake stood on the step, swaying; then he fell forward against the door, knocking it open. He grabbed Jamie for support as he staggered inside.

'I say – say! You're all wet, eh? Been having a bra— brath? barth?'

Jamie dislodged Leake's arms and pushed him away. Leake stood with his feet wide-planted, his head lowered like a bull's, his little, red, drunken, bloodshot eyes fixed on the cloth around Jamie's hips.

'Gird up – gird up thy, they loins for battle, eh?' His voice was even thicker than usual. He lurched forward and snatched the cloth. Jamie stepped backwards quickly. He grabbed his trousers from the floor and pulled them on, but he could not find his belt. He held the trousers up defensively.

Leake grinned. 'No need t' be modest with me, lad. Go on with yer bath; I'll watch.'

'No thank you. I've finished bathing. Now I would like to go to sleep.'

'What – alone? Don' you ever get sick of sleeping alone? By God, I do. Ever since – since Lushy parshed away – alone, ev'y night. Now, what you say? I make it worth yer while – new shirt and trousers, a side o' lamb – what you say? Jus' one night, eh?'

'Mr Leake, I think you should go back to your house. You've had too much to drink.'

Leake scowled, staggered sideways, and Jamie took the opportunity of steering him out the open door of the one-room hut. He pushed him towards his horse, which was quietly cropping the grass around the tank-stand, and hoisted him into the saddle.

'Convict scum!' muttered Leake. 'Who're you to shay I'm drunk?'

Jamie pushed the bunched reins into his hands, and gave the horse a slap on the rump. It would take its master safely to his own door, as it had brought him from the town, without guidance.

When they met again, Mr Leake was sober, and had the grace to look uneasy, even ashamed. But he took a dislike to James Brown from then on, finding fault with his work, once sending him to the magistrate with a request 'to give this man thirty lashes for impertinence and insubordination.' Fortunately the magistrate was Joseph Forbes, who substituted a week on bread and water in the cells, and Leake lost a week's work from him for his pains.

As soon as his year was nearly up, Jamie walked the thirty miles to the neighbouring property of Joseph Forbes, to offer himself as an overseer at £10 a week; but to his dismay, Mr

21

Forbes said he was selling up and leaving the colony.

'The new District of Port Phillip is a better place for sheep, it seems,' he said. 'Many Tasmanian settlers are crossing the Straits, and all the runs nearer to Melbourne have already been taken up. I'd like to take you with me, but – '

'But I'm not allowed to leave the island.'

'I've heard rumours that some of the Patriots are to receive free pardons. The French-Canadians sent to New South Wales have already been returned home, free men.'

'They have? 'Tis only justice, and we should be freed too. There are twelve of us in the Oatlands and Campbell Town districts, all wrongly imprisoned by the British Government.'

'Come, you did take up arms against authority, didn't you?'

'Yes, but I never fired a shot.'

'Only from want of opportunity, no doubt. Tell you what, I'll give you a note of recommendation to Mr Booth, at Sunny Banks station. You're an experienced stockman, I take it?'

'Yes, Mr Forbes. And if I'm not repatriated, when I get my freedom, I'll get to the mainland and ask you for a job.'

'Right. I'll just go and scribble that note for you.'

If James Brown felt anything besides gratitude to young Forbes, it was envy at his lot: scarcely twenty-six years old, tall, dark, fortunate, with a face unlined by privation though browned by the sun, and that indefinable air of authority and ease which came of a secure childhood in a wealthy home. He talked to his men as equals; he never 'bounced' them, yet there was never any doubt who was boss.

Edward Booth was a very different man from Sam Leake. He was cultivated, kept a library of books, belonged to the Natural History Society that met each month at Government House, and made drawings of native birds. On one of his collecting expeditions he shot a rare White Hawk, a handsome bird which he skinned and stuffed. He showed the finished result to James Brown: a fierce, lifelike pose, the claws grasping a branch of wood, the golden glass eyes glaring above a hooked beak.

'You see that, Jamie? It's probably the only white hawk occurring naturally in the world. Not an albino, a freak; if it were the eyes would be pink, as in a white rabbit. Strange that the swans should be black here, and the hawks white! It is getting shot out, of course; being so conspicuous it's an easy mark.'

When he found that Jamie could read and write Mr Booth had invited him over to borrow some books from his library. Reading was a luxury Jamie had almost forgotten. The light of his slush-lamp, made from mutton-fat and a length of cotton wick in an old tin, was scarcely enough to read by, but he made it a practice to wake early in summer and read from four in the morning until he had to go out at six. Now he was getting better wages he had bought himself some cotton drawers and flannel undershirts, besides a real, absorbent towel. The luxury of such things could only be properly appreciated, he thought, by one who had been forced to do without them.

He had heard no more about the free pardons when two of his fellow-Canadians came up from Oatlands, full of the news that bushrangers were in the midlands and a reward and free pardon were offered to anyone who would apprehend them. They asked Jamie to join them. Conway and Jeffs, the two bushrangers, were young men who had been convicts and had taken to the bush. Conway had been sentenced to Port Arthur for eating one piece of bacon and an egg from his master's meat-safe one night when he was hungry. He escaped with Jeffs, and they managed to steal some guns and ammunition from an out-station.

James Brown felt a revulsion at the idea of hunting the bushrangers, who had been oppressed by the same system as himself and were only trying to escape the horrors of Port Arthur. It was a business he did not like. He couldn't blame the others for wanting to regain their freedom, but to go and hunt two other men to their death was something his spirit rebelled at. He told Booth that he was not willing to go, and he was not forced.

Two other stockmen of Booth's were pressed to go and joined the party. After a month of scouring the bush, they noticed one morning that smoke was curling from the chimney of a deserted and derelict shepherd's hut. Creeping up, they surprised the two men at their breakfast, their guns laid

23

by, and they were quickly captured. The reward was £200 between them, a free pardon for each, and a free passage home.

James felt a pang of envy to think that the other men were now free and on their way back to their families. But he was glad he'd had no hand in it when he heard a description of Conway's end. He was hanged at Oatlands. Two days before the date of his execution, he asked for a clean white shirt. It was brought to him.

'No, I won't put it on now,' he said. 'Let it be kept until I'm to be led to execution, for I want it should be clean and nice. I cannot bear to die in this filthy convict's shirt.'

So on the fated morning he ascended the scaffold, dressed neatly in a new white shirt open at the neck, the long sleeves buttoned at the wrist. He walked with a firm step, his face impassive, and died bravely without a struggle. He was only eighteen.

Shearing started on Booth's station about the first of October. The shepherds were pressed into helping in the wool-shed once the flocks were mustered. Jamie was rolling and skirting fleeces on the wool-table, when 'the boss' came by and said, 'Here, I'll take over there; do you try your hand with the shears.'

'I'd make a muck of it, Mr Booth,' he said. 'I wouldn't like to cut one of your valuable sheep –

'Nonsense, it's not difficult.' Mr Booth grabbed a fine, open-wooled wether and wrestled it to the floor of the shearing-shed, where ten men were working with hand shears. 'See, you hold the shears thus, and make a kind of scooping motion – you'll get the knack of going as near as possible to the flesh without actually cutting it – open up the belly, then up the sides and along the back – so that the fleece comes off in one piece. Try it.'

Reluctantly Jamie took the shears and grabbed the wether's legs to keep it motionless. He made an awkward sweep with the shears.

Mr Booth laughed; the shearing was going well and he was in a good mood. 'Go on, Brown; just shove the shears in.'

Jamie took a deep breath and shoved them in – the sheep

gave a grunting cough and expired. The shears were dripping with blood. 'I'm – I'm sorry, sir – I just didn't – '

'Well, that *was* rather deep; I didn't mean disembowel him. Never mind, never mind, we'll have mutton for dinner. I was going to kill one for the cook anyway, so you've saved me the trouble.'

And he made him try again, on a smaller sheep. This he managed to shear with only a few gashes, which were quickly smeared with healing tar. At the end of the day he had shorn thirty sheep.

Booth did not want to leave the station to market his clip, and so, as he had learnt to trust Jamie, he asked him to lead the drive of three drayloads of wool to Hobart, each weighing about two thousand pounds – a bullock-driver and a yoke of oxen to each dray – and sell the clip for him.

At the Derwent the wool had to be ferried across to Hobart, where Jamie's first act was to report to the police and show his safe conduct pass for Hobart, and get a permit for a stay of a week.

Within two days he had disposed of the wool. He ordered some purchases of stores for the station and paid for them, and still had £500 in his pocket. That night he went to the 'Settler's Arms' to celebrate, and there met an American seaman whose ship was in port, ready to sail on the following night's tide. They got to talking over their pints, and in a low voice the sailor offered to take him on board tomorrow night and hide him till they were well away.

Poor Jamie! Temptation swept over him in a wave. He could take the money in his pocket, buy his passage, and be free forever of this accursed island! But immediately came another thought – if he were caught, if anything went wrong, and no doubt the constables were keeping an eye on him – he would have lost everything, his chance of emancipation, his ticket of leave, and he would be sent to Port Arthur for another seven, perhaps fourteen, years! That would be unbearable, after the comparative freedom he had attained. And the money: it belonged rightfully to Booth, who had trusted him. And yet – to be free now, at once! He came to a thousand different decisions overnight. But when the time came to meet the sailor, Jamie was not there. His better judgment prevailed, and he felt a certain relief at not having robbed a man who had treated him with kindness and trust. And he still had hopes of a free pardon.

He crossed the River Derwent once more, loaded the station stores on the drays, and started on the return journey to Campbell Town. All the way he was tormented with the thought: 'I could be aboard that American ship by now. I could be free. Why didn't I take the money, and go?' But when he handed over the money to Booth and saw the quizzical look with which he took it, he knew that the boss had known he was taking a risk; perhaps had not expected he would come back.

'You've done very well, Jamie,' he said in a friendly voice. 'As well as I could have done myself. I'm going to make you overseer from now on.'

This meant that he had a room in the servants' quarters of the big house, and ate in the kitchen – the first good, well-cooked meals he had enjoyed since his arrest in Canada. He never spoke with Mrs Booth or her daughters, who regarded convicts as beneath notice; but just to be in the same room with the cook and the two kitchen-maids – all free emigrants – made him feel he had rejoined society, was no longer an outcast.

He no longer spent his days with sheep, but had the supervision of the farm and its buildings, and directed the gardener and the dozen men employed about the home paddocks, planting turnips and potatoes and lucerne, mending fences and gates, milking cows, and all the other work of a mixed farm. Also he was often asked to fix a window-frame or make a new cupboard door, so that he went into the rooms of the big house and actually trod on a carpet again.

One day, having been sent to Oatlands on an errand, he was idly reading the notices posted up outside the Police Station, when he saw the latest Government Gazette with a list of free pardons; among them was the name of Orrin Smith, the American with whom he had pulled side by side in the stone-cart when he first arrived. Feverishly reading down the list, he saw among the nineteen other names five which were known to him; but his own was not there.

What did it mean? Why were some of the Patriots being

freed, and others not? He had never received a secondary sentence, had been an exemplary prisoner apart from a few minor sins like 'receiving tobacco', 'lighting a fire when not permitted' and 'being out after curfew'. If it was to do with the crime for which they had been deported, all were equally guilty; it was monstrously unjust. And yet, who knew if they meant to free all of them shortly? Hope began to flutter once more in his breast. He went to Mr Booth and asked if he knew why some of the Canadian prisoners had been pardoned, and some like himself were still held.

'Last time I was in Hobart Town,' said Mr Booth, 'I did hear something about it, but I didn't want to raise your hopes too soon. I'm pretty well assured that the Government intends to liberate you all; but it was thought best by the authorities that it should not all be done at once, in case it should create unrest among the other prisoners. They are putting through the pardons six or twelve at a time.'

'Since there were ninety-one of us landed, that is going to take some time,' said Jamie rather bitterly. 'Though of course those who have died would reduce the number. If you knew how we were treated, you would wonder that any of us survived.'

'I know the System is hard –'

'Hard! Mr Booth, there are sufferings which not only rend the flesh, but also try to kill the innermost spirit and every feeling of being a member of the human race. I could tell you tales that would curdle your blood! I'm sorry to be bitter, but when a man thinks of how his spirit was bowed to the dust – how those fiends crushed and broke his manhood, and degraded him to the level of a beast – how can he help the bitterness of his heart?'

'Yes – well – that will do, Jamie,' said Booth uncomfortably. His own wealth and broad acres were based, he knew, upon convict labour. 'Let us hope your pardon comes through soon – though I'll be sorry to lose you.'

Another long month went by, when one day in the autumn of 1844 a neighbouring settler arrived to see Booth. 'Don't you have one of the Canadian exiles working for you?' he asked.

'Yes, my overseer, a good, trustworthy man.'

'I thought so! I've just come back from a meeting of the Executive Council and there are twelve more of that lot to be gazetted for free pardons in the new Gazette. What's his name?'

'James Brown.'

'Brown – yes, I'm sure there was a Brown among them. I should have brought the list with me –'

After his visitor had gone, Mr Booth called Jamie to where he was sitting in the parlour. 'Well, Jamie,' he said, 'I hear that twelve more Canadians and Americans have been pardoned at the last sitting of the Executive Council, and your name may be among them.'

'May be? Do you *know*? Don't play with me, I beg of you.'

'No, I don't *know*; but if you want to be sure, ride over to Mr Connor's this afternoon after work, and ask him to look up the new Gazette.'

He could scarcely do anything for the next two hours, because of the trembling of his hands. 'No, it can't be true,' he thought, and then, 'But it might be; why not?' And then, 'But if it isn't true? How could I bear it? Oh, pray God it may be true.'

At five o'clock, he saddled a horse and turned his head towards Connor's. It was ten miles away following the road, but Jamie set off across country, recklessly urging the horse over low hedges and across streams, until, as the horse stumbled on a downhill gallop, he suddenly thought, 'What a fool you would be to break your neck *now*, just when freedom may be in your grasp! What an irony that would be!' He slowed down at once, trotted quietly back to the road, and continued by the long way round.

Arrived at Connor's, he was told by a servant that the master was resting, but he insisted on his name being taken in and was soon admitted. Mr Connor was sitting by a small fire, with his feet up on a bead-embroidered stool.

Jamie stood before him trembling all over with hope and fear.

'Well, Brown, you are a free man!'

Jamie almost fainted; he closed his eyes, opened them and said, 'No, it cannot be!'

'Pass me that paper there, on the table. Now – you can see

28

for yourself. What is the second-to-last name there?'

He ran his eyes quickly down the list. There it was: JAMES BROWN.

Could it be true? Was his name really James Brown? He held his forefinger on the name, as though it might jump off the paper and disappear. 'Are you sure this is me, Mr Connor? There's no mistake?'

'It is you,' he answered, with a broad smile. 'You are free!'

At last he believed it. Jamie felt his heart swell in his bosom as though it would burst. His whole frame seemed to expand; his coat sleeves became too tight, the buttons seemed likely to burst from his shirt. He was in a delirium of joy.

He stammered some thanks and dashed out to the horse again. He mounted and went wildly galloping round, shouting at the sky, 'I am free! I am free! It is true, I'm a free man at last!'

Mr Booth was delighted for him, when he heard the news, but tried to persuade Jamie to stay another year with him and save some wages. He even offered an advance to £16 a year. But Jamie couldn't wait to get away. He wanted to leave the hated island of Van Diemen's Land as soon as possible. He called at the Police Station at Campbell Town for the precious slip of paper which officially restored his liberty. He was free to leave, but he had not enough for the fare home to Canada. Instead, he would get a berth or a passage aboard one of the small steamers leaving regularly for Port Melbourne on the other side of Bass Strait.

Four

ON THE mainland, Joseph Forbes had settled on the Goulburn River, in the Port Phillip District, where he had taken up a fine tract of bushland with five miles of river frontage. He had paid £10 to the Commissioner of Crown Lands for the right to

29

depasture his flocks on some 30,000 acres. It did not occur to him, or to the Commissioner, that the land really belonged to the Kaieltheban tribe who had hunted over it for thousands of years. Finding that they called the bend of the river where he built his house 'Daralgoon', he gave this name to his station.

The £10 had to be paid every year, besides a small tax per head as a grazing licence for his sheep. In Melbourne he met an older squatter, William Brodribb, who told him he should take up land across the Murray in 'New South Wales proper', which offered a better prospect for men of small to moderate means.

'But you will get on all right here,' he added, 'if you're not afraid of hard work, and have plenty of courage, energy and perseverance.'

Josh was not lacking in energy. He rose with the sun, and as there was no bathroom as yet in the wooden cabin he had built, he would take a dip in the river. In his first spring he saw the feathery dark acacias come out in brilliant bloom, each tree like a ball of gold, reflected like sunlight in the smooth gliding water. He rested at midday, when even the insects and birds fell silent and a mighty stillness brooded through the bush. Then he worked again till sunset, and sometimes during lambing, well into the night.

On summer mornings, setting off in the cool dawn to ride round the cleared portion of his run, he would feel a tremendous surge of well-being. Here he was, a young man, healthy, soon to be wealthy, he hoped, carving a homestead out of the bush in this vast new land. Who could help being an optimist, he thought, seeing the gentle promise of pink clouds against the morning sky?

As the light dew melted upwards, before the sun had dried every vestige of the softening veil of moisture from the air, the distances shone pearly and opalescent through a haze of palest blue. A clean scent of eucalyptus rose from the dried bark and dead leaves beneath the gums.

Only one thing marred his contentment; he needed a woman. It was such a waste to commit the sin of Onan and spill the seed which should be deeply planted so that he might breed sons to inherit his lands when he died. (But that event,

30

of course, was somewhere in the far distant future. Old men died. For himself, he felt that he would live for a hundred years.)

He was steadily building up his flocks. Sheep had fallen in value recently, so he bought a thousand more to add to the flock he had brought with him, and a dozen good rams to improve the fleeces. Besides which his ewes had dropped five hundred new lambs which would soon be ready for shearing.

He had no trouble with the Blacks. Remembering how they had terrorised the countryside in his boyhood in Van Diemen's Land, he was amused rather than frightened at the grave old men who stalked up to his verandah, very erect in their long possum-skin cloaks, to ask for tobacco in exchange for fish: fat golden perch and Murray Cod which they had speared.

He had heard it rumoured that in exchange for a sheep, or even a haunch of mutton and some tobacco, they would provide a brown-skinned girl to share a lonely young man's couch. The girls were trained to obey the Old Men of the tribe. Certainly the number of paler-skinned half-white babies was increasing, and the cause was not, as some simple Aborigines believed, that their lubras had been eating too much white flour.

This was a way out of his problem which Josh would not take. His stern Methodist upbringing forbade it. He knew too well that the primrose path, however enticing to the feet, led to the everlasting bonfire.

He began calling on his next-neighbour-but-one, further downstream on the Goulburn which flowed north-west to its junction with the Murray. Mr Robert Hume had a large well-appointed homestead and a station which spread on both sides of the river. (Josh was not on the best of terms with his immediate neighbour, who, having settled on some poorly-grassed land, cast covetous eyes on the unfenced Daralgoon acres where he often let his sheep stray.)

After calling at Hume's station, Murrundindi, Josh was invited to an afternoon picnic by the river – no swimming, of course, in mixed company – and to dinner back at the house, where he stayed the night. Mrs Hume's father, the Reverend Edward Coggin, had been a chaplain on a convict ship before he settled in Van Diemen's Land. It was a link between them, as she and Josh could reminisce about the days of wild Aborigines and convict labour in the island colony. Mrs Hume was a large, pleasant-faced lady who wore elaborate caps and lace collars and layers of flounced and fringed clothing in dark colours most unsuitable for the climate.

But for Josh the attraction lay in the three daughters, Selina, Betsy and Mary Ann. The younger boys were away at school, and only one son, the eldest, was at home. It was unfortunate that Josh was immediately attracted to the youngest daughter, as the Hume parents were anxious to see the older girls married first.

How could sisters be so different? thought Josh. Selina was tall and slender, with a rather long pointed nose and large teeth, though her brown hair was soft and pretty. Betsy was fair, had good features and a neat figure, and fine flyaway eyebrows above her grey eyes; but her looks were spoilt by a poor complexion. In the dusk, or when her face was shaded by a bonnet, he could feel quite romantic towards Betsy. But then he confessed to himself that he could be interested in *any* female under fifty, provided she was white and didn't have a wooden leg.

Mary Ann was his favourite, with her rich red-brown curls the colour of his chestnut mare, her clear brown eyes like pools in the Goulburn, her creamy complexion. What fascinated him most were her heavy, pale eyelids, like camellia petals half-drooped above her eyes, and a manner quiet and modest – whereas Selina talked almost like a man, and was reputed to be writing a book; not, it was to be hoped, a novel!

Although he now had a substantial house built at Daralgoon, it had few comforts; it was a plain bachelor's establishment, where he lived and ate in the one room from which his bedroom opened. The kitchen and the men's quarters were in a separate building at the back. There were no women servants, though the old lubras sometimes came up from their bark *mia-mias* to do a little work in the garden.

But at Murrundindi he found all the comforts of home. There was even a German piano. Each of the girls could play a little, Selina being the most accomplished, while Mary Ann had a light but charming soprano voice. The younger girls

were delighted that he could play. He accompanied Mary
Ann on the piano in Schubert's *Heidenroslein* as she sang:

> Once a young lad spied a rose
> In a hedgerow grow–ing . . .

Then they played a duet, with much laughter and many
mistakes. She slapped his fingers playfully when he hit a
wrong note, and then blushed delightfully at her own action.

'You must be my tutor, Miss Hume,' said Josh, lifting the
hand that had punished him to his lips.

'*I* am Miss Hume, Mr Forbes,' said Selina tartly, from
where she was sitting at the oval table with her sketching
things, making a formal floral design of irises, those geomet-
rical three-petalled flowers which lend themselves so well to
decoration.

'Well, Miss Mary then.'

'Mary Ann,' said Mary Ann shyly, her eyelids at half-mast.

'I shall call you Miss Marian, Maid Marian – '

'And do you see yourself in the role of Robin Hood or Friar
Tuck?' asked Selina dryly.

'How can you ask?' said Betsy reproachfully. 'Mr Forbes
has not the figure of a Friar Tuck.'

'Some say that our highwaymen are like Robin Hood,
robbing the rich to help the poor,' said Selina. 'But I say that is
romanticising them. They are simply desperate men who have
put themselves outside the law, and must take the consequences.'

'Dr Wardell's murder was a terrible thing,' said Betsy.
'What would you do if bushrangers appeared on the Goulburn, Mr Forbes?'

'Eh? I? Oh!' said Josh, rather confused, for he had been
staring raptly at Mary Ann who was smiling secretly down at
her hands folded in her lap. Selina's rather mocking look
upset him further. 'Well, I would take my gun in self-defence,
I suppose. Just as we had to do in Van Diemen's Land against
both bushrangers and savages.'

'You must have been very young to have been handling a
gun,' said Selina. 'Mamma tells me that they were quite
dangerous when she was a young woman, but they have all

been locked away on an island in Bass Strait for many years.'

'I volunteered to join the "Black Line" against them, nevertheless,' said Josh rather hotly.

'And how old were you?'

'Fifteen. My parents wouldn't let me go.'

'Only fifteen! I should think not,' said Mary Ann, giving him an arch smile. 'You can be no more than five-and-twenty now.'

'I am twenty-seven.'

Mary Ann said, 'The Blacks about here are not very troublesome, fortunately. They seem to be more warlike along the Murray River, where Mr Faithfull's party was massacred.'

'There have been massacres on both sides,' said Selina. 'What about Myall Creek? Men, women and children were shot down there.'

'Yes, and there are rumours of a similar happening on the Ovens River, and at Rufus Creek where I believe a whole tribe was destroyed. But personally I have a good relationship with the local blackfellows. One old chap visits me regularly when he is camping in the vicinity. When he sees the picture of my brother John beside the fireplace, he puts his head on one side and asks sagaciously, "That one brother b'long you, aint it?"'

'You mean you let them in the house? They work in the garden here sometimes, for some flour and tea and tobacco,' said Betsy.

'Oh, yes, they are very clean, in and out of the river all day, either fishing or swimming. I find the old men to be natural gentlemen, with better manners than the average shepherd from the slums of London.'

He was asked to stay the night and left early in the morning to ride back to Daralgoon. His heart was singing with the magpies as they swooped and soared above the river gums, or poised carolling on a bare twig. Mary Ann had got up early too, and come to the garden gate to see him off. He was conscious that he made a fine figure of a horseman on his chestnut mare, with his broad shoulders and well-fitting white moleskin trousers and riding boots. He swept off his cabbage-tree hat; she waved a fond farewell.

34

However, he was in for an unpleasant surprise. Riding back from Murrundindi he was met by one of his shepherds in a great state of agitation. 'I was jest sittin' down on a log, 'avin a smoke,' he said, 'when this great ugly painted savige, nakid as the day 'e was born, comes and taps me on the shoulder. He asks quiet-like for some of me terbacca. I thought I'd best give it to 'im. Well, he took the terbacca with one hand, and me carbine with the other. Then about twenty more Blacks pops up from behind the bushes, and they spears a sheep each.'

'And they took the gun?'

'No, they never. They laid it down a little way off so I could get it after. Didn't know 'ow to use it, I spose.'

Josh did not know whether to report this occurrence or not. His men were frightened, and the loss of a score of sheep could not be taken lightly. He had made a bargain with the old men, that in return for a supply of flour and tobacco, both of which they craved, they would not spear his sheep. He would have discussed it with them but the Aborigines (even the women who usually came about the house to do odd jobs) were nowhere to be seen. He decided to report the spearing to the Protector in Melbourne.

A week later a mounted trooper appeared, in charge of a posse of four black and four white police; with instructions, he said, 'to apprehend all troublesome Blacks, and restore quiet to the district.'

Josh, used to the easy-going life of the bush where usually he wore an open-necked shirt and kerchief, was amused at the officer's military manner and accoutrements as he strode up and down in his brass-buttoned jacket, spurs jingling, sabre at hip, forage cap set jauntily at an angle.

Peeling off his buckskin gloves and smoothing his little blond moustache with a caressing forefinger, the visitor began to deliver a lecture in military terms to this ignorant civilian; his men would 'bivouac' at the station, 'advance in line abreast' on the morrow, 'take up a position' by the shepherd's hut, and 'engage the enemy' as soon as he discovered himself.

Josh could not see that there was much danger from 'the enemy'; where spears were opposed to carbines, the fight must be unequal. However they all set out the next day, having sent a decoy party with a dray and a flock of sheep to entice the Blacks away from the river, where they could immediately dive in and swim away under water.

The troopers hidden around the clearing soon saw a mob of natives, spears in hand, approaching the sheep. With a war-whoop they charged them on horseback. One trooper's horse bolted with him, carrying the rider out of sight; a second was plucked off by the low branch of a tree while his horse went on without him; another went headlong when his mount put a hoof in a bandicoot hole.

The Blacks slipped between the other troopers and made back to the river, but as the last native was leaping from the bank the officer discharged two barrels, putting a bullet through the fleshy part of the man's arm. He fell, clutching his arm. He was seized by the party and, his hands being too slender for handcuffs and his arm being painful, the handcuffs were placed round his ankles.

The man, Mirrandooka, was driven back to the station next day, his ankles freed but a rope around his neck attached to the officer's saddle. From there a wool-dray took him down to Melbourne, feeling sure that he would never see his native woods or his people again.

He was brought to trial for sheep-stealing before Judge Willis, but the judge refused to try him as there was no interpreter who could speak his language, and the prisoner was unable to understand the proceedings or make a plea.

He was kept languishing in jail for a month, while his arm healed, the ball having been extracted by the prison doctor. As Josh was in town looking for an overseer, he went to see Mirrandooka, and found him sick and drooping like a black cockatoo in a cage. He could not live away from his own country, he said in broken English. 'Me soon buggerup pinish longa this one gaol.'

Josh bestirred himself to get the authorities to release him, as it was his sheep the man was accused of spearing, and he said he no longer wished to prefer charges. Then he visited the man in his cell, and told him he was to be set free. 'Mitter Daralgoon!' cried the Aborigine, calling him by the name of his property as the old men often did, 'you *maranooka*, good friend, you kind-fella to poor Mirrandooka. They not hang Mirrandooka no more?'

'No more. You go home longa Daralgoon with me.'

After that they were the best of friends, and no more sheep were speared on Daralgoon.

Five

JOSH HAD still not managed to kiss Mary Ann when he proposed. She cast down her heavy eyelids and would not answer at first. Then she looked up, and those clear golden-brown eyes the colour of the Goulburn waters, with lighter flecks in them like the netted sunbeams glancing on a shallow sandbank, gazed into his ardently. In a moment he had wound his arms round that tiny waist, as he had dreamed of doing, and kissed her full on the lips.

He thought she had fainted at first; she was so still, with her pale eyelids closed. But then he saw the rich colour in her cheeks, and concluded that she just swooned with joy. Her lips moved, and she murmured, 'Yes, dear Josh, oh yes! – if Papa will let me.'

'But surely he will let you, if you love me.'

'Oh, I do! But – but he will say I am too young, and send me away.'

Josh could not believe it, but this was just what happened. They packed Mary Ann off to stay with an aunt in Sydney.

'If your heart is set on the gel,' said Mr Hume firmly, 'you'll wait for her a couple of years, till her sisters are married and she's of an age to know her own mind. She's but seventeen, after all.'

'Two years!' said Josh bitterly.

They wrote to each other every week, at first. Sometimes twice a week. But the flat white envelopes were little consolation to Josh, inflamed by the few but passionate kisses he had exchanged with Mary Ann. On nights of full moon he lay staring out the window at the light-drenched sky, and burned with longing. Mary Ann wrote that she thought of him always, but especially when the first stars came out.

'I look at the two Pointers of the Southern Cross, deep golden, glowing like the eyes of a god, and think that you, too, may be looking at those same stars, though hundreds of miles away. Let us make a pact to go outside each evening, an hour after sunset, and look at the brightest star in that constellation. So our eyes will meet across space, and none will know it but you and I. . . .'

Josh crumpled the letter and dropped it on the floor. Eyes meeting across space! When he longed for her here and now, in the flesh, in his bed! Oh that my love were in my arms, he groaned. And another eighteen months before he would even see her. . . .

He rode to Murrundindi whenever he could get away, as even her family had a kind of charm from being connected with his love. Selina was making a series of drawings to illustrate her book 'My Wild Bush Friends', which described a platypus, a koala bear, a kookaburra, a native spotted cat, and other creatures of the wild. She had found a native cat under her bed one night, spitting and hissing, not a friendly creature at all. Betsy sang the 'Heidenroslein' to his accompaniment, almost as well as Mary Ann. She was envious of Mary Ann, and thought the tall young man with his fine head and wide-set grey eyes the handsomest she had ever met.

When their fingers touched as they went to turn a page of music on the piano stand, something of her feeling was conveyed to Josh. He gazed at the fair hair at the nape of her neck – so straight and fine, like wisps of yellow silk – and a strange feeling came over him. He loved Mary Ann, of course he did, his Maid Marian of the forest. But she was far away, and her image was fading. And here was a warm, living, attractive girl who seemed ready to fall into his arms.

Mary Ann wrote less frequently: chatty letters about parties and afternoon teas and visits to the country, but still assuring him that she loved him and *of course* she would wait for him. Josh wondered a little at the emphasis. Surely it went without saying; they were betrothed to each other, whatever her father might say.

He rode over to Murrundindi. 'Do you hear from your

sister much?' he asked the girls. 'Of course she writes to me every week, but lately – I don't know, her letters have changed. She seems to be having a gay time in Sydney.'

Selina and Betsy exchanged glances; Betsy looked down, a faint smile on her lips. Selina said, 'Her cousin has been squiring her to balls and picnics on the Habour. I think the city has turned her head a little. I wish it were me they had sent away! I long for life, for crowds of people, for bookshops and art galleries. Not parties and balls, just to be at the centre of things! Somewhere the men do not talk *sheep* all the time, and the price of wool! I long for the town, even though it is not London.'

'She might as well be in London as far as I'm concerned,' said Josh sadly.

'Poor Josh!' said Betsy tenderly. He looked at her gratefully. 'What about a song?'

'I don't feel in the mood for music, somehow,' he said.

'Would you like me to read to you? We are reading Scott's *Ivanhoe*. I read while Sel is drawing.'

'Yes! I should like that above everything.'

Betsy read well, with verve and expression. She sat in the padded window-seat, Josh on an embroidered stool at her feet. And as he sat there he became aware of a neat little foot, swinging slightly, protruding from under the hem of Betsy's morning gown. And above the foot was an ankle, and above the ankle a deliciously curved leg, and –. His mind's eye had run away with him, and for the moment he lost track of the story.

Mrs Hume came in to tell them luncheon was ready: cold mutton and tomato salad with boiled potatoes, which was what they had for the midday meal every day of the week except Sunday. This was followed by rockmelon and cream, brown bread, butter and cheese. Mrs Hume was proud that everything on the table, except the salt and pepper, had been produced on the property.

After lunch Josh took his leave. He would ride back home along the river and have a swim on the way, in a pool he knew of with a small waterfall at the top. Betsy came out with him to his horse. He pressed her hand warmly in farewell. Again he felt that electric current of attraction.

Just before he got to the boundary of Daralgoon he came to the pool where he rode his mare Nora into the water while she drank, then tied her to a bush while he stripped and dived in. There was a steep overhanging bank here, and a rocky bar which held the water back in a dark, still pool. Yet it was not still, for the river cascaded over another bar at the top, the clear brown stream dividing into glassy ropes of a golden colour like Mary Ann's eyes, then breaking into creamy foam. Green wattles shaded the far bank, making the water even darker and deeper-looking.

He had swum across the pool and was returning towards his horse when he saw a black stick floating on the water. It was not floating downstream, but seemed to be coming towards him! Almost too late he realised that it was a black snake, submerged for most of its length, and moving with sinuous undulations which did not break the surface.

He splashed water ahead of him to frighten it and flung himself backward in the same movement. The snake veered away. He swam quickly to the bank and got out, shivering with more than cold. Those bright, venomous eyes had looked into his; death had looked him closely in the face.

That night he reviewed his life so far. If he had been bitten today, if he had died, what would he have achieved? He had carved a property out of the bush, but he had no one to leave it to; here he was, twenty-seven years old, with neither wife nor sons, no one to carry on his name. He sat down and wrote to Mary Ann, asking her to marry him at once if he came to Sydney. Her father would accept the situation once they were married.

He had to wait weeks for the slow mails to travel across five hundred miles and back. When Mary Ann's letter came he sat on his bed staring at the single page: in shock; and yet he had half expected what it contained. They had been too far apart for too long. He should have gone to Sydney and taken her in his arms to ask her, not written a letter from a distance.

Dear Josh,
   I am sorry to have to hurt you by writing this letter, but –

As soon as he saw that word 'but' he knew it was hopeless. She had met someone else, she begged him to understand, she

40

would always be his friend, but she could never be more than a sister to him. . . .

'Only I don't want a sister!' cried Josh, throwing the letter on the floor. He went out and paced up and down under the stars. There was the Southern Cross, lying on its side, with the two bright Pointers above; the Mowie, old Mirrandooka had told him, was their name, and the Cross was Mirrabooka, and the Pleiades were the Meimei, seven sisters who brought the cold white frosts in their train. The natives had names for all the stars, and the Milky Way was a river lined with the campfires of the myriad dead.

That other river of light, the shining curve of the Scorpion, was rising above the trees, one of its stars glowing red like a malevolent eye. What did the stars know of human longing, the warmth of human lips and thighs, the pangs of rejected love?

Slowly his mind became calm. The stars were so bright and close, they seemed to be tangled in the branches of the river-gums. Well, he would get over it. But he doubted if he would ever forgive her.

Two months later he and Betsy became engaged, and were married in the spring from Murrundindi Station in a celebration that lasted three days, including a meal for fifty guests at a sit-down wedding breakfast in the wool-shed. There were race-meetings and kangaroo-hunts organised in the next two days, and even a cricket match. Whole families came on horseback and by spring-cart and dray. Men slept in the shearers' huts, women on verandahs shielded by canvas blinds. It was the event of the season on the Goulburn, but Mary Ann was still in Sydney and did not come home for her sister's wedding.

Josh brought Betsy home to Daralgoon after the festivities. Apart from the three-day party at her parents' home and a week's honeymoon in Melbourne, he felt that he could not spare any time away from the station at present, short-handed as he was. It was lambing-time, and he had to be out in the paddocks shooting at crows, trapping dingoes, picking up motherless lambs or occasional twins and bringing them in to be fed by hand. He came home to dinner late, tired, and stinking of sheep.

Betsy, brought up on a sheep-station, knew it must be so, but she wished they had got married at some other time of the year, perhaps after shearing, when they could have had more time in Melbourne. It seemed such a pity – here she was, roused, longing for him, hoping he would come to her in the afternoons when she felt most languorous – and instead he came in after dark, tired and irritable. By the time they had a meal and went to bed, after a brief love-making he would fall asleep and stay sound asleep till morning, when he was up with the dawn and out among the sheep again.

One night – it was full moon, when Betsy always felt romantic – he stayed out very late helping a valuable ewe that was down. The shepherds had summoned him to come and do what he could for the poor creature, with a half-born lamb which had presented wrongly protruding from its crutch. The moon was so bright that they scarcely needed lanterns, though it was well after dark when the dead lamb was delivered from the exhausted ewe.

Betsy waited and waited dinner, and at last ate a few mouthfuls herself and sent the servants off to bed. She decided to have a bath and get into her prettiest nightdress before Josh's return. She would take his mind off sheep for tonight.

The bathroom was on the verandah, and its walls did not go quite up to the roof. She had told the maids to heat plenty of hot water in kettles and fill a bucket from the fountain which remained hot whenever the kitchen stove was alight. She lay in the warm water luxuriously, soaping herself all over with a rose-scented soap.

Suddenly she had an uncanny feeling that she was being watched. She rolled her eyes round, and saw behind her, over the door, huge and black against the whitewashed wall, the most enormous spider she had ever seen. It must be five, no, *six* inches across. Oh God, it was bigger than her hand, a monster. She felt the horripilation of her scalp.

What could she do? She couldn't walk under that door, it might jump on her. She'd had a real horror of spiders since she had been a little girl, and her brother, for a joke – knowing

42

she hated them – had handed her a box from which one had run out and over her hand. She had almost fainted, then had run screaming to her mother, only to be told not to be silly because those big spiders were 'harmless'.

All she knew was that they didn't look harmless. They had big, black, jointed, hairy legs, and far too many of them. They moved sideways, very quickly, like a crab.

This one sat perfectly still, watching her. She knew it was watching her, was aware of her, and knew she was aware of it. She had nothing she could knock it down with.

'Lizzie!' she called, 'Lizzie! Help!' But the maids slept in the kitchen building, on the other side of the house.

The lamp! She had brought a kerosene lamp as well as a candle in a silver candlestick, its base an oakleaf, the holder an acorn cup. She crept out of the bath and pulled on her nightdress without bothering to use the towel, one eye uneasily on the spider in case it moved. She blew out the lamp, wrapped the towel around the hot chimney-glass and removed it. Going as close as she dared, with her eyes half closed, she threw the metal base at the creature. It missed. The spider ran across above the door, and scuttled to the right-hand wall. Betsy screamed again in fear and disgust.

She grabbed the candlestick and her dressing gown and ran through the door, along the enclosed verandah, and into the bedroom, where with trembling fingers she tucked the mosquito-net securely round the double bed. Only then did she feel safe. Josh found her still tense, staring with wide-awake eyes, her fair hair dishevelled and her night-dress damp.

'Oh Josh, oh Josh!' She sobbed out her story, while he held her in his arms. 'It was so *big*. And it kept looking at me!'

'There, there, I'll go and remove the monster if it's still there.' Josh felt big and protective as he held her close.

'You'd better empty the bath, I just left it.'

'I'll have a proper wash while I'm there. I just cleaned up roughly at one of the shepherd's huts.'

'There's an awful smell of kerosene in the bathroom,' he said, coming back. 'Did you drop the lamp?'

'Yes.'

43

'That's dangerous, you might have started a fire. Anyway, it's removed.'

'But did you *kill* it?'

'No, but I put it well out in the bush where it belongs. They live under bark in the gumtrees, you know.'

'I know. But I can't bear them in a room with me.'

'I thought you'd be used to bush creatures, a squatter's daughter like you.'

'I'm sorry, I know they're supposed to be harmless, but when Selina brought one home inside a jar because she wanted to draw it, I was nearly sick.'

'Selina is a sensible girl. You are a very feminine little girl, which is why I love you.'

Betsy was comforted. After that he always removed for her any big spiders that came into the house. But she could never bring herself to use the bathroom at night again.

Six

As THE hated shores of Van Diemen's Land – that place of hellish suffering, a Demons' land indeed – faded away astern, seeming to sink beneath the waves forever, Jamie Brown felt as if he had been reborn. He was once more a member of the human race, wearing clean cotton and flannel undergarments, and free to wander where he liked in the huge continent of Australia. He could not help whistling a tune as he strode the deck.

'I'm a free man!' He kept saying it over to himself. One day he would like to return to Canada, but at the moment he wanted to make a new life for himself and perhaps accumulate a bit of money, so that he could return as a man of substance and wipe out the shame of his departure.

The attempt at whistling ended in a fit of coughing. He had not yet recovered from the terrible privations of his early years as a prisoner, even though the last two years on the farm had been comparatively easy.

He felt a sort of terror at that cough. What if he should die of consumption, just when he was free? The thought was unbearable. The past seemed like some terrible dream from which he had recently awakened, but it had left its mark on him in his physical debility.

'I'm a wreck,' he thought. 'And only thirty-four! I must get a job in the country, in the open air. They say that Melbourne winters are wet and cold.'

He would go to a physician as soon as he landed and get him to listen to his chest.

Within five days the schooner reached the growing settlement on the Yarra Yarra. It was a warm, windy day of early spring, with white clouds flying across a blue sky. Jamie felt his spirits rise. This was his Port of Good Hope; here, in the coming summer, he would make a niche for himself in this great new land. Here he would regain his strength.

As if his luck had really turned, the very next day he landed a job as hutkeeper to a squatter from eighty miles inland in the Port Phillip District. Mr Robert Hume had a sheep station on the Goulburn River, nearly a hundred miles from its junction with the Murray – but these names meant nothing to Jamie.

Mr Hume was leaving immediately for his station, travelling slowly with one of the returning wool drays loaded with station stores.

'You've a nasty cough,' he said doubtfully, looking at the gaunt face and bony frame of his new man.

'Uh-huh. It worried me till I saw the doctor yesterday. He said it was not consumption, and all I needed was a warmer climate; my system was run down, he said, but I had a strong constitution to begin with. The cough won't stop me working,' he added eagerly.

'Can you ride a horse?'

'Sure. I often rode messages for Mr Booth when I was in Van Diemen's Land.'

He had not told his employer his whole history. He had liked at once the small, middle-aged, grey-haired man with his kindly face and his quiet air of authority, but if he

45

mentioned his convict origins Mr Hume might take him for a common felon.

'We have a most healthful climate on the Goulburn. You will soon get your strength back there, Brown. For the present you will be hutkeeping about eight miles from the homestead where there are two shepherds based, looking after three thousand sheep. They are both old hands from Van Diemen's Land, so you will have something in common.' Mr Hume was looking at him quizzically, one eyebrow lifted in the rather comical manner he had.

'Yes – er – well . . .' stammered Jamie. 'The fact is, I suppose you've guessed I didn't leave Canada with some idea of making my fortune in Australia. I was transported, but I'm not a criminal!' His dark eyes flashed. 'It was a political crime, if you like; I joined the Canadian Patriots. We were defeated, and sent to Sydney and Van Diemen's Land by the British officials who run our country. Our leaders were hanged.'

'That's all right, Brown. I'm not interested in your past, and I was sure you were not a robber or a murderer. I suppose you haven't done any shearing in Van Diemen's Land? I'm sure to be short of men next season in the shearing-shed. I pay fifteen shillings a hundred.'

'I *have* shorn a bit, but doubt if I'm up to the hard work at present. Perhaps next season I'll be fit again.' He thought it as well not to mention his first shearing attempt, when he had disembowelled one of Mr Booth's sheep.

'Well, I expect you to bind yourself to me for a year, at least. Did you say you've done some cabinetmaking, joinery work?'

'Yes, but I'm rusty, and haven't any tools. The native woods in Van Diemen's Land were very hard and dense, though there's a King William Pine found on the west coast, a softwood. Then the honeysuckle banksia wood is too soft; bootmakers used it to make their lasts, as it's easy to carve.'

'Our red-gum here is hard and fine-grained like mahogany, and there's wattle and Forest Oak along the Goulburn. We have our own saw-pit on Murrundindi, and the homestead is built entirely of local timbers,' said Mr Hume. 'Have you ever split shingles for roofing?'

'Aye, we used the wood of the peppermint-gum, it's a very free-rifted wood and easy to split.'

Talking thus to beguile the journey, and camping out twice on the way, they almost forgot they were master and man. Mr Hume noticed at once that Jamie did not call him 'sir' or touch his hat. There was something free and independent about him, a fire in his dark eyes which looked at you straight, while he spoke firmly with his soft Canadian accent which had something Scottish about it. They rode on ahead of the dray which carried the camping gear.

'I suppose the trees are very different in Canada,' said Mr Hume. 'Here, of course, our "she-oaks" are nothing like English oaks.'

'At home it was spruce and fir and maple and red pine. Red pine is soft to work, with a beautiful colour and grain; it's often oiled rather than polished.'

'I'll get you to knock up some cupboards for Mrs Hume before you go out to the hut. You'll find some woodworking tools in the blacksmith's shop.'

The station, far from coach-routes or towns, was self-supporting with its own food and clothing store, smithy, harness room, woolstore and shearing-shed, with the huts of permanent employees besides accommodation for travelling shearers making a small village round the homestead. And out on the run were the out-station huts where hutkeepers and shepherds led an isolated life, following the grazing sheep all day, penning them in at night with temporary hurdles. But to men who had had too much of being incarcerated closely with their fellow-men in prison barracks, perhaps chained to each other in a road gang, and forced to rise, go to bed, go to church, go to work, at the behest of a bullying overseer or constable, there was a wild, delicious freedom about station life.

With a well-trained dog to keep the sheep from straying too far, the shepherd could lie in the shade with a book or newspaper if he could read, or just sleep and dream away the hours. Mr Hume had given Jamie a pile of books, which he had time to read in daylight until he had to start cooking the evening meal for the three of them. The rations were generous – for a week: ten pounds of flour, a pound of sugar, two

47

ounces of tea, and as much meat as they wanted. At night Jamie had to sleep in a little outhouse like a sentrybox, with a loaded gun, ready in case dingoes attacked the sheep in the yard of hurdles. The wild dogs would kill thirty or forty in a night just for mischief, going through the flock and tearing out their throats.

So the first year passed, and with good food and temperate weather his cough had almost cleared up. He helped to bring the sheep in for shearing and took a stand in the shearing-pen where his skill gradually improved. At first he found it exhausting and could not manage a hundred sheep a day, though Mr Hume and his son Jim had put them through the sheep-wash to get rid of burrs, sand and grease.

'My neighbour up the river convinced me that it pays to wash the wool first,' he told Jamie. 'I used to send greasy wool down to Melbourne, but it means paying freight on all that useless dirt, and the wool does not bring such a good price. No, young Mr Forbes has the right idea; he first began washing his sheep in Van Diemen's Land, he tells me.'

'Forbes? Not Mr *Joseph* Forbes, of the South Esk district? He is your neighbour?'

'The very one. Not my next neighbour, but the second station further up the river, Daralgoon. Mrs Forbes is my daughter, Mr Joseph Forbes my son-in-law.'

'Good God! I mean – good gracious! He once offered me a job as overseer on his property near Campbell Town. I'd like fine to see him again; he was very good to me.'

'He's an excellent manager, and a good sheep-breeder. Already Daralgoon rams are sought after as sires.'

'No doubt he's busy with shearing at present, but will he and Mrs Forbes be coming on a visit, do you think? I'd aye hoped I might run across him on the mainland.'

'And so you shall, Jamie. I want to send an invitation down for a kangaroo hunt to celebrate getting the wool in. I'll get you to ride down with the message.'

'Thank you, Mr Hume. That'll be great. I hope he won't have left for Melbourne with his wool.'

'No, we'll cut out here first; he has ten thousand to my eight thousand, and is probably short-handed too.'

*   *   *

As he rode down the track that skirted the clear golden-brown waters of the river, Jamie thought of the strange coincidence, that Mr Josh should be living almost next door. Yet not so strange; he had left to take up land in the Port Phillip District, and most of the sheep-runs were along the bigger rivers.

If only he had been in Melbourne looking for men when Jamie arrived! He would still like to work for him, but although his year was up he felt he could not leave Mr Hume as yet, and besides it might cause trouble if the son-in-law took his father-in-law's labour away.

He went round to the kitchen building at Daralgoon when he arrived, tethering his horse outside the garden enclosure at the entrance to the cultivation paddock. Only the male cook, who gave him a surly look while he went on chopping carrots precisely into rounds, was there.

'Would the boss be in his office?' asked Jamie diffidently.

'Don't know. Why don't yer ask at Government 'Ouse?'

The house was of wood, with wide verandas on to which the rooms opened through long glass doors. He tapped at one of these on the back veranda, and a voice bellowed from a small room which opened off the back lobby: 'Who's there?'

'Mailman,' called Jamie. 'At least – I've brought you some mail from down-river.'

He heard a chair pushed back on a wooden floor, then a large young man, with the wide-set, sleepy grey eyes and big well-formed head he remembered, strolled out to the back door.

'Mr Forbes!' he said.

Josh stopped short, and then came forward with his hand outstretched. 'Jamie Brown, by the Lord! I scarce knew you, man! You've lost some weight since I saw you last.'

'Aye, I've had this rotten cough the last year, but it's nearly better. I've a job with Mr Hume at Murrundindi.'

'And how long have you been in the Port Phillip District?' asked Josh, tearing the envelope open carelessly.

'Just over a year. I got a job with Mr Hume straight away. I didn't know you were nearby, and connected to the family now.'

'Yes, Mrs Forbes is Mr Hume's daughter. Do they want a reply to this? Wait on, you'd better come in and sit down in the office while I write it. It won't take me a minute.'

He quickly wrote a note of acceptance and handed it to Jamie. 'You know there's a job waiting for you here, anytime.'

'Yes, but I can't leave Mr Hume, not yet; he's shorthanded, y'see. There's nothing better I'd like than to work for you Mr Forbes, but – '

'I know, and I respect you for it. You always were a loyal worker. I wish you were a book-keeper, these station accounts give me a headache.'

'I'm not that good with figures. I've been hutkeeping for Mr Hume, and doing a bit of shearing. And since I can ride a horse, this week I'm mailman.'

'I'll tell him what a good man he's got, if he doesn't realise it already . . . Well, Jamie, I suppose I have to let you get back to your boss.'

'If I'd known where to find you when I first arrived, I'd have come and asked you for a job,' he said. 'I'm a free man now, with a piece of paper to prove it.' And he pulled out the precious document he carried folded in his pocket.

'I'm delighted to hear it. And Mr Hume treats you all right?'

'Right as rain. Young Mr Jim's a bit impatient, but then he's young yet. I'm even saving some money.'

'That's good. So many chaps go on a bust after shearing and blow their whole cheque on bad grog. Which reminds me; tell the cook – No, wait, I'll tell him myself.'

Jamie followed him outdoors to the kitchen building detached from the house. The cook had the stove going and a kettle simmering, as he prepared the mutton stew for dinner.

'Larsen, give this man a mug of tea with a tot of rum – yes, I know you've got some "cooking rum" in your cupboard – before he goes. He's had a long ride.'

He shook hands with Jamie again, and the cook's eyebrows, which met over his eyes in a single black band, rose towards his greasy black hair. He served Jamie quite civilly with a fresh cup of tea and a generous tot of rum, with a slice of cold 'brownie' pudding.

Jamie left on the long ride home with a warmth in his chest which was not all from the refreshments. Mr Forbes had shaken his hand and said he hoped to see him again when he came up to Murrundindi for the hunt. He liked nothing better than hunting, Jamie knew. This was to be an elaborate, organised affair, with ladies present, and refreshments set out in the bush under the trees.

It was while he was riding through the bush delivering invitations that Jamie lost his pardon. He knew it was only a scrap of paper; it was ridiculous to feel so upset at its loss, for it didn't make him any more free than he was already. But he had treasured it as a memento of what he had suffered, a reminder of what he had escaped from.

Within another year, with his health vastly improved and some savings put by from his wages – for food and basic clothing went with his job, and he had nothing to spend money on but tobacco and a few extra clothes from the station store – he was thinking once more of asking for a job at Daralgoon.

Mr Hume was leaving the running of his station more and more to his son Jim, a young man Jamie found rather arrogant and difficult. The last of the daughters, Miss Selina, had married a member of Parliament and gone to Sydney to live. Jamie had been told by the station cook that Mrs Rushworth, as she was now, had not only written a book but illustrated it herself, all about wild animals and plants of the bush. This book had been a great success in England, and her father was 'like a dog with two tails, he's that proud of her!'

'He's that pleased to have got her off at last, if you ask me,' said Roberta the cook, who had a soft spot for Jamie and often gave him a slice of pie or a scone in her kitchen. 'Her bein' nearly thirty, and not what you'd call exackly a ravin' beauty. Still, she's clever, yer have to admit. I couldn't write a book to save me life!'

Which was true, for Roberta could not even sign her own name.

Once again, Jamie rode up the river with a message from Murrundindi to Daralgoon. When he went to the back door this time, the letter was taken by a tall, black-haired, blue-eyed Irish lass he had never set eyes on before.

'What's your name, then?' he asked, smiling at those blue eyes almost on a level with his own.

'Bridget, if it's any of your business. I'm the nursery-maid. And who might you be, and all?'

'I *might* be Jamie Brown from Canada; I *used* to be Jamie Brown, I know. And as far as I know, I still am.'

'A humorist, is it ye are? Well, I've no time to be talking, with the chicks to be dressed and taken for a walk.'

'Could I walk along with you a ways, d'you reckon?' asked Jamie on an impulse.

Her cool face melted into a brief smile.

'Sure, and why not? Ye can frighten the snakes from our path, it's dead scared I am all the time. There's no horrid snakes in Old Ireland.'

'Then why did ye leave it, lassie?'

Her face darkened; her brow grew stormy. 'Ye may well ask. I'll not speak of it now, indeed I cannot bear to think o' it.'

Jamie hitched his horse to a post and gave it the nosebag of chaff he had brought with him. He walked beside Bridget as she pushed the elegant London perambulator which looked rather out of place in this bush setting. They walked along the wagon-track through the bleached grass, the wild oats white as paper.

Young Hamilton, the eldest, bounded on ahead. Little Jason trotted behind him.

'May I push Ellen, please?' asked the little girl who was holding Bridget's hand.

'Are ye sure ye can manage, Miss Caroline dear? The track's after bein' that rough, ye might tip her up.'

'Of course I can manage,' said the little Miss disdainfully, standing on tip-toe to hold the pram handle. Bridget unobtrusively kept a hand on the side to steady it.

'You haven't been here long?' asked Jamie. 'In Australia, I mean.'

'Ah, no, we come out in the immigrant ship and I went straight into service up here. Me family is in Melbourne, but me eldest brother went drovin', and we don't know where he are.'

'And what made ye leave the Old Country?'

Bridget compressed her red lips; her breast heaved with emotion. She said in a low voice, 'We was driven from hearth and home by British landlords in Connemara. They sent their men to tear the thatch from our roofs and smash the winders. We could not pay the rent, ye see; it was a famine year an' the tater crop failed. . . .' Her lips were trembling. Tears stood in her blue eyes. She dashed them away angrily. 'Oh what a fine country Australia is! What a difference betwixt here and home for poor folks! Ireland is a fine place for the rich, but God help the poor!'

'The bloody British!' cried Jamie, his face dark. 'I'm sorry, Bridget, forgive me the swear-word, but the thought of them makes my blood boil.'

'Never apologise for them words to me. Bloody tyrants, the lot o' thim. Are ye not English yerself, then? Scottish, maybe?'

'Scotch-Canadian.'

'Ah! And for whoi did ye leave Mother Canada?'

'What's "bluddy", Bridget?' asked Caroline, saving him from having to answer.

'Saints preserve us!' cried Bridget. 'What are we sayin' before the childer? Hush, acushla, it manes nothing at all, just that when I cut me finger, as I was after telling Mr Brown, it was all covered in blood, and I had to wrap a spider's web around it.'

'Let me see!'

' 'Tis nothin', 'tis better now. Run on and take Jason's hand, there's me darlin'.'

Bridget seemed to have forgotten her question. Jamie decided to wait till they were alone and better acquainted before telling her his story, and that he had not left home of his own free will. He had become used to talking to women again since he'd worked where there were women servants in kitchen and dairy. He wanted to impress this girl with her deep blue eyes and curly black hair. He could not tell her yet that he had been transported, however unjustly.

The message he had delivered had been to ask Betsy to

bring the children down to see their grandmother, so Bridget went along to help and once more met Jamie Brown when he came to the big house at Murrundindi for the weekly rations.

They had both felt that instantaneous attraction of opposites, the blue eyes to the brown, while their Celtic ancestors and their hatred of British tyranny drew them to each other. They exchanged only a few words, while Bridget stood at the stove in a long apron, stirring the children's breakfast porridge which had to be made just so, or they would not eat it.

'They've niver known want, or what it is to be hungry,' she said. 'There was times back home whin we'd have eaten the pig's swill and bin glad of it.'

'I know. I know what it is to be hungry,' said Jamie quietly.

She gave him a level look from under her soft dark brows. 'Ye must tell me about Canada some toime, and the bitter winther weather with the snow fallin' and the lakes frozen. It's asier for poor folk here, with the warmth o' the sun and the firewood free for the pickin' up.'

'Yes, that's true.' He picked up the ration bags the cook had handed him, wondering uneasily if Bridget had guessed his secret. 'Well, till we meet again, Miss Bridget O'Brien.'

'And I hope that may not be too long.' She gave him a warm smile and turned back to the stove. Jamie rode back to the hut with a strange bubbling lightness in his head and heart.

He was in love, but he did not recognise the symptoms.

A travelling priest came through on horseback, seeking the faithful Roman Catholics along the river. Bridget was delighted when he offered to say Mass for her and two of the men in one of the shepherds' huts. She set a sumptuous breakfast before him in the kitchen, apologising for it:

'It's sorry I am there's no fish, Father,' she said, for it was a Friday.

'Well, now, that's what I call illigant meat,' said the priest, eyeing with pleasure the plate of fried mutton chops and onions. 'Niver mind, my girl, we must take what the Good Lord provides, when travellin'.' And after saying Grace, he fell to with a will.

'Ye're not a Catholic, I suppose?' Bridget asked the next

time she saw Jamie. She felt a motherly interest in this thin gaunt man with his sad dark eyes. He had grown a big dark moustache which, though it hid his well-cut mouth, gave new character to his face. They sat outside the dairy, where the water from washing the milk-pails and cream-pans had made the soft grass grow long and lush.

'No, I'm a Presbyterian if anything. But I'm not really anything any more. Religion was forced down my throat for so long, it's put me off for life.' He was thinking of the Sunday services in the Penitentiary in Hobart, and having to listen to prosy old Reverend William Bedford droning out his sermons, his nose red and bulbous from the port he took with dinner, his belly round from good food. The half-starved prisoners listened to him with impatience. They called him 'Holy Willie'.

Jamie plucked a blade of grass and chewed it, remembering how they used to cook the peelings from under the kitchen window.

Suddenly he found he was telling her all about it, the story pouring from him in a cleansing flood. He had never told a free person the whole story of his arrest and deportation and the embittering years as a sort of ill-fed slave of the Government; of having to pull a cart like a beast, always in danger of the lash; of feeling like something sub-human.

'I cannot tell you the worst of it; 'tis not fit for your ears,' he said. 'I could tell you tales that would make you blush to think men should stoop so low; to think of the barbarity with which man rules over his fellow man on that island . . . Some things are too disgusting, too inhuman, to mention – ' He was shuddering with emotion, his face twisted with remembering.

'Hush, hush, 'tis over now.' Bridget had taken his head in her arms, as naturally as a mother, and rocked him gently. 'Sure ye have suffered at the hands of thim rotten British, just the same as we did, bad cess to them! 'Tis all the same. And all ye did was stand up for your own country, for Canada. And for that they sent ye over the bitter wide sea as they have many sons of Old Ireland. There, there! 'Tis a free man ye are now, anyways.'

'Do ye know,' she said pensively a few moments later, 'I can never forget me old Mother, lavin' her home of forty years. She knelt by the cold hearth-stone, and made the Keen of the Empty Hearth. The roof was gone, and the winders, but the hearth and fireplace stood.'

'I wish you might share a new home and hearth with me, Bridget dear!' cried Jamie. 'I'm no longer a young man, but I'm not very old either, and I'd do my very best to make you happy –'

'You mean marry you?'

He looked up from where his head was still cradled against her soft breast, seeing the flash of doubt in her dark blue eyes. He drew her head down until he could reach her lips with his own.

'Of course, marry you! To love and to cherish, till death us do part,' he said against her mouth.

'Oh, Jamie, and here was I thinkin' ye'd never ask! But we don't have a home, nor a hearth neither.'

'But Mr Forbes would give me a job any time, he said so, and a cottage on the place, and rations. He wants me as a handy-man and carpenter about the big house, not just as a shepherd. My last year's bond at Murrundindi is nearly up, and I'm sure the boss will understand when I explain I want to get married. You could come and live with me up there, but Mr Forbes wouldn't want to lose you.'

'No, I couldn't leave the childer. Which reminds me, little Jason will be waking from his afternoon sleep! I must be off, and so must you, to get home by sunset.'

First he pulled her over in the long grass so that she lay on top of him, their eyes gleaming near together, while his strong hands moved up and down the length of her back, pressing her close. When they rose a few moments later, to go their separate ways, both were shaken by desire.

They were married by the travelling priest in the spring, as soon as Jamie had permission to leave his work and set up home at Daralgoon in one of the cottages near the big house. Betsy gave Bridget some linen from her own linen-closet. They were intensely happy in each other and in their little home by the beautiful Goulburn which talked and murmured over its gravelly bars as a background to their love, all through that first summer. Whenever he was given a bit of spare wood from the sawpits, Jamie knocked up some well-made furniture. Their only sorrow was that Bridget did not conceive, but she said it must be God's will, and Jamie felt that perhaps it was just as well, while she was responsible for the growing Forbes family, to have no little one of her own to tie her down.

Jamie had refused to change his religion, to the scandal of the priest, but agreed that any children of the union should be brought up as Roman Catholics. But by the time they all moved to the Riverina there were still no little pledges for the Church, and Bridget was past thirty. Jamie thought it was because of his sufferings in Van Diemen's Land, that somehow they had dried up his seed and made it non-productive. Or perhaps it was God's will, as Bridget said. But he hadn't much faith in God any more, after the way he had seen innocent men suffer, and cruel and wicked men flourish, in Van Diemen's Land.

Seven

Daralgoon,
February 2, 1848

My dear John,
    (wrote Josh to his brother in Hobart Town):

I have just returned from town after arranging the sale of half my wool clip at 14d per pound. Some of the wool that is of better quality I expect to receive at least 18d per lb net. Sheep are decidedly rising in price. . . .

I should like to buy some portion of my River Goulburn run, but the price of £1 an acre for Crown Land is too high. Much of the land is poor and scrubby and still covered in trees, so I cannot run more than 10,000 sheep. We are obliged to pay £25 to £30 a year for shepherds, hutkeepers and the like. There is a great shortage of labour.

In Melbourne he had attended the Squatters' Ball and danced until dawn, feeling like a gay bachelor again. Betsy was pregnant once more and could not travel with him, so he made the journey on horseback, far outstripping the slow wool-wagons. After the ball and a couple of hours' sleep he was up again to visit the wool-classer's at nine to get a price on the rest of his wool. He left the same day with the advance in his pocket, and made twenty-five miles before camping in the bush at sundown. He was up again at sunrise, and arrived home early in the afternoon, a journey of seventy miles in twenty-four hours. He was tired, but far from exhausted.

He never needed an alarm clock in the bush. The loud rollicking laughter of the kookaburras, the 'bushman's clock', always woke him at dawn. But what had driven him and made him too restless to sleep was seeing Mary Ann again at the ball: a Mary Ann still slender and young, but with an added maturity which gave a new, mysterious charm to her smooth pale face and heavy-lidded eyes.

Dancing light-heartedly in the mazurka, he had caught his breath and missed a step as he saw, across his partner's shoulder, a pile of chestnut curls, a white neck, a tiny-waisted figure in a cream lace gown as they swung past. He guided his partner round the far side of the other couple to be sure; and – yes, it was Mary Ann's unforgotten face, scarcely changed in nearly seven years.

She caught sight of him as the dance whirled her away, and he saw her eyes widen, her teeth close on a rosy lip. He watched when the dance ended and her partner guided her back to her seat by some potted palms. Was that her husband? Insufferable, long-nosed, superior-looking fellow! Josh felt as if he would like to knock him down, if only because Mary Ann was smiling at him as she fanned herself with a parchment fan.

The night was hot, airless, with an electric tension in the air after a day of north wind – the kind of weather when squatters did not like to be away from their runs for long. It was bushfire weather.

After returning his partner to their party, he made his way across the room to Mary Ann's side. He was introduced to her husband, Dugald, shook his hand stiffly, and asked Mary Ann for the next dance as the band struck up a waltz.

As they stood up and she put her small, gloved hand on his

shoulder, he felt his emotions racing away like a fire in dry grass. He had sworn he would never forgive her, but she only had to raise those clear golden-brown eyes to his to make his heart beat hotly under his starched shirt-front. It was a circular waltz, and he felt giddy with the mixture of joy and movement. Like many big men, he was light on his feet and a good dancer.

'And is Betsy well?' she asked, as he 'reversed' expertly and they revolved the other way.

'Very well – at least, she is confined to home as we are expecting another happy event.'

'Oh? You have four already, I think, two boys and two girls? Mamma keeps me informed, but I never hear from Betsy. And then, being in New South Wales, we rarely get to Melbourne.'

She fell silent, and Josh gave himself up to the sensation of the dance, the feel of her supple waist beneath his hand, the fingers of her other hand lightly in his. Mary Ann! She still looked as she had at seventeen, while Betsy had begun to thicken in face and figure, though her complexion had improved as she grew older.

He woke as from a dream when the music stopped. Daringly he asked her to walk on the terrace with him before returning to her party.

'Why, yes, since you are a relative now,' said Mary Ann. 'And the air is so close in here.'

She took his arm and they stepped out into the hot, oppressive night. Lightning was flickering, showing up huge storm-clouds piled over the city, and thunder growled. Thousands of white-ants danced in a cloud round the gas-lamps, shedding their wings in glistening heaps.

'A good thunder-storm will clear the air,' said Mary Ann. 'It has been excessively hot with the north winds, has it not? I long for rain.'

'Mary Ann! Marian! Don't make conversation, don't talk about the weather. You are as beautiful as I remembered, you haven't changed. How could you have been so cruel to me? Why did you do it?'

She drooped her heavy lids above her eyes, looking down at her closed fan. 'I fell in love with someone else. We had been apart for too long, you and I. And I was very young, Josh.'

'When I had your letter, I swore I would never forgive you.'

'And now? You have been happy, surely? And have a fine family.' She spoke sadly.

'Yes, of course. Betsy is the best of wives. She cannot help it that she is not you.'

'And you can neither forgive nor forget?'

The lightning had come nearer. A sudden crash of thunder underlined her words. Josh started, looked uneasily up at the sky.

'I can never forget you.'

'Dear Josh.' She put a hand on his arm. 'I suppose . . . I may be allowed to kiss my brother-in-law?'

Fascinated, unwilling, yet unable to resist, Josh bent his big frame towards her pale, upturned face. There was a flash, a simultaneous crash, and forked lightning sizzled down on to the terrace near the iron railings of the steps.

He grabbed Mary Ann's arm and hustled her back inside.

'What on earth – ? Don't tell me a great fellow like you is frightened of thunderstorms?' Mary Ann looked flustered and angry.

'I am, as a matter of fact. I was struck by lightning once, as a boy, and my pony was killed.'

'Goodness! I've never met anyone before who was actually struck by lightning. You certainly didn't waste any time getting inside.' She rubbed her shoulder, for in his haste he had pulled her arm rather hard, and had lifted her almost off her feet.

'Well, I always like to get under a roof when there's zig-zag lightning about.' He was feeling a reaction against Mary Ann, who was tempting him to be disloyal to Betsy, and who had cold-heartedly jilted him when they were engaged. She must have known as well as he that any kiss he gave her would not be a brotherly one.

'How long are you in Melbourne for? Shall I see you again?' she asked. 'We are sailing back round the coast, and won't be visiting Murrundindi.'

'I'm leaving first thing tomorrow,' said Josh, feeling rather glad that this was so. 'As soon as I've picked up my wool-cheque. And you – I suppose you will want to be getting back to your family.'

Mary Ann looked at him steadily. 'We have no family. Hasn't Betsy told you? It seems that I – I am unable to have children. We're going abroad this winter to consult a specialist in Switzerland, but – '

'Oh, I say!' he stammered. 'I'm s-sorry.'

'So you see I really did you a kindness. If you had married me you would have had no descendants.'

This revelation had filled Josh's mind as he rode homeward to his pregnant wife. What an escape! To think that he might have had a barren wife, no sons to carry on his name, to inherit his land!

He felt a rush of affection for Betsy, who conceived regularly almost every year.

That night over the excellent dinner Betsy provided, he said when the maids had left the room, 'I met your sister Mary Ann at the Squatters' Ball. She is remarkably unchanged in appearance.'

'Oh, yes?' said Betsy, with an edge to her voice. 'And you know why she still looks young? Mamma tells me that she cannot conceive. She has been to all sorts of doctors and charlatans, and is now off to Europe in a last effort to find a remedy.'

'Yes, I know. She told me.'

'She *told* you? Surely it is a rather intimate subject for – '

'After all, I'm her brother now, by marriage at least.'

Betsy was silent. Then she said suddenly, 'Josh, do you love me?'

He looked surprised, even awkward. 'Why, of course I love you, my pet. You are the mother of my children, and a wonderful little wife.'

'Yes, but you never say so.'

'Well, I do.'

And with this Betsy had to be content.

One of his best men was the ex-convict James Brown, who had married the nursery-maid Bridget, a free emigrant from Connemara. Bridget was a wonder with the children; there

61

were now four little Forbeses and a fifth on the way.

Young Hamilton, the eldest, was beginning to look a real little farmer in his round cabbage-tree hat of woven palm-fronds and short coat of brown holland. His younger brother Jason followed him everywhere, his black curls contrasting with Hamilton's straight blond hair. Betsy was teaching them to read and write, but later Josh would have to employ a tutor.

Josh had been enjoying some shooting, though it was so easy to pot the birds that it was scarcely a sport. The gumtrees along the river were in summer flower, and the trees seemed to boil with birds: parrots and lorikeets and honeyeaters which had gathered for the feast and became drunk on fermenting nectar, noisy and quarrelsome as men in a grog-shanty.

Much harder to stalk was the lyrebird, the Australian equivalent of a pheasant. He sent the lyre-shaped tail to his brother for a present, since Betsy refused to have it in the house, and had scolded him for shooting the bird.

'I would rather think of him looking after his hen and chicks, not adorning my drawing-room. Why do you have to kill everything? Parrots, possums, kangaroos –'

'The kangaroos were eating my grass,' he replied sulkily. 'And you must admit that possum skin rugs are soft and warm.'

'And parrot pie is very tasty. But I still feel guilty about eating the gorgeous creatures. They're more like butterflies than birds, such crimson and blue and green! But I'll be glad when the blossom is finished; the noise they make is distracting.'

'That's why it's called King Parrot Creek.'

Betsy had been born in the Colonies. Josh used to call her jokingly 'my Colonial lass'. She had no childhood memories, as he did, of English blackbirds and bluebell woods.

The Port Phillip District was still part of New South Wales, but there were strong moves for separation, led by Mr Edward Curr senior. It was expected that the separate colony of Victoria, with Melbourne for its capital, would be declared not later than 1851, with the course of the Murray River as its boundary, though the separationists wanted it placed further north, at the line of the Murrumbidgee.

Josh began seriously looking for a property north of the river, where Port Phillip landowners like young Edward Curr and John Phillips had taken up land across the Murray. Melbourne remained their nearest city and port; their fat stock and wool all went to Melbourne markets, rather than Sydney.

But it was 'Black Thursday', February the sixth, 1851, that finally decided him.

On that day the outstation at Murrundindi was burnt, and Robert Hume lost a third of his flock and two of his men; at Daralgoon they had spent a terrifying day, Betsy crouching down in a waterhole at the widest part of the river with the children and the servants.

February had opened in burning heat. The bush was tinder dry after the long, hot summer. On Thursday the thermometer, hanging in the shade of the south veranda, showed 105° Fahrenheit at nine in the morning. By noon it was 112°. The north wind had sprung up by then, bringing air like a furnace blast to shrivel the dead grass still further. Then Josh, who had been anxiously watching the sky to the north, saw what he had dreaded to see – a brown-grey stain of smoke spreading upwards into the blue. He could smell the fire upon the wind.

The bushfire had started on the south bank of the Murray, but to the east of the northward-flowing Goulburn. Fortunately for Daralgoon, the fire was so far contained in the angle between the Murray and its tributary, though burning on a ten-mile front. If it did not cross the Goulburn, Daralgoon on the south-western bank would be spared. But the river was so low near the end of summer that it did not make much of a barrier, except in the wider reaches where there were green reeds and beds of white gravel. The King Parrot Creek had ceased to flow.

Josh had already that summer ploughed a firebreak round the weaning-paddock where his most valuable ewes and lambs were now penned. The rest would have to take their chance. But he turned his prize rams into the cultivation paddock, where they would be safe among the green vegetables and melons and lucerne.

'We'd better get some troughs and buckets filled and

standing round, eh, Mr Forbes?' said Jamie. He never called Josh 'sir' and he never, never touched his hat as he spoke, as an employee would have done to the boss in England. He remembered still that brutal overseer who had made him answer 'Yes, sir!' and touch his cap when he was a prisoner. Now he was free, and the equal of any man.

The two 2,000-gallon tanks were attached to the back of the house, and were filled from the broad roof when it rained. Both were rather low at present. A smaller tank stood outside the kitchen, which was filled by the windmill pumping from the river.

Now the crackling roar increased in volume. Tongues of flame could be seen among the smoke, racing up the trees, while glowing cinders rose high on the hot currents of air.

The men kept guard all day, beating out with sheepskins nailed to green branches the small fires that the cinders caused; but the main fire did not cross the river.

Then, late in the afternoon, the wind changed. Betsy and Bridget, crouched praying in a shallow pool of the Goulburn with the children, saw the fire falter, and the smoke bend backward. They could not see the rain-clouds forming for the smoke that hid the sky, but a large drop fell, splat! on Josh's cabbage-tree hat. Soon it was raining, and the danger was over.

'Well, dear, we've escaped this time,' said Josh to Betsy that night as he bathed his smoke-reddened eyes with boracic solution. 'But next time we might not be so lucky. A botanist in Melbourne told me that the Victorian bush in summer is the most dangerous fire area in the world!'

'I'm worried about Mamma and Papa,' said Betsy.

'You needn't worry about their safety, with the river to shelter in. But their stock is another matter.'

No one had thought to look at the temperature that afternoon, but it had reached 118° Fahrenheit. Ten people had died in the fires in Gippsland that day. The hot north winds carried some black cinders right across Bass Strait, to land in Tasmania two hundred miles away.

Betsy's brother rode down the river to see how they had fared and to tell them that the Murrundindi homestead was safe, but that all the sheep on the far side of the river which could not be brought across in time were believed to have perished in the fire. Two hutkeepers living on the far boundary, about eight miles from the river, had not come in when he left, but it was hoped they had escaped.

It was only later, when they visited Murrundindi, that those at Daralgoon heard what had happened.

When the ground had cooled sufficiently – and the south-westerly change had brought a sudden drop in temperature of nearly forty degrees – Robert Hume had set out with his head stockman to look for the men. At the outstation they had found the clay-packed log walls still standing, though charred black, and the roof of bark completely burnt. They poked about inside among the still smouldering ruins, but found no charred bodies as they had feared.

'I pray God they reached the river. They may be at the homestead by now,' said Mr Hume.

'Or burnt somewhere in the bush. We might never find 'em,' said the other gloomily. They were both depressed by the heaps of grisly sheep bodies, their wool melted and crisped and black. There were none about the hut, yet there was a smell like boiled mutton in the air.

They stared at the iron water-tank – buckled with the heat, blackened with smoke – then at each other.

'You look!' said Mr Hume. 'I can't – I daren't – '

The stockman hesitated, then climbed on the tankstand and looked in. . . . He fell back with a yell, and began to retch.

The two men had been boiled alive. They must have climbed into the water when the fire came close, thinking to save their lives. With the intense heat as the hut roof burned the water had begun to boil. They must have been overcome before they could scramble out.

Only a month after the big fires, the gold-rushes began. At first, the Colonial authorities tried to hush up the finds, fearing the effect of a stampede like the one to California earlier: the wholesale absconding of convict and indentured servants, properties left without shepherds and stockmen, cities bereft of policemen. But gold was there in vast quantities, and the fact could not be hidden forever.

When more rich finds were found near Hill End, and then at Ballarat and Bendigo, the stampede was on. Immigrants poured into Victoria and New South Wales. Josh and his neighbours were left short handed on their unfenced runs, without shepherds or hut-keepers. Josh put up short fences across several bends of the Goulburn, thus making sheep-proof enclosures.

The only men not infected by the madness, it seemed, were the Aborigines. They had often found the yellow, heavy metal or seen the gold-dust glittering in watercourses, but did not value it at all. A good sharp flint which would flake into a cutting tool was much more valuable than a lump of the soft yellow stone. When Josh was desperate, he asked help of old Mirrandooka, who gathered some tribesmen to mind sheep in return for a weekly feast of mutton.

Then, on a trip to Melbourne with wool – now averaging 1/6d per pound – he met Mr William Brodribb, who said he was about to buy Wangarella Station, a property of 250 square miles north of Deniliquin, 'quite a large sheep-walk in the western portion of New South Wales, known as the saltbush country, or the blacksoil plains.'

He said that this saltbush, both annual and perennial, would survive through the longest drought, when grass would wither away; and it was safe from bushfire. It had been found to be excellent fodder, the sheep thrived upon it.

Josh made up his mind to move before the next summer.

He knew he had a buyer for Daralgoon in the neighbour who had squatted on such poor land and who had always coveted his pastures. The neighbour had not lost any stock in the bushfires.

Josh found a station property advertised with a thirty-mile frontage to the Edward River – which meant plenty of water, and also somewhere to swim in summer – with a fourteen-year lease from 1852 on 50,000 acres, besides 1,500 acres of freehold about the homestead. Best of all, there were 50 miles of post-and-rail fencing.

The older Humes had now retired to Melbourne and Betsy's brother Jim was running Murrundindi, so she did not mind leaving the Goulburn.

Little Philomena cried when told of the move, because she thought she would have to leave her pet magpie behind, but Bridget reassured her: 'Sure, Miss Philly, he'll be after ridin' on top of the load as proud as a lord, and givin' us a bit of a song in the mornin's and all. We'll be goin' to the banks of another grand river and he won't know he's been moved at all, at all, once we're settled in.'

'But what if he gets off the dray, and gets lost?' She knew he couldn't fly away, for his wing was cut, and he spent most of his time running about the large fowl-pen with the fowls, trying to cluck like a hen. 'Indeed, I think the bird thinks he is just a hen of a different colour,' said Bridget when she saw him first.

But no hen could sing as gloriously as Benjamin, who carolled and warbled an effortless, full-throated, bell-clear song from the top of the woodheap each dawn, then strode off with his strutting aldermanic walk in his white-satin waistcoat and black tail-coat, looking from left to right for a juicy bug or caterpillar.

They decided to tie a string round his leg for the journey, just to be sure.

Josh managed to secure three stockmen to drove his flock of sheep to New South Wales, along the stock-route which followed the Goulburn to Seymour, then crossed the big river at Maiden's Punt. They could travel only seven miles a day and would probably camp a bit longer where the feed was good, so they were not likely to arrive at Tumbudgery Station, sixty-five miles from the border, for at least two months. He knew the men would desert him once they had been paid; they took the job only because they wanted to get to New South Wales and the goldfields north of the river, having failed to strike it rich at Ballarat. The only man whose loyalty he was sure of was Jamie.

He depended on his overseer, Bailey, to stick with him, and to see that the men did not desert the travelling sheep. He had sold his two-tooth wethers and the new season's lambs (too young to travel well) to the new owner, besides some of the older ewes, and had purchased 20,000 sheep with the new property.

He went ahead with his family and the four spring drays

loaded with furniture, servants and children. As they travelled they left behind the green gullies where bell-birds chimed and tinkled, *Chink! Chink! Chink!* from every tree. Flowering paperbarks and river-oaks leant above the clear brown water. Bridget drove one dray, Jamie Brown another, and himself the third; while the last was driven in turn by young Hamilton, now nearly eleven, and an old handy-man and ex-convict, Dan, who was not interested in finding gold.

They made camp at the beautiful junction of the Goulburn with the Murray, where the children watched fascinated as the glass-clear snow waters of the upper Murray were met by the equally clear but peat-brown flow from the southern plains. The two streams ran distinctly side by side before they mingled.

They had been entertained at station homesteads on the way up the Goulburn and had made easy stages, stopping the last night at Sheppard's run, Tallygaroopna. Now they pushed on to Maiden's Inn on the New South Wales side.

After seeing his family installed at Tumbudgery, Josh was going to return by way of Deniliquin (where there was still no bridge over the Edward, as there was none over the Murray) to supervise the crossing of his prize rams and pedigree Merino ewes over the Murray, by either Maiden's ferry or the new one installed by Henry Hopwood. (He had also come from Van Diemen's Land and was said to be an old lag though he never admitted it.) Because of the ferry charges much stock was swum across the river, especially cattle and horses; there was a rate for each wheel of a cart or buggy, and for each animal. People, unless on horseback, travelled free. Josh was not going to risk his prize rams getting drowned, whatever the ferry might cost. Daralgoon rams were sought by stud breeders wishing to improve their fleeces. He had now bred animals which yielded fifteen pounds of wool per fleece.

They travelled north through sandhills enamelled with wildflowers, crowned with forests of dark Murray Pine, which gave way to the more slender, greener cypress of the inland plains. Deniliquin was already a town, five years old, in 1853.

It would be nearer than any town was on the Goulburn when they lived there, Betsy noted gratefully. But when she saw the One Tree Plain stretching away to the north, bare and empty, she raised her hands in horror.

'What a desolate, dreary place!' she cried. 'And so flat! The horizon stretches so far, you might almost be at sea.'

'You've never been at sea except Bass Strait.'

'No, but Grandpa Coggin used to tell me about it, and show me his silver watch that crossed the Equator eleven times, and still kept good time.'

'It won't be like this about the homestead, my dear,' said Josh. 'There are big red-gums along the Edward River, besides Grey Box and Cypress Pine on the sandridges, though some have been cut down for fencing. And we will have –' He took out the letter from the former owner's agent and read:

An eight-roomed brick residence with slate roof, a large cellar, detached kitchen with two bedrooms for servants, men's huts, store-shed 56 feet by 33 feet, stables and cart shed, large woolshed roofed with iron . . .

Betsy was mollified at the thought of the slate roof and the large cellar – an absolute necessity in Australian summers. Fresh-killed mutton could be hung there in muslin bags away from the blowflies and the heat, butter would keep cool, and jellies could be set.

Native-born though she was, she felt strange as they travelled through that wide, weary countryside, flat or gently undulating, with the river and its bordering trees on their left. To the northward stretched the blue-grey saltbush, the dark grey of the blacksoil plains, and over all the bare hard blue of the sky, where crows passed wavering like cinders from a bush fire, dropping their harsh and melancholy *Ahr-ah-ahhr!* as they flew.

Tumbudgery homestead, with its solid buildings and green garden watered by irrigation from the river and fenced away from the hungry sheep and horses by a neat picket fence, was a relief to the eye. A climbing floribunda rose in a delicate tea-rose colour trailed up the veranda posts outside the front door. Galahs in a massive flock wheeled up from beside the house, grey-white backs against the sky, then as they turned, one pristine flash of rose from five hundred coloured breasts. Betsy, who had been depressed by the crows, thought it a good omen. Roses and rose-coloured birds! The future must be auspicious here.

She watched the birds come in to drink at sunset: instead of noisy King parrots there were pale quarrians, green budgerigars in vast flocks, tiny masked finches with the faces of baby owls, while great white cockatoos screeched discord from the river gumtrees.

Since women servants had been almost impossible to get, Betsy had learned from the age of fifteen the arts of baking bread, making preserves, making soap and candles from tallow, roasting meat and baking pies and puddings. Josh knew that he was lucky, that she was a good wife, though after six children – four girls and two boys – she was by now turning grey and had lost her neat figure though she was not fat.

There had been severe flooding in 1852 along the inland rivers, which had left a new deposit of dark river silt around the homestead. This should help to produce outsize melons and potatoes for years to come. Josh had brought some fruit-tree cuttings, some of them buds of those he had brought with him from Tasmania years ago, and proceeded to plant apricots and peaches, though he feared it was too hot for the apples. There was an established grove of orange and lemon trees above the river bank, though some had been washed away in the floods.

The reason the station was on the market (he did not tell Betsy this) was that the previous owners had lost a little girl, a toddler, who had been swept away by the flooded river. The mother could not bear to stay there any longer.

On his return to the Murray, Josh rode one horse and led another with tent and cooking equipment, his tin billycan, frying-pan and spare quart-pot and pannikin jingling merrily as they trotted along. He spent the first night in a camp of bullock drivers, a dozen teamsters all pulled in together for companionship, camping under their drays.

They had a good fire going. He shared their damper and tea

and good fellowship, though one bearded fellow eyed him in a rather unfriendly fashion, and asked:

'You're a cove, ain'tyer?'

'Eh?'

'You're a cove – a station boss.'

'Oh, yes, just bought Tumbudgery.'

'They use horse-teams from there mostly.'

'Could have used boats in the flood, I hear.'

'Yair. She was an Old-Man flood, all right.'

The men, their clothes and faces caked with the dust of travelling behind their heavy-footed teams, were discussing with great indignation a new and officious police constable appointed to Deniliquin. He had charged one of their number who was moving his team along the main street, with 'swearing in the streets'.

All present voted that it was not possible to move a team without swearing at it. No self-respecting bullocky would try, his bullocks wouldn't understand.

'And orl I said was,' the aggrieved driver was telling them, '"shift yer bloody carcasses, you cross-eyed flamin' misbegotten bastards, or I'll bloody well have yer blanky hides for boot-leather!" No one could object to "blanky" now, could they?'

All present agreed that no one could object.

'And I was perfeckly sober, what's more!' added the bullocky indignantly. 'Hauled into court, I was, and fined five bob! My bloody oath! I should've punched that blasted constable on the nose.'

And all present agreed, Josh abstaining from the vote.

He turned in and slept under the stars. The shining Scorpion lay along the East, for the winter constellations were just returning. He had waited till April to start the move, so that it would not be too hot on the road, and the night was clear and crisp. The bullock-bells sounded a hollow, sweetly mellow tone, as the teams moved about in their hobbles after grass. Josh felt supremely content. 'Life begins at forty', they said. Well, he would be forty in another year, but he had never felt so alive and well since he was a young man setting out for his midlands farm in Van Diemen's Land. As soon as the mortgage was paid off, he would acquire another 10,000 acres of

71

backblocks, land away from the river that so far no one wanted, and build big earth-tanks (using horse scoops) to hold the scanty rainfall and the run-off from small creeks. If there was not enough water for washing the sheep, well, he would send greasy wool down to Melbourne.

He must have plenty of land to leave his sons. And he would like to breed some more sons to carry on his name. Only two boys so far, and the rest girls. (Betsy's last two had not lived.) Well, he would work at it when they were settled in their new bedroom at Tumbudgery. He felt his loins stir at the thought. He smiled to himself in the darkness, rubbing a hand over the stubble that was beginning to itch on his chin. Perhaps he would grow a beard. . . .

He rose with the dawn, to a glorious chorus of warbling magpies, and prepared his favourite breakfast: strips of bacon first boiled lightly to remove the saltiness, in the separate quart-pot he kept for the purpose, while his tea brewed in the other, then fried gently till crisp in some mutton fat. He arranged the strips on a hunk of Betsy's delicious bread, fried in the remains of the fat, and washed it all down with a mug of sweet, black tea.

He was beginning to put on weight round the middle, but he had the height to carry it, he told himself. The plaited rawhide belt which kept his moleskins above his hips, dipped below his belly in a wide curve. It no longer circled a trim waist. But for the rest, he was hard, muscular, fit for long days in the saddle or as 'boss of the board' at shearing time. The men liked him because he was not aloof, but would sit down with them in camp or in their huts to share a pannikin of tea or a tot of rum; at the same time they respected him and knew he was boss.

He would soon have 80,000 acres and perhaps 40,000 sheep, depending on the carrying capacity of the backblocks. But if saltbush feed was as good as old Brodribb said it was, he might run a sheep to two acres back there, once the tanks and dams were installed. And if he wanted to sell fat lambs instead of keeping them for their wool, there was the stockroute leading straight down the Edward to Deniliquin, then over Maiden's or Harry Hopwood's punt on the Murray, and so down to the hungry hordes at the Bendigo and Ballarat fields. He couldn't lose. They said there would be paddle steamers on all the inland rivers before long; one boat had managed to get as far as Walgett on the Darling, and two had gone up the Murray all the way to Albury. Soon he might be able to ship his wool from his front door right down to the sea.

Eight

JAMIE AND Bridget settled in happily in their cottage at the new station on the banks of the Edward River. The Forbes children were growing up and no longer needed a nursemaid, for though Mrs Forbes seemed to get pregnant nearly every year, there had been two still-births and several miscarriages. Bridget handed over her charges to the governess Miss Thomas, for whom she did not conceal her dislike.

'Herself expectin' to be called "Miss Thomas" and puttin' on airs and graces like a lady,' said Bridget scornfully. ' "Bridget", she says, "see that the childer've finished breakfast by eight-thirty," she says. "I want them in the schoolroom by nine o'clock sharp." And "You can fetch me tray to the nursery, I'll be takin' luncheon there." No eatin' in the kitchen for her, if you please! And for why should I be workin' me feet to the bone runnin' messages for her that's only a paid servant like the rest of us? Sure, an I felt like tellin' her to fetch her own tray, the lazy cow.'

Jamie laughed at her. 'It's just because she's *not* one of the family that she tries to boss you around,' he said. 'It's because she's unsure of herself.'

'And tellin' the kiddies there's no leprechauns and Little People in Ireland, makin' me out a liar!'

It had taken Bridget some time to get used to their new surroundings. Coming from small green Ireland, she had found the Victorian bush strange enough, but that was a green paradise compared to this! There were big red-gums along the river banks, but beyond the sandridge on which the homestead was built, the empty blacksoil plains stretched to the horizon, dotted with dark clumps of cypress pine. Bridget carried in her bones a feeling for green hills and misty rain. Here the skies were of a hard, polished blue, or filmed with dust; huge white birds with demonic voices roosted in the river gums; dry roly-poly and grey soil and blue-grey saltbush stretched as far as the eye could see. She could not get used to it. But, as Jamie pointed out, it was safe from bushfire; and if he hadn't moved to Daralgoon to work for Mr Forbes, he might have died with the two hutkeepers on Murrundindi.

Then, in the eighth year of their marriage, she became pregnant. In this barren place she had become fruitful at last. Not without difficulty and danger, for she was no longer young, she presented Jamie with a healthy son.

Bridget's happiness was complete.

'Since I may never have any more,' she said, 'we'll give him all the names I've saved up: Thomas Patrick James Brian Boru –'

'Have a heart!' said Jamie. 'The priest will twist his tongue over that lot and never be able to say Mass again. And think of the poor little blighter filling in forms when he grows up, or signing on for shearing. He'll curse us for saddling him with all those names. Just Thomas Patrick –'

'But I wanted to call him after you, me darlin'!'

'Well, Thomas Patrick James then.'

'I'd like fine to have a Brian Boru,' said Bridget wistfully.

'Then we'll have another son.'

But they had no more children, and Thomas Patrick James Brown, born in November 1855, became the only descendant to carry on his father's name in Australia, until his own son was born.

Jamie had long cherished the hope of returning to his native Canada one day. His old parents must now be dead. He had lost touch with them long ago, and anyway as good Presbyterians they would be horrified at his marrying a Roman Catholic, though he had not 'turned'. He began saving for a trip home, but first he would get a pony so that Tommy when he was old enough could learn to ride and take himself to school in Deniliquin. He and Bridget were determined that Tommy should get an education.

Unlike his parents, young Tom breathed the dust of the

western plains from the time he was born. He knew the streaky skies, when the white mares' tails were teased out across the blue, that heralded summer; the magnificent thunderstorms, when the sky turned a dark, bruised colour and the wide expanse of saltbush gleamed with unearthly light; and in winter the clear green and apricot that came after sunset, with a planet glowing low down in the west like a heavenly lamp.

When one of the rare rainstorms came after a hot day, Tommy would run out into the pelting rain, while the gidyea began to give off its peculiar smell. Years later, travelling to Bourke at the beginning of shearing, he put his head out the train window and breathed that nostalgic scent in great gulps.

One of Jamie's jobs was to repair the windmills that raised water from wells to fill the troughs on the backblocks. He would take young Tommy with him in the wagonette loaded with tools. The windmill sails were of wood, which could easily be damaged in strong winds. (Near the homestead, a horse working a whim, walking in circles all day, was a more certain way of lifting water from the river.)

Canvas or iron buckets were used, lifted on huge hempen well ropes. Then someone invented the self-emptying bucket, so that a windmill could be left working, if there was any wind, filling the stock-troughs and tanks without supervision.

Tommy loved to be out on the run with his father, often camping overnight. It was good, too, to return to the weather-board cottage that was home, with its smoke-yellowed walls over which were pasted newspapers, pages of *The Illustrated London News* and *The Australasian*, and any other magazines Bridget could get her hands on. There was no picture of the Royal Family, Victoria and Albert and their numerous children, in their kitchen which was the living-room in winter. Bright parrots cut from Arnotts biscuit-tin lids were nailed on the wall each side of the wood-burning stove. There was an old sofa covered with a faded cretonne, leaf-patterned in blue and brown, and here Tommy loved to lie and watch the glow of the stove reflected on the absorbed, contented face of his mother, on her soft Irish complexion and black hair in which were a few streaks of grey.

*   *   *

Within six years Josh Forbes had doubled his flocks and increased his Tumbudgery run to 150 square miles. His brother John, in small, green Tasmania, was astounded that anyone could need or want so much land. But an acre of Riverina soil would support only half a sheep, and less in the backblocks of the station, Josh explained.

His eldest son Hamilton, named after Kate's family, and young Jason in his long summer holidays, were now doing much of the work of overseeing and mustering, but Josh refused to let the reins of management out of his own hands. Men were beginning to drift away from the goldfields looking for work; his labour troubles seemed to be over, and anyway he had several good part-Aboriginal stockmen who sat a horse with ease and whose families lived in humpies on the river-bank. He paid the men a wage no white man would accept and sold them shirts, boots and hats from the station store.

He had become hard, demanding, completely absorbed in his stock-records and stud-books. His mouth that had once been young and soft was now a thin uncompromising line; his grey eyes had become slits in the leather-brown of his face, and his hair like his father's had receded, leaving a scalp like a brown, polished nut.

Though he was mean about small expenses like new dresses for the girls or riding-boots for the boys, Josh spared no expense to improve the quality of his flocks. The sheep he had bred from the old ewes descended from Tasmanian pure Saxon Merinos, he now improved by selecting his best ewes and mating them with Rambouillet rams. He wanted to breed a larger, more robust, heavier-woolled type with a broad back, to stand up to summer heat. He thought he might produce a ram which would yield a record thirty pounds of greasy wool. He kept careful records of the yields of individual sheep, descendants of Old Grimes and other famous sires. Breeding was carefully controlled so that no stray stock got into the breeding-paddocks.

About the time Jason was nearly ready to leave school, Betsy was feeling unwell, and increasingly estranged from her husband. She had produced eight children, including two infants who died, and had three miscarriages in the eighteen years they had been married. She felt she was being used simply for breeding by Josh, who wanted more sons to work his miles of property.

'Don't go and drop another ewe this time, Betsy,' he had said jocularly, but she was affronted. She hated his obsession with breeding and the prowess of rams. He had become coarse and inconsiderate, and the whole business disgusted her. She kept the girls resolutely away from the breeding-paddocks when a ram was introduced to the ewes. Ram! The very word was offensive. Her father would not have dreamed of discussing such subjects at the tea-table, yet Joseph did.

He came in earlier than usual while they were having afternoon tea, a gathering he usually missed, as he liked to stay out among the sheep till sunset, which now at the equinox was about six p.m. He flung himself down in a brocaded armchair and sat brooding, with his chin down on his chest, staring at the floor.

'Philomena, ring for another cup for your father,' said Betsy. 'What would you prefer, Joseph, China or Indian?'

'Eh? Oh, *tea*!' he said, as if the imbibing of tea was not the purpose of the present gathering, but some exotic subject she had wilfully introduced. 'I don't care . . . Indian.'

'What is the matter?' asked Betsy, not very sympathetic-ally, while the girls looked at him with scared eyes.

'Matter? I'll tell you what's the matter. That new ram, the one I paid the earth for, offspring of Emperor: he's sick, off his tucker. And not performing properly.'

'Oh?' His wife had stiffened her back very slightly. She took the new cup and saucer from the maidservant and lifting the big china teapot, poured delicately.

'Yes, I'm wondering if there's a patch of Darling Pea got into the home paddock, though I can't believe we'd have missed it. If he dies . . . I should have insured against his loss.'

'Can you insure the life of a sheep?' asked Caroline, carefully avoiding the word (like 'bitch' for a female sheep-dog) which her mother regarded as indelicate.

'Of course, if he's valuable. It's just a form of life insur-ance.'

'Perhaps the cold snap has affected it,' said Betsy. 'It will probably be all right in a day or two.'

Josh, irritated at her referring to his treasured possession as 'it', took a shortbread biscuit and dipped it in his tea. 'If you are referring to Rajah of Canally,' he said, 'I hope you may be right; however he is not, in spite of his pedigree, a pampered weakling to be affected by a change in the weather. Good Lord, he yields fifteen pound of scoured wool at one clip. That should insulate him against cold snaps.'

'I feel sorry for the little first-year lambs,' said Eliza, 'without their coats in the cold. Why does the Bible say "The wind is tempered to the shorn lamb"? It isn't, you know. I've seen them huddling in a bit of shelter. . . .'

'Would you rather I turned them all into lamb chops?' asked her father. 'At least they're alive still. And *you* have warm woollen stockings and scarves to wear when you go down to Melbourne.'

'Papa, can we go down to St Kilda for Christmas, it is going to be so hot?' said Philomena, seeing an opening.

Josh frowned. 'I don't see any need for you all to go traipsing off to Melbourne. It will cost – '

'Not nearly as much as your old ram,' said Ellen pertly.

'Wait till I take first prize at the Royal Sydney Show, my girl. Then we'll see who's wasting money. In fact, we'll all go down to Sydney, stay at the Wentworth – '

'When? When?'

'Next year, for the Show.'

'But that's *ages* away.'

'Perhaps Hamilton could take you to the River Murray at Albury for a few weeks. It's not nearly so far as Melbourne or Sydney. And I hear there are some steamers on the Murray now, carting wool and carrying stores, and some have been fitted up for carrying passengers.'

'Wouldn't it be fun if they came right up the Edward to Moulamein and Deniliquin?' said Philomena.

'H'm, it would certainly be a good way of getting my wool down to Melbourne. Echuca is only a hundred and fifty miles from the coast.'

The question of Christmas holidays was dropped for the time being; the ram recovered, and Josh, restored to good humour, announced that they would all go down to Albury after shearing; he would escort them himself. The girls pouted, for they wanted to visit the shops in Melbourne. Still, Albury was the next best thing; it had several good hotels and quite large stores, with a population that had grown from a few hundred to six thousand in the last ten years. And there was boating on the river, and tennis . . .

Betsy, being pregnant again, decided she would not make the long journey to Albury but stay home and keep her feet up. She felt too tired for any activity these days. Each pregnancy, in the long hot summers, seemed to sap her energy more than the last.

'Miss Thomas can chaperone the girls,' she said. 'I have plenty of sewing to do, and Bridget will look after me.'

She did not like Miss Thomas much: a plump, pale-eyed young woman whose mother had come to New South Wales as personal maid to Governor Macquarie's wife. She was well educated, no doubt, but lacking in breeding.

It was as well, Betsy thought, that their father was going along to control young Jason, who would be home for the summer holidays; he was growing to be rather a handful. The boy, with his black curls and rosy cheeks, not yet bronzed to the usual sallow tan of the outback, was like neither of his parents.

He was her favourite, but he could not get on with his father. Fiercely protective of his mother, he had once kicked Josh in the shins when he was shouting at her angrily over some household disaster – the cook on strike, and no bread baked for the shearers who were threatening to walk off the station with half the sheep unshorn.

Josh had rather a bad name with shearers as a tough boss, though not so careful as 'Hungry' Tyson of Deniliquin station which was avoided by swagmen and sundowners looking for a free meal. One disgusted traveller had scrawled on the wood gate:

> You'll get rather thin
> At Deniliquin,
> It's got neither tucker nor grass . . .

At Tumbudgery there had not been enough huts for shearers the first year, so Josh put them up in tents. He had sixteen men enrolled, and half of them walked off, complaining that they should be given proper accommodation. Josh took them to the magistrate's court at Deniliquin and charged them under the Masters and Servants' Act, which provided penalties for shepherds who lost sheep, convict servants who absconded, and shearers who broke their contracts. The shearers were ordered to go back to work, or pay a fine of £9 each.

'That'll teach them!' he said with satisfaction when he returned from court in Deniliquin. But the fact remained that the men were disaffected, kept declaring the sheep 'wet' or the wool 'sandy' and the shearing took twice as long as it should have. Then the rains came and bogged his wool-wagons on the blacksoil plains. Loaded with their square bales of wool, the high-piled wagons leaning into the ruts looked like great galleons crossing the level, waveless sea of the plains. He was using horse-teams, which when the track was good could cover in a fortnight the route which took the bullock-teams a month.

To Betsy the river flats covered with blue-leaved, dark-trunked box trees, the sand ridges topped by thickets of cypress pine, as symmetrical as Christmas trees or candle-flames, began to take on a certain beauty, and the low blue-grey saltbush, seeming so monotonous at first, could be breathtakingly lovely in heavy dew or frost, each leaf coated with sparkling silver. Only the gidyea she could have done without. After the first rains, as the air became damp it gave off a horrible distinctive smell, 'Like a mixture of bad drains and squashed bugs!' as Eliza declared with unladylike emphasis.

It was when the family came back from Albury that Betsy first noticed the change in Miss Thomas. It was nothing definite that she could put her finger on; but there was a new assurance about her, and a sort of sly smiling air which was puzzling.

Then Jason let something fall at breakfast, when Miss

Thomas had failed to appear because of a sick headache and Josh had gone out early to inspect some fencing.

'Huh – she just stayed up too late last night,' said Jason.

'What do you mean? You should have been asleep, anyway,' said Philomena.

'Well, I heard her and father talking on the veranda, and then the clock struck twelve.'

'What was that, Jason?' said his mother sharply.

'Father and Miss Thomas. They were always having long talks on the balcony at the Albury Hotel, too,' he muttered.

Josh was still sleeping in the office since his return. She did not know what time he went to bed.

'Don't gossip, Jason,' said Caroline sharply. 'You shouldn't be eavesdropping.'

'I wasn't. I got up to get a drink of water, and it was moonlight, and I stopped to look out of the window, and I heard them – '

'That's quite enough!' said Betsy firmly. 'Eat up your porridge, and then you can run out to the orchard and pick some oranges for me. Hurry up now!'

She said nothing to Josh, but she began to watch, and notice the little attentions he paid the governess.

The *Pastoral Times* of Deniliquin, announced in March, 1859:

Birth. At Tumbudgery Station, Edward River, to the lady of Joseph Forbes Esq., a daughter.

There was no rejoicing at Tumbudgery. Josh strode about with a brow of thunder, having looked indifferently at the tiny red-faced bundle with its wisp of thin dark hair. He did not conceal his disappointment. Betsy scarcely cared. She did not recover her strength, so the nurse stayed on and Betsy kept to her bed.

The sickly baby wailed and mewled. When put to the breast she sucked hungrily for a while, then threw herself back with surprising strength and screamed with what looked like anger. Her eyes were screwed up tight, her mouth was wide open, her puny fists beat the air.

'I think she's just hungry,' said the nurse. 'She's sucking nothing but air, you don't have the feed for her. We'll have to put her on to cow's milk and water.'

'Let me try again,' said Betsy, but she had little feeling for this scrap of flesh, begotten on an unwilling dam by a sire that did not want her now she was born. If only it had been a son, how different things would have been, she thought. She herself would have been a heroine, pampered and petted, as she had been when Jason was born. Now she felt nothing but a great weariness. She had set out to snare Joseph, to make him forget Mary Ann and marry her instead, and much joy it had brought her! Though she'd been happy the first year or so.

The baby daughter – she had called her Sarah Jane – became smaller instead of growing. Her little belly grew larger, but her arms were like sticks, with the flesh hanging on them in folds. She began vomiting her bottle-feeds, the half-digested curds flying out of her mouth as though shot from a gun.

'Projectile vomiting!' said the nurse. 'I think we should take her into the hospital at Deniliquin, as Dr Scott suggested. She is simply not getting enough to eat.'

Betsy looked at her listlessly. 'You mean she might die?'

'Yes – of malnutrition. She is taking sufficient milk now, but she can't keep it down.'

Betsy unwrapped the little bundle, so quiet and apathetic, and stared at the big, dark eyes in the wizened face. 'Why were you born?' she thought. 'He cares more for one of his newborn lambs.'

She told Joseph they would have to go to the hospital. He grumbled at the expense but got out the buggy to drive her in to Deniliquin. At least, he thought, they could get rid of the nurse now.

Betsy said she would stay in town, while the baby was admitted to the new hospital. But it was too late. The doctor said he could do no more, and within a week Sarah Jane was dead. Betsy felt a numb indifference. She had had no milk for the baby. It was as if her body rejected the idea of mother-hood; her milk had flowed in a fountain for her earlier babes.

When she had recovered from the birth, Josh moved back into her room. She lay and watched him hanging his trousers across a chair, shrugging off his open-necked shirt. She looked at his absurd paunch, so round and full, like a pregnant woman's, above his still lean and sinewy legs. And she found herself thinking, what if it was *he* who had to carry the babies and bear them and see them die; and what if *he* had to carry that uncomfortable burden in the heat and feel sick and heavy-bodied – above all to have to wear the layers of stifling skirts and high necked long-sleeved dresses that *she* had to wear?

'Josh!' she said suddenly. 'I don't want any more babies.'

He stopped with one sock off and one sock on, like John in the nursery rhyme, and stared at her in the lamplight.

'What on earth do you mean?' He looked astounded. 'You're my wife, aren't you? Eh? What d'you expect me to do? Get a black gin to take your place, rear up a lot of yellow brats like you see round these bachelor stations? I won't do it. What's more, I want another son.'

'But I don't.'

She was in tears now, her brief rebellion almost over.

'Aw, come on Betsy, I've been missing you all this time. You still want your old man, don't you? Come on, girl.'

He was in the bed now, edging his weight on top of her, the battering-ram forcing an entry at the closed gates of the citadel. No use. Ram, ram, ram, she thought dully, lying like a log beneath him. Ram me full of another child; you're not the one who has to bear it. Lord Josh of Tumbudgery, champion sire of the district . . . The lady of Joseph Forbes, Esq. has dropped another ewe. I wouldn't mind, she thought, if he had a string of black gins, or if he got a son on that plump little governess, as long as it wasn't me who has to bear this, year after year after year . . .

The son, if it was a son, never reached full term. Betsy miscarried at five months and died lying in a bath of her own blood, hallucinating that she was a sheep going down the race at the abattoirs where someone waited with a knife to slit her throat. She stopped screaming only when she was too weak to utter a sound.

Jason came home from his Melbourne boys' school for the

funeral. Hamilton had already left college to help his father manage the station, and Josh had promised him the back-blocks for himself next year, when he would be nineteen.

'I want to leave at the end of the year, too,' said Jason when he came home.

'But you're only fourteen!' said Hamilton.

'What if I am? You can leave school at twelve.'

'Yes, but Mamma would have wanted you to finish – '

'Don't talk to me of Mamma!' said Jason in a choking voice. 'He killed her, the hateful beast.'

'Jason! You can't – '

'Well, it's true. She'd hardly recovered from the last baby, and he couldn't wait to start another. She wasn't well when we went to Albury. He didn't care about her.'

The girls, swollen-eyed from weeping, were sent down to St Kilda on Port Phillip Bay for a holiday with Miss Thomas.

'I know you will look after my motherless girls for me,' said Josh. He was shocked at Betsy's loss after nearly twenty years of marriage. She had been buried in the Deniliquin cemetery next to the tiny grave of Sarah Jane, in the 'good sandy loam' which Surveyor Townsend had noted in his report ten years earlier.

Deniliquin had become something of a boom town. It was now a prosperous place of more than five hundred inhabitants, on the southern banks of the Edward River. Because there was no stone in the area, two brickworks had grown up. The lock-up and police station were among the most imposing buildings, besides the brick hospital, a large courthouse, and several hotels. Plans were in hand for building a bridge to replace the ferry. It was the centre of trade for stock-markets, both sheep and cattle, and had grown in population as men drifted away from the Victorian goldfields. Locals had made fortunes by selling their town lots, bought for £5 an acre, at up to £500 a lot.

Josh complained that he could have made just as much if he had put his money into town allotments instead of breeding stock, by selling the land and not doing a pennyworth of improvement.

There was now an Agricultural Show held annually in a nearby town at which Josh was sometimes asked to judge the fleeces and the best rams; but this year he wanted to enter himself, as a warm-up for the Royal Sydney Show next year.

Nine

JOSH HAD been one of the first to wash his sheep before shearing, when he was at Daralgoon on the Goulburn. It made a lot of work, but it paid in the higher prices he got for his wool. Now, on the dryer stations along the Billabong Creek, which did not always flow, they were shearing greasy wool and sending it down to the city or to the larger towns to be scoured – which meant of course the bales were heavier and cost more for freight.

In 1860 the freight problems seemed to have been solved, for the first paddle-steamer chuffed and churned its way up the Edward River, and leaving her barge loaded with flour and eight tons of fencing wire at Moulamein, came on as far as the town of Deniliquin. (That was the year 'Big Fellow', the former chief of the Deniliquin tribes, died of old age.)

A message to the effect that the *Moolgewanke*, Captain Johnston, was on the way had been received by the electric telegraph at Deniliquin; also the screw steamer *Wakool* belonging to Captain Cadell, was supposed to be somewhere ahead of her. But it was the hundred-foot *Moolgewanke* with her twin paddles churning the brown river waters, which appeared off Tumbudgery in July.

The girls ran down to the small landing where their father kept a duck-punt and a dinghy, of little use in the dry summers when the river dwindled, but now afloat. They begged Captain Johnston, the big bearded skipper, to let them travel a little way on board.

'Aye, ye can come aboard,' he called down from the wheelhouse. 'And travel all the way to Deniliquin with us, if ye'd like to. That's if we make it, ha-ha! The snags are thick as plums in a puddin'.'

Eliza, Ellen and Philomena ran back to the homestead for permission. Caroline followed more sedately. And Josh, having been sent for where he was out on the run, came galloping back to shake the captain's hand and offer him half a newly-killed sheep for his larder. If the steamers could really make their way to his door, or even as far as Moulamein, it would lower his freight costs tremendously, both for sending wool away and for getting in supplies.

Miss Thomas went along with the girls, since they would be away all night; in fact the way was so impeded with snags that it was ten the next morning before they arrived at Deniliquin, to a salute from the old cannon outside the Courthouse.

The girls disembarked here and booked in at the Royal Hotel with Miss Thomas, who, however, would not allow them to go to the celebration dinner that night for the captain and crew. Jamie Brown arrived in the spring-cart next morning to drive them home again, but not long before they had stood on the bank with the waving, cheering crowd to say farewell to the little steamer. The *Moolgewanke*, with an insolent blast from her whistle, steamed on up (or down – the Edward had no source and no mouth since it was an anabranch of the Murray) the river.

She was much lightened in draught by the unloading of her cargo of fencing wire at Moulamein, and the white flour and sugar and tea she had delivered to stations along the route, but still had to fight her way along a narrow channel almost choked with fallen trees. (The arrival of the *Wakool*, Captain Cadell's boat, four days later was something of an anticlimax. She did not attempt to go any higher, for her screw propulsion was not suitable for a snag-filled river and she had already broken her propeller once.)

Captain Johnston made his way slowly to South Deniliquin Station, now owned by the millionaire 'Hungry' Tyson. He had heard that Tyson had a bridge across the river, which he had built unofficially and too low for steamers to pass under it. 'We'll see about that!' he said, slapping the handle of the axe with which he, along with the crew, had been cutting trees out of the way. The Government of New South Wales had passed a law that 'no obstructions are to be placed in the way of navigation'.

No other steamer was to pass that way again, but Captain Johnston was determined to make his way back to the Murray by going forward. Sure enough they found a wooden bridge had been placed across the stream by the squatter. Soon the sound of axes and tomahawks, swung with a will, brought Mr Tyson down to the bank, shaking his fist.

'You'll never get through!' he yelled. 'And when you come back, you'll find the bridge back again across the river, you rotten mud-pirate.'

But they didn't come back. Captain Johnston and his mate Murphy fought their way on along the narrowing anabranch, startling flocks of white cockatoos from the branches to circle screeching overhead. The 'river' was little more than a forest of gumtrees with their feet in water; it took all day to hack their way along five miles of channel, past snags and over-hanging branches which snatched at the funnel and paddle-wheels.

They eventually re-entered the Murray just below Tocumwal, 460 miles from the Wakool Junction where they had left it, and turned downstream again to pick up their barge – thus circumnavigating a large piece of the western plains, including Tumbudgery Station.

It was shortly after this, only a year since Betsy's death, that Josh called the family together and informed them that he was marrying again.

'I can't live alone,' he said heavily, 'and your sainted mother would not have wanted me to; she would want me to be happy, as far as that is possible without her.' He gave a heavy, rather theatrical sigh. There was a smothered snort from Jason, sitting alone to one side of the girls. Josh looked at him sharply.

'I know you will all be pleased,' he continued, 'that I will not be bringing some strange lady home as your new mother. Miss Thomas has agreed to be my wife.'

'Did you say a lady?' muttered Ellen.

Josh kept smiling determinedly. 'So, what do you all think of that?'

'I think it's disgusting!' said Jason loudly.

'What do you mean by that remark, sir?'

'I mean she's only half your age, and Mother scarcely gone a year –'

'That's why I've not waited any longer. I'm not getting any younger –'

'Father, you can't seriously mean to marry Miss Thomas!' said Caroline.

'Certainly I am serious. We shall be married in six months' time, in Melbourne, after Christmas.'

'I don't want a new Mamma!' said Philomena, beginning to cry.

'It's not a question of what *you* want, my girl, but what *I* want,' said her father, beginning to lose his temper. He had persuaded himself that the children would not oppose his idea, though they might take a while to get used to it.

It was near the end of the winter term, and Miss Thomas went down to Melbourne to prepare her trousseau. The girls said goodbye to her rather stiffly. She would, of course, still look after the younger ones' education, she said, but now she would be one of the family.

'But you aren't one of the family, you're Miss Thomas,' said Philomena obstinately.

'I will not be Miss Thomas when I come back, dear. I will be Mrs Joseph Forbes,' she said with relish.

'I would never have believed it!' said Jason, ruffling up his dark curls despairingly. 'How *could* the Guv'nor fall for that fat, ordinary little piece! And no doubt she'll produce a whole new family of sons and daughters to divide up the property.'

Hamilton whistled. He hadn't thought of that. But of course, that explained his father's action. Miss Thomas was fairly young, healthy, good breeding stock as far as Joseph was concerned. He felt sure his father didn't love her. But no doubt she would fill her role of occupying his empty bed and increasing his progeny well enough. He had no doubt they would come back married in the autumn. Joanna Thomas would be the new lady of Tumbudgery, and in due course there would be a new line of sons and heirs.

'Good Lord! She could go on producing for another – what? twenty years,' said Jason. 'And in our mother's place! It's disgusting. He's just a lecherous old billygoat!'

'Well, I suppose he's lonely,' said Hamilton more tolerantly. 'But he certainly didn't waste any time finding a replacement. She's been making sheep's eyes at him for years, of course.'

'Of course. We must do something to stop it.'

'What can we do? They say there's no fool like an old fool.'

'I'll do something,' said Jason darkly.

It did not occur to either of his sons that Josh, at forty-eight, did not regard himself as an old man at all. To them anyone who was married and had children was one of the older generation – and their father had been married for nearly twenty years. To Jason, passionately fond of his mother, the very idea of remarriage was a betrayal.

Some school friends of Jason's had come up from Melbourne for the summer holidays. Wild pigs had been troublesome on the run of late, coming down to the waterholes in the river to wallow in the mud and dirty the water, then retiring to daytime 'camps' among the thick groves of native cypress and myall, and so Josh organised a hunt. Waiting till the worst heat of the day had passed, they all piled into one of the open drays, Josh driving, the loaded guns laid carefully across a pile of sacks in the back, the dogs running alongside.

The horse pulled them along a scarcely-marked track winding through the grass to the gate of the weaning-paddock. Josh had bought some of the *Moolgewanke*'s load of wire, and now had fences, both wire and post and rail, round most of his run, but the pigs got in somehow. Pigs were far more cunning than sheep.

'There's one now!'

The two dogs were already in pursuit. Josh jumped down lightly, almost before he had pulled up the cart, grabbed a rifle and ran after them, leaping a small ditch in the black-clay soil (now cracked and greyish on the surface) where some moisture still lay and the pig had been wallowing. He got in one shot before the others joined him, but the pig disappeared into a small forest of cypress. Josh caught the dogs and put them on a leash, tying them to the cart.

'Shall we go after him, sir?' asked one of the boys.

'Might as well. If we all spread out he won't get away.' Jason filled his pocket with spare ammunition, cradling his gun on his arm. 'Let's go, then,' he said.

'You two stay in the middle,' Josh instructed the two youths, 'and Jason and I will spread out on each side. Move quietly. We don't want the dogs; they'll only frighten him before we get a chance of a shot. Don't fire till you actually see him.'

They moved in wide formation into the patterned light and shadow between the cypress trees. It had the effect of camouflage, so that their figures lost their outlines and seemed to melt into the tall straight trunks. It would be hard to see the pig if he kept still. Perhaps we should have brought the dogs to flush him out, Josh thought. He heard the crackle of a twig ahead and to the right, and raised his gun. He caught a glimpse of something moving close to the ground, and fired. Almost simultaneously there was another shot from further to the right, and then two more from the lads in the centre, who had not seen the pig but didn't want to be left out.

The pig, unscathed, had run out of the forest and was doubling back past the cart, the dogs barking frantically as they caught his scent. Josh lay on his back between the slender trees, looking wonderingly at the patch of blue far up there between their feathery green tops. Something had knocked him down. He grasped his side, which was hurting like hell, then raised his hand. It was covered in blood. Shot! One of those idiots had shot him!

He groaned, and making a tremendous effort, gathered all his ebbing strength to shout. 'Help! I'm –' which were his last words, for his lungs had rapidly filled and before long he drowned in his own blood.

It was Charles, the lad nearest him to the right who found him, having heard the shout. He urgently called to the others. It was evident that Mr Forbes had been shot, but how? He himself had been firing rather towards the right. It must have been one of the others, thank the Lord.

Clarrie, the other boy, and Jason came running through the

trees at his shout. 'Quick! I think he's dead!' cried Charles. He had thrown his gun down in the thin dry grass under the trees. He was struck by Jason's appearance. He looked almost mad, his face white, his eyes staring, his dark curls standing on end. He flung himself down beside his father.

'Father!' He shook the dead man, as though trying to wake him. 'Father, Father! Say something!' But only some pink froth, followed by a gush of bright blood, fell from his father's lips.

'I'm afraid he's dead, Jason,' said Charles with a shaking voice. 'We'll have to carry him to the cart.'

'Dead!' Jason stared at them wildly, then flung himself on the ground, weeping. 'Oh God, what have I done?'

'It was an accident, old man,' said Clarrie. 'Not anyone's fault. In fact it could have been a bullet from any one of us. We all fired at the pig. At least, I didn't actually see it, but I had a shot anyway.'

'So did I. But it wasn't me,' said Charles.

'It was an accident,' said Clarrie.

They managed to lift him into the back of the cart, but not before another gout of darker blood had issued from his mouth. They drove back to the homestead. The western sky bled crimson, below a long spear of dark cloud which pointed towards the cool blue south.

The *Pastoral Times* announced:

Well-known pastoralist Joseph Hamilton Forbes Esq. died in an unfortunate shooting accident on his property, Tumbudgery, last Friday afternoon. With a party of schoolboys, including his son and his son's friends from Melbourne, he was out after wild pigs when the accident occurred. Mr Forbes whose wife Elizabeth, née Hume, died only last year, leaves a family of two sons and four daughters.

Mr Forbes was known in the Riverina district for his close attention to breeding stock and the fine quality of his Merino wool from the famous Daralgoon rams . . .

Unfortunately, because of the heat and the distance from Deniliquin, and the time it took to get a message through for a doctor and a police sergeant to arrive at the station, there was no time to organise a funeral or to take him to the town cemetery to lie beside Betsy. He was buried on the property as soon as the doctor had made his hasty examination and reported that death was due to a bullet entering from the right side, probably tearing a lung and lodging in the heart.

The police officer took notes and questioned the boys, but because of their obvious distress, especially Jason's, he made the inquiry as brief and informal as possible. Hunting accidents were not uncommon in the bush.

At the Coroner's Inquiry later, it was established that the light and shade in the pine forest made visibility poor, that Mr Forbes had been wearing a dark shirt and the pig was black. He had taken a risk in going out shooting in the late afternoon with three schoolboys inexperienced in the use of firearms.

Verdict: Accidental death.

'But Jason isn't inexperienced in the use of guns,' said Caroline that night to Hamilton. Jason had retired early with a headache, and the younger girls were asleep. 'He's had a gun since he was eleven or twelve years old.'

'Yes, I know.' Hamilton walked over to his father's cabinet and poured himself a stiff Scotch whisky. It had suddenly struck him that he was now Mr Forbes of Tumbudgery, the boss.

The thought of all the responsibility daunted him rather, with his four unmarried sisters. He swallowed the whisky, and shuddered. 'I know, and even the biggest wild pig doesn't stand as high as a man's chest. Not a big man like Father.'

'At least we won't have Miss Thomas for a stepmother.'

'Exactly.'

They stared at each other.

'I am not going to say anything to Jason, however,' said Hamilton. 'And I don't think you should either.'

'Very well. We won't speak of it again.'

Nor did they, until years later when Elaine Forbes asked her father why she had never seen her Forbes grandfather.

Hamilton replied that his father had died before she was born, 'shot in mistake for a wild pig'.

Ten

AFTER JOSEPH FORBES' affairs had gone through Probate and the death duties had been paid, his son Hamilton found that he was a wealthy man. The property had been left to the two boys, but the older brother had the controlling interest and inherited most of the capital after the girls had been provided for with an annuity each.

Jason and he argued interminably over the running of the station. Jason was a gambler, who wanted to take a chance by heavy stocking in good years, while Hamilton was cautious, always expecting a drought. After some years Hamilton decided to sell his half of the property by cutting off the backblocks, which were watered from dams and from the Wakool River, leaving Jason the frontage on the Edward.

Hamilton moved to a new property he had bought on the Murray River near its junction with the Murrumbidgee. Benangal was not a large run, but it was well-watered, with frontages to three permanent rivers and an eight-roomed brick homestead. It adjoined Fergus Macdonald's Rothsay station; the Murrumbidgee was the border between the two runs. Rothsay was one of the show places in the Riverina, where Macdonald, known as 'the Laird of Rothsay', kept up almost royal state. He claimed descent from the Lord of the Isles and Rainhilde, the King of Norway's daughter. When he entertained the Governor he had his own piper to march round the dinner table, and he himself wore the kilt and a Macdonald plaid caught on the shoulder with a cairngorm brooch which an ancestor had wrested from Robert the Bruce. Fergus was a proud and canny Scot who hated anyone with the name of Campbell, but was otherwise said to be a kindly man, who had brought up his orphaned granddaughter as his own child. He never mentioned the other orphan he had cared for, the black boy Billiwidgery. As a young man on the

Hunter River, Fergus had gone with a party of squatters on a punitive expedition after Blacks who had been spearing cattle. The tribe was wiped out, but not before they had put a spear through the crown of Fergus's hat. The lad survived because his mother pushed him into a hollow log, where he was found and taken home by Macdonald.

Hamilton had met him at the Squatters' Club in Sydney, a huge red-bearded man with eyebrows as big as moustaches above his shrewd blue eyes, and a hearty handshake. He had property which was said to be worth a million.

The Forbes girls were by now all married. Eliza lived in Melbourne, but the others had married into the families of local squatters: Caroline was now a McLaurin, Ellen a Macleay, and Philomena a Kennedy. Jason had recently married also, and it was his new wife Rosa who led to the final break between the brothers.

Hamilton could not accept Rosa: a brassy blonde with a voice to match, just out from England in a migrant ship when Jason met her in Melbourne. He felt it was an insult to their late mother to have brought her to Tumbudgery. Jason had objected to Miss Thomas for their father, yet he could marry someone like her, with a loud laugh and awful clothes . . .

So Hamilton moved out, first acquiring some Wanganella rams from the original Peppin stock to put with his own best Merino ewes. He had kept up his father's careful breeding programme, entering each year's progeny in the stud-book. When he won prizes for best ram and best six fleeces at the 1870 Deniliquin Agricultural Show, he thought how pleased Josh would have been.

Jason was impatient with his carefulness, and derided his caution in not stocking up fully in good years. But Hamilton had seen the results of overstocking in saltbush country. The small annual saltbush would come up again after rain, but the old-man saltbush which was so valuable as shelter and fodder would not recover. After eating it down to the ground, the sheep would dig up the roots and eat them too in a drought year. Even the pines on the ridges were being lost as the older trees died and sheep ate the new seedlings.

Jason had been rather upset at the dividing of Tumbudgery, as it meant halving the number of sheep as well, but Hamilton couldn't see that he had any grievance. He was keeping the best land with the Edward River frontage, and the homestead.

'I wouldn't like to sell the half with father's grave on it,' said Hamilton.

Jason gave him a veiled, impenetrable look. Hamilton had never felt quite at ease with his brother since that mysterious accident with the gun.

All Hamilton took from the house, apart from his personal possessions, was a miniature of their mother, besides a large silver watch that had belonged to Betsy's grandfather, the Reverend Mr Coggin. Rosa made such a fuss when he suggested taking some of the furniture that he left it all.

Jason and Rosa's first child, born suspiciously soon after the wedding, was a daughter named (of all things! thought Hamilton) Rosebud Forbes. He decided that when he had a son – and he really should start looking for a wife soon – he would call him Joseph, after his father. It was unlikely, he thought, that Jason would want to use that name.

Eleven

IT WAS inevitable that Hamilton Forbes should meet the vivacious auburn-haired Moira Macdonald, now living with her grandparents at Rothsay. They met at an amateur race meeting held on Poon Boon station, where she backed his horse in a race and he won.

'You see, I am a good judge of horses – and riders,' she said as they drank champagne in the marquee afterwards, Hamilton looking rather dashing in the coloured silk shirt he had worn for the race. It was early spring, and the rivers were beginning to rise. He thought what a gorgeous girl she was with her bright hair and pink cheeks. She wore a long green riding habit and black velvet hunting cap pulled over her auburn curls.

'I hope we may meet again, Miss Macdonald,' he said, refilling her glass.

'I am sure we shall. After all, we are neighbours now.'

Hamilton was physically not as big a man as his father, Josh, but with his large, fearless, straight-gazing grey eyes he inspired trust. He was known to be an honest man, and a man of his word; but most men trusted him instinctively.

'I would ask permission to ride over and call on you and your grandparents, but I have to go down to Melbourne next Friday before shearing starts. I find the best way is to travel by steamer to Echuca, now the railway has come through from Melbourne.'

'Yet there is still no bridge over the Murray. Do you think the railway will ever be extended to Deniliquin?'

'Eventually, yes. There's a sort of pontoon bridge at Echuca now.'

'Have you heard about the plague of rabbits in Victoria, Mr Forbes? It is thought they will never cross the Murray.'

'No, they will never cross the Murray. Anyway it is too hot and dry for them in western New South Wales.'

Hamilton took her small, square, capable hand in his and looked into her eyes, before he made his departure from Poon Boon, mounted on his thoroughbred – a skittish two-year-old that he mastered with ease and skill. A few days later he left for Melbourne.

Was it chance, or fate, or did Moira help fate along a little? Certainly she had asked him which steamer he was catching. When the *Lancashire Lass* stopped at the Benangal landing, who should be leaning on the rail of the top deck but Miss Moira Macdonald and her older companion – a dour Scotswoman from the Macdonald household who had been sent along as her chaperone.

Hamilton looked up and caught his breath as he saw a pair of merry blue eyes looking down at him, beneath a wide straw bonnet swathed in bands of chiffon and tied beneath the chin. He thought he had never seen a more enchanting fashion. Moira always looked her best in white, and she looked cool and charming in her hailspot muslin gown.

96

The long face and heavy jowls of her companion, and her sombre black dress, made Moira's sweet youthfulness more noticeable, but Hamilton had no idea that she was less than seventeen. He was fifteen years older.

'Why, Mr Forbes! What a lucky coincidence!' she called as, having given his bags to one of the deckhands, he made his way to the upper deck. She introduced Miss MacIntyre, who muttered, 'Pleased tae meet ye,' in a tone that suggested anything but pleasure.

'I'm going up to Sydney to visit my mother in hospital; she is not at all well,' said Moira. 'Grandmama lives at Albury, you know, so I shall break the journey there, and then go on to Sydney by coach.' (Hamilton politely concealed his surprise; he had understood Moira was an orphan.)

'It's a tremendous journey for a young lady! And you may have to get the coach to Albury, the steamers are having trouble except on a high river.'

'Oh, I love travelling! Just to go to school, I had to come about six hundred miles overland to Warwick from out on the Bulloo, before I came to Rothsay.'

'Well, I used to go down to Melbourne from Tumbudgery, near Deniliquin.'

'Tumbudgery! Why, I believe I own some land near there; it used to be Breckan Plains. Or shall do when I'm twenty-one.'

Hamilton gazed at her ardently. She was not only dazzling to look at (a more impartial critic might have thought Moira's mouth, though soft and pink, to have rather the shape of a blob, while her nose was definitely snub), but she was an heiress as well!

During the three days' steaming up-river to Echuca, they spent much time leaning on the rail in conversation, while 'the dragon' as Hamilton thought of Miss MacIntyre, sat crocheting in a deck chair nearby. He found to his delight that Moira could talk sheep and wool as knowledgeably as a man; she knew about dry pastures and dam-sinking and the grading of Merino wool from triple A downwards, according to its fineness and crimp.

'My father used to teach me the letters on the wool-bales at Noccunda,' she said. 'That was how I first learned to read, and the first letters I learned were our brand, NOC. Then I learned 'M' for Moira Macdonald.'

Hamilton thought it the most musical arrangement of letters he had ever heard.

'I was brought up in those days by an old native woman, Yeelana, and the station Blacks used to teach me to read tracks in the sand – '

'Really?' Hamilton felt a little taken aback. 'One would never think it, Miss Macdonald. I mean, you are so elegant and, and – '

'And *clean-looking*?' She eyed him sideways, with suppressed amusement. 'I assure you, the house lubras were *perfectly* clean; they bathed every day in the river, unless there was a bad drought and water was scarce. My mother used to give the girls scented soap for a treat, and they loved washing their hair, which was rather light-coloured and quite pretty when well cared for.'

'My father remembered the Tasmanian race in Van Diemen's Land, when he first came to the colonies as a child. Most unprepossessing he said, with tight woolly mops which they cut in a sort of cap. A very primitive type. I believe there are only one or two old women left of the race.'

'How sad!' said Moira, but he did not take that up. It was, in his opinion, merely inevitable.

'My grandfather still lives in Hobart Town; my father took up land in Port Phillip when he was in his early twenties.'

'I should love to see Hobart, and Tasmania,' said Moira. 'I hear it is a most beautiful island. I've seen the apples from there in the Sydney shops – '

'My grandfather, Josiah Forbes, founded the apple industry in Tasmania,' said Hamilton, exaggerating a little. 'My uncles and cousins all have orchards over there.'

They were interrupted by the gong sounding for luncheon. Hamilton helped Miss MacIntyre from her chair and picked up her wool. He could always charm elderly relatives, and he thought she would be a useful friend at court. But when he offered her his arm to help her down the steep steps over the paddle-box, she gave him a glare, gathered up her skirts in one hand and her crochet in the other, and announced,

98

'I'm nae sic' an auld dowf that I canna gae doonstairs by masel'!'

This gave him the chance to go ahead of Moira and help her down, being rewarded by the glimpse of a sturdy foot clad in a white kid boot, and a neat ankle.

By the time they reached Echuca, five hundred river-miles upstream, he knew he was in love, but Moira treated him with an offhand, half-mocking manner which bemused him. She was a well-developed girl, and he still had no idea she was just out of the schoolroom. Yet sometimes she was serious, and her eyes held an indefinable promise which set his pulse racing.

It had been evident when they passed Murrumbidgee Reef, where the steamer had almost to 'walk' on her paddles over the shallows, that there would not be enough water to take her up to Albury, another three hundred miles further on. Hamilton helped the two ladies to settle in at their hotel and book their seats on a Cobb & Co coach for the next day, before he caught the train to Melbourne. Moira pressed his hand and gave him such a sweet smile that his hopes rose.

He composed half a dozen letters and tore them up. At last, when shearing was over and he judged she would be back at Rothsay, he wrote a simple declaration and proposal of marriage, asking her to give him permission to call on her grandfather.

The usual convention was for the young man to ask permission to make his proposal to the young lady, but he judged rightly that Moira as an individualist would resent this. He waited in a ferment for her reply, cursing the slowness of the mails, but it was delivered by hand by a servant riding over from Rothsay. She agreed to be his, 'forever and ever.'

'Wait!' he cried. 'Wait for a reply!' and beaming, told the man to ask for a glass of beer at the kitchen door. He dashed off a few lines beginning, 'Oh glorious, delightful, generous girl!' He came down to earth when he had to write a formal note to Fergus Macdonald asking for an interview. He felt very nervous when he rode up to the imposing front door of Rothsay, but he found Fergus in a jovial mood, while his wife

Janet gave him her blessing and promised to make the bride a wreath of orange blossom from their own orchard.

They were married three months later, just after Moira's seventeenth birthday, though Fergus complained that she was 'ower young in my opeenion.' But he was really delighted to have the adjoining Benangal Station 'in the family,' especially as his young neighbour did not believe in over-stocking, but managed his run sensibly. Also he knew that Tumbudgery was next door to Breckan Plains, which would soon be hers under her grandfather Ferguson's Will; and he knew that Tumbudgery was Forbes property. Fergus, who had arrived in Sydney fifty years earlier with £500 capital, had since acquired millions of acres in Queensland, on the Darling, and at Balranald on the Murrumbidgee, but he was still land-hungry.

Since both Moira's father, Lachlan Macdonald, and his second son Donald were now dead (Donald had been speared by wild blacks when the brothers were on their way to take up Noccunda on the Bulloo River, in far western Queensland) Fergus regarded Hamilton almost as a son. His third son, Alexander, had become a woolbroker in Sydney, and his only daughter Flora had dared to marry a Campbell! Her father never spoke to her again.

Moira's brothers, still at boarding school in Sydney, would carry on the name, but 'the gel has mair speerit than her namby-pamby brithers,' Fergus opined, having memories of an unfortunate visit when Andrew had earache and grizzled all the time, while little Duncan was homesick.

But he and Moira got on famously. He seemed to see something of himself in young Moira, with her bright hair and madcap ways. He admired a girl who could ride and shoot almost as well as a boy. So when Lachie died and Isobelle was incapable of looking after them, he'd suggested to Janet that they bring Moira up as their own, while their grandmother Ferguson took the boys. Janet agreed, if only for the sake of improving Moira's manners. She feared the girl had been allowed to run wild on Noccunda station, with black girls for nurses and companions.

Moira had grown up something of a tomboy, a favourite with the black staff, a crack shot with a rifle and an expert horsewoman. Her governess was rather scandalised by her behaviour, but her father encouraged her. Yeelana taught her 'the language of the sand', so that she could track tiny bush creatures, skinks and hopping marsupial mice and bilbies to their hiding places among the roly-poly bushes or the clumps of spinifex. She could recognise the wide print of an emu's toes, the track of a heron by the waterhole, the sinuous line made by a snake.

She had been nearly three when her brother Donald was born, and named after the uncle who was speared by the Blacks. There was scarcely enough water for his baby's bath, for even the home waterhole had dried out, and the fish were all dead, while the water-birds had departed for the distant coast. Water had to be carted from the nearest big lagoon, twenty miles away, and then it was half mud. It had to be cleared by throwing in Epsom salts and ashes from a boree log. The garden withered, though Ah Fu the Chinese cook managed to keep some vegetables alive. But Isobelle Macdonald, the only white woman for a hundred miles, did not complain. She loved her husband and had given him a son and a daughter. Isobelle doted on their boy, and Lachie on their little girl. By the time Donnie was eighteen months he was a bonnie child, with sunny temperament. It was Moira with her red hair who would fly into rages when crossed, and fling herself down screaming and beating her head against the floor.

Lachie Macdonald had made friends with the local tribes after that first tragic encounter, and for years ran his station with the help of Aboriginal stockmen, housemaids, and nurses for his children. Yeelana, who had lost her own daughter, made Moira her special care. The women came up from their camp in the bend, wearing the bright cotton dresses the Missus had given them, their hair clean-washed with 'chope' – a great treasure. Their families were kept in flour, tea, sugar and tobacco, and they received the left-overs from the evening meal.

One night Isobelle found Moira's bed empty, and Lachie, going down to the Blacks' camp to get help in tracking her in case she had wandered away, found Moira enthroned among green boughs beside the campfire.

The members of the tribe danced past, each touching her little chubby knees with a green twig.

'What's going on here?' cried Lachlan.

'S'alright, Boss.' Yeelana stepped into the circle of fire-light. 'Just little singabout, we singin' the knees, make Missie Moira strong-feller when she grow up.'

Moira herself was quite composed, and seemed to be enjoying the tickling of the leaves on her bare legs.

'You should not have brought her down here without asking. You know Missus is not well. She worry all-a-time 'bout Missie Moira.'

'Aw, me sorry, Boss. We just sing-em knee bilong 'er. Got to be at new moon, while she still little-feller. Makem strong-feller, walk lo-ong way, ridem horse – '

'Orright. I take her back now.' He swung the child up on his shoulders and carried her back to the house. Moira had not been frightened or tearful. She sat astride his neck and thumped him with her heels, crying, 'Gee-up, horsey!'

It was one of Moira's earliest memories. She could recall the firelight, the men decked in leaves and feathers, the way the twigs of leaves tickled her knees and made her laugh.

She had one earlier memory; it was more like a dream though she knew it had happened, of the day when Donnie died.

She had been put down for her afternoon sleep in her mother's room which opened, like all the other bedrooms, on to the long veranda and was screened with a flywire door to keep out insects but admit as much air as possible. It was intensely hot, in the midst of a bad drought her mother told her afterwards. Even the long waterhole in the Bulloo River below the homestead was dry, and water had to be brought by tank and dray to fill the water-barrels for domestic use.

Isobelle was asleep on the big bed and Moira lay on a mattress near the door for coolness. Nurse Binns had put Donnie, who was just walking, in his cot in the nursery while she took a nap in her own room.

Moira woke first, played with her dolls for a while, then growing bored she went along the veranda to the nursery to see if Donnie was awake. He was still asleep. She knew she was not allowed to wake him, as he would be cross and grizzly if he hadn't finished his sleep. Moira picked up a coloured picture-book from the floor, with bright lithographed drawings of a cat sitting on a mat; she could still see the ginger cat and the cyclamen-red rug with yellow fringes in that book, from which she would 'read' to herself.

She had to stretch on tip-toe to reach the handle of the wire door which had latched itself behind her. She went back to Mamma's room and looked at the pictures and dozed off again. She woke to a cry from Nurse Binns: Donnie was missing, was not in his room, must have climbed out of his cot and could not be found . . .

When she was told later that Donnie had 'gone to Heaven' she accepted it as she did when told that Papa had 'gone to Sydney', or Brisbane.

It was not until years later, when Isobelle was confined in a mental institution in Sydney, that Moira learned from her father what had happened that day. Little Donnie had not only climbed from his cot for the first time, but had wandered outside. Though the bed of the river was dry, the water-butts were full. He had clambered on a wooden crate beside one of them, and fallen in and drowned.

Isobelle had never recovered from the shock. A few years later, after the birth of little Duncan, her behaviour became strange. Then one day she filled her dressing-gown pockets with weights, and walked into the deepest hole in the river. It was Yeelana's sister's girl, Jennah, the half-white daughter of a shearer, who saved her.

Moira's governess could no longer cope with her wild ways, so at thirteen she was sent away to a Presbyterian girls' school in Warwick. When her father died in a fall from his horse (which rolled on him after putting a hoof in a bilbie-hole) she went to Rothsay station on the Murray to be brought up by her Macdonald grandparents. From there it was easier to get to the Presbyterian Ladies' College in Melbourne. So she travelled by Cobb & Co coach from Hay on the Murrumbidgee on the 200-mile journey each summer term. She would persuade her companion to sit on the box-seat with the driver, who entertained them with hair-raising tales of bushrangers and murders, of the Headless Horseman who haunted the black swamp on the Old Man Plain and used to spirit the drovers' cattle away; of Jimmy the Whisperer, the quiet-voiced cattle duffer for whose capture there was a £50 reward; and the Ghostly Galloper, whose hoofbeats could be heard on moonlit nights, on an empty road.

These tales lost nothing in the telling, as the team of horses rushed on over the level plain, and stars swam up out of the lake of clear green light lingering in the west. They would stop for a meal at an inn while the horses were being changed: roast mutton and pumpkin, apple pie and custard, or stiff red jelly made extra firm so that it would not melt in the heat.

In winter when the paddle-steamers were running she could travel by steamer from the Rothsay landing down to Echuca, and from there it was only a few hours by train to Melbourne.

At first Moira was homesick for the far inland, where her mother had been the first white woman on the Bulloo River, her nearest neighbour a hundred miles away at Thargomindah. Though the Murray water was green, or brown when in flood, the predominant colour was grey: grey mud-flats with grey-blue acacias (known locally as 'willers' because of their long drooping leaves), grey saltbush and grey-blue gumtrees; wiry lignum swamps and dark green, almost black, Murray pines.

She missed the colours of Noccunda: the orange-red sand-hills, the red willy-willys that would spin and twist against the blue sky on the heat-hazed plain; the cobalt scarps of the Grey Range in the distance, the tall Mitchell grass bleached to paper whiteness in drought years, or enamelled with brilliant wildflowers after rain. Pale gold waterlilies bloomed on the backwaters, and Darling lilies on the orange sandhills. But she never went back again, and had not seen her father's grave, or the little Aboriginal half-brothers that Yeelana's niece bore to Lachie Macdonald each year until he died. And she never told Hamilton of her feelings of guilt when she learned how her baby brother drowned, and remembered how she stretched on tip-toe to open the wire door.

Moira had wanted a honeymoon on a paddle-steamer, perhaps down into South Australia where she had never been. Hamilton thought cabins and bunks were not ideal for a newly-married pair. He compromised with a trip by river down to Euston and back, then they returned to Benangal and the newly-decorated bedroom.

In bed Moira was ardent but clumsy, like a big schoolgirl, but her generous nature denied him nothing. Hamilton was quite infatuated. Her skin was so white, and the fine red-gold mat of her pubic hair so delicate, he could not stop admiring her. As a child he had seen, and shied away from, old naked Aboriginal women in the Port Phillip District, with wrinkled dugs and dark bushes which he felt, without knowing, must hide some obscenity.

Moira insisted on still going riding after she knew she was pregnant, which led to their first quarrel. Their quarrels were spectacular, for Moira yelled at him and threw things.

She had a difficult first birth although she was so young. Only after a long, exhausting struggle was the baby born. This was Elaine, a vigorous, healthy mite with her great-grand-father Macdonald's long Scottish bones and bright red hair. But she had Hamilton's eyes, large and of a dark grey-blue which the nurse said would turn either brown or green as she got older.

Moira, who had always been so healthy, suffered from bronchitis the next winter, and developed a cough which she could not shake off. Two years later when Joseph Macdonald Forbes was born, she was staying in Albury with her grand-mother Ferguson. As the baby thrived, his mother became thinner. Alarmed, Mrs Ferguson wrote to Hamilton that she thought Moira should not make the long journey home at present. When she was stronger she should go on a sea-voyage for her health. Or so the doctor recommended.

Hamilton felt he could not bear her to go even further away. He was missing her terribly, he wrote. As soon as he could get away he would go down to Melbourne where he had to see about the sale of his wool-clip, and meet her there. She could take the train to Melbourne. Her maid would look after her, and she must get a nursemaid for little Joseph and Elaine.

He stayed in Melbourne as long as he could, increasingly worried by Moira's thinness and pallor, and the troublesome cough which Melbourne's changeable climate, first burning hot and then cold and wet, did nothing to improve.

'I dread the heat at home,' said Moira. 'It's funny, I was born and bred in the north-west, I used to revel in that dry, burning, clear, healthy heat. But now . . . Do you know what I should like? I should like to visit Tasmania amd see Mount Wellington with snow on it.'

'Well, it *would* be a sea voyage, though a brief one. But no snow at this time of year, unless they get some freak weather. As a matter of fact, when I wrote and told Grandpa Forbes about the birth of Joseph, he said his dearest wish was to see his great-grandson before he died. And Kate, his wife, would dote on him! She's a most lovable woman, I believe. She was Kate Hamilton, which is where I get my name.'

'Of course! Oh, please let us go!'

'My darling, there's nothing I'd like better than to go with you and see the old people, but you know I can't stay away any longer. The rabbits are spreading and eating us out. They haven't crossed the Murrumbidgee yet, but Jason has seen a few stray ones on Tumbudgery. The good seasons are making them breed all the faster. One could almost wish for a drought.'

Moira sailed for Tasmania, with a new, hectic colour of excitement in her ivory cheeks, promising to come back 'fat and well.'

'Not *too* fat!' protested Hamilton. 'Just well. It's not worth going for less than a month, but I hate it when you are away.'

He went home to rabbit-eaten pastures and dying trees. The dark Murray pines on the sandhills had turned to black skeletons, the sand was in motion, swallowing up lignum swamps and saltbush flats. He imagined he could smell rabbits, even in the house. He organised a band of trappers, paying a bounty for each rabbit skull, and he and his neighbours engaged in massive shoots, but it was not a sport any more, not a social occasion, just a bloody massacre leaving heaps of stinking carcasses which had to be burned, lest they make breeding places for blowflies. He began to hate rabbits. How could anyone make pets of the things?

Lying awake at night, feeling the cold emptiness of the double bed, he missed Moira unbearably. He had a recurring nightmare in which he tried to reach her among a crowd of people, in some large public place, a theatre or exhibition hall. He would call her name, but she never seemed to hear him, and the crowds frustrated his attempts to get near her. Then one night the dream changed. He was in a big hall; Moira at the front on some sort of stage or dais with a stone arch above it. Suddenly he saw a crack appear in the arch. It was crumbling. He screamed a warning, tried to run to her up the steps, but his feet were like lumps of lead. The great stone arch crumbled slowly into huge blocks, which fell and obliterated her white-robed form.

He woke in a cold sweat. Beyond the veranda roof he could see the stars, sharp and white, in the black inland sky. A plover flew over, calling with its ratchet notes. It was a bird the Blacks called the Death Bird, Moira said; it flew over the camp when someone died. Far off, a curlew cried, a bodiless voice under the stars, full of the strange melancholy of this vast and lonely land.

When she was quite an old woman, living alone in one of her father's houses overlooking the blue expanse of Sydney Harbour with its enchanting succession of bays and wooded coves, rocky headlands and sheltered inlets, Elaine would recall the visit with her mother to that other beautiful harbour in the south, where her great-grandparents lived.

She had been only four years old. She had no recollection of Mount Wellington, but she remembered how Great-grandfather Josiah had frightened her, because he was bald. She had never seen a bald man before. Besides, he had a red face and a loud, angry voice. The old man was in fact rather deaf and did not know he was shouting. He now rarely left his home on the peak of Knocklofty, from which he could look out over the estuary of the Derwent and see the ships which carried the apples grown by his sons and his sons' sons to ports around the world.

Great-grandma Kate had a soft voice and a gentle face. But the whole visit was something Elaine remembered only as a dream is remembered, a long period of unreality, outside of ordinary time, when she was homesick for her father and her dolls.

They had travelled from Albury to Melbourne by train, and then by ship across the Straits to Hobart. In the train, her nurse asleep in the top berth with Joseph wedged between her and the wall, Elaine had listened to the train as it racketed through the night; swaying, rocking, braying a wild triumphant note. She had crept to the foot of her berth and pressed her face against the glass, seeing the reflection of dim blue light from a ceiling lamp, and beyond the compartment the rushing landscape, reflections in a pool or stream, a great lighted station where they did not stop but raced through and out into the country again. There were bare slopes under the stars, and a few thin black trees which revolved, curtsied, sank into the ground. The stars swarmed on beside the train, keeping pace with it . . . She fell asleep watching, keeled over on top of the blankets with her thumb jammed in her mouth.

She could not remember anything about the ship but a vision of wild blue water and a strangely slanting horizon, beyond an open doorway. And being lifted up to a porthole in the early morning, to see 'all the little waves with their nightcaps on.'

She was sure that she remembered, and that it was this journey which gave her a taste for travel, and sent her later to India. She always loved trains, and being at sea.

Twelve

MARGARET, MOIRA'S third child, was born the same year that Isobelle Macdonald died in the private hospital to which she had been moved. Moira had taken the children to see her mother, but she was never sure how much Isobelle understood with her clouded mind. She kept calling young Joseph 'Donnie' and Elaine 'Moira', while she seemed to wonder who Moira herself might be. She appeared to have forgotten her sons Andrew and Duncan completely.

Margaret grew up a thin, pale child with fair curls; Hamilton called her 'my little asparagus stalk.' Moira too had become thin, and continued to lose weight. Though her complexion was brilliant, the colour in her cheeks was hectic rather than healthy.

When tuberculosis of the lung was diagnosed, Hamilton insisted that she should enter the Echuca Private Sanatorium which existed for 'the open-air treatment of Consumption'. So Moira lived in one of the luxurious chalets on the banks of the Campaspe, a few miles out of town, on milk, butter and cream produced on the property and freshly processed in its dairy. The dry sunny climate was thought to be ideal for consumptives.

Her health began to improve, and she seemed to be putting on weight. But it turned out that she was pregnant again. As sometimes happened with a pregnancy, the latent disease flared up and became a galloping consumption. She returned home for her confinement, but became too weak to get up again.

Moira was unreconciled to dying young. She clung fiercely to life, and to Hamilton's hand, as if he could keep her from slipping away.

Then on the first day of spring, she got him to help her out of bed and over to the window. Outside was a gusty blue day, no day for dying. She saw the green fronds of the pepper trees, their paper-pink berries against the blue sky, an almond-tree in a cloud of blossom. She stretched out her thin, fleshless arms towards the sun.

This was only the last flicker of a dying fire. At sunset she asked him to bring the children to say goodbye.

They stood round the bed, Elaine with her great eyes in her small white face, and her flaming red hair; Joseph looking solemn in a sailor suit, and little Margaret smiling doubtfully, unaware, yet sensing the others' distress.

Hamilton stood at the foot of the bed, covering his eyes with his hand. The nurse had taken the baby away to feed it.

Moira lay propped on her pillows against which her bright hair was spread, seeming to have a vitality of its own.

'You'll have to be a mother to the little ones, pet,' she said weakly. Elaine began to weep. 'Don't cry, dear. It's only –'

But she was shaken then by a terrible paroxysm of coughing. Hamilton led the children out of the sickroom. They did not see their mother alive again. The baby died soon after.

Hamilton was inconsolable. Remembering how he and the others had felt at his father's proposed remarriage, he swore he would not marry again, even to provide a mother for his youngsters. He wished he had his old nurse, Bridget, there to help; but she and Jamie had gone to Canada and he had lost touch with them.

Elaine, only ten years old, became his housekeeper and a mother to her young brother and sister. Hamilton had sold the Breckan Plains land and put a manager in at Benangal until Joseph should be old enough to take over. He hadn't the heart to carry on; he lost interest in sheep-breeding, though he still sometimes attended the wool auctions in Sydney, and visited the office of his wife's uncle Alexander Macdonald. It still gave him pleasure to delve his hands into the creamy fleece in an opened bale.

He seemed to age rapidly, and by the time he was fifty he looked an old man. His light hair had thinned and greyed, while his face grew fat and round. His large, straight-gazing grey eyes had become rather bulbous. Hamilton was known as a connoisseur of food and wine, a diner at clubs, and had given up riding and all forms of exercise except golf. He was devoted to his children, especially Elaine, who reminded him of Moira.

Just before her twelfth birthday, Margaret, the second daughter, died of the same disease. Elaine, who had nursed her devotedly and had felt more like a mother than a sister to her, announced that she wanted to leave home and train as a nurse.

'If this world of suffering is all there is,' she said (for her religious faith had been shaken by the deaths of her mother and sister), 'then the best thing we can do is work to make that suffering less.'

'There is no need for you to work at all,' protested Hamilton.

'I don't *have* to, but I want to! Do you mind so very much, father? After all, you spend a lot of time at your club.'

'No! I absolutely forbid it!'

But Elaine persisted, and Joseph, now old enough to leave school, backed her up. Hamilton gave in with a sigh. 'Very well, my dear. You know I only want your happiness.'

Fergus Macdonald had outlived his wife and all his children except Alexander.

He was hale and hearty at ninety, and though his hair was grey his beard was still tinged with red. In the drought years of the eighties, he had acquired a portion of the Benangal run from Hamilton. Rothsay Station now spread on both sides of the Murrumbidgee junction, with frontages to three rivers and a shearing shed which could handle 100,000 sheep. Rothsay was the first to instal machine shearing on the Murray.

When rabbits first crossed the Murrumbidgee, Fergus had completely enclosed his run with wire netting rabbit-proof fencing. By digging out burrows and wholesale poisoning, he soon had his properties free of rabbits. They had been introduced by a squatter near Geelong, Victoria, to provide sport for his guns. Now they were in New South Wales, and the twenty million sheep which had taken over the waterholes and driven the Aborigines from their hunting grounds, were being driven out themselves by fifty million rabbits. The huntin' and shootin' squatters had imported their own destruction.

The drought and the rabbits meant the end for many small, under-capitalised farmers, who had taken up 'free selections' on the squatters' vast holdings as their fourteen-year leases expired. (They were referred to scornfully as 'Cockie farmers' as they were supposed to be so poor that they fed their families on baked cockatoo.) Fergus Macdonald and Hamilton Forbes, having plenty of water and irrigated feed paddocks did not fare too badly. They could kill off their surplus stock and ship hides and tallow by paddle-steamer to Echuca for

111

Melbourne markets, or down-river to Morgan for Port Adelaide.

After the flood year of 1890 the rabbits bred in an overwhelming wave. The carrying capacity of runs was so reduced that many big owners had to walk off their properties. Strikes, low wool prices, drought and rabbits had brought them to the verge of bankruptcy. The final straw was the failure of the banks in 1893, and the failure of the winter rains. The overstocked and eaten-out pastures were blowing away in dust.

During the depression in the pastoral industry, Jason Forbes was one of those who went under. Overstocked, and with not enough capital for rabbit fencing, he found his topsoil eroding, leaving a scarified clay surface on which not even saltbush would grow. Tumbudgery was taken over by the bank to which it was mortgaged, and Jason took a job as a station manager. Hamilton refused to help him, feeling that his brother had brought his troubles on himself. But Jason had the last laugh. His daughter Rosebud, a pretty girl with her mother's high colour and Jason's black curls, married young Joseph, Elaine's brother. Hamilton was not at all pleased; the daughter of that dreadful woman to reign at Benangal!

When told of the engagement, he had reacted angrily.

'You can't be serious,' he said to Joseph, who was only eighteen and with his long Scottish head and light sandy hair was a taller, sturdier version of his grandfather Lachie Macdonald. 'The girl is your first cousin, for one thing, and she's a lot older than you –'

'Only four years,' said Joseph.

'– and anyway you're under age. I can forbid it.'

'Then we'll just run away together, and get married when I turn twenty-one. At least I can't be accused of running off with a minor. And her father approves of the match. Uncle Jason –'

'No doubt he does. Since he knows old Fergus has left you one of his Queensland properties in his will. And thinks that Benangal will be yours one day. Well, I won't try to stop you marrying, since you've made up your mind, but you won't have Benangal,' said Hamilton, deciding at that moment.

'I'm going to sell it to young Sandy, Alexander's boy, who'll have Rothsay when the old man dies.'

'Do what you like. I'm going to Queensland, away from the Murray and its mosquitoes. Fergus has offered me the job of manager at Mungurriba till it's officially mine. So we'll be off as soon as Rosebud and I are married.'

'Rosebud!' snorted Hamilton. He sold most of his prize stock with the station, except for some breeding ewes and a champion ram which he gave Joseph for a wedding present. He had already parted with Breckan Plains. He invested the money in harbourside properties in Sydney, going cheap because of the depression.

Young Joseph and his bride set off for the Queensland property near Barcaldine, which had been in the centre of the great shearers' strike of 1891 when the country trembled on the brink of civil war.

Fergus Macdonald, having survived blackfellows' spears, drought, rabbits and free selectors, lived to be ninety-four. There was enough land for all his grandsons, including Moira's brothers, for he owned about three million acres when he died. He made generous bequests to the Presbyterian Church and Scotch College, Melbourne. But he left nothing to Flora's boys, who bore the hated name of Campbell.

BOOK TWO

The Golden Fleece

1870–1930

I've shore at big Willandra and I've shore at Tilberoo,
I've shore at Burrabogie, and upon the famed Barcoo,
At Cowan Downs and Trida, as far as Moulamein,
But I always was glad to get back again to the One Tree Plain.

(Chorus)
All among the wool, boys, all among the wool,
Keep your wide blades full, boys, keep your blades full.
I can do a respectable tally myself whenever I like to try,
But they know me round the backblocks as Flash Jack from
    Gundagai.

I've been shearin' up the Lachlan, and I've dossed on Cooper's
    Creek,
And once I rung Cudgingie shed, and blued it in a week.
But when Gabriel blows his trumpet, lads, I'll catch the morning
    train,
And I'll push for old Tom Patterson's on the One Tree Plain.

Old shearers' song

By a forge near a hut on the Condamine River
    A blacksmith laboured at his ancient trade;
With his hammer swinging and his anvil ringing
    He fashioned bells from a crosscut blade . . .

The smith is lost to the Condamine River,
    Gone is the humpy where he used to dwell;
But the songs and the clamour of his busy hammer
    Ring on through the land in the Condamine Bell.

Jack Sorensen.

One

JAMIE BROWN and his family had gone with Hamilton Forbes when he moved to his new station Benangal, on the Murray. Jamie missed old man Forbes, and he could not take to the young man Jason; while Bridget was as scornful of Mrs Rosa Forbes as she had been of Miss Thomas. She knew 'a real lady' when she saw one, and Jason's wife did not qualify in her opinion.

Young Tom, who had been falling on and off horses ever since he was big enough to climb on the pony's back, rode to school in Balranald township. There in the old bush school a single teacher coped with children at all different stages of learning. He had to give each one his individual attention, and the bright ones, like Tommy Brown, got on fast.

He was a great reader, and would read anything he could get his hands on; he regretted now their old home with all those printed pages stuck on the walls before he was old enough to read them. One of his favourite books which they were reading at school was Kingsley's *Heroes*. When at sunrise he looked out and saw a patch of cirrus, crimped like finest Merino wool, catching the first gleam of gold, it reminded him of the story of Jason and the Golden Fleece.

When he left school, Tom Brown got his first job as a rouseabout on Benangal. Later, he was taken on as tar-boy and sweeper-up at shearing. His ambition, like that of every lad hanging around the shearing shed of a big station, was to become a 'gun' shearer, or at least a 'ringer'. The ringer of the shed was the best shearer of the season.

The shearers looked after their blade-shears with tender care, keeping them well oiled and sharpened. Some were fitted with Hayden's patent thumb-guards and other extras. Jamie let Tom have a pair so that he could get in some practice on an old bare-bellied ewe, and the pet lambs he had helped to rear the year before.

Under his father's instruction Tom felt he was getting the knack of it. There was an art in making a wide, clean blow through the wool with each sweep of the shears, while holding the sheep immobilised on its haunches. It was satisfying to see the wool peel off in one continuous fleece, leaving as few short pieces, or 'locks', as possible. Tom knew all about 'daggy' sheep and 'sandy' sheep and 'wet' sheep – shearers refused to work after a heavy shower of rain, as there was a theory that handling wet sheep all day caused rheumatism in the hands, on which their skill and livelihood depended.

Jamie, happy in his marriage and his job, delighted with his son, had mellowed with the years. He no longer hated the British Crown and did not think Australia should secede from the Empire, but he thought that Riverina should become a new State, separate from New South Wales. In this he was in agreement with most of the squatters, including Fergus Macdonald and Hamilton Forbes.

After a few years Jamie had saved enough for all their fares to Canada, but Tom announced that he didn't want to go. He was eighteen and regarded himself as a man.

'Some of me mates are goin' up to Queensland this season,' he said. 'They reckon they can get a job with a drovin' plant up the Darling, and through Goondiwindi to a station on the Condamine, in time for shearin'. I've always wanted to see the Condamine River,' said Tom.

Bridget was most upset at the thought of 'leavin' him behind us' but, Jamie pointed out reasonably, she couldn't expect to keep him tied to her apron strings forever. Jamie was disappointed too, yet pleased that the lad was showing independence. Tom had always shown a strong feeling for what he called 'a fair go,' and would tackle anyone he saw bullying a smaller boy, so he was often in fights. He was a dark wiry youth, not very tall ('black Irish', said Bridget proudly), but with whipcord muscles and hard fists.

To young Tom Brown, Queensland had a romantic sound. He longed to travel north of the border, where the Condamine cattle-bells came from: musical, mellow square iron bells that sounded as the bullocks moved and fed, 'TONK! Tink-tonk!' in the darkness beyond the campfire's ring of light.

It was from the Condamine that the explorer Leichhardt had set out in 1848 to cross the continent; nothing had been seen or heard of his party since that day twenty-five years ago.

When Tom prepared to leave, his father gave him a new saddle and Bridget said a tearful farewell and gave him a St Christopher's medal to protect him on the road. She said she would pray for him 'ivery livin' day.' He was a strong, healthy lad, but she feared his temperament and his brown, sensitive eyes that could flash with fervour over ideas of liberty and equality, as Jamie's once had over the wrongs of Canada.

She was more worried about Jamie's health, for his old cough had come back. She hoped the sea voyage might cure him. Whatever happened they would be coming back to Australia. It was now their home, and Bridget could never be persuaded to stay in Canada, so far away from her son. To know he was 'knocking around somewhere in Queensland' was different from being separated from him by thousands of miles of ocean.

Two

TOM BROWN was thoroughly enjoying the independence of being 'on the track', away from his mother's anxious care. Crossing the border at Goondiwindi, he felt the dreamy warmth of Queensland in his bones. The Macintyre River wound placidly between its grassy banks; the Noisy Miners scolded from the gum-trees overhead; blue kingfishers darted along the reach.

He had discovered in himself a vein of bush poetry, or at least a facility in making up rhymes. Someone had been quoting Phillip Lorimer's lines:

Queensland, thou art a land of pest,
From flies and fleas we ne'er can rest . . .

119

and he thought he could do better than that. The old Aboriginal names of stations and settlements echoed with ready-made music: Thargomindah, Dirranbandi, Cunnamulla, Goondiwindi, Widgeegoara . . .

'In dreamy Goondiwindi, beside the Macintyre . . .' he began, but got no further. However, he was not one to give up.

He began composing verses in his head, as he lay in his unrolled swag under the stars or rode beside the wagon fitting rhymes to the slow sounds of the turning wheels. The rattling and jingling of chains, the creak of the wooden wheels, and the mournful bleating of sheep, blended into a kind of music inside his head:

> *Rackety-crack! Rackety-crack!* The wagonette complains,
> *We're on the track, we're on the track,* comes from the
> jingling chains . . .
> Spare horses all around us, the dogs high on the load –
> We're off again a-droving on the Dirranbandi road.

Tom wrestled with the second verse, until he had:

> Last trip I swore that nevermore a-droving I would go,
> And scrub and plain in drought and rain no longer would
> I know,
> Farewell ye Bulloo River, and dogs high on the load;
> I'll go no more a-droving on the Dirranbandi road.

He managed two more verses and the chorus, but it needed to be set to music for the hardbitten drovers to appreciate it.

When he stood up by the fire to declaim his masterpiece at the next night's camp, there were some ironical cheers and a few hand-claps, but the head drover growled, 'Ar, put a sock in it, Tommy. Yer've got a voice like an old billy-goat pissin' on a tin.'

Tommy was a little dashed, but his mate Dinny, an older man who had promised his mother to look after him (though Tommy did not know this), patted him on the shoulder and said, 'Good on yer, mate, it's got a real swing to it.'

Tom Brown had found the way of life that suited him. He

never wanted to go back to living in a house again. On the road, he felt a wonderful sense of freedom and independence. Lying awake he would hear, in the silence of the night, nothing but the howling of dingoes, silver-thin, a cry that rose tingling to the glittering stars; the chink of hobble-chains; or the lonely cry of the curlew.

After two months he and his mates with the droving plant delivered their mob of five thousand wethers to Warroo station, and were kept on for the shearing. Tom was still learning, but he was beginning to be an expert when the shed cut out.

He had been shocked at the conditions on stations in Queensland. It was almost like the bad old days when some squatters expected shearers to live in tents, and the iniquitous Masters and Servants' Act made station hands virtually slaves. The rate was £1 a hundred sheep. A gun shearer could earn good money, two or three pounds a day; but for a rouseabout or station-hand, it was only fifteen shillings or a pound a week and his keep. If he wanted jam and other extras such as vegetables, he had to pay for them.

The shearers' huts had earthen floors and the bunks were bare boards, nailed two deep round the walls, leaving just room for a full-length table in the centre with log benches all round it. Sixty shearers had to wash in six tin dishes, or they could bathe in the waterhole where the drinking water came from, and the water for washing their clothes.

The shearers' cook was 'a cranky coot', all were agreed, but he could turn out good tucker when he tried. Some of the men had a habit of tossing the food, untasted, out the door, plate and all, if they considered it not up to standard. Then one night at dinner they found the cook had nailed all the tin plates to the table.

Dinny was a bit of a practical joker. When they were all signing on for the season, he had given his name as 'Walter Schnuthrumpf.'

'How do you spell it?' asked the clerk, his pen poised.

'Be damned if I know!' said Dinny, and laughed madly, passing on.

The clerk turned to Tommy, next in line. 'Can't spell his own name? I've never heard of that!' he said.

121

'That's not his name,' explained Tommy, trying not to laugh. 'His name's Dinny Maloney.'

The shearing-shed was large, with sixty stands, their floors made of grating to let sheep droppings fall through so that they kept clean. There were two men to each pen of twenty sheep, and each four men had one picker-up who took the fleeces to the sorting-table, and swept up the pieces that fell loose from the solid mass of the fleece.

When the shed cut out, Dinny farewelled the cook with an 'Irish blessing'.

'I bear ye no ill-will, but I hope that when I'm dead an' buried me bones is nowhere near to yours, or I'd never sleep aisy.'

With forty pounds in his pocket, and moving always further westward, Tom set out for the dry Channel country. Dinny and the other shearers were making for the nearest pub to 'cut out' their cheques. Some of them intended to go to the coast, Melbourne or Sydney, but few of them ever got there before they had drunk all their money. Then they would camp on one of the permanent rivers, or take a few odd jobs, till shearing season came round again and they were once more – however briefly – in the money. It was a regular pattern which Tom did not intend to follow. He'd been drunk, dead drunk, a couple of times and did not enjoy the experience.

'Once I rung Coondoo shed and blued the cheque in a week,' Dinny used to boast. Young Tom thought it foolish to work so hard and have nothing to show for it after a week but a sore head or an attack of the 'DTs'.

He crossed many rivers whose names were familiar to him, ringing like Condamine bells in his mind: the Balonne, the Maranoa, the Warrego, the Paroo.

In 1874 he was a station hand on Nockatunga, getting experience among cattle, though he preferred sheep. That was the year that Timothy O'Hea (an Irishman who had been a Queen's soldier with the same regiment in Canada that helped to arrest Tom's father thirty-five years before), set out to look for a supposed survivor of Leichhardt's expedition. The search was being organised by an official of the Crown Lands Office. It was to be led by Andrew Hume (a distant relative of Mrs Betsy Forbes), who had been released from prison where he was held on remand on a charge of horsestealing. He knew the Western rivers, and was supposed to have information about a survivor living with the natives.

At Mungindi on the Queensland border these two were joined by Lewis Thompson, another ex-soldier. They stopped for a while at Thargomindah Station, but the shearing being over, Mr Dowling, the owner, was away in Sydney. It was late in the season for travelling; the summer heat was beginning to dry up the waterholes. Tom watched the party leave Nockatunga on the first day of November. What an adventure! He wished he could be going with them into that land of sand and mirage, out beyond Cooper's Creek.

Two weeks later, Lewis Thompson staggered into the homestead, more dead than alive. They revived him with sips of cold lime juice and water, and when he could speak through his swollen lips and tongue, he told how they had run out of water.

They had been heading west for Cooper's Creek and camped on Graham's Creek, which had water in it. Hume would not let him fill the large waterbags there because of the extra weight. They had gone on for three days without striking the Cooper. They cast about desperately, now seriously short of water, until Hume decided to go back to Graham's Creek. By now they were all badly dehydrated, their lips cracked and swollen.

Next day O'Hea collapsed, unable to go on. Thompson, as the youngest and strongest, volunteered to go back and get help or water. He stumbled on a small soak when nearly back to Nockatunga, and came in to get help.

'They were as fine fellows as I ever met,' croaked Thompson through his painful lips. 'Good fellows – good companions. Must take water – find them – before it's too late.'

A search party was organised, with two trackers from among the station Blacks who followed the meagre signs with uncanny skill. Tom Brown volunteered to go with the party. They never found O'Hea, who presumably had died first, and perhaps had been eaten by dingoes. The wild dogs would scatter his bones far and wide over the sandridges.

After ten days they found Hume's body. He had become

completely disorientated, walking in circles, and finally throwing off his clothes as he staggered along, perhaps seeing imaginary water in which he meant to bathe.

Tom Brown never forgot the sight of that body. The man had perished little more than two weeks before, but already the dried, blackened, sun-cooked flesh was parting from the bones. At the end of the withered legs was a pathetic pair of boots. His beard was thrust up at the sky, the cavern of his mouth a home for ants and flies.

They rolled what was left in a tarpaulin and took it back to the station for burial. O'Hea had disappeared forever in the scorching wastes, like Leichhardt before him.

After a searing summer, Tom felt that he'd had enough of heat and drought, and started to make back towards the coast. But first he took a job for a while as station-hand at Noccunda, and stayed on for shearing. Since Lachie Macdonald died the station had changed hands; there was a white woman in the homestead again, and Jennah was banished to sleep in the camp once more.

Lachie had never acknowledged his half-white children; they were their mother's responsibility. But he had treated Jennah almost as a wife, and she missed the boss's bed. She refused all advances from those of her own colour.

The travelling shearers got to know that Jennah was always ready for 'a good time,' that she had no blackfeller husband to make trouble. They urged young Tom to try his luck.

'Go on!' they said. 'Yer've got to dip yer wick some time. And she's not a bad looker, that Jennah.'

Tom protested that he wasn't interested. He was, of course. He was burning with curiosity to know and do and prove himself a man. But, a black woman! Well, she was a half-caste, not so very dark, what they called a yeller-feller in the west. And she was attractive in her thin, gaunt, vital way, with her high cheek-bones and deep-set eyes, her bright rag of a dress which was tight across her jutting breasts and slender hips. Her glossy dark hair hung to her shoulders, swung across her eyes as she crouched by the waterhole, washing out some child's shirt. She looked up under her dark brows, and saw Tom watching her. She smiled. Tom found himself smiling back.

'Eh, you meet me tonight, about moon-come-up?' she asked. 'Be'ind the woolshed. I wait for you.'

'All right,' stammered young Tom. 'Good-oh. I'll be there.'

But when the time came he nearly didn't go. Black velvet! It was a fact of life on most outback stations, he knew. But what would his mother think! She would expect him to wait till he got married, for a start. Well, he wasn't going to. You were only young once, as Dinny used to say.

The moon was rising over the wide plain, the dark mulga-clad sandhills, turning the saltbush to glittering silver bubbles, when Tommy with pounding heart sidled round the back of the woolshed. A low whistle greeted him.

Jennah gave a chuckle as he fumbled with her one garment and she drew him down in the deep shade against the shed wall.

'This first time for you, eh?' she said, and guided him where he wanted to be.

She was fierce, demanding, lithe and active, and came quickly. He couldn't believe it was all over, though it had been a great experience while it lasted. When he went back to the shearers' quarters he had to put up with a lot of teasing and sly jokes from the men.

Next day he felt a certain revulsion. Jennah, perhaps sensing this, gave him a mocking look as he passed by her near the wood-heap. He knew he was young and clumsy and no doubt she had not found him anything special. He left the station soon after, without knowing whether he had increased the number of part-white children (some of them half-brothers of his former boss's wife, Moira Macdonald Forbes) on Noccunda.

He took a job for a while as station-hand at Thargomindah, and there he met a fellow called Blue who had been cutting cane for a sugar farmer up the coast north of Brisbane. He was called Blue – rather than the obvious 'Carrots' – because his hair was orange-red.

'It's hard yakka in the cane,' said Blue, 'but you can make a packet in the season if you can keep your tally up. These Kanakas from the Islands are on daily rates of pay, but white blokes are faster and they're on piecework.'

So Tom saddled up, and loaded his pack-pony with all his worldly belongings, and they set off for the coast six hundred miles away, taking odd jobs along the route.

Tom was amazed to see the green standing cane, the neat square patches of cultivation on the rich red soil, the soft blue of a sky gauzed with moisture from the sea. But he didn't last long with the cane. It was terribly hard work, worse than shearing.

'What a racket!' he burst out to his mate Blue, after he had been talking to the Kanakas in their straw huts. 'D'you know what they're paid? About six bloody quid a year. A year! That's no more than ten bob a month . . . And expected to live on a bit o' rice and porridge, and work a twelve-hour day!'

'Shouldn't be brought inter the country, by rights – takin' jobs from white fellers,' growled Blue. 'That's the whole trouble with coloureds, Chinks and even Dagoes from south Italy, they're nearly as bad. Live on the smell of an oily rag, and get fat on it. No wonder we can't get a decent wage in Queensland. They're cutting back to fifteen bob a week for station 'ands.'

'Should be a pound a week minimum,' said Tom.

'Should be twenty-five bob, you mean.'

Tom tried to 'organise' the Kanakas, to get them to go together to the boss and say, 'More pay, or no work.' Conditions were bad enough for white men, at one pound two and six a week for ten or twelve hours a day working in the mill during the sugar season, and field workers were little better off.

He tackled the overseer first, who remarked impatiently that the men soon got used to the conditions, and were probably better fed and housed than they were on the island homes from which they had been brought (sometimes by force) to work in Queensland. Some worked in the juice-extracting mill, some in the fields.

'Yair, and eels get used to being skinned!' said Tom, walking away. His attempt to get the Kanakas to strike was a failure, as they were soon cowed by the overseer's loud voice, and still more by the whip and pistol stuck in his belt.

The only result was that Tom Brown was told not to come back next season. He couldn't be sacked as he was under contract, but the cane farmer made it clear that no one in the district would employ him again.

'You're a trouble-maker, I know your sort,' he said sourly.

Said Tom, 'There'd be no trouble if your men were properly paid.'

The big, bearded canegrower restrained himself with an effort. He'd have dearly liked to kick Tom Brown all the way to the gate of his property.

Next weekend Tom and Blue were riding into town, when they saw a spring-cart standing in the middle of the road.

'Looks like old Gates', ' said Blue – Gates was the boss.

The back of a man was just visible above the side of the cart. They rode alongside and looked in.

An extraordinary sight met their gaze. Trying not to laugh, they stared at Mr Gates, his hat gone, his hair and his full grey beard thick with molasses, which was dripping down his face. He had evidently been taking in forty-gallon casks for sale, when the chock moved from under one of them and it tipped over on the rough road, causing the bung to come out, and a stream of molasses to shoot over the driver. Apparently he had tried to fill the hole with his thumb, causing the stuff to spurt over him even more, till he was half blinded.

'Help! Can ye find the bung?' he cried, removing his thumb.

Blue groped in the sticky flood in the bottom of the cart, found the bung and replaced it.

'Any w-water near here?' asked the poor man. They led him to a puddle where he washed his head and face clear, and wiped his hands on his trousers. Tom gave him his red neckerchief to dry his face. It was only then, as his eyes came open, that he saw who his rescuers were.

'Oh, it's you, Brown!' he said. 'I suppose you think it's funny!'

And without a word of thanks climbed back into the cart and whipped up the horse.

'Blimey, how's that for gratitood?' said Blue.

When the season finished in Queensland, Blue set out for northern New South Wales where the crushing season started later, but Tom went for a holiday to the coast. He wanted a swim in the sea. But after that he was heading out west again where the grass wasn't this everlasting green, and the air was dry and the skies were clear, not curdled with great masses of steamy cloud.

Cane-cutting was hard and dirty work, but he didn't mind that so much. It was being dwarfed by that giant grass, lost among the stems like an insect, feeling unable to breathe in the humid, airless channels between the rows. Hating the very smell of the cane, he worked like a demon. There was nothing that he liked better than to see a canefield bare at last. He made up a song to an old hymn tune to relieve his feelings:

> The cane was bad, the cutters were mad,
> The cook fed us nothing but liver;
> And I'll never cut cane for that bastard again
> On the banks of the Mary River.
>
> So now I'm leaving this lousy place,
> I'll cut no more for that bugger,
> He can stand in the mud that's red as blood
> And cut his own bloody sugar.

In Tom's second year in Queensland, a letter came from Bridget, re-addressed from several of his last work places, to tell him his father had died in Canada only a week before they were to have caught the ship to return. He'd had a wonderful holiday, but he had felt the cold in his chest, and longed for the warmth of Australia. Bridget was catching the ship they had booked passage on, one of these new fast steamers, and would be home almost as quickly as the letter. She thought she would settle with her bachelor brother Brian in Brisbane, and she was his ever-loving Mam.

It was a brief letter, for as Bridget said herself, 'Faith, it's no hand with the pen I am, at all.' But Tom read between the lines, the bare words telling of Jamie's end, and understood her grief. She said that a cold had turned to pneumonia, and his weakened chest collapsed. It was all over in a few days.

'So at least he lies in the land of his father,' wrote Bridget, 'although the old man was no longer alive to welcome him home. It was for the love of Canada he was transported over the wide sea, and so 'tis fitting he should rest at last in her soil.

He is buried in Vancouver, in sight of the grand mountains, for 'twas from there we was about to sail when the sickness took him. I will never see Ireland more, but it's glad I am that he lived to see again the land where he was born.'

Tom went down to Brisbane to see his mother, finding her aged, still unable to believe that Jamie was gone, but happy to see him. She wept over him a little, then grew cheerful.

'It's thankful to God I am that He gave me a son,' she said, stroking his sunbrowned hand. 'Just to know that ye're there, me darlin' heart; a part of him that's gone.'

'You know, Mumma, I could never stay in the city. It has a fine river and all, but there's too many people. I don't even like the coast, it's too green, and the sea's too salt. In the sugar-cane there, I used to feel like an ant, smothered among those great stems of grass. What a pleasure it was to see it all cut down and crushed.'

'Sure, and it's not fittin' work for a white man, the heat and dirt of it, they say. It's not expectin' ye to stay I am, just to be seein' ye now and thin.'

'I'll come and see you every year after shearin'. That's a promise. But now I'm off out west again. And here are me savings to be goin' on with. I'll only lose it, or get robbed or something; I don't need money in the bush.'

'Ah Tommy, acushla! I don't need it neither. But I'll look after it for ye until ye need it.'

Bridget didn't trust banks. She put the roll of nearly two hundred pounds in notes in a flat tin under her mattress; and each year Tom added to it. He didn't spend much on drink or women, but he loved horses. The only time he asked her to take any money out of the tin was when he wanted to buy a good horse. And sometimes he bought her a present, knowing she would never spend the money on herself.

Three

SINCE HIS mother had settled in Brisbane, where her brother Brian O'Brien was working on the wharves as a stevedore or 'wharfie', Tom went less to New South Wales. He decided that he would start working for better conditions for rural workers in Queensland.

Brian had told him that the wharfies were going to organise themselves into a Waterside Workers' Federation, which would speak for members anywhere in Australia. The miners in New South Wales had started a strike in the coalmines to get their working day reduced from twelve to ten hours.

'Sure, we're all slaves of the big ship-owners and squatters and sugar barons,' said Brian, 'so it's always Us and Them, and Them's not goin' to give in without a fight. So then, we must organise. In the meantime, we can make t'ings a bit more equal,' and he winked at Tom, bending to pat his ankles. 'See them? Them's me pillagin' socks.' He indicated the large, loose woollen socks which he wore under his boots, and which came well up his legs. 'Plenty o' room there for a few t'ings which will not be missed from the cargo. Well now, and what's to be done when a crate splits open, an' the goods is all layin' about gettin' dirty in the hold?'

Tom was rather shocked, and not convinced of the morality of helping themselves in this fashion, but it was an accepted practice and evidently Brian felt no compunction.

Compared to the miners and wharf labourers, Tom found the rural workers apathetic.

'She'll be right, mate,' they said lazily when he approached them. 'Things are gettin' better.'

'Things are *not* getting better!' cried Tom. He found that the one thing which roused the shearers to something like fury was to find when they arrived at a shed that half the places had been taken by Chinamen. For the gold rush to the Palmer in the seventies had brought 60,000 Chinese coolies flocking to

Queensland, including those imported by New South Wales squatters when labour was scarce.

'Last year at McCaughey's station on the Warrego,' one bearded shearer complained, 'I seen nine or ten damned Chinamen a-shearin' in a row. That was enough for me. I rolled me swag and left his scabby station straight away.'

Tom now had a girl in Cunnamulla and another in New South Wales, at Collarenebri on the Barwon. Gertie was a good-time girl, blonde and voluptuous. He had no illusions about Gertie's doings when he was not around. Nancy, who worked on a station out of Cunnamulla, was different. She reminded him of his mother, with her black hair and blue eyes, but she was not so tall and her figure was comfortably rounded, with full breasts and hips – what his father would have called 'sonsie'.

Nancy wrote to him sometimes, and he sent her his latest verses and songs, which she copied out in her neat round hand. Her widowed mother, who had been the wife of the station blacksmith and saddler, was a Lancashire lass with a broad north-England accent. Nancy, as a child, was allowed to attend classes with the governess who taught the boss's children. Later she stayed on to teach the younger ones herself.

When each year the itinerant shearers arrived, there would be competition for the notice of plump, pretty Nancy Beveridge. Tom had to knock down a big, bullying fellow from the south, who regarded Nancy as his property, before she became his. She had noticed Tom as soon as he arrived. When most men wore beards, Tom Brown was clean-shaven, which with his neat compact figure gave him a deceptively boyish look. By now he was twenty-eight, hard-bitten and assured, with a reputation as a tough bare-knuckle fighter: a personable, still-young man with dark hair and bright brown eyes, and a strong, knobbly, determined chin.

When he was leaving for the shearing at Charleville and Miles, he kissed her goodbye and sang in his light baritone,

Oh Nancy, dearest Nancy, pray do not hold me back,
The men have all gone mustering, and I must be on the
track;

So here's a goodbye kiss, love, back here I will incline,
When we've shore the last of the jumbucks on the Banks of
the Condamine.

'Who's trying to hold you back?' asked Nancy crossly. 'That stupid song! With the woman saying she'll "cut off all her auburn fringe, and be a shearer too!" Fat chance! And I certainly wouldn't cook and count your tally and wash your greasy moleskins, men should wash their own greasy trousers in my opinion. Who would want to go shearing just to be some man's slave?'

Oh Nancy, dearest Nancy, [sang Tom irrepressibly]
With me you may not go,
The squatters have given orders, love, no woman may do so;
And your delicate constitution is not equal unto mine
To withstand the constant tigering on the banks of the
Condamine.

'What nonsense! My constitution is just as strong as yours. And fancy that "Willy" saying "the squatters have given orders". Since when have Australian men and women taken *orders* from the squatters?'

'Don't get so worked up about it; it's only a song.'

'Yes, a man's song. If I wanted to come along with you I would, but only as an equal, not a domestic servant.'

Tom laughed at her vehemence, but he liked her spirit. He sang 'Nancy Nancy, tickle me fancy' instead.

When shearing finished in Queensland he crossed into New South Wales, where the season was later.

Travelling from shed to shed, he found himself at Macdonald's Balranald in the western Riverina. Here W. G. Spence, who had led the Victorian miners in a successful fight for shorter working hours, was organising the shearers to form a union.

At an open-air meeting in Balranald township, with a Scottish skill and zeal that Fergus Macdonald might have admired, he exhorted the men to close their ranks and get

132

every shed in Victoria and New South Wales closed to all but Union labour, with no employment of Chinese or Kanakas who would accept low rates. Fergus was among the group of angry squatters who rode round the gathering on their thoroughbreds, cracking their horsewhips and jeering at 'Spence the agitator.'

The Amalgamated Shearers' Union was founded that day, and when the cheering had died down and the squatters had ridden away, Tom spoke to William Spence, a man about ten years older than himself.

'And what about Queensland, Mr Spence?' he asked. 'They seem to be too easy-going up there, don't want to fight.'

'Queensland is next on my itinerary,' said Spence. 'After South Aus, that is. Australia's such a wide country, it's a job to get all the bush workers together; but later they'll all be in it. And not just the shearers, but all the workers: stockmen, miners, wharf labourers, factory workers – an Australian Workers' Union, Australia wide! Think of the power of the worker then! We can do it; we only have to stick together.'

Tom was impressed, inspired. He joined the ASU forthwith and became a foundation member in 1886.

The angry meeting had arisen because the squatters, faced with the cost of exterminating rabbits and a drop in the price of wool, had got together and agreed to reduce the rate for shearing a hundred sheep to seventeen shillings and sixpence, when the standard rate was a pound.

This was the last straw for shearers, already uneasy about the threat of machinery taking away their jobs, for machine shears had been invented and would soon be in use on all the bigger stations. The first showdown had come on Balranald Station, where the men refused to shear Macdonald's sheep. As the wool had to be got off before it deteriorated on the sheep's back in the hot weather, every day Fergus was losing money. At last he had to give in and agree to the shearers' terms. The men gave a great shout of victory.

Tom Brown made up the words of a song and called it 'The Squatter's Defeat'. It became a favourite Union song and was printed in a popular song-book, with its rousing lines,

> You would starve us, devil doubt you,
> But we've lived before without you;
> Take my tip, a blow we'll never cut
> Per hundred less a pound!

It was set to a lively tune that someone remembered and was roared out by the shearers around the fire at night. This was Tom's first attempt at 'political' verse, and it brought him more notice than all the bush ballads of his which had appeared in the Sydney *Bulletin*, some under the pen-name of 'Thomas the Rhymer'.

He took a trip to Sydney to see 'the Big Smoke' and visit the offices of *The Bulletin* in George street, where he met the editor who had been taking the outback verses and 'Aboriginalities' paragraphs that Tom sent him. Travelling out west again by train, he went to Bourke and then followed the Wool Track up the Darling and the Barwon to Collarenebri. Spending a week with Gertie on the way, he picked up two new horses and rode back to Brisbane, crossing the border at Goondiwindi where he had first tried his hand at poetry.

Back in Brisbane, Uncle Brian clasped him in his arms.

'Ye're one of the bards, me boy!' he cried. 'In Ireland the poet is a king. And ye can be after tellin' yer mates that we've got a Wharfies' Union now, and if they're wishin' to fight them squatters, we'll be behind 'em. Sure an' if we refuse to load the woolbales into the ships, what can the squatters do?'

Tom was to remember those words when later the fight moved to Queensland.

He stayed the rest of the year with his mother, doing odd jobs about the house and garden, and persuading her to take some of his savings for board. He noted with a pang how old she was looking, her blue eyes and black hair both faded to grey, her pale clear skin now wrinkled very finely, like crumpled tissue paper.

It was more than two years since Tom had been to Cunnamulla. As soon as shearing time came round he set off from Brisbane, riding his brown gelding and leading his packhorse, a gentle chestnut mare he had bought with his last shearing cheque before leaving New South Wales. She was never any trouble to catch, would come at his whistle like a

134

dog, and would follow even without the lead rein wherever the brown horse led.

She was like a submissive woman, he thought; she seemed to have no will except to follow and to serve. Not like Nancy! *She* was one of these independent types, ready to flare up at the slightest suggestion of ordering her about. And yet she could be loving and submissive, too, in bed. He had found Gertie's aggressive sex unusual and exciting at first, but it began to pall after a while, especially when a man was tired from a long day in the shearing-shed. He looked forward happily to a few weeks in Nancy's company again. How could he have stayed away so long?

He arrived early, so as to have some time with Nancy before the hard work began, and helped with the mustering and penning before shearing. Her room at the station opened off the end of the veranda. He spent the first night there.

'How did you get on the last two seasons without me, eh?' he asked, spreading his bare feet against the iron bed-end while he played with a strand of her dark hair. 'I bet you had to fight off the blokes, all after a beaut sheila like you.'

'They know you've put your brand on me,' said Nancy.

He laughed, pulling her over on top of him.

'Let's make up for lost time, eh? Oh darling, I could do this all night – '

'No, you couldn't. And we must have something to eat . . . Oh God, it's good to feel you there again!'

'I used to dream about being up you, and then I'd wake in some rotten shearers' hut on a hard bunk, alone.'

'Well, you knew where to find me.'

Some time later, Tom woke from a delicious doze, his head pillowed on a soft, smooth breast, to a cry which seemed to come from the next room. A child crying?

'Mummee!' said a high, petulant voice.

Nancy struggled out from under the sheet and put on a wrapper. 'Coming, darling.'

She went onto the veranda and into the next room. While Tom sat up in bed, staring, his arms crossed on his bare, hairy chest, she came back with a baby boy astride her hip: light brown hair, damp with sweat, flushed rosy cheeks, big blue eyes, and a mouth screwed into a protesting grimace.

'This is Charlie,' she said defiantly.

'But – but – is he yours?'

'Whose do you think?'

'Yours and – mine?'

'Of course. Say hello to Daddy, pet.'

The child glared under his brows at the stranger, then turned his face away against his mother's breast, grizzling.

'How old is he?'

'Just on two.'

'Nancy! And you never told me!'

'I was waiting for you to come back. I wanted to be sure you wanted me. I wasn't going to blackmail you into – '

'Blackmail! You crazy girl. I want to marry you anyway. But now more than ever. My son, eh!' There was no doubt he was pleased; a proud papa.

Nancy didn't know about Gertie, and Tom decided that what she didn't know wouldn't hurt her. He would miss Gertie, but he knew now he would not be seeing her again. He was fond of her, but she would not break her heart over him.

The station boss and his wife had been very kind to Nancy, allowing her time off to have the baby and giving her a room next to her own for a nursery. She and Tom were married in the little Methodist church in the nearest township, which was what Nancy wanted. Her mother was in Sydney, and neither of them had any family present at the ceremony. Tom had been brought up a Roman Catholic by his mother, but he had no prejudices and not much time for priests or parsons, his only religion that of 'mateship' – the religion of the outback. He liked to quote Henry Lawson's 'Shearers':

> No church-bell rings them from the track,
> No pulpit lights their blindness –
> 'Tis hardship, drought and homelessness
> That teach those bushmen kindness . . .
> They tramp in mateship side by side,
> The Protestant and Roman –
> They call no biped Lord or sir,
> And touch their hat to no man!

'And I wish *I* had written that,' said Tom.

Four

WHENEVER HE could, in the months until shearing came round again, Tom stopped with his growing family in Cunnamulla. It was a bit like being married to a sailor, Nancy thought. He came and went, and they never had time to get tired of each other. There was now a little girl, Emma, and a baby, Agnes.

Nancy still helped in the big house, so they had been given one of the station hands' cottages. Tom could have got a regular job as a stockman, but the wandering life of a shearer was in his blood. He still intended to buy a place of his own, but couldn't decide which Western town to settle in. Nancy suggested the coast, but he preferred the dry inland, where the climate suited him and his work was to be found.

Charlie was growing into a leggy, sunbrowned small boy, running barefoot and hatless in the sun, so that his hair was a bleached straw colour, streaked with brown. He was inclined to tease Emma, who shed floods of tears.

'Don't waste all that precious water, child!' Nancy would admonish her. 'Go outside at once and cry on the geraniums.'

Emma would run to the dusty patch of garden, and was so tickled with the idea that she was watering the flowers that her tears soon stopped.

Charlie never cried nor sulked. He was a good-tempered and helpful lad, in spite of teasing the girls sometimes; though his mother declared that 'he was never there when she wanted him', but off swimming or catching yabbies in the river. But he could be trusted to mind the baby, and to help Emma get dressed.

Nancy sometimes wrote to Bridget and sent her some photographs of the children taken by a travelling photographer. She had resisted all their grandmother's appeals to have them 'brought up in the Faith, as Tommy was.' It was such a long journey by coach and train to Brisbane that they had not met.

Though Tom had told Mr Spence that Queenslanders were apathetic, it was in Queensland that the hostility between shearers and squatters came to a head. Trouble flared at Aramac Station near Longreach, where the men refused to work under an overseer who employed Chinese.

A Queensland Shearers' Union had been formed in 1887. At Beaconsfield Station the men put up a printed sign, 'This shed under Q.S.U. rules'. The rules stated that no Chinese, Japanese, or Kanakas, or any other coloured race except for Australian Aborigines, should be allowed to join the Union.

When the squatters, like those in the southern colony, voted to reduce their rates to 17/6d a hundred sheep shorn, and to employ Chinese who would accept these rates, there were mass meetings of protest. Speakers told the men they were 'little better than slaves' under the Masters and Servants' Act. At Meteor Downs, Logan Downs and Wellshot, the shearers stood out for Union rates for shed hands. By 1891, more than 10,000 workers were engaged in the struggle for better conditions.

The squatters already had their own union, the Pastoralists' Association. 'They say they only want "freedom of contract",' said Tom, 'to be able to engage whoever they like; and that they "have no wish to cover their shearing boards with Kanakas and Chinamen". But we all know there are stations where the labour's done by Aboriginal stockmen working for just their keep, and where as many as seventy Chinamen are employed for shearing.'

He addressed several meetings in western Queensland. Feeling against the squatters hardened, and in March 1891 a general strike was called by the shearers. The squatters responded by asking the Government to call in the military. One of them got his wool off with scab labour and drove a wool wagon himself down to the wharves at Brisbane. The result was a riot on the wharves; the Riot Act was read, and the maritime unions came out as well. The State Government voted for the use of force.

Defiantly, the pastoral workers formed camps on the inland rivers outside the big western towns. A line of messengers was stationed at twenty-five-mile intervals on billabongs and creeks, to give warning of the arrival of 'free labour'. At

Barcaldine a huge camp was set up on the banks of the Alice River, with tents and a well-organised food supply. Every day, meetings were held beneath a big old gum-tree near the railway station. They sang Francis Adams's 'Fling out the Flag' and Tom Brown's new song, 'The sheds'll be shore Union, Or they won't be shore at all.'

When the shearers' strike erupted, Nancy was still in Cunnamulla with the children, where she waited while Tom followed his wandering calling; she had known it would be so when she married him. But she was not going to miss all the excitement of the fight against the squatters. She packed her clothes and the children's and joined Tom at the camp in Barcaldine. Here she became one of the cooks at the strike headquarters on the Alice River, two miles out of town.

She also helped to run off pamphlets on a copying-machine, including sheets of Tom's songs, 'The Squatter's Defeat' and 'The Sheds'll be Shore Union'.

Tom Brown and Julian Stuart, a red-bearded Scot, continued to write songs and poems to incite the shearers. Soon all work in the pastoral districts was at a standstill. Tom was carried away by his own eloquence. He was among the leaders who worked to get the iniquitous Masters and Servants' Act repealed, and a guaranteed wage of 25s and keep for pastoral workers. Also the banning of coloured labour, and an eight-hour day and a six-day week, with no work on Saturday afternoons.

Feelings ran high in Auguthella, Hughenden, Barcaldine and Clermont. Some shearing sheds were burnt, and sabotage of railways and public buildings was urged. Henry Lawson wrote a warning poem, 'If blood should stain the wattle', while E. J. Brady exhorted them to:

> Close the ranks a little longer,
> Leave the tyrants' sheep unshorn.

There was a heady excitement in preparing for battle. Tom wrote to his mother:

A thousand men are encamped in a regular canvas town here, and from a tree the blue flag is flying . . . The spirit of

Eureka is born again. There is regular 'army' drill, tho' very few have guns. And it's not much use having Johnny cakes in our hands for weapons if they bring up the Army. We won't be the first to fire a shot, but that shot could be the beginning of civil war.

Some hotheads had already been arrested for such things as 'abusive language' and 'disturbing the peace'. Several woolsheds on scab stations were mysteriously burnt down, and it was alleged that men from Clermont camp tried to sabotage the train bringing strike-breaking workers from the south.

Premier Griffith brought in the Army, with a formidable array of Gatling guns and one big Nordenfeldt gun pointing at the camp. A large detachment of soldiers protected each contingent of 'free labourers' as they arrived on the railway stations.

Booed and jeered by the strikers, they had to sleep on the shearing board in the woolshed, with armed soldiers to protect them. Industrial depression was spreading in the southern cities, and there was no lack of men willing to work even under these conditions.

The fight culminated in 'the Clermont riot', when two hundred strikers rode into town and, according to the police 'attempted to take over all the Government institutions, including the railway'. One of them called for 'three groans for the Queen', and an effigy of Griffith was burnt in the street. Then the military arrived, with the Nordenfeldt gun, and the rioters faded back to camp.

'The men went peaceably to camp when the soldiers appeared with the big gun. Their own sense of law and order restrained them, not cowardice,' wrote Tom uncertainly to his mother. 'They deliberately avoided a collision with the Army.'

The following day he was arrested, at the point of a gun, along with all the other strike leaders in western Queensland.

'You will be shot if you move; the Riot Act has been read in the camp,' he was told as he came to the flap of his tent.

His anger exploded. 'Fire!' he said. 'Go on, fire! That's all you're good for, shooting defenceless men.'

He turned aside to comfort the older children, Charlie who was staring wide-eyed at the uniformed soldier, and Emma. 'Run over to the cook-tent and tell Mummy I've had to go away for a while,' he said. 'I'll be back as soon as I can.'

With six other men from the camp he was handcuffed to one chain and put on a coach for Jericho on the western railway. There he was put with fourteen others, some of them brought from Hughenden, in two cells only eight feet square. When he wanted to go outside at night to the closet, Tom had to wear a leg iron with a heavy chain attached and be escorted by a policeman with a drawn revolver. After nine days in the stifling cells, they were taken out to board the train for Rockhampton where they were to be tried. They were fitted with leg-irons for the journey.

As they hobbled towards the railway station, Tom sat down in the road and refused to get up. 'I won't walk another step till these damned irons are taken off!' he said.

'Same here.' And one after another the men plumped down in the dust.

A policeman menaced them with his pistol, but they sat firm. At last the irons were unlocked and they got aboard the train, heavily guarded and handcuffed.

At Rockhampton, they were charged with sedition, and 'imperilling the peace of our sovereign Lady the Queen, her crown and dignity'. They were sentenced to twelve years' gaol each. It was a shock to all of them, such a savage sentence for a political crime. Why, his son would be grown up, a young man, before he saw him again! thought Tom.

He was sent with the other 'conspirators' to the island prison in Moreton Bay known as 'St Helena'. Other inmates were long-term prisoners and murderers, but it was healthier than the Brisbane Gaol.

Bridget, now in her seventies, was felled by the news as by a physical blow. She had dreaded to hear that Tommy was dead, or wounded in the fighting everyone expected to break out. But this was somehow worse. He was condemned to a living death, as his father had been before him.

'Blast thim!' she screamed. 'Blast the bloody tyrants, one and all. God blast the Queen, and the Guvmint, an' the lot av thim!'

Then she fell senseless to the floor. She never recovered consciousness before a second stroke carried her off.

The strike ended in failure. The combination of financial depression, the invention of the shearing machine, and the hostility of 'the lying Capitalist Press' was too much for the Union. A man could learn to shear in a few days with these wonderful gadgets which took the wool off so cleanly. They claimed that the strike had been valuable in bringing the workers together and retired to lick their wounds and to concentrate on getting Union men elected to Parliament.

So arose the Labour Electoral League, and the Australian Workers' Union formed in 1894.

When he was sentenced Tom had told the court passionately that 'he would just as soon go to Hell to look for ice, as come into this Court and look for justice.'

There was a strong feeling abroad that the men had not received fair play; and one of the Labour candidates elected by the Electoral Lobby as Member for Bourke, later made a strong appeal in the House for the jailed bushmen. He described some of those still imprisoned as 'valuable citizens,' and of Thomas Brown he said:

'He is a true Australian man, noble minded, honest to a fault, but one who resents the oppression of the producer by the capitalist. He has more than average intelligence, has written some fine bush verse, and has always conducted himself respectably as taught by his parents . . .'

All this eloquence had some effect, besides the continuing campaign by the Labour newspaper, *The Worker*. At last, in November 1893, the thirteen gaoled 'martyrs' were released.

The Worker brought out a special number with a group photograph of the men sentenced at Rockhampton. They had been imprisoned for two years and six months, and the experience had aged them.

Tom was now thirty-four. He had found prison a good place for composing verses, at first, but after the news of his mother's death from a stroke came through, he spent his spare time brooding. He knew that it was grief that had killed her; he felt that the Government was responsible, as surely as if one of the strike-breaking soldiers had shot her through the heart.

Tom's verse after he left prison became savagely satirical, and was less popular. He looked years older, for his hair had receded and the black beard he had grown while incarcerated already had threads of grey in it. Before he left Brisbane he had his photograph taken with the other 'martyrs' on the lawns in the Botanic Gardens, where they had a Union picnic with kegs of beer and cold prawns, which went on till sunset. It was a hot summer's day in November. Rainbow parrots were screeching among the red and yellow blossoming trees, feeding on nectar, swooping from tree to tree with loud cries of shrill, fierce joy in life. He felt almost blinded by the brilliance of sunshine, white cloud and blue sky, green palms and blazing bougainvilleas, and the purple-blue of jacarandas shedding their blossom on the grass. It was as though he had been dead for nearly three years, and had been resurrected.

And now Nancy was waiting for him, and the children . . . He gazed at a figure in long skirts passing between the trees, two children running alongside. The letters and parcels from Nancy had kept him going. Nancy had lost all chance of returning to her job on the station through her connection with the strike. She now had a job in a Longreach hotel, five hundred miles due west of Rockhampton and right on the Tropic of Capricorn. It was hot as hell in summer, she wrote, and freezing cold (but dry and sunny) in winter. The pub provided board for her and the children.

Tom wrote that she might think hell and Longreach were warm, but a shearer who died in Booligal had somehow got a message to his mates from the next world: 'Can't stand the cold, please send my overcoat to hell.'

'So don't let them tell you that Queensland is hotter than New South,' he added.

A letter from Uncle Brian O'Brien, written in a cramped, schoolboy hand, told him that Bridget had left Tom everything except her bits of furniture, which she had given to him (Brian), and that there was nearly a thousand pounds in old cigarette tins under her mattress when she died. He had only taken a bit out 'to give her a decent funeral.'

Tom now had this money in a roll in his wallet. He took the next train north to Rockhampton, where he booked in at a comfortable hotel on the river-front, overlooking a broad reach of the muddy Fitzroy.

He woke early, and folding back the wooden shutters, lay looking at the calm green-reflecting water, with some water-birds swimming round on it. There was a jingle of crockery in the corridor; a part-Aboriginal girl with a big smile brought him a cup of early morning tea.

Tea in bed! And a hot bath the night before in a luxurious full-length tub. He got up and wandered barefoot on to the grey sun-warmed boards of the veranda which ran right around the hotel at the second level, with a railing of white-painted iron lace. It was rather like the deck of a ship, on which he was sailing along that wide green-brown river . . . Tom felt himself relax, unwind completely, for what seemed the first time in centuries.

He went to the station to book a seat on the train. The line had just been extended to Longreach. He couldn't wait to get home, and 'home' was where Nancy and the children were. Now, with the savings his mother had left him, he could buy a small house for them.

The stationmaster informed him there would not be another passenger train for two days. There was only the 'Mixed', leaving at 5.30 p.m. No sleepers, only a couple of grey blankets to put on the padded seat. Tom almost laughed at him. It would be luxury after his hard prison pallet.

He was on the station by five. The train left ten minutes late. He had bought a couple of meat pies with tomato sauce from the station Refreshment Rooms and swallowed a cup of stewed, near-boiling tea. In gaol, living on stews and skilly, he had dreamed about meat pies and peas.

That was the longest journey he ever remembered. There was no corridor, just a two-seat compartment cut off from the rest of the train; no other carriages, but a long line of goods trucks. A dozen times in the night they pulled up in the middle of nowhere, or stopped to unload something at a tiny siding.

Sometime about midday they reached Barcaldine. Tom didn't know how much time he had, but he jumped off and walked into the main street, looking at the 'Tree of Know-ledge', the big old white-gum under which they had held their meetings daily. It had been an exciting time. Now he just wanted peace and quiet, and Nancy's arms around him.

He ordered a pie with peas and mashed potato, but just as he was going to eat it the train's whistle blew. He had just time to grab the pie in his hand and sprint for the station, cursing as the hot gravy burnt his hand.

While he ate what was left of the pie, he said to himself:

> Passengers could die of hunger,
> On the way to Warrumbunga!
> Iron rations come in handy
> During halts at Dirranbandi.
> Let us toast, before we part
> Those who travel, stout of heart,
> Drunk or sober, rain or shine,
> On a Queensland railway line.

Not only was there nothing procurable to eat on the train, there was not even water in the dusty container in one corner. He seemed to have the whole train to himself, apart from the guard and the engine driver. Western people knew better than to catch this train.

The one light was inadequate, high in the ceiling. When it got dark again he lay down on the seat and pulled the grey blankets up to his chin. Beyond the window he saw that ethereal green afterglow in the west towards which they travelled, as the apricot light faded from the flat land's edge. Clear inland skies! They seemed higher, purer, than on the steamy coast. The sun was brighter, stars were sharper, and Venus as the Evening Star danced along above the plains.

The train stopped with a jolt which threw him to the floor. As soon as he climbed back, it started again with a jerk. The blankets slid from the slippery seat. He gave up trying to sleep, and sat with his forehead against the cold glass . . . Then there were lights ahead. Could this be Longreach at last?

Another lurch, screech, grind of brakes, and they were slowing for Longreach station. It was nearly nine o'clock; he had been on the train for 28 hours without even a cup of tea. He grabbed his bag. There was no one on the station to meet the train, only a few railwaymen to deal with the goods being unloaded.

Feeling flat and tired, all the excitement with which he had boarded the train for the West long evaporated, he stepped down onto the platform, shouldering the bag with his new clothes bought in Brisbane with money the Union had provided. Where was Nancy? At least she might have been here to meet him.

Outside in the long, wide street, someone was tying a horse and sulky to a hitching post: a plump, petite figure, a mass of dusky hair . . . He ran, gathered her in his arms.

'Oh, Nancy, dearest Nancy!'

'Ohh, Tom!'

Then it was a wordless embrace, long and close, in which they seemed to float in some other dimension. All the longing, the loneliness, the separation of three years, it seemed to Tom, were almost worth it for the sweetness of that reunion.

'Where are the kids? Are they all right?'

'All well. A girl-friend is minding them for me. I've been back three times, and then they said the train wouldn't be in till nine.'

'I'm starving. There was nothing to eat or drink on that rotten train.'

'You shouldn't have come on the "Mixed".'

'It was that or wait another two days, and I wanted to get back to you.'

'Oh Tom! You look so thin!' She didn't add, and so old and different I hardly knew you.

'Can we get something to eat at the pub?'

'No, dinner's over; we'd better call at the Greek's and get some steak and eggs. The kids are asleep by now anyway.'

He stared at her under the station lamps as if he couldn't see enough.

'Do you know I've hardly set eyes on a woman for nearly three years?' he said. 'That's one of the worst things about prison, it's so depriving, so unnatural, apart from the lack of freedom. I wasn't bored, I did some writing and they let me have books to read, though not enough. I've read the Bible right through twice . . . What a nasty, vengeful old cove the

146

Old Testament God was, to be sure! I can't believe I'm really here, with you.'

She stroked his silky black beard. 'I wish you'd shave it off, it makes you look older.'

'I *am* older,' he said grimly.

'Well, it's all over now. Come on. I borrowed the sulky; I wasn't sure if you'd be too weak to walk . . . You're all right, Tom?'

'Yes, love. I'm all right.'

Five

FROM THE time when he first went to school, young Charlie Brown became 'Chukka' Brown. The name clung to him, partly because in the game of cricket he could 'chuck' the ball with deadly accuracy, making it whizz about the stumps, and partly because he used the word freely in conversation in every possible and impossible context.

When he was sick he 'chucked up' his dinner, when he asked his sisters to pass the butter or salt, he said 'Eh, chuck us the butter, will yer?' or 'Chuck the salt over here,' though his mother scolded him for such slangy talk.

'You should always use good English,' she said.

'Aw, chuck it, Mum,' he would drawl. 'It's a good Australian word.'

Chukka grew up without a father for a lot of the time, for Tom was in gaol for three years and was often away shearing. As the only boy he became careful and protective of his mother and sisters.

Chukka was fired with the usual ambition to become a gun shearer and perhaps beat the records of Jimmie Power or the famous Jackie Howe (who invented the sleeveless singlet to give his arms more freedom of movement when shearing

147

three hundred and twenty-one sheep with blade shears in less than eight hours).

He knew his father was a good shearer, who had been ringer of the shed more than once. When he was home Tom liked to talk of the great days when the Labour movement was born under the white-gum tree at Barcaldine. (They had a house now at Longreach, and Nancy no longer worked at the hotel.) Tom would take the two girls, Agnes and Emma, on his knee and sing them the songs and rhymes he had composed during the shearers' strike: all about brave fighters for justice and the despised scabs who refused to join them.

'Your father wasn't a scab,' Nancy would put in proudly. 'He was in the thick of the fight, and they sent him to gaol just for sticking up for his mates.'

However, Tom had had enough of gaol, and kept out of the New South Wales fight which culminated in the burning of the paddle-steamer *Rodney* near Tolarno Station on the Darling in 1894. She was carrying scab shearers from the south, when the strikers put a wire rope across the river which she steamed into in the darkness. Eight men were arrested, but they had an alibi proving they were in camp at the time of the incident.

The Wolsey machine with power-driven shears was now used everywhere, except for prize rams which were still shorn with blade shears. If a machine should slip and remove a vital part it would be a costly mistake.

'Careful of his balls!' the anxious boss of the board would beg, watching closely as a lordly ram was divested of his great weight of wool.

At shearing time the big stations had become like factories where the huge sheds employed up to 150 shearers, and the clip was classed, scoured, and baled for export on the property.

The steam-driven machines clicked and whirred, while the men worked with the untiring precision of machines.

Chukka didn't like machinery. After listening to some of his father's tales of the green sugar-land on the coast, he thought he might 'chuck the idea of being a shearer, and have a go at the sugar.'

'You don't want to do that,' said Tom. 'It's hard, filthy work. See how soft and clean my hands are from working with wool? That's the natural lanolin in the wool does that. But cane-cutting! Hell, that's really tough. Your hands get calloused, you're covered in tacky juice with red dust sticking to it, and if you cut yourself with the cane-knife – they use these great big *pangas*, murderous things – it starts to fester in the heat and dirt and you come up in boils. No, I tried cane-cuttin' once, but I gave it away.'

'They burn the cane before they cut it these days. It gets rid of all the trash, and the vermin as well, the snakes and rats – '

'How would you know, son?'

'A bloke was telling me. And there's good money in it. Specially now they're goin' to boot out the Kanakas.'

For he had read in the newspapers that all the Pacific Islanders were soon to be deported to their home islands, as it was found that white men could work in the tropics after all.

'And about time, too,' said Tom. 'Australia for the white man, I say. That's a plank of the Labour platform. Why, when I was in Buderim in '78, I see this big fuzzy-haired feller – he was quite a pleasant bloke, with a big toothy grin – who was married to a white woman! She seemed an all right type, too; but it stands to reason – I mean it goes without saying – that no decent white woman would be livin' with a blackfeller. They had a slab and bark humpy and a garden of bananas and mangoes; Barney was a good gardener, I'll give him that in, and a hard worker. A pity he took up with a woman of that description.'

'But Dad! Perhaps she loved him. It's not unheard of.'

Tom ignored this. He had just remembered something he preferred to forget: his first adventure with a woman, half brown, half white, who had been the offspring of such a union. Jennah! He had even forgotten her name until now.

'A' course,' he said, 'his idea was prob'ly that he won't get sent back with the others since he's married to an Australian. Some of the Chinks get married here for the same reason. But you don't like to see a woman stoop so low.'

'You mean he was an Islander, not an Aborigine?'

'Yair, a Kanaka. One o' them.'

'I reckon they're Australians now, and should be allowed to join the Union. As it is they're just being exploited.'

'They're helpin' the squatters and cane-cockies to exploit

us,' said Tom. 'Living on a handful of rice and sixpence a day! Next thing they'll be bringin' Indian coolies here, they tried it on once at Mackay but the local men wouldn't have a bar of it. There'd have been bloodshed if they hadn't got them back on board the ship, quick-smart.'

'Oh, I dunno,' said Chukka lazily. 'Live and let live, that's my motto. I wouldn't have chucked them out.'

'Bah!' said Tom. 'You don't know anything about it. White men are just better workers, in tough jobs like cane-cuttin'.'

He was disappointed to find that none of his own crusading spirit seemed to have been inherited by Charlie, who was easy-going to the point of being negative. He was a long, lean, slow-speaking, 'typical' Australian of the second generation, fair where his father was dark, his light-blue eyes with their clear whites contrasting with his bony, tanned face.

'A' course,' said Tom reminiscently, 'it's not all a bed of roses when you're shearing, either. Things are a lot better now, though. When I started the big sheep barons treated us men like serfs. We had no showers, no lavs – sometimes there was an open pit for a latrine, sometimes there was nothin', you were expected to go behind a bush or a tree . . . No wonder 'Barcoo Spew' was so common! Sometimes there was no water-tank, no drinkin' water except the nearest creek. During the last drought the flies were like bees in western New South: fallin' into your tea, into the stew. A man had to fight the flies for every mouthful!'

'Well, they're not so bad on the coast, are they?'

'No, the mossies'll get you there. And the sandflies. Bring you up in great weeping lumps till you get used to 'em. They're that tiny you can't hardly see them – but bite! Struth! Wait till the sandflies get you.'

'Mmm,' said Chukka. Later he read out of the Brisbane *Courier*: 'NO MORE KANAKA LABOUR. It has long been felt that the employment of cheap Asiatic and Islander labour in Queensland is not in the best interests of our development. The policy is supported only by those who make capital by the use of such labour.'

'Too right!' said Tom.

After his eighteenth birthday Chukka, like his father before him, left home; not to go shearing, but to become a cane-cutter. He kissed his mother and sisters goodbye on the railway platform, and wrung Tom's hand. They all looked so sad, the girls a bit weepy, that he kept his face solemn till the train left. As soon as it was speeding towards the distant coast, he put his feet up on the seat opposite and let his face relax into a contented grin.

'You'll be sorry!' his father had said at parting. And 'Have a look at the "Tree of Knowledge" in Barcaldine when you go through. And give the courthouse in Rocky a kick for me.'

From Rockhampton Chukka travelled south as far as Maryborough, where he joined a team cutting cane on old Angus Johnstone's property, Chindera, which employed two hundred men in the field and in the juice mill.

Griffith, who had been going to deport all the Kanakas by 1890, and then by 1902, had been persuaded to extend the time limit; and in practice it was to be 1906 before the last were sent back to their former islands, which most of them had long forgotten, and where they were not welcome.

Chukka's costume for working in the cane was much the same as theirs: shorts for hot weather, long dungarees for cold, three Jackie Howe singlets, a pair of heavy work-boots with large, thick socks which turned down over the tops of his boots to keep out burrs, snakes, and centipedes. He had a wool serge shirt for when the sun was too hot on his bare shoulders, and a best shirt for Sundays. A wide-brimmed, flat-crowned felt hat completed the costume.

They worked from daylight till dark, about twelve hours with two smoke-ohs of thirty minutes, and an hour for midday lunch. To add to the discomforts of the work, the bunks in the sleeping quarters were of the most primitive kind, and full of dust and vermin. Only dirty straw or bagasse, the dried refuse of cane from the mill, was provided for a mattress.

The best wages a European cane-cutter could expect were eight to nine shillings a day. After a cold night, the standing cane was often wet with a heavy dew until about ten in the morning, and the cane-cutters were soon wet through too.

The coloured workers lived in straw huts, with no proper water supply and no sanitation. Their meals consisted of rice, maize porridge, and sometimes fish on weekends. Angus

Johnstone had built a magnificent mansion on the profits of sweated labour.

Discontent simmered among the white workers, but while there was plenty of cheap, uncomplaining Island labour, little could be done about it.

From what Tom had told him, Chukka was not surprised at the conditions. What he had not expected was the widespread drunkenness among the white cane-cutters. The Kanakas did not drink, though they gambled a lot at the Chinese fan-tan houses. Chukka, who liked a beer after work – there was nothing to do in the evenings but go to the local pub – did not like drinking for its own sake, just to get drunk. He became friendly with a part-Islander, George Tombua, who was near his own age and not as brown as Chukka, who had been running around barefoot and bareheaded in the Western sun for most of his life, and whose light brown hair had become bleached to the colour of wheat stubble. George's fuzzy hair, unmistakably Islander, was an unusual colour, almost auburn.

One of the first Acts of the new Federal Government (which came into being in 1901 when the Commonwealth of Australia was proclaimed) had been the Pacific Islands Labourers' Act, to end indentured coloured labour.

'Will you have to go when the deportation order comes into force?' Chukka asked George Tombua. 'It's pretty hard, I reckon, on men who were born here, or whose families were born here. The Government's got no right just to chuck them out like a worn out shoe.'

'How right you are, mate! But they'll do it just the same. I'm exempt because my people've been here more than thirty years. I was born here, and besides I had an Australian father – unofficially. Dad brought me up as his, but he must have known. I'm the only one in the family with light skin and red hair.'

George and Chukka remained mates, travelling up and down the coast, following the cane. They joined in the horseplay at the end of the season when the last truck on the cane-tram was loaded for the mill. It was the custom to decorate the end of the train with articles of their dirty work clothes, sticky with sugar and black from soot, which were beyond washing. George put not only his shirt, but his shorts and hat on the truck, and danced along behind it without a stitch on, except for his heavy boots and socks.

After a holiday, they would take a job planting 'setts', or hoeing between the rattoon crop, but 'sucker-bashing' was a last resort – this was slashing and chipping at regrowth in newly cleared land, for the best cane-lands were on the site of what had been 'vine scrubs', or green rainforest, before the land was cleared.

Then the cane would be ten feet high again and spearing, the green stems topped with feathery lilac grass-flowers. As soon as the leaves began to dry it was fired, and the fierce flames crackled through the sugar like rifle-fire, leaving only the blackened stalks standing ready to be cut.

Chukka followed next season by a visit home, when the last of the crushing was over. His mother wanted to hear all about the coast, but Tom, now nearing fifty, seemed to be more interested in the past. He had developed rheumatism in his back – he reckoned it was from so much bending over at shearing – and could no longer work.

He kept harking back to the days of his youth, his first trip to Queensland droving, and the mateship of the shearing shed.

'Though we were all rivals there, make no mistake. Every man had his eye on the man next to him, or the man further along the board who was beating his tally. The competition was fierce. We never let up from the time the first bell rang to knock-off time. And many a shearer would grab a jumbuck just on the bell, and then shear it at his leisure. And of course we all tried to dodge the cobbler, the last and worst sheep in the pen.'

'D'you reckon it was harder work than cuttin' cane, Dad?'

'Not harder. It was different. Unless a man had no ambition, there was this pressure on him all the time to better his score; even if he was the ringer of the shed, he'd be trying to beat his own record.

'A' course, some of them were pretty rough with it, if they thought the boss of the board wasn't watching. My mate Dinny Maloney, he taught me to watch out for the boss's boots. He'd be the only one wearing smart leather elastic-sides, we all wore soft moccasins mostly for shearing. So Dinny'd squint along the board to catch a glimpse of the boss's boots coming. "You want to pink 'em nicely when you see the boss's boots," he said. (You know what pinking 'em is, Chukka; cutting so close the skin shows pink through the short wool.) There's no time to straighten up and have a look round, you'd just squint under your eyebrows, with your head down.

'Well, the boss of this shed – it was Dunlop, out on the Darling – had very big feet, and you couldn't mistake his boots. One day Dinny was working fast to get his ton up, and was shearing a bit rough, when he cut the ewe. He stuck his leg in front to hide the blood, and then he sees, right beside him, the boss's boots.

'Well! He didn't dare turn the ewe, or the wounds would be seen, and he thought he'd be fined for sure. He kept on shearing the one side, pinkin' her nice and pretty, and swearing under his breath, waiting for the boss to move on.

'At last he had to move his leg, and turn the ewe, and then he let his eye travel up from the boots – and it wasn't the boss of the board at all, but a new-chum picker-up waiting for the fleece, and wearing a brand-new pair of number eleven 'lastic-sides.

'Dinny left the ewe, he dropped his shears into the water-pot, and he punched that picker-up on the nose and then threw him down the shoot. "That'll learn the fool to wear the boss's boots!" he said.

'I told that yarn to Henry Lawson once, in a pub in Bourke,' said Tom. 'He used it afterwards in a poem. I wish I'd thought to write it meself . . . Yes, we had some fun in the old days,' he sighed.

Tom did a bit of gardening, cut wood for the stove, grew some tomatoes; but he missed his old wandering life which had suited him so well.

'I can just see it,' he said, 'though I don't go shearing now . . . and I can almost smell the smell of greasy wool,

> For the Western creeks are calling,
> And the idle days are done,

154

With the snowy fleeces falling
And the Queensland sheds begun!

The practical Chukka, who had none of his father's vein of poetry, was rather embarrassed at all this sentiment, as he thought of it, about 'the old days'. Tom had forgotten the heat and dust and flies, the aching right wrist, the tired back, the meals of stringy mutton from old six-tooth wethers. Like all older people, he saw the past in a rosy glow. He had now bought a comfortable cottage in Charleville, three hundred miles south of Longreach, with the savings Bridget left him; but he resisted Nancy's suggestion that now he wasn't shearing they could go and live on the coast. He couldn't stand the dampness and the everlasting greenery, he told her.

Instead he sent Nancy and the girls for a holiday in Bundaberg. Emma got engaged to a young man who worked in the store there, so Agnes would soon be the only one left at home.

Chukka left for Mackay at the beginning of the sugar harvest, with instructions from Nancy about writing once a month, even if it was only a few lines. He agreed easily, even intending to comply, but of course forgot. He was fond of his mother; there was a bond between them from all those years when Tom was away and he had 'looked after' her, but writing letters was something he could never be bothered with.

Tom asked him, if he could get to Brisbane, to visit his old Uncle Brian O'Brien, who though younger than Bridget was now well into his eighties. When Sir Thomas McIlwraith – a former Premier of Queensland who had helped to crush the shearers' strike and tried to introduce coolie labour to the canefields – died under a financial cloud in 1900, Uncle Brian had pronounced a farewell in the bar of the South Brisbane pub where he used to drink since his retirement:

'Faith, they may say what they like about Sir Thomas, but he was a man! He mightn't have had much honesty, if there was big money to be had, and he liked his gin and tonic strong an' frequent, an' he had a rovin' eye for the wimmin; but outside of them matters, he was pure as the drivellin' snow.'

Six

GEORGE TOMBUA had met an Islander girl who worked at the Maryborough Hospital as a nurse, though she lived at home.

'May's a bonzer sheila,' said George. 'I dunno, Chukka, what came over me, but I've asked her to marry me.'

'Fair dinkum? You're not just chucking me a line? 'Struth, I can't imagine you settlin' down, with a whole row of kids.'

'I s'pose in the Islands, I'd have married long before this. The kids grow up quick there.'

'But you're half white, I mean, er, Australian or English or whatever.'

'Yair, and I've got this gingery hair to prove it. But it's got the Island kink in it, you notice.'

May Efate had told him that she needed to be better, quicker, more efficient than the white trainee nurses, to pass the Matron's sharp critical eye. She would not let Aboriginal girls train at all.

George had no doubt that the young doctors at the Hospital found May sufficiently attractive, with her smooth brown face and liquid dark eyes, and the neat fuzz of her hair which fitted her head like a dark cap beneath the starched white Probationer's cap she wore on duty.

When George went to meet May's family, he took Chukka Brown with him for moral support. He was dead scared of meeting May's mother, a pillar of the Presbyterian Church and the daughter of a parson. Her husband, Joseph Tula Efate, had been kidnapped from the Loyalty Islands when he was only fifteen, and then married, in Queensland, the fair-haired daughter of the Scottish missionary for whom he had once worked as a house-boy on Lifu. He was now sexton at St Andrew's Church.

Fiona was May's older sister. The only surviving brother, Tula, had gone back to the Islands as a missionary to his own people.

Fiona was lighter in colouring than her sister, but with the same large eyes. And she was not just pretty, Chukka told himself, but intelligent; she had topped her class at the local school and had applied for a job at the Shire Library. She was also involved in the fight for ordinary human rights, and welfare benefits for Aborigines and Islanders, who were second-class citizens under Queensland law. Not only were they not allowed into hotel bars, she told him, but they could not drink alcohol even in their own homes, without risking prosecution; and those who lived on Reserves had no control of the money they earned, which was kept for them by the white Superintendent, or by the local police officer if they worked in a town. And they had to get a written permit to leave even for a day.

Chukka sat on the edge of his chair in Mrs Efate's front parlour, clutching a delicate china cup in his big, scarred brown hands. Joseph, May's father, managed his cup easily, but his feet were bare, his toes curled comfortably round the rung of his chair, and in place of a shirt he wore only a snowy-white singlet.

While George talked easily with Joseph Efate about cane-cutting, Chukka desperately made conversation with Fiona and her mother. Mrs Efate had been distinctly cool in her greeting to George, he noticed. She was a fragile-looking woman, with pale yellowish-grey hair that had once been blonde. She showed Chukka the silver mantel clock that her father had brought out from Scotland to Lifu.

'I was born in the Islands, you know,' she said. 'And my brothers too; but none of them survived . . .'

When Chukka tried to tease Fiona gently about her crusading for the Aborigines, who were not even her people, she flared up at once. He was fascinated by the old-rose glow which came up in her pale brown cheeks, and the fire which flashed from her dark eyes. 'Lightning reflected from still water,' he thought, surprising himself, for unlike his father he was not given to poetic comparisons.

On the way back to the plantation where they were working, Chukka said musingly, 'She's rather beaut, isn't she?'

'May? I told you she was!'

'I meant Fiona. I've asked her to go to the pictures Saturdee night.'

'Gosh, you're a quick worker. But her Ma will be watching like a hawk for you to come home. Apparently she's always been afraid they'd be got into trouble by some white feller, and she's very strict.'

'I wouldn't mind getting into trouble with Fiona,' said Chukka fervently.

'You'd think Mrs Efate'd be more pleased about May and me, gettin' married proper. I reckon she was hoping they'd both marry white. She's probably got you lined up as a husband.'

'Not me, mate! I'm not the marryin' kind! Not yet, anyway.'

He did not know how chance had taken a hand in his parents' marriage, or that Thomas had 'made an honest woman' of Nancy two years after he was born. Chukka had 'been around', as he put it. He'd had various encounters in Sydney and Brisbane, where the tough seasonal workers down from the north had a certain glamour.

But he found Fiona unexpectedly determined. On the way home from the pictures, as he told George next day, he never got anywhere with her, though he'd made a jolly good try.

'Have you made it with May?' he asked curiously.

' 'Course I have. But she's not up the creek or anything.'

'I'm goin' to a meeting of the Abos' and Islanders' Advancement, or something, next week. Fiona's making a speech.'

'Cripes, Chukka! You have got it bad.'

Only Fiona knew how close a thing it had been, as she struggled fiercely with Chukka to preserve – not her virginity, that had gone years ago, but her self-respect. She had given in once before to a travelling cane-cutter, and perhaps just because he was her first man, fell madly in love with him. He had made her believe he felt the same – oh, he was smooth-talking, eloquent, convincing. She waited with longing for the next season, and when it came round, sat at home waiting for a knock upon the door. He had not written, except for one postcard just after he left. The knock never came.

His name was Reynard. Reynard the fox. She never saw him again.

But Chukka didn't have any smooth-talking line. She liked his thin, bony, honest, sun-browned face with the laughter crinkles round his mouth and eyes, and his straight, streaky blond hair. It had been easy to see that her mother liked him, too.

However, when 'in a moment of madness,' as he told George, he asked her to marry him on the way home from the CIAA meeting she did not at once accept. She was suspicious of his motives, not believing that he really wanted to marry her.

George Tombua, inspired by his engagement to May, saved hard the next season and with his other savings had enough to buy a small-holding for growing sugarcane. He would be his own boss next year. Chukka, more easy-going than his mate, could see that it was the sensible thing to do. Once the land was cleared and planted, you just sat back and waited for the profits. As George said, 'The stuff grows itself.'

Going north again the following season, he found himself thinking of nothing but Fiona. The train was crowded with cane-cutters coming up from Brisbane and Sydney for the start of the season. They slept along the seats, in the luggage racks, on the floor of the compartments, even in the corridor, ignoring the complaints of the guard who had to step over their outstretched forms when he came to punch tickets. The train swayed and rocked slowly along its narrow-gauge track. One group had made a table of their luggage and played cards on it. Beer flowed down dry throats, empties were tossed out of windows.

'Fiona, *Fiona*, Fiona, *Fiona*,' muttered wheels to sleepers, or was shouted suddenly in narrow cuttings of stone that flung back the sound redoubled. Absence had certainly made his heart grow fonder. He was determined that Fiona would marry him straight away.

'Hell, you'll have to chuck up this job when we get married,' he said as soon as he'd managed to get her away from the library where she worked and the disapproving eye of the female librarian. 'I can't stand it when you're not around. And when we have kids – '

'Who says we're getting married?'

'I do, and that's flat. What's more I had a word with your Mum at her place, and she's all for it.'

'I bet she is! Poor Mum, she always worried herself sick about me. She'd watch me in the mornings, and if I looked a bit pale or got sick after breakfast, she'd nearly have a fit! She'd never ask, but I know she kept thinking I might be pregnant.'

'Well, now she won't have to worry any more.'

'And I'm not even sure I want a family. Everyone wants to have kids, but they aren't always a blessing. My Mum had four of us; lost one as a little boy, poisoned by arsenic; and then her other son broke her heart by going back to the Islands. Mum's old man, who was a Scottish reverend, never got over her marrying my Dad, a Pacific Islander. I believe it killed him. So you see – '

'Don't worry, you'll get broody later on – '

'Chukka! I'm not a hen!'

'No, you're a much nicer shape than a hen, especially your bottom,' he said, clasping that part of her firmly. Fiona sighed and relaxed against him.

'All right,' she said. 'You knew I'd give in, in the end, didn't you? But what will your father and mother feel about me?'

That rocked him for a moment. He had not considered his parents' reactions.

'They'll love you just as I do,' he said warmly. But he was remembering Tom's words about the married couple he had seen on Buderim Mountain: 'No decent white woman would marry a black . . . You don't like to see a woman stoop so low.' Would that be his opinion of Fiona's mother? He only had to meet Emily Efate to see at once how wrong he was.

'And even if they didn't,' said Chukka, 'it's me you're marryin', not them . . . And you'll like my Mum. She used to teach, you know, till she chucked it up to get married. And I oughter tell you, my Old Man was in gaol once, when I was little.'

'Oh!' Fiona, granddaughter of a stern Churchman, was a little shocked. 'What – what for?'

'Standing up for his rights. Sticking to his mates. He was in the big Shearers' Strike in '91, and they arrested him as one of the leaders. He used to write these revolutionary songs – the words, I mean – '

'Not *the* Tom Brown? Not "Thomas the Rhymer" of the *Bulletin*?'

Chukka grinned with embarrassment. 'Yair, that's the one.'

'But he's a poet! One of the real bush poets – and you're his son!'

Chukka, who at school had always tried to keep dark his connection with someone who did anything as odd as writing poetry, nodded shyly.

'How marvellous! Wait till I tell them at the library. And he was one of the martyrs in the big strike, too!'

'Yair. They let them out after three years, but.'

He decided not to go into the fact that his grandfather had been transported and was technically a felon too, though he also had been imprisoned for political reasons. It was, thought Chukka, a bit too much of a good thing. The old man had died in Canada, and Chukka had never met his grandfather.

Fiona regarded him with her wide brown shining eyes, 'like pools in a paperbark swamp,' Chukka had told her.

'Oh, Chukka! No wonder you have sympathy for our fight to get a bit of land of our own on Fraser Island. My sister-in-law Maud is an Aboriginal, you know, and it was she who got me into the Council for Islander and Aboriginal Advancement. You'll be able to help me with my speeches – '

'Not me, love. I'm no good at speechifying and that. You go for your life, chuck the words around as much as you like, but don't count on me. I only came to that meeting to impress you.'

'I know you did, you rotten bastard. If only I didn't love you! I ought to give you away after that.'

But her soft eyes belied her words.

Chukka, who never wrote letters, sat down and composed a short note to his family to let them know he was getting married. He didn't go into details – what they didn't know wouldn't hurt them – but mentioned for his mother's benefit that Fiona's grandpa had been a Presbyterian minister. Nancy, brought up in a position that was not quite menial on the station where her mother and father worked, was enough of a snob to be pleased about this, he knew. And she might influence his father to accept the other grandpa – a full-blood fuzzy-haired Loyalty Islander, one of the 'Kanakas' that his father's Union excluded from membership.

He had liked Joseph Efate at once – big, slow-talking, with a calm certainty of his own worth, and a ready smile breaking in his dark face like the white water spreading on a coral reef. Fiona had those same big, strong, even teeth.

Seven

IT WAS not until their eldest daughter, Anna, was three years old that Chukka took his wife out West to meet his parents. Nancy wrote to warn him that he would find his father changed, grown old before his time.

Tom was slowing up. Though still on the right side of sixty, he tired easily, seemed to be losing interest even in gardening, and felt the heat far more than he used to. He'd had one strange giddy turn, but it passed and did not recur. All the same, she worried about him. She hoped the coming visit, and seeing his grandchildren, would revive his spirits.

'Hell, I didn't know my old man wasn't well,' said Chukka, reading this aloud to Fiona.

'But your mother says the visit will cheer him up.'

'Yair . . . perhaps. But . . .'

'Chukka! It's me, isn't it? He's going to get a shock when he sees me! Haven't you *told* them, for God's sake?'

'Well, not exactly, no. Y'see, he's an old Union man, and they were dead against imported labour, wanted the Kan— the Pacific Islanders chucked out, sent home, long before the Government got round to it. It wasn't colour prejudice really, more an economic thing. But I know when he actually sees you, he'll accept you for what you are – a lovely girl and the mother of his grandchildren.'

'Who have brown skin and fuzzy hair.'

'Go on! They're not as brown as me.'

'Yes. But yours is sunburn.'

Anna and the twin boys, Frank and Freddie, were too young to appreciate all the implications of that disastrous visit. But they felt the tension in the air, and played up accordingly. Because Fiona was nervous and anxious for them to behave well, she jumped on them for making a noise or any small misdemeanour and so made them worse. Fortunately their young Aunt Agnes was good with children, and took them out of the house as much as possible.

Not that Tom Brown was openly hostile to his daughter-in-law. He was unfailingly polite, but his smile was insincere and his courtesy chilling. Fiona got on well with Nancy, who spoilt the children and laughed with her over their antics. The two women worked companionably in the kitchen. It would have been a pleasant visit but for Tom.

Then one day when little Anna, who was used to getting her own way, had been carried screaming to the bedroom, Fiona heard him complaining to his wife about 'that damned spoilt Kanaka brat'. She went to find Chukka, who was putting up a trellis for his mother in the garden, and insisted that they leave the next day. She couldn't take any more of his father's veiled hostility and dislike.

'Well, I'll say goodbye tonight, then,' said Tom, looking obstinate and miserable, as Chukka told him they would be leaving on the early morning train for the coast. 'Why didn't you give us some warning, son? Prepare us for the shock a bit?'

'What "shock"? Listen, Dad, my best mate George is half Islander, and he's a lot harder worker than me, and owns his own cane-farm while I'm still a poor bloody labourer. And Fiona's mother is as white as you, and a real lady. In fact a lot whiter. Have you looked at yourself in a mirror lately? Sure you didn't inherit a bit of Australian Abo from somewhere?'

'Don't be stupid,' said Tom. 'I'm "black Irish", like my Uncle Brian O'Brien.'

'Well, you've got no cause to chuck off at Fiona and the kids just because her father's a Kanaka. He didn't want to come. He was chucked into a blackbirding vessel by some Queensland skipper, and brought here against his will. And anyway, she's my wife, and I won't have her insulted, and we're goin'. So put that in your pipe and smoke it.'

'It's just that they shouldn't have been brought here in the first place. "Australia for the white man" – '

'Yes, that's what your bloody *Bulletin* has on its masthead, the most racist journal in Australia. What about the Abos who were here first? We pinched the country from them, chucked them out of all the good coastal land, took over all the old camping grounds, and made sure Australia was for the white man!'

Chukka kissed his mother goodbye, but he couldn't bring himself to shake Tom's hand. Easy-going Chukka had at last been made angry.

The following summer Fiona received a medal from the Royal Lifesaving Society for diving overboard from the Keppel Island tourist launch to save an elderly man who had fallen overboard. She was a superb swimmer and kept him afloat in the choppy sea till the launch could circle round and pick them up.

Chukka sent a cutting from the Rockhampton *Star* to his parents but did not write. There was no reply from Tom, but Nancy wrote warmly to congratulate Fiona. She said that Tom's health was still deteriorating, and she felt that whatever was wrong with him was affecting his mind as well. He was losing his hair, even his eyebrows and the hair on his chest, and he spent a lot of time dozing on the veranda. He seemed to have lost all zest for life. (She did not elaborate, but she meant he had lost all interest in her, though they still slept in a double bed.) She wondered if it was all the aspirin he had taken for the rheumatism that was having some effect.

Since Charleville was much nearer to Brisbane than Longreach and had been connected with the capital by rail for more than ten years, Nancy could leave Agnes (a capable girl, though rather plain) to look after Tom while she went to visit Emma and her children. But it was Charlie she missed; he had never once visited home since that time two years ago when

Tom had given his wife such a chilly reception. Fiona wrote to her sometimes.

Tom never mentioned Chukka's family, which now included another little girl, Ellen. Yet Nancy thought they were beautiful children, with their black curls and big brown eyes like their mother's, and complexions more ivory than brown – in fact many degrees lighter than Tom's sunburnt visage, which seemed to be darkening more and more as he got older. She had persuaded him to apply for the invalid pension, which when it first came in he had been too proud to accept.

In 1911 the Amalgamated Workers' Association of Queensland called a general strike in the sugar industry. They demanded a minimum wage of thirty shillings a week all found in mills and fields, with an eight-hour day and 'time-and-a-quarter' for overtime.

Camps were formed at each strike centre up and down the coast, with an effective system of picketing. When strike-breaking labour was brought up from the southern States, the Unionists 'persuaded' most of them to join the strike. Collections for the strike camps were taken up all over the West; shearers and shed-hands who remembered their own struggle contributed to the funds. After three months, the Transport Workers' Union decided to back the strikers. The Associated Sugar Producers, who had refused to have anything to do with the Union, now gave in and asked for a conference. The result was that all the demands were met.

'It's like 1891 all over again!' Tom Brown wrote exultantly to his son. He had followed the course of the strike in the newspapers, reading between the lines of what he guessed were biased reports, for didn't the bosses own the newspapers?

The six thousand men living in camps at Bundaberg, Childers, Maryborough, Bauple, Gin Gin, Mackay, Proserpine, Burdekin, Ayr, Mossman and Herbert River, celebrated with a great binge on Bundaberg rum and local beer. Chukka sent a postcard to his parents, with the words 'We've won!' scrawled across it.

Chukka had gone along with his mates in the strike, and yet

he could see the point of view of the cane growers as well; especially the smaller growers. Wasn't his mate and brother-in-law George Tombua one of them? He himself still hadn't amassed enough for buying his own cane-farm, though Fiona nagged him about it sometimes. She now lived, with the children, at Keppel Sands, near Yeppoon, about halfway up the coast along which Chukka travelled throughout the winter months. It was also near her sister May, since George's farm was in the Yaamba-Farnborough district – rather too dry in some years for a successful crop.

Tom was disgusted at the two words sent home by Chukka about the 'great struggle'. He remembered the long, descriptive letters he used to write to his mother from Barcaldine during the shearers' strike.

'Charlie seems to have no feeling for words,' he mumbled.

'You know how easy-going he is,' said Nancy. 'He'd never get worked up about a strike, he'd just go along with his mates.'

'You'd never think he was a son of mine,' said Tom.

Sitting idle in the sun on the veranda, he began to brood on this theme, until he convinced himself that he was not Chukka's father.

'Why don't you admit it?' he said bitterly one night. 'You knew all the time Charlie wasn't my kid. He's nothin' like me – fair and blue-eyed. It stands to reason –'

'Oh, for God's sake, Tom. You're not going to start imagining things in your old age? You know perfectly well that he's yours.'

'Go on! All those shearers out for a good time – don't tell me you never gave in to one of them, like you did to me.'

'Not after I met you, Tom. Honest! I won't say I wasn't tempted,' she added rather smugly. 'When you were in gaol, I mean. You get lots of propositions, working in a pub. But then I'd think of you suffering at St Helena for your principles, and I couldn't do it. I've been true to you, Tom.'

He looked unconvinced. 'That's just it, Chukka doesn't seem to have any principles! He just drifts. Not like me at all. Not like my son, and the grandson of a Canadian Patriot.'

'And Emma and Agnes? I suppose you think they're not yours either.'

'Of course they are! Aggie's the dead spit of me, and Emma takes after you.'

'Well, I assure you they all had the same father.'

Tom continued to brood over the past, taking little interest in his present life after a brief flare of enthusiasm over the sugar workers' strike. Nancy and Agnes tried to 'take him out of himself', organising picnics to the banks of the Warrego.

The great Artesian Basin of subterranean water had been discovered in the West, giving a new lease of life to the pastoral industry, and providing towns like Longreach and Charleville with seemingly endless supplies of warm, mineralised water. Though it was not much good for drinking, stock thrived on it. Instead of a few dusty geraniums, Nancy now had a garden of flowering shrubs, hibiscus and poinciana and other exotic, heat-loving blooms.

Tom said suddenly one night – at least he didn't come out with these things in front of Agnes, thought Nancy, but waited till they were in their bedroom – 'You know I don't blame you entirely, dear . . . After all I had another girl for a long time. Her name was Gertie; she worked at the pub in Collarenebri.'

'Oh, Tom! It's all in the past now, anyway. You didn't see her after we got married, did you?' she added with a stab of retrospective jealousy which surprised her.

'Well – a couple of times when I was shearin' in the district . . . and I'd had a few drinks. But I told her I was married,' he added virtuously.

'A lot that would worry her, I'll bet.'

'She didn't mean anything to me. It was just, sort of a habit.'

'Oh, was it! It's a habit you've got out of lately, even with me.'

'Yes, I know.' Tom sighed. 'What wouldn't I give to be young again! I just seem to be tired out all the time . . .'

'But Tom, you're not an old man! What – fifty-six? Old Ogilvie was still getting sons at eighty.'

'He didn't have a bad back. And I reckon there's something wrong with me blood. Perhaps I ought to see the quack.'

'Perhaps you ought. Ask him for a good tonic.'

But Tom couldn't make the effort to go to the doctor.

In the summer of 1912, with the great drought beginning to take effect over the inland grazing country, and hot winds drying up what little grass and moisture was left, Tom seemed to be affected by the heat more than usual. He complained that he didn't sweat, so that his skin was always hot; his lips were dry and cracked. Then one morning he got up from his chair in the warm kitchen, and pitched unconscious to the floor.

'I knew there was something wrong with Dad!' exclaimed Nancy, distractedly trying to revive him. 'He wouldn't see the doctor . . . Has he had a stroke, do you think? His mother died of one, I know.'

'Perhaps it's just a heat-stroke, Mum.' Agnes smashed bits of ice from the block in the ice-box to put on his head. His face looked dark rather than pale.

'But it's not all that hot!'

When he did not come round they sent for the ambulance. Nancy blamed herself for not making him go to the doctor before. She had been impatient with Tom lately, scolding him for sitting around staring vacantly in front of him, or 'getting under her feet'. He moved slowly, and his hair had become thin and grey. She could not recognise the virile young shearer she had married.

Tom woke in the Charleville Hospital, unable to remember how he had got there. He stared around bemusedly, while a young nurse took his temperature and tidied the sheets. Looking up at the wall beside the bed, he saw in large letters the word 'PAUPER'.

This was an incomprehensible insult to Tom. He had always paid his hospital dues to the Union while working; every shearer had paid a pound a week out of his earnings in every outback centre where he worked. He had his savings and owned his own home. And here they had branded him a pauper!

The nurse didn't seem to understand his distress. When the doctor came he felt so weak and upset that he cried a little. The doctor seemed to realise the magnitude of the insult and promised he would be moved to another bed in the ward.

His main symptoms were giddiness and a bad headache when awake, but mostly he was drowsy and half asleep. The doctor made a provisional diagnosis of 'heat-stroke', but his temperature stayed up, and when he did not improve, he was moved by train and ambulance to the General Hospital in Brisbane.

Nancy travelled down to the city with him, but when after a month he was still in hospital with little change in his condition, she returned to Charleville. She and her daughter Emma were too much alike to get on well for long. They argued about minor things, like whether school sores were better left alone or bathed daily, or the proper diet for one-year-olds, and as they both held strong opinions neither would give in.

As it happened, Tom had a rather rare and interesting condition, at least from the medical point of view. Three young doctors were brought in by the senior surgeon to look at him, and to prod the painful part of his chest and abdomen, where they seemed interested in some brown freckles, and even in the small amount of his pubic hair.

The doctor in charge of his case, as it was his first encounter with the disease, took a case-history from Tom while he was still able to speak. By now he was too drowsy and uninterested to care, but he wished they would leave him alone. He passed water when requested to; he used the bedpan regularly; he ate his meals; he slept and woke. They spoke of a 'sugar-free diet' and something with a long, incomprehensible name which he had.

The doctor afterwards wrote a complete report on the case, and asked permission to do an autopsy after he died. He called his report, which was later published in a medical journal:

A Clinical Study of a Case of Haemochromatosis,
(or 'Bronze Diabetes')

Case History
Thomas Brown, 57, married (three children). Retired shearer. Has not worked for four years. Becomes very tired

on exertion. Hot sun causes headache and dizziness. On admission he was cyanosed and drowsy. His temperature was 102.4 F. On 20/2/12 he was transferred by ambulance to Brisbane. The strange pigmentation of the face and arms was noted. Diagnosis: Haemochromatosis with possible heat stroke.

Pigmentation has been present for two years; he considered it was due to the sun.

Previous Illness: None. Has always been healthy, apart from a rheumatic condition affecting the back.

Family History: Mother died at 76, father at 64. No history of diabetes. Son alive and well. Two daughters alive and well. Patient was an only child.

On Examination: An elderly man, dark-skinned, lying quietly in bed. Very drowsy. Very difficult to get a clear history from him. Easily becomes tearful and upset.

Abdomen is soft; liver edge palpable, tender on excessive manipulation.

Pigmentation is most marked on the face and neck and exposed part of the arms, especially backs of the hands. The colour of the pigmentation of head and neck is dark brown. The skin is dry to the touch.

The external genitalia are pigmented, and there are freckle-like marks over the abdomen.

Hair of the head is dark grey and wiry-looking. Pupils a little dilated; *arcus senilis*.

Progress of the Case
Temperature
After admission, the temperature was above normal; it was irregular, reaching 104 degrees F on the third day, after which it fell abruptly, being normal the next morning. It rose again to 101 F during hot weather, but fell again to normal after a cool change. Throughout the heat the patient showed no sweating.

Further Investigations
Special tests showed increasing blood sugar to 42%. The diabetes was difficult to control.

Last Days
On 23/3/12 the patient was very drowsy and somewhat irrational, and eating poorly. During the night he had risen

from his bed, wandered about, and fallen over. That evening his temperature was 100.8 F. On examination next day it was 102.4 F.

On 31/3/12 his temperature was 101.4 F, his pulse not palpable, and respiration 40/min. The lower limbs were cyanosed, with dilated venules. He vomited up some dark brown vomitus, and at 4.30 p.m. he died.

Subsequent (post-mortem) Examination

Liver shows a rather fine hobnail cirrhosis. Section shows advanced portal cirrhosis and gross pigmentation.

Skin: The epidermis shows considerable dark-brown pigmentation outlining the cells in the basal layer of the epithelium.

Cause of death: Failure of liver function from the internal fibrosis.

Commentary on the condition

Haemochromatosis is not a common disease. It is not known to occur before twenty, with increasing incidence up to fifty-five.

Pigmentation of the skin occurs eventually in 80% of cases, often as a first symptom, with loss of weight, impotence, enlargement of the liver and diabetes. It is characterised by the presence in the tissues of two kinds of pigment, haemosiderin and haemofuscin. The pigmentation is largely due to the melanin content of the deeper layers of the epidermis.

Death on the average occurs within two years.

So died Thomas Brown, far from the dry outback that he loved, in the neat white island of a hospital bed set in shiny seas of linoleum. Strike-leader and poet, father of Charles, grandfather of Anna and Ellen, and great-grandfather of the writer Maggie Pinjarra, he was buried in a South Brisbane cemetery beside his mother, Bridget.

By a double irony (his name being Brown) he died with a skin as dark as that of the Melanesian races he affected to despise, and considerably darker than that of his own part-Islander descendants. A simple pigment called melanin, a protein containing sulphur and oxidation products of aminoacids, and deposits of haemosiderin, from the breakdown of haemoglobin in the blood, had turned him from a white man into a brown one.

Eight

ANNA BROWN and Johnny Tombua were out fishing in the family dinghy at Emu Bay. Johnny was down for the summer holidays from his father's cane farm at Farnborough, near Yaamba. By afternoon the sea would be choppy in the regular south-easterly, but for now it was glassy calm.

'Reckon we could row right out to the islands?' asked seven-year-old Johnny, looking at the shapes of Great and Little Keppel on the horizon.

'Don't be mad! It's ten miles,' said Anna scornfully. 'My Mum could swim out there though, I bet.'

'Bet she couldn't.'

'Well she got a medal from the Royal 'Saving Society, so there. For when she rescued that old geezer that fell in.'

'P'raps she'd row us out there, then. Wisht we had an engine.'

'Billy an' David have got a boat with an engine. They take Auntie Maud over to the islands, fishing.'

Anna stared over the turquoise sea to the cobalt shapes painted on the pale sky like the backdrop of some vast stage.

'I'm goin' to be a ballet dancer when I grow up,' she stated, winding in her line thoughtfully. The bait was gone. She threaded a small, translucent prawn on the hook, swung the handline round a few times and cast out expertly.

'Go on! What makes you think you can dance?'

'I practise every day in front of the mirror. And then later on I'm goin' to Brissie for lessons.' She was only eight, and given to fantasies. She had a picture of Anna Pavlova as the Dying Swan, cut from a magazine.

'Huh! Who's goin' to pay for you to live in Brisbane and do ballet? And anyway, ballet-dancers in pictures all·have smooth hair and toe-shoes. You couldn't dance on your *toes!*'

'Bet I could.' But Anna scowled. She had tried to get up on her toes, with and without shoes, but had found it painful and indeed impossible.

A sudden tug on her line and it went racing out, the stick on which it was wound rattling in the bottom of the boat.

'Hey! That's a big one,' said Johnny enviously. Much of the catch so far had been Anna's.

Over the side came a fine silver bream, looking bigger than it was because all the spines along its back were erect in terror, like a man's hair standing on end. Anna closed a hand firmly over its gills, removed it from the hook, and slipped it into the wet sack which now held half a dozen fish.

'That'll do,' said Johnny. 'Don't bait up again.'

He began to row towards the beach where the small waves broke in a regular pattern. He sang:

'Speed, bonny boat, like a bird on the wing,
    Onward! the sailors cry;
Carry the lad that was born to be king
    Over the sea to Skye . . .'

'Grandma Efate taught me that,' he said. 'It's a Scottish song, she said. You can really hear the rhythm of rowing in it, can't you? She said her mother told her the islands off the coast here look just like the Hebrides in Scotland where she was born. I'd hate to live away from the sea.'

'So would I.'

Johnny looked over his shoulder to judge their approach to shore. 'I'm goin' to take Ellen with me next time I go out,' he said. 'You get all the fish, is the trouble.' He saw a bigger wave approaching, and prepared to catch it.

' "Courage!" he said, and pointed t'ward the land;

"This mounting wave will roll us shoreward soon" – That's by Tennyson. I'm learnin' a new song, "Wind of the Western

Sea", and the words are by him. Only here the sea's eastern, and –'

He rowed madly. They caught the wave just as it poised to break, and surfed smoothly to the beach. The wide sandy deserted beach stretched for miles.

'You're always spouting poetry, and singin' songs,' said Anna. 'What are you goin' to be when you grow up?'

'I dunno. A cane-farmer like my Dad, I expect.'

'I'd like to live on an island.'

'Like the Pinjarras? They just about own Pandanus, I reckon. They're all blackfellers over there, aren't they? And they're just about all related to old Nyora. Anyways, how could you live on an island and be a ballet dancer?'

She sighed. 'I s'pose I couldn't, really.'

They cleaned the fish on the beach, throwing the pieces to the fiercely-squabbling gulls, then fixed a kedge anchor to the boat and left it there while they took the fish up to the house. Normally the boat was kept under the house, which was set on high wooden stumps behind the dunes.

Fiona was taking the children down to Brisbane for a treat, on a long weekend late in July. They were going to see the Botanical Gardens and ride in a tram. She promised Anna she would take them across in the ferry to Stradbroke Island in Moreton Bay. Brisbane people, who had only a mangrove-lined river for swimming in, liked to go to Stradbroke on weekends.

'And can we go to the ballet?' asked Anna.

'What ballet? There isn't any ballet in Brisbane, silly. You'd have to go to London, or Paris, to see one of them.'

But Brisbane, with its electric trams, its shops, its gardens bright with blood-red poinsettias, was excitement enough. The most exciting of all for Anna was the excursion to Stradbroke Island.

Fiona dressed the five-year-old twins in identical sailor suits, with navy-blue ribbon ties and little white caps sitting jauntily on their dark curls. The girls were in long stockings and button-shoes, their dresses demurely covering their knees, their shady straw hats lined with frilled net. Fiona, conscious of the looks which said 'Kanaka children', was careful to dress them smartly when they went out. She understood now why her mother Emily had always made them wear shoes when they went to town, even though lots of kids went barefoot.

It was a bright sunny day, though with a strong south-east wind, and the ferry was crowded. As many as possible got on the top deck in the sun, and on the sheltered side out of the wind. Ahead, the long shape of Stradbroke was misty against the sun. To the north, separated by a channel, was Moreton Island. It was midwinter, the coldest time of the year. Fiona took the children inside where she could keep an eye on them, and the glass windows protected them from the cold wind. She handed round a picnic lunch of cheese rolls and chocolate lamingtons. Anna was almost dizzy with joy. She loved to be on the sea, and to be having a picnic, to have all the family together; except Dad, of course, but he was always away cutting cane.

No one quite knew how it happened. One moment they were sailing along with a slight list to leeward, with spray flying up and breaking over the bows. Then someone saw a porpoise – or was it a shark? – off the port side where most of the passengers were gathered, and everyone else crossed to that side as well. As they shouted and pointed, a large wave hit the starboard side. The launch heeled over, hung suspended for one sickening moment, then turned over on her side. Screaming passengers were flung into the sea.

Frank and Freddie had wandered to the stern and were standing looking at the wake when she went over. In the last moment Fiona saw them fall into the turbulence from the still-turning propeller. She grabbed both girls, climbed through an open window on the high side, and jumped. 'Swim!' she cried. 'Swim away from the launch before it sucks you down.'

They were both like fish in the water. Anna, the elder, was the stronger swimmer. But they were not used to deep water and big waves. Fiona swam despairingly to the stern of the foundering boat.

'Freddie! Frank! Where are you?'

People were floundering and sinking all round her. Others were still trapped inside the glassed-in deck, their eyes goggling like those of fish in a bowl. But she could think of nothing but her own children.

'Frank! Freddie!'

There was no answer; but floating past she saw a little white sailor-cap.

'Oh God! Where are my boys?' And then she remembered the girls. At least she could save them. The launch began to go down by the stern; she swam strongly against the suction.

'Mummy! Mummy! Mummy!' Ellen was screaming in terror, swallowing water. Anna, sensible girl, was saving her breath for swimming. An elderly man grasped Fiona by the shoulder, pulling her under. She flung him off, and saw his silly eyes staring, his mouth open to cry out as he sank. She could feel nothing for him. Her sons had not even lived yet!

'Now Ellen, stop screaming and keep your mouth closed. Breathe through your nose. Rest both hands on my shoulders while I swim, and kick your legs just enough to keep them up. Right? Anna dear, are you all right?'

'Yes, but I'm f-frightened.'

'Of course you are, but you needn't be. You've swum in water over your depth before. Just because we're in the deep sea doesn't make it any more dangerous.' Except for sharks, she thought, and sent up a quick prayer. 'Just tread water for a while.'

The launch had sunk before any life-buoys or jackets could be given out. A ring of passengers clung to each of the floating seats threatening to make them sink with their weight. People were calling, crying and drowning all round them. No other vessel had seen the disaster, apparently. And the water was cold. Anna's teeth were chattering, partly from fright.

A current was setting in from beyond the bar, and they were being swept away from the island, back towards the shore they had left. How would a rescue boat ever find them in this choppy sea? Fiona felt a chill foreboding like a cold weight in her chest.

'Mummy . . . Where are – are Freddie and Frankie?'

'I don't know, dear. Perhaps they're floating on a piece of wreckage, somewhere.' But she knew they were not.

Anna began to cry. 'We'll all be drowned!' she sobbed.

'Anna! Now listen to me. The worst thing you can do is panic. And you're frightening little Ellen. Now rest your hand on my other shoulder, I'm going to try and swim ashore with the current. Whatever you do, don't let go and get separated from me. Ellen, are you all right?'

'Ye-ye-yes. I'm cold.'

'I want you both to unbutton your shoes and kick them off. I can't get my boots off now, the laces have swollen and I can't get them undone. But I can slip my skirt off. Tread water now, while I get ready. I will get you to shore.'

Her calm voice reassured them, though the shore three miles away looked terribly distant. Fiona began to swim.

She had made about a mile when she suddenly found she could make no progress at all. She stopped swimming, and immediately they were carried back out to sea. The tide had turned, and the current was setting the other way.

Nine

WHEN THE inquest was held on the ferry disaster, no blame was attributed to the designers of the vessel. She was not normally a top-heavy craft, and in ordinary circumstances and even rougher weather than that encountered, she should have remained stable. But the Coroner reprimanded those in charge for letting passengers cluster on the top deck and the leeward side, and not anticipating the danger from a sudden rush to that side by the rest of her passengers. The heavy loss of life, almost fifty people, including many children, was due to swift tidal currents and the fact that no large vessel to act as a rescue craft was in the area at the time.

Among those who died were the Brown twins, Frank and Freddie; their sisters Anna and Ellen were among the rescued.

Remembering the ordeal afterwards, Anna said that she was most conscious of a feeling of helplessness – that the sea was so large, and they were so small. 'As though we were ants,' she said, 'fallen into a huge pool, without even a stick or a piece of leaf to clamber out on. And how would anyone see us?'

The worst moment was when the tide turned and the current began to sweep them out again into the Bay. But by now there were rescue boats looking for survivors. They were swept swiftly past one of these, while Fiona called despairingly and tried feebly to wave.

They were not seen. Later, another boat – a launch of the Water Police – came slowly towards them. Fiona's voice had by now become a croak.

'Call to them, children,' she croaked. 'Shout "Help!" as loud as you can.'

They shouted, and the launch altered course slightly. It slowed, almost stopped; then a blue-clad arm plucked Ellen from the water, then Anna. But when they reached down for Fiona she was gone. With the last of her strength she had lifted the girls high so they could be seen, and then slipped unconscious beneath the waves. Two policemen dived and searched, but the tide was setting strongly now and it was hopeless.

The girls sat huddled in each others' arms, wrapped in one blanket, too shocked and exhausted even to cry.

Chukka Brown, shocked and disbelieving, came down to Brisbane to collect what remained of his family. Their Auntie May and Uncle George Tombua offered to take them while Chukka was travelling with the cane. His sister Emma did not offer. In spite of her message of sympathy, he felt sure she shared his father's views on 'Kanaka brats'.

The children stayed with May while they went to school, and during holidays Chukka took them west to Charleville, where Nancy spoiled them and they were kept in order by Aunt Agnes – who was small, bustling, dark-eyed and sharp-tongued. Chukka said a bit of discipline wouldn't hurt them,

178

and at least Aunt Agnes was always fair in her distribution of punishments.

Inland, on the sleepy Warrego, they almost forgot the sea. But Anna was of Island blood; she felt fully alive only when she could smell its clean salt tang. She liked best the holidays when her father stayed home at the wooden house set among the dunes like a stranded ship. He used to take her out fishing, trolling for mackerel in the dinghy. Ellen wouldn't come. She had such a horror of the sea since her ordeal that she hardly went swimming any more, only paddled on the edge.

Then the World War broke out, in August 1914, and was to take the lives of 60,000 young Australian men. After the tragic and heroic Gallipoli landing, where Anzacs died in their thousands trying to take an impossible position from the Turks, Chukka felt he ought to join up. In 1916 he volunteered for service with the AIF. There was no conscription; the whole Australian contingent was a voluntary force.

Nancy had recently married again, a widower who now shared her home in Cunnamulla, so Agnes came to the coast to look after the children while Chukka was away. He disappeared from their ken for more than two years. He came through the bloodbath of the trenches with no visible wounds, but after his return in 1918 he rarely spoke of his experiences. His eyes held a haunted look, and at any sudden loud noise he would jump and tremble.

He had been invalided home with shell-shock. Even thunder upset him, or a backfire from one of the new motor vehicles. The shell that had knocked Chukka down had blinded his mate, who had been facing the blast. At Returned Servicemen's meetings on Anzac Day, Chukka avoided looking at him: a big, cheerful fellow with a pair of glass eyes set in watering lids in his healthy red-brown face.

As his nerves gradually recovered, Chukka bought one of the latest Model T Fords, a 'Tin Lizzie' with a starting handle at the front. The engine was mulish in starting, but once started, Lizzie refused to stop. When the engine was thoroughly warmed up by a journey, she would go on coughing into life after the ignition was switched off, at last thudding doggedly on on one cylinder.

In the May school holidays their father offered to take the

179

girls camping down the coast, perhaps to Bundaberg where they could meet their cousins, Emma's children. Agnes wanted to make a trip to Charleville to see Nancy and her new husband. Ellen had almost forgotten her own mother, but Anna still mourned her loss; and on the anniversary of her death would make a wreath and throw it into the sea.

The girls helped Chukka to pile everything into Lizzie: mattresses, folding stretchers, bedding, towels, a kerosene stove, tinned food and 'ports' of clothing. The dog perched on top, with the saucepans, frying-pan and billy-can. She was a kelpie cross, an intelligent yellow-eyed bitch called Angelina.

The packing had taken so long that it was already afternoon, but Chukka would not wait till the next morning to make a start.

'We can't stay here, there's nothing left in the house,' he pointed out, for they had packed all the perishable food as well as a supply of canned goods.

So the girls climbed aboard, and Chukka began to turn the starting handle . . . and turn . . . and turn . . . and turn. Chukka swore mildly. Angelina barked encouragement.

Half an hour later he was still cranking, and his language was growing more lurid. The only life the engine had showed was to backfire with a kick that bruised his hand.

'Won't it start, Daddy?' asked Ellen unnecessarily.

Chukka exploded. 'Get down from there and go round the back while I swear properly!' he shouted. 'I'll chuck this rotten heap of metal in the sea, I will. All it's good for is an anchor.'

At four o'clock he gave up. The girls crept back to see him wearily unpacking their bags and some of the bedding.

'We'll have to camp in the house tonight,' he said.

Anna and Ellen thought it rather a lark, but their father never forgave the car for its temperamental performance. In the morning he gave it a good kick, pumped some petrol into the carburettor, turned the handle, and she started instantly, and ran forward and knocked him down. (Fords were always slightly in gear.) He chased the car and got aboard just as she was chugging out into the road.

The girls played on the beach with their little cousins, and

Chukka found that he got on well with Emma's husband Jack. Jack persuaded him that he ought to buy a boat with a petrol engine, so that in good weather they could visit the islands. He took it back to Yeppoon on a trailer.

It was on a trip to Pandanus Island that Anna met Bert Pinjarra, son of Nyora, a full Aboriginal, and a Portuguese sailor who had jumped ship in Queensland. Bert was a strikingly handsome young man, lithe and dark with smooth brown hair and a wide laughing mouth. He was not like his heavy-browed sister, Elsie, or his thick-bodied, dark-skinned older brother, Morgan.

At sixteen Anna was a romantic. She parted her hair in the middle and slicked it down with water, and tying it back with ribbons, tried to make it look like a sleek ballet-dancer's coiffure. She thought her eyes and fine dark brows had the look of a ballerina. She listened dreamily to the Swan Lake music on her cousin Johnny's little portable gramophone, holding her arms in artistic poses. Johnny spent all his pocket-money on records. He even had one of Caruso singing, and Australia's own Dame Nellie Melba.

As soon as Anna's hair was dry again, the obstinate wiry curls sprang back into place. Sometimes she felt like tearing out her hair, or cutting it off close to her head, especially after she had been teased about it at school, called a 'Fuzzy-wuzzy' by the other girls.

But when she left school and met Bert, who told her he liked her hair as it was, she stopped worrying about it. She gave up her ambition to be a dancer, or even a nurse or a teacher. All her aspirations were forgotten the first time Bert Pinjarra walked her along the beach at Pandanus Island, in the moonlight, with his arm round her and his hand cupping her breast. Nothing else mattered any more. When she slept, she dreamt of him; when awake, she daydreamed about him. Each night she summoned the memory of his caresses before she went to sleep.

Bert came across in his fishing-boat on a regular trip to the fish market on the mainland, and each time he managed to meet Anna among the sandhills. By the time she was seventeen her first baby was on the way. Aunt Agnes was scandalised, Grandma Brown resigned, Nyora amused, her father not much upset but declaring that the young things must get married right away.

'I don't know what your mother would have said,' he remarked worriedly. 'She would have looked after you better. Aunt Agnes thinks you should go away somewhere to have the baby, and let it be adopted. She's horrified at you going to live with an Aboriginal fisherman on an island. She reckons you're reverting to your Kanaka ancestors.'

'Perhaps I am,' said Anna seriously. 'And anyway, it doesn't matter, Dad. We love each other and we were going to get married anyway.'

She kissed his cheek, now deeply lined and grooved, and each year growing more tough and leathery. His nose had grown more bony and sharp; his light blue eyes were like cold, slitted daybreak between banks of cloud. It was a face entirely devoid of softness, pared down by hard living and human suffering to its elements of skin and bone; yet it could fold suddenly into a warm, engaging smile.

For the first time a typically *Australian* face had evolved. Chukka might have posed for a national portrait, of the Australian Digger, the typical hardbitten soldier of the AIF, the bronzed Anzac, the Returned Serviceman of the Red Cross stamps.

He gave his daughter away at the ceremony in the Presbyterian Church in Rockhampton, where her cousin Johnny Tombua sang 'The Voice That Breathed o'er Eden' most beautifully. Now that his voice had broken, the Church was going to pay for him to have singing lessons in Melbourne, where it was hoped he might get a travelling scholarship to go abroad. He had asked Ellen to marry him. Chukka went back to cutting cane. Under the Repatriation Scheme a grateful government had decided to give him a small piece of land of his own, on which he could just make a living with backbreaking toil; he would become a 'soldier settler'. Meanwhile he went on working to get a bit of capital for improvements.

Envious eyes had been cast on the small cane farms owned by former Kanaka labourers like George Tombua. They were prosperous only because they worked hard, for long hours, which many of the easy-going white Australians would not do. But they put pressure on the Government, and before the

War an Act had been passed forbidding Chinese or Pacific Islanders from acquiring cane-growing land, and offering a subsidy for sugar grown by white labour.

Ten

EARLY IN the morning, Anna Pinjarra walked on the silver-gilt beach on the sheltered side of Pandanus Island. There were no other footprints on the firm sand: just a few crab holes with the tracery of their pointed claws all round. Toe-dancers! thought Anna, smiling to herself. They could run effortlessly on their tip-toes, while holding their front claws above their heads in various poses.

Where the tide had receded, small waves had left their own calligraphy. A pattern of delicate curves like a pencil drawing of folded hills or the petals of a huge rose, was sketched in the sand. In the hollows of tidal pools, wind and water had cross-hatched the surface with finer lines. For this was not a coral island with soft coral sand. Its hilly centre was made of granite, which broke down into clean, shining grains of quartz and mica.

Tucking her short skirt into her drawers, Anna stepped into the clear emerald shallows, feeling with sensitive toes for the smooth shapes of shellfish under the sand. Now the tide had turned they were feeding near the surface. Morgan, Bert's older brother, had showed her how to find the live cockles which he called 'worwongs'.

'That the blackfeller way,' he told her, demonstrating a kind of hip-twisting wiggle which sank his feet deep in the wet sand. 'You kinda churns and churns th' sand, till you feel somethin' hard and smooth with your toes. Then you grab 'im quick, before he digs in deeper. That's the best bait out, worwongs, or eugaries; but they gotta be fresh. Good tucker, too.'

He showed her the great heaps of whitened shells where Aborigines had feasted and thrown the open shells away for ages past. Nyora cooked them these days, into a kind of chowder.

She was minding the children, Marie and Dan, while Anna was out looking for worwongs.

'You go an' get some fresh air,' Nyora had urged her. 'You lookin' a bit pale and peaky. They good kids, no trouble to their ol' Gran. Eh?' she said, chuckling, as she picked up the smaller of the children and tucked him on her ample hip. Little Dan laughed and grabbed a fistful of his grandmother's hair. 'Ow! Leggo, you little bugger, you pullin' me hair out.'

When the wet season came round with its occasional cyclonic storms, the skies were less pure but more interesting than in the clear, dry winter months. On the beach in the afternoons, while the little ones had their sleep, Anna would feel nearer to the sky than the earth. She would watch the solid whipped-cream clouds towering round the horizon, seeming to rise like a dream of fair white women from behind the veil of blue mist that hung above the sea. Endless shapes formed and dissolved again: a chubby orator raising a white fist; a marble Venus with blue-shadowed breasts; a great bird with trailing pointed wings, and once, frightening her, a huge grey beast which reared up slowly and devoured the daylight moon with ragged jaws.

Anna was two generations removed from her Pacific Island ancestors who might have had a legend about a beast that devoured the moon. She was closer in spirit to her Aboriginal relatives by marriage: Nyora, her mother-in-law, and Morgan, with his dramatic stories of Hairy Men and Bugeens and beautiful Water-Lubras (daughters of the Rainbow Serpent) and Devil Dingoes and Old Women who turned into islands in the sea. Called 'Dingbat' in his youth by the other kids at the Mission school because he was 'bats' about the old stories, the name stuck to him and he was known affectionately as 'Uncle Dingbat Morgan' to all the younger generation.

The Aboriginal people on Pandanus Island were nearly all related by ties of blood or marriage. They regarded the place as 'their' island, and though this was quite unofficial, it was true that their ancestors had probably lived there for some twenty thousand years. The few white people who drifted there, unless they married one of the locals, were made to feel intruders and usually left before long.

As soon as she was old enough, Ellen Brown, Anna's sister, had married her first cousin Johnny Tombua (much to the scandal of the Aboriginal in-laws: this was equivalent to incest in their view, almost as bad as a man marrying his tribal sister.) But they had gone off to Townsville away from their Aboriginal connections, while Johnny had even changed his name to 'Harold Brown' for his professional career. Once his voice was discovered and trained, he had gone south, and had even made a trip to America.

Anna did not see much of Ellen these days. She felt that her sister had become a bit stuck-up since her marriage and Johnny-Harold's success; while Harold Brown had no doubt forgotten how, as Johnny Tombua, he used to go fishing with Anna in the dinghy. She still loved fishing, casting with a hand-line or a rod and reel from the beach.

Fishing in the afternoon with the worwongs she had found at low tide, she would usually get enough for their evening meal. The patches of blue sky would become smaller and smaller until all was a swirling mass of grey, rent here and there by gashes of lightning, growling with continuous thunder. By the time she got back to the cabin above the beach, the solid, heavy monsoon rain was falling. By midnight the sky would be fair with stars, and the dawn came up in a sky that was clear, without trace of storms. Then the first creamy masses showed in the north-east, and the daily cycle would begin again.

It was during the cyclone season of 1927 that Bert was lost. Even inside the Barrier Reef the seas had been mountainous, enough to tear off great chunks of living coral and toss them up on the fringing reefs above the reach of normal tides. Bert was impatient to get back to his fishing. He had a contract with a fish shop in Rockhampton, where his catch was taken in a Model T Ford with an ice-box built in the back. He'd had a bad year, and if he did not put his full quota through the Fish Board for the year he could lose his licence.

Morgan waited for the seas to go down. He enjoyed fishing, but in his own good time. Whenever he passed the Old

Woman rock near the point – a rounded pinnacle of granite – he would lift his old felt hat and say, 'Good-day, Old Woman.' Anna thought perhaps he was placating all rocks, 'getting in good' with them so that they would not damage the keel of his cutter.

Bert set off early, ignoring the Old Woman, his inboard engine chugging noisily as he left the shelter of Sheoak Bay. When he had not returned by the next day, Morgan went to look for him without success. Then a full search was organised.

Nyora knew he would never be found alive. She knew he was drowned when she heard that Death Bird, the plover, fly over. And when she 'saw' him afloat, face-down and tangled in his own fishing net, she knew what had happened. And this was how they found him. His unattended boat had drifted far out towards the outer reef, without going aground. It was towed back safely.

Nyora did not tell Anna what she knew in her heart, for the girl still hoped, but she stood ready to comfort her when the body was found. After the funeral they went back to her house.

'There, there,' she soothed, holding the sobbing Anna against her generous bosom and stroking her short, dark curls. Nyora herself had given way to a wild paroxysm of grief at the open graveside of her son, wailing and tearing her hair and flinging herself on the ground. She did not cut herself with a stone knife as her tribal people would have done. But the ritual expression of extravagant sorrow for the dead had eased her pain, and now she was the comforter.

'You be a brave girl, now,' she admonished. 'You still got them little ones, they's part of him. An' maybe Bert – maybe he's left you one on the way, eh? So part of him still alive.'

'I don't care!' said Anna fiercely. She sniffed, and gulped a rising sob. 'I don't want any more, if Bert is gone . . . A lot of fatherless kids! I don't want any more.'

Anna had hoped when her first child, Marie, was born that her daughter might become a dancer, and fulfil her old ambition. But the moment she saw the baby's broad button nose, big feet and tight-curling hair, she had known it was not to be. Marie was built like a Pacific Islander, a Melanesian, without the slender hands and feet, the smooth hair, the long-legged grace which had attracted her to the part-Portuguese Bert Pinjarra. Marie grew into a solid, chunky child, strong-willed and fearless, but definitely not artistic.

Daniel, her brother, looked more like his Uncle Morgan than either of his parents, as Aboriginal in features as Nyora. No doubt he would become a fisherman, or at least follow some trade connected with boats and the sea.

She was still trying to get over her deep depression after the loss of her husband when Nyora urged her to take a holiday: 'Get away, girl, you wants to get right away for a while.'

So she left the two children with Nyora and took the coastal train, then the bus, to a beach resort just north of Bribie Island. The mainland beaches stretched for miles, backed by tangled thickets of tea-tree and paperbark.

She hired a surf-rod and would often go fishing in the early mornings, walking far from the town; and there, between the dark scrub and the empty sea, she felt at peace.

She saw the black yacht one morning just as the sun was rising, anchored halfway to the horizon on a tranquil sea. Somehow it made her heart beat fast, her breath catch in her throat. There was something strange, almost sinister about it. She declared afterwards that what she felt was a premonition, an inkling of the death that was to overtake her only a few years later.

As she watched it, preparing to make her first cast into the surf, the long bank of cloud along the eastern horizon, above the sea, became outlined with a fine edge of fire. The sea felt warm about her ankles, holding a stored memory of summer. She sent a long, expert cast into the patch of white water beside a promising gutter. There might be some chopper tailor there. After a week of off-shore westerlies the Pacific was living up to its name, breaking in gentle waves which spread, white-lace-edged, and sank with a hissing sound into the yellow sand.

As the sun cleared the bank of cloud she felt its growing warmth on arms and shoulders, like a bath beginning to heat up. The sun picked out the long black hull and bare masts of the yacht at anchor. The sea turned blue.

A quick tug-tug on her line, then nothing. She reeled in, to find the bait gone. She selected a small pilchard and threaded it on the double hook, then cast exactly into the same patch of water.

She was so intent on her line in the next five minutes that she did not notice a small dinghy coming shorewards, until it reached the line of breaking waves and hovered waiting to catch a surge. Just as well she was wearing her swimsuit; she often sunbathed here without it. There was a tentative tug at the bait, and then – there! The rod bent nearly double as she began reeling in. The fish zig-zagged wildly and pulled like a horse. She brought it ashore, flapping and frantic, just as the black-painted dinghy crunched into the sand.

Anna felt an absurd twinge of pride that the stranger had seen her make the catch. And what a catch! A golden trevally, at least two pounds in weight. She despatched it quickly and wiped the blood from her knife in the sand.

'Sa–ay, that's a mighty fine fish you have there.' The man, tall, brown and tough-looking, but with a boyish mop of salt-tangled, sunbleached fair hair, wore nothing but a pair of faded shorts which might once have been blue. 'What is it – trevally?'

'Yes. I thought I had a tailor when I hooked him.'

She stood up and brushed the sand from her bare knees, keeping the knife in her hand. This was a lonely strip of beach.

'D'you know you're wearing a watch? Won't it rust up some, or is it waterproof?'

She laughed, reassured at his tone, but still wary. 'It rusted up long ago. But it was a gift from someone, and I still wear it as a sort of charm. It doesn't tell the time.'

'Wa–al!' he drawled. 'If that don't beat the band! A watch that don't tell the time! You must've been keen on the guy gave it to you!'

'I didn't say it was a guy.' But it was Bert who had given it to her, when they were first married, Bert whose heart had stopped forever like the rusted mechanism of the silver watch. She wore it always.

'Have you just come down the coast?' she asked now.

He looked at her with amusement in his brown eyes. He said, 'We have just come from the U–nited States of America.'

'From the States! In that little tub – all the way across the Pacific? And this is your first landfall?'

'Not quite. We did hit New Zealand in between. I came ashore to ask you for our bearings. No doubt we'll pick up a light tonight. Are we near Moo-loo-lah-ba?'

She laughed. 'Mooloolaba. The accent is on the second syllable. You're about twenty miles off course, which isn't bad after a voyage of about six thousand miles.'

'We–ell, I guess Australia is a mite too big to miss. Should we head north or south?'

'North. The next river mouth you come to is the Mooloolah River. Moreton Bay lies south.'

'Yes, it must have been the Moreton Island light we saw last night, but I didn't believe it. I was allowing for the two-knot current setting down this coast from Fraser Island.'

'You've certainly been studying your charts.'

'Not much else to do at sea. This last few days has been slow work, tacking against those goddam westerlies. Anywhere around here we can get fresh provisions?' He gazed at the long, empty beach, the dark tangled scrub of tea-tree and honeysuckle banksia.

'There's a general store at Caloundra, but I wouldn't advise taking the yacht over the bar, or even the dinghy. There's a tide race out from Pumicestone Passage. The local fishermen treat it with respect, I know.'

'We're a bit sick of canned beans,' he said.

'I suppose I could let you have the fish,' she said reluctantly.

'No, that's OK. My mate's probably caught something by now.'

She had made another cast while they were talking, and now hauled in a fine silver Dart, flashing like minted metal in the sun. He grasped its gills firmly and unhooked it for her.

He sniffed at his fingers. 'It's sure got a funny smell. Good eating?'

'Very good, grilled whole and eaten off the bone. It's a Swallowtail, or Dart. The smell goes when they're cooked. But you wouldn't get them out where you're anchored, only in the surf. Would you like to try it?'

'That's mighty nice of you, Ma'am . . . I can only thank you with a kiss.'

The fish fell unheeded on the sand. She found herself pressed to a bare brown chest, while a hard mouth encompassed her own. If she started to struggle, she thought better of it. His arms were like iron bands. When he let her go she swayed, feeling dizzy for a moment. The rising sun behind his head outlined his light hair with a halo of gold. It seemed so long since she had been kissed, since her cold and empty bed had held Bert's warm, vital presence. Yet it was only three months.

'Goodbye,' he said softly, moving backward and picking up the fish as he went.

'Wait! What's your name? Who are you?'

'Just one of those knights that pass in a ship,' he laughed, blowing a kiss and beginning to lope towards his dinghy.

'What ship?' she called after him.

'The *Black Witch* – out of California.'

As he rowed out to the yacht Anna stood watching, shading her eyes, filled with an extraordinary sense of loss. She turned the bracelet of the silver watch on her wrist. A stopped clock. That was how she had felt since Bert died.

She began cleaning the trevally, standing ankle-deep in water to wash it. She looked up and saw him reach the yacht and climb on board. He waved something white towards the land. She waved back, waiting to see the sail run up, but nothing else moved on board. Perhaps they were fishing.

The weather stayed calm and perfect. The westerly dropped overnight, there was scarcely enough wind to take them north. In the morning the sea, still calm, was beginning to curl in a gentle south-easter. With a sense of excitement Anna hurried away from the town towards her fishing-spot just after sunrise. The black yacht was still there, and her heart leapt absurdly at the sight.

Soon she saw the black dinghy put out from the stern. What if they both came ashore – ? Two men who had been at sea for months, who had scarcely seen a woman in that time. But that young man did not seem like a rapist.

Pretending to be interested only in fishing, she made a poor cast, slamming the bait off the hook. The dinghy was rowing straight towards her. There was only one man in it. With trembling fingers she began to bait up again. He caught the next wave and beached the dinghy, pulling it high above the reach of the tide. She stared as though hypnotised as he came towards her, unconsciously reeling in her line. He walked up close to her, smiling, took the rod out of her unresisting hands, and fixed it upright in the sand. With an arm round her waist he led her towards the tea-tree shadowed sand-hills.

'I couldn't bear to sail away without seeing you again,' he said. 'I told my crewman I was coming to get another fish. But I'm afraid he guesses what's keeping me here.'

'You mustn't stay,' she said faintly. 'It's not a safe coast. If this south-easterly gets up you'll be on a lee shore, and you mightn't have time to get out.'

'Don't worry, we'll be gone within the hour.'

His hand had slipped up from her waistline to her breast, and cupped it gently as they walked. She began to lean on him, feeling herself grow weak. Not a word, not an endearment passed between them as they lay in the mother-of-pearl hollow between two ridges of silvery sand. Her swimming costume, his faded shorts were the only impediments, soon cast aside, to the deepest, most complete meeting she could ever remember. He had come to her like a merman, straight from the sea. Their movements were like the rhythmed breathing of the waves upon the sand.

One sharp cry was forced from her, echoed by the cry of a gull. Then she became aware that he was gently withdrawing, standing up, leaving; he picked up the tattered shorts and was gone. She lay for a long time, motionless, bemused, at peace. Then the sun rising above the tea-trees beat down on her upturned face and roused her to move.

She went to the edge of the sandhills and looked out to sea. The black hull with its white sail was dwindling away to the northward.

Though she had told Nyora she didn't want another baby, when her third child was born Anna felt a great tenderness for the little mite, with her wisp of straight dark hair which stood up in a tiny crest from her scalp. She looked vaguely like Aunt Agnes, Anna thought. Remembering how her auntie had told

191

them her name meant 'Lamb of God', she decided to call the baby Agnes.

It was after Agnes was born in 1928 that Anna developed the incurable blood disease – none of them had ever heard the word 'leukaemia' before – that was to kill her in a few years. When it became known that her case was hopeless, Anna's sister Ellen came to the island and promised to do something about the children's schooling when they were older. Meanwhile there was the Mission school at Keppel Sands.

Agnes, or Maggie as she called herself, grew into a beautiful, slender child with creamy-brown skin and softly waving hair which Anna never tired of brushing, until she became too weak to make the effort. She spent much time lying on an old sofa under a shade of woven pandanus fronds beside the house, from where she could watch the sea.

'Hullo, I'm Aggie,' little Agnes would introduce herself. Gradually it became 'I'm Maggie,' and she was known as Maggie Pinjarra. (It had been Pinjaró when Nyora married her Portuguese sailor, but as they rarely wrote things down it had changed over the years to the more Aboriginal-sounding Pinjarra.)

Little Maggie had so many aunties and uncles, besides motherly old Nyora and her older sister Marie, that she scarcely missed her mother when she died. Meanwhile the great Depression had spread round the world, and thousands left the cities where there were no jobs for them and joined the army of itinerant workers tramping the bush. Among them was Maggie's grandfather, Chukka Brown.

Sugar was a luxury, and the demand for it grew less. The Tombuas managed to hang on to their cane-farm, but Chukka, whose soldier-settlement block was too small and had poor soil, could not keep going when the price of sugar fell. The area was too dry for cane-growing; he'd not had a profitable crop for years, and was in debt to the bank. He sold his car, and the bank took over his mortgaged house and land.

Chukka walked off his block and went back to cutting cane. But at nearly fifty he was not fast enough to keep up with younger men. There were a dozen workers competing for every job, even when the farmers could afford to employ help.

He rolled a few clothes and some bedding into a grey blanket, added a frying-pan, a camp-oven, and a billy-can for tea, and set out to walk with his swag on his shoulder. The grandson of Jamie Brown the Canadian Patriot had become a swagman, 'waltzing Matilda' over the dusty roads and camping beside the dry watercourses of inland Australia.

BOOK THREE

The Rainbow's Gold

1853–1933

To the West, to the West, to the land of bright gold,
Where the man who buys shares is never once sold,
   To the West, to the West, where there's plenty of fun,
Where the quartz fifty hundredweights goes to the ton . . .

'The Coolgardie Miner', 1895

Damn Coolgardie! Damn the track!
Damn it there and damn it back!
Damn the country! Damn the weather!
Damn the goldfields altogether.
Old diggers' song

One

LIKE Joseph Forbes King, his ancestor Samuel King was born under the sign of the Scorpion, almost exactly a hundred years earlier – in November 1849. He was the youngest son of a country solicitor who had emigrated from Aylesbury in Buckinghamshire to a copper-mining town in South Australia which was said to be booming.

Early in life Sam saw the piles of copper ingots, stained with blue and purple and green like rainbowed gold, stacked ready to be railed from Kuldunda to southern ports for export overseas. South Australian copper was so fine that it commanded the highest price on the market. But Sam King's first love was to be not copper but gold. He was to say in later life that the sweetest sound on earth was the tinkle of small nuggets falling on to a banker's gold-weighing scales.

Sam did not think much of the earth when he arrived on it, head-first and bawling, towards midnight at the beginning of summer in the southern hemisphere. His twin brother, Albert, apparently thought even less of it, for he closed his eyes almost immediately and did not open them again, but died quietly without a whimper. His mother always felt that Sam had more than his share of energy, will and determination – as though, surviving, he had inherited all the vitality that would have been Albert's had he lived.

The plump, handsome Henrietta, an Edmond from Ivinghoe, had already borne three children before they left for the new land. Arthur, Henry and Caroline were born in England, and Bessie, James, Albert and Sam in Australia.

Robert King did not find enough work in his legal practice, for copper miners (mostly Cornishmen) seemed to be more law-abiding than was usual among mining communities. So he started as well a hardware store to supply mining tools and equipment. Later, when the mines began to fail, it was to sell farming machinery and provide a living for one of the sons.

As Sam and his brother Jim grew old enough for school, they all walked off together each morning, the biggest in the lead, the young ones trailing behind, along the white dusty road with its green pepper-trees. They were a close-knit family, and no one ever 'picked on' young Samuel or James King, as they knew they'd have their big brothers to reckon with: Henry and Arthur. Caroline and Bessie, disdaining the company of 'rough boys', kept apart, stepping sedately along in the pinafore dresses and shady sunbonnets which they wore to protect their delicate complexions from the Antipodean sun. The boys were made to wear cloth caps, but as soon as they were away from the house they tore them off and stuffed them in their pockets, already bulging with pen-knives, cata-pults, 'useful' bits of wire and string, and glass alleys (plain green marbles from lemonade bottles, and valuable 'cats' eyes').

By the time he was five years old, young Sam had seen a fall of rain only as many times as he could count on the fingers of one hand. It rained so rarely, and so briefly, in this dry northern part of the province of South Australia that the children would run outside, laughing and excited, to stand in the falling rain when thunderstorms at last broke the long drought. The rain was warm, and there was no sweeter scent than the smell of dry grass and parched earth receiving the caress of rain; no sweeter sound than the steady drumming of rain on the corrugated iron roof.

'D'you hear that, lads?' their father would say, holding up his white, well-shaped hand towards the fancy moulded ceil-ing. 'That is money falling on the countryside. This land depends on the farmer and the grazier, and everyone benefits when the rain comes. Everyone in this town, and even in the city, knows that it's good for business. The man on the land –'

'What about the miners?' asked Sam.

'Well, yes, mining is very important to the economy, and it's not affected by droughts and bad seasons. But primary production – wheat and wool – that is the solid basis on which South Australia is built. Don't you know the State's coat of arms? On one side, a man holding a sheep's fleece, and on the other, a woman with a sheaf of wheat and a cornucopia, the horn of plenty; and between them the Sun that makes everything grow. Why, last year the export of wool alone brought in nearly a million pounds! And wheat and flour as much again. Not bad for a little province that's only existed for less than twenty years!'

Their father liked to read them 'improving' books, history and geography in heavy tomes bound with calfskin and marbled endpapers, but their mother, growing larger and heavier every year though still handsome and fair-haired, would read them fairy-stories after they were in bed. One night she read a story about the Crock of Gold at the end of the rainbow.

Sam was fascinated. 'But why hasn't somebody found it and dug it up?' he asked. 'Marmee? Why hasn't they?'

'Well, someone did find it in this story, didn't they? But the next day it had turned to dirt and leaves, because it was only fairy gold.'

'I'd like to find some fairy gold,' said Sam, thinking that it would be finer and more beautiful even than the gold in the wide band of his mother's wedding ring, and her brooch set with amethysts.

Sam had never seen a rainbow, except in the picture-book. Then one day, when he was six years old, a rainbow arched above Kuldunda. It shone in the eastern sky one afternoon as they were coming home from school. One end disappeared into the low bare hills to the north-east; the other seemed to curve down in front of the dry creek – dignified by the name of 'river' – which ran only after heavy rain, and which bordered the town's outskirts to the south and east. The mine-workings lay to the west.

Sam thought he had never seen anything half so beautiful. He'd never particularly noticed such things as sunrise or sunset or moonlight. He loved the beauty of things he could hold or touch, like his mother's amethyst brooch with its three big stones. And he liked pieces of translucent quartz picked up by the roadside, or blue-green copper ores from the mine.

But the rainbow! The lithographed picture in the book had shown hard bands of colour, as if the rainbow might be made of jewels, or enamelled wood. Nothing had prepared him for this glowing pure colour, soft yet brilliant. He said the colours over to himself: red, orange, yellow, green, blue, indigo, violet. And at its foot was the shining Crock of Gold. Which end was the foot, though? He hadn't thought of that; the rainbow had two ends. Marmee had said that rainbows did not last long, and that was one reason why it was so hard to find the gold. He didn't have time to get to both, so he would make for the one by the river.

Without saying a word to his brother, Sam went and got his father's shovel – it was taller than he was – from the tool-shed and, dragging it behind him, set off to dig up the gold at the end of the rainbow.

The unusual misty rain which had caused the phenomenon was drawing off towards the east. The rainbow still hung before him, beckoning. Though the ground was damp on the surface, the air was clearing overhead. The dry wild oats, white as paper, soft as feathers, bowed before a gentle breeze. Sam toiled along manfully, still in his school uniform of short grey pants, shirt and tie, long knitted socks and lace-up boots.

He was tired and hot before he reached the last of the town's wide streets and neared the line of gumtrees marking the course of the river. And then, looking up from stumping along with his head down, he saw a strange and disturbing thing. The rainbow had moved! It no longer reached the earth in front of the trees, but beyond them, still further to the east. It seemed to have grown more brilliant in colour, and there was a faint reflection beside it, a ghost, a shadow of the rainbow.

He reached the deeply-eroded river bank, lined with dead prickly weeds, above one of the chain of pools left from the last heavy rain. He and his older brothers used to come here fishing for yabbies, small freshwater crayfish, with a lump of meat tied to a piece of string. He moved along the bank till he came to a bar of ironstone rock holding back the pool. The shovel scraped and rattled behind him as he crossed and climbed the far bank.

When he came out from the trees on the other side of the river, he stopped in consternation. The rainbow did not end just behind the trees, as it had seemed to do, but was even further away across the treeless plain. He pushed on, his little legs beginning to ache. He looked over his shoulder. The sun was setting, sinking behind the river-side gums; but still that bright and beautiful promise hung in the sky, one end plunging into the earth ahead. He could see the very spot where he would dig. He fixed it by a washaway just to the left, and to the right an outcrop of dark rocks, of the same ironstone as the bar in the river bed. He put his head down and pressed on, dragging the now ton-heavy shovel behind him.

He looked up again to get his bearings, and stopped with a choked cry. The rainbow was fading, dissolving. First all the right-hand bow disappeared, then the arch at the top, until nothing was left but the glowing pillar of coloured light ahead. He began to trot forward, abandoning the shovel. Once he had marked the spot to dig, he could come back and get it.

He ran till he was exhausted, and then, with a shock, realised that the end of the rainbow had moved again, beyond the gash of clay and the black rocks which no longer shone through it, but were in front of it.

So it was magic, then! You would have to be a magician and work some kind of spell to keep the rainbow from always retreating ahead of you . . . Then, as if to mock him, the whole thing simply disappeared. There was nothing but grey sky and empty plain.

Sam stopped in his tracks. The light was fading, and looking round at the now distant trees, he saw that the sun had set. Doggedly he went on to the mark he had fixed; there was the clay ravine, there the outcrop. Between them was ordinary reddish clay soil, baked hard except for the rain-moistened surface. He scuffed at it with his boot. It would be too hard to dig in, even if he had the shovel, even if this was the right place.

Suddenly the excitement which had carried him on left him, like the dissolving colours of the rainbow. It was getting dark, and he was far from home. There was no lingering twilight here as in the cooler climes from which his parents had come to Australia. A brief afterglow of orange light in the west, turning to a clear pale greenish tint, then darkness. Though tired, he began to trot back towards the river. Then he remembered the shovel.

How far back had he dropped it? Was he following the

same line? When he judged he was at the right distance, he began casting around and up and down, hoping to stumble on it in the growing dusk. But he could not find it. If only he had been able to stick it upright in the hard ground! Then he might have seen its silhouette against the fading sky. Though frightened of his father's anger over the loss of the shovel, Sam gave up and hurried towards the river, marked by a frieze of black lace, the thin-leaved eucalyptus traced against the last brightness in the west. But in casting about for the shovel, he had moved out of the line which led to his former crossing place. He was too far to the right, and even further from the area where the river curved close to the town, where the bridge and the swimming-hole were.

Stumbling and falling, the high lace-up boots beginning to chafe his ankles, Sam was close to sitting down and giving himself up to tears. But boys didn't cry; only girls cried. By the time he came to the river the western glow was gone; he had no further guidance from that direction. If he had known the constellations he might have recognised the Scorpion, setting now in the west, and plunging head-first below the horizon so that it looked like a big fish-hook, like the pot-hooks he made in his copy-book when learning to write. Or like a huge yabbie with its tail curled under.

The river was strange, a ravine of deep shadows with a glint of water in the bottom. This was not where he had crossed, this long waterhole with no bar across it. Should he be further to the left, or to the right? He moved to the right, looking for a break in the pale gleam below. Then, when he found it, he had to struggle through prickly bushes and giant wild tobacco to get down to the bed. The other side was so steep he had to crawl on his hands and knees, sharp shale bruising his chubby hands. He reached the top, and looked in vain for the lights of the town. Unknown to him the river had made a deep loop, and he was now facing away from it.

Sam knew that once he left the river he would become lost. He could follow it one way to the town bridge, in the other, down-stream, to the railway crossing. Either way he would be able to walk back either along the main road, or along the railway line. He picked up a smooth pebble, spat on one side of it, and tossed it in the air.

Wet for left,
Dry for right.

He felt about for it where it fell. Wet side up! He started off, walking along the top of the river-bank, towards the bridge.

When it got dark and there was still no sign of young Sam, a mild panic set in at the King home. The lamps were lit, the table was set for dinner, but nobody sat down. Henrietta, her usually rose-pink cheeks as white as chalk, walked distractedly up and down the dining-room, wringing her plump hands.

'I've called from the veranda, and rung the bell . . . Oh Robert!' wailed Henrietta. 'Where can he be?'

'I can't think, my dear. He came home from school with Jimmy, who doesn't remember seeing him after that. Do you think he might have gone yabbying?'

'Without telling anyone? What if – if he went to the swimming hole?' This was a deep, permanent water under the town bridge.

They stared at each other, unable to put their fear into words.

Robert King turned on his heel. 'I'll call Storr, and we'll go to the bridge. I must take a lantern – we'll need two lanterns.'

Storr was the handyman and gardener who occupied a cottage in the corner of the grounds, and spent his time clipping the delicate blue flowers from the Plumbago hedge, watering the dusty geraniums and mowing the small patch of lawn. He willingly left his meal to come and search for 'young Sam', who was his favourite among the boys. Sam liked to listen to his tales of mining, when he was a digger on the fabled Ballarat and Bendigo fields.

He had come from Victoria to work in the Kuldunda copper mines, and now, laid off to make room for younger men, he gardened for a small wage and his keep. There was also a housemaid, and the cook-general, Jinnie, who said that Master Sam had come to the kitchen to get a piece of cake after school. (He was a favourite with the cook, too.)

Storr and Robert King set off for the river, each carrying a lantern. They collected several men on the way, until a search party of eight had been gathered. James had wanted to go too, but his mother would not let him; he was only eight. Henrietta hugged him on the veranda as she watched the lanterns dwindle into the distance, feeling his solid warmth, but thinking more of her lost lamb. The bigger boys were both away at boarding school.

'We seen a rainbow, coming home from school,' said James, looking at the dark sky.

'*Saw* a rainbow,' said his mother automatically. 'Jimmy, what did you say? A rainbow!'

'Yair – it was real pretty. Just like the one in the fairy-story. Didn't you see it, Mama?' (Sam, the youngest, was the only one who called her 'Marmee'.)

'No – I was down in the cellar, counting preserves. Oh – !' Her head went to her breast. She knew where Sam, the independent, had gone – on an expedition to find the end of the rainbow.

'Jinnie!' She went to the kitchen. 'You give the young ones their dinner, will you? And Hannah, come with me, and bring another lantern. We're going to look for young Sam. I know where he's gone.'

'Yes,'m. Shall I top it up with kerosene?' asked Hannah.

'Yes, but hurry!'

Since the sun would have been fairly low in the west by four o'clock, the rainbow would have shown in the east, towards the line of trees marking the river. Henrietta walked quickly in that direction, holding in one hand the folds of her long, full skirts above the dusty road. Hannah carried the lantern.

How much rain had there been; was it enough to make the river flow; how deep was the chain of waterholes ahead? Please God, not very deep! Sam was a sturdy child, but he had not yet learned to swim.

They had not gone far when they saw lights flashing off to the right, and heard voices. It was the group of men returning. And leading them was Robert with Sam astride his shoulders: a grimy Sam, with a tear-stained face, but smiling happily. Papa hadn't even been angry about the shovel – said something about he could get a new shovel from the store, but where would he get another Sam?

With a cry, his mother ran forward, forgetting to hold her skirt out of the dust. In a moment he was in her arms, her face buried against him, her warm tears making his collar damp. 'I wasn't lost, Marmee,' he said. 'I was makin' for the main road, but the river bends so!'

That night he was thoroughly scolded by both parents for going off without telling anyone, for crossing the river alone. Not a word was said about the lost shovel.

'You were trying to find the pot of gold at the end of the rainbow, weren't you?' said Henrietta, stroking his golden head.

'Yes, and Marmee, I couldn't catch up with it. It kept gettin' furver and furver away.'

'Tomorrow, young man,' said his father, 'you are going to have a lesson in prismatic light and the properties of the spectrum. Then you will understand why *no one* ever reaches the end of the rainbow. And since he has such a literal mind, my dear,' he added with a smile at Henrietta, 'I think you should read this lad factual stories in future.'

Though he didn't tell Sam so, Robert King was quite impressed with his son's navigating ability. Sam's tired and scratched legs soon recovered, but his mother made him spend the next day in bed (much to his disgust), for it was a long walk to school. On the week-end he led his father unerringly to where he judged the shovel would be, picking up the twin landmarks of a dead tree on the river-bank and the ironstone outcrop among the clay. And there was the shovel, right on Sam's line.

'H'mm,' said his father. 'This soil's too hard to dig in, anyway. Didn't think of that, did you?'

Sam hung his head, his pride deflated.

'You'd need a pick or a mattock. But in fact if you want to find gold, that ironstone and shale would be your best bet. It probably has traces of copper, too. They're often found together. Sometimes there are gold-bearing veins of white quartz through the rock. But remember, all is not gold that glitters.'

'Can we go an' look now, Papa?'

'No, Mamma wants us back in time for lunch. But we'll all come on a picnic to the river one day, and you can stop here and take a sample. We'll take a good sample of the rock home for crushing. You ask Storr, he'll show you how to use a dolly-pot and a panning dish.'

'Gee-whiz!' said Sam, his blue eyes alight. 'When can we?'

'Not next weekend, but soon. Meanwhile, why don't you try washing the sand in the creek that runs by our back paddock? You might find some specks there, I reckon. If you can find a pool with some water left in it for your panning dish.'

Sam had been disappointed to learn that the beautiful rainbow wasn't real at all, that the colours his eyes saw as the sun shone through the drops of rain were there all the time as the components of white light. To illustrate the principle, his father unhooked one of the crystal prisms from the small chandelier in the hall and let Sam look at a beam of sunlight through it.

'That is called a spectrum, not a rainbow,' said his father. 'It is the same row of colours exactly as you see in the sky: red, orange, yellow, green, blue, indigo, violet. The rainbow is always opposite the sun, because it is really the sunlight refracted through a million drops of water, each one acting as a tiny prism.'

Sam looked about him through the glass prism. Every object was haloed with coloured light. He felt as if he were holding the rainbow trapped in his hand, in the smooth, clear, three-sided piece of glass that had such magical properties. After that, he was always begging to have a prism unhooked so he could look through it.

Two

By the time he was eight, Sam already had a small collection of fine gold-dust and flakes in a glass jar. His elder brothers jeered at Sam's 'gold mania', and James did not share his interest, though he would come on his gold-seeking expeditions just for company.

Sam never forgot the lesson he learned from his first try at finding alluvial gold.

He had begged the biggest iron frying-pan from the kitchen, and every afternoon after school he was 'up the creek', carrying the pan, and in a knapsack on his back a glass jar for specimens, a pair of his mother's tweezers, and a bottle of drinking water. Very often he used the drinking water to wash a pan of sand in his impatience, before he got to the one small waterhole above a bar of rock, surrounded by some short green grass showing where it had shrunk by evaporation until only a scummy pool, alive with waterbeetles, remained.

From here he moved upstream – though there was no stream at present – as Storr said that gold, being heavy stuff, would be dropped wherever the creek was checked in its flow by an obstruction across it. The very first day he actually saw flakes of gold glinting in the sand before he washed it! Trembling with excitement, he panned off a quantity, slowly swirling the water and turning the dish with a small, shaking motion, just as Storr had showed him. The trouble was, the gold wouldn't stay in the 'tail', as it was supposed to, but was in such thin flakes that it actually seemed to float. He sorted it out and transferred the glittering flakes to his screw-top glass jar with the tweezers. Soon he had the bottom of the jar lined with gold. There was still more gleaming in the sand, but the sun was low, and he almost ran back to the house with his treasure. Storr said that somewhere further up, where the creek began, would be the reef that shed the gold found lower down.

'Storr! Storr! I've found gold! Lots of it!' he cried, before he'd even got to the old man's cottage door. Storr came out and turned the jar in his gnarled fist, squinting at the grains which showed bright gold in the last yellow rays of the sun. 'Aye,' he said, 'looks real pretty, don't it, with the sun on it? But it ain't gold, young feller. Wait till you see it inside, in the morning light. More silvery than gold, and more brassy than either. That's fool's gold.'

'Fool's gold!' Sam remembered his father saying, 'all is not gold that glitters.' 'But – but it's metal, and it's yellow, and –'

'And it's pyrites, that's what it is. Not iron, but copper pyrites, I'd say, what looks nearer the real thing. O' course there's lots of copper round in these hills. But b'leeve me, if there'd bin that much gold in the crick, some fossicker would've found 'er long since. I don't say there ain't *any*, mind, but not that easy ter come by.'

Sam was crestfallen. 'I was dead certain it was gold.'

'Tell yer what,' said Storr. 'I'll take yer down the river on Sundee mornin', and show yer how to pan for alluvial. There's a knack in it. If there's any danged gold in that riverbed, we'll find some.'

'I have to go to Sunday school,' said Sam. 'And church after.' As if five days of school weren't enough, to have to spend Sunday morning indoors always seemed to him the height of injustice. He would shut his ears to the boring sermon and fix his eyes on a beam of sun coming through a panel of gold in the stained glass window over the altar.

'We'll go Saturdee arvo, then,' said Storr.

They didn't have much to show for their expedition, but Storr, spreading the tailings with his big thumb, showed Sam a few flakes which he said were gold. Sam picked them out carefully with the tweezers and transferred them to his jar, in which he kept an inch of water on the bottom.

Later he was allowed to go down with Jim – as long as they didn't go near the swimming-hole – and one day, swirling the dish with a professional action, Sam realised that the fine yellow dust at the tail, which he thought was just sand, was in fact gold dust – gold in grains as fine as mustard, which his new-found skill had separated from the dross.

After the promised expedition to the outcrop beyond the

river with his father, Sam had taken Storr his first specimens of ore. The old man's eyes lighted up at a gleam of what might be gold. 'Aye, gold is queer stuff,' said Storr. 'I've known a man to starve when 'e 'ad a small nugget in 'is money-belt. Used to sleep with it under 'is pillow, and take it out and rub it to make it shine under the lamplight. Couldn't bear to part with it for money.'

The ore was in lumps of amorphous white quartz with a rusty vein no thicker than a knife-blade. In places it was greenish, with flecks of shining metal, probably a mixture of copper and gold. Storr showed him how to smash and powder it in an old iron pot, using a flat-ended crowbar; then to wash the dirt in the shallow frying-pan.

'When you've dollied 'er, and panned 'er, and got the bit o' colour what you think is gold, then you drop 'er into a spoonful of Spirits of Salt – that's acid, see – and fizz! all the copper's gone, and what's left, if there is any left, is gold.'

Sam thanked him and after an hour's work came up with two specks of undoubted gold: small ones, what Storr called 'fly specks', less than a grain in weight. He added them proudly to his collection of fine dust from the river bed.

When they were old enough, it was the turn of the two youngest, Sam and Jim, to be sent to boarding school in the city. Because their father was a Methodist, they went to a Wesleyan college on the edge of the parklands, with broad playing-fields and imposing buildings. Its motto, carved above the Gothic doorway, was UBI NON EST SCIENTIA ANIMAE NON EST BONUM, which Sam, who had little Latin, translated for himself as 'It's no good having animals without science', which would have made quite a good motto for an agricultural college. Unfortunately, though most of the boarders came from the country, the only lessons in agriculture they received were from the Georgics of Virgil.

Sam hated it, except for Geology and Chemistry, his favourite subjects. He lived for the long vacations, when he would go on long rambles among the mineral-rich outcrops around Kuldunda, taking his geologist's hammer and a sugar-bag for specimens. Soon he had a good collection of crystals: gypsum, amethyst, clear white quartz, galena, iron pyrites in square metallic crystals, lumps of white marble and beautiful,

veined green malachite, carbonate of copper; and his favourites: diamond-shaped, sea-blue copper sulphate crystals. He
also picked up tektites, those strange little black buttons said
to have come from the moon.

The copper mines were fading in the town, the second
boom of 1872 had moved to the west coast and his father did
not even consider making Sam a mining engineer, his obvious
vocation. Because he was good at figures it was decided that
he would become an accountant.

So Sam studied figures and bookkeeping and read books
about gold-mining and geology in his spare time. He kept his
precious specimens of gold in his room. Spreading a newspaper over the bed, he'd uncork the little bottle, holding it
upside down over the paper and tapping the cork against the
bottle to shake off the last particles clinging to it. Then he
would sit and gaze at the small, shining heap. He dreamed of
one day finding a nugget, a monster like the 'Welcome
Stranger' which had hit the headlines in 1866, and weighed
2,284 ounces. But that was in Victoria, in alluvial gold
country. And the trouble was, there was no science about
finding a nugget; it was as much a matter of chance as the spin
of a roulette wheel. Sam preferred science. He studied 'The
Gold-Finder of Australia' and wished he could trace a rich
lode, or even a 'dab'.

As soon as he was home again he was out prospecting. A
'dab' was where two gold-bearing veins met and enriched
each other, shedding traces of gold into the surface soil. By
careful panning, the direction of the dab could be found,
perhaps by striking one of the veins or stringers that led to it.

'You need the patience o' Job to trace her down,' Storr had
told him. 'If you break the stringer, you're sunk. It's like a
piece of string leading down into the rock. But I once saw a
bloke take three buckets of ore from a dab, that crushed 1,000
ounces of gold. I reckon it's hungry country round 'ere,
though – you won't find nothing like that, or I'd be lookin'
meself.'

Sam, the gambler in him aroused, went back to the ironstone outcrop beyond the river where he had followed the
rainbow. What a lark if there really *was* a pot of gold, or its
equivalent, hidden under the soil at that very spot! He had

found small traces of gold in the samples taken on that family picnic long ago – not enough, Storr said, to indicate there was more. And yet . . . Sam decided to test the spot again.

There had been an unusual, heavy rain with a thunderstorm the night before he set out. Sam had to wade the river, carrying his tools. The sun was shining, frogs chorused, brown doves were cooing among the leaves, a crested bell-bird chimed: *Pan-pan-panella*! The sky was a clear-washed blue like Sam's eyes. He whistled happily as he began to work.

The surface of the rock was washed clean, the soil about it softened. Sam knapped some pieces of rock carefully with his hammer, scraped some of the soil from the crevices and panned it with water from the waterbag he carried. Soon he found fine gold like shiny mustard appearing in the dish. And then he saw it – a thin, sugary quartz leader like a string of small glass beads, the gold among it in small rough pieces. When he dug them out they had pieces of ironstone and quartz clinging to them.

Cautiously he traced the stringer down. The rock became harder. He used a small charge of dynamite far enough away from the stringer to do no more than shake it. He pulled out the loose pieces; he was still no nearer finding a dab. He followed the vein down until at last it petered out. Still, at the end of the day he reckoned he had at least four ounces of gold, about twenty pounds' worth.

'And it isn't fairy gold, either,' said Sam to himself with a grin. He washed his tools in the big pool in the river where he had carried the ore in a sack, and turned for home.

'You *are* a clever boy!' said his mother admiringly when he showed them the result of his week-end's work.

'H'm, I hope you haven't been working on the Sabbath,' said his father.

'This wasn't work, Papa! This was fun!'

From that time on he was hooked. Gold had him in thrall; he became a gold-seeker and fossicker as some men become alcoholics. All his life he was to chase precious metals, below and on the surface of the ground. He was to go through several fortunes, while his brothers ran the family hardware business, or carried on the legal firm of King, Foyle and King (his eldest brother, who had done Law, was already engaged

211

to a Miss Foyle), or acquired large sheep-holdings further to the north.

It was no good Storr telling him that it was a fool's game, that he had never known a prospector, even one who had made a lucky strike, to die wealthy.

'I seen an old bloke once, at Bendigo,' he said, 'and there was real gold there, you could kick it out of the ground with your boot, in the early days. This chap stuck his pick into a hundred-ounce slab o' pure gold. Well! He sat down shaking like a leaf, and started to cry . . .'

'I ran into 'im later, down and out, in front of the Salvation Army's old men's home in Melbourne; 'e asked me for a deener for a drink.'

Storr was an old man now and did little but clip the front hedge and prune the fruit trees; the starved lawn scarcely needed cutting. Hannah had got married and been replaced by a succession of housemaids, some of whom were pretty enough to attract Sam's eye now he was of an age to notice such things.

By the time Sam had passed his Accountancy exams, a prolonged drought had struck the North, drying up the 'permanent' waterholes, while starving stock scratched despairingly at the stony ground, digging up even the roots of the saltbush to eat them. The saltbush, which absorbed moisture from the air and could exist for years without rain, had been the staple support of the woolgrowing industry outside the ten-inch annual rainfall line. Now, through overstocking and intensive grazing, it was almost killed out. A financial depression set in, for copper prices were falling even if rain was not; and all the easily-worked ore had already been taken out of the Kuldunda mines. Miners were laid off, and stockmen drifted into the town looking for jobs.

As there were no positions available for a young accountant, Sam was unemployed. His father gave him a job, at a nominal wage, looking after the books of King, Foyle and King.

Sam, now bigger than his father, had inherited his mother's handsome features and tall frame. He was beginning to cause his parents worry. His mother, taking out a lock of golden hair from her youngest's head (it had now darkened to light brown), would gaze at it and marvel that the last of her babies had grown into a man. He was courting young Mary Tregona, the black-haired, dark-eyed daughter of a Cornish mine foreman, who seemed a nice girl. It was to be hoped she would prove the good influence she seemed to be, and help to snatch this young brand from the burning.

For his mother knew that Sam smoked cigars and drank at the Miners' Arms with a rather wild lot of young men. Worse still, he had been involved with a girl of bad repute, one Ida Ryan, known to the townspeople as 'You tellin' Ida', as this was her favourite expression. Ida always knew what was going on and had the news of births, deaths, and prospective marriages before anyone else; if anyone offered her such a piece of news she would retort scornfully, 'You tellin' Ida! I knew all about that last week.'

James, only two years older than Samuel, never gave his parents cause for worry. He was always neatly dressed, ambitious and industrious, and he was successfully running the store, selling mining equipment and machinery. It was not his fault if the fall in the price of copper had made business slack.

Samuel, on the other hand, often failed to wear a tie or a cravat, forgot to polish his boots, went without a jacket on hot days, and was difficult to get out of bed in the mornings. Robert King was thinking of sending him north to one of his brothers' properties as a jackeroo or as bookkeeper. But the drought had killed so many sheep, and so many more had been railed to the stock paddocks in the south to be sold as mutton, that the wool industry was almost at a standstill and neither stockmen nor office workers were needed.

Sam kept telling himself that he must stop seeing Ida, for if Mary once found out that he had not given up the other girl she would refuse to marry him. And last week they had plighted their troth, though it had not been officially announced as yet. Sam was nineteen and Mary just turned seventeen; it was time they thought about settling down. It was going to be hard enough to wait for his wedding day. Nice girls like Mary did not understand how it was for a man, and that girls like Ida existed to help them through the period of waiting for legal matrimony.

Sam told himself that he must say goodbye to Ida anyway, so it would not hurt to see her once more and tell her it was all over. He knew that Ida was fond of him. Even if he had no money, and he never had by the end of the week, she did not mind lying down and spreading her legs. He looked approvingly in the mirror at his burly, broad-shouldered, six-foot frame, his bright blue eyes and cheeks pink with health. Yes, he would definitely break it off tonight. Casting about for a present for her, he found a coloured silk kerchief a missionary aunt had sent him from India. He stuffed it in his pocket.

' 'Ullo, dearie,' Ida greeted him outside the Miners' Arms, where she was talking to some of the Kuldunda boys.

'Come in and I'll buy you a drink, Ida,' said Sam. 'Yesterday was pay day, you know.'

'You tellin' Ida! I was wonderin' when you'd be along.'

He bought her a rum and drank a rum himself with a beer chaser. Ida looked at him fondly. 'You still workin' for your dad? You want to get out on your own, like your brothers have.'

'Yeah. The old man doesn't pay very well, that's for sure.'

'You don't want to go working for him for nuthin'.'

'He doesn't expect me to work for nothing, but with the wages I get I don't see how I'll ever save enough to get married.'

Ida's green-grey eyes opened a little wider. She fluttered her lashes at him coquettishly.

'Why – you thinkin' o' getting married?'

Sam smiled, a small, tight-lipped, self-satisfied smile. 'Well – who knows? I might be.' He put his arms round her and lifted her down off the bar-stool. She leant against him for a moment, her tangled reddish curls on his shoulder.

'Let's get away on our own,' she murmured urgently. 'Down by the bridge? Or in the haystack?'

'What, already?' He was amused at her importunity, but it stirred his desire. They walked out with his arm round her waist. The lads in front of the Arms laughed and cheered as they sauntered off down the street. The haystack, belonging to the innkeeper, was in the vacant block alongside, and beyond it was the office building where Sam worked. It was a two-storey weather-board building, built right up to the fence line.

Sam led Ida around the far side of his father's office, so that no one would see them approaching the haystack from the street. He climbed the wooden fence, pulling her after him. The haystack had been partly pulled away on this side for forage for the horses of guests at the inn.

'Gosh, you're so strong,' breathed Ida admiringly as his hands gripped her under the armpits and lifted her easily – though she was a solid girl with big, voluptuous breasts and hips. 'Let Ida see your muscles,' she murmured, unbuttoning his shirt . . . 'Oh, Sam'l, love. Oh – ! That's good. Oh, that's so good. Oh – ! Sam, you're better'n any of the boys. I dunno if you're longer, or rounder, or what, but you're just what the doctor ordered. You and me fits so well together.'

Sam felt his ardour a little damped at this artless comparison, reminding him how many of his friends had shared his present felicity. But he responded nobly to her well-known charms and tumbled her vigorously in the hay.

Afterwards they lay quietly while she tickled his neck with a straw. She looked up at the yellow stars, rather dull tonight with a haze of smoke or dust.

'All them stars,' she murmured. 'Sometimes I fink there're people up there, lookin' down at us with their yeller eyes – fousands of people, all over the sky.'

'Nonsense, Ida, the stars are balls of fire, just like the sun. It's just that they're a long way off.'

'Balls of fire! You tellin' Ida stories? If they was balls of fire they'd burn up, wouldn' they, and go out?'

'They *will* burn out, eventually, in millions and millions of years. So will the sun, but we don't have to worry about that yet. Ida . . . I wish I could give you something, but you know how short the Old Man keeps me, damn his eyes!' He pulled out the silk kerchief and tied it round her neck. 'Here, this is for you – a goodbye present.' He kissed her.

'Goodbye! Eh, whatyer mean?'

'I have to stop seeing you, Ida. It's been good fun, but I have to think about settling down – having a family . . .'

'I fought p'raps you was going to marry me.' She was pulling pieces of straw in half, savagely.

'Marry you!' Sam was so astounded he started to laugh. 'My dear girl, what would my parents say if I said I wanted to marry the town bike!'

She sprang to her feet in the soft hay, nearly over-balancing, and threw an armful of it in his face.

'*You – bloody – barstid!*' She said through her teeth. ' 'Ad your fun, 'aven't you, so now poor old Ida can get lost. I always liked you best, an' I thought you liked me, and – and . . .' she began to sob.

'I do, I do like you, Ida. I'm sorry I said that, it just slipped out. Stop crying now. I'm sorry.' He tried to pull her hands away from her face, but she struck at him wildly.

'Leave me alone. And don't never come near me again.'

She straightened her clothes in offended silence. He helped her back to the top of the fence, lifting her down and kissing her in the shadowy yard of the lawyers' premises. She pulled away and stalked ahead of him back to the Miners' Arms. He walked behind her, pulling tell-tale pieces of straw out of his hair.

'Let me buy you a last drink,' he said as they reached the building with its wooden veranda posts and sign of a crossed pick and shovel.

'No fanks. I don't want nuthin' from you,' she said in a low voice. 'And who was you finking of marryin', pray?'

'Mary Tregona. We'll be announcing it soon. And you'll know about it first, so when someone tells you you can say, "You telling Ida? I knew about that last week." '

She smiled unwillingly, then tossed her head. 'Huh! A miner's daughter! *She*'s not up to much!' She walked on to the veranda and put her arm through that of a young man leaning against a post. 'Come on, Bill! Drinks on Ida.' She went into the bar without a backward look.

In the early hours of the morning the fire-engine was heard clanging past the Kings' home, its bells clamorous. Getting up and sleepily looking out the window in the direction it had gone, Sam saw a glare in the sky. He felt half-inclined to go and see the fun, but instead went back to bed. It seemed to be somewhere in the vicinity of the Miners' Arms.

Then there was a banging on the front door. His father went down in his dressing gown, the boys crowding down the stair

216

after him. It was one of the Foyle partners from the law firm.

'Quick, the office building is on fire!' he cried. 'They think it started in the haystack next door. All our records will be gone, except those at the bank.'

Sam went cold all over. The haystack! Had he smoked a cigar while he was there with Ida? No, he was sure he hadn't. She had left so precipitately, he hadn't had time to think of a smoke.

By the time the King men got there, the fire was under control in the building, but the haystack and part of the fence were destroyed. Sam and his father and lawyer brother, when it was cool enough to go into the building, began sorting wet and blackened papers into Manila folders. It was a mess.

There was great indignation about the fire. The innkeeper, who had lost all his hay in a drought year when fodder was like gold, was particularly vociferous; so was his wife. A Justice of the Peace and twelve citizens gathered at the Miners' Arms next day for a Citizens' Inquiry on whether the fire had been caused 'by accident or by malice aforethought'.

The *Kuldunda Morning Herald* reported the proceedings on its front page:

Evidence had been given that Ida Ryan 'a person of doubtful character', had been drinking with the town youths, among them Samuel King, during the evening before the fire. Ryan testified that 'Sam was half-slewed' and boasted that he would set fire to his father's premises in the night, 'cos his old man wasn't giving him enough for his work in the office.'

The barman, called to give evidence, said that he had not seen young Mr King drunk, and he'd had only one beer. No one in the bar had heard him utter threats. Neither had any of the group on the footpath outside.

Mr Robert King said that he knew of no one who would light the fire deliberately to spite him. Also he had spoken with his son at 11.30 when he came home and went to his bedroom. He lay awake after that and did not hear Samuel leave the house again.

The innkeeper's wife (who did not like Ida and felt she gave their hostelry a bad name) said that her husband owned the haystack. She had seen Ida in the light of the flames, looking on with an expression 'like the cat what's eaten the cream'. Others had also seen her outside the burning building.

Robert King said he felt there was no need for his son to be called to answer such a preposterous charge. Ida Ryan, recalled to the witness stand, said she had been nowhere near the bloody fire. Yes, she had slept in the haystack earlier, on other nights. Last night she was sleeping under the bridge and knew nothing about the fire till the morning.

The JP decided that it had not been proved that the fire was lit deliberately, nor by whom; that Ryan, however, had been seen in the vicinity and was presumably up to no good; and that he was indicting her for wilful perjury for her remarks about Mr King Junior. So the Establishment closed its ranks.

Sam, however, did not get off without a severe reprimand from his father. 'Let this be a lesson to you,' said Robert King when he had called Sam into his slightly fire-blackened office. 'You cannot touch pitch and not be defiled.'

'She's not all that bad, really. She could have dobbed me in with Mary, and she didn't.'

'That was your scarf she was wearing – the one sent you from India by Aunt Ada?'

'Yes, it was. I wanted to give her something, when I told her I wouldn't be seeing her again.'

'You had broken it off, then? And that was the cause of her malice towards you?'

'Yes, but I never dreamt she would go to such lengths.'

'Hell hath no fury like a woman scorned,' said Mr King, who was rather given to such aphorisms and had already told Sam, on an earlier occasion, that 'a fool and his money are soon parted.'

'How long will she get for perjury?'

'At least twelve months, maybe more. And serve her right.'

Sam felt sorry for the woman, but he believed, along with everyone else in the town, that she had deliberately lit the fire.

'You have brought shame on your mother and me, apart from the destruction of papers in the office. It's a poor bird that fouls its own nest,' said Mr King.

Sam felt that he couldn't wait to get out of that nest and have a home of his own; he contented himself with saying, 'I'm sorry, Father. I only hope that Mary will have me after all this.'

'If she won't stick by you, son, she's not worth having,' said his father.

Sam did not see Mary until Sunday morning. Both families went to the Methodist chapel. For the King family it was an ordeal, knowing the whispering and pointing that was going on behind their backs, for the fire and its aftermath were the talk of the town. Henrietta wore her best hat and held her back very straight.

Mary's father was a rather straitlaced Cornishman with a small goatee beard as dark as his bushy eyebrows. His wife was a round, merry, black-eyed, rosy-cheeked woman, full of life, always laughing and good-humoured. Sam remembered what one of his uncles had told him: 'When choosing a wife, my boy, look at her mother. That will tell you what she'll be like in twenty years' time.'

He felt he could not go wrong with gentle Mary, who was quieter than her mother, with a very much slenderer waist, and a winsome expression that reminded him of his own mother. But to blue-eyed Sam, whose family were all fair, Mary's dark eyes, large and luminous, were fascinating. She used to tease him by keeping her lids obstinately cast down, until he said something to make her look up, when he felt he could drown in their shining depths.

Her father had read Mary a lecture about the ways of wild young men and said he would not like his girl to throw herself away on a young wastrel who was known to drink too much and had apparently been indulging in other vices 'which I won't specify; but he who touches pitch is sure to be defiled,' said Mr Tregona, echoing Mr King's words to his son.

'Promise me, lass, ee'll give un up,' he said, not doubting that she would.

'That I'll not,' said Mary stoutly.

'If ee's thinking of snatching a brand from the burning, 'tis a noble sentiment, but a wrong one. Thee'll only get tha fingers burned, lass.'

'Would you have me abandon Sam just when he needs me?

We are engaged, Father. I am promised, even though we hadn't asked your permission. I was sure you'd be happy about it.'

'Happy! Aye, they're a respectable family enough, and well thought of, seemingly; but it's the lad's character I worry about. I like the lad, a fine manly-looking chap, can't help liking 'un, but broad shoulders and blue eyes be'n't everything. Oh! Mary, think! The miseries of drink and unrighteousness – '

'Samuel is not a drunkard, Papa, just a normal young man. What does Mamma think?'

'She's on tha side, I fear. But as thy father, I can forbid it; I do forbid it.'

Mary, for all her sweet, merry looks, had a streak of iron-hard obstinacy. 'Then we'll be married without your permission,' she said calmly, 'so you had better get used to the idea.'

Both her parents were Cornish. Her mother's people, the Harrises, had come out to the Burra mine when her mother was a little girl. She had met Dan Tregona when both were on a seaside holiday at Glenelg with their families. The two mining men had got on famously, and were delighted when later their Daisy and Daniel decided to get married.

There was a simplicity about the Cornish miners, and a deep religious feeling combined with a belief in the supernatural. They were fine figures of men, most of them, sturdy if not tall, and 'active as cats, and strong and brave as lions,' as one mining engineer described them.

The Burra mine had yielded 50,000 tons of copper, nearly all dug out from either deep shafts or open cuts by Cornishmen, yet by 1880 both the Kuldunda and Burra mines were to be exhausted. The miners said there were still copper ores hidden below, but that 'the knackers' were angry for some reason and so begrudged their copper.

The knackers were little men who, the Cornishmen believed, lived in the deep mines. Whenever they heard the sound of their goblin picks and hammers they knew rich ore lay near. They used to leave choice bits of pasty from their lunch cribs for the knackers, and listen for their warnings of danger underground. Some declared they had heard them singing away on Christmas Eve, but since those who heard the songs had been celebrating rather heavily, not everyone believed them.

Three

SAMUEL KING and Mary Tregona were married in the Dissenting Chapel at Kuldunda, with the rather restrained blessing of their respective families. Mr Tregona had been induced to an unwilling agreement, while Sam's mother, like doting mothers everywhere, felt that her tall son with his commanding good looks which he had inherited from her, could have done better than marrying the pretty, ordinary daughter of a Cornish miner.

Her parents, perhaps conscious of this sentiment on the part of Mrs King, spared no expense for the wedding and the bridal gown, though Mrs Tregona was shocked at Mary's insistence that she wanted to be married in palest lilac taffeta rather than the traditional white, with a white silk fringe around the hem. She knew that it was useless to argue with Mary. Sam had given her an unusual engagement ring of a large amethyst he had found himself and had cut into a square stone, so Mary dressed to match the ring.

Both families had to admit that the young couple seemed ideally happy. In just over nine months, in the hot month of March 1869, their first son William was born. Sam decided while the baby was still in his wicker cradle that he would become an engineer, preferably a mining engineer such as he would like to have been himself, or else perhaps a geologist.

Mary bloomed in her motherhood. Her cheeks glowed, her dark eyes shone, her hair gleamed with glossy highlights, and her petite figure rounded to a fashionable hourglass shape.

She was disappointed when the next two babies were girls, Ada and Alice. When Alice was born her father was away in the hills south of Adelaide, prospecting.

Mary had written in her diary, on her second wedding anniversary, 'The two happiest years of my life!' Now she began to realise that her big, handsome, blue-eyed Samuel, who was never to lose his physical attraction for her, would always go his own way regardless.

It was better than being married to a drunkard, yet in some ways similar; Sam had the gold fever in his blood, and his feet itched to take him to every new strike. 'Goldseeking is like drinking,' Mary confided in her mother, 'and Sam cannot leave it alone.'

This third birth was a difficult one, and Mary felt frightened and alone. Her mother was bedridden at the time and could not stay with her daughter; Sam was away, as usual; the local doctor was busy with an emergency operation, and Mary was ministered to only by the midwife, while her mother-in-law Henrietta took William and Ada out of the way to her own home.

Sam justified his fossicking by finding some payable gold at Echunga. He sold his mining lease to a syndicate on the strength of samples assaying two ounces to the ton, with the possibility of a rich mother-lode nearby. Now that he was married, with a growing family, he had to find a better income than the one he gained from an occasional auditing job in the town and the uncertain possibility of finding gold. Encouraged by an older brother who had already taken up land further north, he bid for three sections of Crown Land bordering the low ten-inch rainfall areas. The Government was making these marginal lands available for farming and grazing for a small down-payment, the balance of £1 an acre to be paid in five years' time. By then he fully expected to have found a fortune.

His property was so covered in round limestone rocks – known locally as 'gibbers' – that he christened it ironically 'The Boulder Run'. He reckoned he had more white boulders than sheep to the acre most of the time. It was part of the old Bundaleer run, now opened up for selection, near the recently-surveyed town of Jamestown. Sam ran some sheep

222

and planted wheat and barley before the good rains of 1873 and 1874. He built stockyards and sheds beside the small but solid limestone house, part of an outstation which was there when he bought the place.

The house was enlarged two rooms at a time with the local stone; that was one thing he had plenty of. In the new home Mary, with help from a local farmer's daughter, coped with the growing family, producing two more daughters and a son, James. She could attend the Methodist church in town and borrow books from the Institute library. While Sam stayed home, she was content.

Sam King was strong and energetic, but his energies were not concentrated on farming. His property was pitted with deep and shallow holes, dug wherever a quartz outcrop appeared. The whole countryside from Ulooloo in the south to Oodlawirra in the north was highly mineralised, he knew: manganese, silver, lead, copper, magnesite and gold were all to be found.

When the £1 an acre became due to the Government for freehold title he did not have the money. Robert King came to the rescue, taking over the property for £1,000 mortgage, and leaving Sam there as manager.

Sam was busy gathering stone near the Terowie railhead which went more than an ounce of gold to the ton, but it was hard work for little return in the stony ground.

Mary meanwhile had a miscarriage; it would, the doctor told her, have been a boy had it lived.

Pretty, merry, plump Mary seemed made for motherhood, yet she was to bring only one son to maturity, and him she was to lose to distant lands, to the sweltering plains of central India. It was James, her second son, on whom she doted. Unlike Willy, who took her own dark colouring, James (named after Sam's favourite brother) was like a new edition of his father: angelically fair, blue-eyed and sturdy.

James at four years had such an equable temperament, such a winning smile, and such transparent, silken skin that sometimes, looking at him, she caught her breath in a spasm of fear. So many children 'went to Heaven' before their time; so many parlour poems referred to pale little angels, tender buds plucked by God for His garden. But she watched over him lovingly, and though the heat of the summer made him pale, it was a dry, healthy heat.

She had seen the others off to school without a qualm, but she worried all the first day when Jimmy went to school, riding 'donkey' on his elder sister's pony. Willy, who was a good rider, was expected to walk.

'What are you fussing about, Mother?' said Sam. 'He's got his sisters and his older brother to look after him, just as I had my brother Jim to look after me. He's no milksop, thank goodness. And you know that Willy has his head screwed on the right way.'

This was an understatement, as Willy in fact was very bright, excelling at Arithmetic and Chemistry, the only science subject at the local school. His other attainment was drawing; he could do a pencil sketch of a building, a dam, a bridge, or copy an etching with great skill. Perhaps he should be an artist, Mary suggested. But that was not a life's work in Sam's opinion.

Sam did not have the temperament for a small farmer. He was too much a gambler, too impatient for quick returns. He gambled on good seasons and rising mutton prices – over-stocking his run – and lost. Drought seized the north of the Colony – drought, indeed, was its normal state, it was the 'good' seasons which were abnormal, but no one realised this as yet. The land shrivelled, the soil blew away from between the stones. Starving stock stood listlessly, heads hanging, and fell where they stood.

Sam pinned his hopes once more on gold. He was not going to sell his property, with farmers abandoning their land on all sides and prices ridiculously low. He had found a promising show in the Oodlawirra area, and had pegged it carefully. He was still looking for 'the reef that shed the gold'.

The high-ceiled stone house remained cool through the autumn months, but as the week-long heatwaves of summer followed each other, with every day around the century mark, the walls began to take on the character of a bush oven.

Sam had dug a cellar under the kitchen (not being able to resist 'washing' some of the dirt he extracted for gold, just in case) and it was the children's task to go up and down the cool slate steps all day long for butter, lemon syrup, cool home-made ginger beer, meat and milk. Even in the cellar the meat and sugar were not safe from ants; Mary stood the legs of the fly-netted safe in tins of water, to keep the ants at bay. She would not put down the purple powder which was used for poisoning them by other housewives, being afraid of it somehow getting into the food or being picked up by the children or pets.

There was no ice-box, and of course no ice-cream such as they used to buy for a penny a cone in Kuldunda. But there was a little Italian in Jamestown who made his own to a special recipe and drove around the streets in a tiny cart pulled by a tiny pony, ringing a handbell which attracted the children as if he had been the Pied Piper. His creamy, custardy, Vanilla mixture also attracted flies when it was sitting in cans waiting to be frozen. Mary had forbidden the children to buy his product, as she believed it was dirty and probably contaminated.

William at fourteen would be leaving at the end of the year and going to school in the city in preparation for his University matriculation. Sam didn't know how he was going to pay the fees, but he was determined that his eldest son should be an engineer. And there was no doubt Willy would pass his exams all right.

Towards the end of the last term, the November days were clear of dust but burning hot. As the two boys were walking home from school – the older girls had left at thirteen, and the younger ones were not yet attending – they came upon the little ice-cream man's cart, bowling along with its enticing bell ringing. It stopped at the corner, hailed by a group of children. Jimmy stared wistfully.

'I've got my penny pocket-money left,' he said. 'Couldn't we just have one ice-cream, Willy? Mumma won't ever know.'

'No! She said we must never ever buy one.'

'Aw–w!' Jimmy dragged his feet disconsolately. Willy looked back at the cart, where the other kids were luxuriously licking their cones of yellow home-made ice-cream.

'Well – ' said Willy, weakening. 'I suppose one little old penny one wouldn't hurt us. And it's such a hot day,' he said, justifying himself.

Jimmy bolted off at once, dragging his penny from the pocket where he had three glassy marbles stashed with a catapult and a smooth stone. He had got his ice and was already licking it when William came up. He bought a penny cone and the cart drove off, the bell still ringing, calling all children to follow.

Jimmy had walked on, and turning to run after him, William stumbled on a rough stone in the white road and went headlong, his schoolbag flying over his head. The ice-cream landed face down in the dust of the cart-tracks. He got up in a rage, and kicked the remains in his disgust.

'Hey, Jimmy! Give us a lick of yours,' he called, pursuing his small brother. Jimmy, whose angelic appearance belied his normal six-year-old's nature, hastily bolted the rest of his, and crunched up the edible cone.

'Can't. All gone,' he said, smirking.

William scowled. 'Pig! What if I tell on you?'

'Pig yourself! You can't, you bought one too.'

'Anyway, I've got another penny. I'll get one tomorrer, and you won't get even a lick, so there.'

'Don't care.'

'What was it like? Good?' he asked, weakening.

'Bonzer! Like frozen custard, only nicer.'

'Cornish pasties for tea!' said Mary, who in spite of the heat had been baking all the afternoon. Her pasties were a treat they all looked forward to, and they were economical too: the merest scraps of mutton, but large quantities of potatoes, leeks, onions, turnips cut up small and baked all together in a short pastry crust, in their own juice.

'I'm not very hungry,' said Jimmy. His mother looked at him sharply.

Jimmy did not eat his tea that night, and by eight o'clock he was writhing and groaning with stomach pains, dehydrated with continuous vomiting and diarrhoea. William thought it was probably the ice-cream, but felt rather smugly that Jimmy was being punished for his greediness in not sharing.

But the punishment exacted for that one act of disobedience was a terrible one. By nine o'clock Mary had extracted from the boys the fact that they'd bought ice-creams, and Willy had not eaten his. She sent at once for the doctor. He was an hour in coming, and he looked grim. Eighteen other children in the town were affected by the 'ptomaine poisoning', as he called it. There was little to be done at this stage but to give sweetened fluids, if they could be kept down. Hot-water bottles might help relieve the abdominal cramps, which by now were agonising. By midnight Jimmy was too weak to vomit any more: he sipped some lemonade but seemed unable to swallow – it ran out the side of his mouth again. His mother, terrified, held his head, the sweat-damp golden curls, the clammy, pale cheeks against her breast. His transparent blue-veined lids closed over his sunken eyes.

He opened them again and whispered, 'Mumma – I can't see! Where are you?'

'I'm here, dear, holding you. Look, there's the lamp – can't you see it?' she asked in dread.

'Yes . . . but it's all blurry.'

Another cramp shook him, but he passed nothing but a trickle of water and mucus, blood-stained. 'Thirsty,' he muttered.

'Sam!' Mary's voice was hysterical. 'You must go and get the doctor and come back – quickly!'

Sam, who had been tip-toeing helplessly in and out of the room, went at once. There was no hospital in the town. The one doctor, exhausted, was just sitting down for a cup of tea. Sam asked would it be worth taking the boy on the long drive to the Kuldunda Hospital?

'Not in his weakened state. He wouldn't survive the journey. It's a very virulent form of food poisoning; I must tell you I've lost one patient already tonight, and he was a teenager.'

Sam told him about the blurred vision, the recurring cramps. The doctor shook his head despondently.

'I'm afraid the prognosis is not good.'

'What do you mean, man?'

'I mean your son may die.'

Sam staggered, and sank into a chair. 'If – if you could just come and see him, again, it would relieve my wife's mind . . . Just to know that everything possible had been done.'

'Yes, well . . . My horse is having a feed and a rest. I've

been out on calls all night. If you'd like to drive me – '

'Of course.'

The other children were asleep, all but William. He tossed and turned, listening to the weak crying from the front room where they had taken Jimmy. William felt guilty. He was older, he should have known better, he shouldn't have bought an ice-cream or let Jimmy buy one. If it hadn't been for the accidental spilling of his, he'd be suffering too, which would have made him feel less guilty.

He got out of bed and went to his mother's room. She was holding Jimmy's head, but he was squirming restlessly, his eyes closed.

'Is he gonna be all right?'

His mother gave him a distracted look. 'I don't know – I'm afraid – I wish the doctor would come.'

All over Jamestown that night mothers were sitting up with their pain-racked children; sometimes two and three in one family had been affected. A ten-year-old girl was the next to die. The doctor came and felt Jimmy's threadlike pulse, his clammy forehead, and listened to his sighing breaths.

'I will administer a stimulant,' he said, 'but it's a forlorn hope.'

By sunset the next day Jimmy was dead, 'gone to Heaven', as Mary told the silent, stricken girls. William had rushed out of the house and gone striding off across the paddocks, alone. Mary sat like stone, still grasping her young son's cooling body in her arms. 'Gone to Heaven.' Yes, of course he had. He was already picking flowers in the heavenly fields, among God's angels. What she held in her arms was no more than a shell. Ah, but she loved that physical shell, blood of her blood, flesh of her flesh. She could not see him angel-bright in heaven, however earnestly she tried.

She got up, went to her work-box, and with her sewing scissors cut off a bright, curling tress of his hair. She was suddenly terribly tired. Sam led her gently away from the soiled, disarranged bed, the smell of sickness, and made her lie down in the girls' room while, with twelve-year-old Ada, he washed the small body for burial.

The sexton was busy next day, for no less than eight children of the small town and surrounding farms had died.

The little ice-cream maker huddled in his cottage, crying and wringing his hands; if he had stepped outside he would have been in danger of lynching. There was to be an inquest at which a Government inquiry into the hygiene of all premises used for food preparation was proposed. Mr Georgio, the ice-cream maker, left the town for good, before the mass funeral attended by the whole district.

Mary announced that she wanted to leave the vicinity of Jamestown.

'What irony! – *Jamestown*, James's town! Yes, it's his now; he will occupy a patch of its soil forever. My little Jim! I can't bear to stay here, where everything reminds me of him. I keep thinking I see him coming up the steps, curled up in a chair, running along the veranda.'

'My dearest heart, you must go away for a while. Down to your mother's at Kuldunda, or even to the city. We'll manage somehow.'

'No! I don't want to be away from my family. I just want us to move. Anywhere, away from this house, this place.'

She turned for comfort to her *Favourite Poems of Gifted Bards*; it was almost as if 'Little Jim' had been prophetic:

> With hands uplifted, see, she kneels
>   Beside the sufferer's bed,
> And prays that He will spare her boy,
>   And take her life instead.
> She gets her answer from the child,
>   Soft fell these words from him –
> 'Mother, the angels do so smile,
>   And beckon little Jim.
> I have no pain, dear mother, now
>   But oh! I am so dry;
> Just moisten poor Jim's lips again
>   And, mother, don't you cry.
> Tell father when he comes from work
>   I said "goodnight" to him,
> And, Mother, now I'll go to sleep' –
>   Alas, poor little Jim.

Alas! Poor little Jim had not said 'Goodnight', or 'Mother, don't you cry', or 'now I'll go to sleep'. The last clear words she had heard him say, before he became comatose, were, 'It's all blurry.' And then a fretful murmur, which sounded like 'Thirsty – thirsty.' She had, at Sam's suggestion, wet a muslin cloth in cool water and placed this between his lips, since it seemed he could not drink. He had not spoken again. If the angels beckoned him with smiles, he showed no sign of seeing them.

After reading this sentimental ballad, however, she always wept and was obscurely comforted by the story of the poor miner's only child. In time she forgot the reality of that dreadful night, the sickly smell, the blood and vomit, the terror and helplessness she had felt, and began to believe that Jim, forever young and fair, would be waiting to greet her when she died:

> In Heaven, once more to meet again
> Her own poor little Jim.

Sam tried to comfort her in a more practical way.

'We'll have another son, dear heart,' he said. 'I know he can never replace Jimmy, but at least it will fill the empty space at table. I miss him too, you know.'

'Yes, but Ada is your favourite, you know she always was. The girls can get around you the way the boys never could. And . . . I'm afraid to have another – what if we lose him too?'

'God wouldn't let that happen again,' said Sam, who did not feel as confident as he sounded. He thought of the stricken mother in Jamestown who had lost both her sons to the poisonous ice-cream. One had been a classmate of Willy's, a big boy of thirteen. They could be thankful at least that William had escaped, it seemed by luck. Yet the ways of God were mysterious; perhaps it was ordained . . .

In due course Mary got over the worst of her grief. The first anniversary of Jim's death was the hardest. She became pregnant once more and prayed for a son.

Sam was off prospecting again when the baby arrived, a month early. William, who was home from the city for the long summer holidays, went for the midwife and took the younger children out for a picnic to get them out of the way. But they had to come home again when the 'brickfielder' blew up.

The baby had come before his time and did not live.

The hot, stinging north wind from the deserts of the interior had brought a towering, palpable cloud of sand and red grit like a Sahara sandstorm; it became dark in the house, the sun at midday turned a strange blue colour in the red sky, the sand seeped in everywhere under doors and windowpanes.

'And where were you?' said Mary when at last Sam returned, fixing him with a reproachful stare from her dark eyes, still large and beautiful but surrounded by a network of fine wrinkles from the heat and dryness of the North. 'Where were you when I needed you? It's all very well for the man, you come home and take your pleasure, and then off you go again on your jaunts and journeys, and the poor wife has to stay at home and bear the result. It's bad enough being big and heavy with child in this heat, but to have borne it all in vain! In vain!' She began to sob. 'And the ground almost too hard to dig his grave, tiny though it is.'

'Mary, my darling, you know I have to go prospecting. It's our only hope, to find gold in payable quantities – the land is valueless unless the drought breaks.'

'I don't care! You are never home.'

'And I'm the one who has to find the means of feeding the new mouths we bring into the world; I'm responsible for you all,' he said, thinking that though he'd have liked another son, perhaps it was no bad thing not to have another mouth to feed at present. 'So don't reproach me, dear heart. I'm doing what I'm good at: finding minerals. Already they're beginning to say, "Sam King can smell gold." '

Mary turned her face to the wall.

When she was up again Sam once again tried to persuade her to go for a holiday to visit her parents.

'No! They didn't approve of my marriage, and I'm not going crawling back there to have them say "I told you so", and anyway my mother's not well, and who would look after the children here?'

'Well, take the two youngest, and go and stay with my people.'

'Have you forgotten? They've let their house and gone on a trip to England for at least a year. We had a postcard from your mother, showing her in her travelling dress, remember? They sailed on the 18th of September, in one of the new steamships.'

'Yes, of course. But please go to your mother, just for a week or two.'

'No. I have no wish to go away.'

'I don't know!' Sam ruffled up his moustache and appealed to the children. 'Wouldn't you say your mother had the prettiest, sweetest face imaginable?'

'Yes, she has.'

'And do you know she is obstinate as a mule?'

Mary smiled unwillingly, but she remained obdurate.

Just when their fortunes were at their lowest ebb, and Sam was wondering how on earth he would find the fees for Willy's boarding school in the city – let alone his University fees later on – just then the drought broke, washed the dust from the surface rocks, and showed Sam the lode he had been looking for.

He sank a shaft on a beautiful white quartz reef of milky stone like marble, veined with copper and gold. The values continued good for twenty feet and then cut out. He drove a horizontal winze for a few feet, then struck upwards again. Gold once more appeared among green stains of copper in the quartz. He knew from experience that you seldom saw free gold in payable quantities until the ore was pulverised and panned. This reef must be very rich. He knapped and dollied for a week, finding that samples were going about 8 oz to the ton. He had found the reef that shed the gold.

The drought was over, the follow-up rains were good, and the price of land recovered as the inland pastures clothed themselves with waving green and dancing wildflowers in the miracle of a good season. Sam pegged a rough claim, then took out a mining lease and sold 'The Golden Hope' to an eager buyer for more than he had paid for the whole property. He was able to sell the land for twice what it had cost, pay back his father, and move to the capital city to live on the proceeds of his goldmine. It was the excitement of finding gold that appealed to him. Let other men work at digging the stuff out . . . It was time, he said, that Mary had a bit of comfort. They settled in the green foothills of Adelaide at the beginning of the southern winter.

Worn out with childbearing and miscarriages, of which she'd had three more in four years, Mary welcomed the move. But Sam began to spend a lot of time at the Maid and Magpie Hotel, spinning tales of his mining exploits and shouting drinks at the bar. The money had gone to his head.

He knew now what he wanted to do with his life, and it was not to be either an accountant or a farmer. He would be a prospector all over the world, wherever a new 'rush' began.

Four

SAM SET off for South Africa, where gold had been discovered in 1884. Water cost £1 a bucket, the life was hard, but Sam had been bred among heat and drought. He left William at home to look after his mother, attending school by day but sleeping at home. He was only seventeen, but by that age his mother had already married. Mary had her own cheque account and controlled the finances, running the home frugally with the help of the four girls, Ada, Alice, Elizabeth and Mae. Ada was engaged to a squatter's son who had been their neighbour in the north, so she should be well provided for. Frances was still a baby, but Mary wondered how they were to find husbands for so many daughters. At least they had left behind the heat and dust of the outback, which had been ruining their complexions.

Mary never forgot her first spring in Adelaide. The rounded hills, sheep-grazed to a turflike smoothness, shone brilliant green after the winter rains. Wattle blossom was just finishing, and groves of almond trees dropped their blossom like snow. Flowering plums in the garden floated like pink clouds against the white clouds sailing in the blue. Flying fleecy clouds, cool air, no dust, green grass; it was like a dream, with the nectar scent of blossom, the cool song of English blackbirds in the dew, the transported blue of forget-me-nots and hyacinths along the garden paths. It was not like Cornwall, she supposed, and anyway she had been born in Australia. The Adelaide plains were flat and the hills behind them not high, yet she felt some vestigial memory stir in her blood.

When Mother King returned to Port Adelaide from her trip abroad, she declared that the Adelaide hills reminded her of nothing so much as the chalk hills of Buckinghamshire, around Ivinghoe, green and smooth where the forest had been removed.

Sam returned from South Africa not much the richer, except in knowledge of reef gold and its occurrence. Though beautiful quartz reefs remained his first love, he knew now that the most unpromising looking rock, brown ironstone and haematite, could hide gold in various forms and chemical combinations. Any fool could kick nuggets out of the dust and wash free gold from sandy creekbeds, if it was there; but he preferred to find the mother-lode by persistent, careful detective work. It was not true, of course, as they said, that he could 'smell gold', but there was something more than luck, and less than science, in the hunches which he sometimes followed with spectacular success.

He leased a rocky section of hillside and valley near Waterfall Gully and sampled rock from every foot, mostly bluestone, quartzite, and metamorphosed slate. He made little more than a living. Then he ploughed some of the rich silt at the bottom of the gully and planted fruit and citrus trees. This time he had struck gold of a different order. The apricots grew big as peaches, the oranges hung in golden globes among the glossy green foliage. Irrigated from the creek which ran only after winter rains until he made a series of small dams across it, the orchard was a success.

Mary was contented as she had not been since James died. She had both her men at home, William helping to work the orchard and pick fruit in the long summer vacation. Though the house they had moved to was rather small, it was built of the local bluestone with foot-thick walls that kept out the

heat, was shaded by cool trees and looked out upon greenness. They built wire-meshed 'sleepouts' on the verandas
which in that temperate climate could be used all the year
round. After the heat and the dust of the North it seemed to
Mary like Paradise. The word, she had read somewhere, was
from the Persian for an oriental walled garden. Their garden
was protected (not from the winds of the desert as in Persia,
but from cold winter westerlies) partly by natural walls of rock
– the gorge formed by the waterfall as it had cut back for
thousands of years through the quartzite hills.

The garden also had a high wall of brick all round it, for the
property had been settled in the early days when the local
Aborigines were troublesome. Now there were only a few
left, living in humpies along the Murray River, or in a camp on
the Patawalonga not far from the city. The wall had sharp
pieces of broken glass set in the top to keep out the now-
vanished black man. Weathered and lichen-covered, the old
wall made a foil for the dark, glossy green foliage of the
orange trees.

It was not long before Sam developed itchy feet again. The
rush to Hall's Creek had begun in the far north of Western
Australia, following the Pine Creek stampede to the
Northern Territory. The only way to get there was by packhorse train, after taking a small coastal steamer to the tidal
port of Derby on the west coast. But since the overland
telegraph line had been put through from Adelaide to Darwin, right across the centre of the continent, Sam couldn't see
why it should not be followed on horseback: the trail was
already made, and there were stations on the way at places
like Oodnadatta, Alice Springs and Newcastle Waters.

He gathered a party of three out-of-work miners from
Cornwall (sturdy workers though no bushmen), a deserter
from a ship at Port Adelaide, and two young brothers who
wanted to see the inland. With Sam to lead them, the party set
off to ride across Australia from south to north over nearly
two thousand miles of hostile territory.

Passing through Kuldunda on the way north, Sam left his
companions while he went to visit his brother Jim, now

running the hardware store stocking solid, practical things like farm machinery and posthole diggers instead of mining equipment. Sam had much more in common with Jim than with his lawyer brother, the stuffy and pompous Arthur. He asked his favourite brother to come on the adventure with him, but James only laughed and shook his head.

'My wealth is in my family,' he said, smiling at his plain but pleasant-faced wife, 'and I don't want to leave them for all the tea in China – or all the gold in the Territory . . .'

Sam's party left for the far north as soon as the summer ended, when the temperatures would be a little less scorching in the stony deserts about Lake Eyre. They spent their last comfortable night at Henry's sheep station near Lyndhurst, where Sam's brother told him that he had never grown up – 'still chasing the pot of gold at the foot of the rainbow.'

'You'll see!' said Samuel calmly. 'One day I'll have enough to buy you up, and Arthur and James too. I'll make a fortune, and I'll live to be a hundred.'

Next day they set off across saltbush and spinifex country, crossing steep sandhills which lay from east to west across their route. They rode across stony deserts of purple and magenta pebbles, and the salmon-coloured sands of the dreaded Depot Sandhills, crossing the wide dry sandy beds of the Alberga and the Finke. They had to carry water with them over the many dry stages, for there was a danger of being speared if they used Aboriginal waterholes. They lived off salt beef, flour, sugar and tea, and the onions which Sam always took with him on an inland journey to take the place of fruit and green vegetables. Sometimes a station-owner let them have a haunch of beef, as well as flour and sugar from the store; sometimes they 'borrowed' a steer which wandered into their camp. Sam, a good cook, made the lightest of dampers and johnny-cakes from flour and water and a little rising. At Newcastle Waters they met six diggers coming from the east coast, a gaunt cavalcade, and the magnificent seven became the ragged thirteen. By the time they reached Hall's Creek in the middle of winter 1886, there were two thousand men ahead of them on the field.

In the dry season there was no water to spare for washing gold. Sam devised a cradle or shaking-box from the wood of an abandoned dray, which separated out the heavier ore while the dust blew away in the wind. It was a dirty and inefficient system. At the last stage the powdered rock had to be held in a tin dish close to the face, and gently blown upon until only heavy metal was left, the glitter of galena or the glow of pure gold.

There were few rich patches of gold on the field. Many diggers did not find enough to cover the cost of their long trek from distant coastal cities. Many died from fever and dysentery, or perished on the track before they got there. Temperatures stayed in the hundreds. Flies and dust were all-pervading. Most of the diggers' songs, sung round the cooking-fires at night, were mournful: a wheezing mouth-organ would begin, and a nasal voice take up a song:

Take this package and this message to my mother far away,
And tell her that the boy she loves sleeps 'neath Australian clay,
 Give her this gold for which I've toiled, while in the grave I lie,
'God bless you, mother, farewell mate', was the digger's last goodbye.

Sam cast round for a new lead, but found none. On the way up the track, at Barrow Creek and Tennant Creek, the telegraph repeater stations, he had seen promising jump-ups of red-brown haematite, but his mates would not let him stay to search there; in their eagerness to get to the new find, they had been like thirst-crazed cattle who smelled water. Sam and his three Cornish mates were now scarcely making a living.

Then, towards the end of the dry season, Sam noticed that his eyes seemed always full of grit. He bathed them with water and salt, but they got worse, and his vision was affected. He realised that he had the dreaded condition of Sandy Blight, the trachoma of the dusty north.

Sam set off with a party leaving for Broome, three hundred miles away, but by the time he left he was so bad that his horse had to be led. While he waited for the ship at the little pearling port, the Roman Catholic nuns nursed him and put drops in his eyes to relieve the maddening sensation of sand beneath the lids. When he left he gave a donation to the Mission. The rest of the gold he had won went in paying his passage home, and for treatment at the Adelaide Public Hospital.

'I'm cured, Mary my love – in every sense,' he told her when he came home. 'There's some wonderful country in the Centre, but out there in the North-west it's sheer hell. I must have been mad,' he said, looking appreciatively round at his green, walled garden. 'From now on, I'm staying home.'

'That I will believe when I see it,' said Mary.

Five

FOR NEARLY four years Sam stayed home. Ada was married, and Alice had decided to become a nurse in an Adelaide private hospital. Elizabeth and Frances were at school and Mae helped in the house. Then one day young Frances came to her mother and said, 'Sam has got his maps out on the dining-room table. He's on the rampage again.'

'Frances!' said her mother sharply. 'Don't let me hear you speak in that disrespectful way of your father again . . . Oh dear! Are they overseas maps, or local?'

'They are maps of Western Australia.'

'Oh, no!'

Sam had been doing a little fossicking at weekends at Dashwood's Gully in the nearby hills. Last weekend two young men, William Goodman and a mate, had been working there too without success. Like line fishermen watching enviously as another, more lucky or more skilled, pulls fish from a nearby gutter, they watched Sam panning off a little gold and transferring it to his bottle. They wore high-collared white shirts and were obviously newchums. Sam, naturally generous and seeing that they were having no luck, gave them some tips on dollying and washing and where to expect 'pay dirt' in the shallow gravelly soil.

The three men worked companionably for several weekends, netting no more than about £5 worth of gold. Then in early spring, when the wildflowers were out in yellow and lilac drifts over the hills, a friend rode out to see Goodman, with a copy of the Adelaide *Register* under his arm. It told about Bayley and Ford's recent strike near Coolgardie, Western Australia, 'where the gold sticks out like raisins in a plum pudding.'

This was enough for Sam. Goodman was soon persuaded that if there was as much gold as they said lying about on the surface, the underlying reefs must be stupendously rich. And if they were there, Sam would find them. Goodman's brother was a financier, so he underwrote the venture, to the extent of their steamer fare to Esperance in Western Australia and mining equipment and supplies to take up north with them to the new strike.

Sam King had embarked on his greatest adventure, and it was to meet him in the same hot, dry difficult conditions he knew so well.

Mary wept when he told her he was leaving. Sam promised to send her enough money very shortly for her to employ a man permanently in the orchard.

'Don't cry, my love,' he said soothingly. 'This is my big chance; I feel it in my bones.'

'What *I* feel in my bones is the beginning of arthritis,' said Mary, quite sourly for her. 'I hope you don't expect me to be out picking fruit in all weathers; yet we can't just let it rot on the ground, I suppose. The girls will just have to learn to be roustabouts and handymen, since William has to go to his lectures.'

Sam King and William Goodman enjoyed the trip by coastal steamer to the Golden West. The Great Australian Bight for once was calm; they saw whales wallowing and spouting far out over the satin-smooth sea. Sam spent much of the time playing cards, at which he often won because of those mysterious hunches like the ones he followed when seeking gold. Sometimes it seemed to him that he actually 'saw' the other player's hand in his mind's eye, however closely his opponent breasted his cards.

Saloon and steerage were packed with passengers, all men, the hold and deck with mining equipment and mail for the western goldfields. A wake of empty beer and whisky bottles floated behind the ship. As soon as he had made a win at cards, Sam would spend it all on shouting drinks at the ship's saloon bar. He was popular with other men, but did not need to buy his popularity with free drinks: large, with the firm aquiline features of his mother, a hearty laugh and a hearty appetite, he would set the table in a roar with his stories of mining camps round the world: of Jo'berg and Kimberley, the deserts of Central Australia and South Australia's parched north. Like the one about the fellow who, at Oodlawirra after a very dry summer, saw the dark clouds of a thunderstorm piling up, and, going outside the tent, soaped himself all over in a fine frothy lather with all the water he could spare in a tin. (He used to be very touchy about being called 'Dirty Harry'. 'Dirty!' he'd say, 'I'll have you know I washes meself once a fortnight, on principle, whether I really needs a wash or not!') The lightning flared and streaked, the thunder cracked – and the clouds blew away, leaving the poor man dancing with rage under a blue sky. The wind of the dry thunderstorm had stirred up a cloud of red dust which stuck to the drying soap.

'Poor Harry,' said Sam, laughing, his strong white teeth gleaming agreeably in his sunbrowned face. 'He looked like a Red Indian for a week, until it wore off. And swear! You never heard such language . . .'

He liked to read Bret Harte and Mark Twain and was not above incorporating some of their tales in his own reminiscences.

At Esperance the two friends disembarked with many others heading for the same destination, though some were going on to Perth, to travel to the Murchison field further north. They bought a spring cart and horse in the port. Tent and bedding, cooking utensils, picks and shovels and hammers and maps, lengths of fuse and packages of dynamite, all were loaded on the cart. Once they had left the coast at Esperance the going was almost level, but it was all the horse could do to pull the load. Sam and Bill trudged beside it in the white dust, fine as flour.

As they left the higher rainfall belt and the blue waters of the Great Australian Bight behind them, the track became dustier and hotter. They learned to walk ahead of the cart to avoid the cloud of dust from its wheels. Two canvas water-bags were slung under the wagon at the front. Though the bags were coated with dust, enough water evaporated through the canvas to keep the contents cool. They camped in the hottest part of the day, sitting in the shade of the cart, and rose before dawn to travel in the cool of the morning.

Their first gold they did not win from the ground, but came across it in a rather gruesome way. Scouting around in the hope of finding water, where a clump of trees indicated at least underground water not far away, they came upon the skeleton of a man. A few bones were scattered about, as by dingoes, and in the shelter of a hollow tree lay his still-preserved boots of tanned leather, and a bleached skull. And beneath the skull a small leather bag with a draw-string, uncannily heavy. They opened the rotting bag carefully over a piece of cardboard: it was full of gold dust.

'Look at that!' said Sam, in a subdued voice. 'I 'spose he would have given all his gold for a single billy of water.'

'Perished!' said Bill. 'He's been here for years, by the look. Wonder if he found Hannan's Kalgoorlie find first, and never made it back to the coast?'

Musingly, they examined the scattered remains – no piece of cloth, no clue to the name of the departed stranger.

'We ought to bury him, away from the dogs,' said Bill. They took their picks and shovels off the cart and set to work. Bill paused as they were about to shovel dirt over the few dry bones, the pathetic boots. 'What about the gold?'

Their eyes met above the shallow grave. 'No point in burying it with him,' said Sam. 'Not much use reporting it to the police, either. They can never trace his kith and kin.'

They made a rude cross of two small boughs tied together, stowed the gold carefully in a screw-top jar which had held flour, and went on their way.

They had rationed themselves to only one quart pot of tea a day. The bulk of the provisions was packed in the wagon below the heavy tools and canvas, while they kept a box of daily needs on top. At one of their last camps, after making a big brew with the very end of their tea ration, Bill stood the boiling billy to cool under the shade of the cart, to which the horse, munching in his nosebag, was still harnessed.

'Look out!' cried Sam inarticulately, choking on the piece of 'damper and push' he was eating.

Bill turned round with a mighty oath as a neat round dollop of yellow dung, landed fair in their brew of tea. Reckless of scalding his hand, Bill fished it out and flung it away.

'You filthy, four-legged, stupid bloody monstrosity!' he addressed the innocent animal, still munching unawares. 'I'm damned if I'm going to throw away our pot of tea. I was so looking forward to that brew,' he added mournfully, staring into the fire-blackened billy where bits of metamorphosed straw which had gone a journey through the equine intestine now settled gently among the tealeaves on the bottom.

He poured himself a mug, fished in it with one finger, then added plenty of sugar 'to disguise the flavour'. Sam decided to drink plain water instead.

The two friends were too late to claim any of the fabulously rich quartz country round Bayley's Reward. Arthur Bayley and his mate Ford, searching further out into the dry country beyond Paddy Hannan's Kalgoorlie bonanza, had camped beside a waterhole soon after some heavy showers. When they woke, free gold was gleaming everywhere in the morning sunlight. It was like a dream of riches. Gold was lying on the surface, just waiting to be picked up like mushrooms.

Bayley and Ford pegged on a narrow ridge of golden quartz, and quartz was the known mother-rock of gold. They took back to Southern Cross £800 worth of gold, and though they left town again quietly they were followed. They had started a rush to Coolgardie.

Sam and Bill Goodman had a demonstration of the richness of the Bayley's Reward quartz. After they had seen some crushed in a small dolly-pot and panned off, they sat disconsolately in their tent on the outskirts of the new field.

'We've missed out,' said Bill gloomily. 'Just a few weeks earlier, and we might have been able to claim just a bit of that quartz ridge. The alluvial's all been picked out by now.'

'It's beautiful gold,' said Sam wistfully, turning in his fingers the little piece of white rock he had been given as a sample. There was free gold in the quartz, like a gold bracelet resting on white satin. 'But there must be more around here somewhere; it's auriferous country, all right. Perhaps those ironstone hills yonder might be worth a try. I know that sometimes the iron cap covers the golden head.'

Few prospectors of the time and place could recognise the 'gossan', the ironstone cap of a rich mineral deposit. But Sam King had studied geology, and he saw the possibilities of those dark-topped hills with their outcrops of diorite and veins of iron, which the other prospectors had passed over. He had the knowledge and experience, but above all he had a 'feeling'. He lay on top of the roundest highest hillock, his felt hat tilted over his eyes, a straw between his lips, and let himself relax, breathing deeply of the warm dry air under the clearest and purest of skies.

There was no wind to stir the dust, and no cloud. The leaves of the sparse salmon-gums glittered in the sun, exuding their oil of eucalyptus, while their deep pinkish-orange trunks and boughs were as smooth and rounded as the limbs of women. Over all was that perfect arch of blue sky, stretched like taut translucent silk above his head. He felt in his bones and blood that gold in vast quantities lay somewhere below. He had only to find it.

He got up and, walking a yard or two to the north, peered into a crevice in the diorite ridge. He saw the gleam of gold. He fell on his knees and began knapping specimens to show his mate, who started off for Coolgardie with samples as soon as they had pegged a 24-acre lease and sunk a small shaft. Under Mines Department laws, a claim had to be pegged at each corner, with short ditches outlining the direction and line of the boundary. The soil was so hard and stony that instead they made a line of stones. The lease had to be rectangular, with the longer sides not more than twice the length of the shorter sides.

Almost immediately they struck more gold.

The ironstone was veined with extraordinary richness: it was almost impossible to fracture a piece of rock without seeing free gold. After dollying a few samples Sam declared that it would go at least 8 oz to the ton. 'A blacksmith's shop on top, but a jeweller's shop beneath,' he exulted. Their rough method of taking a condensed milk tin of crushed rock, which equalled about a pound weight, washing it, then estimating the weight of the gold 'corner' panned off from this and then multiplying it, gave an idea of the amount of gold to the ton.

The ironstone became richer; it was indeed a case of the black cap hiding the golden head. Underneath was a hill of almost pure gold, which came to be known as 'Sam's Hill' and was talked about round campfires wherever prospectors met. They had discovered the richest mine in the whole of the Golden West: the beginning of the fabulous Golden Mile.

Bill asked what they should call the mine when registering their claim. Thinking of his first stony property, and the rounded shape of the golden hill, Sam suggested 'The Boulder' or 'The Great Boulder'. While Bill went in to Kalgoorlie to register the find, Sam went on to discover the Lake View and Ivanhoe mines, the Three Australias and the Royal Mint. In the end they had nearly 500 acres of gold-bearing country under lease.

It was too late for other prospectors to muscle in on the ironstone and greenstone deposits they had ignored. King and Goodman held the best ground on the field.

Back in Adelaide, Bill Goodman's brother floated the Boulder Perseverance, and formed a syndicate, the Ivanhoe Venture Gold Mining Company. He advanced a substantial reward to Sam and Bill. Sam sent Mary £5,000 to put in the bank, 'and that is just the beginning, Mary dear. We have a fortune, and I will buy you the biggest and most comfortable home your heart could desire. You deserve it, dear heart. My best love to you and the girls.'

He wrote again to Mary: 'The Gold is there on all sides, by hundredweights, staring one in the face; fine and coarse and on every side, the stone so rich that all the stone has to be put in for crushing as soon as loosened, with results up to 1,000 oz of gold to the ton . . . I have never in my life seen so much at one time, gold sticking out of the stone, gold shining out of the shaft wherever we looked, thousands of pounds' worth of it! In another 5 years this place will be a city . . . Not one of our claims has turned out to be a shicer, they are all good, not a duffer among them . . . My acquaintances over here seem to have no surnames, or at least they don't use them. They're known as Big Jack, Bluey (for a redhead), Bill the Diviner, IronBark Bob, Fungus Fred, Sweet Pea Sam (I won't tell you how *he* got his name), Timber Dick and so on . . . Water still terribly scarce . . . I notice the publican keeps his hand firmly on the water-bottle, doesn't worry about the whisky.'

And indeed, in the next two years Kalgoorlie and Coolgardie shot up on a fountain of champagne. The market for mining shares was insatiable. The wide streets were alive with carts and carriages, wagons and camel teams and men on bicycles or horseback. From the single bough camp at Great Boulder, roofed with gum-boughs and spinifex, rose a smart Hotel and the beginning of Boulder City, a city set in the sandy desert. Great stamp-mills vibrated through the air day and night, crushing the rich ore.

The Boulder lodes had turned out to be phenomenally rich; the area was christened The Golden Mile. Big companies from England bought up the richest mines and proceeded to drive the shafts downwards – 1,000, 2,000 feet – and the further they went the more gold they found.

Sam was not there to see the result of his prophecies and discoveries. He was always interested in finding new gold-mines, not in getting the stuff out of the ground, or even in making profits.

He had moved further south and discovered rich lodes again near Norseman, which had been overlooked in the mad rush to Hannan's Kalgoorlie find. The Leviathan, the Lady Mary, named after his wife, and the Golden Horseshoe were almost as rich as Lake View and Boulder. When the assayer's report came in on the Golden Horseshoe, he trundled some gold along in a wheelbarrow to the blacksmith's shop in town, and had him make four golden shoes for his horse, and galloped him up and down the main street, shedding flakes of gold against every pebble.

He 'shouted the bar' every night for a week. 'King's shout!' came Sam's genial roar. 'Once more, gentlemen. Shout the bar!' and the drinkers would cheer and hastily down their drinks in readiness for the free round.

A few of the prospectors, and many of the early explorers, had used camels successfully to cross the arid parts of Australia. Although the goldbearing country was not true desert, it had no surface water and a man could perish there if not careful.

Sam decided to do a survey of the new lands opened up by the prospectors, who had moved out ahead of the official map-makers. He went to India, from where his missionary aunt had sent him the silk scarf he gave to Ida long ago; travelled north to Afghanistan and brought back camels with their Afghan drivers, to put his name on the map of Western Australia with 'King's Survey'.

He had enjoyed pitting his wits against the desert, finding waterholes by following the flight of birds at sunset, taking his bearings by the stars. He knew the constellation of the Scorpion by now, and though he took no account of astrology and suchlike superstitions, he felt in some way that this was 'his' constellation. The stars were magnificent out in the desert winter nights: Orion striding down the western sky, Scorpio rising in its glittering curve, the Milky Way giving off a soft effulgence which was almost strong enough to read by.

Though he found no more great fields in the desert, he sampled rock and sand wherever he camped. He was an expert in 'dry-blowing', letting the fine sand and crushed rock tip from one dish to another on the ground while the wind carried away the dirt.

Most of the features of the land were already named, for he was far from being the first white man to cross the droughty south-west inland of Western Australia; but he had named Mount Thirsty on an earlier trip, and now, pushing north through a desolate area of dry salt-pans, he saw a rounded blue peak with a pointed nipple in the shape of a small outcrop on top. He climbed it, but found no gold. He marked it on the map as 'Mount Ida'.

Now he longed for home. It had been exciting, buying champagne by the bucketful in Kalgoorlie's Palace Hotel, drinking from the slipper of a local dancer of international fame, meeting British investors who had travelled all the way to the fields to see the fabled mines they had financed, attending meetings at the open air Stock Exchange, gambling and bragging and lighting cigars with five pound notes. But nothing had exceeded the moment when, after wheeling a barrow half full of gold from his hotel, he had heard it clunking onto the scales at the bank.

And in spite of his wandering, he loved his family and longed to see Mary and the girls again. He had not, of course, remained entirely faithful during his long time away; that would have been unnatural, he told himself. He had found, or bought, his way into the bed of the glamorous dancing star and had occasionally availed himself of the favours of The Mountain Maid, who had set up shop on the goldfields and whose name, according to the miners, should have been spelt 'The Mountin' Maid'. And it was not just physical need that drove him to seek her company. In her earthy, forthright manner and brazen good looks she reminded him of his first girl, Ida of Kuldunda. He sometimes wondered what had become of Ida, whether she had done any more terms in prison and where she might be now.

Six

WILLIAM SAT in his room drawing careful pictures of massive arched bridges, railway tunnels, dams. To Sam's disappointment he was not interested in metallurgy or mining. He wanted to be a civil engineer, building imposing structures which would far outlast his own lifetime. It was, he felt, a form of immortality.

He had been haunted by mortality ever since James's death. If he hadn't fallen and dropped his ice-cream, he could so easily have died too. Or Jimmy might have been the one to fall and drop his ice-cream in the dirt. Or he might have shared the remaining sweet with his brother; then both might have been very ill but both might have survived. It just seemed a matter of random chance.

William was now attending the University of Adelaide where his grandson Vincent King, as yet unborn, was later to study Law. He was living at home in the eastern suburbs of Adelaide, only four miles from the University, and riding or taking the horse tram to lectures in the classic buildings on North Terrace, set among green lawns which sloped down to the small but pretty River Torrens, and the Parliament House where his grandfather King now sat as a Member of the Legislative Council for his northern electorate.

If Willy had not inherited from Sam his gambling instincts and his gold-fever, he had the same interest in travel and adventure. Because of his boyhood in the far north of South Australia, he had a liking for hot climates and sun, and a tolerance for dust and flies. And he loved horses and riding. They actually had a Hunt Club in Adelaide, which would ride to hounds on winter Saturday afternoons across the smooth green paddocks: complete with red coats, black velvet skull caps, and even a real fox. For these pests had been imported, along with the English rabbit, to make the English gentry feel at home in their new country.

William had a big grey hunter, which he would ride to meets over the carefully simulated 'fences' which property owners had arranged for the Club: solid log or soft brush, set into the dangerous post-and-wire fences which were so hard for a horse to see, and judge, the height of the jump.

In the North they used to breed remounts for the British Army in India – tough brown horses used to a harsh summer climate and hard-baked, bare soil. William planned to travel as soon as he was through his BE course at the University, with the thousand pounds he would inherit from his Edmond grandfather when he turned twenty-one. From childhood memories of the coloured silks and engraved brasses donated by a missionary great-aunt, and the row of ebony elephants sent home by his father from India, his imagination settled on that country. India, he felt, was peacocks and ivory, blue and golden silks, Maharajas in jewelled turbans and caparisoned elephants: a fascinating land, exotic and mysterious.

One day, of course, he would like to see London, and the chalk hills of Buckinghamshire which his ancestors had come from, but India was his first choice.

Willy enjoyed his lectures, to which he would ride as far as the horse-tram terminus, along the banks of Fourth Creek, fording Third Creek at the village of Payneham. He left the horse in a stables and picked him up again at night. Now that Sam had struck it rich, he could have lived in one of the North Adelaide colleges, but he loved his home and enjoyed the daily ride. Then there was the walk along elm-shaded North Terrace to the University grounds, past exotic Jacaranda trees (were they Indian?) which dropped their blue-mauve flowers in a ring on the green lawns. And then in autumn, coming back down the opposite pavement, he would crunch the crisp fallen planetree leaves beneath his boots, while the westering sun painted the backdrop of the Adelaide hills with red-golden highlights and viridian shadows.

Even better was the field work, going out with theodolite and chain, measuring imaginary dam-sites and surveying new roads and weirs for the Engineering and Water Supply Department; studying soil samples and basic rock formations.

His work gave him a sense of power, for civil engineering was the branch of human endeavour by which the forces of Nature were tamed and brought under the control of man. Rivers could be turned from their beds, valleys filled, hills levelled, all by human ingenuity. In Western Australia the Chief Engineer, D. Y. O'Connor, had planned a huge pipeline to pump water 346 miles to the goldfields Sam King had helped to discover.

Ever since ancient times, from the irrigation systems of the Nile and the Euphrates to Roman roads and aqueducts, up to the Suez Canal and the great irrigation works of the Indus valley, man had been planning and designing and altering the face of the earth.

In construction, iron and steel were coming into their own: the Eiffel Tower had been built in Paris, entirely of prefabricated wrought iron, and Monier had pioneered reinforced concrete as a building material, which was being used for building construction in Chicago. It was an exciting time.

He received his degree at the age of twenty-three, and in 1895, after a year's experience with the E & WSD, he set off for India, where he had applied for a job with the Government in the Public Works Department as a junior engineer stationed in Bengal. He was anxious to get away, for he had become involved with the bridesmaid at his sister Elizabeth's wedding, drifting into a pattern of picnics and tennis parties where he was her accepted partner. He knew quite certainly that he did not want to marry her.

After the wonderful news and the first draft of money had come from Western Australia, Mary had indulged in a shopping spree. She was happy and excited and could afford to employ servants and workers for the orchard, so William was able to leave home before his father returned. But when it was time to see him off on the mail-steamer from Outer Harbour, she became tearful. If it had only been England he was going to, even though that was further away, it would not have seemed so bad. At least that was a civilised place, with proper food and sanitation!

In India, she told him, he would be in danger from all sorts of horrid diseases, malaria and dengue fever and cholera and goodness knew what else. Sam had written and sent some addresses in Calcutta. He was pleased that Willy was going to see the world, and he could well start with India, 'and tell your mother that it's not as dangerous as she imagines. Why, Aunt Ada Edmond, Grandma's sister, was there as a missionary thirty years ago. And she has only just died in England, well into her seventies.'

Before his ship sailed, William had to assure his mother that he would be very careful, and never eat ice-cream from native stalls.

He disembarked at Madras on the Coromandel Coast, so that he could travel by rail to Calcutta and see the countryside. It was a flat, barren, sandy shore that welcomed him to his imagined India, but once on land he found the city attractive, with its impressive artificial harbour and Marina, its great citadel of Fort George, its flowering trees, and parks full of bright splashes of colour.

From the station, once out of the poor slums where emaciated goats and cattle wandered on the line, the train began to speed up. Spires of wayside temples appeared through the branches of peepul trees, buffaloes wallowed in muddy dams with children tending them. A Rebecca stood at a village well, clad in a coloured sari, with a pitcher on her head and a naked brown baby on her hip, waiting her turn to draw water. Tall cranes stepped through the fields on long legs, following the primitive wooden ploughs drawn by hump-backed oxen.

India! He sat on the end of his bottom berth, staring out at the sky, the occasional wayside station, long after the sun had set redly beyond the windows, and the other passengers had left for the dining car.

William did not have to take up his appointment immediately. He planned more travel first, but as he had an introduction to the Calcutta Club and his horsemanship gave him an entrée into racing circles, he began to find life in Calcutta very pleasant. It was the so-called 'cool' season around Christmas. He was introduced to the Crosley-Sheridans; he played polo on the Maidan and rode in the Gentleman's Purse at the racecourse, having acquired a workmanlike brown horse, Sahib, which had originally come from Australia; he won the Calcutta Point-to-Point and carried off several minor trophies.

He had meant to leave for Delhi by the Grand Trunk Road and visit the Red Fort and go on to see the Taj Mahal and perhaps get some tiger shooting in the Upper Pradesh. All these plans came to a halt when by chance his eye lighted on an advertisement in the *Times of India* just as he was throwing it in the waste-basket at his hotel. It was for a State Engineer to the Maharaja of Gorobhunj, an independent feudal State adjoining the State of Orissa to the south. He went to see the Chief Engineer of the British PWD in Calcutta, and asked if he would mind if he applied for the job. The Chief said he would be glad to recommend him; it would be excellent experience for a young man. But the post, he pointed out, was for a married man.

So William had frequented the Crosley-Sheridans' drawing room and paid court to the statuesque daughter, Diana. But he found her rather cold and silent, except on the subject of dogs. She had two pedigree Pekingese with their own Ayah to look after them. She showed more animation when talking to these animals, in a sort of baby talk, than in human company.

'Didums want its ickle tum-tum tickled, then?' she would croon. And 'come to Mummy,' as she lifted one of the snuffling, flat-faced creatures on to her lap or draped it over her shoulder. 'Who was a good boy, then? A veddy, veddy good boy?' and 'Aren't they *sweet*?' she would demand, stroking their silky heads.

Though her own nose was bony and aristocratic, unlike their snub features, like theirs her teeth showed constantly below her short upper lip. She was tall, elegant, and had a delicate English complexion as yet unaffected by the Indian climate. Also, as her father's only daughter, she would have independent means one day. Not that this carried any weight with him, Willy told himself, yet he felt that compared with Sam with all his unmarried daughters at home, Mr Crosley-Sheridan had been lucky in this regard.

However, when he compared his own mother with Diana's – sallow, complaining, always having trouble with her horde of servants – when he thought of round, rosy-cheeked, good-natured Mary, who still baked delicious Cornish pasties on Fridays though she now had a cook and a kitchen-maid, he knew that Sam had been the lucky one, and not only in finding gold.

Seven

IN THE West, not everyone was making fortunes. Those who were making the most were the canny 'mining experts' who took advantage of the mad gold fever to float worthless mines, selling their own shares before the bottom fell out of the boom. Many credulous investors lost their life savings.

Water was so scarce on the fields that it cost two shillings and sixpence for a bath at the hotel. Miners were rationed to two gallons a day for all their needs.

Women were even scarcer than water, about one to every ten men. Most of the men were young and without ties, but the married ones were reluctant to bring their wives to the hot, dusty gold towns. If there was little water, there was plenty of champagne. Hundreds of bottles were being chilled every day in the crowded hotels, for successful prospectors, or for promoters' dinner parties. At one of these an Irish toast was proposed by one Murphy who had been sampling the champagne beforehand:

'I gives you the toast of the Prospector. The prospector goes out with his pick in one hand, his shovel in the other, and his life in the other. He goes out into the bush where the hand of man has never set foot, and before he comes back he finds his bones have been picked clean by the dingoes . . .'

Some men died of thirst on the track, some of typhoid and some by their own hand. There was no proper hospital. The nurses in the little bush clinic battled with cross-infections, inflamed wounds, and terrible burns, when men, dead drunk, rolled into their campfires in the night, broken noses from bare-knuckle fights, dysentery from bad drinking-water, and venereal disease for which there was no certain cure. Sometimes they lost a patient who committed suicide rather than go back home and tell his wife he was infected. The inquest always gave the reason as 'insomnia'. The nurses stuck by their patients and gave evidence of minds deranged by lack of sleep.

But Sam King and William Goodman were not among these unfortunates.

Goodman's brother in Adelaide, who had formed the Coolgardie Gold Mining and Prospecting Syndicate, floated three new companies. Members received one-tenth shares in Ivanhoe, Great Boulder, and Lake View, which between them (had the original shareholders only known it) were to produce a hundred million pounds' worth of gold. Sam King and William Goodman were given three shares each, and became wealthy overnight. But to Sam it was no good being wealthy just on paper; he wanted tangible assets. He wanted to live in style, to have people say when they passed, 'There goes Samuel King, Esquire, who found the Golden Mile and made a fortune.'

He sold his shares for an immediate return of £200,000 – shares that would have made him a millionaire in a few years. With money like that in his pocket, though, who needed to worry about the future? He returned home to his family and commenced to make the money fly. He installed Mary and the girls in a seaside hotel, sold the hills property and bought an ocean-going steam yacht for which even the curtains at the portholes were specially commissioned. Then he looked about for a suitable house to become his private mansion.

It happened that just at the time Sam made his big find, the Eastern States were going through a financial crisis. Banks closed their doors, companies went bankrupt, merchants went out of business. Robert King lost his whole fortune in the crash of the Bank of Adelaide, in 1893, for besides having his own money in the Bank, he was on the board of directors and a guarantor of its funds.

Sam was able to help him with a gift of five times his father's earlier advance on the Jamestown land, but the shock of his loss left the old man weakened in body and mind. He died the following year, and Henrietta went to live with Arthur and his wife.

She was now an impressive figure of a woman, still handsome, big all over, and clinging to her costumes of the 1870s: two-tiered edifices of black velvet and taffeta, fringed and flounced like pieces of furniture. Her head was crowned with a white lace cap, like snow upon the summit of this woman-mountain. Mary, though she admired her mother-in-law, had always been a bit intimidated by her and was glad she was to make her home with Arthur in Kuldunda and not with them.

Because of the universal depression – except in mining stocks in Western Australia – land values had fallen. Many big houses were coming on the market, put up for sale by those who could no longer afford their upkeep.

Flowing through the foothills and across the Adelaide plains were five crystal creeks, coming from the Mount Lofty Range and descending to the blue waters of the Gulf to the westward. Here a few market gardens, vineyards and orchards were already established in the red Bay of Biscay soil which sloped towards the western sun. The most fertile areas had been taken up first, along the largest stream, the Torrens, which had overlaid the red clay with rich black river silt. But on Fourth Creek were some large holdings where the pioneer cottages of the first settlers had been replaced by imposing storeyed mansions in English county style, surrounded by shrubberies and parks.

Sam bought the largest available for a mere £3,000. Later he acquired six acres of adjoining land, and irrigated it from the creek. He had the painted ceiling in the drawing-room touched up with real gold leaf.

Mary was a little bewildered by it all. She had been born in a simple Cornish miner's cottage – though her father had later become a 'Cap'n' in charge of one of the underground mines – and she let Sam do most of the ordering: the lengths of plum-coloured brocade for the tall windows, with rings of carved cedar on cedar poles; the Japanese silk screen with its embroidered cherry blossom and long-legged birds; the expanding table for the dining room, with its twelve carved walnut chairs upholstered in red Morocco leather, each with a different sign of the Zodiac on the back. (Sam always sat in the winged 'carver's chair' bearing his sign of Scorpio.)

Mantlepieces of Italian marble, handcarved rosewood chairs, inlaid tables, ornamental mirrors, and a whole set of oil paintings bought from an antique dealer, graced the lofty rooms. Even the chamberpots in the bedrooms were of Royal Doulton.

A governess and a visiting music-master were engaged for the younger girls, and Sam bought a black japanned baby-grand piano for them to play on. He liked to sing after dinner in his rich baritone,

> Nita! Juanita! Ask thy soul if we should part!
> Nita! Juanita! Rest thou on my heart . . .

and

> In thy dark eyes' splendour,
> Where the warm light loves to dwell . . .

which always made Mary feel sentimental, though her brown eyes were by now rather faded and did not appear as large and lustrous as before.

Sam waved his golden wand and transformed the land around the house. He planted a thousand vines, three hundred peach and apricot trees, and two thousand oranges and lemons. An old muscatel vine grew round a trellis between the veranda posts, bearing fat green muscatel grapes in summer. Inside the house, cases of French champagne filled the cellar. Mary drove out visiting (though she had few friends in the city) in a white-painted trap with a pair of white horses to pull it. They had a patent Coolgardie Safe in the kitchen, based on a miner's invention: wet cloths covered its walls and cooled the contents by evaporation.

The younger girls, Fanny, Harriet and Sarah, had the fun of playing in the shallow creek, at night lying in bed listening to the wild gully-wind flapping the canvas blind which kept the afternoon sun from the western balcony, listening to magpies carolling in the early morning, playing croquet on the lawn, gathering round the piano to sing. They picked wild lilac along the creek and brought in armfuls of gumleaves and native pine and white-flowering thorn bush to decorate the house for Christmas.

Elizabeth had married someone she met on a visit to her cousins in Kuldunda; William had gone to India, and Alice had left to continue her nursing career in England. Mary felt that her nest, now so large and commodious, was nearly empty. There were only Mae and Fanny now, besides the two youngest.

Mary, who had produced four more girls – two of whom did not live – mourned the sons separated from her by death and distance. The anniversary of James's death she always spent in her room, with the blinds drawn and a damp cloth over her eyes to keep out the light. She would emerge the next day calm and cheerful, as though the day before had not occurred.

Mary had passed the change of life while Sam was in the West: 'Thank goodness!' she said. 'I am tired to death of having babies, Sam. Do you know I was actually relieved when the last one didn't live? It seems terrible, but I just have no motherly feelings left, after eighteen pregnancies. I always hoped for another son, but it was not to be.'

Her father had died, and her mother had gone back to Cornwall. She had lost touch with her sisters and brothers since coming to the city. Without her children she would have been terribly lonely in the Adelaide hills, but at least while Sam was away she could not fall pregnant again.

Now he was home, and she could welcome him without the constant fear of conceiving. She was nearly forty-five years old, plump as ever but not as pretty, though to Sam she was still the Mary he had married when he was nineteen. Sam was busy, happy, active, improving the property, or taking sailing parties down the Port River and out into Spencer's Gulf in the glamorous yacht he had christened, perversely, 'The Tub', or on week-long fishing excursions for whiting down around Kangaroo Island, which ended only when the flagons of port and crates of bottled beer ran out. Once they had all fallen asleep after a party and woke next day, or so Sam declared, to find 'ice in the rigging and 'bergs off the starboard bow', for the yacht had sailed all night and half the day by herself, making due south towards Antarctica.

He bought a dinner suit and a black tie, a stiff, frilled white shirt with black pearl studs, and had a sample of ore from Bayley's Reward – a gemlike piece of silky white quartz veined with gold – set in gold wire and hung from his gold watch-chain.

He still loved the look and feel of pure gold, just as he used to love stroking his mother's wide gold wedding-ring when he was a child. And he still felt a lift of spirits when he saw a rainbow. He had found the magical Pot of Gold; he was rich for life, and there was no chance of his fortune melting away and turning to dirt and stones. It was not fairy gold; it was real, and Sam King had found it.

Eight

ELAINE HAMILTON FORBES, a great-granddaughter of the pioneer Fergus Macdonald of Rothsay and Balranald Stations, had a first name that suggested a romantic figure like the Lady of Shalott. Yet she was a forthright, energetic, practical girl who loved healthy exercise in the open air: a third-generation Australian on her mother's side.

Her untamed red hair refused to be drawn into the flat, demure, parted-in-the-middle Victorian style which was the fashion when she left school. Her eyes were more green than brown and far too large; in fact they were inclined to bulge a little like her father Hamilton's. While in him the effect was rather repellent, her eyes only added an air of intensity to Elaine's pale face and strong features.

With a doting father and a mother who died when she was still a child, Elaine was able to do much as she liked. But first she became a mother to her little sister and brother, Joseph. She learned to run the household in Sydney for her father, to manage housekeeping money and staff, and to nurse childish ailments. She had inherited from her mother, the auburn-haired Moira Macdonald, not only the rich red curls that went so well with her white skin and large greeny eyes, but also a Scottish practical sense.

When Elaine was seventeen, her younger sister Margaret died of the tuberculosis which had killed her mother. With Joseph away at school, Elaine had nothing to do but go to tennis parties, picnics and balls for which she had no heart. Margaret's death had shocked her deeply. Besides, the out-ings' real purpose was for young men and women to meet, to pair off, to marry. Elaine, who had no intention of 'marrying and settling down' as so many of her friends were doing, decided to train as a nurse.

By chance her room-mate at the nurses' home in the Sydney hospital where she trained was Lucy Bainbridge, who was set upon being a missionary in India. After her un-requited love for a surgeon at the hospital, Elaine too decided on missionary work in a far country, for she longed to travel. She saw herself working among lepers, perhaps contracting the disease, being brought home with fingers and toes in bad shape, to be operated on by the famous surgeon who would notice her at last.

She did not even know that there were lepers in her own country, among the Aboriginal population in the far north. It was a subject kept hidden, as the leper colonies were kept hidden in remote areas or on islands off the Queensland coast. She knew that leprosy was a disease of overcrowding and poor diet in a subtropical climate, and that it was rife in India: a disease of the skin and mucous membranes for which large doses of Chaulmoogra oil given subcutaneously were effective. The important thing in India was to teach that leprosy was the result of infection by a bacillus, *Mycobacterium Leprae*, and not a punishment for displeasing the gods; that lepers, in fact, were simply ill.

Elaine had been inspired by the story of Father Damien and his work in the leper colony of Molokai in Hawaii. Robert Louis Stevenson on a visit to Sydney had written a spirited account of his life and a defence of the priest in his 'Damien Letter' to the *Australian Star*. But it was a Roman Catholic mission on Molokai, and Elaine had been brought up a strict Presbyterian. She decided on the Church Missionary Society, which ran a hospital for the poor in Calcutta.

She sailed in 1894 when Queen Victoria was still Empress of India and the British Raj was at the height of its pomp and power. Her white caps and starched bibs were packed in a round yellow tin hatbox marked on the lid 'Not Wanted on the Voyage'. It had accompanied her great-grandmother Janet Macdonald from Scotland seventy years earlier.

As the P & O liner sailed up the Hooghly river, one of the streams of the Ganges delta, Elaine had her first glimpse of India: coconut palms and rice paddies, green against a soft blue sky filled with steamy clouds. Calcutta's approaches were impressive, such beautiful Botanic Gardens on the left bank, such great white houses set among flowering shrubberies in parklike grounds, and the pile of Fort William symbolising British might.

This was the 'front door' of the city. When they were tied up, and she ventured ashore by way of the steps up from the jetty where they were anchored in the tidal river, she found herself undoubtedly in the East. So many people flowed along the Strand: foot-passengers and cyclists, ox-carts and horse-drawn gharries and tongas, hand-carts drawn by men. She saw a coolie, who might have been any age, drawing a heavy cart. His eyes were fixed before his feet, his face was set in a grimace of endless, brutalising toil. She saw a driver beating a horse about the face and head. Another horse passed, with its bones sticking almost through its hide, an open sore showing beside the collar. While she stood staring, sickened, a faint voice whispered beside her, 'Memsahib! Memsahib!'

She felt a gentle tug at her skirt.

A woman was crouched on the ground, in a colourless cotton sari, a sickly-looking infant cradled inside the fold of cloth across her thin breast. 'Memsahib! Husband dead, very many children, no food, baby sick. *Bucksheesh*! I cannot feed my baby, Memsahib, he will die. One anna for food. A few pice . . .'

The murmuring went on without expression. The baby stared from great dark eyes in a wizened face.

'I'm sorry, I have no change – no Indian money. I came ashore without any – from the ship down there. Wait! Here –' She struggled to remove the plain gold bracelet which she'd had for years, now growing too tight to pass easily over her big, capable hand.

'Here, I say! Is this woman pestering you? Be off at once! *Jow*!'

A passenger from the ship, an Anglo-Indian who had been rather attentive to her on board and was just getting a coolie to carry his luggage up to his waiting carriage, stopped beside Elaine. The woman cringed, but did not move. Her eyes were fixed on the bracelet.

'No, no, she is not pestering me! It's just that I have no rupees.' The bracelet slid off, painfully. She held it out. The woman took it swiftly, made a gesture of gratitude with her palms pressed together before her forehead, then slipped away into the crowd.

'You shouldn't have done that, you know,' said her acquaintance. 'She won't know its value, some dealer will only rob her. I'd have given her a few pice for you, my dear Miss Forbes. I must warn you, it's no earthly use trying to help all the beggars in Calcutta. It's a way of life with them. Once they get to know you, your life will be made a misery as soon as you step on to the street.'

'I know. I'll try to be firm in future; it's impossible to help everybody. But she had a sick baby.'

'And when you get to your hotel, there will be a blind boy waiting at the steps, and his brother perhaps with one arm, because his parents removed the other when he was a baby to get sympathy.'

'Surely not!'

'I'm afraid so. They are hopeless heathens.'

'All the more need for the missionary work I shall be doing.'

'Calcutta is the worst. Thank goodness I am going to the Hills . . . Can I get you a carriage?'

'No, thank you, my friends are calling for me on board.'

He escorted her down to the jetty again and back to the ship. The English officer on duty at the gangplank saluted her with a smile. She had got used to the Indian crew on the voyage and decided that she liked them: the Lascars who worked willingly at loading and unloading, washing decks, chipping rust; the Goanese stewards in the dining saloon, quick and efficient and unobtrusive. Such handsome features, such sympathetic brown eyes, such grateful smiles for a kind word! The coolies who acted as bath-wallahs and key-minders were small and brown as monkeys, but how energetically they washed out the big baths, ran hot saltwater from the huge silver taps, and filled the tub of fresh water which rested on a board fixed across the bath! The cabin steward was elderly and self-effacing. She had heard that some Englishwomen, sleeping topless in stifling nights going through the Red Sea, would not bother to cover themselves when the steward brought their fruit juice and early morning tea, since in their minds the Indian stewards were less than men.

Coming up the Hooghly she had seen the style of the English residents in the Garden Reach suburb, where they lived in feudal splendour with about twenty servants to a household. The Mems all stayed inside in the heat of the day, so the bright gardens appeared deserted, but, as Elaine was to learn, they would issue forth at sunset, bathed and dressed in fresh white linen for the evening parade of carriages. They would never step outside, even into the garden, without a shady hat or parasol, and they never ventured outside the grounds on foot. Some of the younger women rode horseback in the evenings, each attended by a syce whose only job was to attend his mistress's horse.

A member of the Church Missionary Society had now arrived to convey to Elaine the welcome of her fellow-workers in the medical missionary field. He offered to take her to see the headquarters on the edge of the unfashionable native part of the city to the north, as her friends would not be calling for her until it was cooler, towards dinner time. These were relatives of the Hamiltons, her paternal grandmother's people in England, who had asked her to stay for a few weeks while she became acclimatised. 'It won't hurt you to have a little taste of luxury before you begin your slumming,' they had written.

The Reverend Mr Chandler was gaunt and sallow-faced from the heat of the sweltering Bengal summers, for unlike the British Government officials he did not go to the Hills for regular leave in the hottest months; he could not afford it. He wore a khaki suit with clerical collar and lifted a solar topee from his damp brow.

'My dear Miss Forbes, how fresh you look!' he exclaimed almost involuntarily, as Elaine came to her cabin door to greet him. She was in a freshly-laundered white hailspot muslin blouse, with a tussore silk skirt of the natural pale fawn colour produced by Indian silkworms. Some of her rebellious red curls had escaped from the upturned hair and smooth bun on top of her head, and the humid heat had made them twine in soft tendrils about her forehead. But it was the complexion, the clear pale skin of a girl from a hot but less enervating climate than the delta of the Ganges, which had struck poor Mr Chandler so forcibly, used as he was to the washed-out yellow faces of his wife and fellow workers. (Elaine always cleaned her face with oatmeal rather than soap, and when she was at home bathed it in the whey from soured milk.) She was wearing a new hat with fawn silk roses which she had bought in Sydney.

He had hired an Indian gharry with a terribly thin horse and an equally emaciated driver. Cutting through to the North Circular Road, they passed the Chitpore Road bazaars, with wares displayed right on the street under awnings. Elaine stared with her great eyes, drinking it all in; the dust, the noise, the colour, the smells, the teeming crowds.

'I had expected Indian costume to be very colourful,' she said, looking at the booths where bright silk, scarves and saris, hung for sale, and thinking of the high-caste Hindu lady with her red-painted forehead and exotic saris who had travelled on the ship. 'But the crowds are so drab!'

The uniform of the general populace was a dingy off-white cotton, the men's *dhotis* looped between their legs like a badly-anchored baby's diaper. The turban or head-cloth was of the same no-colour cotton, and sometimes a European shirt was worn over the top. The women too, though many wore glass bracelets and bangles and nose rings, were mostly swathed in colourless cotton. 'They are unbelievably poor, and dyestuffs cost money,' Mr Chandler explained.

The Mission compound lay in the northern part of the city, where the ornate homes of wealthy Indians rubbed shoulders with the hovels of the poor. The streets were narrow, with open drains. The smell was scarcely salubrious. Low-ceilinged shops and workshops lined the streets, with no lighting but from the open door in front, and with the family living quarters above.

'But you will not be working in this area,' said Mr Chandler. 'Your work will be at the hospital, which is near the Old Mission Church off Chowringhee Road, at the other end of town. We have only a dispensary here. There is an excellent Medical College in Calcutta, where even high-caste Hindus doing their Med. course will perform an autopsy without turning a hair, in the cause of science.'

When she looked puzzled, he explained, 'To touch a corpse is considered defiling for a Hindu. That is why only the Untouchables go down to the river below the burning-ghats and sieve the sand mixed with the remains of cremated bodies for any jewellery that they might have been wearing.'

'Really?' Elaine felt slightly sick, but no doubt it was the smells of the open drains – more like sewers – which were at their worst in the heat of the afternoon. The humidity, too, was building up towards evening.

Mr Chandler, seeing her looking rather green, patted her hand as the gharry drew up before a group of low white buildings set among peepul trees and mangoes in the Mission Compound.

'There, there, we'll get you a cup of Indian tea in a moment, and you can sit down in the cool.' He paid off the driver and escorted her in to meet the staff.

'I assure you I'm not squeamish usually,' said Elaine,

mortified. 'In fact, I'm hoping to work among lepers later on. It is just the heat, and – '

'My dear Miss Forbes,' said the Missionary, laughing, 'this is the *cool* season. It's as well you didn't land in the Monsoon.'

'But I am used to the heat! At Benangal in the west it was sometimes 112 degrees Fahrenheit in the shade, and we often had a week over a hundred in summer. But it was a dry, clear heat. I find this much more enervating.'

'Of course. But you get used to it.'

The missionaries were a married couple, the man tall and ascetic-looking with steel-rimmed glasses, his wife painfully thin; and two sturdy young English girls who reminded Elaine of her friend Lucy Bainbridge, who had intended coming with her and then had to stay behind at the last moment to nurse a sick father. The women wore what seemed to be a uniform of plain high-necked white blouses and dark blue serge skirts.

Then they took tea, with small, sweet cakes. The Indian girl from the dispensary joined them, one of the 'new women' still wearing a sari but taking her place in the world like a man. She was a converted Christian, or she would have been forbidden by her caste from taking food in company with unbelievers.

The rooms were cool, white, high-ceilinged. Vashti took Elaine on a tour of the buildings, including the Christian chapel and the prayer-room for other faiths. Besides the dispensary there was an office, a schoolroom, and a small library of religious books in Hindi, Bengali and Gujarati.

When she went out into the street again with Mr Chandler, the heat hit her in the face with a palpable blast.

'You do not have a sunshade, Miss Forbes?' said Mr Chandler, looking at her hat which was a mere pile of muslin and flowers. 'I suggest you invest in one to protect that complexion from our Indian sun.' He hailed a gharry outside the gate.

'It is no stronger than the Australian sun, I assure you,' said Elaine rather crossly, wishing she had worn a more sensible hat of straw. 'But a sunshade cumbers the hands too much. I shall be too busy, I hope, to be bothered with one. I shall buy a pith helmet like yours, with a length of veiling.'

'Most eminently sensible.'

The friends who called for Elaine towards six o'clock were very different from the missionaries. The perfectly cut pale silk suits of the ladies, their fashionable hats and lacy cotton gloves, drew a glance of admiration from the Sydney girl. Mrs Crosley-Sheridan and her daughter Diana were 'County' English, and in India followed the same interests and social life as they would have at Home: attending suppers and balls, polo-matches and race-meetings.

There was a rich and splendid social life among the Europeans, with their gracious homes and troops of cheap servants, in what used to be the headquarters of the East India Company when it ruled the country and was now the administrative capital of India.

With a few sharp words in Hindi Mrs Crosley-Sheridan directed her servants where to stow Elaine's bags in the barouche while Elaine proceeded to over-tip the coolie who had carried them up to the quay. Then she was taken on a sight-seeing drive round the impressive public buildings, Government House with its four pillared verandas and central dome, the Bengal Club, the green Maidan, the two Cathedrals, the elegant new theatre with its Grecian columns, and the buildings of the East India Company, of which Mr Crosley-Sheridan was an official.

It was a different world from the narrow, ever-crowded, humanity-choked streets of the northern part of the city. Only the burning-ghats where the Hindus cremated their dead reminded of the East.

After a circuit of the open space between the Esplanade and the Racecourse, they came back along the wide Chowringhee Road to the suburb of handsome private houses which Elaine had glimpsed from the ship, and where the Crosley-Sheridans lived.

'I am overwhelmed,' said Elaine, leaning back against the padded leather seat, looking at the spotless white turbans of the coachman and the groom in front, and at the beautiful gardens and houses like white marble palaces – though they were actually of brick covered with white stucco – passing on either side. 'I did not expect Calcutta to be such a splendid European city as well as an Indian one.'

'Of course the native quarter is very different,' said her

hostess. 'It is quite repulsive, with its dingy streets and low population – some of the men half naked, or even entirely so. And then the noise, the open drains, the native hovels, the beggars – ! The Indian has no conception of segregating the classes, so that even in the better Indian suburbs you have wealthy mansions overlooking the filthy huts of the poor. Quite appalling.'

'Appalling for the poor, you mean?'

Mrs Crosley-Sheridan looked at her as if she had not heard correctly.

'I mean, being overlooked like that,' Elaine went on. 'I have been in the native quarter of the city this afternoon, with my missionary friends. I found it all extremely interesting, I must say. If your suburbs are segregated, white from black, rich from poor, you become insulated from the needy, you can put them from your mind.' She spoke rather heatedly, and her pale face flushed. Her hostess's easy assumptions of superiority over a race and country from which her own countrymen were busy making their fortunes, annoyed her. 'Do you have no social contact with the Indian people, then?'

'Oh, of course the higher-caste Hindus – and the Muslims too – have positions of trust in the Company, and in Government departments. My husband brings them home sometimes. But I never meet their wives. I have an Indian doctor, too, a splendid little man who trained at Edinburgh.'

'Yes, that's probably the best medical school in the world. But I hear there is now a good Medical College at Calcutta University.'

They passed a tree-shaded cemetery. Frangipani and tulip-tree dropped their pale stars and red blossoms on the graves, some with elaborate marble monuments. It was picturesque, but Elaine could not help feeling that the Indian custom of cremation was far more hygienic than burial, in a country where cholera and typhoid were endemic.

Soon the carriage and pair turned in between gates in a high stone wall, and swept along a gravel drive between flowering shrubs and trees set in rather sparse, dried-up lawns to a big house set well back from the road. An arched veranda ran round the second storey. A porch under which the vehicle could drive sheltered the front door, held by a bowing, white-robed and spotlessly-turbanned butler.

'My dear, you will want a cold bath before anything. Diana, go with Miss Forbes and show her the Chintz Room. It has its own bathroom attached. I will send Ayah to help you unpack. Drinks on the upstairs balcony at seven-thirty, dinner at eight.'

The slender and silent Diana led her up the stairs, answering in monosyllables Elaine's excited chatter. She was stimulated by all she had seen, and felt full of talk. However, Diana left her on her own as soon as she had ushered her into a bedroom on the third floor, with chintz-curtained windows looking over the front garden. She showed her first the stone-floored bathroom with its zinc tub, bowl, and brass jars of cool water for rinsing, and the 'thunderbox', a chamberpot set in a wooden commode.

Elaine pulled back the tattees, the straw blinds, and looked out at the afterglow shading upward into a peacock blue sky, too bright for stars. In the brief twilight, the delicious garden plants were breathing out their perfumes so essentially tropical, which had a peculiarly languid effect upon her senses at that hour.

She felt herself longing for . . . something, was it romance, the delights of love, the touch of a man's lips on her bare shoulder? She shook herself, and went to the bathroom and splashed cold water on her face. In the bedroom, she looked at herself in the long mirror on the *almirah*.

She was above the average height, yet so slim that patients at the hospital where she trained, not knowing her name, would ask for 'the little nurse'. But she did not have red hair and a determined chin for nothing. While still a probationer she had dared to argue with the theatre sister over the number of swabs in the bucket after an operation. Sister tried to intimidate her, with 'My count is twenty-seven, Nurse,' to which Elaine steadily replied, 'Twenty-six.' (There were always two separate counts kept, to prevent the disaster of a blood-soaked swab being lost inside a patient before he was sewn up.) The surgeon had raised his eyebrows above his mask, probed with a forceps, and 'Twenty-seven!' he said, dropping the swab into the bucket.

While Elaine was still staring out the window at the darkening sky, the elderly, diminutive Ayah, in a plain white sari edged with dark blue, came in. She laid out Elaine's evening dress for dinner, and hung the rest of her things in the *almirah*.

'*Dhobi*, Memsahib?' She picked up a soiled blouse and stockings from the linen-bag.

'Yes, thank you,' said Elaine.

She supposed she would not be allowed to wash her own things. Ayah made the *namaste* gesture as she was leaving, palms together before her forehead. She paused, her hand on the painted china door-knob. '*Mukkar . . . Diwali . . .* Tomorrow night,' she said. 'Lights . . .'

Elaine smiled and nodded. She had no idea what the woman meant, and she resolved to learn Hindustani as soon as possible.

Ayah smiled and went. She had faded brown eyes and a grey streak through the black hair twisted in a bun low on the back of her head. She had been Diana's nurse when she was a baby and had been with the family ever since.

Elaine dressed and went down the wide stone stairs to the second level, where arched doorways led out to the veranda. Her host, red-faced and black-moustached, was in dark braid-striped evening trousers, but with them he wore instead of a jacket a starched white shirt and bow tie, and a cummerbund of brilliant Indian silk – which seemed to her a rather charming compromise with the climate. He greeted her gallantly. He was a real *pukka sahib*. If he dined away from home Mr Crosley-Sheridan would swelter in a full evening jacket.

In the dining-room there was a pleasant breeze, even though the night had been stifling on the veranda where they took drinks. Looking up, Elaine saw a wide band of material, almost the width of the room, swaying back and forth above the table. A silken cord attached to one end disappeared into an alcove where the punkah-wallah sat on the floor, regularly pulling the rope to and fro while the *sahib-log* ate. Sometimes, if he was lazy (Mrs Crosley-Sheridan remarked) he would tie the cord to his toe and lie down while working; and then he would invariably fall asleep, and they would have to throw a napkin-ring or a walnut at him to wake him up.

Fortunately Elaine liked curries, though her eyes watered and perspiration sprang to her forehead at the spicy hotness of the second dish. The curry was served with slices of cooling melon and cucumber.

She was getting used to luxury. She was woken next morning by a bearer bringing her *chota hazri*, her little breakfast, on a tray complete with English china teapot, watery pale-looking milk, and perfectly made toast, with butter in a separate dish with a piece of ice. On the drive yesterday they had showed her the great ice-houses where ice brought all the way from North America was stored, ready for delivery to private houses.

In the bathroom last night she had dropped her blouse and skirt on the floor, and then spent so long in the tub cooling off, that she had to dash down to dinner and leave them there. When she came back they were gone. Clean towels had been hung in the bathroom, the chintz bedspread had been turned back, and the brass jars refilled with cold water. So had the drinking-jug on her bedside table.

Sitting at the round table near one of the windows, she ate her breakfast in the faint, perfumed morning breeze. There was a knock at the door and Ayah came in with her clothes on hangers, freshly laundered, starched and pressed. Thanking her, Elaine felt abashed. She had carelessly left her things where they fell, and they had not only been picked up, but restored to freshness while she slept. It was part of the unobtrusive service on every level which made the British Mems, in spite of the heat they endured, among the most pampered women in the world.

Mrs Crosley-Sheridan had told Elaine that the Diwali Festival of Lights was a fantastic sight which she was lucky to be in Calcutta for; it occurred only once a year in November.

'We will take a later drive tonight, taking in some of the native quarter,' she had said at tiffin. 'Then we will go to the Gardens to watch the fireworks over the river.'

All the same, Elaine was unprepared for the fairy transformation of the city in honour of the Goddess Lakshmi, wife of Vishnu. The house servants, of whom there were twenty, had each set their own lights on the balustrades of the veranda: little *chirags*, shallow earthenware dishes containing oil and a cotton wick, or half a candle.

As they drove away from the house in the open landau, Elaine could see it outlined in twinkling lights; and every house was the same. Every wall, parapet, window ledge and even footpath edge in the city was fluttering with lights. The poorest beggars who slept wrapped in a bit of cloth on the pavement, or those a little better off who had webbing *charpoys* to sleep on, each had a light fixed in 'their' place, or a whole cluster of lights where there was a shopkeeper who could afford them. Shops, stalls, bridges were all decorated with the tiny lamps.

When they crossed the Howrah Bridge and looked back across the river, they saw quays and steps and embankments dancing with light and reflected in the ripples of the river.

Then the official and unofficial fireworks began. The sky was lit with coloured chrysanthemums and exploding stars, followed by drifting spiders of smoke. They watched from the carriage the rockets reflected in the dark Hooghly, and the rows of lights outlining all the barges, lighters and native boats at the long jetties.

Even the great banyan tree in the Gardens, big as a house, had lamps twinkling among its huge roots, as though it too were someone's home where Lakshmi was welcomed.

For two weeks of luxury, Elaine lived the life of a pampered Memsahib. She found her hosts rather dull company, but the city itself, with its magnificent Botanic Gardens, its riverside drives, its imposing public buildings, and the beautiful green garden filled with flowering shrubs which surrounded the house – all these, with her daily lessons in Hindustani from Ayah, filled her day with interest. Yet she was marking time. Her real life in India would begin at the Mission Hospital.

So far she had seen no lepers; except in the country and in the native States they were segregated in leper colonies, yet she felt a call to work among these outcasts of the human race. After she had completed a year at the Hospital and was fluent in the *lingua franca* of northern India, she would ask for a transfer to one of the outer areas.

Nine

Since her mind had a scientific bent, Elaine laughed at astrology and predictions based on the conjunctions of the moon and planets of her birth. Yet, picking up a book on astrology that had been left on the bedside table, she could not resist looking up her fate; she was a Scorpio.

The Scorpio woman has one secret regret; that she was not born a boy. She realises that this would have meant less restriction and more opportunity. She can be overbearing and domineering; but she is never wishy-washy. She can often recognise a future mate at first glance. She wants one with civilisation and courage and intelligence.

Scorpios have no fear . . . The average Scorpio faces pain, ridicule, failure, with confidence.

'That is me!' she thought approvingly.

Was it because of that ridiculous book that she noticed the stranger so particularly? It was her habit, after a long day in the wards, to spend an hour at the Old Mission Church, in Mission Row off Dalhousie Square. It was an attractive stone building set among giant Neem trees. It was cool in the Church and under the trees. She would sit relaxing in one of the pews, not praying, just contemplating the coloured light through stained-glass windows of blue and green and gold. Then she would wander out under the trees, in her white uniform and starched white bib and apron, the conical cap set atop her luxuriant hair which seemed the more vivid for the pure white of her costume.

The man was seated on a section of wall, once whitewashed but now grey with the universal mildew and mould of India, sketching the façade of the stone church on a wide sketchpad held on his knee. He was sparely built, dark-eyed, with finely marked black eyebrows and a thick dark moustache, but otherwise clean-shaven. Something about his bright, sensitive glance as he looked from paper to subject, from his subject to the paper, attracted her at once.

He looked up and caught her gazing at him. Immediately she looked away, and walked back into the church. He had caught her staring, like 'an ill-bred Colonial' as he would no doubt regard her if he ever heard her speak. The British! Did they really have an inborn sense of superiority, or was it just the ones who visited the Colonies, and more especially those who lived among coloured Colonials (those lesser breeds without the Law) who developed it?

She peeped out from the porch and saw that he was folding over the cover of his sketchpad and walking away. He was tall, held his shoulders well back, yet walked with an easy stride as if used to long distances, the sketchpad under his arm, one hand slipped into the side pocket of his white duck jacket. He placed his feet with an easy assurance that the earth would present no roughnesses before him.

What arrogance! she thought.

And next moment, *I hope I see him again.*

It was not in the churchyard they met again, but at a weekend luncheon at the Crosley-Sheridans. She had not seen them for a month, being immersed in her work at the hospital where she had her own cell-like quarters in the grounds. It seemed that her father was worrying about her, and had asked the Hamiltons in England to write to their relatives and ask if they were keeping an eye on the young girl from New South Wales. So the Crosley-Sheridans' coachman dropped a note at the hospital with a warm invitation to stay for the weekend.

It was too hot for drinks on the veranda in the middle of the day. The drawing-room was dim with tattees across the windows, though the shutters were folded back, so Elaine did not at first see the tall stranger in his neat tussore silk suit. Her host introduced them: 'Miss Forbes, here is someone you'll be int'rested to meet: allow me to present – '

(He's a doctor, Elaine thought at once, a doctor at the English hospital.)

' – Mr William King, who's in Calcutta on his way to the Orissa district, and an appointment with the Maharaja of Gorobhunj. Miss Forbes is from Australia,' he added.

She half expected the man to say, 'Australia? Where's *that*?' but instead he took her hand with the most charming and gentle smile, and said 'How do you do? The nurse's uniform did not do you justice, but I recognised you at once by that pile of auburn hair.'

He looked appreciatively at her frilled white muslin dress with its large leg o'mutton sleeves.

'I see you are a diplomat,' she said, laughing. 'My hair, by any standards, is red. *Are* you in the diplomatic corps? And your voice – it's not English, nor yet quite Australian.'

'That is an Adelaide accent, if there is such a thing. I come from South Australia – '

'And you're an architect!' she finished for him eagerly. 'And you're going to design a palace for the Maharaja of wherever it is, and you were sketching the old Mission Church because you are interested in the form and proportions, not because you're an artist. Am I right?'

Her prominent, large green eyes were fixed on him hypnotically, just as they had been across the churchyard. Her gaze made him uncomfortable. He cleared his throat nervously. 'Not quite, Miss Forbes. The truth is more prosaic. I am a civil engineer, and what I am going to build for the Maharaja are drains and bridges. Excuse me.' And he turned to speak to Diana, who stood at his left hand offering a *chota peg*, a small whisky and soda, from a tray borne by a resplendently starched and turbaned bearer. Elaine felt snubbed. However, at tiffin she was seated on his left, and without her direct, disconcerting stare he found her a stimulating companion after the almost silent and statuesque Diana on his right. English girls could be charming, of course, but he found his fellow-Australian's cheerful outspokenness refreshing.

As she had been living on vegetable curries and *dahl* for the past weeks, Elaine studied the printed menu eagerly.

'Mm, salmon mayonnaise *and* pigeon and mushroom pie!' she murmured. There was cold capon and cold ham and salad too, she noticed, and trifle and fruit to follow.

'I'm so hungry I could eat a horse!' she confided to her neighbour.

He was amused. It was the fashion for young ladies to pick at their food and declare they had no appetite in the heat. There was in fact a pleasant breeze from the labours of the punkah-wallah with his giant ceiling fan.

'You might change your mind if you had ever actually eaten horseflesh,' he said.

'Why, have you, ever?'

'Yes, indeed; but not from choice. I was exploring out from Beetoota, in the northern part of the State where my father had a property. It is very dry, almost waterless country. After a long day's ride without water, my horse, smelling a water-hole, made a bolt for it; put his hoof in a wombat-hole and came down, breaking his leg.'

'You had to destroy him? How horrible.'

'Yes. I had a pistol with me, but of little use for game. Even birds were scarce after the long drought. So after I shot old Luther I cut up some of his carcass and dried it in the sun. It was the toughest thing I've ever tasted. But I knew I had to stay put till someone came looking for me, or it rained.'

'And what happened?'

'It rained, a most unusual occurrence. So I was able to get back on foot. I remember there was a rainbow late in the afternoon, a rare sight in that country. It seemed like a promise of succour. I remember my father telling me how he tried to find the end of the rainbow when he was a little boy. He had hardly seen rain before he was five years old.'

'But you said you came from Adelaide?'

'Yes. We moved there after Sam found the pot of gold.'

She did not follow that up, but said, 'My grandparents had a property in western New South Wales. It's very dry there too. But at least there are rivers.'

'We have rivers and lakes, all marked in blue on the map. I remember learning to draw them and colour them blue in geography at the Jamestown school. The trouble is, there's no water in them.'

'Not like this part of India! The Ganges must be a tremendous river away from the delta. I long to see it. And the Himalayas, and the Hindu Kush –'

'Nanda Devi, Mother of Snows . . .'

'What is that?'

'Just a mountain I read about. You can see it from Mussoorie, in the Hills. But tell me about your work. You are a trained nurse, and you work at the Church Mission Hospital?'

'Later. I must do justice to this delicious food.'

In fact, Elaine did not want to think about her hospital work just then, or about the other side of her life at all. India fascinated and appalled her, what she had seen of it. She had a sense of complete unreality at first, coming to visit in the ordered streets, the palatial homes, of the English quarter. She felt guilty just sitting down to tiffin, with half a dozen courses. She shut out of her mind's eye the emaciated forms, the gaunt cheeks, and sticklike arms which lifted in appeal from hospital stretchers.

She was haunted by the sight of two beggars she had seen near the Mission compound: a boy about six, entirely naked, with a scrotum so swollen with elephantiasis that it hung as big as a football between his legs; and a man with no legs who propelled himself with extraordinary agility through the feet of the crowds, on hands and backside, with the quickness of a spider. Then there was the blind boy with the beautiful smile, who was touted round by his sighted brother, begging for alms; and the body of an old man she had found, wrapped in his *dhoti*, lying in the gutter like a dead dog, with flies crawling into his mouth and the unheeding crowds passing him by. The Crosley-Sheridans were insulated from all this; their servants were comparatively well-paid and well-fed, and they did not visit the native quarter, that vibrant, sprawling, spawning other India! Where the bazaars were full of bright cloths and strange sweetmeats, dancing monkeys and swaying cobras moved to the rhythm of drum or flute, dancing-girls swung past in their bright skirts, jewels flashing in their nostrils, and high-caste Brahmin ladies picked their way to the vegetable market, attended by a servant with a beautiful handwoven basket over his arm.

It was the children in the hospital who upset her most. The cases of malnutrition and beri-beri, the small distended stomachs and wrinkled limbs, the old-looking faces of children who had never known what it was to be really well. Children with yaws, with deformed limbs, with no eyes, with tuber-culosis, with cancer . . .

There were lighter moments in her day. Like the time she had tried to wash a difficult Mohammedan patient who had just been admitted, in his white calico pantaloons and over-shirt. An orderly had removed the pantaloons, and the patient sat moodily on his bed, dressed in nothing but his shirt.

Elaine pulled the sheet discreetly up to his waist, and asked him to remove the shirt. 'I want to sponge you,' she ex-plained.

'I say no!'

'Off with your shirt, please. I can't wash you with it on,' she said, pulling at it.

'I say no!' he cried, pulling the shirt down again and sitting on it.

'Good fellow, Ali, off with your shirt now.'

'I say no, no, no!'

In the end she had to get the Indian orderly to wash him; his modesty was outraged at the thought of an infidel woman performing such a service . . .

Elaine applied herself determinedly to the second course. It would help no one if she refused to eat what was already prepared, and she must keep her strength up so that she could continue to do her bit, however small, to help a few of the suffering millions.

That night Elaine stayed with her friends. In her third-floor bedroom she let down her long red hair and took off her blouse and camisole. It was hot, but a warm breeze drifted in from the garden, bringing languorous scents of frangipani and magnolia. She sat in front of the mirror contemplating her breasts, which seemed fuller and more relaxed in the heat. As she brushed her hair, with her left hand she touched herself gently.

Insects drifted in the open window along with the night scents. They soon made a grisly pile about the lamp. She blew it out and looked from the high window at the yellow stars that seemed so close; there was the Scorpion, high in the zenith, the red star in its head glowing like another Mars. Her star was in the ascendant; the Scorpion ruled the midnight sky.

She got into bed in her cotton nightgown. The sound of one of the servants playing a *sitar* in the distance came to her on the breeze, and the *tim, tom, tam*! of a small hand-drum. She lay staring into the warm darkness, thinking of William King, thinking of the astrology booklet:

The Scorpio woman can often recognise a future mate at first glance. She wants one with civilisation, courage, and intelligence . . .

Yes, indeed! She had met her fate in a Calcutta churchyard.

Ten

WHEN WILLIAM had met Elaine Forbes for the second time – after the first encounter in the churchyard – it never occurred to him that she might make a suitable wife, though she had such striking good looks. He had felt a sympathy with her at once, simply because they were both Australians in a foreign country. But those enormous eyes, that hypnotic stare, had rather put him off. And she did have rather a lot of freckles, no doubt due to the Australian sun and her very pale creamy complexion.

He still called dutifully on Diana, but could not make up his mind to speak. His father had been lucky, but how many miserable marriages there were, people who jogged on in double harness which chafed them both unbearably, and so on for a whole lifetime! He meant to choose carefully.

Then Fate, as it seemed to him, took a hand. His gharry-driver took a sort of fit just as they were passing near the Church Mission Hospital. He managed to get the fellow inside, and who should receive him in the office but that red-headed Miss Forbes! She looked tall and stately in her uniform and was brisk and efficient in taking down details of what had occurred.

'He just keeled over, with his eyes rolled up in the top of his head and his mouth open. I managed to grab the reins and guide the horse here, as we were passing. By the way, if I could bring the vehicle inside and let the animal have a bit of shade under your trees – ?'

'Of course. Doctor's not on duty at present, but I'll do what I can meantime. He must be admitted for treatment. The horse cannot stand in the heat for hours.'

William went out and drove the gharry in under the big shady trees. He found an empty tin and a standpipe from which he filled it and gave the horse a drink. It looked as emaciated as its master, but he had nothing in the way of fodder for it.

Miss Forbes came out on the hospital veranda while he was gingerly removing the horse's bridle, for it had wicked-looking yellow teeth and was rolling its eyes, showing the whites in terror – no doubt used to being struck in the face by its driver whenever he came near.

'You have quite a feeling for horses, haven't you?' she called.

He flushed. 'You mean, more than I have for human beings?'

'Not at all. Many people would have simply hailed another gharry, and left the man to expire in the road, not brought him to hospital.' She came down the two shallow stone steps and patted the gharry-horse's thin neck. 'He's come round, by the way. He'll be all right.' She rubbed the horse between the ears.

'I think he might bite,' said William. 'But I see you're not afraid of horses.'

'I have ridden almost since I could walk,' she said. 'At Benangal they used to let me go out mustering, but of course I had to ride side-saddle. Such a bore! I wish women could go in for races and steeplechases. Though I have been in the Horses-in-Action at the Sydney Royal Show.'

'Really!' William beamed at her. She liked horses! She was an accomplished horsewoman!

'And you, I hear, have won the point-to-point this year.'

From then on the friendship flowered. He had no idea that Elaine Forbes had already made up her mind to marry him, but after they had been riding a few times on Sunday evenings, or early in the morning when she had a weekend off, he wondered why he had not seen what a wonderful girl she was to begin with. Then her second name was Hamilton, and her relatives were the Scottish Macdonalds who owned several sheep stations in western New South Wales and southwestern Queensland; her parents were of the Forbes pastoral family. For an Australian, she was very well-connected; the squatters, 'graziers' as they were called, were the nearest thing in Australia to the landed gentry of England.

Not that this weighed in the slightest with him, he told himself, but it would make the innocent snob in Mary happy. His mother, he knew, was aware that with all their new-found wealth and private yacht and magnificent home they were not socially acceptable in the tight little world of Adelaide. Grandpa might have been a big frog in Kuldunda, but he was nobody in the southern capital.

Also, it seemed that Elaine was Hamilton Forbes' only surviving daughter, and she, like Diana, could expect to be financially independent one day. He had not committed himself to Diana, fortunately, or at least not in words. She had never shown any particular preference for him over her other suitors, and all of them came a bad second to her dogs.

Apart from his rather tepid affair with his sister Elizabeth's friend Anne, William's experience of girls was limited to kissing one or two at Engineering Faculty dances, or rather after the dances when seeing them home. He had found it a pleasant experience, but compared with Sam at his age he was an innocent. On board ship coming out to India the competition had been too fierce, as men outnumbered young women five to one. Mothers of daughters liked him instinctively; they felt that he was 'nice' and tried to tell their daughters so, but in the perverse way of young women they preferred their own judgment, and the flashier young men that their mothers distrusted, to the quiet and dependable Willy.

He was a little disconcerted, as the Crosley-Sheridans had been, at Elaine travelling so far from home without a chaperone, or at least a companion of her own sex. Still, she was what was called a 'modern' girl, and next thing no doubt women would be smoking and wearing trousers!

He told her of the work he hoped to do at Gorobhunj, of his ambitions in life. She began teaching him Hindustani, in which she was already proficient.

'Though India has so many languages,' he said. 'They have books printed in at least ten; and where I am going, I believe they speak Oriya; though Hindustani will be understood by the house servants.'

'At least you will be away from the horrors of Calcutta,' she said, her wide, intense eyes upon him. 'Sometimes it is all too much for me.'

'You are overtired,' he said tenderly, feeling an urge to put back the heavy red hair from her white brow. 'It's the hot season beginning – '

'No, I mean that the tiny bit we can do, in such a great sea of suffering, seems scarcely worth while. Every moment there are more children being born to a life of malnutrition or an early death from starvation or disease. I feel so guilty sometimes, and so helpless.'

William saw his opportunity. 'My dear, dearest Miss Forbes . . . Elaine! At Gorobhunj, which is a small independent State, you could be of enormous help, and see the results of your efforts. Medically it is very backward, I believe, apart from the Maharaja's one Indian doctor, and a dispensary where the peasants come for medicines, there is nothing. If you would only marry me . . .' He took her hand.

Elaine flashed him a brilliant smile. 'Why, of course, dear Willy! I thought you were never going to ask me.'

He was so taken aback by her lack of maidenly reticence and hesitation, that he quickly took her in his arms to cover his own confusion. They were almost of a height, and their bodies met like two halves of a perfect whole, like a Filipino almond in one shell, he thought fleetingly. Then he kissed her, and found that the merely pleasant experiences of his student days were as nothing. He had come all the way to India to find an Australian girl who was to be the one woman in the world for him from that time forward.

Eleven

SAM KING had his portrait taken at a leading Adelaide studio, in stiff shirt and black bow tie, with the pearl studs. His hair was still abundant, but with two wings of silver which lent his rather florid face an air of distinction. 'Samuel King, Esq. of Kingsland Hall' he wrote on the back of the photograph with schoolboy vanity and sent one to each of his brothers.

For a time, his wandering and prospecting days seemed to be over. Of course he could not resist panning and washing a bit of sand in the creek. Mostly he strode about his new estate, admiring the growth of the shrubs he had planted: flowering camellias and Japanese ornamental plums, and a stand of Californian Papershell almonds which had blossomed already, almost before the winter was over.

He had repeated his success at Waterfall Gully, planting oranges on the level acres of good soil. They flourished so that he began to wonder if he should call the place 'Orange Grove'. The scent of orange blossom drugged the air, with the promise of golden fruit next winter. Mary suggested 'Golden Grove'.

'Enough blossom to make wedding wreaths for all the girls,' he said. Yet Mae and Alice had no suitors, and only Elizabeth and Ada had as yet worn orange blossom. Frances was still too young, and Harriet and Sarah were in the schoolroom.

William wrote from India that he was getting married; he also had an interesting appointment as engineer to the Maharaja of Gorobhunj, the ruler of one of the feudal States in the Orissa district, south of Calcutta. He and his new wife would be provided with accommodation, and the salary, compared with the Government PWD rate for a junior engineer, would be 'princely'.

Mary was delighted with the news of the wedding. Now that

she could produce no more children herself, she began to long for more grandchildren.

'How I should love to go to Calcutta for the wedding,' she sighed.

'But of course you can, my love. We can all go, if you wish. We can do anything we like.'

But stay-at-home Mary, who had never gone with Sam on any of his wild prospecting journeys, could not get used to the idea. She 'rather thought' she would just send a wedding present when the time came, and hope that Willy would bring his bride home for a visit.

'I doubt very much if he'll be able to get away for so long, when taking up a new appointment.'

And so it proved. William sent a silver-printed invitation from the Crosley-Sheridans, friends of his and the bride's who would entertain for her. Her father was coming out to India to give her away; he was Hamilton Forbes, of the well-known pastoral family of New South Wales. She was beautiful, tall and red-headed, and was working as a trained nurse with the Church Missionary Society when they met. He did not mention that she hoped to work among lepers when they went to Gorobhunj to live.

'It is a small and very *jungli* State, but with great possibilities,' he wrote. 'The young Maharaja is full of progressive ideas and wants a railway line and good roads, which of course mean bridges. His former tutor, an upright Englishman by the name of Cadell (who is married to an Australian, by the way), is still a power behind the throne. So we should get on all right.'

Sam sent off a set of silver goblets to the young couple. He had already ordered a set for himself, as well as a silver-gilt claret-bowl and claret ladle, with his and Mary's initials entwined on the handle. (Mary had embroidered 'MEK' for Mary Ellen King on all the new cushions, towels, and pillow cases; she said that the second Mrs King – for she was sure that Sam would outlive her – would have a terrible time unpicking them all after the wedding.)

'I don't like the sound of all that jungle,' sighed Mary, reading William's letter for the fifth time. 'It is probably full of cobras and tigers and leopards and things.'

'He doesn't mean "jungly" in our sense, exactly,' said Sam. '*Jungli* is one of those Anglo-Indian words like *pukka* and *gharry* used in northern India. *Jungli* just means a bit low-class, peasant-type, countrified and so on. The Orissa area has a lot of open country, I think – rice and hemp fields, and so on.'

'Well, I hope so, dear.'

Just when everything seemed perfect: no money worries, a beautiful home, William about to be settled with a most suitable girl, a new trouble lifted its head. Elizabeth, the third daughter, wrote hinting that all was not well. She had settled in Kuldunda with her husband, a man twenty years older than herself who had not been married before.

'Oh Mamma, I am so terribly unhappy. I cannot tell you what I have been through; I doubt if I can ever bring myself to tell you. Certainly I could never tell Father or Arthur.'

Mary wrote at once asking her home for a visit. She came on the very next train, travelling alone as her husband was busy with his store. She was overwhelmed by the size and grandeur of 'Kingsland Hall' and ran from room to room like a schoolgirl, exclaiming over everything and chattering 'nineteen to the dozen', as Mary said to Sam. Then, leaning on the wooden balustrade of the upstairs balcony and staring out at the golden globes of ripe oranges hung among dark leaves in the orangery beyond, she suddenly fell silent. Two large tears coursed down her cheeks and dropped unheeded off her chin.

Mary put an arm round her and drew her golden head down on her shoulder. She had been shocked at the first sight of Elizabeth: the wide, strained eyes, the shadows beneath them, the pale, thin cheeks. Was she going into a decline? Such things were not unknown with young girls. Pernicious anaemia, tuberculosis . . . Her mother's heart contracted in fear.

'What is it, dear? You can tell me. You're worried about your health, is that it?'

'Yes . . . no, that's not it.'

'I thought you would have had a little one to bring home to see us by now. Is anything wrong? Are you and Reuben not happy? There is Ada with four already.'

'*Happy*! Oh, Mamma! You told me I had to bear with

whatever he asked, that I would even come to like it! But he is revolting, I shrink when he touches me. I go to bed first, and pretend to be asleep, but it's no use. He – h – he . . .' She began to sob against Mary's capacious bosom. The younger girls peeped out curiously from the french windows.

'Go and ask Bessie to make some afternoon tea, girls,' said Mary briskly. 'I want to talk to Eliza alone . . . Now, dear, tell me. Is it so painful and unpleasant always? You must see a doctor. There are women doctors now, don't look so horrified. Someone like Dr Violet Plummer can help you. A simple operation called dilatation may be all that's needed.'

'Mamma, I couldn't tell a doctor about it, even a lady doctor. I can't speak of it.'

'Now, now child. It's perfectly natural –'

'That's just it! It's *not* natural, I'm sure. He makes me . . . with my back turned . . . and in the wrong place. And it hurts! Oh Mamma! It's disgusting, horrid. And then afterwards he expects me – in my mouth! He makes me do things I can't believe, looking at him so neatly dressed and respectable in the store next day, being civil to the ladies. And he's a beast! A beast! A beast!' She began to sob.

'There, there! There, there,' Mary rocked her in her arms, trying to find something to say. 'You poor child. What you have had to put up with! And you've never had – what would be called normal relations – even at the beginning?'

'Never! From what you told me, and some physiology books I have read. That is why I have never conceived, I'm sure.'

'You are not going back to him,' said Mary decisively. 'You are to come home to us. I am sure this is grounds for divorce, or better still, annulment. Fortunately your father can afford the best lawyers, and we will keep you out of court if possible.'

'I would rather die than stand up in court and tell what I have just told you.'

'Yes, dear, yes. I'll have to speak to Sam about it and see what he thinks.'

'Don't tell Father! He is a man too, and it seems to me that men are vile.'

'Not all of them, dear Eliza. Nor most of them. You have just been very unlucky. As you say, he *looks* so respectable!

But I fear that, while remaining unmarried, he has got into bad habits, visiting low women, and even young men, who would accommodate him for a fee.'

'Young *men*! Mamma, what on earth can you mean?'

Mary patted her shoulders. 'Never mind, you innocent child, I was just thinking aloud. Now wipe your eyes, and come and have a cup of tea. Bessie has made butterfly cakes especially for you.'

Mary, faced with telling Sam of their daughter's problem, felt some embarrassment in spite of her matter-of-fact attitude with Elizabeth. But in the blessed intimacy of the double bed which they had shared now for some thirty years, she told him about it, and of her determination that Elizabeth should never go back to her husband.

'Of course she needn't!' said Sam heartily. 'I never did like that fellow, I remember he had small, mean eyes, for all his fancy manners. Every orifice but the right one, eh! I should say he really prefers boys to girls.'

'I tried to tell her that, but she was even more shocked at the idea.'

'Yes, well, you come across it in a community of men only, as on the goldfields for instance. In South Africa they actually encouraged it. The Bantus were brought to work at the Jo'berg mines without their families, and kept there for years without seeing their wives. What were they supposed to do? I believe the white authorities thought it would even up the population a bit.'

'*That* is shocking,' said Mary.

'It's also true. I've a good idea: why don't we put a manager in here, and all go on a world trip? Of course 'Liza must free herself of this so-called marriage first.'

'Sam, she couldn't face a court case for annulment. If he will agree to a divorce, on the grounds of his adultery – and presumably he would rather that than have all the sordid details come out – it would be best. Though I doubt she will want to marry again. She said all men are vile!'

'Poor little kid! She doesn't know anything about it really, does she? What an insensitive bounder the man must be. Heavens, she was scarcely out of the schoolroom! *You* don't think men are vile, do you, my Mary?'

'Not you, anyway. Though I did get tired of having all those babies. Women do get the thin end of the stick, it seems to me.'

Sam roared his great uninhibited laugh and gathered her to him. 'Come here!' he said. 'Thin or thick, you know you like it. Don't you? Don't you?'

'Yes,' said Mary submissively. And then more strongly, 'Oh, yes, yes, yes!'

Twelve

THEIR TRIP to Kashmir for the honeymoon was something Elaine never forgot. In her memory the place was unreal, like a country visited in a dream: so beautiful, so incredibly 'picturesque' in the truest sense; wherever you looked the landscape made a picture.

She could close her eyes and summon up a vision of the calm blue expanse of Dal Lake on which their houseboat was moored. The pale pink of lotus blossoms clustered round the verge; the flower-sellers' boat heaped with blossoms, the snowy line of the Karakoram Range, beginning of the Himalayas, reflected like clouds in the still water: and over all a perfect windless calm, a sifting of sunlight, and the clarity of atmosphere that comes above five thousand feet; all *luxe, calme, et volupté*.

They had travelled by way of Delhi and Rawalpindi, so William saw all the places he had wanted to see. Then they had a week in Rawalpindi at the headwaters of the Indus, staying in a luxurious bungalow in the garden of Flashman's Hotel. Here Elaine saw her first mongoose, and was charmed by the little creature she had read about. Peacocks paraded and long-tailed birds with two trailing tail-feathers perched in the flowering shrubs.

Then there had been a rather hair-raising ride into the

Valley of Kashmir with landslides blocking half the road in places, while in others the outer edge of the road had slipped down into the valley. Once there was a fallen tree blocking the whole road and they had to wait while it was pushed aside.

There were parties of workmen all along the road keeping it in repair. They stopped overnight at a *dak* bungalow on the two-day journey and arrived tired but still cheerful at Srinigar, where houseboats were a way of life.

Their houseboat, with an elaborately carved wooden balcony in front and a kind of roof-garden with awnings on the top deck, was moored on the far side of the lake. They were paddled across by a handsome Muslim lad in the *shikara*, a luxurious canopied vessel with embroidered cushions and curtains, which belonged to their houseboat. In this they were paddled every day along winding waterways lined with lotus blossom, gliding as in a dream, while reflected clouds and mountains swam past below.

From the jewellers' boat William bought her a silver bracelet to replace the gold one she had given away, a curious two-headed snake of beaten and engraved silver with no catch: it just bent to fit the wrist. Made for a slender Indian hand, it refused to slip over Elaine's until William forced the two heads further apart.

The Shalimar Gardens were a little withered and dusty, the intricate waterfalls and cascading streams which came from natural springs were scarcely flowing. Elaine did not mind. The whole place enchanted her. She bought Numdah rugs for their new home, pieces of lacquer ware with Moghul hunting scenes, and exquisitely embroidered cloths in patterns of kingfishers and chenar leaves.

On the owner's boat moored behind, all the meals were cooked, delicious lamb and vegetable curries and rice dishes, brought on board by the Muslim owner's sons. The youngest, Abdul, was fascinated by the colour of her hair and tended to heroine-worship after she had bound up his foot with bandages from her first-aid kit when he cut it. He became their guide for gardens and bazaars.

'You are going?' he would inquire, bright-eyed and eager, as they called up the *shikara* paddled by his brother-in-law. 'I am going also? *We* are going?'

She hadn't the heart to refuse him, though William, in an absurd display of jealousy, said he would really like his bride to himself for a while. She pointed out that he had her to himself all night, every night, for once the dinner things were cleared away the houseboat servants all faded discreetly back to their own floating home.

Sam and Mary King and their five daughters set off on their world trip, calling at Calcutta first to meet William and his bride, who travelled up from Gorobhunj to see them. Elaine was pregnant already, she told Mary privately. She and Mary, so different in looks, temperament and background, took to each other at once.

Sam hired a suite at the Great Eastern Hotel and entertained William's Jockey-club friends, and anyone else he could persuade to accept his over-flowing hospitality. The Crosley-Sheridans, to Elaine's secret relief, were on leave in England. She found her exuberant father-in-law vastly entertaining, but she could imagine Mrs C.S.'s lifted eyebrows, and her husband's British accent: 'The fellah's like all these damned Colonials, splashes his money around in a rather vulgah way, don't you know.'

Sam, who had been to India before, enjoyed showing off his bit of Hindustani to his family. He chaperoned them in strings of rickshaws to the Botanic Gardens and other sights of the city, while dispensing handfuls of *bucksheesh* to the poor.

Elizabeth had not gone back to her husband. Mary had agreed to the trip mainly to take her daughter's mind off her troubles, while Sam thought they might find a husband for the rather plain and mousy Mae on their travels. Arthur's legal firm was handling Elizabeth's divorce, agreed to by Reuben who had paid a woman to help him provide 'evidence'. As Sam told his wife, buggery was a crime in the Statute books, and even though a wife was not supposed to give evidence against her husband and though they knew that wild horses couldn't drag Eliza into court to testify, the man would be too scared for his skin to refuse a divorce on the grounds of adultery.

The divorce was expected to go through by the time they returned. Elizabeth had become a different girl, lively and laughing, walking round the decks arm-in-arm with her sisters. As soon as the ship cleared Port Adelaide and the Outer Harbour and the coast of South Australia with its hateful memories was left behind, she seemed to forget the past. Only sometimes she would fall silent, her eyes wide and staring; then she would blink them swiftly as if trying to shut out some picture too unpleasant to contemplate. She and Mary never spoke again of the cause of her unhappiness, while she avoided being alone with her father, knowing the things he must have told the lawyers to make Reuben agree.

Sam had thoroughly enjoyed the sea voyage. He always liked being at sea: the open bar, the yarning on deck, the games of cards in the saloon. He was soon known as a high bidder, a reckless gambler, and a good loser. He would bet on anything: the relative speeds of two albatrosses following the ship, or the time they would first sight land, or the length of the ship's daily run. On any voyage he became a personality, known to everyone, including the stewards, who remembered him for his generous tips.

From Calcutta they sailed on to Colombo and then to England through the Suez Canal, a wonderful time-saving route which had been opened since their families made the long journey round the Cape of Good Hope by sailing ship. In England, Sam went to Buckinghamshire to look for family graves at Aylesbury and Ivinghoe. Perhaps he hoped to find some titled ancestors who had once occupied a home like Kingsland Hall. All he found were yeomen farmers in the parish records and a few centuries-old graves, but then, he reasoned, how did the family get the name 'King' in the first place?

'Perhaps one of them was called King of the Moock-Heap!' said Mary, laughing at him.

They stayed in an expensive hotel at Marble Arch, seven of them and the governess. Mary went down to Truro to visit her mother's grave, for she had died about the same time as Robert King.

'Now,' said Sam, after they had 'done' the sights of London, 'shall we go to the Continent, or the New World: the

United States, Canada, the Rocky Mountains, Niagara Falls – '

The girls rather wanted to see Paris. Mary felt she'd had enough of 'foreigners' in India and would prefer somewhere the people spoke English. So Sam took the girls for a week to France, while Mary did some shopping and packing. Then they all set sail across the Atlantic, Mary and Sam taking a stateroom for the voyage. It was to be the last time that Samuel lived like a king.

Elaine and William were alone in the warm, scented darkness, where huge yellow stars hung in the sky. At first she had insisted on wearing the high-necked, long-sleeved muslin nightdresses from her trousseau, but William argued that they were unnecessary, hot, and restricting.

'But I couldn't sleep with *nothing* on!'

'Why ever not? The thing was up round your neck all night last night, anyway.'

'Really, William!' But she laughed. That night she slipped into bed without a nightdress and discovered a new freedom. He kissed her all over in gratitude. She thought of the night she had sat by the open window at the Crosley-Sheridans, admiring her own breasts.

'You know, we are taught to have a horror of nudity,' she said. 'All the nursing procedures which involve a doctor examining a woman are complicated by sheets that have to be bound and pinned around, above and below, with just a teeny opening for him to get at the part he wants to see. Even bathing in hospital – we had to keep a sheet over the patient having a sponge bath, so her top end was covered while we were washing the bottom end, and vice versa. It really is ridiculous.'

'Did you never feel embarrassed at having to bathe men patients – all over?'

'Oh, we just washed down to the waist and up to the buttocks, and then handed them the flannel to finish off the more intimate parts themselves. Unless, of course, they were too ill to manage, and then it didn't matter.'

'No, I suppose not. Did your patients ever fall in love with you?'

'Yes, occasionally. It's an occupational hazard. But hospital romances are like shipboard ones; they rarely last once the voyage, or the hospitalisation, is over. Nurses fall in love with doctors, too. I had a terrible infatuation for a leading surgeon in Sydney. He had a beautiful wife and three children, and I knew it was quite hopeless.'

'Are you sure you're not still in love with him?'

'*Quite* sure. Though it's one of the reasons which made me want to come to India, where I would never see him again. I used to turn faint and tremble all over when he walked into the ward. I was furious with myself, it was so stupid, but I couldn't help it.'

'Did you ever turn faint when *I* came into the room?' asked William jealously.

'No, silly. With you it was all calm and perfect and right. I knew the first time I met you that I wanted to marry you, and no one else. And when I saw you, before that, in the grounds of the Mission Church. It was truly love at first sight. And then, when you kissed me, I knew for certain.'

'Like this . . . ?' His kiss deepened and became more insistent. She felt herself expanding like a flower.

'Oh, yes!' And then, some time later, gently caressing his bare foot with hers as they lay flung apart on the hot tumbled bed, sweating, relaxing in the still, airless Indian night, she said, 'I think marriage is the most wonderful invention ever made.'

By the time they left Calcutta, the weather was building up to the season of monsoon rains. On the train, the restaurant car could be reached only by braving the heat of the platform, and the dinner was the standard one: mulligatawny soup, roast chicken, and caramel custard.

Though glad that she was pregnant, Elaine would have liked a year to adjust to her new position, to get used to the servants, to running the house. She had always been a good housewife, but she knew little about running a home in India. Mrs Crosley-Sheridan had given her some advice, however: 'All drinking water must be boiled; even what you clean your teeth with. Make sure that no night-soil is used in the vegetable garden. Have the salad vegetables washed in Condy's crystal solution just in case. And keep all your food supplies under lock and key. The cook must come to you to unlock the pantry when he needs supplies.'

Elaine thought the first three conditions were sensible ones, given the incidence of typhoid and cholera in the country. But she refused to keep kitchen supplies locked up, and to have to unlock the pantry whenever the cook needed some flour or rice.

'I intend to trust the servants,' she told William. 'And I believe if I treat them well they won't cheat me. Even if they do, it won't be for very much, and it must seem to them that we have such a lot of everything, and they have so little.'

Mrs Cadell, whose husband had been tutor to the young Maharaja when he was growing up (when after his father's death his widowed mother, the old Maharani, had wielded the power behind the throne), still had great influence at the Palace. She was also very kind to her fellow-Australian, Elaine, and helped her to engage servants. She said that she had never kept her store-cupboards locked and had never been robbed. She engaged to give Elaine lessons in Oriya each afternoon at siesta time; another thing they both agreed on was that sleeping in the middle of the day was a terrible waste of time.

Elaine had thought that she might make do with only two or three servants, but soon realised that this was not practicable in India. Each servant kept strictly to his own duties: the coachman, the groom and *syces* would have nothing to do with anything but horses; they would not, on the other hand, stoop to sweep out the stables, which must be done by men of the 'sweeper' caste. Again, men of low caste had to be employed to clean the bathrooms and empty the commodes.

Slightly higher in the hierarchy came the gardener and his assistant, then the house-servants, not only cook and kitchen man, but bearers to carry the food to the dining-room, serve drinks, take children (when there were any) for walks, and clear away, though they would not wash up. The butler ruled over the kitchen staff and presided over the ordering of meals: a portly Hindu in resplendent white suit and immaculate turban, from which starched ends fluttered in the breeze of his motion. And, essential to comfortable meals, the lowly punkah-wallah to sit in the archway into the dining-room and pull the rope of the giant fan.

Women were not employed very much, except as personal maids or as *ayah*s, nursery-maids for young children.

Altogether there were a dozen house servants, some with wives and children, including William's valet Hoitri, who was in charge of the bedroom, and saw to it that the baths were prepared and the master's clothes taken to the *dhobi*. The washing was done on the shore of the lake below the palace, where there were some shallow rocks, and here men and women rubbed the clothes with yellow soap, in the plain cold water, then lifted them high and bashed them against the rocks to remove the dirt. Spread to dry on the grass in the sun, they came back clean and sweet-smelling.

The living quarters consisted of a large bungalow, all on ground level, with its airy, high-ceilinged living-rooms opening through white-plastered arches into each other to give a feeling of spaciousness. The floors were tiled for coolness, the windows shaded with *tattees* and outside shutters. But as William remarked, there were drawbacks to the convenience of living on ground level, with only two steps up to the veranda: they were safe from thieves and *dacoits* inside the grounds, but there was nothing to stop wandering snakes from invading the bedrooms. It was to be hoped that with so many servants they would be detected at once and removed.

However, he had a nasty experience with a krait in their first few weeks. Taking the rolled-up *Times of India* which had been lying for some time unopened, he cut the binding and gave the paper a flick to unroll it. He saw the slender, deadly snake fly out of the other end. 'Quick! Get up on the table!' he commanded Elaine, who hopped up at once, drawing her long skirts away from the edge. Then he proceeded to despatch the snake with a long ornamental sword which hung on the wall, a present from the Maharaja (who had explained that it was a ceremonial sword which once was used for disembowelling faithless priests). After that William opened his papers very gingerly, and kept a pronged stick in the corner of every room. The statistics for snakebite were horrifying: in one of the outlying villages, in 6 months four people had died from drowning, two from tiger attacks, and fifteen from snakebite. Crocodiles were probably involved in the drowning cases. One which was killed was found to contain several undigested silver bangles and anklets from women victims.

Other creatures invaded the house. On her very first night at home, Elaine was luxuriating in a cool tub after the heat and dust of the long journey by train. Trickling water down her back from a soft sea-sponge, she gave a sigh of content. Then she looked over the side of the bath and the sigh became an indrawn breath of horror, then a piercing scream.

William, already in bed in the adjoining bedroom and impatiently awaiting her, leapt up as though he had been stung. Grabbing his riding crop, the only weapon handy, he rushed into the bathroom.

Elaine was pointing a trembling, wet arm towards the floor.

'What is it? A python? Or a cobra?' he cried.

'No, no, look! The most enormous – horrible – disgusting – cockroaches you have ever seen! Eekh! Look at them scuttle! I daren't get out of the bath in my bare feet! Do something!'

William flung the riding crop down on the cement floor.

'Really, Elaine! Cockroaches! What a ridiculous fuss. I thought – ' He looked around for something to swat them with, and picked up the sweeper's heavy scrubbing brush.

'No! No! Don't squash them! I can't bear the smell. Just carry me out of here.'

William saw that she was genuinely upset. He took a bath-sheet, lifted her wet, slippery form and wrapped it, then carried her like a parcel to the bedroom, where he dumped her rather unceremoniously on the bed.

'I'll get some insect powder in the morning. It's just that the house hasn't been used for a while.'

'I'm sorry, Willy dear. You will think me an idiot. But I cannot *bear* the things. We had them in the old hospital in Adelaide where I was training, and they gave me the horrors. But these – ! They're as big as mice!'

'And just as harmless. Dirty things, I agree, and we'll get rid of them. But I thought it was a snake. You gave me a fright, screaming like that. You're usually such a sensible girl.'

'Even sensible girls can have phobias. Some women are terrified of mice, you know, or of bats getting in their hair, or of spiderwebs. Personally I had far rather meet a snake in the bathroom than a cockroach. Please close the sliding door so they can't come in here!'

He did so, grumbling. 'All the same, I bet you'd scream the house down if you saw a cobra in the bathtub.'

'I would not! I've shot plenty of brown snakes at home, and they're just as deadly. Tiger snakes, too. And red-bellied black –'

'All right, all right, you're not frightened of snakes.'

It led to their having a shooting contest the next day with William's Express rifle. When Elaine hit a bottle at fifty yards, he agreed that she probably *could* shoot a snake – even a moving one. He set up a small copper *pais*, the size of a farthing, and pierced it with his third bullet. It put him in a good mood for the rest of the day. The sweeper sprinkled all the cracks in the bathroom with insect powder, and William put down baits of borax and sugar.

After that Elaine saw nothing but a few grisly bodies, which she draped with tissue-paper so that they were out of sight until the sweeper removed them in the morning.

Besides being frightened of cockroaches, Elaine was nervous of elephants when she was standing on the ground near them. Their intelligent eyes, appearing small and knowing in the vast grey wrinkled expanse of their foreheads, seemed to her to have a conscious, considering look, as though they were deciding whether to pick her up in their trunks or trample her into the ground. She knew of course that they were thoroughly domesticated and that the Mahouts looking so small up on their necks could control them with just their voice and a small pointed stick; but still she was illogically afraid. 'They're just too big!' she said to William.

Sometimes they went touring by elephant, when the country was waterlogged from the Rains. In the dry season they went on shorter picnic excursions. Riding down an empty river bed of soft sand, they would see the elephants' great feet sinking out of sight at every step. As they returned late in the afternoon, the sun made flecks of mica in the sand sparkle like thousands of pink diamonds.

Elaine climbed very gingerly up to the howdah of the kneeling elephant on which they were to ride. Mrs Cadell, with the contempt born of years of familiarity, would ignore the steps and the offer of helping hands, and taking a firm grip, climb up the elephant by its tail like a mountaineer going up a rope. None of them ever objected to this indignity.

On Sunday morning the mahouts brought the Maharaja's dozen State elephants into the paved square in front of the palace, to salute him with uplifted trunks and a unified trumpeting. Soon after Elaine and William moved into their bungalow nearby, Easter arrived, the first for both of them in the strange land. On Good Friday they were still in bed when a tremendous trumpeting sounded outside the front door. Grabbing a cotton housegown, and putting her feet in slippers, Elaine ran to the front veranda. William hastened after her, rubbing his eyes. There in their front garden, arranged in a perfect line on the lawn with their heads towards the front door, were the twelve elephants: toenails polished, skins gleaming with oil, foreheads decorated with coloured paint. Each mahout gave a signal, and in perfect unison the elephants raised their trunks in a salaam.

It was a charming gesture from the Maharaja, his personalised greeting from the Palace to the bungalow.

Before she grew too big for travelling in comfort, Elaine went on one of William's surveying trips to the south, into tiger country. They arrived in a village where the people were still alarmed over a tiger which had taken a village woman two days before as she went alone for water. It was growing dusk, and William and his assistant explained that they could do nothing that night, but if the people would build a tiger-trap and tether a goat near it, they would deal with the tiger once caught. Elaine was indignant. She thought it unfair to the tiger, to shoot it in a trap, but even more unfair to the goat which was to be used as live bait.

That night Elaine slept very little. She got up and put chairs under the handles of the flimsy doors of the *dak* bungalow. She kept waking and fancying she heard the pad of great paws on the wooden veranda. By morning she was feeling less sorry for the tiger, which after all was a known man-eater, or rather woman-eater. William, who had seen the bloodstained sari and one torn-off arm belonging to the unfortunate woman, was not sorry for it at all. He could scarcely sleep for excitement, and for Elaine prowling round to make sure the shutters were fastened and the chairs firmly fixed under the door-handles.

It was a bit of an anti-climax to find in the morning that there was nothing in the trap. The tiger was evidently too wary a beast to be fooled in such a fashion. The villagers were in a state of excitement, for the tiger had taken one of their working bullocks from the compound during the night. In their poverty, this meant even more than the death of a woman. The beast was a daring one and would probably strike again. They pointed to the drag marks in the sandy river bed, leading toward an island with only one large tree in the middle. On his touring elephant, William waded across to the island and there found the mutilated bullock under the tree, and the pug-marks of a large tiger.

He ordered a webbing bed to be fixed in a fork of the tree as a makeshift *machan*, or shooting platform, with a ladder of twisted vines which he could pull up after him. Before sunset he prepared to spend the night alone in the tree. After he had stepped from the elephant's back to the swinging ladder, the mahout took her away out of the danger zone until morning. Elaine stayed in the *dak* bungalow and worried about William.

He told her afterwards that it was the longest night he ever spent. Mosquitoes sang about his ears, large red ants crawled over him, moths flew against his face, but he had to stay motionless, utterly silent, and keep wide awake. Jungle creatures rustled in undergrowth, night-birds called, but there was no sign of the tiger in the bright moonlight. He may have dozed, but he did not think so. There was no movement that he saw, no sound, not even the rustle of a leaf, but there suddenly was the tiger, on the far edge of the clear space beneath the tree. It looked round lazily, evidently quite unalarmed, and yawned like a domestic cat. It was a male, a magnificent beast, its striped coat blending with the moonlight and shadow on the sand. Then it strolled across to where its left-over dinner was waiting.

His heart beating suffocatingly, William fired. The tiger gave a mighty spring, turned in the air, and landed on its running feet. Before William could load and fire again it was gone. He heard it splashing through the water to the far bank of the river, and shouted 'Damnation!'

In the morning when the elephants came back with daylight, he searched the ground but there was no sign of blood. He had not even wounded it. William was disgusted with himself. The villagers, however, said at least he had frightened it away for the time being. William said that if it came back, the Maharaja would organise a full *shikar* with beaters. Only Elaine felt rather glad the tiger had escaped.

The bungalow drawing-room was elegant, with its baby grand piano and kerosene bracket lamps on the walls: brass with pale pink china shades like fluted waterlilies which made a soft glow. Elaine would play after dinner, in a low-cut evening dress, her piled red hair gleaming like fire in the warm pink light.

The big dining-room through an alcove held the locked gun-rack, ornamental swords, and some of William's trophies of the chase; a stuffed pheasant, a fan of peacock-feathers, and the head of a bear with glass bead eyes. Here William took Divine Service at ten on Sunday mornings, when all the staff were expected to attend: Christian, Hindu and Moslem joining in the hymns in their own language, while Elaine pedalled the harmonium.

The favourite drive in the evening, or when there were visitors to be shown round, was in the open landau with the four-in-hand trotting sedately out the gate, down the avenue of sal trees, round the end of the lake and past the leafy Mission compound, to the huge grove of mango trees with their thick canopy of shade, where the State buildings were, including the Public Works building where William had his office. His first job had been to design smooth new roads to and from this area, and now the landau bowled along them in fine style. Though it was not 'the thing' to drive yourself,

William sometimes took the reins from the coachman on the way back, for the horses were a joy, perfectly matched and with mouths like silk.

From the office square a wide dirt road led on to the scattered villages and farms, and eventually to the jungle, the forests of teak and ebony, and the Magasani Hills on the horizon. In the other direction, past the Palace, the village, and the bazaar, were the wide paddy fields of rice, the paddocks of jute and maize, on the fertile floodplains of the Great Python River, and the swamps where crocodiles, cobras and tigers lurked.

Visitors to the Palace were always taken on a tiger-hunt, usually by elephant, to bag the magnificent Bengal tiger, largest of the Indian big cats. No one thought for a moment that the tiger might one day become almost extinct, while the men and women he preyed on would proliferate on the face of the earth till there would be scarcely room for other living creatures.

All was green, lush, fast-growing, abundant: waterlilies on the lake, flowering hibiscus and tulip tree in the garden, ripe mangoes falling in the grass. Sometimes William thought of the dry plains about Beetoota in far-off South Australia, the empty watercourses and the drifting sand. Apart from the heat, it might have been on another planet. He said to Elaine that he would like to travel in the Deccan, and in the desert regions beyond the Indus, towards the borders of Persia and Afghanistan.

'Sometimes I long for a nice, clean, empty desert,' said William. 'There is such an *abundance* of life here, from leaves to flowers to people. And of course, though it looks like the Garden of Eden, it's crawling with serpents.'

He had not forgotten his brush with the krait in the rolled newspaper. It was also cobra country.

One night in bed they were having one of their quite vociferous arguments over the meaning of some word, when Elaine jumped out of bed in her bare feet to go to the bookshelves in the dining-room for a dictionary. Because of the cockroach incident, William took little notice when he heard her scream.

But she came staggering to the bedroom door, her face

between the long red cascades of her hair white with shock.

'Willy! Willy! I've been bitten . . . by a krait. It was on the floor in the shadow of the bookcase and I trod on it. Look, look!' And she pointed to the two red puncture marks, oozing dark blood, on her instep.

Without hesitating William gave a quick draw on the cigar always in his hand and jammed the burning end against the bite. Elaine screamed again, and fainted. One of the servants was sent for Dr Gupta, and when she came round Elaine found that William had tied an efficient tourniquet above her knee and had tracked down the snake and killed it. William poured some whisky and water between her chattering teeth.

Dr Gupta, when he came, praised William's presence of mind; though Elaine had a nasty burn and would bear a scar for life, the cauterisation performed within seconds of the bite had stopped the poison from spreading. The doctor had a wide experience of snakebite, and after dressing the wound assured them that they had nothing to fear.

'And there is no need to walk her up and down and keep her awake,' he added. 'That has always been a fallacy. She should rest completely with the foot raised.'

'Thank you, Doctor.' Elaine gave him a wan smile. 'I'm sorry to have called you out in the middle of the night.'

Their first dinner at the Palace was something of an ordeal for Elaine, though the old Maharani did not appear. She had to call on her first in the Zenana, the women's quarters of the Palace, built around a marble-paved courtyard in which white peacocks strayed among fountains and flower-beds. Maharani Vashti was a small, very erect figure in white widow's dress of plain sari, without jewels or border or ornamentation of any kind. She had dignity but little conversation. Her women attendants, in coloured saris, handed sticky jellabies and other sweetmeats on a brass tray.

There were long pauses while Elaine sought desperately for something to say to this strangely magnetic person, wise in the ways of men and affairs, yet wholly cut off from the great world beyond. She sat erect, her hands folded in front of her, a gracious smile fixed upon her rather purplish lips, her dark eyes slightly ironic in their expression. If it had not been for her daughter, Diwa – gorgeous as a parrot in her orange and blue sari edged with gold, a diamond twinkling from her left nostril, sapphires in her ears – the silences would have been unbearable. But once she came in, bringing her pretty little niece Devi, things brightened up at once. She spoke animatedly: 'You come from Australia, too, where Mrs Cadell has come from? What a coincidence, isn't it? In all my life I have met only three Australians: you, your husband, and Mr Cadell's wife. It is a large country, like India? But not, I think, nearly so hot!'

'It can get *very* hot in the interior,' said Elaine. 'Weeks over a hundred degrees – months in some places, like Marble Bar in Western Australia. I come from eastern Australia, from New South Wales: Mr King from South Australia, where it is very hot in the remote parts of the State. And dry. Those beautiful blue lakes you see on the maps are dry salt-pans.'

'Then how is it most different from India?'

'In the people! I don't mean the difference in race, but in numbers. We have about four million people, you have a hundred times as many. It is what strikes me at once about India, the numbers of people everywhere, in the streets, in the bazaars, even in the country! In Australia you can travel six hundred miles without coming to a city; two thousand miles if you travel through the centre.'

Devi, whose mother had spoken no English so she had learnt very little, pulled at Elaine's hand. She wanted to show her the pet spotted deer she kept in a grass-covered courtyard at the back. Then the dancing girls, who had no English at all, led them up to the flat roof for a game of badminton.

Devi was very good at this, moving as quickly as a young panther, batting the shuttlecock vigorously; but her sari would keep blowing in the wind, getting in the way, which made her cross. Her black, oiled, gleaming hair lay in a heavy plait across her shoulder. She was so slender waisted that she looked as if she might break in two if roughly handled. The dancing girls giggled with delight whenever they managed to make a stroke, which was not often.

Then they all trooped back to the Maharani's sitting-room for afternoon tea. Diwa brought her embroidery and asked for help, for she wanted to learn some new stitches from Mrs

Cadell. Elaine helped to untangle the knotted skeins of silk. She was impatient with embroidery. It was too 'fiddly', like the tatting which her great-grandmother had once tried to teach her.

Tea was now served by the waiting-women, first to the Maharani and then to her guests. Elaine took a sip from her cup and put it down again. The tea had been made with rose-water, which gave it a sickly, scented taste. She drank it all out of politeness, but refused a second cup.

Diwa was questioning her eagerly once more, about her home in Sydney. She had been in purdah most of her life, and though she had been to Calcutta, she longed to hear about the world beyond the Zenana.

'And you have trained as a nurse, isn't it? In a hospital, with men doctors?'

'Yes, and I have made a study of leprosy. I should like to start a clinic where lepers could be brought for treatment, not shunned and feared – '

'And what makes you think, Mrs King, that we have leprosy in Gorobhunj?' interposed the Maharani silkily. 'This is a very advanced State, we have our own Medical Service apart from the British. As my son will tell you.'

Elaine was abashed, but she replied spiritedly, 'Because leprosy is endemic in India, and until superstition is replaced by education – '

'We also have village schools, subsidised by the State.'

'I mean education of the village people, the adults, so that they know how to avoid infection, so that children are not infected by their families. For it is not a very contagious disease.'

'It is not a very pleasant subject, either. Please take a sweetmeat, Mrs King.'

Elaine took the hint, and kept off the subject of leprosy clinics at dinner; but she resolved that with the help of Ruth Cadell she would get the Maharaja's ear and ask for help in her project. For of course there *were* lepers in Gorobhunj; she had seen noseless faces and fingerless hands among the beggars outside the Mission Compound.

William worked on drawings in his den, and read up the requirements for earth-fill dams (which had been used in

India since ancient times) in Craig, Justin's *Engineering for Dams*:

> A large bank of earth usually with side slopes battered at
> 1 in 2½ to 1 in 3 and with base very wide in proportion to its
> height . . . the design most suitable where the foundation
> is of earth as the load per sq ft. brought to bear on the
> foundation is considerably less than would be the case with
> a gravity dam of heavy rock construction. The dam itself is
> rendered watertight by provision of a central core of im-
> pervious materials, formed of selected silt and clay fill,
> 'watered in' as the dam bank rises. . . . This is most suited
> to the climate of India as the shrinkage of soil during the
> hot season and expansion during the following monsoon,
> sets up forces destructive to solid-core walls . . .

The next on the agenda would be the light railway, involving
several wooden overpasses across ravines, to the back country. This was a project dear to the Maharaja's heart. He had
been educated at Calcutta University and had travelled on
railway lines built by the British Raj, which fascinated him.
The Maharaja was also very keen on chess.

William, whose favourite sports were riding and shooting,
was impatient with games, needing all his spare time from
work for reading, riding and driving, and was often away on
surveying trips. Elaine found herself summoned to the Palace
to play chess with the Raja on his exquisitely carved ivory and
ebony set – hand-made in Gorobhunj, which got much of its
wealth from the export of these two materials, besides the sale
of working elephants brought in from the back country and
trained by his own mahouts.

She had realised at once that the Maharaja, for all his sad
face and melancholy eyes, was a ladies' man who could no
more help trying to impress a presentable woman than a
peacock could help displaying before a hen. He paid her
subtle compliments and touched her hand during play more
than was necessary. Fortunately she was not attracted,
though he exuded an aura of powerful sexuality. Yet every
game became a kind of sexual contest. He had a compulsion

to win, to dominate, to subjugate her, and would move his pieces to the Checkmate position with an arrogant smiling deliberation and sweep her Queen from the board with his smooth brown hand. She did not allow herself to win too often, for when she did he sulked. Mrs Cadell, sitting close under the lamp to do her embroidery, the necessary chaperone on these occasions, would give Elaine the smile of an accomplice, and would jolly him back into a good mood.

When a Palace party went riding, complete with attendant syces, or on a partridge-shooting expedition, the same thing happened: Elaine, excellent horsewoman that she was, would gallop ahead, the streamers of her puggaree'd helmet flying in the wind. He always whipped up his horse and passed her – for he had the better mount, a beautiful white Arab bred in the State – with a triumphant, conquering look from his dark eyes. Elaine, secure in her love for William, her coming motherhood, quite enjoyed his attentions. Though she soon had to give up riding because of her condition, she continued to play chess with him, and was not above using her charm to get his approval for the leprosy clinic.

As soon as she mastered Oriya, she had gone out and spoken with the outcasts begging in the village streets: in rags, casteless, more shunned even than the Untouchables or Harijans of the lowest caste. At first they could not believe that a memsahib – a white lady who rode in a carriage – was actually talking to them, and in their own tongue. They were bewildered and scarcely answered her. But gradually she gained their confidence, told them that she was trained in medicine and in the use of Chaulmoogra oil, the new miracle treatment which would arrest their terrible piecemeal decay. They promised to come in for treatment as soon as she had a refuge built for them. She was to be helped in her work by two English ladies of uncertain age, who had come as missionaries to the State and were running a Christian school for village children with the blessing of the broad-minded Hindu ruler.

Elaine wrote home to her father:

You asked if we ever dined at the Palace, and if so what did we have to eat. Occasionally when there are European visitors to the State we dine there . . . What we had to eat on the few occasions I have been there might have been anything: it was very spiced and hot. Great dollops of this curry affair were put on enormous platters, one in front of each guest, and round the platters were little bowls of all the things that go with curries – sweet chutney, rice and so on.

The second course was a sweetmeat of some kind, but just as hot and spiced as the first. Our throats were burnt, I almost felt steam coming out of my ears! Then came a juicy-looking slice of pineapple, exactly what we were wanting – until we came to taste it and tears started out of our eyes.

'Do you always curry your pineapple?' I asked the Maharaja's cousin who was sitting next to me.

'No,' he replied quite affably, 'but we rub it with a chilli to make it taste more pungent.'

When a servant came round with finger-bowls of scented water I felt like drinking it instead, to soothe my poor throat.

Thirteen

THE MAHARAJA of Gorobhunj had great charm for most Europeans who met him. He was always courteous; he spoke beautiful English with the slightest of foreign accents; he had a melancholy smile but on occasions could laugh like a schoolboy. He wore gorgeous gold-embroidered tunics of white silk over fitted white trousers, or in cooler weather velvet tunics trimmed with gold braid and precious stones, and on his head an embroidered velvet cap, or a white turban with jewelled aigrette.

Elaine liked to see men dress up like peacocks; it was so much more interesting than the plain business suits at home: two stovepipes and a square jacket, with a bowler hat above.

Here the Governor would sometimes arrive from Calcutta, resplendent in whites with golden epaulettes and a gold-spiked pith helmet trimmed with white cocks' feathers. William went about in khaki work clothes of shorts and bush jacket, and a solar topee. He would change into a tussore silk suit for dinner, and Elaine had bought him a brilliant cummerbund which he had so far refused to wear.

On jungle or swamp journeys he wore long trousers and riding boots as an insurance against snakes and leeches. He had found the roads dangerous, deep in dust which hid the pot-holes; and one with such a deep hole, still full of water, that there were waterlilies growing in it. But the ruler's first priority was a series of dams and tanks.

With permanent water close to each village, women were less likely to be taken by tigers or crocodiles as they went down to the river with their washing, for the village wells were only for cooking and drinking-water. And the dams could be used for irrigation when the monsoon failed, as in the dreadful famine year of 1865. William felt that the Maharaja sincerely wished to use his great wealth to help his people to a better life. Already he had established schools in the outer villages.

Ram Chandra Gobind, product of centuries of fine breeding, ruled over an area of nearly four thousand square miles: swampy coastal plains, inland mountains, and forests which provided wealth from ebony and elephants, teak, and wild silk from the tussar silkworm. Elaine found him a fascinating study. During one of his frequent absences in Calcutta she asked Mrs Cadell about him. Ruth Cadell, a motherly person in her fifties, had known him as the 'Minor Maharaja' when he was still a lad.

'He's very fond of his children,' said Elaine, 'especially Devi. But what happened to their mother?'

'She died of smallpox; there's a monument to her in the Palace gardens. She was very young, very beautiful. She was only fifteen when they married.'

'It seems unnatural for such a vigorous, handsome man to live alone.'

Mrs Cadell smiled, and pressed her needle through the base of an embroidered leaf. 'He doesn't live alone, exactly. He has a wife in Calcutta, and a concubine in the Palace.'

'But – !' Elaine's mouth had dropped open in surprise. 'But why Calcutta?'

'Ah, my dear, it's a long, sad story. When he was a youth studying at Calcutta University, he fell in love with a very intelligent, very emancipated girl. Selmi was the sister of one of his student friends. The affair lasted several years, and they were regarded as engaged; but she was not an orthodox Hindu, and because of that, and caste differences, the State and the family opposed the match. They insisted he should marry a Hindu girl of high caste and produce an acceptable heir.'

'How romantic! So he gave up the love of his life for the throne.'

'He gave it up through a sense of duty to his people, I think. This had been bred into him very strongly, and then he had so many ideas he wanted to carry out – for schools and hospitals and better roads and so on. He asked my husband's advice – for he regarded George as a father – and he told him he should put Gorobhunj first.'

'And Selmi?'

'Never loved anyone else. She refused all offers of marriage, much to her father's disgust. Three years after Gobind's first wife died, they were married, but she was still *persona non grata* in the State. She could never come here to live, nor her children. He has built her a beautiful home in Calcutta and, in defiance of opinion at home, calls it Gorobhunj House.'

'How long did she wait for him?'

'Fourteen years.'

'Wouldn't you think, after they had waited so long and he'd provided a Hindu heir for the State, they would have let him marry the woman of his choice?' said Elaine.

'No, the forces of religion and custom were too strong.'

'And even though she's his legal wife, he can't bring her here?'

'Never. His mother would not receive her.'

'Do you know her? Is she beautiful?'

'Yes, I've met her in Calcutta. She's very lovely, but with a sad face.'

'The things that are done in the name of religion! And he is still officially Hindu?'

'Strictly so, when at home, probably not when abroad. Here, he eats no meat and no food that has not been prepared by a Brahmin cook of the highest caste. But he has made a study of comparative religion, and I believe he is as much a Christian as a Hindu, and as much a Buddhist as either.'

During religious festivals the people would gather in the main street to watch him pass, borne aloft on a silver chair by his retainers. He would be dressed in a ceremonial coat of pink and silver brocade, with ropes of pearls about his neck and diamonds flashing from the clasp holding the osprey to his turban. He held his head high and his back straight, every inch a regal figure, while caparisoned elephants trod behind. To the poorer people, the simple peasants, he was almost a god.

Elaine determined to build a clinic for the lepers herself from the money her father had given her for a dowry, since William agreed. She broached the subject of the leper asylum to the Marahaja when he was in a good mood after winning at tennis. A week later, as she was leaving to go to her own quarters after a game of chess, he bent and picked up a calico bag which propped back one of the big double doors of the reception rooms. The bag was quite small, but heavy, as Elaine knew from having kicked it once, quite painfully, in her evening slippers when the doors were open. She imagined that it was full of river pebbles.

'Here, take this for your lepers, Mrs King,' said Ram Chandra, pushing the bag towards her.

She took it awkwardly in two hands.

'Untie it,' he said.

She undid the tapes and pulled open the drawstring with her strong, white, capable fingers, and upended the bag on the corner of an inlaid marble table. Out clattered a double handful of stones: not quartz and flint pebbles, but rough rubies and sapphires, round and uncut, garnets and topaz and emerald, all gleaming dully in the lamplight.

Elaine stared, her prominent greeny eyes seeming about to start from her head. Mrs Cadell smiled. The Maharaja laughed at Elaine's astonishment.

'There! Will that suffice?' he asked lightly.

308

'But – but they're jewels!' she said stupidly.

'Of course they are jewels. They would be worth a great deal more when cut, but a merchant in Calcutta will pay well for them.'

'You are too generous, sir.'

'Not at all. They will do more good building a leper asylum than propping open a door.'

When Elaine showed them to William, who had been away with a road survey party, he grumbled, 'I wish he would untie the purse-strings for the Public Works Department! Some of the roads I have to travel over are appalling – a foot deep in powdery dust, with potholes and washaways so that they're not safe for horses. Our cart of equipment had to be drawn by twelve coolies. They're delighted to have the money, of course. And I couldn't bear to see horses trying to struggle over those roads.'

He was stretched on the cane lounge, smoking a cheroot.

'But how generous it was of him! And how trusting. How does he know I won't get some of the gems cut for my own use?'

'Because he has read your character, dear heart. Not just that you're as honest as the day, but he knows you are the least grasping of women, and wouldn't have even wanted an engagement ring if I hadn't insisted.'

It was true. She usually lost jewellery or gave it away before long, though she still had the silver snake bracelet and necklet from Kashmir, and the pair of round silver earrings set with turquoise that William had given her as a housewarming present when they moved into their first home.

William had heard from his mother that Sam had bought an orange orchard and a ranchhouse in California, where they were now living, while he did some fossicking in the worked-out goldfields nearby. The manager, she said, wrote from South Australia that the orange crop had failed that year, all the fruit being affected with rust, and that the funds they had left him were getting low. William worried a little about his feckless father. But surely he couldn't have run through two hundred thousand pounds already?

'How nice it is to have you home again,' said Elaine,

stroking his dark hair and smelling the masculine scent of his cigar.

'And how nice that you haven't lost your waistline yet.' He looked appreciatively through the wreaths of smoke at her tall and slender figure in a black dress sprinkled with jet.

'I've had to start letting out my skirts at the waist already. I'll soon be big as a house!'

She spread the jewels on a cane table-top, licked one stone and held it up to the lamp. A blue, crystalline gleam showed.

'They're so big, these stones. They must be worth thousands!'

'Don't forget they're a lot smaller when cut and faceted. The buyer will make provision for losses and possible flaws. All the same, we must make a trip to Calcutta and get an expert to assess them before you try to sell them.'

When they came back from their trip to Calcutta – where Elaine saw the English doctor at the Mission hospital, who confirmed that her pregnancy was going normally – they found the Palace in gloom and confusion. Little Devi, eight years old, had contracted typhoid. Fortunately her brother, the Minor Maharaja, was away at boarding school, attending the Ajmir College for Princes in the Hills.

The Maharaja was distracted. The little Indian doctor, Das Gupta, was terrified the father too would catch the disease, for he was always in her room and would not rest. Elaine went at once and offered her services as a nurse, turning out the weeping Ayah who was too distressed to be of any use.

The child was dehydrated, burning up with fever, racked by spasms of dysentery. Elaine knew the importance of hygiene in these cases, the imperative need for burning or disinfecting all waste from the sickroom, or they would have an epidemic on their hands. It was thought that Devi had contracted the disease while staying with her cousins, the children of the Maharaja of Cooch Bihar, another feudal state where there was now an outbreak.

'She is far gone, I'm afraid,' Elaine told William. He had remonstrated with her for overtaxing her strength and risking infection at such a time.

'He has had such a sad life, and he dotes upon that child,' had said Elaine in defence.

'And what about our child? What if you lose him – or her – through doing too much? What if you get typhoid?'

'I promise you I shan't get it. I'm very careful. And besides I am so well and strong. I *must* do all I can to save her.'

But there came a time when Elaine and Dr Gupta could do no more. The little Indian had tears in his eyes as they left the Maharaja alone with the frail wisp of girlhood, sunk into a coma from which she would never rally, her thick plait of blue-black hair looking incongruously healthy against her yellow, pinched little face.

The Maharaja came out without a word when it was over. Only his deeply shadowed eyes and reddened lids showed his feelings. He pressed both their hands and went to give orders for a great collection of flowers for her funeral procession. There was soon a whole carpet of flowers in the courtyard; and ever afterwards the pungent scent of marigolds was associated in Elaine's mind with death.

After the funeral, before he left for Calcutta to take his grief to Selmi, he said to Elaine, 'Your leper asylum shall be her memorial. We will call it the Shri Devi Leper Asylum, and I will have a memorial pillar engraved for her, to place at the gate. I will never forget how you nursed her.'

Later he wrote from Calcutta to Mrs Cadell, 'For a while it seemed to me that I could not accept the Divine Will which took my child from me. And yet perhaps sorrow is a blessing in disguise. It was in the moment of deepest sorrow when my mind could find no rest except in a passionate cry to God, that I heard distinctly a Voice . . . Suffering is a sacrament. He who realises this holds the key to the enigma of the universe. We are no longer the playthings of blind fatalistic forces, but the offspring of God after his own image.'

Though William adored his wife, and admired her warm humanity and her nursing skill, in his heart of hearts he would rather she had stayed at home like other European wives and contented herself with bridge and tennis and visits on Saturdays to the Indian ladies in purdah. He was a little embarrassed by her, in fact. And though he approved in principle her work among the lepers, which had been so desperately needed, he thought that now the London Mission had sent out workers and the asylum was in working order, she might forgo her regular visits there.

She had explained to him that leprosy, like tuberculosis, could only be transmitted by long and intimate contact with an infectious case, as in the home. That was why children of infectious parents were taken away and sent to special 'clean' schools until their parents had been cured. When she came back from her visits she always bathed and disinfected herself, changing all her clothes and putting them to soak in a solution of phenyle just to be sure. Yet William felt a sort of reluctance to kiss her or make love to her on those days.

Elaine had now managed to bring in and isolate all the infectious cases in the area. The asylum was run by two workers sent out to India by the London Mission to Lepers, and their Indian helpers. Non-infectious cases were treated at the clinic or in their homes. At the asylum there were now dormitories for men and women, besides the helpers' quarters – buildings paid for by the ruler's gift of jewels. Elaine had built a clinic and dispensary. There had been some heartening cures, and best of all the lepers no longer had to live in the street as outcasts, wailing for alms, displaying their dreadful stumps of hands and noseless faces to get sympathy and *bucksheesh*.

There was a prayer-room for the various religions, and a permanent catechist for the Christians among them.

Elaine still thought marriage a marvellous institution, but she valued her own individuality as well: she was herself, not just Mrs William King. Yet she realised that she had changed through living with someone else. She did not like shooting and killing things, and kept away when one of the hens was being slaughtered for the pot. Yet hunting was second nature to William. He never went out without a gun and would bring back dead pheasants and beautiful blue peacocks which she ate at dinner, trying to pretend to herself that the rather dry, white meat was the flesh of turkey. It seemed wrong to eat the flesh of what had once been a mass of shimmering splendour. Gradually she had become hardened, just as she had adapted to the climate of India.

She talked about it with Ruth Cadell. They agreed that one lost as well as gained from marriage.

'It's like trying to press two circles together,' said Elaine. 'You lose the perfect roundness of personality belonging to each, when they become flattened along one side where the two circles meet. If they *don't* become flattened they never really meet, and you end up with unhappiness and separation. Where they do join perfectly, you get a distortion of both.'

'Perhaps it is only necessary to meet at a small segment of the circumference,' said Ruth Cadell, taking up her image. 'And that is enough to keep them together.'

'You mean the physical side – bed and children? Yes, it probably is enough to keep most couples together, providing it is a good "join".' She laughed at the double meaning of her remark. 'I mean, if they love each other at that level, and love their children.'

'It would not be enough for me.'

'No, of course not. And anyway, once your children were grown up, they alone couldn't bind you together; and that leaves only bed, become perhaps just a habit – '

'A very pleasant habit!'

They both laughed this time. Ruth Cadell shook her head, laughing. Her strong, curly hair was 'salt and pepper', but still more brown than grey. Her eyes were a warm brown in her tanned face, which wore an expression of contentment, not cowlike but lively and pleasant.

'One has only to look at you to see that you've been happy,' said Elaine. 'No, I sometimes think the very best thing about a double bed is being able to wake up and talk, in the middle of the night, and share your thoughts and ideas and fears and hopes with another human being. Do you suppose if two women slept together they would feel the same? Companionship is so important.'

But this was too advanced for Mrs Cadell. She looked slightly disapproving and changed the subject.

Elaine valued the friendship of the older woman and had found her advice from her thirty years' experience in India invaluable. Mrs Cadell was neither Australian nor English, but one of that distinct breed of Anglo-Indians; those who had lost their insularity and reserve, who regarded India as their second home, and felt friendship and respect for its people. George Cadell was a fascinating study, too. Elaine thought of him often as just 'The Englishman', as he seemed to her to personify the best and the worst of that extraordinary race. His manners were impeccable; his accent was pure Oxford. He wore a neat moustache and an Edwardian beard (though the Prince was not yet on the throne, his influence on fashion was profound), and he was never seen without a jacket, however hot the weather. He treated the Maharaja as an equal, and all lesser mortals with a calm assumption of superiority by virtue of his British race.

George Cadell had a good seat on a horse. Like William he loved shooting for its own sake, bringing home piles of beautiful dead peacocks and pheasants, besides organising 'shoots' for tiger and leopard. Yet she had seen him take a letter he was writing outside, starting all over again on a fresh sheet of paper, rather than kill with his pen any of the multitude of tiny, shining green beetles, attracted by the moist ink, which swarmed on the page.

His integrity was unquestioned, and his wrath formidable when he uncovered a case of corruption among village officials or prison officers in charge of the district *thannas*. Prisoners, sitting on the ground for inspection, would grasp his feet, his ankles, as he walked past them, begging him to intercede with the Maharaja for them, for he was known to hate injustice. Once when he found the inmates of an outlying jail all suffering from beri-beri and malnutrition, because they had not been given their monthly addition of fish or chicken to the prison diet of rice, he lost his temper and threw a tin plate at the Head Constable and warned him to mend his ways.

'The great Sahib is angry,' the prisoners told each other, grinning.

With his uncompromising gaze, Mr Cadell would look at a defaulting Sirdar, and the man would feel those eyes going right through him and penetrating the secrets of his soul.

Fourteen

Two MONTHS before the baby was due, Elaine left for the healthier climate of the Hills. During the hot season one of the Calcutta nursing homes run by a British matron closed down and reopened in Darjeeling. Here she had booked a room well in advance. Mrs Cadell accompanied her as far as Calcutta, where she engaged a well-recommended ayah. Mrs Cadell put them on the train for the overnight journey to Siliguri Junction, where they transferred to the tiny toy railway, with two-foot gauge track, for the steep climb through the foothills of the Himalayas. Even with two engines, one to pull and one to push, the little train was unbearably slow. Ayah brewed tea on the kerosene stove they carried with them. The journey took hours, and Elaine suffered from indigestion. She longed to get out and walk, for she could have gone as fast as the train as it corkscrewed among tea estates and across bridges over rushing mountain streams.

Exhausted, Elaine went straight to bed when she arrived at the boarding house just across the road from the little hospital building. She woke refreshed by the cool, clear air at 7,000 feet. Every day she walked along the steep streets where the summer residences of British Army and Government officials nestled among fir trees.

At the highest point, where the land dropped away into a great valley, there was a panorama of mighty peaks, Kangchenjunga among the highest, seeming to float like clouds in the ethereal blue. The cold, clean snow-wind blowing from them seemed to deny that the teeming squalor and dirt of Calcutta existed, down there in the steamy delta of the Ganges – 'Mother Gunga', born from these same pure snows.

Six weeks after her arrival, Elaine developed a sore throat, then a cough which turned into bronchitis. The doctor came from the hospital to visit her and prescribed a linctus. But she still coughed. Because her stomach was displaced by the growing foetus, every time she coughed she vomited. She began to lose weight. Ayah, thinking to cheer her, made her a *dalli* – a necklace of marigolds. But Elaine could not bear the smell of the flowers. She began to feel lonely and frightened; she wanted William, but he could get only a few days' leave because he was in the midst of a big dam project, and was coming later to take her home.

Elaine had her midwifery certificate; she knew all the things that could go wrong in this remote station in the Himalayan foothills. She began to wish she had taken the time to go home to Australia for the birth.

The doctor warned her jokingly not to have the baby on the night of the Bachelors' Ball, the social event of the season, or he would not be present.

As it happened he was not present, as he was operating on a tea planter with acute appendicitis at the time the baby's head appeared. Matron managed quite well without him, but the baby was a wizened little thing, only six pounds and with skinny arms where the flesh hung in folds on the bones, like a little old man's. He was also quite bald, and suffering from jaundice and malnutrition. Elaine looked at him doubtfully. This was not what she had expected her son to look like!

Ayah thought he was beautiful, however. Matron persevered patiently till she had Elaine breast-feeding him, but though the doctor ordered supplementary feeds he did not thrive. After a fortnight in hospital Elaine was preparing to return home, but the doctor said, 'the Babe is not fit to travel.' He told her he had sent a telegram to her husband telling him to come at once if he wished to see his son alive.

Elaine's heart seemed to stop, and then start again painfully. She had feared something of the sort. They had agreed to call the baby Stanley if a boy, Anne if she was a girl. She had originally wanted to call him James, but William had frowned and said it was an unlucky name. Now she thought he had better be baptised as soon as possible. Elaine wrapped the quiet, lethargic child in blankets and shawls and with Ayah carrying him they walked to the nearest Church and had him christened.

As the minister dipped his finger in the font and made the

sacred mark of the Cross on the baby's forehead, the cold water startled him. He opened his mouth wide, and screamed. He continued to scream for the rest of the ceremony.

It was the most wonderful sound Elaine had ever heard. Since his birth he had not once cried in a normal, lusty way.

As if there had been some magical property in the holy water, from then on he began to improve. He put on weight and yelled when he was hungry. But he did not seem to digest his feeds properly and often brought them up again.

By the time William arrived, having organised leave and made the long journey by train, Stanley was out of danger. They waited another week and took him back home together.

'It's like a miracle!' said Elaine, but she added that the doctor was a very experienced one, and Ayah a most devoted nurse, or the baby would not have survived.

They rested briefly in Calcutta on the way. It was a place to keep out of in the hot season. Elaine consulted a specialist about the baby's digestion. He suggested that as soon as he was weaned he should be put on acid milk, or artificial curds and whey.

Elaine's old Mission friends came to see her. Mrs Crosley-Sheridan arrived at the hotel with flowers and a jacket for the baby. If she had ever felt any hostility towards Elaine for appropriating Diana's admirer, she had forgiven her now. She was inclined to patronise her, as one whose only connection with a title was the friendship of the ruler of Gorobhunj, a mere Indian prince. For she was full of Diana's recent wedding in London to a Viscount no less, the son of a belted Earl.

'I feel for you, my dear, living in that primitive, *jungli* State so far away from Calcutta,' she said.

'Oh, but it's not so very *jungli* these days. The Maharaja is a most progressive man; there are schools and clinics throughout the country, and he is getting William to build a light railway and lots of new dams and roads and bridges.'

'But the snakes, the insects –'

Elaine admitted that she could have done without those.

Before they left Calcutta Elaine bought Ayah a length of new material for a sari, and a silver anklet, for helping save the baby's life.

317

Already Stanley and his father were absurdly alike. His cheeks had grown chubby as he put on weight, so that Elaine declared if only William's face was a bit fatter, and if only baby had a moustache, it would be difficult to tell them apart.

'He's a real chip off the old block; there's certainly no doubt who the father is!' said the Mission ladies, smiling and unconscious of any innuendo.

('I should hope not!' said Elaine to William. 'What on earth did they expect? A mulatto?')

'I consider I'm a better block than he is a chip,' said William. But he was really intensely proud of the baby, as if no one before had ever fathered a son.

The baby slept in the nursery, securely tucked inside a mosquito net to keep out snakes and insects. Ayah slept on her low webbing *charpoy* beside him; she preferred it to a European bed and mattress because it was cooler. She would bring him to Elaine for his 2 a.m. feed, and take him back to his cot when he had finished, so that Elaine scarcely had to wake up to feed him, and would go straight back to sleep again. When he was weaned she missed those intimate moments with her son, when, his greed for milk satisfied, he played with the nipple like a lover, nibbling and caressing it with his tiny mouth.

'He will be a great horseman, you'll see,' said William, admiring his long-boned feet and slightly bowed legs. And almost as soon as he could walk, he bought Stanley his first pony. But Stanley was a sickly child. He lived almost entirely on curds and whey, for everything else he ate seemed to give him asthma. It seemed unlikely that he would grow up to become a champion rider.

Wearing a long-sleeved white blouse with leg o'mutton sleeves and a cream serge skirt which daringly exposed her ankles, Elaine was playing tennis on the rather sparse grass court in the grounds of the Cadells' imposing residence near the Palace. She had found she was putting on weight after the birth of the baby, so she began playing in the cool of the mornings.

She was partnering Mr Cadell – a brown, fit fifty-five – in a doubles against Ruth Cadell and the Maharaja. On some mornings she played singles with George Cadell. William said that he had never liked tennis at school, and he preferred polo. He liked to go down to the stables in the morning and visit the horses: his two polo ponies, Elaine's Arab mare, Charmian, the four matched Burma carriage horses and the two walers.

Elaine's complexion was not of the sort which would tan. The sun made her freckle, so she wore a wide shady hat tied on with a veil. Mrs Cadell, who was of Welsh extraction and dark in colouring, wore only a bandana handkerchief over her curly hair. She had told Elaine how once, when she was on a visit to Australia without her husband, an officious immigration inspector at the Port of Melbourne had tried to stop her.

' "You think I'm black, don't you, just because I've come from India!" I told him. "Well, have a look if you don't believe me." And I pulled up my skirts and showed him the white skin at the top of my stockings. He nearly fell over with shock.'

Thinking about this, Elaine said to Ruth Cadell as they sat in the shade for the next set while the men played a singles, 'It's a bit difficult to explain, this xenophobia in Australia, don't you think? You know there was nearly a riot in Queensland when they tried to bring in some Indian coolies to work in the sugar cane. My Indian friends are puzzled by this.'

'I suppose it's a hangover from the time of the goldfields riots against the Chinese.'

'Yes. I remember when I was at school there was a song:

"Rule Britannia, Britannia rule the waves!
Chinamen shall never, never enter New South Wales."

But why is it that the British seem so much more relaxed about it?'

'Certainly a wealthy Indian can feel perfectly at home in London,' said Mrs Cadell. 'I once saw the Maharaja of Mysore installed at Claridge's; he took the whole floor, with all his servants and his Brahmin cook.'

'Perhaps it's because Australia is so new, we've only just wrested it from the black people who lived there. And we are so isolated really in an ocean that's full of coloured nations. Perhaps we feel threatened.'

'Surely not by the Aborigines! I don't believe I've ever seen one.'

'I remember them as a child, when they were camped in the river bend below Benangal. They were perfectly harmless then, but one of my great-uncles, Donald Macdonald, was speared in western Queensland. There were quite a few massacres of whites in the early days.'

'No, I think it's as you say, the feeling of being an outpost of empire, like the British at Kabul.'

'I suppose we're an outpost here, for that matter,' said Elaine. 'Yet we never feel insecure.'

'Not now, perhaps. But do you know that George's life was threatened more than once when we first arrived? The favourite ploy is to shoot someone in mistake for a tiger or a bear.'

'Not really?'

'Yes, indeed! And once when we were giving an official dinner for the Governor – he had brought his own servants with him from Calcutta – I was just about to serve the sweets course when the cook asked to see me urgently. He had just found that the sugar was doctored with powdered glass.'

'Good heavens! And I thought we only had to worry about snakes!'

'Mind you, that was a long time ago. There is less disaffection now. But the Bengal babus will stir it up again. It is the failed BAs of Calcutta University who hate the British being in India; yet the country would fall apart without them.'

'Nevertheless, the Indian patriots will take over one day.'

'Yes, I suppose it must happen, though not for fifty or a hundred years. Then they will have the benefit of the British judicial system, British railways and roads – and sound engineering. The bridges built by your husband will still be in use when the British have left India . . . Oh, good shot!' She applauded a forehand drive by Ram Chandra Gobind which had aced George.

Elaine had always been good at tennis. To play well, to beat the men, was considered unladylike, but her serve was a stinger and she was a lively and effective net player.

'Game and set!'

The Maharaja, being the younger man, had won the vigorous singles match. He was wearing a white European shirt today over his fitted white trousers, and a puggaree wound about his thick dark hair. He strode off the court like a conqueror, smiling with the delight of victory.

He's still like a schoolboy in some ways, thought Elaine as she congratulated him.

In that, and in the generous way he liked to distribute his wealth, he had something in common with her father-in-law, the exuberant Sam King.

The latest news, according to William who corresponded regularly with his mother, was that he had set off for the wilds of Alaska and the Northwest Territories of Canada, leaving Mary and the girls to fend for themselves in the city of Vancouver. There was a new stampede to the Yukon and the Klondike in this year of 1897, and of course that was something Mr King senior would not be able to resist.

'Come, you must be my partner next time, Mrs King,' the Maharaja was saying. 'We are an unbeatable combination, are we not?'

Fifteen

SAM KING was in his element while travelling, shepherding his flock of women to and fro across the North American continent. When Mary complained that she would like to stop in one place for a while, he settled in California – the former site of a great gold rush – and bought a large furnished house in an orange grove to make her feel at home. But before long he uprooted the family again and they set off across the United States by train, occupying nearly a whole carriage with their 'travelling circus', as Mary called it.

They visited New York and Buffalo, where Sam hired a

fleet of carriages to take them on a picnic to see Niagara Falls. From there they travelled north to Toronto, over the Canadian border, and boarded the Canadian Pacific railroad for Vancouver.

The girls spent a lot of time in the Observation car, staring out at the wide inland sea of the Great Lakes, more fresh water than they had ever seen in their lives before. The train stopped the first morning at Thunder Bay on Lake Superior, where there were some flat-topped islands in the Lake, but the farther shore was invisible. After they had crossed the wide flat Prairies, which reminded them of home, they came to the deep, winding river gorges which the railwayline followed right down to the coast through the snow-capped Rocky Mountains – sometimes dashing across dizzying bridges to the other side, or looping round on its own tail like a sinuous snake.

Fanny did not want to leave the observation coach even to go to the dining car to eat. It was all so exotic, so different – the thin, tapering spruce and fir like dark green candles, the gold of birch and aspen sprinkled through them, as the panorama of the northern Fall sifted slowly down the slopes; and then, as the gorge narrowed, the swiftly-flowing, cold green river gliding between its rocky walls.

She was sitting alone in the back seat of the observation car, where she could twist to look back along their tracks and up at the mountain peaks, as well as out the side and through the front windows. A fresh-faced young man she had noticed in the dining car on the three-day journey came up the steps, and with a look asking for permission, sat down beside her. They began to talk, and he was intrigued with her accent and her nationality.

'Australia!' he said. 'I've never met anyone from there before. Though I believe there are lots of Australians, as well as men from all over the world, pouring into Canada at present, into the Northwest Territories. There's a stampede on, to the Klondike.'

'Oh, dear!' said Fanny, looking depressed.

'Why? Don't you approve of gold fever?'

'It's Sam – that is, my father. He can't resist the lure of a new gold-field. We're supposed to be sailing from Vancouver in a fortnight for Sydney and Adelaide. Let's hope he doesn't hear about it!'

The young man, who hailed from Vancouver, told her she would need at least a fortnight to explore its beauties and to visit the large Vancouver Island across the narrow strait from the city, and its capital, Victoria. They were chatting animatedly when without warning the train glided into a tunnel, and all was black. Fanny gave a small scream; it had startled her. He put out a warm, firm hand and held both of hers till they emerged into daylight again.

He removed his hand at once, but they looked long into each other's eyes with startled solemnity.

They met again that evening in the car to watch the sun setting behind the majestic peaks ahead. Before they had reached Vancouver the next afternoon, he had proposed and been accepted – on condition that her parents did not oppose the match.

Sam and Mary demurred at first, but when they had met the young man and learned of his credentials – he was a dentist, returning from a course in the East, whose father was going to set him up in practice in Vancouver – they agreed.

John McNaughton, as he was called, did not say a word to Sam about the gold strike in the Yukon Territory. But as the train glided down along the estuary of the Fraser, where great rafts of logs floated from the logging camps upstream, they came to the Vancouver wharves. All was a bustle of activity, ships loading and unloading, and on one wharf Sam saw a pile of green canvas bags guarded by armed men – a great heap of bags, which could contain nothing but gold!

At the bar in their hotel that night he heard 'the Klondike' and 'the Yukon' on everyone's lips. Those who had money to invest – and even those who hadn't – were buying shares in new goldmining ventures. It was like the Golden Mile all over again. To Sam it was irresistible. There was the challenge of the Frozen North, the land of the Mounted Police, where men were men; and there was the challenge of gold still to be found.

Within a week Sam had his family settled in a comfortable twelve-roomed stone house in one of the better suburbs of Vancouver, with a view of the mountains behind and the bay in front. He waited only for the official engagement party for Frances, and to buy some warm clothing and boots in the stores, before he was off on his new adventure. He took passage in a small coastal steamer, laden with stampeding miners, for the newspapers had taken up the story of the bags of gold on Vancouver's wharf, with headlines like, 'One Ton of Gold Arrives from Klondike!'

They sailed up the west coast of Canada by the 'Inside Passage', sheltered most of the way by islands, and on the starboard side a succession of deep, narrow fjords with walls thousands of feet high where they could anchor in bad weather. They had to make the deep entrance to Skagway before winter sealed it with ice. Besides being overloaded with human freight, the steamer carried a hundred dogs, and the stalls off the dining saloon were occupied by horses, which gave a stables-scent to every meal. Several icebergs were sighted as they sailed further north.

To get to the Klondike they would have to cross from Alaska into Northwest Canada, over the frightening White Pass to the headwaters of the Yukon's tributaries, then travel by lake and river to Dawson, where the Klondike River joined the Yukon.

Sam had found two mates on board the little *Williamette*: they were travelling together, a professional gambler called Dandy Dan Diamond (who hoped to make a fortune in the brand-new town of Dawson) and his friend One-Eyed Reilly, who was a rough diamond, as big and tough as his friend was small and dainty. They were landed with their gear on the cold, grey gravel beach behind which the cold white mountains towered. In Vancouver they had all stocked up with warm fur coats, sheepskin-lined boots and mitts, waterproof sleeping bags of quilted down and a two-man tent. Sam, to save weight, had decided to sleep out.

On the first night the flickering lights of a hundred camp-fires made the beach look less desolate, rum rations were broached and there was a picnic feel about the whole venture. Then all set off to walk across the forbidding coastal ranges to Lake Bennett, where men were feverishly building boats from spruce and pine hacked from the hillsides. The ship had brought horses, though there would be no fodder for them in the coming winter; they would have to be shot, once they had done their work of packing supplies inland to Lake Bennett. Sam bought a packhorse for an exorbitant sum to carry his supplies of flour, dried beans, hardtack and tea and sugar. He also had a twelve pound sack of onions.

Even though Dan's pack was the smallest, Sam and One-Eyed Reilly had to help him up the last of the steep trail to the top of White Pass. There, as they sat on their packs to get their breath back, Sam had his first sight of the cold and silent North. From here they were going right to the borders of the Arctic Circle. He contemplated the barren, wind-scoured waste of rocks, the walls of stone which separated the sea-shore from the inland lakes, and felt something he had never felt in the Australian desert. There, the land seemed vast and indifferent. Here it seemed positively inimical: 'sinister, savage and baleful', the poet Robert Service had described it. It was a place where Man was not wanted and would not be long tolerated. Snow lay in sheltered hollows, although this was the end of summer, and the Fall was just beginning; the brief 'open season' when the Yukon was not frozen into icy silence, lasted only from the end of May to the middle of October.

Four days' march and forty miles from Skagway they came down to Lake Bennett, a long, steel-grey sheet of water which led on through a chain of lakes to the Yukon, the highway to the Klondike. Here the men who had arrived ahead of them, told them that the Redcoats, the Canadian Mounted Police, had set up a post further on (for they had crossed the border of Alaska and were now in Canada). The police had taken charge of the mad stampede, turning back any man who did not have a winter's supply of food with him; otherwise there would be famine in the little settlement of Dawson.

Sam and his mates sat down gloomily to discuss the matter. Sam wandered among the boat-builders, and seeing what he took for a Scot in a bright plaid lumber-jacket who was directing a group of three men, he spoke to him and offered to 'buy in' on their outfit, 'and we'll help you work on the boat and get away quicker.'

The leader, who said his name was Macrae, thought about it for a while. 'How many of you?' he asked.

'Three. Two of us good, strong workers, the other's a little cove who won't eat much. And he'll put in a share of the finances too.'

'Done!' said Macrae. 'We've got plenty of stores, but if we don't get this blamed boat finished soon, we'll find the river freezing up around us.'

So Sam and Reilly worked at sawing and hauling timber, while Dan hammered nails into the soft spruce boards. Macrae had thought to bring plenty of nails in his pack. He could have sold them for fifty cents a pair, but he used them all to brace the hull with extra-strong ribs. He had heard about the White-horse Rapids and the dangers of Miles Canyon, where the river for two miles tore along between high cliffs, with a sharp bend in the middle which formed a whirlpool. A dozen men had already been drowned in this stretch of water when their boats or rafts crashed into the sheer walls and disintegrated or were capsized.

Macrae had decided to build a small skiff as well as the larger boat, thinking to take it separately through the more dangerous passages, so that he would not be stranded if the big boat came to grief. It could tow behind while crossing lakes.

When he saw Dandy Dan's equipment, which Sam had packed in on his horse, he laughed shortly. 'Enough blankets for a hotel!' he snorted. 'And throw away the tent and all them dishes – who's goin' to wash them, anyway? D'you think you're travelling by Pullman coach?'

Dan insisted on keeping the tent. 'If you're goin' to Dawson you have ter learn to rough it,' said Macrae.

Each day the sun rose a little later and set earlier, describing an arc round the southern horizon. There was still warmth in it in the middle of the day, but the nights were bitterly cold. Sam, nearly fifty, felt the cold in his bones. But during the six hours of darkness he was snug in his sleeping bag.

When all was ready and stowed, they launched the boats by hitting them with a bottle of rum, being careful not to break it. They ran up sail for the long lake crossing, with six men aboard and two tons of food: flour, rice, beans, bacon, coffee, sugar and condensed milk. The start was auspicious: the lake between its banks of grey gravel lay calm and blue, reflecting the sky, the snow-capped peaks, and a few motionless white clouds on its broad bosom.

Sam realised that beans, bacon and coffee would be his bush tucker on the Klondike, instead of salt beef, tea and onions. Damper, the flour-cake leavened with baking powder which was the bread of the bush, was not the same as the sourdough of the American backwoods. He found that bushmen here were called 'sourdoughs' because they baked and lived upon it. Sam had his own camping equipment of skillet frying-pan, camp oven, quartpot or billy, and enamel mug; a good sharp knife, a couple of spoons – and for the rest, 'fingers were discovered before forks', as he was fond of saying.

The one luxury he had missed when camping in the outback was butter; for fat of any kind simply melted away to oil in the heat of the desert, sometimes up to 140 degrees. Here he was able to carry a tin of butter for special occasions. He had also brought along a plum pudding and a bottle of whisky to open when he celebrated his birthday.

Camping and travelling again in the free and easy world of men, he felt young and happy. This was the life for Sam King! He took his turn at the tiller, wondering if these men would believe him if he said he had an ocean-going yacht sitting in harbour at home.

They took to the heavy oars to enter Caribou Crossing, which dropped them down to the next lake in the chain, Tagish. By moonlight they pulled for shore to shelter from the fierce wind that met them head-on as they entered the notorious Windy Arm. Here the surrounding mountains funnelled all the winds down on to Tagish. Fretting at the delay, for the lower river would soon be starting to freeze over, they had to wait two days while the wind blew with unceasing ferocity, whipping up a heavy cross-sea.

Beyond Tagish was Lake Marsh; from there the waters tumbled into the fearsome Miles Canyon.

Macrae was a lumber man and knew all about rapids. Sam, coming from a land of flat or undulating desert, was horrified at the welter of white water, breaking in peaks like rows of ravening wolves' teeth.

'I'd rather walk, if you don't mind,' he said. 'Don't you

think we should portage the goods, anyway, and let two of the men take the big boat down empty? We stand to lose less that way.'

'No!' said Macrae. 'We haven't time to mess with unloading and portaging. The next party will be upon us soon, and I wouldn't fancy a traffic jam in that there canyon. You just sit tight, and I'll take her through.'

Sam thought his last hour had come. At first he shut his eyes, but the violent motion of the heavy boat over the lumpy, swirling water, its dives into whirling hollows and climbs over watery mounds that concealed submerged boulders, made him feel as if he were going over Niagara Falls in a barrel. They shot out of the canyon with its menacing walls into a smooth, swift-gliding stream of green snow-water. But no sooner had he got his breath back than they were in the grip of Squaw Rapids, where sharp rocks stood up in midstream waiting to destroy them. Macrae, with superb skill, worked the rear sweep and guided them safely through. The small skiff followed.

Next they were rushing through the mile-long chute of White Horse Rapids, dodging among manes of spray, where sheer rock walls closed in again to less than thirty feet apart. It was like being in the midst of a stampede of a thousand wild white horses. Sam clung to a stanchion till his knuckles were white. If the boat sank here, there was nowhere a man could clamber out, even if he made it to the bank.

As they shot out into wider and calmer water, they saw the bones of several wrecked vessels on the rocks, and lost equipment scattered for a mile downstream. They had moved so fast that the terror was over in a few minutes; but as soon as a flat sandbank appeared, they had to pull in to shore and spread their spray-soaked clothes and equipment in the sun to dry. Dandy Dan surprised them by bringing out some fishing gear, and providing a feast of grilled mountain trout. Next day was one of Indian Summer, almost hot. They spent it in a leisurely crossing of Lake La Barge, the last of the chain of lakes. Then there was 'only' four hundred and fifty miles of easy downstream travelling, their boats carried by the current on to Dawson.

Rolled in his warm sleeping bag, dressed in his long woollen underwear and all his clothes but for his outer coat and britches, Sam lay in the lake-side camp and stared up at the glorious panoply of the northern sky. He was wearing a woollen cap pulled down over his ears, and had only the top of his head out. Later he would pull the hood of the sleeping bag over his head, and sleep as snug as a bug in a rug.

Somewhere, during his life of adventuring, Sam had lost the simple faith of his childhood. He was not sure what he believed any longer, but that Man was the centre of the universe and of God's anxious care, that he could not believe. He had seen dried-up bodies of perishers in the desert, the flesh parting from the bones as water sheers away from rock in a waterfall; men who had died, sometimes, within a few miles of water that would have saved their lives. Men died by chance, by accident, just when they had every reason to live; like the old fellow at Hall's Creek, a battler all his life, who sank his pick into a nugget and promptly fell dead of a heart attack.

And all those stars! What if there really were people in other universes beyond our own, or nearer still in other worlds in our own solar system, looking out with awed and puzzled eyes at the overwhelming splendour and extent of the visible heavens?

He remembered Ida's artless prattle as they lay in the haystack – how many years ago now? It must be thirty years! She had imagined that the sky was full of people looking down with their yellow eyes, and he had scoffed at her. And yet . . . it was almost as if they spoke to him, those myriad dots of light. He did not feel alien, but somehow a part of it all, of something far vaster than his own consciousness. His life was nothing but a moment, a less-than-a-second's tick in the aeons of time, and yet he was aware, and could contain in the tiny receptacle of his human brain, or soul, or mind, these immensities of time and space.

His own constellation, the Scorpion, was no longer a reversed question mark as it sank in the west, but right-way up: the dazzlingly bright curve of stars, with the double star in its tail clearly visible to the naked eye. All about it was a soft effulgence from the millions of stars in the Milky Way. He tried to find the Pole Star, but succeeded only in tracing the

Big Dipper, Ursa Major. There was nothing in the northern hemisphere's sky to compare with the jewelled Cross of the south.

But, as the campfire died down and darkness became complete at ground level, Sam held his breath. The height, the clear, cold air, the lack of any dust in the atmosphere or of distracting lights on earth, made the sky as brilliant as he had seen it in Central Australia on moonless midnights on the track. There the Milky Way glowed with a pale luminescence which it was almost possible to read by. Now the familiar sky was changed, turned around, and held strange constellations he had known only by their names but had never seen before.

It was long before sleep overcame him and he drew the hood of the sleeping-bag in front of his eyes and buried his face in the blankets. The new beard he was growing prickled his chin. His last drowsy thought was that he was glad the dangerous rapids were safely past. It would have been ironic if, after all the times he had escaped perishing for lack of water, he should now die of drowning.

They had congratulated themselves too early on their progress. Below Lake La Barge they found themselves in a ten to fifteen-knot current, where the silky gliding of the cold, green water was deceptive. They brought up on hidden sand bars, and had to work like beavers to get themselves water-borne again; islands appeared in mid-stream; sudden rocks and boulders challenged their route. Macrae at the stern sweep desperately guided them through, but at the end of the Thirty Mile Rapids he was exhausted. They were all dripping wet from being over the side pushing, the goods were damp again from flying foam. In spite of the rapid current, it had taken them nearly five hours to do the thirty miles. The sun would soon be setting. They spent a miserable camp in their wet things, and made a late start next day after waiting for the sun to dry their clothes.

'I'll lay five to one we make it to Dawson in a week – that is, seven days,' said Sam to Dandy Dan in the morning. He had been assured there really were no more rapids, by a party camped along the bend which contained seasoned sour-doughs, who had made the trip to Dawson before.

'That's sixty miles a day!' said Dan. 'You're mad, old chap.'

'I'm told you can do seventy a day, easy, from here on.'

'Huh! That's what they *tell* you.'

Sam got a couple of other takers, and put up his five hundred pounds against their hundred, which they put in between them in dollars. At first it looked as if he would win easily, as they slid rapidly down with the steady current, the river seeming to hurry as though it sensed the end of its journey, still a thousand miles away, in the Arctic Sea; or that the end of its free flowing was near, and it would soon be bound in the icy silence of winter. After the junction of the Pelly River, the temperature dropped to near freezing. Lumps of pancake ice, brought down by northern tributaries, began appearing in the river. Then one morning they woke to find the boats frozen to the bank.

Sam was among the hardest workers as they chopped the big boat free (the skiff had been pulled up on the bank overnight). Not that the hundred pounds meant much to him, but he wanted to prove he was right and win his bet. The centre of the river where the current was strongest still kept clear of ice, but rim-ice held them up again on the fourth day. They had to chop their way for almost a hundred feet to get to clear water. Sam's heart sank.

Then a tributary came in from the south, and the river temperature rose again. On the sixth day, late in the morning, they swept round a bend and everyone raised a cheer – even those who had lost their money.

Below a steep mountainside dark with a thick forest of spruce and fir, the beginnings of fabled Dawson City lay on the right bank: a cluster of buildings and tents lying under a sprinkling of fresh snow.

Sam collected his hundred pound winnings, resolved to spend most of it on one great drinking spree to celebrate their arrival. By good fortune, two supply steamers had just made the last trip upstream before the winter, and there was plenty of grog available. That night he 'shouted the bar' in all the saloons in town.

Sixteen

USED AS he was to roughing it in the bush, Sam King was to find that the sub-Arctic cold and frozen streams of the Yukon made life just as difficult and uncomfortable as heat and lack of water had done in Western Australia.

To begin with, there was no running water for washing dirt or cradling during the winter. Though there was plenty of water, it was all frozen. The soil itself in the Running Creeks area between the Klondike and the Indian rivers, was frozen solid all the year, below the first foot. The only way to drive a shaft into it was by lighting fires and melting it half a yard at a time.

Dandy Dan soon fell on his feet in Dawson, as miners came in with their pokes full of gold-dust to spend, and ready to gamble on anything. The route to the nearer creeks was easier to negotiate in early winter, because the frozen Klondike made a highway for part of the way into town; in summer it had to be crossed by ferry. As soon as the rivers froze over, men began arriving on foot and by dog-sled, with the gold in which they had been paid for 'mucking' and sluicing.

That first winter of the rush, Dawson had but two commodities in abundance: gold-dust and whisky. Gold was almost as plentiful as the snow-crystals that hung in the frozen air like a silver-dusted curtain. The only other goods in plentiful supply were flannel shirts. When these became too dirty, men threw them away and bought new ones.

The versatile Dandy Dan, who had brought in some exotic supplies like dried raisins and soy sauce, made up a big batch of HP ketchup to his own secret recipe, and bottled it in empty whisky bottles. It sold like hot cakes to miners bored with a diet of corned meat, beans, and jack-rabbit stew. Dan wrote down the recipe and gave it to Sam, telling him not to let anyone else see it.

'You might like to try it one day,' he said. 'It's a blamed

good recipe. Only I can't get all the right ingredients here, y'see. Don't you lose it now.'

Sam folded the bit of paper and put it in his wallet.

For the next six months the town would be cut off from the outside world. There would be no more steamers up the river, or stampeders floating down it, till next May or June when the ice broke up. It would be July before the first steamer arrived from the distant mouth. Meanwhile, nails were bringing twenty-eight dollars a pound, and shovels twenty dollars each. Eggs, a rare luxury, sold for twelve dollars a dozen. Women were the scarcest commodity of all: one dance-hall girl auctioned herself as a bed-warmer for the winter, and collected a fee of $5,000 in gold.

Day and night the dog-teams swung up and down the main street, their sled bells jingling in the icy air. They were bringing the last gold from the summer clean-up, and taking firewood and stores out to the camps.

Dawson was ringing with the exploits of 'Klondike Mike', a huge redheaded Irish-Canadian who was as light on his feet as a ballet-dancer, could high-kick better than a girl, and use his feet to deadly effect in a fight. He was now planning a solo journey back to Skagway with his team of huskies, carrying mail for the 'outside' at a dollar an ounce. Sam wrote a letter to Mary in Vancouver, telling her that he was safe and well – he did not add, happy as he had not been for years.

As the winter closed in and the sun disappeared, except for a brief appearance on either side of noon in the southern sky, night and day ceased to have meaning. The nights were rarely black, the days scarcely light. There was a grey twilight or a luminous darkness lit either by moon and star-shine, reflected from white snow, or by the weird filmy curtains of the Northern Lights, pulsing across the sky and dimming the stars as with a veil.

A continuous air of Saturday-night gaiety pervaded the town. Men wandered in at any time of the clock and always found the bars open. They were the only places of public entertainment and the source of all news and rumour – though before long there were to be two newspapers.

Sam had always felt at home in a bar. This man's world of hard-bitten sourdoughs and hard-drinking newcomers fitted him like a comfortable suit. His experiences in outback Australia and South Africa provided him with endless yarns. As someone who had found Lake View – one of the richest lodes in the world – he was respected as an experienced prospector. Among the seasoned miners who had travelled to the Klondike were men from all over the world, including Australia, who knew of Sam King's reputation and how he'd found a hill of gold in the Coolgardie rush. There were plenty of offers for him to go into partnership.

But he was in no hurry. Little could be done in the way of prospecting till the worst of the winter was over. No sluicing and very little washing and panning were possible until the first thaw. By arriving as he had just before the river closed to traffic in both directions, he would have time to talk to those in the know and assess his chances for staking a worthwhile claim in the spring. His plan was to establish a likely prospect, then build a cabin near the claim so that he could winter at the mine.

As soon as the river was open a new influx of stampeders would arrive from outside, and prices, already high, would soar out of sight. So he began laying in timber and nails, window glass, and fodder for the horses he would need on the trail next summer. Last year, hay had gone up to $1,400 a ton.

Everyone was waiting for the break-up with more than ordinary interest. Once the clean-up of the winter stockpile of wash-dirt was complete, and the fine gold began to pour into Dawson, men would pour out in the opposite direction, rushing to the most promising locations.

In early November Sam went with One-Eyed Reilly up to the junction of Bonanza Creek and the Klondike River, now frozen over. Bonanza was lined with diggings. Reilly took a job 'mullocking' in one of the shafts at $17 a day, or an ounce of gold-dust. It was good pay, but to Sam it looked like hard and dirty labour. He was not going to slave in someone else's mine.

He was disappointed to find that there was little country-rock visible, nothing that could point the way to a reef, and not just because of the snow but because a thick band of glacial moraine – clay and pebbles – lay over the bedrock like a frozen blanket. He visited a few mines where the clay was being dug out by the slow process of lighting fires in the pits to melt the soil.

After a good look round he decided to go back to Dawson and make enquiries about steam boilers and pipes. A team of pack-horses would be needed to bring them out, in sections, to wherever he had decided to locate. But if the first shaft indicated gold at depth – and the average depth to bedrock seemed to be twenty or thirty feet, with the alluvial gold spread in a layer on top of this – it would be worthwhile using steam because of the saving in time and labour.

Between them, he and Macrae had sufficient capital for a big venture. He respected Macrae's ability, his Scottish determination and canniness. If he did not want to come in as a partner Sam would go it alone and offer him the job of overseer, for he would need to employ numbers of men.

Back in Dawson he talked at every opportunity with miners who came plodding in along the frozen trails, fed up with the hard life of the Creeks, to thaw out in the bars and spend their gold. Sam shouted drinks for all. His easy hospitality and ability as a raconteur had made him once more a popular figure.

There were those who resented his social success in the small community, especially Big Ole, a Swedish-American, also known as Yankee Ole, who had been a hero the previous summer when he came in with a thousand ounces of fine gold from Bonanza.

'Yes, it was so hot around Lake Eyre,' Sam was saying, as he leant back on the bar and looked easily around his audience, 'that the metal of the stirrup-iron would burn the skin off your hand. The birds were falling dead out of the trees. It must have been fully 150 degrees in the shade –'

'Vot, you think ve stoopid, belief' all that? It never vos that hot.'

Sam paused, took a drink of whisky, and went on: ' – in the *shade*. God knows what it was out in the sun. We managed to camp under some desert oaks that day, and travel on at night. The air seemed to burn your lungs as you breathed it, like a furnace blast. Lake Eyre, of course, was bone dry – just a saltpan filled with beautiful blue mirage.'

'I doan' belief it!' Yankee Ole, burly in checked wool jacket, a fur cap pulled halfway down over his big ears, banged his glass down on the bar. 'See, the drinking-vater she vould have dried up too, the horses vould be dead –'

'Australian horses are bred to take outback conditions,' said Sam mildly. 'That's why they're used by the military in India. And we carried canvas water bags to keep the water cool, apart from what was in the screw-top cans on the packsaddles.'

'Yah! Tell us another vun, ho-ho!'

'Are you calling me a liar?' asked Sam dangerously.

He was on the verge of losing his temper at these interruptions.

'Vy, vos you vanting to make something of it?'

Sam, though he'd had a good few drinks, had no desire to make something of it. He was old enough to let discretion rule over passion. Though the blood had come up in his cheeks, and his blue eyes bulged ominously, he controlled himself. The man was mean-looking and twenty years younger than himself, though they were of a like size, both being broad-shouldered and over six feet.

But before he could turn away and ignore Ole, the men he was drinking with shoved him forward with encouraging cries. He bumped the other man's drinking arm and spilled his drink. Ole swore.

'Good old Sam, don't take any of his lip!'

'Go on, Sam, what you waitin' for?'

'It's a fight, fellers! Come on, outside everybody. Who'll be seconds? Come on, you two!'

The truculent Big Ole needed no urging. But Sam hung back, arguing. 'I can't fight him, my back's crook,' he said, for he'd had a bit of rheumatic pain in his back since sleeping out on the cold, wet journey from Skagway.

'Yer can't pull out now!'

Sam saw that this was so. He thought quickly. 'Right-oh. I challenge him to a duel. Pistols at dawn.' (He thought that everyone would have forgotten by morning, including the drunken Ole.)

'Be buggered to that,' said his mates. 'Yer gotter fight him now, everyone's waitin'. Sam'll fight a duel!' they shouted.

'Duel to the death!' –

'No, first blood wins.'

'Who's got a pair o' guns?'

Ole looked alarmed, but the crowd took up the cry. 'Pistols at twenty paces! They're gonna fight a duel.'

'I not fight duel. Fist fight.'

Sam began to feel anxious. The boisterous crowd reminded him of a Roman mob thirsty for blood outside the arena. Butchered to make a Roman holiday . . . Why had he ever suggested guns? He had feared being beaten-up in a bare-knuckle fight. But better a broken nose than a bullet through the heart!

Ole said obstinately, 'I not fight with guns.'

'You haveter. He has the choice of weapons.'

Ole took a deep breath, and scowled at Sam. He said:

'Orright, it vos that hot. I belief you.' Then he pushed his way out into the night, to the jeers of the crowd. He was not popular, being known to be a bully who picked fights with men older or smaller than himself. The men, who had scented blood, muttered angrily, but Sam shouted double whiskies all round and peace of a sort was restored.

Through the long, dark winter the Northern Lights crackled and purred in the heavens, wavering their pale green and pink and oatmeal-coloured streamers in front of the stars. Later, a sort of perpetual dawn played behind the southern mountains. Mid-winter passed, with week-long celebrations of Christmas and New Year.

As soon as he had recovered from his hangover, Sam announced that he was off to the Running Creeks for a 'look-see'. He was bunking in Macrae's cabin, which had been built from the timbers of the big boat. It was warmed by a Yukon stove, a wood-burning affair packed in rocks and insulated with clay. Once it had been burning for several days, the rocks became heated through and even if the fire went out during the night, kept the cabins snug and warm. One-Eyed Reilly stayed with Dandy Dan when he was in town, in rooms behind one of the gambling dens attached to the saloons.

Here Sam was a regular patron, and because Dan was his friend he was allowed to win as often as he lost.

Macrae was interested in a partnership, but he wanted to wait for the full spring thaw before starting on a prospecting trip, as it would then be possible to travel by water first down the Yukon to the mouth of the Indian River, and then upstream, following it westward to the headwaters of Dominion Creek. He was a timber and raft man rather than a born prospector like Sam.

The sun began to stay longer above the horizon and, when it set, left behind the clear hues of crimson and gold which Sam remembered in winters at home; only they lingered much longer.

For $25 he hired a passage on a dog-sled going up to Grand Forks with supplies for the small settlement of miners at the junction of Bonanza and Eldorado. The dogs followed a hard-packed trail over the frozen Yukon and Klondike and along the banks of Bonanza Creek. There were now rough road-houses every ten miles or so along the way for those who made the journey on foot.

Dawson lay behind them as they skimmed along through the frozen world. At midday the sun crept above the mountains to the south, and flooded the trail with warm pink light. The cold white scene was transformed. The snow took on the tint of sunset clouds on which the long blue shadows of the loaded sled and the steadily-trotting dogs were thrown. Every tree and bush glittered with a coloured iridescence of frozen drops. During the dark of afternoon, as they approached the Forks, he saw the full moon with a perfect rainbow round it; caused, it was said, by high-level cloud formed of tiny ice-crystals.

The promise of the rainbow! Sam felt his heart lift.

> My heart leaps up when I behold
> A rainbow in the sky . . .

he muttered to himself. He had always liked those lines when he was at school, had memorised the verses once for a task, and whenever he saw a rainbow remembered them, and his first escapade after the Pot of Gold. The crystals of ice were each like the prism his father used to let him look through at home, when he was small.

From sheer high spirits he began to sing:

> Too weak to break the chains that bind me,
> I need no shackles to remind me
> I'm just a prisoner of lo –ove . . .

and because they were all free men in a man's world, the other two men laughed and applauded.

Sam had grown a strong brown beard in contrast to his greying hair. The eyebrows were still dark above his blue eyes, now rather bloodshot from the effects of desert travel and Sandy Blight and occasional heavy drinking. Two pouches of puffy skin had formed beneath them. 'Life begins at fifty,' he thought contentedly, stretching his feet in their soft, warm boots. What a celebration he would have for his half-century next November! He had no doubt that he was on the way to find another fortune.

His boots were of caribou-leather, his socks of rabbit skin with the fur turned inside. He had a warm parka with a fur-lined hood, and felt ready to tackle the trail to Dominion on foot. At the Forks there were some guesthouses and eating places for men who were working winter claims, piling up the melted muck they had dug out in readiness for the thaw when sluice-boxes could be used for washing out the gold. It occurred to Sam that it would be possible to work a 'wet shaker box' with riffle boards on the bottom, as a substitute for a sluice box, by using melted ice before the creeks were running. Where water had been scarce in the West they had found that a 44-gallon drum of water would put through quite a lot of dirt. Firewood would be the only problem.

He stayed the night, then got up in the darkness of the winter day to travel on up the banks of Bonanza, packing his blankets and sleeping-bag in a swag on his back, with a small frying-pan, a billy, and a spirit-stove. He had no snow-shoes, but there was less depth of snow than he expected, for precipitation around Dawson was fairly light in most years and the winter so far had been mild.

Twenty miles brought him over the Dome and down by a

series of ridges between snow-filled gullies to the valley of Dominion Creek, where there were signs of workings along the creek-bed, mostly old. But no one, he noticed, was working the 'benches', the slopes on either side. He resolved to be one of the first back here in spring. On the way back he engaged two hard-up sourdoughs, whose upper Bonanza claim had proved a duffer, to cut 250 cords of wood by the spring, to be delivered to Dominion at $15 a cord. It would cost more than that, he knew, to get it freighted out from Dawson by dog-sled. He paid them half in advance, and they looked doubtfully at the strange, new dollar bills. Everything on the creeks, and even in town, was paid for in gold-dust.

That year of '98 the ice went out early, in the first week of May. Sam stood on the banks watching with fascination as the frozen Yukon cracked across, the cracks shooting over the ice like forked lightning with a series of loud bangs. The broken mass heaved, and the centre of the stream began to move, while the banks still held their ice. Then the shore ice began to join the flood. It roared and cracked and groaned, till at last the whole Yukon was in motion.

He watched until after nine at night, when the sun dipped briefly out of sight only to reappear in a few hours. He knew that as soon as the upper river was navigable the Skagway stampeders would arrive, and in another month or two the up-river steamers would bring more. A dog-sled musher coming from Skagway had brought news that there were 3,000 boats, rafts and canoes waiting at Lake Bennet to leave for Dawson, and traffic jams on the White and Chilkoot Passes. Sam was ready to leave at once, before this gold-hungry mob arrived to stamp the trails into slush and take up every likely-looking prospect. He already had bought his horses for the trail, and booked a passage on the ferry to cross the Klondike.

First to arrive on the still dangerously ice-strewn river was a detachment of the Royal Canadian Mounted Police, resplendent in their red coats. From now on Dawson, which had never been such a wicked town as Skagway, would be more orderly. Considering the amount of gold and whisky circulating that winter, it had been fairly quiet.

Sam bought a barrel of whisky and added it to the stores,

'for medicinal purposes' he told Macrae, who was not a drinker. The team of twelve horses was now loaded with stores, including hay for their own sustenance, kerosene for lamps, picks, shovels, saws, axes, hammers, nails, even two small panes of glass for the cabin, and extra clothing and blankets. Sandy Macrae had come in on a half-sharing basis, though he did not like Sam's idea of the expensive boiler and steam pipes. He was a tall, gaunt, rawboned Canadian who had led a tough life in logging camps since he was twelve years old. He had sold his timber-mill back in Ottawa to invest everything in the gamble for gold.

Sam King and Sandy Macrae set off on the fourteenth of May. One-Eyed Reilly, now an experienced mucker, came with them, though he was not in partnership as he had little capital. He would be working for wages with the other labourers they hired – that was, if they struck gold. Sam would have made him foreman, but as he could not read or write he would not be able to keep account of the wages.

The sun rode high in the blue sky. Darkness was something that happened briefly around midnight. The deathlike silence of winter had given way to the murmur of life, the rustle of spring: everywhere sounded the ripple of running water, the drip of thawing icicles. Willows and aspens along the river were bursting into bud, sap was rising in spruce and alder, wild geese passed honking overhead in long formations. The brilliant cerise of fireweed carpeted the ground.

The *Klondike News* had printed a small copy of the map supplied by the Canadian Department of the Interior, since there weren't enough of them to go round. Sam had one of these and a magnifying glass. It showed the maze of creeks and ridges, the trails and workings along the creeks, between the Klondike and the Yukon. Nearly every creek showed a rash of dots, like measles, marking the registered claims along their beds. The first proven claim was called 'Discovery', and the claims were numbered from there as so many 'below Discovery' or 'above Discovery'. So whatever fancy name a miner gave to his claim, it would be known to everyone as 'six above' or 'forty-five below'.

Arriving at Dominion Creek after two days' travel, Sam looked around carefully and staked two bench claims just below Discovery. The claims along the valley floor had been staked out last summer, and some were already worked out. There were a few mud-and-pole or wattle-and-daub huts, insulated and roofed with moss, with tiny windows made from pickle jars and bottles thrust through the clay in a square pattern, or a bit of thin canvas made translucent with bacon fat.

'We'll have to costean down to bedrock,' said Sam. 'It's as well I have that wood cut and ready.' When the two men he had employed delivered the cords of wood to the claim, using the partners' horse-team, they laughed at the site, well up on the bench below a high ridge.

'You won't find no gold there, chum,' they said.

Sam only smiled in his beard and employed the two men, Stan and Merv, to help dig out the first pit. First they dug out the foot of soft topsoil, then it was a business of lighting fires every night in the hole to melt the next foot or two of permafrost. Macrae and Reilly (who had lost his eye when chopping a piece of hardwood that flew up and hit him in the face), set to work to put up the cabin and stove, after cutting logs for the walls.

As the first buckets of melted dirt came up, Sam panned a sample from each in icy half-melted snow water, but he saw not a gleam of gold. Macrae and Reilly started a second shaft, complaining that the ground was worthless but they might as well dig anyway. Sam went back to Dawson to register the claims he had staked with the Gold Recorder's Office. This took longer than he expected because no one had ever tried to register bench claims before, and there was no provision for it.

By the time he got back the first shaft was nearly down to twenty feet, still with no gold showing.

'We might as well throw our hand in, Sam,' said Macrae. 'Everyone says there's no gold on the slopes. We should have got here a year earlier, and located in the creekbed.'

'There's an old saying, "Gold is where you find it",' said Sam. 'There are no set rules for gold; it's queer stuff. But I have a hunch we'll bottom on some rich stuff here. Back home they used to say, "Sam King can smell gold." '

'Well, you're the expert,' said Macrae.

Next day the first shaft bottomed on rock at eighteen feet. There came a muffled shout from below. Sam, who had agreed to do the cooking for the camp, leaving the work of digging and winching-up mullock to the younger men, strolled over from outside the cabin where he had been washing and peeling potatoes and onions in half-frozen water.

'Holy Mackerel!' came the voice from below. 'Comanava-look at this! Just lookatit!'

Sam climbed down into the pit, his heart beating high with hope. Merv, the labourer who was working in the bottom, made way for him, swinging his lantern. The whole floor was gleaming with golden streaks. Sam picked up a handful of dirt and held it to the light. It seemed to be smeared with yellow butter, the gold was so thick and fine. His hunch had been right. He washed a few pans at once with the potato-water, for there was only a trickle in the creeks as yet. Each pan produced more than a dollar's worth of gold. They melted more water and from fifty buckets of dirt put through the 'wet shaker', produced $2,000 worth of fine gold and small nuggets.

Macrae was ecstatic. He did a wild Highland Fling around the claim, a dance which he said his Scottish grandmother had taught him, though he'd been born in Canada. Sam had only expected it, though he was delighted at having been proved right.

Next day the second shaft reached bedrock, the men working in shifts for twenty hours. Once again the whole bottom was 'lousy with gold', according to the jubilant Macrae.

'We must go into this in a big way,' said Sam that night over the onion stew, to which a snowshoe rabbit shot by Reilly had been added. 'I'll get the steam-boiler I ordered, brought out from Dawson by horse-team. Or we could use our own horses, they're eating their heads off here and the hay's nearly gone . . . First thing is to get some more workmen and put them on cutting more firewood and driving across the top of the bedrock. Doesn't matter what it costs, the important thing is to get the stuff out and washed before the freeze-up. Let's see: we'll want 600 feet of steam pipe at five dollars a foot. Freight on the boiler, unless we bring it out ourselves – '

'Too dear!' said Macrae. 'We've got the whole winter ahead of us, man. I suppose if the equipment was broken up into small sections it could come out with dog-sleds easier.'

'Too late!' said Sam.

Back went Sam to Dawson City, riding easily over a trail where the snow was now gone from all but the most sheltered gullies. He mentioned not a word to those he met of the bench strike below Discovery on Dominion. In town he hired a foreman to manage the camp, a cook, and eight workmen with tents to house them. The bank manager looked dubious at the amount of money he was spending, till Sam threw a caribou-skin poke of gold-dust on his desk, and told him that much was coming out of the mine every half-hour. Then he lodged the $2,000 worth in the partnership's joint account, and went to see about the boiler.

But Sam had not reckoned with the queer mechanics of the rush or stampede. The wild geese flying over must have carried the news, it seemed. Perhaps someone deduced the find from the way Sam was spending money. By the time he set off again for Dominion, a great line of men and animals was strung out along the trail, all eager to stake out the formerly despised 'bench' land along Eldorado, Bonanza and Dominion. It was the first chance for the new arrivals, just in from the outside by way of the Chilkoot and Skagway, to stake a worthwhile claim, for all the likely locations along the creek valleys had been taken up long before.

Sam called his find 'Eureka'. When he got back to it he found Macrae fending off wandering prospectors. 'I've paid two thousand dollars for the boiler,' said Sam. 'Now all we have to do is get it out here.'

Macrae suggested taking it by boat down to Indian Creek and then poling up to the junction of Dominion, but Sam did not trust boats. They could sink, and all the expensive equipment would be lost.

Macrae had rigged up a sluice-box with riffle-boards in the bottom, over which water flowed which came through wooden flumes from a creek on the higher level. Already the two shafts had yielded another 4,000 dollars' worth. Every kind of alluvial or placer gold was there: from 'mustard' or 'flour' to dust, to 'fly-shit' or specks, to wheat-grains, to small

344

nuggets. Sam spread it out on a rug and lovingly stroked the nuggets spread on a piece of paper.

'There's nothing quite like gold,' he said. At that moment he had forgotten Mary, the girls, William, his new grandchild in India, his beautiful home and orchards back in Australia. The gold lured him like a fascinating and mysterious woman. The money it represented was a secondary consideration.

'Hell!' said Macrae admiringly. 'We've sure been dealt a royal flush this time!'

Loading up the pack-saddles with the new gold, Sam and Reilly set off again for Dawson through the bright, endless summer days.

When they got to Dawson they found the place seething with discontent. Because there had been so much confusion and recrimination along the Creeks since the new rush, the Gold Commissioner's Office had been closed to all bench claims, which could not be registered.

Rumours were rife. Notices had been posted saying that Dominion would be re-opened for prospecting in July, but only with special permits. The date for obtaining permits was set at July 11. Hastily loading up his pack-horses, four of them hauling the boiler on a kind of dry-weather sled and the rest carrying stores and lengths of pipe, Sam prepared to start on the morning of July 9 to beat the expected rush. But on the night of the eighth there was a sudden exodus on the Bonanza trail. The rumour was that permits would not be necessary. Next morning a notice, dated July 8, was posted at the Gold Commissioner's Office to this effect.

'Je–sus wept!' cried Sam. He swore and stamped around, calling down maledictions on all dithering officialdom. When he and Reilly set off in the early hours, they found the trail already clogged with men and equipment. They were reduced to the plodding speed of the slowest in the queue. The ground underfoot was churned to slush for miles. The passage of so many men and animals – the main body of the rush was later estimated at about four thousand – had warmed the surface so that the permafrost below started to melt. Water held in the frozen soil was released, to reach the surface as a long, muddy lake.

Sam fumed with impatience. Near the headwaters of

Bonanza they negotiated the notorious Carmac's Bog, where blackflies and mosquitoes drove the horses nearly mad, and men's faces and necks were bitten till the blood ran. As they came out on the higher land leading to the Dome, Sam called a halt.

'I can't stand any more of this slow travelling,' said he. 'Let's camp here off the trail till they go past.'

They pulled off the trail, gave the horses a feed of hay, and lit a fire to fry some beans and bacon for lunch. They didn't have to worry about getting in by nightfall; there was no night, and the day was clear and sunny, even hot.

Looking down from the rise at the never-ending stream of men moving like ants over the vast Yukon Territory, Sam was reminded of something – something long ago, in his childhood . . . What was it? The memory eluded yet tantalised him. With it came the memory of a taste: wax, wax candles melted into sweet cake . . . Of course!

He'd been given a magnificent birthday cake for his fifth birthday, a double edifice of sponge cake with coconut flakes pressed into the creamy icing. The five coloured candles had started to melt by the time he blew them out with one breath, which was supposed to be lucky. The icing near the candles had tasted of melted wax. November was not the hottest month, but it was already summer, and the cake had been shut in a kitchen cupboard away from the flies.

Sam ate too much, and could not face any more for a week. Then he went to the cupboard, and noticed a long, dark, moving line of ants leading to a crack in the cupboard door, and another leading out of it.

'Marmee! Look at the ants!' he called.

'Oh dear! They'll be after your cake.'

His mother came and opened the cupboard door. She took out the cake and set it on the kitchen table. It looked all right on the outside, but when she cut it with a knife the whole remainder was seen to be tunnelled through, mined by the industrious ants. They had stopes and shafts and winzes, just as in the Kuldunda Copper Co. mines.

'They haven't eat it all,' said Sam hopefully.

'No, but it won't be any good.' Henrietta cut him a fat slice, from which ants fell without apparently being hurt, however far they fell. He pulled a piece of cake off and shook it, then put it in his mouth. Erkh! It tasted not of wax, or sugar, but of ants. A strange, pungent, acidy smell and taste filled his mouth. He spat it out.

'I'm afraid we'll have to throw it away, Sam. We should have put it in the meat-safe down in the cellar,' said his mother . . .

Now Sam, lost in a dream, looked at the moving black specks below. In the same way, busy lines of men were coming ashore at Skagway and Dyea, toiling up the slopes of White Pass and the Chilkoot, making their way to the Klondike and the Yukon, then up the creeks, to dig holes and cart the spoils away. Grains of gold, grains of cake and sugar icing . . . And for what? What was the point? Suddenly Sam remembered his home, his magnificent furniture and luxurious yacht, Fourth Creek rippling musically over its stones . . . He must be mad! Living in muck in a wooden hut in the howling wilderness! He resolved that this winter was the last; he would pull out, go home. He would sell out his share.

There was still no break in the long line of men and pack-horses coming up the trail.

'It's no use waitin', Sam,' said Reilly. 'They'll be just as thick at midnight as they are now, by the looks.'

Sam spread his map out against a pack-saddle and said, 'Look, we can take a different route from here, bypass the trail and make a short cut down Caribou Creek to Dominion. If we follow this ridge here . . .'

'I'm game if you are,' said Reilly. 'I'm sick of this mob.'

Sam spat on a flat stone and tossed it in the air. 'Dry for right,' he said, picking it up.

The ridge they turned along tended south-west, in the right direction. The sun with its circling round the sky was confusing. Sam depended on his compass to keep his course. 'I hope this map is accurate,' he muttered, glancing at it again. 'It's pretty rough.'

In the top right-hand corner was a blank white area marked 'unexplored'. He'd like to do some prospecting there one day. Two creeks flowed through it to the Klondike River, the 'All Gold Creek' and the (ironically named?) 'Too Much Gold'. Another trail led down to Sulphur Creek, further to the west, so they could hardly go wrong, for both Sulphur and Caribou flowed into Dominion. He expected to come out on the lower reaches of Dominion Creek, and follow it upstream to the claim. There was little snow to impede the laden horses. They seemed in good heart after their rest and food.

All went well until, after a few hours, they left the ridge and descended into what seemed to be an endless bog. Covered in an inviting green carpet starred with wildflowers, it was a sea of muddy water from which the mosquitoes, which had been breeding in the long warm days of early summer, rose in shrilling clouds, mad for blood.

The two men beat frantically at their faces and had to swathe themselves right up to their eyebrows in scarves and spare sweaters, in spite of the heat. The horses plunged frantically, whinnying and shaking their heads, getting deeper into the bog. The high whine of the millions of insects filled them with panic. Sam, taking off a glove to beat them away from the leading horse's eyes, saw the back of his hand instantly covered in a dark fur of blood-sucking insects. The horse's eyes were ringed as with a line of kohl, with voracious black bodies. He brushed them off, but they returned at once. He had to put on goggles to defend his own eyes.

Stumbling, tangling themselves in their harness, the horses pulling the boiler became hopelessly bogged. The heavy pipes on the others came loose from their lashings and toppled sideways, pulling them down. The two leaders had got through but now they stopped, uncertain. Sam rushed to them to urge them on, but they would not move till he pulled the lead reins. Then he realised that they were blind. Their lids, horribly swollen, had covered the whole eyeball.

'Leave it be!' he cried desperately to Reilly, who was trying to get a fallen horse to its feet, half-blinded himself with his one eye being bitten. 'Help me to lead these two out. These bastards of mosquitoes will kill us all if we don't get a move on.'

The horses, down in the water and mud, presented their undefended heads to attack. The first two horses were led to firm ground beyond the swamp, where a slight breeze kept the mosquitoes at bay.

'We can't leave them like that,' said Sam. 'The machinery's

done for, and so are the horses. We'll have to shoot them.'

They each carried a rifle. They plunged back into the horde of singing, stinging insects, and within a few minutes the stricken horses were out of their misery, and the swamp was stained with red.

'Well, now we know,' observed Reilly, rubbing at his eye.

'What?'

'Why the track don't come down by Caribou Crick.'

They led the two blinded animals along the banks of a small creek. Reilly, who having lost one of his eyes dreaded blindness, bathed his eye and helped Sam bathe the horses' eyes with cold water. Then they each led one of the horses, which stumbled and baulked, unable to see where to put their feet. It was hours before they came out in the valley of Dominion, and saw beyond a shoulder of hill upstream the smoke of a miner's fire.

Seventeen

So FAR, Sam King had led what might be called a fortunate life. Happy in his childhood, happy in his marriage, lucky in finding a fortune before he was fifty – perhaps it was inevitable that it could not last. Perhaps if he had died on the Yukon at the height of his career . . . but few people die at the most appropriate time, after all.

It was certainly bad luck that the next winter should be one of the most severe for many years, that the trails should be blocked with snow, and that the claim should keep being buried under new falls. The loss of the steam boiler meant that the work was much slower and much of the gold still remained below ground when the creeks froze over once more. Since the pipes would have been useless on their own, it was at least fortunate that the two horses that survived the journey were carrying essential stores and food.

349

'It'll take us a lifetime to get the gold out at this rate,' grumbled Sam.

'Well, if you hadn't lost the boiler . . .' It was the only reference Sandy Macrae made to the disaster since the two men had arrived, exhausted, with their tale of woe and two remaining horses, whose eyes gradually recovered.

The work of firing, thawing, and mucking went on through eighteen hours of the day; the muck, thick with gold, was brought up to the surface by windlass in a bucket. They were now driving along the top of the bedrock, and this was where steam would have been so useful.

There was a long wait after each firing for the shaft to cool down and the carbon monoxide to escape. Sam started another shaft on a new claim higher up the hill, below an overhang of rock. The gold must be nearer the mother-lode, he reasoned, and also nearer the surface. He had one of his hunches about it; it would prove richer than the other two put together. Although it was staked out, he had no registration number and no papers to prove his claim, but there was no need to defend it; the flood of stampeders had faltered and stopped. Many, disappointed at not finding any gold on the benches, had returned to town: and then a new rush started in the opposite direction, to Jack Wade Creek eighty miles west of Dawson City. There was something particularly frenetic and mindless about the Klondike rushes, as if men, driven to desperation by the cold and discomfort of the surroundings, felt an urgent haste to beat the weather as well as each other to each new location.

In September the first snow fell, the beginning of that awful winter. By October the creeks were frozen, but by then Sam had reached bedrock, using men in two shifts throughout the day. The first panful from the bottom washed out at $1.50 the pan. It was the richest gold he had seen since Lake View. In November he celebrated his half-century and his new find by broaching the barrel of whisky and opening a canned plum pudding they had been going to keep for Christmas.

'Sam King's shout!' he cried, and the men cheered and gathered round to drink his health.

There was now a new mullock-heap waiting to be washed. Sam resorted to the slow method of melting snow in a

44-gallon drum over a fire and pouring it through the wet-shaker box. Colours were no longer showing in the first claim, so all hands were set to enlarging the new shaft, even the cook.

The day after New Year, when the celebrations of Christmas week were over, Macrae, who did not drink, set off alone for Dawson to lodge the new gold they had washed and register the new claim with the Gold Commisioner's office. He left Sam and Reilly nursing their hangovers, but made sure the foreman had the men back at work before he left. He took the two horses and, as there was no longer any forage for them, said he would sell them in Dawson and come back by dog-sled.

Because of the value of the load he carried he took his rifle with him. Sam did not dream that he would not get through safely; it was only forty-odd miles, and just over half that to the nearest settlement. Dominion itself had been deserted since late December, as men drifted back to Dawson for Christmas – those who had not already left to get caught up in the new rush to Jack Wade. One of the severe blizzards that plagued the north that year blew up soon after Macrae left.

Next day Sam invited Reilly to help him finish off the last of the whisky. The men were all working up the hill on the second claim, shovelling fresh snow away from the workings and the cords of wood while the brief twilight lasted at midday.

Sam and One-Eyed Reilly drank another toast. They sang:

In a cavern, in a canyon, excavating for a mine
Dwelt a miner, forty-niner, and his daughter, Clementine . . .

They each downed another whisky. The cabin was warm from the Yukon stove burning in the corner. They felt somnolent and content. Poor ole Macrae, out there in the snow and darkness – but he'd be in Grand Forks by now, having a hot feed.

There came a muffled Whumpf! from up the hill, and the cabin shook.

'Whatsh – that?' asked Reilly in a fuddled way.

351

'Wass – what?' asked Sam, concentrating on emptying the last of the barrel into a jug.

'Dunno – felt the floor shake.'

'I thought it was me shaking, ho-ho!' said Sam. 'Here y'are – where's your mug? Bottoms up!'

They drank again, agreeing that the amount left in the jug was not worth saving. When they'd finished the whisky they both fell quietly asleep.

Sun struggled above the southern peaks, lurid among long grey clouds, just on noon. Sam woke, shivering, for the fire had gone out and even the stones were cold. The outside world was strangely silent. He was used to the deadening effect of snow upon sounds, so that nothing echoed clearly. But there was not the slightest clunk of shovel or distant shout from the men. Were they all asleep? It was the foreman's job to keep them at work, to roust them out of the bunkhouse that had been built for them.

Sam tottered outside, feeling the back of his head open and shut. He picked up a handful of snow to quench his raging thirst, rubbed some against his bloodshot eyes.

All was as still as death. He went behind the cabin and pee'd in the snow, watching his urine turn to a heap of yellow frozen crystals. He looked up the hill to the dark heap of mullock, the windlass, the shaker box. They were not there. He rubbed his eyes again. Nothing. Just a huge white mound, featureless, a mountain of new snow. Had there been another blizzard while they slept, then?

'Hey, Reilly! Come and look! Something's happened!'

He began to walk up the cleared track, on which no new snow had fallen. Then something made him look up, to the overhang above the mine. It was bare of snow, the rocky moraine showing dark and glistening. The whole snow-cap had descended and wiped out the camp.

Reilly followed him. They stood gaping. Then they ran, their hangover forgotten. Only the handle of a single shovel stood out of the snow, near the outer edges of the mound. Sam grabbed it and began furiously to dig, while Reilly began scraping with his hands. They shouted, but there was no reply

352

from below, and they had no idea where to dig. The snow was powder-snow, soft and fine almost as flour. They floundered about in it until Reilly's foot touched a shovel. He scooped it out and they both dug like madmen. The marking-pegs, the winches, the shaker box and eight men including the foreman – all had disappeared in the great white mantle of snow, big as the hill it had fallen from.

'The men in the shaft – they'll be alive still!' said Sam. 'There might be some air trapped there . . . only . . .' He faltered. 'How long is it since they were buried?'

They both thought back, remembering the muffled 'whumpf', the shaking cabin. 'Yesterday afternoon, was it? Oh God, how long did we sleep? It could have been two days ago. The fireplace was cold.'

Reilly flung down his shovel, panting. 'It's no good, Sam. They're done for.'

'We can't just *leave* them there! And the mine. Eight men, Reilly! Eight men, and a fortune in gold, buried under there.'

If it hadn't been mid-winter, with most of the miners back in Dawson for Christmas, they might still have organised a working-bee to dig the men out. But they were on their own, till Macrae came back. They went on digging till they were exhausted. Then the weather turned again and another blizzard raged across the Dome and down the gulches, re-filling the holes and trenches they had dug above the buried mine. They hadn't a horse or a dog to take them in to Dawson City to report the disaster.

'We'll have to wait till Sandy comes back with the dog-team,' they told each other, huddling about the fire in the hut. Firewood was getting scarce, they would have to go out and get more, though all the near timber had long been cut out. As the blizzard ceased, the awful silence of winter reigned, except for the howling of timber wolves at midnight and 3 a.m.

It was a sound which made Sam's hair stand up on the back of his neck; a sound which seemed to rise, thin and filled with wordless longing, sheer to the glittering stars which shone so indifferently above.

*   *   *

When Sam finally came out of the Yukon Territory on board a steamboat for Vancouver, he was in worse shape than when he was led out of Hall's Creek, blinded by Sandy Blight and weak from scurvy, in '87.

He and One-Eyed Reilly had waited three weeks for Sandy Macrae to return; weeks in which the temperature fell to 55 degrees below freezing; weeks in which they dug out the snow, only to have it fall again the next day and fill in what they had dug. Then they had to conserve their strength for cutting wood and hauling it back to the cabin, no easy task when the air was so cold that every breath hurt, and icicles formed on their beards from their frozen breath.

At last, turning their backs on the silent grave beside Eureka, they closed the cabin, and drawing two hand-sleds they had rigged, loaded with stores and sleeping-bags and a tent, they set off to follow the snow-blocked trail back to Dawson City.

On the headwaters of Bonanza they found three miners wintering it out in a cabin, and spent the night with them. They had made a successful bench claim, but were thinking of turning it in and going back to the bright lights.

'I s'pose Christmas ud just about be over, though?' said one of them anxiously.

'Christmas *and* New Year,' said Sam. 'It's about the third week in January, nearly February.'

They told the news of the tragic avalanche, and asked about Macrae. They had not seen him pass. For the first time a pang of doubt went through Sam about his partner.

He had been carrying in the pack-saddles 4,000 ounces of gold, 150 pounds on each horse, worth nearly $70,000. Yet he could not believe that the upright Scotch-Canadian would have shot through with his share and Sam's. And where could he have gone? There was only Dawson, where the partnership was known. Sandy was a good bushman, but that series of blizzards would have wiped out the trail. If he had crossed the wrong ridge and followed the All Gold Creek instead of the Bonanza, he'd have ended up in that blank space marked 'unexplored'. Even so, he could scarcely miss the Klondike . . .

As they headed round the shoulder of Queen's Dome, bad

weather blew up again. They put up their tent against the swirling whiteness, the stinging sago-snow. Then more bad luck: Sam, going outside to scrape his dixie, absent-mindedly licked his knife clean. Instantly it froze to his lip and tongue. He screamed as he pulled it away, bringing a strip of skin with it. Then in the morning Reilly knocked over the can of spirits when going to fill the spirit stove. There was only enough left in the stove for one more meal of beans and coffee. Sam could scarcely eat anyway for the pain in his lip and tongue.

They stayed in their sleeping-bags, conserving warmth, for two days until the weather cleared. Then they got up in the cold greyness of the winter night and went on, little fortified by a handful of half-frozen cooked beans. 'His' constellation of Scorpio was moving round the south-eastern horizon, dimmed by streamers of high-level cloud; and looking at it, Sam saw its separate stars slowly fade, blotted out by the drifting cloud-wrack.

He felt a stab of superstitious foreboding.

At every step they sank into two feet of soft snow. Sam felt that the circulation in one leg was not working. It felt numb, and pricked with pins and needles when he walked. He could not feel his toes at all.

It was a nightmare journey till they reached the first outlying cabins, then the almost civilisation of Grand Forks. Here Sam was put on a stretcher, after a night's rest, and carried by dog-sled for the last fifteen miles. Reilly went straight to the Mounted Police post to report a double tragedy, for Sandy Macrae had not arrived, and after nearly four weeks, must be presumed lost. The Mounties set out on snow-shoes to search, and to confirm what had happened at the mine. The men must be long dead and there was no point in trying to recover the bodies before next summer.

Sam lost one of his little toes; he was lucky not to lose his leg. It had stiffened so that he could no longer straighten it properly. He walked from then on in a dot-and-carry fashion, and his hair was permanently grey.

As he convalesced a letter was handed to him from Mary, with an enclosure from the manager at Kingsland Hall. The place was heavily mortgaged, and unless funds were forth-coming at once, would have to be sold.

Sam felt as if an avalanche of troubles had fallen on his head. But his most painful interview was with his bank manager. As they went through his statements one by one, they showed the credit balance falling steadily. He had less than $500 to his name. He arranged to take his half of the partnership funds, while the balance was kept in trust for possible claimants on Macrae's estate. But of the $6,000 worth of gold they had paid in, nearly half had gone on the boiler, steam-pipes, and horse-fodder, and the rest on wages and wood. There was a little over a thousand left in the account.

Sam was stunned. Sick and in pain, he admitted that the Yukon had beaten him, as it had poor Sandy Macrae. Whether he had taken a wrong turning and headed off into unknown territory, or the horses had gone through the ice on one of the creeks and they had all been drowned, nothing was seen of him again. Somewhere out there were the body of a man and two dead horses loaded with a fortune in gold-dust. The Redcoats did not rule out foul play, as with gold worth nearly $70,000 Macrae might have been murdered and the gold taken by dog-team straight down to Skagway in Alaska. But it was thought more likely that he had been buried in a similar ice-fall to that which had obliterated the mine, for there had been a big earthquake in Alaska at the time, causing disastrous ice-falls and avalanches.

Sam took a passage on a dog-sled for Skagway himself, by the trail which now had roadhouses strung all along it, while there was a railway over Chilkoot Pass, and a permanent settlement at White Horse. He could not afford to stay in Dawson. He might have borrowed some money from his old friend Dandy Dan, but he had made his pile and left the summer before. Sam could not wait till next summer, he was too ill. He just wanted to get out of the North, away from the cold. The pegs with which he had staked the new claim would be gone, and he had no title to the buried mine. Only he and Reilly knew its value. He sold the rights in Eureka No. 1 to Reilly for a thousand dollars, plus another thousand owed to him in back pay.

Sam limped aboard the little coastal steamer at Skagway as soon as the port was open. Stuck in the frontier town which had now grown larger and wickeder, with gambling dens and dance halls on every corner, he had been tempted to gamble with the little money left once he had paid his passage, but some vestige of good sense remained to him, and he placed it in fixed deposit at the bank until the date of sailing.

He had lost weight, for the cold-burn on his mouth had turned septic and for a long time he could not eat without extreme pain. The doctor told him not to drink alcohol.

Altogether it was a chastened Sam who saw at last the ship that would take him away from these disastrous shores, coming up the Lynn Fjord between the towering peaks still covered with snow: the spring sun glittering on the whitecaps as a cold breeze whipped up the Sound and trailed the smoke from the funnels out sideways.

He had written to the agent to sell his yacht at once, but to keep for him the beautiful hand-made curtains. No doubt the orchards would have to go too. They might just be able to take out a second mortgage on Kingsland Hall and hang on to the house.

As soon as some funds arrived they all went south to California while Sam recovered in the blessed warmth. Mary did not reproach him. She had scarcely recognised him when he stepped off the boat, looking old, thin and shrunken. Yet by the time they sailed for Sydney, second class, he had bounced back to good health and optimism.

'I had a fortune in my hands, Mary,' he said. 'It was in my hands, and then it was all swept away. Bad luck! It was just bad luck, that's all.'

'At least you're alive,' said Mary, 'and have come back to us.' She had not much minded her stay in Vancouver, in a comfortable house in a good suburb, with a married daughter to visit. Frances now had a baby daughter, and William and Elaine had four children in India, beside Ada's growing troupe in South Australia. Surely Sam, ten times a grandfather, would now settle down, she thought.

She'd had the South Australian newspaper, the *Register*, sent to her regularly, and one news item described how Bill Goodman, Sam's partner in Western Australia, was now sitting with peers and baronets on the boards of twenty different companies in London. In 1897 he had been paid a fee of £10,000 to revisit the Great Boulder and Lake View for a syndicate, and report back to London. The twin towns of Boulder and Kalgoorlie were thriving. The lodes on the Golden Mile had proved phenomenally rich, living down to well below 500 feet. Up to date the six mines had produced more than a ton of gold each.

One-Eyed Reilly was to retire from the Yukon with a fortune made from Eureka No. 2, which he pegged himself the following summer, going out with the police party that went to bury the lost miners. Sam had left him an address, but as he could not read or write there was never any communication from him.

'Well, it was all experience,' said Sam philosophically. 'And I was lucky, Mary. I could have been buried alive with the others.'

Eighteen

WHILE SAM was losing his fortune and his health on the Yukon and returning to Australia to lick his wounds, his son William had provided him with three more grandchildren. The only girl, Anne, was born in Sydney while they were home on leave; Elaine called her 'my little Aussie'.

Except for the long separation from parents when they went to school, the younger generation of Kings had a happy and interesting childhood. The distances were so great that they had only one holiday a year, three months long, from the Hermitage School in Darjeeling. They kept through life that rather precocious assurance of Anglo-Indian children, which came from being waited on hand and foot by a host of adoring servants from the time they took their first breath – also from much travel, first within India and then, when they went to boarding school in Australia at the age of nine, sailing first class with P & O and bossing the Goanese stewards and the Lascar crew in fluent Hindustani.

At home they each had their own Ayah or bearer in attendance, and a groom or syce when they made excursions to the village bazaar on horseback. They kept pet frogs and lizards in the bathroom and nursed young tiger-cubs orphaned when the Maharaja shot their mother. The boys led the lives of little princes, never having to help in house or garden. But William insisted that they should oversee the feeding and grooming of their own mounts.

Anne, being the only girl, was spoilt by her adoring Ayah, who never complained if her charge pinched her arm or gave her a good push when she had to have her hair done and the comb caught painfully in a knot. But the boys kept Anne in her place by teasing her and laughing at her when she cried.

Stanley as the eldest was the natural leader in their games, but he was thin and not very strong, often confined to the chaise-longue on the veranda with an asthma attack. The second boy, Stephen, the only one who took after his mother with her red hair, soon grew taller and sturdier than his brother. Harry, good-natured and a natural follower, never quarrelled with either of them.

When the first two had gone off to school in Darjeeling, Elaine went with them to see them settled in, for they were only five and six years old. At first they found the train journey exciting, but after two hundred miles through the hot, humid Ganges valley they were both tired. Then they had to change to the little narrow-gauge railway to wind round the foothills of the Himalayas, passing terraced tea estates and patches of jungle with little yellow monkeys in the trees.

At first they kept rushing from side to side to look out the windows, but at last they fell asleep with rugs tucked round them, for the mountain air began to be cool, then cold. They arrived after dark, both tired and cross.

The Hermitage School, built on the lines of an English public school, was one of the biggest buildings in Darjeeling, a massive stone pile. The bathroom windows were covered with wire, because the big, cheeky grey Himalayan monkeys would climb up to them and steal the soap with their long arms. The children used to pelt them with fir-cones to drive them away, but the monkeys would pick up the cones and return them with interest.

Matron seemed to Elaine a kindly soul, but it was with a pang that she left her two sons to the tender mercies of schoolmasters and schoolboy teasing. She knew they would miss her at first, and the nightly prayers they said at bedtime, pressing each side of her lap as they knelt by her low chair in the nursery, the armless rocker in which she used to sit to feed them from her breast.

Stanley had been able to ride almost as soon as he could walk, just as he could talk in Hindustani with the servants before he could speak English properly. Mummy was always busy, with visits to the Mission ladies and the lepers, the Indian ladies in the Zenana, or playing tennis. She had taken him with her to the leper asylum once, but even though the catechist's wife gave him delicious Indian sweetmeats, jellabies and rasakoolies, he refused to go again. The dreadful deformities of the patients had given him nightmares.

The only time he had his mother to himself was at bedtime, before she went down to dinner, and then he had to share her with Stephen. But he loved to lean against her long skirts, burying his face in her lap and smelling the clean, cool, lavender scent she gave off after her bath. Ayah and the Indian ladies were just as clean, but they always had a musky incense-smell from their sandalwood-scented hair and saris.

As he grew older he was allowed to go with his syce for a ride outside the grounds on his pony Silvertail (who at breakfast time would come up the two steps to the veranda for a lump of sugar). The syce was not much more than a boy himself. One morning, walking ahead down a grassy track beside a small stream, he idly picked up a piece of white paper which had fallen there – part of a large official envelope – and folded it into a paper boat to amuse the young Sahib. Stanley was having trouble with Silvertail, who was backing and sidling and refusing to go forward, however much he kicked his plump sides with his heels.

Stanley plucked a switch from a tree they were under, and gave him a sharp cut across the rump. The pony jumped, stiff-legged, then set off at a gallop down the bridle-path. As he came to the bend by the stream where the syce was waiting, he suddenly saw the white paper boat moving in front of him. He shied violently, sending the boy out of the saddle.

Stanley's foot remained caught in the stirrup. As he hung below the horse's belly, he received a kick in the chest that winded him. His head bumped along the track as the pony turned and made for home. By the time the syce caught him, Stanley was unconscious, with a gash in his head from a rock on the path. Tying up Silvertail, the man released the foot, bathed the blood from the boy's head with water from the stream, then putting him across the saddle led him home. Seeing the limp body, the syces in the stables set up a cry that young Stanley-Sahib was dead.

Elaine, hearing the outcry, was just sending a bearer to find out the cause when a mournful procession came up the steps to the veranda. Stanley's syce was in tears, the others were moaning and wailing.

Elaine did not cry out nor faint. 'Stop this noise at once and tell me what has happened,' she said sharply, taking Stanley in her arms.

'The pony bolted – the young Master caught his foot – his head has hit a stone. It was fate!'

'Nonsense.' She laid him on the couch, sent for brandy, cold water, bandages. A servant went for Dr Das Gupta.

She felt for Stanley's pulse, dreading that he was already gone. She held him and poured a little brandy between his pale lips.

'Stanley! Stan dear, can you hear me? It's Mummy. Tell me you're all right.'

His eyelids fluttered open. 'Hullo, is it bedtime?' he said clearly.

'You had a fall, and it knocked you out.'

'My head hurts.'

'Yes, darling, it will ache for a while.'

'Did I fall off Silvertail? I don't remember. Is he all right?'

'Yes, and yes.'

The muddy imprint of a horse-shoe showed on his shirt front. She opened the buttons and saw the hoof-shaped contusion, wondering if any ribs were broken, if they might pierce a lung.

'Does your chest hurt?'

'A bit. When I breathe.' His voice was faint, his breathing shallow.

'Oh! *Where* is Dr Gupta?' cried Elaine. She saw the symptoms of shock, and probably concussion.

'Make some sweet, strong tea,' she said to the servants gathered round. She gave Stan another sip of brandy. 'And send to the Public Works Department for the Sahib.'

'Yes, Mem.'

When the doctor arrived he found no ribs broken, only slight concussion, and predicted a complete recovery in a few days of rest. 'He has a good, thick skull, luckily,' he said, feeling among the boy's dark hair.

'An important requirement for a steeplechase rider,' said William, who had hastened back to the bungalow.

'It was my fault,' said Stanley, who did not want the syce to be punished. 'I cut Silvertail with a switch, and he's not used to being beaten.'

William saw that the boy had not lost his nerve. Within a week he had him out riding again. 'But in future you must go on a lead rein, unless Mummy or I are with you.'

'Oh, Fa—ther!' protested Stanley, but William remained adamant.

Stanley King bore a scar for the rest of his life, a small white patch where the hair would never grow.

The year before he went away to boarding school overseas, during his school vacation there was a prolonged rainy season in Gorobhunj. Stan's asthma became worse. Elaine thought it had something to do with the mould and mildew which grew even on clothes in the cupboards and on Stanley's boots. The doctor suggested a change of air, either to the Hills or at least further inland to a drier climate.

William suggested Ranchi, a semi-Hills station in neighbouring Bihar. It was not in the Himalayas and was only 2,000 feet above sea level, but the climate was supposed to be dry and healthy. Besides, they had Army friends there that Elaine could visit, though they would stay in one of the excellent European boarding-houses.

Ranchi was a Government headquarters in the hot season, with tennis courts, polo grounds, and a European Club. It had a hospital and a European doctor. Life in Ranchi was very social, with moonlight picnics, dinners and dances during the season; but by the time Elaine and Stanley got there, Government and its entourage had departed, and Ranchi reverted to being a normal Hills town.

Almost as soon as they climbed to the wide Ranchi plateau in the little train that branched off the main Patna line, Stanley's health began to improve, his tight chest loosened up and he was able to run and climb without losing his breath. It was a happy time for him, one he always remembered, for he had his mother to himself, while next year he and Stephen, aged eight, would be packed off to boarding school in Australia. Clarrie, the baby, was still in his bearer's care.

It was near the end of their stay, and they were visiting friends of Elaine's who lived in one of the spacious bungalows in the Army cantonment for lunch, when just before the meal something strange happened. The silver and glasses on the table jingled as though on board a moving train, and a hanging lamp swung against the wall. There came a weird rushing, moaning, rumbling sound as of a great wind in the distance. It rapidly came nearer while the guests looked at each other wide-eyed; then the floor beneath their feet began to heave up and down. There was a crash of something falling in the kitchen.

Elaine grabbed her son and held him close while the shock passed. They tried to run outside, but it was impossible to move without falling down. Their legs seemed turned to jelly.

'I think it's an earthquake,' said Elaine through clenched teeth. 'It will stop soon.' (Please God!)

'Mummy, I want to cry!'

Elaine told him firmly to be brave, 'because if you cry I shall.'

After what seemed an age but was less than a minute, the worst of the shaking subsided. They all stumbled out into the grounds – their hostess (whose husband was at his officers' mess) – and the servants and guests. The servants wailed as they gazed in the direction of the bazaar where their homes were, and where a great pall of dust rose lazily and hung in the air. A second shock, not as severe as the first but lasting longer, shook the ground, which undulated beneath their feet like a deep-sea swell.

When it was over, Elaine said, 'I must see what I can do to help. Stanley, you be a brave boy and stay with the ladies – '

'*No*, Mummy! I don't want you to go,' he wailed.

'Stan, I am a trained nurse, and it's my duty to help. I don't want you to see it. Joyce, will you – ?'

'Of course, my dear. But do you think you should risk it?'

'I know I should.'

As soon as the minor tremors had stopped, Elaine went to fetch her first aid kit from the boarding-house, half-expecting to find it in ruins. Though full of plaster-dust and badly cracked, it was still standing. Then she went to the bazaar area where most of the Indian population lived in mud-brick houses in narrow streets.

On the way she passed the polo grounds, now unrecognisable. The smooth field was broken into sharp-edged, terraced steps, like a ragged paddy-field. Underground water spurted up in fountains, making small craters of mud and sand. At the edge of the bazaar a great crack appeared: the earth had fallen seven feet, and houses above it had been swallowed up.

The women had nearly all been indoors cooking the midday meal, and few of them had escaped. Those in the narrow streets had not fared much better. Dust and rubble and half-obliterated bodies choked the streets. Women were wailing, men plucking at the rubble of what had been their homes. A man in a dust-covered, dun-coloured *dhoti* was wandering in a daze, like a sleepwalker, with the body of his young daughter hanging lifeless in his arms. Another, weeping, crouched holding the hand of his wife. Only her arm and head were visible, and she was obviously beyond help. One of the servants from the bungalow where Elaine had been visiting came and begged her to do something for his old mother, whose leg was broken.

Rough operating tables had been set up and the doctors summoned to give pain-killing injections and perform emergency operations, but there were not enough doctors. Elaine did what she could: splinting broken limbs, binding up gashes, speaking encouragement to those still waiting to be disinterred.

That night she and Stanley slept in tents outside, in the grounds of the compound, in case after-shocks should bring down the already-weakened walls. Stanley, who had not seen the horrors of the bazaar, looked on it all as rather a picnic as they ate in the open by the flickering red light of charcoal braziers. But nearly all the servants had lost a member of their families, and the wailing over the dead and missing could be heard from the direction of the bazaar. Later they heard that other places in Bihar, such as Muzzaffapur, had been almost completely destroyed. Railway lines had been bent and twisted like ribbons; the earth had turned to a kind of liquid mud which sucked down houses and people.

'We got off very lightly, considering the magnitude of the earthquake,' Elaine wrote in her diary for William to read. (They were leaving for home, their holiday cut short. Because telegraph poles were down and communications cut, William had spent an anxious time after the news of a major earthquake filtered out.) 'But it was a most terrifying experience, to feel the solid earth moving in waves beneath your feet . . .

'When I realised what was happening, my first thought was, I brought Stan here for his health, and now he is going to be killed. (I resolved to protect him with my body as much as possible if the roof fell.) Instead, he seems to bear a charmed life.

'The poor servants all lost someone, for in those narrow streets where they live there was nowhere to run to. Some of the bungalows fell, but the occupants were out in the garden by then. I saw trees uprooted, houses which had sunk into the earth, water spouting from what had been dry ground, and great fissures as if a pair of giant hands had torn the ground like cardboard.

'I have never had such a feeling of impotence, of being at the mercy of forces so absolutely beyond human control; I suppose one would get the same feeling in a tornado or a typhoon. We might have been so many ants, or beetles. Truly God holds us in the hollow of His hand . . .'

Only Anne among the children was as accident prone as Stanley. When she had finished her schooling and returned home, she woke one night to find a python coiled around the lamp on her bedside table. Leaping out the other side of the bed and running for help, she ran into the doorpost and knocked herself nearly senseless. Fortunately the commotion woke her old Ayah who got help to remove the snake, which was not very large for a python – but 'in the dim light I thought it was a cobra!' said Anne, trembling, as she felt the egg-sized bump on her forehead.

When a visiting Hamilton aunt offered to take her back to England for a year 'in society', her parents saw her off in Calcutta about 8 p.m. and returned to their hotel. Around midnight there was a tap on their bedroom door. William opened it, and Elaine, half-asleep, saw the white, ghostlike apparition of her daughter, shivering and dripping water, at the foot of the bed. She sat up with a cry. But the apparition was real. The mailboat, caught in a tidal rip in the treacherous Hooghly River, had struck a sandbank and overturned. There were plenty of tenders about and everyone was picked up, though some of the engineroom crew drowned.

When she eventually got to England, Anne liked it so much that she married and stayed on in the country her great-great-grandparents had come from.

Nineteen

BACK HOME, Sam King attempted the impossible task of making a living as a gardener, digging potatoes instead of nuggets. The land was good, but every acre was heavily mortgaged. He could not keep up the interest payments or pay workers to pick the orange crop. In 1900, six months after their return from America, the property was put up for sale: 'Residence and 160 acres of splendid land, known as the Kingsland Estate'. The house, land, and most of the furnishings – except for the carved Zodiac dining chairs, the piano and the monogrammed silver-ware – were sold for

£8,000, half of which went at once to pay off the mortgage. They moved to a modest house at the seaside, not far from Sam's favourite pub near where his yacht used to be moored. He enclosed one of the verandas with glass, hung the curtains from The Tub, and, sitting there in the sun, would imagine he was steering her down around Kangaroo Island again.

He now had a new idea for regaining their vanished fortune, or at least making enough to keep the home together. He had dropped out of mining circles; his name was no longer remembered in connection with the Golden Mile, and his venture to the Klondike had ended in failure. He had forgotten his book-keeping of his young days. He told Mary prospecting was too uncertain, and for the time being he would stick to something practical. He had what amounted to a goldmine in his wallet.

Unfolding a grimy piece of paper, with the inked letters upon it almost faded away from the folds, he spread it on the table as reverently as if it had been a map of buried treasure.

'But Sam – ! It's only a recipe!'

'That's right.' He smiled smugly. 'That is the goldmine. Dandy Dan Diamond's own secret recipe for ketchup – he gave it to me on the Yukon, and warned me to keep it to myself. It's a superlative ketchup, I tried some in his gambling den once; but up there, of course, he had trouble getting the right ingredients.'

Mary and the girls were horrified. A backyard factory for making sauce! This was a terrible come-down from Kingsland Hall, the carriage and pair, the music lessons and French lessons, the conservatory, the stables . . . As it was, the new dining-room was scarcely big enough to take the long table and the twelve carved chairs with their backs of Morocco leather. But soon one end of the table was to be stacked with bottles of sauce waiting to be marketed.

'Why not a factory?' said Sam reasonably. 'I was always a good cook, you know. It's not as if I mean to hawk the stuff around myself; I'll sell it to one of the big grocery chains in bulk. And it's something I can do while this stiff leg is loosening up a bit.'

'As long as you don't go drinking all the profits,' said Mary rather sourly, for Sam was spending a lot of time at the local pub, where she suspected him of 'shouting the bar' just to show off, when he could no longer afford it.

'Now, now, Mary, don't throw cold water,' he admonished. He had kept his good temper and his equanimity throughout the traumatic experience of the sale, which had caused Mary to go to bed with a sick headache and the girls to resort to smelling-salts. He had loved owning a mansion and broad acres, but it had all seemed unreal, too good to be true. He felt like Cinderella after the coach turned back into a pumpkin at midnight – disappointed, but not really surprised. It was the yacht he missed most, with the chance to go off with a party of men on a roistering trip round the coast, drinking and fishing and living off delicate, fresh King George whiting transferred straight from the sea to the pan – there was no delicacy like it in the world. Yes, if it wasn't for Mary and the girls, he'd have sold everything else and kept the boat; and he still could have lived like a King.

However, they couldn't go on living off their slender capital indefinitely. He invested in some large copper pans, a lot of empty bottles, and beeswax for stoppers, and installed a gas stove in a large old shed in the backyard. Then he bought huge quantities of spices, brown sugar, vinegar, onions, soy beans and all the other ingredients for the secret recipe.

The first setback came when Mary told him he couldn't cook vinegar in a copper pan, unless he wanted to poison everybody. They would have to be cast iron or stainless steel pots. Then the first batch was over-cooked and came out in a sticky consistency more like thin toffee. Besides, it was bitter.

He threw it out and started again.

The girls, under protest, helped fill the bottles, using a funnel and a jug for pouring. Mary remarked that it 'smelt good, anyway', so they all tried it on their corned beef at dinner and pronounced it a success. Now all that was needed was a market.

Here Sam ran into trouble. The big Rosella company, with a bright rosella parrot for its trademark, had all the markets tied up. They produced their sauces and soups at a large factory in Kent Town in such quantities, and with such modern assembly-line methods, that Sam could not compete in price. He would have to sell at a loss. He went to see the manager, taking a bottle of his best batch of ketchup; he took with him a piece of bread and corned beef and insisted that the man should taste 'Dandy Dan's Home Recipe Ketchup' then and there. Amused, the manager did so. He agreed to pay a lump sum for the secret recipe. On the way home Sam bought a bottle of champagne and that night they celebrated the closing down of the ketchup factory.

His only assets now were the house and the remains of the Kingsland Hall furniture. The girls, Sam decreed, would have to find work. Sarah and Harriet were indignant; Mae pointed out that she already worked at running the house and doing the cooking, for Mary's health was failing. She'd had what seemed to be a slight stroke which had slowed her speech and movement. She lay often on the couch in the sitting-room, protesting that she 'should be up helping Mae,' while continuing to lie down.

Harriet had always been interested in clothes – like her grandmother Henrietta King she was tall, big-boned and handsome, but dark-eyed like her mother – and now she got a position in the fashion-buying department of a city store, and found that she liked it. Sarah, still protesting, became an assistant at the local Post Office. Like her sister Alice, Elizabeth now did her training as a nurse, 'living in' at the Adelaide Public Hospital.

Mary was only fifty-eight when she died. She had been married to Sam King since she was seventeen years old, and it had not been easy. She had borne nine living children and nine that did not live. As she lay paralysed by the final stroke she kept trying to say something, it sounded like 'Woolama-line'. It was only after she was buried that Sam realised she had been asking for 'William and Elaine'. He had sent a telegram to William, but of course he could not be expected to come all that way to his mother's deathbed. And from Elaine's letters it seemed that she was worried about his health. William had a bad cough and sore throat.

Sam, shattered by the loss of his partner of more than forty years, sold the last of the Kingsland Hall furniture to pay the hospital and funeral expenses.

'At least Mother was spared this,' said Mae tearfully, as the auction crowd gathered for the advertised sale:

On the premises, Sale of extremely choice and superior Household Furniture, the pieces including carved walnut dining suite with twelve chairs upholstered in Morocco leather embossed with the signs of the Zodiac, and massive extension table . . .

The costly marble clock, the Doulton chamberpots, two Dresden figures, and the Soehne piano; all were put up for sale with the last of the French chairs and the Queen Anne bedroom suite which had been Mary's pride and joy. He kept only the monogrammed silver cutlery with their twined initials.

Sam divided the proceeds among the five girls. Mae and Sarah left home to rent a cheap cottage in Norwood together. After a few more years the youngest girl, Harriet, got married, and Sam set off for the stony hills south of Adelaide to look once more for gold.

Since his return from Canada he had not been in touch with his wealthy brothers. He let them think he had settled overseas, too proud to ask them for help or to admit his failure. As Mr S. E. King of Echunga he was an anonymous figure. Then the store-keeper who had grubstaked him decided to take him on as an assistant to work out what he owed, and ended up giving him the store to manage when Sam, tired of a single life, offered to take on his plain unmarried sister as a second wife. Pearl was thirty-five years his junior, solidly built and broad-faced. Her virtues were mainly negative ones: she was not stupid, and she was not a shrew.

Living in the country, they were scarcely aware of the Great War. But he had kept in touch with William, who sent the sad news that both Harry and Stephen had been lost. (Four of Sam's grandsons died in that war, World War I.) His daughter Alice had nearly lost her life in the War, when she enlisted in England as a nursing sister with the Queen Alexandra's Imperial Military Nursing Service. The troopship in which she was travelling was torpedoed off Alexandria. Alice, to the hysterical rage of her cabin mate, refused to leave till she had put on her full uniform and regulation panama hat. They were picked out of the sea just as their overloaded lifeboat was sinking.

One of the men she nursed later aboard a troopship off Gallipoli was William's third boy, her nephew Harry King, then dying of typhoid. 'I'm too young to die!' he had told her.

William still kept in touch with his father. He wrote to say he had not been very well, and the doctor had advised him to give up smoking. Elaine, he said, had taken the loss of her two boys very hard. The eldest, Stanley, was not strong and had been advised to leave the enervating climate of India. He was returning to Australia to settle in Adelaide.

The next communication Sam had was from London: a brief, sad letter from Elaine to say they had come to England so that William could visit a specialist. The verdict was, an inoperable cancer of the throat.

Sam's first thought was, 'Well, Mary was spared this, too.' He wrote to the girls to tell them. He did not see them nowadays; they had disapproved violently of his second marriage to 'that awful woman', an insult to their mother in their stern young judgement. The new Mrs King returned their dislike with interest: 'your stuck-up daughters', as she referred to them.

Unlike Mary, she was ready to accompany Sam on his various journeys in search of a new fortune. They went to Coober Pedy in 1920 and lived in an underground dugout home to escape the heat. Pearl opened a store for the miners – she was almost the only woman on the field – which brought in more than Sam's prospecting. His heart was in gold, not precious stones; but they went on to the White Cliffs opal field six hundred miles west of Sydney, and when someone found a huge blue sapphire at Reward Creek, near Anakie in western Queensland, Pearl (who had been named after a precious gem) nagged him until they went there too. Here Sam rigged up a cradle, or dry shaker box – for there was scarcely any water to be had – and putting the gravel through this re-covered enough stones – both yellow and blue, and the green ones known locally as 'emeralds' – to keep them in comfort for a year or two. He liked the clear dry heat, the burning blue of the sky; the only liquid sound the crested bell-birds' musical chime: *Pan-pan-pan-ell-a!*

But Pearl grew tired of living in a tent, in the dust of the dry

Reward Creek. They sold their stones and took a ship to Tasmania, the island State where the apples grew that was supposed to be as green as England. He did some fossicking about the old mines at Fingal and Mathinna, and then went west to Mount Lyell. But it was too cold for his ageing bones. They sailed for Melbourne, wandered to Ballarat and Stawell, then returned to South Australia.

Sam now applied for the Old Age pension. He said he had worked all his life and paid his taxes, and now the Government could keep him. He knew that to the girls this would be the final shame, their father an old age pensioner! He did not really miss his daughters except for Ada, and he had not seen much of her anyway since she married.

Twenty

STANLEY KING, like William, became a fine horseman. After getting a job in a Calcutta bank, he won the Calcutta Point-to-Point as his father had done before him. But after a severe bout of fever which recurred annually, and with increasing shortness of breath due to asthma, he was advised to leave India for a drier and healthier climate. He applied for a position in Adelaide, the city his father had come from as a young engineering graduate.

So when his parents left for England to consult a specialist for William, there were no Kings left in Gorobhunj. Before long the Maharaja too was gone, 'shot in mistake for a tiger' when he climbed down too soon from his *machan* during a shoot. He should have been more careful. An ambitious cousin, an orthodox Hindu with many heirs, was waiting to step into the Rajbhati Palace in his place.

Stanley, who still loved riding, joined the Adelaide Hunt Club, but after the first season he found the cold winter winds affected his chest. Instead of riding to hounds the next winter, he took up an invitation to visit his mother's relatives, the Macdonalds, at Balranald station in the sunny, dry west of New South Wales. There he happened to meet his first cousin, Rosetta Macdonald Forbes, on a visit from her father's station in Queensland.

Stanley and Rosetta went riding together, and by the time she left to return home they were engaged. He was tall, very thin – almost gaunt – but she was impressed by his manners and an air of Indian Army about him, though he had never been in the military.

After their marriage Stanley entered an Adelaide insurance firm as assistant manager, and soon rose to be the top executive. But the long-standing asthma had affected his heart, and he still had recurring bouts of fever. He attended race-meetings, but only as a spectator.

Rosetta, who had money of her own, imported her raceday outfits, complete with shoes and gloves, from Paris. She became a leader of local fashion: what she wore to the Adelaide Cup or the Oakbank Picnic Races was always reported in the social pages of the local newspapers.

Stan wondered how she would get on with his mother when they met. Elaine cared little for clothes and much for good works, though she always looked neat in her plain skirts and high-necked blouses. Since his father was now undergoing radium treatment for cancer in London, they had not come to Australia for the wedding. Elaine had sent the bride a beautifully-carved box of ivory from Gorobhunj. Now they were on their way home by mailboat.

Stanley went down, alone, to meet the ship at Outer Harbour. He had known from Elaine's letters that his father was very ill when they left, but a few weeks later a cable arrived to say that William had disappeared from the liner in the Indian Ocean, and was presumed drowned . . .

Stanley wondered about this, as he waited in the cold dawn for the *Multan* to berth. Visitors would be allowed on board at 7 a.m. The big black and buff-coloured ship towered above the wharf. Stanley exchanged a few words in Hindi with a little brown man in blue working denims who looked over the stern. He was sharply reminded of schooldays, of the first trip to Australia in the P & O liner, sister ship to this one, which had brought him and Stephen to Sydney. And now Stephen was buried in Flanders, far from home. Harry had died of typhoid off Gallipoli, and Clarrie, the youngest, was working among sheep somewhere 'up north' or 'out west' in Queensland.

On board at last, Stanley found a steward to show him to Elaine's cabin on 'B' deck, along a gleaming polished corridor humming with the hidden power of great generators; the warm air had that indescribable below-decks smell he remembered. Cabin-stewards hurried past with armfuls of linen or trays of food. There was an untouched tray of breakfast in Elaine's cabin, he noticed, as the door opened to his knock.

His mother was pale but composed. All the formalities of reporting the death had been gone through in Western Australia, at the first port of call. The tall figure in a grey tailored suit, the large eyes in the pale face, sallow after many Indian summers, the red hair – she had scarcely changed, though nearing fifty.

'My dear, dear Stan!'

'Mother!'

They held each other closely, and when she lifted her head her eyes were wet. She took his hand and led him to sit beside her on one of the narrow ship's beds.

'He wanted to come home to Australia when he knew how little time he had left,' she said. 'But after we sailed, he became worse. He was in constant pain. The doctors had given him at most three months to live.'

'Poor Mother! Dreadful for you, too.'

'Yes. To see him thinner each day – unable to eat – his voice a whisper.' She raised her head and looked out the porthole. 'I think that was why – it was to save me from having to see him suffer to the end; me, a trained nurse, and unable to do anything to help! He was the bravest man I've ever known.'

'He was always fearless. I remember watching him jump, riding bareback at full gallop.'

'This was a different order of courage from steeplechasing. To leave me, and the world, before he had to, and without seeing his boys, or Australia again! A few days before we got to Fremantle Willy said, "Didn't you have an uncle buried at sea on the way to Australia?" I should have known what he was planning then. It was a Great-uncle actually, the youngest of Josiah and Kate's family; and his name was Will.

'That night, he got up after midnight. He could never sleep for long. I was half asleep. He bent over and kissed me.

'He pressed my hand to his poor hollow cheek – his fingers were still strong! – and whispered, "I'm just going for a walk on deck, and I may be some time." I must have dozed off again, and when I woke the dawn was just coming behind those huge Indian Ocean clouds, dark as ink above the sea. Willy's bunk was empty.'

She had rushed out in her bathrobe, searched the deserted decks right up to the boat-deck and down to the poop-deck in the Second Class, where she looked back along the foaming wake. Then she came back by way of all the public rooms, but she had known, as soon as she woke, that he was gone.

Her first instinct was to run and give the alarm to a ship's officer. Instead she had gone back to the cabin, put a 'Do not disturb' notice outside the door, and locked it. Then she sat staring through the porthole at the sea until she heard the ship's siren blow its midday blast. Only then she went to report what had happened.

'Didn't the Captain question you about why you didn't raise the alarm earlier?'

'Yes. I said that I slept in.'

(The Captain had in fact been inclined to get angry, and go on about its being his duty to search for passengers who fell overboard. 'But he didn't fall, Captain Stephens,' Elaine had said, and he stared at this calm, pale-faced woman with the dark shadows under her great tragic eyes. 'And he would not have wanted you to turn the ship around and inconvenience the passengers. Besides, he could not swim in his weakened state. And it has been twelve hours.')

Elaine said, 'He asked me if your father might have been dazed with pain-killing drugs; he knew he had a terminal illness. I told him that Willy refused to take any. He said he wanted to be fully conscious for whatever time was left to him . . .

'I had to make a deposition to the police in Fremantle, of course.'

Stan pressed her shoulder in wordless sympathy.

As the ship was not sailing for Melbourne till next day, he took her home to stay for the night. She had thought to leave her luggage on board and travel overland, for shipboard life was painful to her now, but decided that it was too much trouble. There were only a few days left of the voyage.

Rosetta was quite tactful, for her, and left mother and son alone to talk once dinner was over. Later, Elaine sat at the piano and accompanied herself in a song:

> Full fathom five thy father lies,
> Of his bones are coral made;
> Those are pearls that were his eyes,
> Nothing of him that doth fade,
> But doth suffer a sea-change
> Into something rich and strange . . .

feeling her own eyes, hard and tearless, turn to pearl, or stone.

Stanley King did not see his mother again until several years later, when she passed through in a mailboat on her way back to India to take up her work once more among the lepers. By that time their only son Vincent had been born, so they took him down to the Outer Harbour to meet his grandmother.

Twenty-one

THE SECOND Mrs King had never taken the place of Mary in Sam's heart, though she was a good companion. Pearl liked to come with him to the pub – though not allowed in the bar, quite rightly in his opinion. She did not object when he stayed till closing time at 6 p.m.

To earn a little extra Sam made batches of toffee and sold it to a corner candy store as 'Macrae's Clan Toffee'; it was a recipe Sandy Macrae had from his Scottish grandmother, which he'd once made on the wood fire at the cabin in Dawson. It was good toffee, but as the recipe used a lot of butter, which was expensive, it was not really profitable.

'My word, Pearl, I wish we had some of those tenners I used to light my cigars with in the old days,' said Sam. (Actually he had sometimes used five-pound notes, not tens, but Sam never spoilt a story for lack of extravagant detail.) 'Did I ever tell you about the time I fought a duel in Dawson City? Thousands of ounces of gold were bet on the result . . . Who won? I did, of course. I'm alive to tell the tale, aren't I?'

Pearl was forty-four, and Sam was nearly eighty, when he learnt to his horror that she was pregnant. He couldn't help feeling rather proud all the same, of his ability to father a child at his age, but he had thought, or hoped, she was too old to conceive. Now here was a to-do! He didn't feel very pleased at the idea of a young baby in their small house, quite apart from the expense.

His daughters somehow heard about it, and were suitably disgusted. Not that they feared being disinherited by a new family, for by now he had nothing to leave. But Sam need not have worried about having to provide for a child. Poor Pearl was overweight and not in good condition, being rather too fond of her favourite drink, port and lemon. Her kidneys became affected, and she died before the baby could be born. The doctor told him that it would have been yet another girl.

Sam, aged eighty, set off once more for the bush. Though he missed Pearl, he could never help a feeling of self-congratulation when someone younger than himself was carried off. He had outlived his brother James, and Henry and Arthur had died years ago: his son William and his daughter Elizabeth were both gone, and of course Mary, and several of his grandsons . . .

'I'll live to be a hundred,' Sam told himself.

Once again Sam was fossicking in the stony hills south of Adelaide, camped on Bull's Creek near Echunga. On pension day he would go into town, picking a flower over a fence on his way to the pub, to put in his buttonhole. His white, pointed beard was neatly trimmed, an old felt hat sat on the back of his head, and he carried a small shopping-bag to hold a bottle of sherry and a pack of shredded tobacco, for he could no longer afford cigars, but rolled his own cigarettes.

Breasting the bar, he would drink steadily through his pension cheque. One day a newspaperman on the lookout for a 'human interest' story dropped in at the country pub with a photographer. The next weekend Sam's picture appeared in a weekly journal:

> Mr S. E. King, discoverer of the Golden Mile at
> Kalgoorlie, Prospector for more than 60 years.

There followed the story, more or less authentic, of his adventures in Western Australia and on the Klondike.

On pension day, stumping in on his bent leg, old and white-haired and rheumy-eyed, he unfolded the newspaper on the bar. After a few drinks he began to re-live his days of glory.

'Shout the bar!' he cried. 'Sam King's shout! Once more, gentlemen – *shout the bar!*'

The few farmers and road-labourers who had drifted in from the heat outside, regarded him curiously. The barman smiled pityingly. He knew how much Sam had to spend each fortnight, and that it would not stretch to shouting even the few customers in the bar that day.

He passed over another of Sam's usual, and picked up the paper.

'This you, is it?' he asked indifferently.

'You can see it's me, can't you? Read it!' said Sam. 'Why, I had enough to buy this pub once, and all its stock. I had a grand mansion with a park, a carriage and pair, and an ocean-going yacht – '

'Yair?'

'Certainly I did. I had shares in Lake View and Great Boulder and – '

'What 'ud ya do? Gamble it all away?'

Sam looked startled. 'Yes, I suppose you could say that. But not on the horses. It just seemed to melt away, like Fairy Gold.'

'Yair?' The barman filled his glass again and pushed it across.

'Pour one for yourself. Go on, I can pay. And I'll tell you the story of my life.'

From then on the locals realised that they had a celebrity in their midst.

Apart from his pension, Sam found enough gold to keep him in tobacco and sherry, and the cheap cuts of meat – sometimes varied by an ox tongue – which he would make into a nourishing stew with onions, potatoes and carrots sometimes lifted from a farmer's field. He had a tent, a sleeping bag and blankets, a billy-can for tea, and a big, sturdy iron pot which served both as a container for stew and as a dolly-pot when he found some likely-looking quartz to be crushed with a crow-bar.

Sitting beside his campfire in the gumtrees' shade, stirring his stew, taking a perfectly-baked damper from the ashes, setting his billy of tea to cool, Sam wanted for nothing. He still had his health, which many a millionaire might envy. And as he stirred the pot, from which a savoury smell arose, his thumb caressed the handle of the ladle.

It had once belonged to the bowl in which he made claret cup at Kingsland Hall. It was a heavy ladle of sterling silver gilded with 18-carat gold. On the handle were entwined the initials SEK and MEK, the monogram of his wife, Mary Ellen, and of Samuel Edmond King.

BOOK FOUR

The Conquering Hero

1933–1949

Call across the blazing deserts of the Never Never land!
  There are some who will not answer yet awhile,
Some whose bones rot in the mulga or lie bleaching in the sand,
  Died of thirst to win the land another mile.
Thrown from horses, ripped by cattle, lost on deserts . . . drowned
  in floods
  These are men who died to make the Wool Kings rich.

Henry Lawson, 'The Men Who Made Australia.'

I am the family face:
Flesh perishes, I live on,
Projecting trait and trace
From time to times anon,
And leaping from place to place
Over oblivion.

Thomas Hardy

One

'YOUR FATHER,' says his mother firmly, 'must not be dis-
túrbed. Run outside and play, Vincent.'

Reluctantly leaving his game of sliding in his socks on the
polished brown lino which runs from the kitchen past Flo's
room to the back door, Vincent King sidles along the wall,
going, yet protesting silently as he goes. Beyond the flyscreen
door the garden wilts in the heat.

'And put on your sandals, child. Don't go outside in your
good socks.'

Vin makes a swift run back to his sandals, lying on the
gleaming wooden floor of the hall: slides towards them and
scoops them up as he passes. Speed, speed! He is a skier
swooping down a slope of snow. He is a speedboat skimming a
lake. He goes out in a skating movement through the front
door, letting it bang behind him. Sits on the edge of the porch
steps to put on his yellow leather sandals. A line of ants issues
from a crack in the stone steps. What are they telling each
other as they pause a moment to touch feelers, then hasten
on?

Experimentally he treads on one. The others rush round in
a frenzy, communicating urgently with their feelers. Then
they begin to lug the body away.

'Silly ole ants!' One ant, what did it matter among all the
others? Suddenly he is aware of a great stillness about him.
The sky seems brooding, enormous. If a giant foot descended
through the clouds . . .

He squints up at the sky, deliberately frightening himself,
then shakes it off and wanders about the big garden . . .

Vincent King was not exactly ashamed of his parents, but he
knew they were different. He had been asked to a children's
party when he was four, and when the other parents came to

call for their children, he saw that the mothers were pretty and young-looking, the fathers jolly and brown-faced. His own parents were old. His father walked leaning on a cane and had trouble with his breathing. He could not remember his mother without grey hair. His father was often sick, lying down with one of his 'attacks'. Other boys' fathers took them to the beach for a swim on Sundays. Or they had brothers and sisters to play with. He had no one, not even a dog. His mother kept a cat, but she didn't approve of dogs: they carried horrid diseases like hydatids, she said. Dogs were only good for working sheep; they always had dogs on the station when she was a girl, but they did not make pets of them.

Sometimes, out of sheer boredom, Vin tormented the cat. Now it kept out of his way. He scuffed the gravel of the drive with the toe of his sandal, looking for diamonds, or at least some clear crystals of quartz among the white and grey stones. Gold was sometimes found in pieces of white quartz, his father said. Dad's Grandpa had been a prospector and had once found a whole hill of gold.

But there were no diamonds or bits of gold, only some tiny, tough, amethyst-coloured flowers, like miniature irises, growing among the gravel. Vin rolled on the level front lawn, working off some of his excess energy. The grass was limp and soft in the sun. Rolling over on his face, with his nostrils buried in the short stems, he breathed a scent of greenness and heat. A motor-car on the main road hummed by on a rising note, dropped down a gear. The sun slid out from behind one of the great, solid clouds. Its rays beat on the back of his neck, shafts of heat pricked his shoulders through his thin shirt.

Suddenly he knew that all this had happened before. He had a most vivid memory – or was it foreknowledge? – of a grassy sward where he lay, while waves of sound washed over him: falling, rising to a thin high-pitched note of tearing silk, then fading into the distance. And his heart began to beat with a strange excitement.

'Vincent!'

He clung to the timeless moment, ignoring his mother's voice. Shut up, shut up, shut up, he said silently into the grass.

'Vincent! Do you hear me? Don't lie there in the sun

without your hat, you'll get sunstroke. Here, put on your washing-hat at once.'

She came to the edge of the steps and tossed him a faded grey cotton hat. He reached for it with his heels and put it on to get rid of her.

There was no sound any more but the hum of a car passing on the main road two blocks away. His heart slowed down, yet he retained something, a hint, a trace of that exultation, like the fading glow of an electric lamp when the current is switched off. What had he half-remembered?

That was his mother, always fussing with sunhats and sunburn cream in summer, woollen caps in winter. Other boys went bareheaded, carefree, sailing past downhill on their bicycles with their hair blown back from their wind-keen faces. He had begged for a bicycle. No; too dangerous with all the cars on the road. Roller-skates, then? Or a tricycle? But he was not allowed anything with wheels, anything with which he might play on the road.

'You're all we have, Vin,' his mother would say, smoothing back his straight, light-brown fringe which she kept cut to the level of his fine, slanting eyebrows.

He had rebelled over the knitted cap, though. He remembered the thrill of asserting himself, even while he was afraid of his mother. He found that his will was as strong as hers.

'He takes after you, Rosetta,' his mother's relations always said when they saw him, and his mother would agree. 'Yes, he has the Forbes nose.'

She never smacked him for disobedience; she just bore down opposition. He had thrown the cap into the prickly front hedge, 'lost' it in the street, let it fall in the river. She just made him another one. She made a whole set. She was waiting in the hall to pull one of the hated things down over his ears when he went out. He pulled it off. She put it on again, less gently.

Then he dropped it down the lavatory – it fell, he said – and blocked the waste pipe.

'I believe the days are getting warmer,' she said, though winter was only half over. 'You needn't wear a cap any more.'

He had looked at her with his bright, dark grey eyes which already, at six, held a hint of precocious mockery in them;

what his teachers called his 'cheeky look'. His eyes stared into her grey, rather cold ones, and she looked away. She turned and moved off majestically like a ship in full sail.

She was a high-bosomed, big-boned woman who held herself and walked with conscious dignity. She could be generous with Vin, even doting, but sometimes when he defied her there was ice in her glance.

Rosetta Forbes, elder daughter of Elaine's brother Joseph and grand-daughter of Jason Forbes, was proud of her family's pastoral background. Though her husband Stanley was 'in business' rather than 'on the land', which made her position a little less acceptable in society, he was her first cousin and his antecedents were much the same as hers. They had met when both were on a visit to their Macdonald relatives in the Riverina district. She was nearly three years older than her cousin, but it was Stanley who had become a semi-invalid, old before his time.

Their home in a foothills suburb was set on a large block and was elegantly furnished by Rosetta and slightly exotic with Indian rugs, ebony carvings and inlaid brasses brought home by Stanley from Calcutta. Vin liked best the little ivory box, carved as fine as lace, which opened with a golden key.

On Saturday afternoons, if his father was well, they would all go to the Parklands Bowling Club, of which King was a member. His wife was an associate, but did not play; she liked to play tennis on Sunday mornings at a friend's private lawn court. Although the climate was so dry, with a long, hot summer, all these games were played on smooth green swards, kept alive by constant sprinkling.

Vin was desperately bored at the bowling green, but they would not leave him at home alone. Flo the maid had every other Saturday off, as well as Sundays. The only thing he looked forward to was the glass of lemonade, fizzing and sparkling, which his mother would buy him at the open-air window of the club bar. It was not like lemonade at home, which was flat, and the barman broke the ice from a big piece into clear, jagged lumps. They were like miniature icebergs, and he loved to look at the ice and crunch it between his teeth, one of which was getting wobbly and ready to fall out.

Today it was very hot, but dry and clear. His father was out on the rink in his cream flannels and fuji shirt, a floppy white cotton hat on his balding head. Vin watched for a while the dark, polished wooden bowls curving towards the little white kitty. Sometimes they collided with an audible click. But it was a terribly slow, dull game. He swirled the ice in his glass and made it tinkle against the sides.

The ice was beautiful, pellucid, and streaked with tiny silver bubbles. The glass, which had a solid base and a narrow waist, the sparkling lemonade, and the piece of ice were all of the same colourless colour, like crystal.

He fished in the glass with his small dimpled fist and pulled out the ice. His teeth crunched on it but it was slippery as a fish. It shot out of his grasp on to the close-cropped green of the bowling-rink. The green was sunken below the level of the surrounding path.

'Eh! Get that kid off the green!'

He clambered up again with the retrieved ice, which had pieces of mown grass sticking to it. He dropped it back into the lemonade. The pieces of grass floated off.

'You can't drink that now, Vin, it's dirty.' His mother's hand descended from that higher level where big people lived, and whisked away the glass. It was put on the shelf of the bar-window high above his head. He threw himself on the ground, kicking and screaming.

After a while he got up and wandered off in a huff, as no one was taking any notice of him. He was bored, bored. The bowlers moved incomprehensibly on the green among the black shining bowls – making strange gestures, kneeling on mats. They might have belonged to some unknown religion.

Vin climbed a tree and leant disconsolately in the fork, pleased to see that his white sailor-suit was getting dirty.

His mother was calling him from over by the clubhouse. She had a new glass of lemonade in one hand, and in the other his cotton hat. He submitted to the hat and accepted the lemonade. Once more he fished out the ice and tried to crunch it between his teeth. The loose milk tooth came out, with a small taste of blood. He tied it carefully in the corner of his handkerchief. It was worth sixpence from the Tooth Fairy.

When he had drunk the lemonade he lay down on the green bank that surrounded the rink and stared up at the sky, where a few rounded clouds were roaming its blue fields like a flock of sheep, all drifting towards the west. The sun bathed his limbs, as it gilded those sky-lambs. The gentle progression of clouds made him drowsy. His eyes closed. The voices of the bowlers seemed to come from a long way off, drifting, fading . . .

'Come on, lad. Time to go home.'

He was lifted, carried in strong arms. Then he was in the car, in the front seat between his parents, feeling the mystic unity of the three of them through his bones and flesh. His mother's arm was round him, her breast beneath his cheek was wondrously soft. Her hand played gently in his hair.

'Brrm! Brrmm! Varoomm!' Uttering loud automobile noises, changing gear with his voice, eight-year-old Vincent sped along the passage, in one door of the kitchen, round the table and out the other. Up the passage, once round the hall, and back to the kitchen once more. He had lapped all the other cars, and was now a whole lap in front.

'Really, young Vin!' complained Flo, who was washing up at the sink. 'That row gives me a headache.' She flapped the teatowel at him: the chequered flag. Vincent King was the winner!

He rounded the table, reducing revs as he went, and glided to a stop. 'If you've nothing better to do, you can give me a hand to dry them dishes.'

'Okay.' He was feeling pleased, expansive. His mother and father were both out, and for once he could run and make a noise. He grabbed the teatowel from Flo's wet hand and began lifting plates down from the sink with care and concentration, polishing each one till it gleamed.

He was a perfectionist in everything he did. He piled the dry plates, smelling pleasantly of hot china, on the table and left them for Flo to put away.

His parents had gone to the races, the Adelaide Cup. Rosetta dressed with as much care as for a garden party, with her wide-brimmed hat exactly matching her broderie anglaise blouse, her pleated silk skirt. His father wore with his morning suit an impeccable tie of grey silk and a grey top hat. It was a social occasion where they went to see and be seen, yet their interest in the horses was genuine.

Stanley King had grown up with horses in India, had a scar on his head from a bad fall when he was a child, and had won the Calcutta Point-to-Point when he was only twenty-one. To calm his nerves before a race he had become a heavy smoker. Now his lungs were wrecked. He had emphysema, complicated by asthma, and could no longer go riding; the slow game of bowls was all he could manage.

The medicines he took for asthma, and the strain of inadequate oxygen, had affected his heart. He refused to give up work, though he could have retired on his wife's money and his own investments. He pretended to himself that the whole Insurance firm depended on him, though he knew that if he dropped dead tomorrow, it would go on quite well without him.

He had hoped that his son would follow his interests and become a champion rider one day. But Vincent, who had an irrational fear of horses with their long teeth and hard hoofs, had successfully avoided even learning to ride. The first time he was put on a horse he developed violent hay fever. His allergy was so strong that he could not go near a stables, or even someone who had been riding.

Rosetta, who had no sisters, would have liked a girl, but after Vincent, and two miscarriages, and Stanley's increasing ill-health, she decided that it was wiser to have no more children. All her hopes and ambitions were centred on her son. She wanted him to study Law when he grew up, as there was a tradition of lawyer Prime Ministers of Australia, and she felt sure he was destined for high office.

As for Vincent, he did moderately well at school without being brilliant. He was good at anything competitive, brought home several swimming trophies, and won the under-twelve tennis championship. But he could never learn to like football, where he was only one of a team.

His favourite subjects were Mathematics and Chemistry. The other subject he was most interested in was Girls. Without help or guidance from parents or teachers, he made the usual experiments and discoveries, and was given the usual inaccurate information by his school-mates.

But his over-riding passion was for automobiles, cars of all makes and sizes, and especially fast racers. His heroes were Nuvolari and Caracciola. By the time he left school he knew what he wanted to be: a racing driver like them.

Two

After matriculating, Vin was enrolled at the University of Adelaide for the four-year course in Law, which his mother had decided on for him almost as soon as he was born.

Apart from Latin and Psychology, which he rather liked, he found many of the subjects boring, the textbooks dry and dull, the lectures soporific.

Then in the third year he had to become an articled clerk to a firm of solicitors, as well as attending lectures.

This meant working for a pittance at such chores as delivering Unsatisfied Judgement Summonses, taking Deeds to be stamped, posting mail, and carefully destroying the contents of the wastepaper baskets of the senior partners. In fact he did almost everything but 'polish up the handle of the big front door'.

Bored with *The Law of Torts*, he began skipping lectures with two kindred spirits and roaring off to the beach in the little MGTC his mother had given him for his eighteenth birthday. The War they had just been too young for was over, petrol was no longer rationed, and they were full of the impatient exuberance of youth.

They lived for the present and took no thought of the morrow. Stanley King, who wished he'd had Vincent's opportunities to study, found this attitude reprehensible.

While his parents were in Melbourne for a Caulfield Cup meeting, and Ethel the present maid had gone home for the weekend to nurse a sick mother, Vin and his two fellow

Law-students threw a magnificent party that lasted the whole weekend.

By Sunday night the big house was a shambles. Every bed and most of the couches had been slept on. Bottle-tops had been trodden into hand-woven Indian rugs, beer had been spilt stickily on the polished hall floor, half-empty glasses stood on the stairs. There were glass-rings on top of the piano and full bottles in the bath, which had been filled with ice. Cigarettes overflowed from inlaid brass ashtrays.

With his friends Peter and David, Vincent started a frantic clean-up about 9 p.m. on Sunday, after turning reluctant couples out of bedrooms upstairs and down. Ethel was due back in the morning, and Mr and Mrs King on Monday afternoon. But to the boys' uncritical eyes it all looked pretty good by ten o'clock. Broken glasses, empty bottles, crumbled potato crisps had been cleared away, the carpets vacuum-cleaned, the beds made.

'Thanks, chaps,' said Vin as they finished the last of the beer evicted from the bath. They sat down in the kitchen to a big plate of scrambled eggs each.

'She was a beaut party,' said Peter. 'But what if your parents find out?'

'They won't. Mother might count her glasses and find a few missing, but she's not going to throw a blue fit over that.'

'Pity about the standard lamp, though.'

'Oh, I'll get it fixed tomorrow . . . More eggs, David?'

'No more for me, thanks. I'm full as a boot.'

They helped him wash up and left the plates to drain, mopped the shiny brown linoleum of the kitchen floor, and left. Vin, scarcely waiting to undress, fell into bed and was asleep almost before their car wheels had left the gravel drive.

He was awakened minutes later, it seemed, by a banging on the front door. Groggily he made his way downstairs. Hell, were parents back already? He had wanted to check the place in daylight first. He opened the door and blinked at the too-bright sunlight flooding the eastern veranda.

A dishevelled figure of a man with a large, fair moustache stood there, trembling.

'Burton! What the hell – ?'

'King, you've got to let me in! Woke up in the garden jus'

now, and this great – savage – butterfly went for me. Huge eyes! Black. Horrible.' He rolled his own bloodshot eyes over his shoulder. His usually cheerful round face was lugubrious.

'Come in, Burton, you drongo. You've got the DTs. Scared of a butterfly! I'll make you some coffee.'

'It was after me, I tell you.'

'Actually, it's just as well you woke me. Must open the windows and try to get the smell of grog out of the carpets. Ethel will be back any minute. D'you want some food? Cornflakes? Crispies? After that you'd better get going, old chap. There's a tramline on the next block.'

'Food!' Burton gave an elaborate shudder. He accepted the coffee with shaking hands.

'I feel all right, strangely enough,' said Vin. 'Perhaps because I had a good feed before I went to bed. It took us ages to clear up.'

'I'll bet! It was a great party.' Burton had stopped trembling.

After seeing his last guest safely off the premises, Vin opened all the downstairs windows and turned on the exhaust fan in the kitchen. He took a shower and got dressed. When he came down Ethel was in the kitchen.

'Hullo, Ethel, how's your mother?'

'She's better thanks, Mr Vin.' She took flour from a tin, 'I'm making a batch of biscuits. You had breakfast yet?'

'Yes, thanks. At least I wasn't hungry. Just coffee.'

'H'm. Thought you wouldn't of left my kitchen as tidy as this. It's funny, though.' She opened the china cupboard. 'Everything's in the wrong place.'

'Eh?'

'All them glasses. The tall ones go on top, the crystal goblets go in the sideboard in there, the coffee mugs are where the teacups oughter be. You bin throwin' a party?'

He grinned. 'Well, you know, when the cat's away! How's the place look?'

She went round the downstairs rooms, her long face growing longer. 'Terrible. The hall floor's all smeary, the drawing room smells of beer and tobacco, the lamp's broke, and' – she retrieved a half-full glass from under a chair – 'you haven't cleared up properly.'

'Look, be a sport Eth – don't tell Mother. You can make it look all right by this afternoon.'

'What if there's broken glasses? She'll think I done it.'

'Tell her I had a few friends in, and dropped a tray.'

'A few friends! That'll be the day.'

She was polishing the hall when Vin left for morning lectures.

'What's been going on here? Place smells like a beer parlour.'

Stanley King stood in the hall, moustache bristling, sniffing like a beagle.

Ethel, summoned to explain, said she'd only got back that morning, but she believed Mr Vin had a few friends in for a drink, like, some of his mates from University . . .

'And how did the standard lamp get broken?'

'I dunno. Don't ask me!'

'That boy,' said Mr King to his wife later, 'will never make anything of himself while he hangs around with that 'Varsity crowd, young Peter Whatsisname and Burton and Co. All they think about is cars and girls. You should never have given him a sports car, Rosetta. They all think he has money of his own, so they follow him round and encourage him in drinking and playing up. He must learn to settle down and keep a clear head for his studies.'

He sat down and wrote a long, admonitory letter to his son, pointing out the difference between 'playing up' and 'settling down', and the desirability of the latter. He left it on Vincent's dressing table. Vin rang to say he would not be home to dinner, and deliberately came home late after his parents were in bed. He read the letter and turned his eyes impatiently towards the ceiling.

Vin had joined the Sporting Car Club as soon as he got the car. Though his mother feared it was dangerous, she proudly arranged on the bureau the cups he won for hill-climbs and trials. His little MG was nippy around corners, and he had several times won Fastest Time of the Day.

For the midsummer meeting at Hillview he had the car in perfect tune. The motor roared sweetly as he revved the engine, the straightout exhaust crackled and popped, but there was no raggedness anywhere. He was third in line for the start. The marshall held the electronic device, like a golfclub wired to a battery, against the front tyre of the first car. He gave a nod. It shot off in a clatter of pebbles, leaving a streak of melted rubber. It bucked over the slight switchback and disappeared. Soon it reappeared higher up, like a blue bead threading the trees.

There was a crackle over the intercom, then a voice from the finish line: Masters, Austin Seven . . . One minute, three seconds.'

Over the minute! If he couldn't beat that . . . The second car was off, driven by his friend Burton. He scarcely watched. His stomach felt weighted with lead, yet fluttered as if a thousand butterflies were crawling there. He was next, he was now. His hand trembled as he engaged bottom gear and moved to the start. Sweat beaded his upper lip. Then he was off, his wheels pressing the automatic recorder which would give his time. He was flying up the hill, the wheels touched here and there, sometimes four, sometimes only two. He slithered round the Wall of Death, rocketed through the S-bends, braked hard for the hairpin, straightened out and gave her the gun over the last steep pinch to the top; then slowed, turned, and stopped under the trees where he could overlook the track.

The loud-speaker was announcing, ' – magnificent display of cornering . . . not be surprised to hear . . . 57 seconds and three tenths. The 60 seconds well and truly broken.'

As the procession of cars returned down the hill he felt the sun shining on, reflecting from his golden helmet. Vincent King, here I come! There had been a 58.5 run, but his fastest time held. There was some ragged applause from the watchers gathered under the shade of the great gumtrees, or sitting on the dry grass above the track.

They lined up for the second run.

The first man bettered his time. The second, Burton, did slightly worse. They counted the best of three runs for the trophy. He would have to reach ninety on the straight below the Wall of Death to improve his run.

The starter gave his nod.

He was off, the lead weight lifted from his stomach, the

butterflies banished. He kept his foot hard pressed to the floor. He seemed to be stationary in the midst of a narrow, dark tunnel of trees that went howling past. He lifted his foot from the accelerator and wrenched the wheel round.

There was a faint bang, the wheel turned loosely in his hands, and the car kept straight on.

For a moment he felt nothing but blank surprise. Then something like regret. Well, this was it. Vincent King, promising young driver, bought it on the Wall of Death at Hillview hill-climb. A pity . . .

A heavy sandbag seemed to fall on his head from nowhere. Some time later he found himself under the car, his feet inextricably wedged among the twisted pedals. He felt no pain. Shock, of course. In a minute the agony would begin, he would know where he was hurt. Not his arm, please God! Not lose an arm!

With great concentration he reached up to turn off the ignition-switch. Battery-acid was dripping on the ground beside him . . . or was it petrol? Oh God, why didn't someone come, why didn't they lift the thing off him before it caught fire? More than anything he dreaded being burnt alive. At least his harness had held, and the roll-bar had saved him from breaking his neck. He was suspended upside down.

There was a metallic thump above him, and a crack of light appeared against the earth.

'Easy . . . Easy now. Don't twist his legs. Get his feet free first. We've got you, mate. You're OK . . . You're all right now. Is he out to it? No . . . Well, stand back and let the ambulance chappies have a go.'

They had him out, free, in the blessed fresh air, under the open sky. He refused to lie down on the stretcher. The two Ambulance Brigade men supported him to a fallen tree trunk and he sat there, feeling fine. How did his head feel, they asked. Was his vision normal? His left elbow was hellishly painful, already puffing and turning blue. Just a sprain, they said cheerfully.

'I'm quite all right, really I am,' he told them earnestly. He wanted to go back to the group gathered round his wrecked car. When at last he got there he found himself talking at a great rate. He was euphoric, filled with wellbeing and excited as if he had been drinking a heady wine.

'– couldn't think what had happened, she handled perfectly on the first run, and then –'

'This is your lucky day, mate.'

'I'll say. For a moment there I thought –'

'Better buy a ticket in Tatts.'

'– steering seemed to lock. Just didn't respond at all.'

'– saw him upside down, with the wheels still spinning.'

'– trapped underneath there. We were worried about fire.'

'*You* were worried? How d'you think I was feeling?'

'The Ambulance Johnnies are delighted; meeting after meeting they come out here, and nothing happens.'

'Damn lucky he missed the trees.'

'– the old MG's had it, I'm afraid. Complete write-off.'

'Might be able to sell the engine as is. We'll get you a tow.'

'I must have been doing all of ninety when it went. I reached for the pick and just hung on. There wasn't time to do anything, only think –'

Suddenly the bright blue sky, the grey-blue leaves of the eucalyptus trees, the red earth at the side of the road, the men's faces, all lost their colour. It was as though the whole scene were on colour film, and it had been dipped into a bleaching bath. The voices receded to a far distance . . .

The voices receded, came back again in waves. He was drowsy, lying on the grass at the Bowls Club in the sun.

'He looks so peaceful, we won't disturb him.'

His mother's voice. He was lifted gently, carried in strong arms. Then he was in the car between his parents, the living link between flesh and flesh. His mother's arm was round him; his head was heavy on her breast. He opened his eyes and stared out the side window of the car. It was late and very dark. The street lights were out, and all the stars were shining.

No! The stars were shining at him through a sort of skylight above his head. He couldn't remember a window in that position. *Where was he?* Shadowy shapes failed to identify themselves as known pieces of furniture. He was in a narrow, high bed in a small room. A faint bluish light showed beyond a half-open door. He was lying utterly flat and the bedclothes were tucked round him like swaddling bands.

Then he remembered the accident, the strange fading of colour from the landscape. Was he dead? Was this the morgue? At the thought he tried to start up in terror, but the bedclothes held him. The frightened leap of his heart in his breast, like a great hooked fish, convinced him that he was alive. Adrenalin pumped through his veins; he tingled all over, and his left elbow began to ache unbearably.

He groped with his right arm for a bedside lamp. He must be in hospital. Something fell to the floor with a crash. At once the light was turned on, and a young nurse glided up to his bedside.

'Oh, you're awake,' she said. She popped a thermometer in his mouth, took his wrist and began to count his pulse.

He glowered at her. He was boiling with questions, demands, wants, and he had to keep his mouth shut on her footling thermometer. She leaned over and removed it briskly.

'Temp. normal, pulse-rate up,' she murmured, making a note on a little pad dangling from her waist band, in which her waist looked impossibly tiny, like an ant's. As if she might break in two if roughly handled.

'Of course my pulse-rate's up,' he grumbled. 'I wake up in a strange room, don't know the score, don't know if I'm minus a couple of limbs, and all you do is come in and take my temperature! Where am I, anyway?'

'Private room 26, Concord Hospital,' she said. 'I'm your "special". I have to watch over you like a dragon and you have to do what I say.'

'Like hell.' But he regarded her with less hostility. She wasn't bad looking, either. He tried to sit up.

'No, you don't!' She held him down firmly. 'You have to lie flat until we've checked the X-rays. Doctor's orders. It's just routine, but it's safer for you to keep on your back for now.'

'My back!' Did they think his back was broken? He licked his suddenly dry lips. 'What I need is a drink.'

'There's lemon and glucose in your jug. I'll get you another glass,' she said, picking up the broken pieces. 'You have a sprained elbow and probably nothing worse, except a touch of concussion. I'll bring you the bottle.'

He waited impatiently. She brought a silver contraption with a long neck and a handle on one side.

'And what am I supposed to do with that?'

'You should know. It's designed especially to fit the male anatomy.'

He took the thing sulkily. 'You'd better go and get the glass. Nothing'll happen while you stand there waiting. I'm a man, not a machine for producing water.'

'Producing water.' Wee-wee, his mother had called it. Nothing so scientific as urine or forthright as piss. How he had resented her superior strength when he was little, when she had forced him to sit on his chamber pot! His mother, of course, was a wonderful woman. She was strong-minded, handsome, upright, uncomplaining in her role of an invalid's wife, though so full of vitality herself. She still played tennis like a champion, did most of the gardening, organised bazaars and fêtes, and drove the car better than the old man, who fussed too much at the wheel. Vin couldn't help admiring someone who drove as well as his mother.

'What's the time?' he asked the young nurse when she came back and held a glass for him to drink.

'Three a.m. You'd better go to sleep again. I'll be waking you for a wash at six.' She shook the bottle and said, 'That's a good boy.'

He snarled at her. How women loved to get a man helpless! He'd be out of here in two shakes of a bee's whisker, just as soon as he could get hold of his doctor. She was just trying to frighten him with the talk of X-rays. The silly bitch had better make the most of it, it was the last chance she'd get.

He began to feel weak and drowsy. He was asleep almost before she had put out the light.

'Put out the light,' Irene had murmured close to his ear. He didn't want the light out; this was the first chance he'd had to examine a woman's anatomy closely, and he found it fascinating and scientifically interesting. What a complicated arrangement of folded flesh! And how wonderfully, wonderfully adapted to its purpose.

He felt himself ready to test it again, and groaning slightly he put out the light. This was different from the fumblings in the back seats of cars which had been all his experience up to now.

'You're so soft!' he murmured deliriously. 'So soft!' Even her name was softly luxurious: Irene.

Next morning he had woken early from dreaming that he was in the family car, going home late at night with his head on his mother's breast. It was a recurring dream. The first thing his eyes focused on was a curtain of old-rose brocaded silk, with tiny points of sunlight gleaming through the web of the material. The soft breast beneath his cheek was bare. Without moving he rolled his eyes upward. Good god! This wasn't his mother, though in the morning light she looked old enough. And it was not a dream. He was no longer a child. Indeed, he was now a man, and had proved it in bed with a mature, married woman.

He slid out of the bed backwards, like a lobster. She was older than he had thought. He was only nineteen, and she must be all of forty. He dressed quickly, his back to the sleeping figure in the bed. He had a distinct impression that she was awake, but didn't want to face him in the morning light. Her make-up was smeared; her tousled hair looked brassy. No doubt it was enough to have to face her mirror in the mornings, without a pair of clear, young, judging eyes as well.

But she was a good sort, Irene. Gay, amusing, travelled, a little world-weary. Her husband had gone to the States for three months on business. At the party the night before she had looked after Vin, stopping him from drinking too much, and heading off other predatory women. Then she had said, too casually, 'If you like to run me home, I'll fix you some coffee.'

Looking round to see if he had left anything, he saw the pink roses on her dressing-table, reflected in the mirror. He broke one off above the thorns – not a bud, a full-blown beauty – and put it in her half-open hand, curled outside the bedclothes.

He bent and kissed her quickly. She smiled with her eyes shut. 'Goodbye, darling,' she muttered.

It was just after six as he let himself out into the cold bright early morning. As he had been moving noiselessly through the thick-carpeted hall, a clock there whirred and struck the hour and he jumped, feeling like a burglar.

His car waited along the street like a patient beast. ('Not outside the house, darling. I have snoopy neighbours.')

He had driven home, coasted into the drive and silently let himself in with his key. He took off his shoes and was slipping through the polished hall in his socks . . . his socks . . . 'Vincent! Put on your sandals, child. Don't go outside in your socks.' His mother's voice.

He made a swift run back to his sandals, slid towards them and scooped them up as he passed. Speed, speed! He was a skier swooping down a slope of snow, he was a racing driver whizzing round the circuit . . .

'Vincent! Oh Vin, you gave us such a fright.'

His mother was bending over his bed; he was in hospital, and his elbow throbbed painfully.

'Hullo, Mother. Hullo, Dad. I'm feeling fine except for this rotten arm.'

'Well, at least it's not broken, thank goodness. Nothing broken, according to the X-rays. Does your head feel all right now?'

'It's fine.' He shook it experimentally. 'But I've been sleeping a lot, and dreaming . . .'

'The sleep did you good, the doctor said. He wouldn't let them wake you to wash you this morning.'

'Bet that annoyed them.' He grinned, 'I've got a bossy nurse.'

'Women are all like that, son, when they get you helpless.' His father's tired, faded brown eyes in their folds of skin smiled into his. He took the bony hand and felt a rush of affection and fellow-feeling. What it must be like to be never really well! Even a week in bed would be more than he could stand.

'You've had more experience of nurses than I have,' he said. 'How's your asthma been, Dad?'

'He was much better, weren't you, Stanley? But the shock of hearing about your accident brought on an attack. I've had him sitting up gasping for air half the night.' His mother announced this with a sort of pride, as if counting points towards a trophy for suffering.

'You shouldn't worry about me, Dad. I've got a skull like a Stone Age man, almost unbreakable.'

'That's what an Indian doctor said about mine, once.'

Vincent saw that his mother's eyes looked tired too, and her face was pale. He felt contrite.

'It must have been very worrying, I know. I promise to drive more carefully in future.'

His parents exchanged a look. His mother shook her head slightly, warningly. He explained that the accident wasn't really anything to do with his driving, or lack of judgement on his part. The steering had gone and there was nothing he could do but hang on. 'The car's a write-off, though I'll get something from the wrecker; the engine is still good, and the wheels. But I'll have to get another,' he said airily.

There was a short silence.

'When you've saved enough to pay for another, no doubt you'll get one. I can't stop you,' said his father. 'But we shan't buy you another. Also, you'll be starting work with my firm as soon as you get out of here.'

'Oh.' He had guessed this was coming, but it was still a shock. When last year's results came out he had passed in only two subjects. He sat for the supplementary without really working for it, and did no better. His father had looked grim, and said it was a waste of money sending him to University. (He was not in college, but attended lectures from home.) His father's firm! Insurance! He made a grimace of distaste. His mother took it for a wince of pain.

'Stanley, we shouldn't tire him with all this now. He has to be quiet for a few days. We'd better go and let him rest.'

The nurse came in with a jug of iced water.

Rosetta King made herself pleasant as only she knew how to on occasion, and the nurse was charmed. Vin's father gave him a mock salute and walked out. His mother hesitated at the door, came back. 'Don't fret about the car, dear,' she said in a low voice. 'We'll work something out.' She bent and kissed his forehead.

'Good old Mother,' he murmured. 'If I had two good arms I'd hug you.'

'That elbow's pretty painful, eh?' said the young doctor, sitting on the edge of the bed and manipulating the arm slightly. Vin winced and bit his lip. 'Yes, a sprain can be almost as painful as a fracture, but it will heal much more quickly.'

'As long as it won't affect my driving? It's my gear-change arm.'

'Not in the slightest, old chap. I'll order you some stronger sedatives for the pain. You had slight concussion as well. You were damned lucky, if you ask me. I understand the car is a wreck.'

'Yes, I was lucky that I rolled and stopped in a ditch, instead of going full belt into the trees. Can I go home now?'

'Tomorrow, probably.'

After he had gone the pert nurse brought in two capsules in a tiny dish, and waited while he swallowed them. He went to the bathroom, and when he came back sank into such depths of sleep that he didn't even dream. When he woke it was dusk. The nurse came in with her inevitable watch and thermometer. As she stood by the bed shaking it down, he was only dimly aware of her through a fog of sleep. He rolled on his side, his good arm fell over the edge of the bed and brushed her knee. By a sort of reflex action his fingers gripped the stockinged flesh, then relaxed. The nurse stepped back quickly.

In the morning he was surprised to have a visit from matron before her usual morning rounds.

Matron was in her forties, but she had no middle-aged spread. She was thin all over: thin arms, thin lips, thin eyebrows, a flat figure under her starched uniform.

'Mr King,' she said, closing her lips firmly over each word in case it might get too far away from her, 'I will not have my nurses harassed.'

'Good for you,' he nearly said, but only lifted one eyebrow inquiringly.

'Nurse Everett has complained that you made an attempt to get fresh with her yesterday evening, when she was taking your pulse.'

'What on earth – ?' He sat bolt upright, amazed. 'Whatever are you talking about?'

'Do you deny that you fondled her knee?'

'Good God!' he burst out. 'I was under sedation, I was half asleep. I remember I turned over . . . if her knee got in the way of my hand, I'm sorry. But it certainly wasn't intentional.'

'Well, Nurse Everett was upset, and reported it to me. I have assigned another nurse to your case.'

'I assure you, you needn't have bothered. Nurse Everett has no particular charm for me. Good Lord, I'm not that hard up!' He thought of Irene, and if he hadn't been so angry he would have laughed in the Matron's face.

'Well, Mr King, Nurse is very young and inexperienced; she may have interpreted your action wrongly,' Matron was clearly having second thoughts, 'but I must protect my staff –'

'Not from me,' said Vin. 'I'm going.'

He got out of bed and began collecting his things from the bedside locker. 'Just get them to call me a taxi.'

'I'm afraid you can't go till Doctor gives his permission. I couldn't take the responsibility –'

'Too bad. I'm discharging myself, now, this morning. I'm not staying where the word of a neurotic, hysterical girl is taken against mine.'

'Mr King! Get back into bed at once.' She put out her hand to hold him. He swung his good arm against her slight figure, and she flew back against the wall. He strode out, and without waiting for the elevator went down the stairs and out into the morning. Free! He waved down a taxi and went home.

Three

It was Vin's first day in the insurance office, and he wasn't liking it a bit. To his surprise he found his father remote, autocratic, an absolute ruler in his own kingdom. Ignoring the expensive call-button on his desk, he would summon his secretary with two sharp claps of his hands, as he had done with servants in India.

Vin had been used to seeing Stanley King defer to his wife in most things. Now, summoned to his sanctum to stand before a large, intimidating desk with several telephones and a brass inkstand in the shape of a falcon's head, he realised that even his father's secretary regarded the Chief with something between awe and hero-worship.

As the son of the boss he had not expected to be treated like the veriest office boy. After a week in which he'd done nothing more interesting than run errands, take the mail to the Post Office and buy stamps, he was bored and disgruntled. But when the Paymaster came round on Friday with a buff envelope containing the first real money he had earned, he felt better. He decided to spend it on a meal in a good restaurant instead of going home after work. Everyone rushed home from the city after work; it was known as the 'rush hour' – so perversely Vin would stay.

He often drove his father in the big car, but tonight Stanley was going to some Club dinner, so Vin had the car. It had a roomy back seat which was better than the MG for perving, but that was all it was good for. It was a heavy American sedan with too much chrome, sloppy steering and soft springs. He longed to feel again the hard bounce of a little English sports car, the crisp change of a stubby, floor-type gear lever, the direct steering which would respond to the touch of a finger. He would like to go out now and look at sports cars . . . except that he had just enough money for one good meal. He rang his mother and told her he was eating in town.

'Then I'll just have a snack, dear, since it's Ethel's afternoon off. Dad's going to take a cab home, is he? Now see you have a proper meal, Vin. A growing boy – '

'I am not a growing boy, Mother. I am grown.'

'I know, dear, but I keep forgetting. And Vin, about the new car. It will be all right, but don't say anything to your father yet, it would only upset him. Of course, you could borrow on your expectations from my father's estate when you turn twenty-one, so I might as well advance it.'

'Good old Mother. That's marvellous. I feel like a crab without a shell at present.'

'As soon as you're twenty-one it will be much simpler. Have you decided what sort to get?'

'Well, second-hand, to begin with. I thought a blown Jaguar sports or a Triumph – '

'Blown! It sounds horrid, like fly-struck sheep.'

' "Blown" means supercharged. Later I can go for the big stuff – a 6CL Maserati or an Alfa Romeo.'

'Did you have a good day at the office?'

'Huh! I hate it. I'd rather work in a garage, or teach old ladies to drive.'

At five o'clock he was free. He didn't rush downstairs with the other slaves. He hated the jostle of humanity, the slow clotting of people outside the elevators, the being jammed against them on the way down.

Instead, he went up to the roof. He leaned on the sunwarm parapet, looking down at the little black figures pouring out of the giant termite-heap of a building. Like ants they hastened up or down with an obsessed purposefulness, sometimes colliding, sometimes stopping to confer with one another, then hurrying on. Now, if some cosmic disaster should obliterate them all . . .

He'd had this feeling of detachment before, watching a Sunday crowd from a cliff-top above a Sydney beach. The tiny specks bobbed about on the very edge of the vast Pacific, like ants on the rim of a tub full of water. Just one wave bigger than the rest, and hundreds would be swept away and drowned. Oh yes, it sometimes happened. On Black Sunday in 1938, when three hundred were swept out to sea at Bondi Beach . . .

He imagined the reports of disasters in an ant-world news-paper, if there had been such a thing:

A sudden flood rising in East Lawn this morning swept away the ramparts surrounding two Ant Communities, and drowned many of the inhabitants, including those workers who tried to mend the breach in the walls. Loss of life is believed to reach the thousands.

Or:

A large cavity appeared suddenly at the very doors of South Garden Community yesterday, followed by an earth-fall of many micro-tons. One entrance was obliterated completely. Fortunately the Queen was safe underground, and the Workers managed to clear the entrance by night-fall.

He was now one of this world of ants, but he felt sorrier for all those wretches down there than for himself. He was free; he could always leave. They had wives, commitments, mort-gages, hire purchase payments to be met. They seemed resigned to their fate, but that made it no better.

The pale-faced crowds pouring into the buildings in the morning, the tired, pale crowds pouring out again at night, jamming the streets, clogging the trams and trains at the routine hour for the ant-nest to empty: indeed, ants had more purpose than these. They were not toiling for the common good, but for the weekly pay packet. And two weeks' holiday a year. It was terrible to contemplate.

When the crowds had thinned he took the elevator down to the street level. He had the oddest feeling that he was only an eighth of an inch high. Far above towered the buildings, and over them an arched and brooding sky . . .

He hurried round to his favourite restaurant and ordered soup, grilled Murray Cod steak, and a bottle of Chablis. Soon he began to feel the right size again.

Going straight home after a good dinner and the feeling of mild expansiveness that went with it was rather a waste, but it was a bit late to ring a girl at this hour. He started the old man's car and gunned the engine. At once he felt his ego expand to fill not only the car but the whole area through which its exhaust note echoed. He revved the engine unmercifully, went up to forty-five in second, made a racing change into top. Immediately he felt more alive, more entirely himself. He wound down the side window and put his head out, gulping great draughts of pressurised air, roaring along the suburban roads towards home.

'Vincent King, here I come!' he shouted at the street lights flashing past. He was himself, V. King, no longer one of the ants. He leaned far out to listen to the sweet sound of the powerful engine racing at the top of its bent.

Vin ate a chicken sandwich and drank a cup of coffee tasting of the waxed-paper cup, then lay in the short grass beside the track, letting himself relax completely before his next race.

It was surprisingly warm for April, he was quite hot in his white overalls. He had come to Melbourne for the Easter holidays to get a new car, without saying a word to his father. In Melbourne he had competed successfully in the Templestowe hill-climb, getting the feel of his new fast Special before today's meeting at Albert Park.

The grass was limp and soft in the sun. It smelled of greenness and heat. He lay still with the sun beating on the back of his neck.

The sound of passing cars on the circuit washed over him in waves: approaching, rising to a crescendo, then retreating, with a sudden change of note as the drivers dropped a gear . . . then once more approaching, rising to the high note of tearing silk.

His heart beat high and full, flooding his long, inert body with wellbeing. Somewhere, vague at the back of his mind, was the feeling that all this had happened before, just exactly so – the hot sweet smell of wilting grass and burning alcohol fuel, the passing sound of circling cars. Even as he thought he had the memory pinned it slipped away like a fish and was lost in the turbulent sea of the present.

He came a worthy fifth in the big race, though his car was

outclassed and it was the first time he'd driven it in a road race.

There was a party after the meeting, at which a great deal of beer was drunk and also spilt on the floor at the Sporting Car Club's rooms. It needed an enormous amount of beer to make Vin drunk, and he was still sober though very slightly elevated when he met Jeanne.

She came from his home State, it seemed, and was something of a fan of his. She was a pale metallic blonde with one of those long, elegant faces, a small self-satisfied mouth and highly arched brows, as though she were perpetually being surprised at her own beauty. Her figure was superb. The dress she wore – of white linen with a long zip-fastener from hem to neckline, ending in a great brass curtain-ring arrangement – fitted every curve.

She gazed wide-eyed at Vin over the rim of her glass.

'I've always wanted to meet you,' she said, 'since I saw you win the under 1500 cc. in that little MG of yours. I've got an MG myself.'

'Have you now? A TC, or the latest model?'

'The latest model.'

'I had an idea it would be. You're fairly streamlined yourself.'

'Thank you.'

He put down his glass and fiddled with the curtain-ring at the neck of her dress.

'This arrangement,' he said, 'is most tempting. What would happen if I pulled it?'

'Here and now?'

'Here and now.'

'I should feel obliged to scream.'

'And if – er – there was no audience?'

'Well, it wouldn't be any use my screaming then, would it? Besides, I doubt if I'd want to.'

She smiled into his eyes and moved off to join another group, leaving him amused and tantalised. He must find out where she was staying, or look her up when he got back home. He badly needed a warm and willing girl at present.

Later in the evening, when the Car Club party had reached the noisy stage of reminiscence and post-mortem over the day's meeting, after the presentations and the speeches had been made,. he found himself sharing a narrow chair with Jeanne, one of his arms round her slim waist to keep her from falling off.

She crossed her beautiful knees and the short white dress rode up, showing her white lace slip about her thighs.

'God, do you know what you're doing to me?' he groaned.

She smiled and patted his hand.

'You poor darling,' she said, and then, 'Where are you staying?'

He grimaced. 'At the Savoy-Plaza. It's handy to Spencer Street Station.'

'You mean you came over by *train*?' She spoke as if such a method of transport was unheard of.

'It's cheaper than flying. Then I'm driving the new Special back home.'

'Oh! Could I come with you? I'd love –'

'Sorry! It's a monoposto. Only one seat.'

'Of course; silly of me. You know, I've just thought . . . I'm staying at the Savoy-Plaza also.'

Vin knew very well that if she was staying anywhere it would be somewhere expensive, like Menzies' or the Oriental. He looked into her wide-open eyes and saw that they were green as a cat's.

He said: 'I don't know about you, but I've had a long day. In fact, I'm ready for bed.'

She smiled. 'So am I.'

Jeanne couldn't be much more than twenty, but she had the poise of a woman ten years older. 'I'll meet you in the lobby at the Plaza,' she said. 'I have to go round to Menzies' and pick up some things.'

He got held up by a drunken and argumentative friend near the door on his way out. When he rushed back to the Savoy-Plaza her cab was just pulling up at the kerb.

'Look, you've got a single room I suppose?' she said at once. 'It would be better if you go on up. Give me your room number and I'll join you later.'

He paid the taxi-driver who had kept his face carefully blank during these arrangements. She had only an overnight bag and a vanity case. He got his key at the desk and went up to his sixth-floor room. The plain furniture, the bed with its green candlewick bedspread looked suburban and unexotic for a love-nest.

He undressed, put on a bathrobe and waited. Every time he heard the elevator stop his excitement rose; he waited for her tap on the door. After fifteen minutes had gone by he felt his ardour cooled. He longed for bed, but now he was merely sleepy. To wake himself up he had a stinging hot shower. He was rubbing the dark spikes of his wet hair afterwards when she knocked. He wrapped a towel round his middle and opened the door.

'Why, Vin, how domestic!' She ran a hand over his wet hair. 'Mm, you smell nice, like a baby, all soap and – what is that nice smell?'

'Soap!' Vin regarded perfume for men as effeminate.

She stood in front of him. 'You wanted to pull the ripcord, remember?'

'Why the hell were you so long?' he grumbled, but he hooked a finger in the brass ring and pulled. The long zip-fastener slid to the hem and the white dress dropped back from her sunbrown, perfect shoulders. He removed the lace slip and struggled with the three hooks at the back of her brassiere, beginning to feel distinctly out of temper.

'Everyone should dress in nothing but a toga, or a towel,' he said, removing the one round his waist. 'And these girdle-things should be abolished by act of Parliament. Look at the mark it has made here – '

He ran one hand the full length of her slender body, and lifted her on to the bed. He began to kiss and take the measure of every curve and hollow from ankle to chin, from shoulder to ear. At last he reached her lips again, but as her mouth opened beneath his he realised to his horror that he was no longer ready. He had drunk too much, he had waited too long, she had kept him waiting, it was all her fault . . . A wave of shame and nausea swept over him, and he bolted for the bathroom just in time.

When he came back, Jeanne was damping a handkerchief with iced water from the bedside carafe. 'I may not be that good,' she said, 'but I've never made anyone actually sick before.' Vincent grinned ruefully. 'Sit here,' she said, patting the bed beside her. She did not look upset, but wore her usual expression of faint amusement. She wiped his face, then pushed him back on the pillow and put the cold cloth over his eyes and brow.

'Gosh, I'm sorry, Jeanne. I don't know, I must have drunk more than I realised. It's never happened to me before.'

'I believe you. Now just lie quietly and go to sleep.'

She lay beside him and put a motherly arm round him. He groaned. 'It's such a waste . . .' he muttered. He no longer felt sick, but he was deathly tired. He expected she would leave now. He drifted off into sleep.

When he woke some time in the night, the memory of his failure swept over him in a wave of disbelief. Ah, if only she were here now . . . He flung out an arm, and there was this wonderful, smooth, warm shape in the narrow bed beside him. He gathered her into his arms. They came together naturally, like the two halves of a perfectly fitting machine, twinned, twined and bedded.

It was long before they slept again. Jeanne was insatiable, skilled, wonderful. He hadn't known such girls existed. He wondered at the back of his mind what it would be like to be married to her. All right for one night, but – ? In the morning they made love again; he drowsed off and woke once more to find her gone. A folded note had been slipped beneath his pillow. 'No wonder you are tired! It was marvellous – Jeanne.'

The Special went like a bomb all the way back from Melbourne, cruising comfortably at 80 and nudging 100 mph on the straights. There was a different thrill about driving fast on the highway, apart from the fact that he was breaking the speed limit. He always preferred a 'round the houses' circuit to one built specially for racing. It was more interesting. On a run like this there was a spice of danger from traffic, the possibility of coming over a rise to find a great semi-trailer blocking the way. He would love to drive in a *Mille Miglia* in Italy.

He drove all night without fatigue. He was keyed-up, alert, feeling tremendously alive after a satisfactory weekend.

There was a kind of languorous wellbeing in his lower limbs

after his night with Jeanne, and the car beneath his hands was obedient to his lightest touch like a loving woman. He straightened out the road, cutting corners where he had a clear view, taking up the exact line that was shortest and never deviating from it. He was exulting in his own skill.

He stopped for breakfast on the outskirts of the city, picking up the morning paper to read while he ate a big plate of steak and eggs and fried potatoes. He was drinking his coffee when he turned to the sports page, knowing there would be little about the car meeting in Melbourne. Each State had its own newspaper devoted mainly to State news, and besides there was a kind of jealousy between the capital cities which suggested nothing interesting ever happened in Melbourne (except, of course, the Melbourne Cup), if you lived in Sydney or Adelaide.

The headline hit his eye at once. 'Hillview Marred by Tragedy'. The report of the Easter hill-climb was dominated by the story of a fatal crash. Burton! Ian Burton had rolled his car on the Wall of Death section. That was on Good Friday. His spine was fractured, but he had lived till Saturday.

Vin found that his hand was clenched on the coffee-mug, its knuckles white. He felt physically sick. He turned back to the front page, which he had only glanced at before. There was a picture of the mangled car. Local meetings only got on the front page when someone was killed.

He used a pay phone to dial Peter's number.

He answered sleepily.

'Sorry, Pete, I know it's early hours for you – '

'Thass' all right, I've got an early lecture, anyway. Had to get up.'

'Listen, I've just come back from Melbourne and read about Burton in the paper.'

'Yes. Burton bought it on the Wall of Death, just about the same place where you went into the bindi. By God, you were lucky . . . He wasn't. I went to the funeral yesterday.'

'They said his spine was fractured.'

'What they didn't say was that his breathing muscles were paralysed. He breathed for two days with his stomach muscles, until they got too tired. His parents wanted to put him into an iron lung, but he refused. Didn't want to live in a tin tank for the rest of his life.'

'No. Understandably.' Vin was appalled. Death was a fine abstraction, until it came close and leered with its hateful face over the shoulder of a friend. 'What a way to go!'

'Yes . . . Did you do all right in Melbourne?'

'Not bad. I got a fifth in the under 1500cc., and a bronze medallion at Templestowe. Bought Anderson's Special.'

'I'd give up hill-climbs if I were you. Too bloody dangerous.'

'Yes. I think I might . . . Poor old Burton. What rotten luck.'

He went slowly to his car, in a brown study. He was glad he'd missed the funeral. But he would have to send a note of sympathy to Mrs Burton, and to Janet, Ian's girlfriend. Had she stayed with him to the end? How could she stand it?

He was not sleepy, he had pulled to the side of the highway and taken a cat-nap in one of the rest areas last night. He left the new car in a friend's garage and caught a tram round to their street. It ground along the rails, made long pauses with its generator ticking over. What an incredibly slow method of transport!

At the sound of his step on the veranda his mother called to him through the French windows of the drawing room. She opened one like a conspirator. 'Come in, dear, but be quiet. Your father's having one of his attacks. For some reason he bought Saturday's Melbourne *Age* – wanted to read the finance page I think – and saw your name among the competitors at Albert Park. He's very upset, as you can imagine.'

'Oh Lord, Mother! I'm sorry.'

'And then there was the news in our paper about Ian Burton being killed at Hillview. Did you know –'

'Yes, I heard.'

'I've had a terrible scene with him. He says you'll waste all your money on fast cars, if you don't kill yourself, and that if it had rested with him he wouldn't let you have a penny of your grandfather's money until you were much older and more sensible. I suppose we should have told him about the car.'

'It was for his own good, to stop him from worrying, you said. I'd better go and see him and make the peace.'

'No, no! Wait till he's calmed down. It will only lead to a quarrel if you see him now. It might be fatal with his heart. I won't tell him you're home yet. Have a shower in the downstairs bathroom.'

Next day, Stanley King was still not fit to go to the office. Vin went off feeling like a criminal, still without seeing his father. He was depressed by Burton's death, and the feeling that his father's illness was all his fault. While those two had been fighting for breath in their separate agony, he had been enjoying himself in Melbourne.

He rang at lunchtime to ask how his father was. Rosetta King sounded distracted.

'Oh Vincent! I was just going to ring you. Your father's been taken off to hospital – '

'To hospital!'

'Yes, they've put him in an oxygen tent. He has to be kept absolutely quiet, you can't see him. But I'd like you at home.'

His mother was pacing up and down her bedroom, a small inadequate handkerchief balled in her hand.

'I blame myself, Vin! I blame myself! We shouldn't have deceived him.' Her chin was quivering, her prominent nose was red.

He put an arm about her well-padded shoulders and led her to a chair. 'Now, Mother, it's no good getting worked up. If it's anybody's fault it's mine. You just sit down and I'll get Ethel to fetch you a cup of tea.'

He put her in the armchair, placed a footstool at her feet, and settled a cushion behind her shoulders. Like most big-framed, strong-minded women she occasionally liked to be fussed over and treated as if she were small and fragile. She submitted to being ordered about by her big strong son, and even smiled tremulously.

'I've put the new medal on the shelf with the others,' she said. 'Since Stanley knows about your Melbourne trip there's no need to hide it. Now tell me about the new car.'

'Wait, I'll see about the tea.'

In the kitchen Ethel was scraping carrots over a bowl of water, a worn kitchen-knife in her pink wet hands, the sleeves rolled up from her bony wrists. She looked up mournfully, her hollow cheeks where she had lost her back teeth, drawn in even more than usual. She paused with her elbows on the edge of the bowl, the knife and carrot pointing upwards in an inverted V. Her worried-looking eyebrows sloped in the same direction.

'You're home early, Mr Vin.'

'Yes, Mother's worried about my father going to hospital. What about a cup of tea for her, Eth? I've persuaded her to sit down and put her feet up.'

'Good for you. She hasn't sat down all morning. She's been pacing up and down ever since the ambulance come. Wouldn't have a bite of lunch. You had yours?'

'Yes, I had a meat pie at the office.' He sat on the edge of the kitchen table and took a piece of the clean washed carrot lying ready for chopping on a board. 'Did he look very bad?' he asked casually, munching.

'My word, he looked somethink awful,' said Ethel, drawing her long face out longer. 'He was blue as ink about the mouth, and his eyes looked sunken-in like. He was asking for you.'

'He *was*?'

'Yes, he kept on saying, "Where's Vincent? I want Vincent . . ." '

Vin swallowed the raw carrot half-chewed and went in one bound off the table and out of the kitchen. In the bedroom he confronted his mother angrily.

'You didn't tell me Dad was asking for me!'

'Who says he was? He didn't know what he was saying, he was delirious.'

'Don't beat about the bush. He was asking for me, wasn't he? Did you tell him I was back from Melbourne? He must have wondered why I didn't come in to see him.'

'No, I didn't want him to upset himself any more. He doesn't even know you're back.'

Vin turned on his heel. 'I'm going!'

'Going? Where?'

'To the hospital.'

'To the hospital! But they won't let you in. They won't let you see him.'

'They'd better.'

At the hospital, he asked the nurse in the little glass box at the entrance to the ward for Mr King. She gave him a startled

415

look and asked him to wait. She came hurrying back, followed by a grave-faced Sister.

'Mr King? You are Mr Stanley King's son? I'm afraid I have some bad news for you, I was just about to send a telephone message to Mrs King. Your father has gone into a coma, and it seems unlikely that he will recover consciousness again.'

'What!' Vin felt furiously angry. This was part of the same conspiracy to which his mother was also a party, to keep him from seeing his father.

'What a pity!' said the Sister in more human tones. 'He was asking for you earlier, if your name is Vincent.'

'Let me see him! I'm sure he'll recognise me.'

'Impossible, I'm afraid. But come this way.'

In room 59 a great cumbersome iron cylinder with pressure gauges stood at the foot of the bed. His father was lying motionless under the transparent plastic canopy of an oxygen-tent. His face was waxen, with dark blue shadows under the eyes. His breathing was almost imperceptible. The blue veins showed through the yellowish pallor of his long thin hands, lying limply outside the covers.

Vin put a hand under the canopy and took one of them in his strong young brown fist. He willed with all his might that some of his own abundant life and wellbeing should myster-iously flow to his father. But the hand remained limp and clammy.

'Dad! Can you hear me? It's Vin, Vincent. I'm here, Dad. Can you hear me? It's Vin.'

But it was like talking to a waxworks image. The strong dark moustache, still scarcely touched with grey, looked as out of place on that pallid countenance as if it had been gummed on for a disguise.

Vin looked at the Sister with tormented eyes.

'They didn't tell me how ill he was. I would have been here if I'd known. I've just come back from Melbourne,' he muttered. He felt furious with his mother. Why had she deliberately kept him away? And now it was too late.

The nurse brought him a chair and the Sister went away, saying she would ring his mother. She had already summoned the doctor.

After five minutes there was not the slightest change.

Then the doctor arrived, and Vin had to go out.

'At least he will have a peaceful end,' said the doctor when Vin was able to see him. 'I tried adrenalin injected direct, but his heart is just worn out. His brain is not getting enough oxygen to function; in fact to all intents and purposes he is no longer with us.'

'You mean there's no chance that he might recover enough to recognise me?'

'Not the slightest, I'm afraid.'

White and stunned, Vin wandered outside where he had parked his new Special. It was not really suitable for the city; he'd have to get a little runabout. And then the thought popped into his mind that now – when his father died – he would be able to buy whatever car he wanted, almost. He would not have to work in the office; his mother would be well provided for. And he was an only child.

But how would he forgive himself for having caused this fatal attack?

He drove his mother back that night in the family car, the big cream sedan, and they sat mutely on each side of the bed, waiting for a sign. There was no change.

At three in the morning, when they had gone home to bed, the telephone rang. Rosetta King had the telephone by her bed. As Vin came to her door she stared at him wordlessly, putting a hand up to her throat.

'Mother! Is he – ?'

'He's gone. Passed away in his sleep.'

That is romanticising his end, thought Vin, to make it more bearable. There was nothing of sleep in that ghastly stupor.

He had said no more words of reproach, and they tacitly dropped the subject. He walked over and put an arm round her shoulder. He sat on the bed beside her. She stared silently at the carpet; then her eyes overflowed. She groped under the pillow for a handkerchief.

'I'll go and make you a cup of tea,' he said.

'Yes; don't wake Ethel.'

In the kitchen he heard a noise at the uncurtained window, and for a moment his heart contracted in superstitious fear. A white face was at the pane, two dark eyes stared at him. Then he relaxed.

'Zircon, you old devil!' He opened the window and the cat jumped down to the floor by way of the draining-board and the sink.

Zircon weaved in and out of his legs, purring throatily, lifting his narrow head graciously to a caress. How strange that a mere cat was still here, still alive, and his father was gone! The stove, the kettle, the kitchen table, a chair sitting firmly on its four legs – they existed still in time and space. His father existed still a little while in space, but he had fallen out of time into nothing.

Vin filled the kettle and set it on the lighted gas.

How pathetic the Egyptian custom of mummifying the dead, preserving the helpless remains in the hope of prolonging the spirit that had inhabited them! The Egyptians had even preserved their favourite cats.

He bent down and picked up Zircon and draped him over his shoulder, where the cat settled comfortable and heavy with two front paws on his shoulder, body looped around the back of his neck. He liked to feel the cat there, breathing and purring close to his ear. He stood carefully erect, not disturbing him by any sudden movement. He put up his left hand and stroked the silken paws.

The silken paws, the little white-velvet noses of cats . . .

He used to tease Zircon's predecessor when he was a small boy, but he got on well with the handsome Siamese with its startling blue eyes.

The kettle began to whistle. He turned off the gas, poured boiling water on the tea, and got a bottle of milk from the refrigerator, moving stiffly so as not to disturb Zircon.

He put the cat gently on the floor, filled a saucer and added a drop of boiling water to take the chill off the milk for him.

His mother was calling.

'Coming, Mother.'

He had made a second cup, but suddenly he had a most violent desire for a glass of lemonade. Strange, he didn't like its sweetness usually.

He opened the refrigerator again, found a screw-top bottle and poured some lemonade into a glass. Then he smashed an ice-cube into jagged pieces and dropped them in the drink. The ice was angular, pellucid, with fine silvery streaks and bubbles. He fished a piece out and crunched it. Then he put the glass and the cup of tea on a tray and carried it to his mother's bedroom.

He had rung the undertaker, sent an advertisement for the 'Deaths' column of the morning paper, made all the gruesome arrangements for disposing of a body. Then he went to the hospital and asked to see his father.

The cylinder and the oxygen tent had been taken away.

A sheet had been pulled up over the face of the still figure on the bed. All the 'last offices' had been performed, the nurse told him, hovering in the room. Some people didn't like to be left alone with a cadaver, it made them nervous.

'I should like to be alone if you don't mind,' said Vin.

When she had gone he turned back the sheet and took one of the clay-cold hands. How long since he had kissed his father? Not since he was a child. He bent over and kissed the dead cheek, marble cold. How very dead the dead did look, to be sure. This was already no longer a man, but a thing. This was the dead branch from which his own green life had sprung.

He felt almost the guilt of a murderer. If he had not bought the Special secretly and raced in Melbourne, his father might still be alive.

He bent his head. 'I'm sorry; I'm sorry, Dad,' he whispered.

'I'm sorry, Dad.' Vin hung his head so that the straight dark fringe swung out from his brow like a curtain. His little ears were red. He stood with his toes slightly turned in, the picture of guilt.

'I've told you not to touch the car, haven't I?'

'Yes, Dad.'

'And this is not the first time you've disobeyed me. Now you've left the ignition on and the battery is flat. But that's not why I am angry. It's dangerous for you to play in the car until you're big enough to drive it. You might touch the starter, and if it was in gear the car could leap forward and perhaps knock

419

someone down, or it could run into the house.'

'Will you teach me how to start it, then?'

'What! You're only seven.'

'But I just want to turn the 'nition, and push the button, and hear it start. I PROMISE I won't ever touch the car when you're not there; I'll never ever touch – '

'Well, we'll see. I can't teach you now, anyway, because the battery's flat and the engine won't turn over. But get in and I'll show you where the gears are. At least you can't start it by accident now. Your legs are too short, aren't they? I'll have to push the clutch for you. Now, these are the forward gears: bottom . . . second . . . third . . . top. Here is reverse – can you do that – ?'

He stopped, watching the passion of concentration with which the child manipulated the gear-lever, the solemn joy which lighted his chubby face, the firmness of the little hand where the row of baby dimples still showed across the wrist.

He would have to keep the car locked, there was nothing else for it. Vincent was unable to keep away from it; he would inevitably yield to temptation again.

Punishment – being sent to bed, deprived of an outing, locked in the bathroom – had no effect. He was drawn to the car as by a giant magnet.

'I tell you what, Vin. Punishing you doesn't seem to do any good, so I'm going to get you a car of your own, a pedal car, and then you won't want to touch mine. It will have a forwards and backwards gear and a steering wheel and tyres and everything except an engine. How's that?'

'Gee!' said Vincent. 'I promise I won't touch your car again ever. I'm sorry about the battery, Dad.'

'I'm sorry! I'm sorry!' The nurse found him with his arms resting on the side of the bed, his face buried in them, sobbing.

'Mr King – I'm sorry – the undertaker is here, and he wants to –' He suffered himself to be led away as docilely as a child.

Four

BRIGHT INTERNATIONAL flags, set round the course on tall flagpoles, patched the sky with living colour. The green crescent of Islam, the blood-red and blue and white of the Union Jack, the green, white and red of Italy, and the seven stars on a sky-blue ground of Australia, land of the Southern Cross, all fluttered against the blue.

Canned music blared brassily from the loudspeakers, with now and then a crackle of information. The graceful curve of palm trees, fronds waving in the warm breeze off the sea, made exotic a horizon that was misty with heat and humidity.

Vincent King was the unknown quantity among the visiting drivers. Since his arrival in the Malay Peninsula for the car racing at Johore, he had acquired the ex-Kirracachorn Maserati. The smooth-faced, smiling little Thai, Prince Kirra of Bangkok, had a new and untried car, an Oska. There was some official betting on Kirra and on the British champion in his BRM.

At practice on the day before, Vin had taken it steadily, learning the course, still getting the feel of the new car. Its powerful six-cylinder motor roared satisfactorily when he 'gunned' it at the start. He felt it vibrating right through his chest and arms, rather than hearing it with his ears. He was used to heat; he felt comfortable and relaxed in his white overalls with the embroidered crown and V on the pocket. The circuit went partly through a rubber plantation of gloomy trees, partly between banks of bright red soil, past attap houses on stilts and gardens with ragged banana trees.

For the big race the cars were placed according to their practice times. Vin found himself far back among the riff-raff while the other fast cars, including Smart, the English driver with his green BRM, and Kirra in the gleaming silver-blue Oska, were placed near the front.

He gunned the engine in short bursts to stop the spark-plugs from oiling up. Deafeningly the cars revved all round him. Their engines blared and faded, blared and faded, like the roaring of great impatient beasts held in check. Vin wiped the sweat from his palms on the sides of his overalls and donned his gloves. He felt his stomach crawl and flutter with nerves.

An amplified horn-blast sounded. Ten seconds to go. The starter's arm lifted.

Go! The flag dropped, the cars leapt forward with a screaming howl of engines and smoking rubber. The acceleration pressed him hard against the seat-back.

The Englishman shot out in front; then came a small group with Kirra in the lead, then the rest of the field in a bunch. Vin was in among the slower cars, trying desperately to find an opening. He passed McCall in the New Zealand special.

By the end of the first lap they had sorted themselves out. Smart was being closely followed into the corners by Kirra. Franz Diamond and his Australian-owned Alfa led the bunch of four cars just behind. Then came Vin with the blue Maserati, rapidly leaving the slower cars in his wake.

On the second time round the positions were much the same, except that the tail-enders were more strung out. Vin had moved up to just behind Franz Diamond. There he decided to wait for the time being, letting Franz set the pace. He was a bastard on the track and hated to let anyone through.

The flag marshal, seeing Vin close behind him, leapt out with the blue flag: 'Another competitor following you close-ly.' Franz took no notice. He was giving Vin no chance to get through on the inside. Vin hadn't quite the speed to go out wide and pass. For another lap he bided his time, pushing Franz from behind, hoping to get him rattled enough to make a small slip and let him through.

Next time round he was nudging Franz so closely on the pit straight that the marshal waved the blue flag frantically: 'Another competitor is trying to overtake you.' Franz stayed in the middle of the track and took his usual line into the next corner, but he went into it a shade too fast, and his controlled drift became a helpless slide. He lost the rear end as the wheels touched the dirt at the side of the track and spun off into the straw bales.

Vin saw all this out of the corner of his eye. He did not slacken speed for a moment or let the mishap affect his cornering in the slightest; but leaving the brakes until the last split second, and taking up the position he knew would bring him through on the correct line, he felt the car entirely and perfectly under control.

This was a far greater thrill than hammering it down the straight at full bore, greater even than catching and passing another fast car. To have all that powerful machinery obedient to his lightest touch, to know within half a mile an hour just how fast he could take the corner without going into a spin, just how late he could leave his braking, just the right moment to touch the throttle again and feel the razor-edge balance between track adhesion and the centrifugal forces trying to throw him off; there was science in it, and the deep joy of doing something as well as it could possibly be done.

He now saw Smart's dark green car ahead; he must have spun or had a 'moment' somewhere, and Kirra was in the lead, with three other competitors in a close string behind him.

He found himself overtaking Smart with surprising ease. There was an unhealthy crackle from the engine of the other car, then the driver's hand went up to signal a pit stop.

Once again Vin's brain recorded this as though he were sitting there watching a newsreel of the race. It was outside, beyond the real world, which was here inside the blue Maserati, with the crescent of the wheel just in front of him, the long curve of the bonnet, and the track whizzing past just below.

The crowd of spectators was a blur; he saw nothing off the track but his own pit crew, and each time he came round they were holding up a board with his lap times. He was keeping a steady average, but to get up in front he would have to improve his time. Either that, or every car ahead would have to blow up or spin out. He couldn't improve his cornering; he must make it up with more speed down the straight and a faster line through the dicey S-bends.

The car was going like a dream. As he wound up, its resonant baritone rose to a clear tenor note, a steady high-pitched sound that streamed out behind like a banner. He watched the rev-counter, the oil pressure, the temperature gauge, flicking his eyes over these dials which told him mutely, All is well. He was doing a hundred and forty down the long straight. He'd have to screw some more mph out of her.

Franz must have been back on the track in half a minute; he was already ahead of the slower field again and coming along behind the blue Maserati. Approaching the straight next time round Vin put his foot down flat, well before he was out of the corner. He went roaring along at full bore, seeing Franz's red Alfa dropping back in his rear-vision mirror. Then he was braking, leaving it till the last moment, for the corner ahead.

Through the Esses and up the back straight he caught and passed three cars, and saw Kirra and the New Zealander close ahead, having a private tussle. Better to keep out of that till they'd sorted themselves out. He moved up to third place and settled down to a steady circling. He lost the sensation of speed. He seemed to be cruising without effort, or sitting in a mechanical car while a mechanical track was wound steadily back beneath his wheels. Yet all the time his nerves and muscles were taut, eyes flicking over the instruments, ears listening to the engine note, hands holding the wheel with a firm grip, nose smelling for smoke or overheating, brain noting the position of the car ahead, the lap number – now it was nine, six laps to go – being held up at the pits as he went past, his time-keeper making the thumbs-up sign.

It was intensely hot in the cockpit of the car, under the tropic sun. His woollen flameproof long-johns under his overalls were soaked with sweat, but he was not conscious of the heat. He was as much a part of the perfectly-functioning machine as the steering wheel, the pistons pounding up and down under the bonnet, the valves opening and closing like the valves of his own heart.

Now McCall, the New Zealander, made a mistake. Following Kirra closely down Pit Straight, he had left his braking a shade too late at Palm Tree Corner. Vin had a glimpse of the car going end-for-end, and a cloud of bright red dust rising, but he didn't turn his head. Now was his chance.

Kirra was driving a new car, and though it was faster than his old one he hadn't quite the confidence in handling it yet;

he was inclined to nurse it into the corners and make up by his superior speed on the straights.

Vin caught him at the Hut Bend by leaving his braking late and diving through on the inside. But as they turned into Pit Straight, Kirra was after him and passed him again.

This was what the crowd liked to see. They roared their excitement.

Two laps to go. Vin knew how slight was the edge he had on the other car; he couldn't afford the slightest misjudgment. A spin, even a wild wobble, would cost him seconds he could ill afford.

A kind of power and certainty descended on him like a mantle. The slower cars he had lapped more than once slid backwards as in a dream. There was only the blue Maserati bonnet in front of him, and Kirra's silver-blue Oska just ahead. He had left Franz and the Alfa behind.

Vin repeated his manoeuvre at Hut Bend and was ahead once more. At the right-angle bend before Pit Straight he went out wider than usual and started accelerating earlier, his outer wheels flinging up dust on the edge of the circuit. He wound up to 160 mph before he had to brake, and this time Kirra couldn't quite catch him.

Through the Esses he was still ahead, and he gained another fraction at Hut Bend. Yet on the last lap Kirra was still close on his rear wheel, and the flag marshals were going frantic with blue flags. As if he didn't know that 'a competitor was trying to overtake him'.

By God, he was nearly home! Come on, you beauty! he shouted silently at the car. It was hurling itself along the track like a rocket, a blue streak.

He couldn't see Kirra; he could just feel him there off his nearside rear wheel. Then ahead, the pit marshal leapt out with the chequered flag. Black and white flashed before his eyes momentarily and then as he began to slow at the end of the straight he heard the cheers.

He had won. He had conquered.

When the laurel wreath twined with frangipani blossom and purple orchids had been placed round his neck, he drove slowly round the course, Kirra and Diamond following. He felt as if his chest would burst with pride and joy. He was never to have another moment like it. Not even the Grand Prix he was to win at Surfer's Paradise, Queensland, by half a lap was to equal the thrill of his first international win.

He arrived back at Raffles Hotel in Singapore in time for a celebratory dinner, sharing a taxi with two other Australians. Once over the Causeway the Indian driver, impressed by the victor's wreath stowed in the back, drove as if he thought he was at Le Mans, weaving in and out of the fast traffic in a terrifying manner.

Vin's room was on a balcony above a large and peaceful courtyard, where Travellers' Palms like great feather fans waved in the languorous breeze, and the frangipani blossom fell to the lawns like scented snow.

He was sticky with sweat and grime, tired and hot and aching. He longed for a cool shower. In his adjoining bathroom, large as a railway-waiting room, the bath was three-quarters full of cold water. He frowned, pulled out the plug, turned on the shower taps. Nothing happened.

He banged in the plug against the retreating water and rang the bell.

The Indian room-steward who came at once looked apologetic. He smiled sadly, his long dark eyes melting with sympathy.

'Sorry, sir, is no water. All must come over the Causeway from mainland. Singapore Island very short of water; no baths after eleven ay em, isn't it? So I fill your bath this morning while the water is turned on.'

'My God, I've let most of it out again. Why didn't somebody tell me?'

Still smiling imperturbably, the steward pointed to a small hand-printed notice on the wall:

HOURS WHEN WATER AVAILABLE

Vin cursed loudly. 'I want a shower-bath!' he cried. 'This is supposed to be one of the best hotels in the world, and I can't even get a shower.'

The steward shrugged. 'Tomorrow morning, sir. You are

leaving early, isn't it? Water will be available, but you are asked to have short shower only.'

He went away, and sulkily Vin let his sinewy length down into the remaining cold water in the tub. Soon he was clean and refreshed. Rubbing himself down with a snowy towel as big as a bedsheet, he felt his good temper return.

The wilting wreath lay on a chair, its gold-printed ribbons dangling. The memory of his win rose in his throat like bubbles in champagne.

He dressed in the light-coloured tussore suit he'd had tailored in two days by a Chinese. He walked along the balcony where the air-conditioners muttered at the entrance to every room, then downstairs to the arcade of shops attached to the hotel, where silver and silk from Thailand, saris from India, sapphires from Burma could be bought, all duty-free.

He bought a set of silver soup-spoons for his mother, and for Jeanne a small silver bracelet inlaid with coloured enamel.

He hesitated over the engraved silver rings, but he didn't want to give her anything that might suggest marriage or any permanent liaison. Marriage, a home, a string of kids, wet nappies, babies yelling – no, this didn't fit anywhere into the mental picture he had of the future. A villa in Rome, a beautiful Italian mistress, a stable of sleek racing cars; this was more how his imagination ran.

He had enough now, with the small bequest from his father (who had left most of his estate to Rosetta) and the inheritance from his Forbes grandfather, not to have to work at a regular job. But he was very far from the millionaire playboy class. He meant to make a profession of driving, get the backing of a big firm even if it meant driving their make of car exclusively.

Already he had been offered a handsome sum for using one brand of sparkplugs and racing fuel. They were advertised in the Press and in programmes of Australian meetings. His picture, looking grim and determined under the gold helmet or behind the wheel of a racing car, was becoming well-known among followers of the sport. *Wheels* had run an article, 'The Uncrowned King of Motor Racing', featuring his Special and listing his growing line of successes.

His friend Franz Diamond had ribbed him about it. 'Hey Vin, have you been Dicing with Death lately?' and 'How's the Uncrowned King of the Moock-Heap?' he would cry, slapping Vincent on the shoulder and smiling the winning, film-star smile which made him so many conquests among women.

'How is the Ace Racing Driver?' had countered Vin, and from then on he called Franz 'Ace', short for Ace of Diamonds, and Franz called him 'The King', or sometimes 'King Vin'.

Ace was an accomplished womaniser. He had been married once, but now had been divorced for some years. He left a string of broken hearts and illegitimate children behind him, and had his own emotions perfectly in control. Most women found him irresistible. He had made money in various dubious ways, from black-marketing in smuggled watches to sly-grogging after hours with the help of a taxi licence. He drove the cab on weekends, and knew exactly where to take his customers whether they wanted a brothel or blue movies, or just an illegal drink. If he had an ethic, it was, 'You don't do the dirty on a mate.' Anyone else was fair game, but mateship was the one thing he believed in, and he never took down his friends or seduced their girls, however tempted.

His eyes were light, clear and hard, like chips of blue ice; his longish, straight hair was yellow as brass; his nose was rapacious as the beak of an eagle. He reminded Vin of the brass falcon's head which once did duty for an inkwell on his father's office desk. Ace had the panther grace of some wild jungle creature, and his instincts were those of a bird of prey.

'Hey, wait for me, King Vin!' A nasal yell from the far end of the covered way, and Ace came loping along, his arms full of parcels. 'What's up, have you got a swelled head already after your big win? By God, if I hadn't spun off into the bales you wouldn't have won. Where's the victor's wreath, eh? You'd better put it in the bath to keep it fresh.'

'There's no water in the bloody bath,' said Vin. 'Not till tomorrow morning.'

'I know. I went and had a Turkish bath at one of these Chinese joints. They have girl masseuses.' He winked.

'Have you heard how Tony McCall is?'

'Yes – concussion and a broken leg. He'll recover.'

'Aren't you coming in to dinner?'

'Yes, I'll just pop these things in my room,' said Ace. 'What have you got there?'

'Oh – a present for my mother.'

'Yair? And who else?'

'Well, a bracelet for Jeanne.'

'I thought so. You be careful, King. She's a nice girl, but she's got her eye on you. I know their form. You listen to your Uncle Ace; before you can turn round you'll find yourself engaged or married or something.'

'Not me! Don't worry.'

'Well, don't say I didn't warn you. Give us your things and I'll put them up in my room with these. Go and order me a Tom Collins, will you?'

'Will you have dinner with me tonight?'

As soon as he was back Vin had phoned Jeanne and asked her out. He'd had a good time in Singapore and Malaya but he felt a physical longing for her which increased the nearer he got to home.

He called for her at home, and she dragged him in to meet her mother, who turned out to be an old schoolfriend of Rosetta King; they had both attended a fashionable boarding-school in the mountains. That meant, probably, that his mother would approve of Jeanne.

After a moderate meal of steak and salad, with which Jeanne insisted they order a bottle of champagne to celebrate his win after the event, Vin laid down his knife and fork with a sigh of content. 'And there I stop,' he said. 'After the fleshpots of Johore and Singapore, I won't be able to get under the wheel of the Jaguar soon, let alone the Mazzer. But you have something else, old dear. Peach Melba? Crêpes? Come on, there's room for some flesh on those hollow cheeks.'

'It's not my face where I put it on, unfortunately.'

'The rest of you is perfect as it is. What size is your wrist? I've brought you a present.' He patted his top pocket.

'Oh! Let me see!'

He took out a twist of tissue-paper and unwrapped the dainty silver bracelet. 'Hold out your arm.'

'Why, thank you Vin! It's charming.' She knew it was an inexpensive trinket, but it was pretty, with small enamelled figures of dancing girls. 'I thought you might forget me, over there among those glamorous Eastern girls.'

'Well, Franz did a bit of prospecting, and I had a dance with a hostess in a *cheong-sam* slit up to here – ' He indicated a point at the top of his thigh. 'But you see I didn't forget you.'

What she saw was the reminiscent smile he could not keep from his lips.

'Do not forget me,' the Chinese girl had said, but it was only part of her work. She had a huge beehive of black hair, stiff with lacquer, a face like a pale mask, and brilliant slits of eyes. Her mouth was tiny and red-painted, her figure small but voluptuous. With her and another girl he and Ace had spent a weekend at the Port Dickson hotel, on the low cliffs overlooking Malacca Straits.

They had swum, when the tide was in, on the narrow beach in the shade of coconut palms, in a sea like warm green milk. When the tide was out they had walked to the little mangrove islands – that is, he and Franz had. The girls were definitely not outdoor types. They were like fragile China dolls, who could eat, sleep, talk, sing in their tinkling childish voices, and perform other agreeable acts, but they seemed scarcely real with their stiff hair and painted faces.

The four of them would sit under the shady trees in cane planters' chairs, drinking Tiger beer or gin-and-tonic, watching the majestic procession of monsoon clouds towering silently above the sea, with storms hidden in their snowy curves as in the breasts of temperamental women. Ships moved along the horizon in a painted frieze above the glittering sea.

The girls were undemanding and equable, their whole lives were bent to pleasing men. Lotus Blossom would sing to Vin while he lay naked and sweating under the ceiling fan, in her tinkling voice:

> Bom–de–bom–de bom–de–ay–ay
> I love you more than I can say–ay

and when it got cooler they would make love under the mosquito net, while the tock-tock bird counted unpredictably in the warm darkness beyond the shutters.

Jeanne's mother was a social lion-hunter, so she had been delighted to meet Vin, having read of his success in Johore. A mere Australian Grand Prix would not have counted, but the glamour of being photographed with a Prince of Thailand in a Rajah's palace clung to him now. British titles were rather out of fashion in Mrs Burgess's set, but the East was 'in'. Her curtains were of Thai silk; her mantel was decorated with carved wooden figures from Bali and she burned incense in brass jars.

She was a wealthy woman whose husband had inherited money and property from a well-known cattle baron, who had made his fortune by clever cattle-duffing in the early days of the colony. This meant that their money came from the land and hence was socially respectable. Though Mr Burgess had never branded a calf in his life, he had invested in the wholesale meat business and doubled his fortune. He was 'in a big way', and Mrs Burgess did not even know the wife of the corner butcher, who was in the same business in a small way.

Mr Burgess had known Vin's father through the Jockey Club (for horseracing was also socially acceptable). He collected racehorses, while his wife collected visiting celebrities and literary lions.

Since Art was fashionable she attended the opening of all the new art shows, wearing a different new hat to each. She usually managed to get herself in the Social pages with a picture of herself and her youngest, most photogenic daughter, posed before one of the paintings. (Jeanne was the eldest, and so far showing no sign of getting married and leaving a clear field for her sisters.)

Mrs Burgess had a lively if rather lined brown face, and dressed expensively and well. Tonight she wore a dark-blue linen sheath simply and dramatically saddle-stitched in white, with a string of real pearls gleaming on her tanned throat.

'These chaps all write or paint or something, do they?' asked Mr Burgess, who usually avoided his wife's parties but had been persuaded to stay home tonight from his usual poker game. He looked around, not sure whether to be admiring or contemptuous. It was notorious that artistic people were poor business men and often impecunious; they were also immoral, and if they didn't go about seducing other chaps' wives, it was only because they were impotent, or else queer. 'Who's that feller there – the one that looks as if he needs a wash and a haircut?'

'Well, he's not exactly a writer, at least not any more. He sells books instead of writing them. He tells people what they ought to buy. You must have heard him on the radio. And it's a very arty bookshop, not an ordinary one.'

'And that one with the grey hair who looks like a managing director, or perhaps a wordly archbishop – don't tell me *he*'s an artist?'

'He's a well-known poet, he's published two books of erotic verse. I was very lucky to get him. And the one over there with the kindly eyes and the world-weary expression is the editor of *Perception*. He has a persecution complex, and he hates *everybody*. The one next to him runs the Tynte Street gallery. He hates art critics.'

'H'm, odd-looking lot, I must say.'

'Now you must come and meet Rapolzcki. He is that handsome Pole with the beard, he wants to do a mural for us on the landing.'

Mr Burgess trailed after his wife, hearing scraps of conversation: 'The novel is dead. Who reads Thackeray or Dickens any more?'

'He's still painting gumtrees and blue hills, for God's sake!'

Jeanne was circulating dutifully, handing round savouries and salted nuts to help the hired drink-waiters. She had decided that Vin was beginning to take her for granted and needed a little competition to stimulate him. She kept gravitating back towards the handsome Pole, who had the profile of Christ in a mediaeval painting. His own work was avant-garde; he preferred to work in baked enamel with touches of gold and bronze, and he had a knack of flattering wealthy ladies who might commission murals for their homes. He was at present cultivating both Jeanne and her mother towards this end. As far as the daughter was concerned, he had hopes of a pleasant liaison. He admired her tall, fair beauty, and the expensive tan gained from swimming in summer and skiing in winter made her seem exotic.

With Vin, they'd had a three-sided conversation which was not a success. Rapolzcki was indignant when he found that Vin did not know his work. 'I am not what you call "a painter",' he said stiffly. 'Zis is for house-decorators. I am a creator of forms in space.'

'And Vincent sends forms *through* space, at great speed,' said Jeanne.

'Ah yes, you are ze racing-driver, no? It seems to me very boringk, zis circling round in ze one place for hours.'

'Boring is one thing I have never found it,' said Vin dryly.

'Oh, no doubt. Eet is highly dangerous, eet takes courage to –'

'It's not just a matter of courage, it takes skill and judgment. People who had more courage than judgment are no longer with us.'

Jeanne stepped in with her cool drawl: 'You see, Vincent is also an artist in his way, Wladys. You two have a lot in common.'

Was she mocking him? Vincent suddenly found her cool smile, her arched brows, unbearable. And as for this bloody Balt, with his subtly insulting manner – !

He emptied his glass and made it an excuse to go and look for another drink. The Polish artist's antagonism had got under his skin, not because he was unduly sensitive about his driving, but because he felt its hidden cause in Jeanne. She was deliberately playing them off against each other, it excited her. Well, she was welcome to him!

Some time later Vin was sitting on the floor, leaning comfortably against the wall and discussing the future of Europe with a melancholy Latvian and an extroverted Czech who specialised in four-dimensional paintings, or '4-D'. He painted raised designs on long scrolls which could be unrolled a little each day, while the earlier part was rolled up. So, he claimed, his pictures had an extension in time as well as in space.

They had all reached a stage of semi-drunken solemnity, where they appeared to listen with tremendous seriousness to each other's contributions to the discussion, while actually thinking of nothing except their own next argument.

Reaching out for his mug of beer, Vin saw a pair of trim ankles at the same level – indeed he had almost clasped one by mistake.

Letting his eyes follow their natural inclination to travel upward, he saw calves and knees to match the ankles, and swelling thighs under a short, full skirt. He came to his feet in one long, graceful movement and stood before her.

'Hullo!' he said. 'I've been looking everywhere for you.'

'For me?' She lifted her dark, feathery eyebrows quizzically. Her face matched her limbs, as he had known it would.

'Yes. I have been looking for you all my life.'

She smiled into her glass, not looking at him.

'Hullo, Maggie.' The Czech artist looked up from the floor. 'When is the new book coming out?'

'I don't know. Before Christmas, I hope. But you know publishers!'

'She writes stories. She is a very clever girl,' he said to Vin.

'Oh, shut up, Alex.'

'But you are, you do.'

'You know this beautiful girl?' asked Vin. 'Introduce me.'

Alex got laboriously to his feet, hanging on to Vin's tall frame for support. 'Maggie, allow me to present Australia's ace of speed, Mr Vincent King. Vince – this is Maggie Pinjarra, authoress extraordinary.' He had great trouble with the pronunciation of the last two words. He subsided back to the floor.

'How d'you do?' said Vin formally, looking down at her searchingly. Pinjarra, he thought, must be Italian, a New Australian. But she doesn't have an accent, except for a local one. Must be a daughter of migrants, went to school here. Her skin was a luminous dark honey-colour, flawless and smooth; her eyes were large, dark and lustrous. Perhaps it was reaction against the Chinese girls' lacquered beehives, or from

Jeanne's impeccable blonde coiffure; but Vin thought he had never seen anything pleasanter than the way the hair fell about this girl's shoulders, waving softly back from her brow so that her face seemed to have a forward movement like that of a bird in flight.

'Let me get you a drink,' said Vin, taking the empty glass from her slim fingers. He rounded up a drink waiter and got her a glass of sparkling Burgundy from one of the few bottles left. Most people were now drinking beer or Australian whisky as the Scotch was all gone. Jeanne seemed to have disappeared, and making a quick check Vin noticed that Wladys Rapolzcki was also missing. Well, that figured.

She thanked him and took the glass, burying her nose in it and looking at him over the rim with soft, glowing eyes. She screwed up her nose at the bubbles. 'They tickle my nose,' she said, and laughed. Vin had rather a shock. Her teeth were so large, so white, that they made her face look browner and smaller. They were much too large, but certainly healthy looking.

'So you write?' he said. 'Tell me the titles of some of your books. I suppose I ought to know them, but I don't.'

'There's only one, besides the new one. It is called "Little Brown Brother".'

'Oh! A children's book?'

'No. It is *not* for children. The title is satirical.'

'Oh, sorry! But it made me think of a story in my first reader. It was about a pair of little brown seeds in the ground, and one of them started to sprout and the other didn't. So the first one grew up into the sunlight and left its brother behind, all alone in the earth.'

'My stories are not sentimental.'

'I suppose it does sound sentimental, but d'you know I used to lie awake brooding over that little seed left on its own? I was rather a lonely kid, and used to wish I had a brother to play with.'

'I had a sister, and brother, and cousins and aunts, a big family. Yet the first story I ever made up, that I remember, was about a lonely violet perishing in a drought. Of course, I'd never seen a violet, we lived in the tropics, but I'd read nothing but English verse and stories. I had a chaffinch singing in one of them, too. I still have no idea what a chaffinch looks like.'

'Where in the tropics?' asked Vin. 'I've just come back from the Malay Peninsula, and in Penang the air was like a stifling wet blanket. Not so bad in Singapore.'

'I was born in Queensland, almost on the Tropic of Capricorn, and the air was wonderful. I've just been back for a holiday.'

'Ah, that accounts for your suntan. It's so even and perfect, I thought it came from a bottle.'

Maggie buried her nose in her glass. There was a faint rosy flush in her brown cheeks as she raised her deep eyes to his.

'So you like my colour?' she said rather mockingly.

Even then he didn't wake up. 'Yes, yes, and I like this goldy-coloured dress, it suits you.' He slipped two fingers inside the sleeveless armhole, pretending to feel its texture, but feeling only the silken skin of her shoulder against the back of his hand. Her eyes met his calmly. She did not smile, nor did she step back out of his reach. He dropped his hand.

'I suppose I should have known your name,' she said, 'but I never read the race reports, or even have a bet.'

'Not *horse*-racing, car-racing,' said Vin, horrified. 'I loathe horses. Besides, they have no brakes, and a very inadequate steering mechanism.'

'Oh, cars . . . I like driving fast, with my head out in the wind.'

'Then let me take you for a spin. I have my sports car here, and we can put the roof down. Drink that up, and let's get to hell out of here.'

'Are you always so – ?'

'Impetuous? Well, I'm not given to beating about the bush. Come on.'

As they were pushing through the throng where the decibels of sound were rising steadily, he came face to face with his hostess. He thanked her for the evening; he looked vaguely around for Jeanne, but she was nowhere in sight.

'Vincent King!' cried Mrs Burgess, grasping his hand in both of hers and starting back to the length of her arm. 'You're not going? Why, I haven't *seen* you yet. Broad shoulders and snake hips! I knew it! You can never tell in those bulky old overalls.'

'Yes, would you say goodbye to Jeanne for me? Maggie here has a headache, and I offered to drive her home.'

'But have you signed my book? You must sign the visitors' book.' She dragged him over to a small polished table. 'And Maggie dear – I want a signed copy of your new book, don't forget.'

Maggie muttered in his ear as they went out, 'She expects a *free* copy, of course. Why did you tell that lie?'

'What?'

'About my having a headache. I can tell my own social lies, thank you.'

'Sorry. It just seemed to pop out. Does it matter?' He was puzzled at this small prickliness in her. She did not reply as they went out into the cool autumn night.

'Don't forget you're having dinner with me on Thursday,' said Vin, bringing her back to the city address she directed him to. They had taken a swift run to the hills behind the city, Vin expertly taking the right-hand corners on the winding road too fast, so that she was swung against his shoulder.

They had stopped at a lookout where they could see the lights of the city spread out on the plain below, from north to south, and beyond it the blank dark line of the sea. The lights were green and amber and diamond-yellow, a sifting of jewels over black velvet.

'Sown and seeded and beaded with grains of light,' murmured Maggie. 'Now, how did I think of that? And do I mean sown, or "sewn"? It's strange how associations work. Seed-pearls, pearl beads, bead-seeds, embroidery – '

Her voice trailed away as his mouth came down on hers in a hard, insistent kiss. 'Don't talk,' he said, raising his head. 'Just let me look at you.'

Her eyes were darkly luminous in the reflected light of a thousand suburban streetlamps, seeming more numerous than the stars which flickered overhead. He stroked her feathery eyebrows, delicately, with one finger. As he kissed her again his hand slipped inside the sleeveless dress and encountered a soft globe, a hardened pointed nipple. He was pursuing his advantage when Maggie said in a stifled voice, 'I think I would like to go home now.'

'But Maggie! You want me. I can tell.'

'Please, Vin. Take me home.'

Her voice was firmer than before. 'Okay.' He released her and started the car. The lights swept round over satiny gumtree trunks, pale with dew, like the torsos and limbs of naked women. Though she sat primly away from him, at the first bend he swung her neatly against his shoulder. A long arm wound about her waist. A strand of her hair blew across his mouth.

'Is that safe?' she asked.

'You are safer with me, driving with one hand, than with most men driving with two. That is, you are safe from vehicular accident. I won't deny that I have designs on you.'

'You're a quick worker. We've only just met.'

'I feel I've been looking for you all my life. Where have you been?'

'I told you. In Queensland. Living on an island.'

'A coral island? How romantic! I loved reading Ballantyne as a boy.'

'No, it's a high island, but with a coral reef round it, and the most beautiful silver sand. Coral sand is soft and crumbly, horrid to walk in. I get homesick for Pandanus still.'

Back in the city, he stopped at a high wooden gate in a paling fence at her direction. But when he would have escorted her inside she put a restraining hand on his arm.

'No, Vin. I'd rather you didn't, I don't want them snooping.'

'Them?'

'The other girls. You see, I live in a hostel. A hostel for Aboriginal girls who work in the city.'

There was a brief silence while Vin digested this. She stood very still, awaiting his reaction.

'Of course!' he said, snapping his fingers. 'That explains what you were doing at the Burgesses'. I mean, your book's not a best-seller; but anything Aboriginal is *in*. You're fashionable, my dear child. I expect Mrs B. was among the society matrons who mobbed poor old Namatjira when they brought him to the city.'

'You're absolutely right. Except that my book *is* almost a best-seller in Australia. The first edition sold out, and it's being reprinted. It's because the stories were written by someone of Aboriginal blood, I fear. Curiosity value.'

'But why didn't you tell me? I thought you were Italian or some other New Australian. Instead you're an Old Australian.'

'Only partly. My father was half Aboriginal, half Portuguese. My mother's mother was part Scottish, part Pacific Islander. She married a white cane-cutter in Maryborough, where she was born. My mother was born at Farnborough north of Yeppoon. They used to grow sugar there in those days. My Dad's people had settled on Pandanus Island; the Pinjarras are very clannish. And my Efate cousins all lived near, except Uncle Davey, who's in Melbourne. He used to be a champion boxer.'

'David Efate! I've heard of him.'

'So I'm a quarter Aboriginal, a quarter Scottish, one-thirty-second English, nine-sixteenths Pacific Islander, eleven thirty-seconds Portuguese, and –'

'Here, hold on! That doesn't add up. But I see why you look so – exotic.'

'I didn't tell you all this, because I wanted you to like me, and I was afraid . . . you'd take me for an easy lay.'

'Maggie! What a thing to say! I do like you, very very much.'

Leaning against the car, he lifted her right off her feet so that she was suspended against him, her mouth level with his own. Like this they fell into a kind of sensuous trance, from which they woke to stare into each other's eyes, wide and dark with shock.

'Christ!' said Vin with reverent blasphemy. 'It's – I don't know. I've never felt this way before. You felt it too?'

She nodded, unable to speak.

He kissed her again and let her slide down till her feet touched the ground, while he ached with tenderness and desire.

'I expect it's something chemical,' he said lightly, 'plus the amount of alcohol we've drunk. The biologists could reduce it to a formula – '

'Oh, don't be smart about it, *please*!' Maggie sounded near to tears. 'I didn't believe it could happen like this, but it has. To think that I didn't even know you yesterday. And I nearly didn't go to that party.'

'Me too. It was only because Jeanne – '

She stepped back. 'Are you one of Jeanne's conquests? She collects men the way her mother collects celebrities. It is a great help to have money.'

'Stop that!' He silenced her with a kiss. 'Bitchiness doesn't suit you. And Jeanne has moved on to other fields. Maggie – ? Don't go in yet. Let's go somewhere we can be alone. Darling, darling – '

For a moment she was limp with acquiescence in his arms, then she thrust him away.

'No,' she said wisely. 'Tomorrow we're both going to have a reaction, we're not going to believe we felt like this. And then what would you think of me? Goodnight, Vin.'

He sighed. 'Dinner on Thursday then, remember. I'll pick you up at work.'

Vin still made the gesture of going to work, because he still felt guilty about his father, and he knew Mr King would have approved. The weekly pay cheque no longer meant very much; he did not have to wait till Friday to take himself out to dinner, and he had an Italian racing car and a van with which to tow it to meetings on a trailer, besides the Jaguar C type he drove to work. But on Thursday he would borrow his mother's sedan in case it was raining.

Five

MAGGIE WAS waiting for him in the shelter of a big stone pillar in front of the City Bank where she worked as a stenographer. Maggie, one of the ants! Who would have thought it? He held back among the crowd to study her unselfconscious face. She had her hands in the pockets of a beige-coloured car coat, over a straight brown skirt and sweater. Her pale-brown face was touched with only a trace of lipstick. The hair flowed back from her brow and face in a smooth wave.

'She has sports-car styling,' he thought. 'None of this over-upholstered luxury body and sloppy chassis.' Her face, her body with its long legs had the flowing, forward-looking line of a silver mascot or a figurehead on a ship.

He stepped quietly round the pillar. 'Miss Pinjarra,' he said quietly, close to her ear, 'this is not a snap judgment, but a considered opinion: you are beautiful.'

'Oh!' She jumped, then laughed. Her laugh was whole-hearted, and her teeth were very large and white. He took her by the arm and felt how slender it was inside her coat sleeve. 'You have the bones of a chicken!' he said tenderly, working his fingers under the sleeve till they encircled her wrist, imagining he felt the delicate pulse there.

In the car, Maggie was glowing, breathless, bright-eyed, talkative, much more animated than she had been the other night.

'You look as if you've won the Lottery,' he said, taking her hand as he drove, heading for a restaurant on the south coast road. It went in for ye olde copper, imitation oak beams and dim lights, but the food was good.

At table, he noticed she hesitated a second before taking up her eating utensils, with a swift glance from under her dark lashes to see what he was using. She buttered a whole slice of bread in the air and bit into it, gnawing healthily at the crust.

441

His mother, he knew, would hold these things against her if he took her home to dinner.

Chasing a hard piece of fried potato with her fork, she made it bounce off the plate on to the floor.

'Oh shit!' said Maggie audibly.

He laughed at her look of little-girl guilt. To put her at her ease he asked her to tell him about her island. Just now, she said, in the season of south-east winds, the weather would be perfect: the mornings clear and calm, the wind building up each afternoon, never bringing rain.

'I get homesick in the winter here.'

'Well, I hope you're not going to tear off back to Queensland just when I've found you.'

She smiled. 'I can't. I have to work . . . I'd never left the island till I was eight years old. I cried and cried when I had to go to school. After my mother died I lived in Rocky with my married sister. Then when my Uncle Harold Brown did so well at singing – he married my Aunt Ellen – they asked me to stay with them in Townsville, and I went to High School there.'

'Harold Brown, the tenor? I've heard him sing.'

'Yes, he makes a wonderful Otello. His name was John Harold Tombua, but they used to call him Yellow Johnny at school, until he got so big they were scared to. I think that's what made him work so hard at singing, the need to prove himself to those white boys who used to tease him. When he married my Auntie he took her surname.'

'You're quite a distinguished family with a writer, an opera singer, and a famous boxer in your ranks.'

'Johnny was sent away by the local Church people to study, and then he got a musical scholarship to study abroad. And every time one of us achieves something, the way Albert Namatjira did in painting, it's not just for ourselves but for the whole race. It doesn't alter fundamentally the prejudices of an old bitch like Mrs Burgess, she still feels we're on a lower plane even when she's crawling for an autograph.' For a moment her face looked hard, contemptuous. 'But each successful concert, each work in an art gallery, each book published means a little grain of sand washed away from the wall that shuts us out.'

'Do you see me on the other side of a wall, Maggie?'

'I did at first. There's always this feeling of Us and Them. But the other night, when you kissed me beside the car, I had the strangest feeling. I dissolved. All my molecules seemed to become part of something else, beyond myself, like the solution of a solid in a liquid. You know?'

'I know. It happened to me too. But I felt like a river which has reached the sea. Wonderfully at peace.'

'You are the one who should be writing books,' said Maggie.

He took her hand under cover of the cloth.

'I can't stand this,' he said. 'Eat up darling, and let's get out of here where I can have you to myself.'

As they were leaving he heard his name called softly. It was Jeanne, dining at a discreet table for two behind a potted palm. She had rung him once since the party, but he had pretended to be busy. Now she beckoned him over. Maggie walked on and lingered by the door.

'Don't tell me you're dining alone!' he said. 'What's wrong with the young men of this town?'

'No, silly, Wladys has just gone to have a pee. Vin! Who's the new girl? I know her face. And I'm desperately jealous.'

'Yes?' He raised one of his slanting eyebrows quizzically. 'I met her at your party the other night, her name's Maggie Pinjarra and she writes books.'

'Oh yes, the Aboriginal authoress.' Her eyes flicked over Maggie in the distance. 'Someone should teach her how to dress.'

'Now, Jeanne! Claws in. I can't stop to talk now . . . Bye.'

He hurried after Maggie, paid the bill, and found when he joined her that she was angry and trembling.

'How could you leave me to walk out alone like that? What was that Burgess girl saying about me?'

'Steady on, darling. She's an old friend –'

'You were discussing me. What did she say?'

'For heaven's sake. She was just curious, that's all.'

'I felt so conspicuous, standing there. You don't understand, once it took all my courage to walk into a restaurant in Townsville, never sure if they would refuse to serve me.'

'I'm sorry, honey. It is hard for me to realise what it must be like in the Deep North. You're not there now. Relax.'

'No, you don't realise. What it was like to go to a white school, to sit alone and eat my lunch because I was supposed to be "dirty". Once I walked up to a group of girls and one of them said, "It looks like rain! Black clouds hanging around." I went up and slapped her face.'

'Good for you.'

'I got into trouble. I was told I was "uncivilised", but that girl never teased me again. She was scared to.'

Maggie laughed, her good humour returning as suddenly as it had left her. 'That's one reason I prefer the south, in spite of the cold winters. You don't get that open prejudice, though it's there underneath, a feeling of superiority that some white people seem to be born with.'

'I don't believe they're born with it. Small children will accept a child with no arms, or with a dark face, quite naturally. They pick up prejudice from their parents. I remember my mother telling me when I was quite small, "Don't eat the banana skin, dear. That banana could have been dragged along the gutter by a Chinaman." Of course most fruitsellers in those days were Chinese. But I got the distinct impression that both gutters and Chinamen were dirty.'

'Yes, it is a sort of brainwashing, I suppose.'

On the way back to the car they passed a lighted fruit stall with bunches of violets for sale among bananas and shiny red and green apples. Vin stopped to buy her a bunch. 'There! And not a lonely violet among them.'

Maggie sniffed them rapturously. 'No one ever bought me flowers before.' She looked at the pineapples, and coconuts in their brown fibrous coating. 'Those remind me of home. Bananas don't look the same, we always had them in great bunches, or bought them in "hands" – that's a row of "fingers" joined together. But the coconuts – we used to husk them and then peel off the fibre with our teeth.'

'With your teeth! No wonder yours look healthy!'

'Yes, they're strong.' She laughed, her teeth flashing white as the flesh of fresh coconuts. 'We'd pick them green, too, and drink the milk. They could be quite dangerous if they fell. Uncle Dingbat Morgan was asleep under a palm one night, when a nut fell and nearly broke his nose.'

'What a beaut name!'

'He's my uncle. He is a fisherman, and he has a wooden leg. A shark got the other. I used to go out to the big Reef with him after coral cod and parrot fish. He said I was good as a man in a boat.'

He took her hand and tucked it under his arm, pulling her along with him. 'I'm glad you're *not* a man. And I like your name, Maggie Pinjarra.'

'I like Vin, but not "Vincent". It sounds too all-conquering: Vincent King! Who chose your name?'

'My mother, you bet.'

'If I were superstitious I would say it was tempting fate a bit. Like calling a girl Prudence or Verity.'

'Or Virginia? I take the point.'

They were both slightly light-headed with wine. They felt happy and invulnerable and absurdly pleased with themselves; they said anything that came into their heads and felt they were having 'an intelligent conversation'.

As soon as they were in the car they stopped talking and fell into each other's arms, regardless of passers-by. Vin looked deeply into her eyes.

'Maggie – ? Shall we go somewhere I know of? "I know a bank where the wild thyme blows" – '

She giggled. 'So do I; a bank where the time-clock goes, and I have to be there at nine tomorrow. I mustn't be too late tonight.'

'That's tomorrow. There's no need to think about that yet.'

'Soon we'll come to the place I'm looking for.' Vincent was driving with his attention divided between the road, the farmlands opening up on his right, and Maggie's shapely knees in the glow of the dashboard light. The car was roomy, but he wanted her out under the stars and rising moon. Now he saw what he was looking for: a half-demolished haystack standing back from the road behind a four-strand wire fence. No farmhouse was in sight. They got out, and he held the spiky barbed strands apart for her while she crept through.

They walked with arms entwined, stumbling over clumps of grass and dried cowpats, stopping often to kiss.

They climbed the haystack from the broken side and lay on top in the moonlight, gazing silently into each other's eyes. The hay smelt sweet as honey in the dew. Her face was etherealised by the pale light; her eyes were dark smudges with a glitter of white fire in them.

Slowly, with a kind of inevitability, they came together. He was gentle with her, tentative, instinctively forbearing, as though she was still a virgin. This was their true marriage. A ceremony could only set the seal on what was already accomplished. He did not care if there had been others. It was accomplished, he was there, he had entered in unto her like one of the Kings of the Old Testament, Ahasueras with Esther, David with Bathsheba. She was his, now and forever.

When at last they walked back towards the road, still with arms about each other, they moved hip to hip like Siamese twins, for Maggie was a long-legged girl. The bright moon had almost reached the zenith. *Queen and huntress, chaste and fair*! Vin looked up at that cold, flat face and felt that the moon did not look benignly on such lusty goings-on, in spite of the romantic songs. He felt a little premonitory shiver at the base of his spine.

There came a sharp neigh from somewhere behind them. Four black horses came cantering up, tossing their heads, the whites of their eyes glistening in the moonlight.

Vin stiffened. He hated and feared horses. His father had tried to make a horseman of him, had insisted on putting him up on a big horse when he was no more than five. He had screamed with fright.

He still didn't like anything about them, from their long, dangerous-looking teeth to their hard, lethal hoofs. He forced himself to walk quietly, not to run. His arm tightened about Maggie protectively. She looked over her shoulder uneasily.

'Vin, is it all right? Why are they following us?'

'*Don't run*!' he whispered fiercely, but it was to himself. 'Take no notice; just keep on walking. They're just curious.' He began to sneeze. His eyes watered.

It seemed an interminable distance to the fence. The horses kept close behind them, snuffling and snorting. Vin felt his spine cold, his hair creeping on the back of his neck. Then they were at the fence.

He disciplined himself to wait, to let her through the parted wires, though he was longing to fling himself over. Her skirt had caught in a barb of the wire. He bent to unhook it and seemed to feel a black horse rearing behind him, iron hooves crashing down on his skull like fate or retribution . . . He put one hand on the top wire and vaulted over to safety.

The safety straw-bales scattered on either side. Iron hooves crashed down upon his skull. He opened his eyes to find himself sitting in the Maserati, which was jammed solidly against a tree. Gumtrees – bushland – a curving slope of bitumen – yes, he was at Mount Panorama circuit at Bathurst, New South Wales, and he had just spun off the course into a tree.

Yes, yes, yes . . . It was while he was trying to make up time after refuelling, he had taken a downhill corner too fast, and too late had tried to correct the skid. In over-correcting he had gone the other way, straight into the bindi . . .

Refuelling! Petrol! He snapped open the safety-belt and struggled out of the car. It seemed almost to cling to him like a garment which he couldn't shake off quickly enough. He imagined he could smell gasoline fumes in the air, as he started to run, and his leg crumpled under him. The pain was so intense that he almost passed out again.

He started to crawl, sobbing and swearing, using his elbows and his one good leg, dragging the other leg over spiky grass and small stones. In the distance he heard the scream of the ambulance siren, the roar of cars still circling.

'Don't you fellows take me to hospital,' he begged as the Ambulance Brigade men put him on a stretcher. 'I can't stand hospital. I'd rather go to gaol.'

'Well, there's a good gaol in Bathurst,' quipped one of them.

'You're just asking for hospital, aren't you mate?' asked the other. 'Driving round in one of them Grong Pree cars. What do you expect when you prang at about a hundred and twenty mph? Slight abrasions?'

'I suppose it looks dangerous,' said Vin, 'but actually you're a lot safer on a closed circuit, with everyone going the same way, than on the roads these days. At least you know when you crash that it was your own fault. Just stupidity, nothing else.' Then he quietly fainted. He dreamed confusedly of Maggie, of great black horses in the moonlight, of his unreasoning fear. They meant no harm, he knew . . .

'I knew I was going into that corner too fast,' said Vin. He had managed to get himself discharged from hospital after having his leg X-rayed, set, and immobilised in plaster; it was not a bad break, though both the tibia and the fibula were involved. He was lying on the bed at his hotel, where Franz and Giulio had helped him, being questioned by the Ace of Diamonds.

'Then why the hell did you, old chap?' asked Franz, expertly knocking the cap off a bottle of beer at the bedroom handbasin. He poured from the cold-frosted bottle a glass full of amber liquid with a collar of creamy foam, handed it to Vin, and poured himself another. Then he sat on the side of the bed, absent-mindedly tearing the metal bottle-top in half with his bare hands.

Vin drank in silence, frowning thoughtfully. He set his glass down empty, with a sigh of pleasure. 'Ah, that tasted good . . . Why did I? I don't exactly know. But just sometimes I get an overwhelming urge to go into a corner too fast. I have to force myself *not* to do it. Haven't you ever felt the fascination of the fact that just a tiny twist of the wheel and you'll crash? It's like the feeling of standing on the edge of a precipice, with the sea hundreds of feet below, or on top of a building, looking down at the street. It seems to draw you down, while the sensible part of you is dead scared and keeps you away from the edge.'

'Not Franz Diamond, thank you. I never felt the urge to jump over a cliff or try a damnfool thing like giving the wheel a twist at a hundred and forty. No sir! I want to live.'

'You mean that perhaps I want to die?'

'Christ, no! Why should you want to die? Unless you're a nut, and you're not.'

'No. Silly of me. I guess my head's still a bit woozy from the pills they gave me.' But he was thinking, something he had read about a subconscious death-wish? Yet how could it be subconscious, when he could bring it into the light of day and discuss it? No, it was nonsense. Apart from the throbbing of his leg, he'd never felt better, more alive. Even the pain was a part of life, he would rather suffer than be dead and feel nothing.

Ace struck a pose and chanted extempore:

> 'Unless you're a nut, and you're not,
> You must understand what is what:
> You drive for the thrill,
> And not to get killed,
> And not even for money, you clot.

The middle rhyme's not too good, but never mind.'

As he poured himself another beer there came a tap on the door, and Giulio Mosca bounced in, a bottle of Chianti in one hand, a bunch of green grapes in the other.

'*Vincente, amico*, 'ow are you?' he cried, flashing his white teeth. '*Come sta?*'

'*Benissimo*, thanks Giulio. Have a beer.'

'Welcome, Giulio, you look like Bacchus himself; if only you had a few vineleaves in those greasy locks of yours,' said Ace mockingly.

'Ah, Franz must always 'ave 'is yoke,' said Giulio, mildly. 'No, I will open the *vino* if I may, Vincente? *Si? Va bene?*'

'Go ahead.'

Giulio pulled a corkscrew and a spare glass out of his overalls pocket. He placed the bottle between his knees and withdrew the cork with a slight pop, poured the glass three-quarters full of red wine, saluted Vin with glass held high, and tossed it off.

'To your verra soon good 'ealth, my friend . . . And now, what hoppen? Tell Giulio.'

'What hoppen? He hit a tree, didn't you know?' said Ace.

'Yes, I know this. But why? I 'ave been over the car most carefully. There is nothing wrong with steering, brakes, suspension – *niente*, except what the tree has done. Then, why?'

'Poor judgment, I'm afraid. I tried to take the corner too fast.'

'But you 'ave been over this corner many times in practice, and in the race. You were not being pushed by nobody, you 'ave a comfortable lead. For what you go too fast?'

'I tell you I don't know. I just misjudged. Giulio, just let it rest, will you? You're an A1 mechanic, there was nothing wrong with the car, it was going perfectly and I made a boo-boo. That's all there is to it.'

'Well, I no unnerstan'. You mucha too good a driver, make a mistake like this.'

'Well, I made it.'

Giulio shook his head, rinsed Vin's glass at the handbasin and poured wine for him and another for himself. He looked inquiringly at Ace, holding up the bottle.

'Thanks, I'll stick to good old Aussie beer,' said Ace. 'You can have that Dago plonk on your own. I no like the veeno.'

Vin frowned slightly, Giulio shrugged. Vin was fond of his two friends, but Ace was always trying to needle the Italian. Giulio didn't like Ace much, and no wonder.

Giulio was an inspired mechanic. Like a good doctor he could diagnose ills just by listening and looking. He would drive a car a few blocks and announce that there was three thou' of wear in the cylinders and new rings were necessary, or that it had a crook crankshaft or its timing was out, and he was always right.

His English was not perfect, yet expressions like 'piston-slap', 'gear ratio', 'spark-advanced', 'valve-bounce', 'exhaust manifold' tripped off his tongue as though he had been native born. Instead he had come to Australia from the little town of Pescara in Italy, on the shores of the Adriatic, where he had once seen the great Carracciola win the *Gran' Premo d'Italia*.

'In Italy,' he told Vin once, 'the racing-driver is king, *veramente*. At Pescara the people they hang out on their balconies their most beautiful tapestries before a big race, and long, what-you-call, banners, saying "Viva Carracciola" and "Viva Fangio!". One day perhaps they say "Viva Vincente King!" '

'They may, at that,' said Vin soberly. 'I mean to get to Europe and drive on the big international circuits before I'm too old. I'll drive at Monza one day, and at the Nurburgring, at Berne and Monaco . . . Just their names are enough to give me goose-pimples.' His bright, deepset eyes gleamed fanatically.

Giulio nodded, 'I believe it also. I believe you will not only drive in Europe, Vincente, but you will win.'

'Yes! It's not just a matter of luck, or chance, but of will. I *will* go to Europe, and I *will* become the World Champion. It's just a matter of concentrating on what you want most.'

'What you want now is a good rest,' said Ace, picking up the empty beer bottles and motioning to Giulio with his head. 'Let's leave the wounded hero to have a sleep. I'll get them to send you in something to eat. What would you like?'

'Nothing much. At least, something I can eat easily. A cup of soup and a chicken sandwich.'

Six

HE MANAGED to get to the phone in the office, since there was none in his room, and rang his mother to tell her about the crash. He persuaded her, by speaking brightly and minimising the pain in his leg, that there was no need to come rushing over to Bathurst.

'At least I'll be grounded for a while,' he said. 'The car is a bit of a mess, and the leg will take three months, they say – though it's a clean break, no complications. I'll be in plaster for a good while yet.'

He also rang Maggie at the Hostel that night, outlining his plan for her to come over on a weekend as soon as possible, and drive him home in his own sports car.

'But it's nearly eight hundred miles!' she cried, when she had managed to hear by covering her other ear against the noise in the hostel's community room.

'Well, you could catch a flight early Saturday morning, and be here before lunch. Then if we left early Sunday morning,

451

and drove all night, you'd be back in time for work on Monday.'

'Vin, you're mad! I'm not used to your car, and what if something went wrong, and I didn't get back in time for work? Unlike you, I need my job.'

'Then you'd better give it up and marry me.'

'What? I can't hear a thing. It's so noisy here.'

'I said MARRY ME. M,A,R,R,Y. M for Maggie, A for aye sir, double R for right-you-are, Y for yes.'

There was a long silence, till Vin thought the line was cut.

'Hullo? Are you there?'

'Yes.' Her voice came faintly. 'Vin, did you say – Are you asking me to marry you?'

'Thr-ree minutes. Are you extending?' came the operator's voice.

'YES, for Christ's sake. I mean, Maggie, are you there? What about it?'

'I d-don't know, I haven't had time to think about it.'

'Your voice sounds faint. Are you going to come over and get me?'

'Vin, I can't. You'll have to get someone else to drive you. Can't you fly?'

'It's a bit difficult getting up and down a 'plane ramp with this leg. Guilio's already gone, with the Mazzer on the back of the trailer, and the van. I'll have to wait till he can come back again.'

'Is the car badly damaged?'

'Bodywork mostly. It slammed sideways into a tree – no engine damage. Like my leg, nothing that can't be mended in time.'

'I miss you.'

'I miss you too.'

'If I could afford it, I'd fly over anyway. Just to hold your hand.'

'Well, do that. Next weekend, okay? I'll pay your fare this end and they can telex it through.'

'But Vin –'

'Don't you want to see me?'

'Yes, of course –'

'Well, then. I think the three minutes are nearly up,

darling. Goodbye. I'll expect you on the mid-morning 'plane Saturday.'

'Goodbye. Be careful on those crutches.'

' 'Bye.'

Maggie arrived on the next Saturday, and spent the rest of the morning in the single bed in his room. Vin had pulled her straight into bed with him with his strong arms. 'Nothing wrong with the top half of me, thank God!' he said cheerfully, though he had been awake half the night with the pain in his leg. She rather liked him helpless like this, so that she had to be the active one, fitting herself to him, adapting herself to his need. At first she was frightened to move, fearing to hurt his leg, but he told her that it was safely encased in the plaster and was all right if he didn't move it. She lay above him, taking her own time, and surprised herself with the intensity of her reactions.

Later he asked her to go with him round to the garage, within walking distance, where the C-type had been left. He had decided, he told her blandly, that if they left straight away, this afternoon, they could break the journey at one of these new motels – you could drive right up to the door of your room, no elevators or staircases to contend with – and get home comfortably the next night.

'You won't even have to drive fast,' he said.

She was aghast. 'But I've got my return ticket –'

'That can be cancelled.'

' – and I'd be scared to drive your car all that way. I know you've let me take the wheel sometimes, but I'm just not used to it. I'm not a good enough driver.'

'You will be by the time we get there. You'll have an excellent instructor.'

'You'll get mad at me. And I hate driving at night.'

'I told you, we won't have to drive much at night. And if we average 40 we can do it in twenty hours.'

'*Average* forty? You're crazy. And what about meals?'

'We'll take sandwiches and chocolates. Come on, drive me back to the hotel,' said Vin impatiently. 'We have to pack up and get going.'

He leant his crutches against the roof of the car while he opened the door. They immediately slid to the ground.

'Bloody things! I hate them.' He got himself inside and lifted his cumbersome leg, plaster from knee to ankle, after him. He winced.

'Vin, I don't think you're well enough to travel all that way. You'll get cramp, your ankle will swell –'

'Shut up and get in.'

She did as she was told. She actually liked him ordering her about. But she dreaded the thought of the drive ahead.

Once they were out on the highway she felt better. She had bungled the start, stalling the engine, while the car bucked protestingly till it stopped. Now they were sailing along the black road, down through the hills and on to the western plains. Starting from Bathurst, inland from the Blue Mountains, they followed the Mid-Western highway. There was a lot of weekend traffic in the towns, but there were not many large semi-trailers on the road.

By the time they had reached Hay and Narrandera, with the Murrumbidgee winding somewhere through the endless plains over there to the right, the car had wound up to a steady eighty miles an hour almost without Maggie noticing it. The movement was so effortless, they seemed to fly along like a bird just skimming the surface of the earth. The road was straight and flat, bordered by dry grass and stunted brush. She loved this empty country, vast sheepgrazed paddocks where the back fences were too far off to be seen. (Vin's great-grandfather had owned large tracts of it.) There were few other cars. Sometimes they passed a big trailer loaded with living sheep, going towards Sydney. The animal scent of dung and dirty wool floated back to them. They had crossed the Condamine, the Murrumbidgee and the winding Wollondilly. The road seemed to flow like a river through the shallow valleys of pale grass, round the feet of indigo hills.

Approaching the town of Hay they came to a bend in the road after a long straight. Maggie, though she slowed down a little, did not allow for the long drive at high speed which made fifty miles an hour seem slow. She went into the corner too fast, correcting wildly, and cornered on the wrong side of the road. The car slewed, two of its wheels in the dirt, then righted itself. When she had wrestled it back into line she pulled up on the side of the road, trembling.

'Yes, well, you've learnt something by that, I hope,' said Vin calmly. 'You misjudged your speed, didn't look at the speedometer to check. At least you didn't try to jam on the brakes, that would only have put us into a skid.'

'I could have killed us both!' Maggie was near to tears.

'This is a very forgiving little car. You can do foolish things and it will right itself, it's very hard to tip over. You did very well, here we are pulled up, on the right side of the road, with no dents.'

'I was driving too fast.'

'We all make mistakes at times. Get a can of lemonade out of the back, will you? And look the other way, I'm going to have a piss out the side of the car.'

Still shaking, she opened the can, took a sip and passed the rest to him. She started off again very circumspectly, until at last he had to urge her to drive faster.

'Yes, we all make boo-boos sometimes,' he said thoughtfully. 'That's why this damned leg is in plaster. But there's no excuse for me, I should have known better. You learn to drive by the seat of your pants. You feel the tension, the centrifugal force, the gravitational force, and know exactly what the car is doing, would know if you were blindfolded. I also knew that I had to keep the car on exactly 96.5 miles an hour on that corner, or I'd lose it. That's 4,500 revs on the tachometer. The car was only just retaining its adhesion to the road; I could *feel* it, a sensation like driving on a frozen lake. Yet something made me try to go through at 97. It was as though I was daring myself to do it. And so of course I pranged.'

His steady voice soothed her; she began to feel her confidence come back and to enjoy the feel of the lithe little sports car with its stubby gear-lever. It was not exactly comfortable; the ride was bouncy and the springs were hard. Vincent groaned as he shifted the position of his leg. There was plenty of room to straighten it out, but it needed to be elevated. They stopped and wedged one of their travel-cases in front for him to rest it on, with a thick sweater on top to cushion the weight.

'God, I wish I could drive,' he complained, 'but the accelerator would go right through the floor with this weight on it.'

455

Ahead, the dark ribbon of bitumen unwound and slid away behind. Indigo bands of distant trees on the horizon dipped out of sight again without coming any nearer. Pale, dry grass on the road's verge waved them on. All was flux, yet they drove at the calm centre to which every movement was related, like the hub of a vast wheel. Trees danced by in stately measures, bowed and retreated and sank into the ground. The sky moved like a great closing shell of pearl, to shut upon the sun.

By the time they stopped for the night Vin was exhausted.

They found a small one-storey hotel in a wheatbelt town on the edge of the flat mallee country. Among the low, sprawling buildings rose one tall shape like a fairytale castle, pale in the moonlight; it was a wheat silo for holding bulk grain. Maggie had never seen one before. She thought at first she must be imagining it, for her eyes and brain were so tired that for the last hour, on a perfectly level road, she'd had the illusion of plunging steeply downhill.

In the morning they made a dawn start, without breakfast, and reached Adelaide late on Sunday afternoon, coming down through the hills with a great flood of Sunday tourist traffic.

Maggie was terrified, but Vin praised her driving. He directed her straight to the hostel. He would get a taxi home and ask Giulio to pick up the car.

He saw that she was grateful for this. He knew she would not want to meet his mother for the first time like this, grubby and tired out from a long drive. Also she would be in time for the evening meal at the hostel, and it must seem like a week since she'd eaten properly.

'There's one good thing about Australia's wide empty spaces,' she said, pulling thankfully in at the kerb. She misjudged the width of the car and scraped a hub along it; Vincent winced. 'Anyone learning to drive can count on at least five hundred miles between one capital city and the next.'

She took her luggage in through the gate. By the time she came back he had hailed a cab, waving a crutch imperiously from the roadside. His face was hollow-cheeked and drawn with pain; his eyes had dark shadows under them.

'You must go straight to bed!'

'Don't worry, darling. My mother will love having a chance to fuss over me. I'll ring you at work. And thank you for driving my car back. It wasn't too terrible, was it?'

'I might have wrecked your car.'

'But you didn't. You'll make a good driver yet.'

She waved as the cab pulled away.

Vin, leaning back and resting his injured leg along the seat, reflected how strange it was that they had just spent their first night together, flaked out unconscious in separate beds. But after two days in her company he knew for certain he wanted to spend the rest of his life with Maggie. She was different from any girl he had ever met. And nicer than any of them.

Seven

AT LAST Vin's leg was out of plaster, and it was warm enough for him and Maggie to go swimming at weekends. By mid-November the temperatures had reached the high nineties, and the city recorded its first century before Christmas. The grassy hills burned brown and yellow as toast. Now the pale, streaky skies of early summer turned the deep hard blue of baked enamel, with a few motionless clouds which looked, Maggie thought, like best bank paper cut out and pasted against the blue.

Though the sea was colder here, the beach reminded her of home. In north Queensland they would swim all the year, in spite of sharks and stingrays and deadly sea-wasps that looked like innocent boxes of jelly, but trailed below them fifteen-foot filaments which could kill a man in three minutes. On her island, inside the fringing reef it was fairly safe. Beyond, the Pacific Ocean stretched all the way to America, but the Great Barrier Reef broke the ocean swells thirty miles further to the east.

Maggie missed the warmth and colour, the rainbow lorikeets screeching among flowering poinciana and tulip-tree, pandanus palms spreading their clusters of spiky leaves above a sea like green glass. Sometimes she felt numb for all that colour and light. Hunching her shoulders against the cold south-westerlies in winter, she thought of the island, the dear dark kindly people of her father's family, and her aunties and uncles on her mother's side all of whom had the tight curling hair of the Pacific Islander. There were no picture-shows on the island, and though they had a radio, mostly they made their own entertainment. There was always a card game going on the beach under the shade of the palms, and at night there was singing and dancing in the open.

The men danced all kinds of dances: stamping Aboriginal ones, Maori *haka*s which a visiting New Zealander had taught them (his sister Ilona was married to Maggie's brother Dan) and Island dances full of the swaying undulations of the sea.

Before his voice was discovered and he was sent off to study, Harold Tombua on his visits from Rockhampton was in great demand to lead the songs. Maggie's big sister Marie had taken her into 'Rocky' to hear Harold sing a solo in the Town Hall. It was a ten-mile boat journey, and then another twenty-five miles by road. Maggie, who before had seen only the small seaside town of Yeppoon and the Church Mission school at Keppel Sands, was overwhelmed by the city.

'I'll never ever leave the Island again,' she said on her return. She flung her arms round Grannie Nyora's fat brown neck and buried her face in her ample shoulder.

'Ah, go on wit' you, what wrong wit' Rocky? That a good place, plenty shop, plenty picture-show, mobs of people. Wisht I'd a gone in the boat 'stead of you. Was just wasted on you, girl.'

'I didn't know there was that many white people in the world.'

'Lots more than that, love. Wait till you see Brisbane, and Sydney, and Melbourne, and all of them.'

Marie, on her next visit to her grandmother, said she wanted to take Maggie back with her and send her to school in Rocky. She was 'runnin' wild like a blackfeller' on the island. Half the time she stayed away from the Mission school because the weather was bad, or the launch wasn't running.

Maggie had looked at Marie in her smart sundress and gold sandals, and from her to Nyora in her shapeless cotton dress dipping at the hem, a man's felt hat pulled over her grey hair, and bare feet.

'Can I wear gold sandals if I go to school?' she asked.

'Well, not to school, love. You'll have to wear lace-up shoes in the winter. But you can have some gold sandals for weekends. You can dress up to go to Church – '

'I'm fed up with sermons and psalms and hymns.'

'Not Mission church, but a big Church of England, with these big windows of coloured glass that the sun comes through all red and blue and gold, and an organ with pipes as high as a palm-tree, and a minister in a white surplice with real lace. That's the church where Harold used to be a choir-boy.'

'Gee!' said Maggie.

'Harold sang "Amazing Grace" in St Paul's Cathedral in Melbourne for a big crowd. They couldn't clap because it was in church, but the papers said he sung lovely.'

'I'd like to sing in front of a great crowd like that.'

'You! You couldn't sing for nuts.'

'No, but if I could. To have everyone quiet, listening.'

'Besides, you're too shy. Dead scared of the crowds in the streets, and I could hardly get you into the shops.'

'I know.' She hung her head. 'But it would be diff'runt – just you and the music – and the people beyond the ring, outside, yet sharing it with you.'

'Where does she get these ideas from?' asked Marie of Nyora.

'I dunno. She's alwus coming out with these things . . . But if she goes to the city she'll marry someone that'll go far and fast. Yairs, far and fast.'

Maggie looked up into the dark face, the cloudy eyes staring out through the palm-trees at the blue coral sea. Her grandmother was known to have the seeing eye to foretell events, usually tragic ones. And she knew when someone, away on the mainland, had died. She said quite seriously that a bird told her.

When Maggie's father had disappeared while out fishing in his small trawler, she had said he would be found tangled in his own fishing-net; she had 'seen' him floating face-down in shallow water. And so it was. Everyone else had been sure a shark had got him, or he had gone down with his boat, but his mother knew.

Nyora's much older son, Morgan, had been badly mauled by a shark when he stepped into his fishtrap before the tide had properly gone down. He managed to beat it off with the gaff and drag himself to safety. He would have died of loss of blood if Nyora had not sensed something wrong and sent the men out in the ketch to look for him. They roughly bound up his leg and sailed straight for Yeppoon, whence he was taken to the Rockhampton hospital; but the leg had to be amputated. He had a peg-leg of fine-grained blue gum which he had carved himself, fitted below the knee.

'And I'd like to see a shark try to sharpen 'is teeth on that,' said Dingbat Morgan, slapping the wood with the palm of his horny hand. He pretended cheerfully that the stump was an advantage to a fisherman, making him immune to sea-wasp stings and stonefish and other horrors of the sea.

His boat was a sea-stained, fish-scale-scattered wooden craft with sails and a wheezing auxiliary engine. He knew the waters between the island and Emu Bay like the back of his own hand, and could safely traverse the reefs further out, some of them lurking just below the surface. He would come back with great catches of coral cod – scarlet fish with beautiful blue dots on their skins – Parrot and Sweetlip and Red Emperor. These were all magnificent eating, and with coral trout – even more delicate – and lobsters were the mainstay of the family larder. He also caught 'rubbish fish' in great quantities for the fish-shops in town: doggy mackerel, and small golden trevally, and even small sharks which sold, fried in fish-shaped steaks, as 'flake'.

He was a jolly, proud, and independent man. He had built the boat himself and bought the engine from his savings while working on the railways for a year. He despised the young fellows who were content to hang about the town or the Mission, supported by the State or cadging the price of a drink from white men outside the pubs. When Morgan's wife, Theresa, died of a heart attack, he was inconsolable. For a while he became morose, but gradually his natural good humour asserted itself. Maggie was his favourite niece. He showed her how to bait a hook, how to thread a sliver of fish-flesh on the shank, with a tempting tail of skin hanging down. Sometimes he would take her on his fishing expeditions.

When he caught a small shark, he drove the gaff expertly through its brain before tossing it into the well of the boat. Even so its nerves made it leap and quiver as it died. Maggie would sit with her bare legs drawn high up on the gunwale out of the way. Dozens of small trevally were despatched by a quick knock on the head so that they would not damage each other in their struggles, and dropped into a wet sack.

It was a ruthless, bloody business. But if human beings didn't eat the fish, she reasoned, other fish would. It was the law of the ocean; eat or be eaten. A visitor trolling with live mullet for mackerel off Emu Bay, had unwisely taken the handline several turns around his wrist. His wife saw him on the deck one moment; the next, when she turned at his cry, he was gone. There was not even a swirl in the water. He had just disappeared. The man was never found, but next day a twelve-foot shark was seen in the Bay by a patrolling aircraft.

'When I have to kill a fish, I can be as bloody-minded as a cat,' said Maggie. She and Vin were travelling in the Jaguar with the roof down, along the south coast road. Her hair and her skirt fluttered in the wind of their movement.

'What brought that on?'

'About killing fish? Oh! I was thinking about the Island, and going out in Uncle Dingbat's boat. That blue sea brought it on, I suppose.'

As they came over the first hill beyond the suburbs, the coloured landscape had opened like a fan: strips of brown fallow, wheatfields deep ochre, and golden grassy hollows crowned with summer sea.

'Why don't you wear shorts over your swim-togs?' asked Vin as the skirt flew up around her waist.

'I don't know – my legs are too skinny.'

'Your legs are beautiful.' He held the skirt down for her with one hand, and she felt the sweet molten flood of love and

461

desire as though the burning touch of his fingers had made her melt and run, like whitemetal, like gold in a crucible. She closed her eyes against the sun, reflecting unbearably bright from chromium and glass. Vin wore sunglasses which made his face mysterious, the deep-set grey eyes hidden, the finely marked eyebrows he could lift one at a time. His face was almost as brown as hers, while his hair had bleached with the sun: he never wore a hat.

'I love you,' she said, opening her eyes to look at him. He smiled and removed his hand to change down for the turn-off to the secluded beach he knew of, reached along a rough track. And there below lay the wide, cool sea.

They ran over the salt-white sand, so hot that it burned their bare feet. Then they swam and floated in the zircon shallows, where the netted sunbeams made patterns on the sand below, but never too far out from shore. Maggie's eyes turned uneasily in her head, looking for dark shapes in the water. It was sad, when these southern beaches were so clean and beautiful, with their cold, clear water rolling all the way from Antarctica, that there should be sharks: bronze whalers and white pointers, known man-eaters. And she had been conditioned from childhood to a fear of sharks in open waters.

It was not possible to stay in such cold water for long; she soon became chilled. They waded out and lay close together on the dry sand at the back of the beach, in a sensuous, dreamy contentment. The tiny drops glistened like crystal beads on Vin's bare chest. Maggie licked them off, then tasted the dried salt on her own bare arm. With her eyes close to the sunlit skin she could see its satiny texture, the pattern of its cells. Time telescoped: she was a child again bathing on the island beach, in a pink knitted costume that smelled of warm, wet wool.

She rolled on her back, so that her closed lids became blood-red shields, and felt the rhythm of the sea through the sand. The waves came in steady and slow, great glassy rollers that toppled and crashed in a mile-long bar of foam. Like the rhythm of the blood, the thudding of an enormous heart. Life was colour and warmth and light, and the nearness of his lean body. She propped herself on her elbows and let the fine quartz sand run through her fingers as through an hour-glass.

The whole day was like a clear bubble of glass about them, and through it the sand was running, imperceptibly running out.

She sighed. 'I wish this day could last forever.'

'I want us to be forever. You know that. You still haven't said if you'll marry me.'

She was silent. He lifted the wet costume away from one breast. 'It's so nice that you don't have a ghostly white patch here, underneath.'

'Let's have lunch now,' she said quickly. She didn't want to think about marriage just now. 'I love picnics, don't you?'

'No. There is always sand in the sandwiches. Crunch, crunch!'

'A bit of sand is good for you.' She kissed him and popped a ham-and-tomato sandwich into his mouth.

When the water had turned amethyst and viridian, the sky a luminous yellow-green as the sun sank, the last of the other beachgoers went home. Vin took off the clothes he had donned when he felt himself starting to burn; his Scottish ancestors had bequeathed him a fair skin, and though his face and forearms were brown from many summers, he did not have Maggie's natural immunity to sunburn. He peeled off her scanty costume and carried her down to the sea and dipped her in the glowing waters. The colours of the sea were infinitely varied. It was like swimming in the midst of an Impressionist painting, a Monet or a Renoir.

They ran back up the beach to the warm dry sand and there, on their spread towels, they consummated the day.

When Maggie became conscious of her surroundings again, the sky had turned a luminous blue-green like the tail of a peacock, embroidered with eyes of golden stars. The Scorpion was setting in the west, head-down to the horizon like a giant reversed question mark set with diamonds.

'There is a legend in some of the Pacific Islands,' she murmured, 'that Scorpio there is the great mother-of-pearl fish-hook which the god Maui used to fish up the islands from the ocean.'

'Yes, it does look like a huge fish-hook.'

'But the claws, the pincers, are hidden below the horizon now. No, I can't see it as anything else but a Scorpion.'

'Maggie, you wonderful girl. Was that as good for you as it was for me? Are you happy?'

She nodded serenely. 'I think there may be some sand in the works, but it doesn't matter.'

'I told you butter wouldn't suit the works!'

'But it was the *best* butter.'

This was a private joke. She used a copha-butter pessary with her rubber diaphragm as a precaution against conception. Still, she panicked sometimes when her period was late.

'You're so different from other girls. So quiet. You don't care a bit that I'm an "ace racing driver", do you? That's not why you like me.'

'No.' She looked at him dreamily, tracing the line of his lips with one finger. 'I like the shape of your mouth. I like the funny way your eyebrows grow. And the back of your neck, and the way your ears are fitted to your head. I feel weak all over when I look at you.'

'I do want to marry you, Maggie.'

She was silent. She sat up and traced the healed scar on his elbow. 'But – your mother?'

'Oh, to hell with my mother!' Immediately he felt a twinge of conscience. After all, she was his mother; a boy's best friend was his mother; a mother was a lovesome thing, God wot . . . 'I mean, she's tried to dominate me all my life, but I'm damned if she's going to choose my wife for me.'

'Perhaps she's right. After all, we are very different, our families, and, and – I can understand how she might feel about the grandchildren.'

'Grandchildren! Good God, you are leaping ahead.' He laughed easily. 'They'd be partly descended from her precious Forbes family, anyway. The Forbes brothers didn't exactly come out with the First Fleet, nor in a convict ship, but they've been here since about the 1820's. They made their money by squatting on land that they didn't either earn or inherit. While your people, my dear Maggie, or the Aboriginal fraction of them, have been around for twenty or thirty thousand years. They certainly had more right to the land than her squatter ancestors. Let her try and get around that.'

'Please don't say such things to her, Vin! She will dislike me enough without that.'

Maggie had so far refused to come home and meet his mother, always finding an excuse, but now he said, 'You are coming to afternoon tea next Saturday. That's official. She wants to meet you.'

'Oh no! You mean she wants to look me over.'

'She won't bite, you know. You don't have to sound so terrified.'

He kissed her drooping lids and trembling lips.

'It doesn't have to be straight away this minute, but she'll get used to the idea of us getting married.'

' – and if she doesn't? You may have to choose between us. Which is why you mustn't marry me till you're absolutely sure.'

'I *am* sure!'

They drove home with her head on his shoulder, while the stars moved with them in stately progression behind the trees. The Scorpion had sunk from sight, and the hunter Orion stood above the eastern horizon, the summer constellation with sword and jewelled belt: the sky-striding hero, broad-shouldered and invincible, who seemed to her to personify the man at her side.

Eight

'SHE'S TERRIFIED of meeting you,' Vin had told his mother before going to call for Maggie. 'Try not to be too overwhelming, darling.'

'I don't know what you mean, Vincent.' Rosetta King had a clipped, English accent. She finished her sentences as though snipping through a thread. She clasped a double row of cultured pearls about her still-handsome throat. Vin studied her reflection in the dressing-table mirror: the softly waved silvery hair, the discreet make-up, the formidable nose.

'I mean, you don't have to put on your finery. She's quite impressed enough already.'

'And I don't know what you call "finery". I'm wearing my second-best twinset and a plain skirt. I had my hair done because tonight is my Bridge Club. The pearls are to give *me* courage.'

'Oh nonsense, Mother.'

'I mean, meeting an authoress! I shan't know what to say.'

In the elegant drawing-room where Vin had abandoned her, Maggie sat perched on the edge of a carved chair. She forced herself to relax and sit back, but the carvings hurt her spine. She gazed at the baby-grand piano, the soft gold-coloured carpet, the silken curtains at the long French windows. After her tiny room at the hostel this one seemed enormous. She felt herself diminished. On Pandanus, under the enormous blue sky, surrounded by the vast Pacific, she had never felt thus. She had been a part of it all . . .

She was still sitting on the edge of the chair when Vin came back with his mother. She started up, wondering if she should hold out her hand first? Vin saved her by coming over with his hand outstretched, taking her fingers in his, and holding his mother by the other hand so that he drew them close.

'Mother, this is Maggie!'

Mrs King informally clasped her free left hand. They stood joined in a circle like children playing ring-a-roses.

'Well, my dear!' she said neutrally.

'How, how do you do, Mrs King?' For a mad moment Maggie had thought of saying 'Owyergoin', orright?' which was no doubt how Mrs King expected her to talk.

'Vin has told me about you. So your name is Maggie? I shall call you Margaret.'

'But I was christened Agnes. Apparently when I was little, I kept telling everyone "I'm Aggie" and gradually it became "I, Maggie".'

'But Maggie sounds a bit like a brand of soup-mix, don't you think?'

'Her name is Maggie and I love it,' said Vin. 'Also it is

getting quite famous: Maggie Pinjarra. You should read her books.'

'Oh yes, you write, don't you?' said Mrs King, as one would say, You're a pole-sitter, aren't you? 'And Vin tells me you're working in the city. Your parents aren't here with you?'

'No, my mother is dead. She had a lovely name: Anna. My Dad was lost at sea, and after Mum died my auntie brought me up . . . and I went to school in Townsville.'

'A Mission school, I take it?'

Maggie flushed. 'I went to the High School like everyone else.'

'Everyone who was bright enough to pass the Junior Certificate, that is,' added Vin.

'Quite. Well, do sit down, my dear. I don't know why we're all standing around. I'll just go and see if Ethel has made tea.'

'Oh, *Vin*!' In one movement Maggie flung herself on to his lap where he sat on the velvet-covered couch. Her arms went round his neck like a child's. The formidable stylishness of his mother, her cool and calculated rudeness had sent Maggie's self-possession reeling.

'You're my girl,' he said comfortingly. 'Don't let her browbeat you, Mag. When you are Mrs King she'll be only the dowager, and *you* will be the reigning King's wife.'

She managed a faint, strained smile at his little joke, but she felt sick. If Ethel brought the afternoon tea, did she speak to her or just pretend she didn't exist, as she had seen people do with servants in films? Mrs King would despise her if she did the wrong thing. No, she couldn't just ignore a fellow human being. She would smile and say, 'Good-afternoon, Ethel.' That would be best.

She was so clumsy, she feared she would drop crumbs on the gold carpet, or worse, she might knock over her whole cup. She went hot all over at the thought. She buried her face in the angle of Vin's shoulder, breathing the scent of his hair where it grew down the back of his neck in the way she loved. Too late she heard the rattle of tea-things and a step on the bare polished boards of the hall. She jumped up to return to her own chair, but his mother had seen her sitting on Vin's knee like a child in search of comfort. She felt her face burning. She longed to run from the room, to fly back to her sunny peaceful island and never leave it again.

Mrs King had brought the tea-things herself. Behind her stalked a cream-coloured cat with seal-brown patches, and the most amazing clear blue eyes. Maggie knelt impulsively and called it. The cat came to her rescue. With uplifted tail it minced gracefully over and raised its sleek head to her caress, narrowing its blue eyes with pleasure.

'That's Zircon,' said Vin. 'Zircon, you old smoodger! You haven't even spoken to me.'

Maggie lifted the cat and sat down with it on her knee.

'What beautiful blue eyes!' she murmured. She'd had time to recover, but she felt nearer to the half-wild creature on her lap than to Vin just then. Almost she hated him for making her come and meet his awful mother.

'It's a Siamese cat. Haven't you ever seen a Siamese before?' asked Mrs King patronisingly. 'Here, Vincent, hand this to Margaret and remove that pampered beast. Margaret, will you have a scone, or a tea-cake?'

'A scone, thank you. But my name is Maggie.'

There was a short, electric silence. Vincent gave her an approving look. Mrs King poured another cup, her lips pursed. 'Vincent,' she said, 'your Great Aunt Ada and Aunt Mae are coming down next Sunday. You really should be home to see them, dear. You know they haven't seen you since – the funeral.'

'Oh, Mother!'

'And Alice has not been at all well. In fact, she may have to go into hospital.'

'You mean a home for inebriates, don't you?'

'Really, Vincent!'

She looked furious, but Vin was unrepentant. He had effectively stopped the family-gossip line which he knew his mother had taken up to exclude Maggie from the conversation.

'There's an afternoon and evening rally next weekend, and I've asked Maggie to be my navigator. I can't win if I don't go in for it, Mother, and I only have to get five more points for the Gold Star.'

'What is the Gold Star?'

'The award for the year's best driver. Come, you know you'd like the Gold Star to sit on the bureau with the other trophies.'

He indicated the arrangement of silver cups, medals and shields, some won by his father years ago for steeplechasing, most of them his own car-trophies.

Maggie went over to examine them, thankfully setting down her fragile cup in a safe place.

Mrs King smiled unwillingly. She didn't really expect Vin to give up his Sunday to his elderly relatives, but she was jealous of the girl. She admitted to herself that however suitable had been the match, she would have found it hard to like Vin's choice. But this – this result of miscegenation, this upstart from the wilds of Queensland; what if Vin actually insisted on marrying her! And he might have married *anyone* if he had wished.

No, it was too much. Her tea tasted bitter, though she knew it was freshly brewed. She set down her cup with a grimace.

'Maggie will be the best navigator I've ever had,' said Vin.

Maggie smiled at him gratefully. Mrs King poured a saucer of milk with a little tea in it and set it down on the carpet for Zircon.

'He only likes Indian tea; he's a real connoisseur,' said Vin.

'He's a beautiful beast,' said Maggie.

Zircon pretended to ignore the saucer, daintily licking at a paw that was already clean.

'"Nay, look not down, and lick thy dainty wrists",' Maggie quoted. 'Keats, on a favourite cat.'

'That's good. That feminine word "wrists" . . . Cats are always so dainty,' said Vin.

Mrs King said nothing. The silence was intimidating.

Maggie sat down again and swallowed the last of her tea with an audible gulp. She set down her cup and saucer.

'Vin, I think if we are going for a drive – '

Vin jumped up. 'Yes, I'm giving Maggie a lesson in navigating and map-reading. We must go.'

'But you haven't had a piece of Aunt Mae's shortbread. You know how you always like it.'

'Or did when I was ten years old,' muttered Vin, but he

took a piece to eat on the way. 'Goodbye, old thing. Don't wait up, we're going to a party after.'

'Goodbye, Mrs King, and thank you,' said Maggie. Mrs King smiled and inclined her head regally. She did not say 'Come Again', but she did get up and escort them to the front door. She'll remember her manners even if it kills her, thought Maggie. Looking up as she reached the bottom step, she saw on the older woman's face a look of such bitter despair that she was shocked. She will never accept me, much less like me, she thought. Never.

'Vin, it's no good!' she said in the car. 'Your mother made it quite clear where I stand with her. I believe she'd rather you married Ethel.'

'Ethel! Oh no!' At the thought of Ethel's long, sallow face, her hollow cheeks and bony frame, he gave a great yelp of laughter. 'You haven't *seen* her! Besides, Ethel's got a follower.'

'Yes, but she's white, you see.'

Vin turned from the wheel to stare at her appraisingly. She did not like him to look at her like this, as though trying to see what made her tick, as if he could not fathom her character. 'White, brown, pink, brindled, what does it matter?' he asked impatiently. 'Is Giulio white or brown? He's a damn sight darker than you. For goodness' sake, Maggie, I didn't think you had a complex about your colour. I thought you were too intelligent for that.'

She shrank from the reproof in his voice. She felt like a sea-anemone in a tidal pool, expanding in the waves of his love and admiration, glowing and confident; and then at the slightest touch of criticism, shrinking back into a tight little defensive ball. In that drawing-room she had felt all folded up and closed inside herself, unable to show at her best in the hostile environment Vin's mother created. Why couldn't he understand?

It was the first rift between them. The second came when she travelled with him to Sydney for an autumn meeting, for the Australian Grand Prix.

* * *

470

The air was filled with the sweetish smell of burnt alcohol fuel. The fluttering of bright flags, the scratchy voice of the public-address system, the hum and whine of car engines, crescendo and diminuendo, fed a deep communal excitement sharpened by danger.

Tense with the same excitement, Maggie leant on the Pit-counter, stopwatch in hand. The blue Maserati was circling steadily, lapping in one minute thirty-two seconds. The Sydney sunshine beat down on the pits in the humid air, and in the stands and along the safety fences bordering the track, young men in shorts and slacks had taken off their shirts and were soaking up the sun.

There was something Islander, or Polynesian, in the way the casual Sydney crowds stripped off their clothes at the first touch of warmth. Surely in no other Western city in the world, thought Maggie, could so many young, handsome, healthy torsos be seen, so many bare sun-tanned chests, away from the beach.

The Maserati came hurtling down the straight past the pits, no more than a flash of blue, a scream of exhaust, and a glimpse of a calm, brown face under a gold helmet and plastic visor. Passing a slow car that he had just lapped, Vincent raised one hand in salute. 'He's waving heem goodbye,' said Giulio, chalking the number of the new lap on a board, ready to hold up on the car's next time round.

Vin was now lying third, with two visiting British drivers ahead and another car close behind. The cars rounded a bend and disappeared in a series of zig-zags towards the back straight, diminishing to toy cars with clockwork engines. An observer on the far side of the circuit traced their rapid return through the esses, giving a running commentary.

Among the crowd were connoisseurs of the art of driving, who watched with knowledgeable and enchanted eyes, just as there were connoisseurs of ballet and opera and bull-fighting. It was like an arena, a Roman circus, a corridá of cars. If Vin had not been out there, one of the challengers of death, Maggie might have enjoyed it simply as a spectacle.

Now once more the cars were heading back to the Start/Finish line, threading through the chicane which artificially lengthened the course.

471

They came flying out of Dunlop corner at the beginning of Pit Straight, two cars in English racing green, then the blue Maserati looking as steady as if it were running in a groove, followed by Ace Diamond in his red Alfa doing a dangerous wobble as he came out of the corner and took off after Vin. Ace was right on his back wheel as they reached the next bend. To Maggie it looked a confused jumble, but the No. 2 mechanic gave a shout: 'Nudged him, by God!'

In a moment Ace had cornered on the inside of Vin and was first into the esses. 'He's shaking his fist, he must be ropable,' said the mechanic, who appeared to have eyes like binoculars. 'By Christ, he won't let Ace get away with that! He'll catch him and leave him for dead.'

Giulio looked worried. Glancing apprehensively at him, Maggie saw that two deep creases had appeared in his usually smooth forehead.

'I no lika thees,' he muttered. 'Vincente will tak-a the chance, he will be angry, not calm. That Ace, he should be flagged off . . . '

A crackle from the loudspeaker, and the observer's voice came, rising with excitement:

' – and King is all out after Diamond, the Alfa and the Mazzer' are having a great dice down here! And he's got him – ! King now in third position as they come out of the esses towards – '

Maggie held her breath as the cars came round again, past Dunlop corner: Ace's red car, now in second place, two in English green, but no blue car with a number 4 on the side. Just before the scream of exhausts drowned out the voice, she heard over the loudspeaker – 'had a slight shunt at Leger Corner . . . car seemed to go out of control . . . however, he . . . '

Across the circuit behind them, a column of dust rose and hung in the air. Maggie looked dumbly at the other members of the pit crew, seeing in their strained faces the reflection of her own. The confused unintelligible gabble of the loudspeaker was lost in a ringing that began inside her head. A black contracting cloud obscured her vision.

'No, Signorina, please – ees no need to faint.' Giulio was steadying her with one arm round her waist. 'Vincente is good driver, too good a driver to be in trouble on slow corner like Leger. Somet'ing on the car 'as broke, ees all. You will see, Giulio's always right, *sempre*.'

Maggie shook her head to clear it. She lifted her chin, and stood up straight. 'It's all right now, thanks.'

Then over his shoulder she saw a tall figure in white overalls, a gold helmet beneath his arm, striding across the bare paddock to the competitors' enclosure. It was Vin, taking a short cut back to the pits. She began to run, cannoning blindly into people in her way. He climbed over the high fence, and in a moment she had her arms round him.

'Oh Vin! I thought – I thought you were – ' Tears rolled down her face.

'It's all right, Mag,' he said, hastily putting her away from him. 'Don't make a scene, now. I'm all right, and so is the car, apart from being undrivable.'

'You're sure you're not hurt?'

'Positive. All my arms and legs, see?' he said, waggling them. 'I'm bloody mad about the car, though. And that crazy bastard Diamond – '

She was amazed to hear him that night at the after-race party, in amicable discussion with Ace over a glass of beer:

' – a wishbone went, and the wheel just folded under. One of the front wheels is dented, is all.'

'I knew you were out to get me, before it happened.'

'Yes, you nudged me, you rotten bastard.' But there was no acrimony in his voice.

Ace gave his attractive grin, quite unabashed.

'All's fair when you're out there dicing,' he said.

The newspaper phrase 'dicing with death' had been taken up ironically by the drivers, who would say: 'Well, better get out there dicing,' when a race was due. Maggie stood by, silent and unnoticed, unable to join in the technical conversation which developed. She didn't even know what a wishbone was, except on a fowl. Ace was talking about gear ratios and some trouble he was having with a crown wheel and pinion. Pinion – feathers? She was back to fowls again. She felt an unreasoning jealousy of Ace, and of the easy masculine camaraderie from which she was shut out.

Giulio was her refuge at these affairs; he was always willing to talk to an attractive girl, and his wife did not travel with him but stayed home to mind their large family. Giulio was telling Maggie about a racing car he once worked on, which had a fly-wheel of solid gold.

'Solid gold? Not really?'

'Si, *veramente*. The driver, 'e ees very rich.'

'He's pulling your leg, Maggie,' said another driver. 'It was only sprayed with gold-leaf. Gold would be too heavy.'

'I would verra much lika to pull the Signorina's leg, eet is beautiful, bella, bella! So long, so naice.' Giulio's black eyes rolled wickedly.

'Ah, you're a dirty old man, Giulio. What about your Missus?'

'My wife, she has-a the good legs, too, but – I have seen them!'

There was a burst of laughter from the group around Ace Diamond. He had a wild sparkle in his clear blue eyes; his perfect teeth showed in a laugh; the straw-bright hair fell over his forehead in a boyish lock. Yes, he's attractive all right, mused Maggie. His latest girlfriend, Raylene, wandered up, holding an empty glass.

'Ace, he is telling the funny stories,' said Giulio. 'But you no' allowed to hear.'

'I call him Franz,' said Raylene, making the name sound like a tin lid belted with a length of angle-iron. 'Ace suits him all right, I suppose, but he's too swell-headed already. Ace of Diamonds! He said he'd like a diamond-studded safety helmet. Whatever next!'

'Well, Vincente' as a solid gold one, *non é vero*?' said Giulio with a mischievous glance at Maggie. 'And a corrown embroidered on 'ees pocket.'

'That reminds me – where's me bead bag?' cried Raylene with a little shriek. She dashed back to the corner where she had been sitting.

Vincent came over, a glass of beer in his hand, and put an arm round his chief mechanic's shoulder.

'Giulio, what do you think? Ace thinks we should put a

two-stage blower on and double the boost. More power, but less reliable, eh?'

'Molto, molto less reliable. You melt piston, break valve, blow up, boum! Even eef you have a blow-off valve, maybe it don't always work. I no lika two-stage supercharge.'

As Vin stood in front of her, Maggie reached out and took the empty glass from his free hand. She held his fingers unobtrusively in hers. Vin looked down and smiled.

'Hullo, Mag! Enjoying yourself?'

'Why? Are you interested?'

'Oh Lord, I'm sorry, darling. Look, we'll go in a minute. I just want another word with Ace, then I'll come.' He dived back into the group.

'Aren't men awful?' asked Raylene, coming back. She was a small blonde with over-large earrings. 'That Franz should be looking after me; he brung me.'

'Yes; awful,' said Maggie with feeling. She thought of the night before, when they were staying away across the Harbour at Manly because it was easier to find room there for the cars which made up their stable. Last night Maggie had helped prepare Vin's car for today's race meeting.

She had crouched by the Maserati's back wheels, polishing the finned aluminium brake drums so that they would keep cool in the race. Black with metal-dust and white with Silvo, her fingers sore, she worked at this menial task while the men fussed over the engine.

'Well, that about wraps it up!' said Vin at last, straightening his back. 'I'm going to turn in.'

He put an arm round Maggie's neck and moved his fingers up through her mane of hair. 'Thanks for your help, old thing. Just look at those brake drums gleaming!'

She had smiled happily, knowing quite well that there were plenty of men eager to help, but she was glad to have been made to feel useful.

Back at their hotel, excited by the strange surroundings, she could not wait to get undressed properly but threw off her top things and jumped into bed in her slip, after turning back the hotel's sumptuous purple bedspread.

Vin pottered about for a long time in his pyjamas, winding his watch, hanging up his clothes, laying his clean overalls across a chair ready for the morning, even giving his helmet and goggles a quick polish.

Maggie waited impatiently. 'Aren't you ever coming to bed?' she complained. When he came at last she opened her arms gladly, her heart beating suffocatingly with joy.

Vin leaned over and kissed her hard on the mouth. She became a molten mass of longing. All day she had waited for them to be alone together.

Then with enormous and chilling surprise she heard his firm, 'Goodnight, darling.' He turned away and hunched the bedclothes up to his ear.

There was silence but for Vin's regular breathing, and what seemed to Maggie the deafening thunder of her own pulse. At last it slowed, and she ventured a timid 'Vin – ?'

'Yes? What is it, I was nearly asleep.'

She curled close to him. 'I thought – I thought it would relax you to make love to me tonight . . . wouldn't it?'

'I'm sorry, dear, I thought you knew – not before a big race, a GP. You do understand?'

'Of course,' she said stiffly. She retreated to the far edge of the double bed and lay quite still, almost holding her breath till she was sure he was asleep, being careful not even to cry.

Before they left to return to Adelaide, Vin and Maggie drove round South Head Road to the suburb of Vaucluse. They were going to see Elaine King, Stanley King's mother and Rosetta's aunt. Vincent had not seen his grandmother since he was a small boy. He remembered a visit to the Outer Harbour to meet a mailboat, a ship which seemed to tower above the wharf, big as a cliff. And waving from the rail was a tall lady in a long skirt and red piled-up hair, who was his grandmother.

He had heard since from his father the story of her courage and determination: how she had started a leper asylum in a small princedom of India, using all her patrimony on her favourite charity, and working among the lepers herself. After being left a widow she had returned to Australia to live, but had gone back to India to work in another leper colony.

476

There she had contracted the disease, and was cured only after long and painful treatment.

Once, in India, she'd had a palatial home and twenty servants. Now she lived alone, with a woman to come and clean once a week, in a house overlooking the Harbour that her father Hamilton Forbes had left her. A widowed daughter lived near, but was away at present. Vin had phoned to say they were coming. He wasn't sure what he expected. A little white-haired old lady, perhaps, bent over a cane: a stage grandmother. When the door opened to their knock, however, he recognised Elaine at once. A tall, commanding figure in an old fashioned gabardine suit, a mass of red hair pulled into a chignon, and large greeny eyes that regarded him calmly and observantly while she pulled him inside and kissed him. She gave Maggie her big, cool hand and a warm smile.

'Bless you, my dears. It's lovely to see you.' She looked at Vin. 'Yes, you are more a Forbes than a Macdonald. And this is Maggie?'

'Yes. Maggie is my best girl, and we're going to be married.'

'Then this is for you, dear. My husband gave it to me when we were on our honeymoon in Kashmir.'

She was twisting off her wrist a solid silver bangle in the form of a two-headed snake, engraved with a pattern of scales. Bending the head apart, she passed the bracelet over Maggie's slender hand and bent the ends together again round her wrist.

'There! Don't ever take it off – I never used to, and it makes a black mark around your wrist – but if you keep bending it open it will break, and that will break the good-luck charm.'

'Fatigue of metal,' said Vin scientifically.

'Thank you, Mrs King! I'll wear it always.'

'I thought I'd better take it off at last, or they'll be burying it on me.'

'Nonsense, Grandma,' said Vin. 'You'll live to be a hundred.'

'I hope not! I've already outlived most of my children. Stan flew over for my seventieth birthday, you know. He was very like his father. And that was the last time I saw Clarrie.'

When they were all seated in the window-seat, below a

wide picture-window that overlooked a vista of Sydney Harbour, Elaine said, 'Your great-grandfather King lived to a great age. Did you ever meet him?'

'I don't remember him. Was he the prospector?'

'Yes, the man who discovered the Golden Mile. He was quite a character. But in later years, perhaps not respectable enough for your mother.'

'I knew vaguely that one of my ancestors was a prospector. But they didn't tell me –. Discovered the Golden Mile, eh?'

'So he always claimed. Willie had some newspaper cuttings about him. He certainly had a fortune for a while when he came back from the West. I had a letter from him when William died, but the last time I saw him was in India, when he was taking all the girls, complete with governesses, on a world trip.'

'I remember you brought me a brass stork from India, a little model bird with coloured inlaid enamel. I loved it. But I lost it eventually.'

'Well, I'll send you something big for a wedding-present, that you can't lose. I'll get Anne to choose something for me, I don't go out much any more. For our wedding, Sam King sent us a set of silver-gilt goblets; I think they got left behind in Gorobhunj. Anne is always scolding me for giving things away . . . No, she didn't want the bracelet,' she added, seeing Maggie's look. 'She hates snakes. They were always getting into the house in India. I think the two-headed snake may actually have been worn as a charm against snakebite.'

'I shall treasure it, Mrs King. And thank you again.'

As they rose to take their leave, Elaine placed a hand on Maggie's shining dark head as if in blessing.

'Goodbye, Pretty-hair,' she said, kissing her.

If only, thought Maggie, Vin's mother had been more like her mother-in-law, the elder Mrs King! But Vin had told her they didn't get on, and had met only once or twice since William King died.

'What a marvellous old lady,' she said with a smile as Vin carefully shut the gate of the overgrown, tree-filled garden behind them. They got into the car and sat gazing along the leafy road through the windscreen.

'Yes! Incredible. And her hair is still red. She must be well over seventy.'

'And doesn't even wear glasses! I could see her giving me very keen looks, trying to work out my ancestry, before you told her that I was an Aboriginal writer.'

'And you notice she didn't even blink. She was used to all sorts of races and religions, of course. Dad told me she was a great friend of the Maharaja of Gorobhunj and later of his widow. The one who was shot in mistake for a tiger. She nursed his little girl through typhoid, or cholera or something. And then her son, Uncle Harry, died of typhoid in the first World War.'

'Poor woman, to have outlived her husband and all her sons! What happened to your Uncle Clarrie? He didn't die in that rotten war?'

'No, he was killed on Aramac Station when his horse threw him. Perished, actually. He was miles from the homestead or the nearest waterhole, with a broken leg. I believe he crawled quite a long way before he died.'

'Yet she seems so cheerful and alert.'

'I think she's a devout Christian, and that must be a strength. To be quite sure of meeting her William and her four boys again in Heaven . . . Fancy my father ever having been her little boy!'

Vin turned the ignition key. As they drove off, Maggie smiled suddenly.

'D'you think her great-grandchildren will have red hair?'

'Could be. One of my Aunt Anne's boys is a redhead, I believe.'

'No, I meant – '

'Here, hold on, Mag! We can't go having a family as soon as we're married. It's just not possible!'

'No, I know. But we'll have to produce a girl some time for me to leave the bracelet to. Won't we?'

Nine

'Do YOU want a sandwich?' asked Maggie with her mouth full. She had brought a picnic lunch in the car, but so far they had not had time to eat it. This was her first Mountain Trial, a miniature Alpine Rally where cars were eliminated simply by the conditions if the weather was bad. The trial went across country by back roads, many without signposts, mostly unsealed, and points were deducted for late arrival at controls, so the navigator's role was all-important. Maggie was the navigator.

'Not for me, thanks,' said Vin. 'And I advise you to concentrate and never mind about food. You remember what I told you, now? You must be ready for every fork in the road before it comes up, so that I don't have to stop while you work it out. Right?'

'Right. What's this "grid" marked on the strip map?'

'That's a sheep-grid, iron bars over a pit instead of a gate. Saves a lot of time opening gates, and keeps the sheep in because their narrow hooves would fall between the bars.'

'Will there be any gates?'

'Sure to be. And they have to be closed behind us. Bad form to leave a gate open. And the farmers might refuse to let us through next time. Now, you'll find everything listed in the strip map as well as on the Ordnance Map an inch to the mile.'

Maggie thought she was quite capable of following the track on the map, but she had navigated for Vin only in a short afternoon trial. She pored over the Ordnance Map, with contour-lines, blue outlines of creeks, and tiny black, red and green dots to be interpreted. She was all right as long as the light lasted. At dusk they were climbing in mountain country through a forest of giant eucalyptus trees.

Vin handed her the flashlight fixed to a magnifying glass, and with this she managed to map-read as he wound along the gullies and ridges. Though he was so skilful at the wheel, cutting corners to shorten the line whenever he had a clear view, making no sudden corrections or tyre-screaming corners, the torch swung from side to side over the map.

Maggie began to feel hot, then cold, then hot and cold at the same time. Her brow was dewed with sweat, she shivered and yawned. Oh God, she was getting the 'flu or something and would be useless for the rest of the all-night, all-day trial. Boughs seemed to snatch at the car like menacing arms. She saw faces in clumps of leaves, in the patterns of peeling bark. Vin, relaxed at the wheel, turned smiling towards her in the cosy glow of the instrument panel. Tachometer, temperature gauge, oil-gauge, amp-meter – his eyes flicked over them and saw that all was well.

'You're very quiet, Mag.'

'Yes, I –. Vin, I don't know what's wrong with me, I feel awful. I think I'm going to be sick.'

He negotiated a long sweeping bend. 'You do look a bit green about the gills. I'll find a place to pull off the road.'

When he stopped Maggie had just time to get the door open and stumble down a slope among damp bracken before she vomited. Her head felt heavy and dopey. Vin was unscrewing the Thermos flask when she came back. 'Here, have some coffee with a drop of rum.'

'Vin, I couldn't! The very thought – !'

'Nonsense, it'll make you feel better. Drink up.'

She took the cup, sipped once, then thrust it back at him and bolted. When she came back he was looking impatient.

'Look, if you weren't well why didn't you say so? What's up with you?'

'I don't know,' she said miserably. 'Do you think I could be car-sick? I never have been before.'

'Of course! It's probably the map-reading. But you've done that before. It could be something to do with the darkness and using the torch.'

'Yes. It started as soon as it got dark.'

He looked at his gold wrist-watch. 'We must get on, I've got to check in at the next control in fifteen minutes. Can you stand it till then?'

'I guess so.' She was keeping her lip stiff, but she felt nausea sweeping over her in waves.

They drove on.

'I've never even been sea-sick,' said Maggie. 'Even going out to the Reef in Uncle Dingbat Morgan's cutter, which was quite small – '

'Wait a minute, was that the turnoff? Are we on the right road?'

'Oh help! I wasn't watching.'

'Well, for God's sake be more careful! Here, let me see . . . No, I'll have to stop.' He braked violently, and took the map from her unceremoniously. 'Hell! That *was* the turnoff! We'll have to go back.'

He slammed the car into reverse and went screaming back with protesting gears. Maggie's neck jerked painfully as he stopped opposite the turnoff and the car leapt again into forward. 'I'll be lucky to make it without losing points. Damn and blast!'

She fell silent, feeling both guilty and rebellious. It wasn't her fault that she felt like this, as though her head were stuffed with cotton-wool right down to her neck, where it was gagging in her throat. She unzipped the side-screen and put out her head against the flow of cold fresh air, gulping down oxygen in an effort to push back the rising nausea, to hold it down until they reached the control.

She tried to look at the map again, but instantly felt worse. Peering ahead, she saw the trees leaning over the road with goblin-gestures and grimaces of evil, snatching at the car-roof with thin leafy arms.

A wombat ran across the road on stumpy legs; Vin swerved to avoid it. She was flung against his shoulder, and at the touch of her arm Vin looked at her again as if she were a human being, not just an inefficient machine for navigating.

Then over the next rise they saw the bonfire and the parked car of the control. Maggie had their card ready as Vin pulled up with a jerk, one minute late. The card was checked, the time of arrival entered.

'You're the first car to have lost points on this section,' said the moustached and tweed-capped official, rubbing his hands together as though pleased. 'You've got the horror-stretch ahead, and then the halfway stop. Good luck, mate!'

'Thanks.'

Vin's car shot off into the darkness again, while Maggie, shivering, looked back wistfully at the golden petals of the fire flowering beneath the trees.

'I'm sorry, Vin,' she said. 'It's my fault we were late. If I hadn't been sick – '

'If you'd kept your eyes open at the turnoff, we still might have made it. I lost nearly a minute there.'

'Well, I said I'm sorry.'

'All right. Just watch out now, will you?'

Maggie had checked the route ahead while they were stationary. The road had reached a plateau at the top of the ranges, and was fairly straight for a few miles. Refreshed by the brief stop and the cessation of winding movement, she began to feel better.

'Look out!' she warned. 'We turn off down here somewhere, sharp to the left.' She peered through the side-curtain. 'The track appears to run alongside a creek, and there's a small bridge just before we turn . . . Here it is.'

They crossed the wooden bridge and Vin wrenched the car round to take a 45-degree turn back the way they had come. The road they had just left was graded metal; now they were on a dirt track, studdied with large stones and badly eroded by water. He straddled a deep washaway that ran down the centre of the track. They bounded over small boulders and potholes, skidded round bends. Maggie grasped the bar on the dash and held on, biting her lip. She was now not so much sick as frightened.

Most of the field was ahead of them. The track had been cut up by the slithering wheels, and it was steep as well as rough.

They rounded a bend and saw, blinking in the car's headlights, a small pale creature sitting up as though begging, its forepaws held in front, its pointed snout lifted anxiously.

Maggie screamed. Vin braked hard and the car slithered forward and sideways. The animal disappeared beneath the wheels with a dull, horrid thud. The car slid off the track into the scrub, and ended up against a tree which stopped it from hurtling further down the slope.

Vin was out of the car almost before it stopped, examining it tenderly for damage.

'Broken front axle! That's finished us,' he said at last.

Maggie said nothing. She had bumped her head on the windscreen and was feeling shaken. After a while she took the torch from Vin and went back up the track. She bent over the pale furry shape on the red ironstone earth.

The animal was as big as a small dog, but with longer hind legs. It was a bandicoot, and it was dead. Its eyes stared glassily, its pointed mouth was open and its brains had been knocked neatly out between its long front teeth. Spilling from its belly, among a mass of blood and excreta, were four more pale shapes, exact replicas of each other. They were embryo bandicoots, still without fur, their eyes closed and tiny paws folded.

'Oh!' cried Maggie in distress. 'Oh, Vin! She was a mother.'

She touched one of the front paws compassionately, feeling the digging-claws close about her finger.

'What?' Vin had followed her and stood looking down with distaste at the dead creature.

'She was a mother! Look, four of them still in the pouch – what a shame? They're all dead.'

'Eckh! How can you bear to look at it – to touch it?' He covered his mouth with his hand. 'It makes me feel sick to my stomach.' He turned away.

But Maggie could not bear to think of the other cars coming swerving and crashing down the track – little more than a creek-bed or a washaway leading to the valley – and mashing the tiny creatures into the earth.

She fetched some green twigs and wove a mat so that she could slide the broken body and the four embryos on to it. It was messy, but she managed. Then she stumbled into the undergrowth and placed them gently by a fallen log, among a clump of heath.

'There's nothing for you to wash your hands with here,' said Vin coldly. 'Do you mind not touching the inside of the car? We'll have to sit in it and wait till someone comes along and bum a ride with them – hope they've got a back seat . . . Well, bang goes the Gold Star this year.'

'Bad luck,' said Maggie formally. She wiped her hands on leaves and then on her handkerchief, rolled it into a ball and pushed it out of sight under a bush. They had killed five inoffensive bush creatures at one blow – the little marsupial mother and her four young.

'I always wanted four babies,' she said softly, half to herself.

'I shouldn't have tried to avoid the thing, there was no hope of missing it. Anyway it was only a bandicoot, the things are pests. Why did you scream like that?'

'She was a mother,' Maggie said again.

Vin walked away and rooted in the front of the car and brought out the flask. 'Rum?'

'No, thank you.'

'By God I feel like getting drunk. What rotten, beastly luck. If it was my own fault I wouldn't mind so much, but this wasn't caused by bad driving or bad judgment. Who'd expect a bloody bandicoot to be sitting in the middle of the track, praying?'

'They shouldn't have run the trial through here. It isn't a road. The animals wouldn't expect fast cars through here.'

'Nonsense. There has to be a knock-out section to eliminate the weakest among the cars. Otherwise you'd have everyone getting through without loss of points. It certainly eliminated us.'

He kicked gloomily at a tyre and downed his rum from an aluminium beaker. He poured himself another. 'There's still some coffee in the Thermos flask if you want it.'

'No, thank you,' she said again.

She stood with her back to him, leaning an arm on a slender satin-trunked tree. The beams of the car headlights, slightly crossed, penetrated the prickly, inhospitable bushland.

She was deeply hurt. His brusqueness, his tendency to blame her for everything, his lack of sympathy with her sickness and her distress over the dead bandicoot, had alienated her.

He was a stranger, this man who had held her closer than she had ever been held before, who had been admitted to her most secret places. It was obvious that he no longer loved her; he despised her. She had been too easy, too passionate . . .

Vin was watching her, outlined in the diffused glow of the lights: her small rounded figure in the tight pants and the turtle-necked sweater, her slender fine-boned hands and face looking more fragile against the rough knitted wool.

He rested the empty beaker on the car-hood, came over to her, and took her roughly in his arms.

The rum was coursing through his veins, warming and exciting him and dulling his disappointment over the trial.

'Well, we might as well make the best of it,' he said. 'It may be some time before another car comes through, and there's a rug in the back. Come on. There must be some level ground here somewhere.'

She stood stiffly in his arms. He kissed her and then leaned back to look at her in puzzlement as he felt the hard unyielding line of her lips.

'What's the matter, darling?'

'Everything's the matter! And you expect to make love to me just as if – as if – '

'Oh, come on Maggie. I'm sorry I was a bit abrupt. You know I love you.'

'You don't! You don't! You just wanted to see what I was like in bed, and, and – ' She began to sob.

He dropped his arms. 'For God's sake don't make a big scene, Maggie! Haven't I told you I want to marry you? Does that sound as if – '

'You've *said* so, but I don't believe it. Your mother would never allow it, and you know it. You'll say you can't hurt her feelings, you'll have to wait until she's come round a bit, she's still upset by your father's death.'

Vin was silent, uneasily aware that this was exactly what he had been thinking. Of course he wanted to marry Maggie eventually, but marriage didn't enter into his plans at present.

Her tears flowed faster.

'Maggie, will you for Christ's sake turn off the waterworks?' he cried, exasperated.

'Certainly.' She gulped back her sobs. 'Do you have a handkerchief? I threw mine away.'

He brought one out of the pocket of his wind-cheater. He was wearing a knitted Balaclava helmet to keep his ears warm; it covered his hair and forehead and chin, so that his face, with the eyebrows hidden and the firm chin covered, looked suddenly thin and mean. He was hard and cruel; he had murdered the mother bandicoot; he felt nothing for her but desire, and she hated him.

The sound of a car slithering down the track was a relief to both of them. They turned their faces towards the wildly swinging beams of its lights. Vin stepped out on to the track and held up his hand. The car skidded to a stop. It was a big, old sedan, rugged and powerful, with two men wrapped in scarves and greatcoats in the front seat.

'Can you give us a lift to the next control? Our car's out of action – broken front axle.'

'Right-o. Hop in.'

'Quick, Maggie, don't hold them up,' said Vin sharply. She clambered silently into the back seat and sat pressed in her corner, as far away from him as she could get. The navigator turned round and offered her a piece of chocolate.

Ten

'Chocolates, Vin? You know I shouldn't! I'm trying to cut down on my weight. Not that I'm fat, of course, but I have these big bones – '

'Go on, Mother, be a devil for once. I'm going out for a smoke.'

She smiled at him and began to open the glossy bright orange box he had dropped in her lap. 'Old Gold' dark chocolates – her favourites.

Vincent had brought his mother to the theatre for her birthday. She was greatly enjoying the outing, being escorted by her tall son, who had Stanley's upright carriage and long, narrow head, but unmistakably bore his mother's features. Yes, he was a Forbes, she thought complacently, like Joseph, her father, and his great-grandfathers Jason and Hamilton.

She had written to her mother-in-law, of course, when Stanley died, but had not seen Elaine for years. Poor woman, thought Rosetta mechanically; all her four sons were dead. But the truth was she had never like Aunt Elaine and resented the closeness which she sensed between mother and son when she came back from India and stayed with them that time after her husband died.

Rosetta selected a soft cream centre and sank her teeth in it with pleasure.

'I just had to get out for some fresh air,' Vin apologised as he came back at the end of the interval. 'There's something claustrophobic about all these bored, frustrated Russians in their country houses.'

They were watching a talented amateur production of 'Uncle Vanya'. Vin was getting more and more restive towards the end – it seemed that everyone on the stage moved and spoke slowly – but his mother was enjoying it. She gave a violent start at the pistol-shot off stage and sat with her hand to her breast till the curtain went down.

As the lights came up she rearranged her fur cape and complacently patted the lace dress over her large bosom. Her chin folded comfortably into the soft fur as she looked down at this visible extension of her personality, which assured her that she herself was real, as real and solid as the pillars supporting the roof, and not a mere figment of a dead author's imagination.

Since Stanley's death she had felt the need of reassurance. It was as though the digging of his grave had shaken the solid earth beneath her feet. Sometimes at night she woke with a start, quite disorientated, not knowing who or what she was, her bed as strange as a lonely boat sailing an unknown sea. It was only for a moment; memory and personality came back with the recalling of her name, Rosetta Forbes King. Of course! This was her bed, her house, her name.

Yet her certainty that death was something which happened to other people had been badly shaken. Now she wished to see herself perpetuated in grandchildren; if only Vincent would marry suitably!

At least he seemed to have broken with that impossible girl from Queensland, yet he showed no particular interest in any other. He had taken Bette Burgess's girl Jeanne to a cabaret one night, and she had hoped . . . He was such a goodlooking lad! Not conventionally handsome, of course, with his big bony nose and deepset eyes, but he was tall and brown and healthy. Proudly she laid a hand on his muscular arm as they moved slowly with the crowd from the dress-circle. He looked moody and impatient, hating the crowd for its slow movement and its anonymous bodies impinging on his. She remembered how he would walk up flights of stairs rather than use a crowded elevator.

Ahead, a stream from the right-hand aisle was converging on theirs at the top of the staircase. A girl in a ruby-red velvet theatre coat caught her eye; she had rather nice hair and the colour did something for her sallow complexion and dark eyes . . . Rosetta King squeezed her son's arm, hoping to distract his attention. She knew that face, too well.

'Vincent, did you pick up the box of chocolates? I only ate two.'

'Yes, Mother. I –' His voice trailed away. He was looking up at Maggie Pinjarra, already near the exit. Maggie looked down at that moment, almost as if she felt his gaze. Her glance did not waver. Her large eyes looked at him and through him, calmly and coldly.

'Wasn't that Miss Pinjarra?' asked Mrs King casually, keeping a tight grip of Vincent's arm. She felt his muscles tense as if he would spring up the steps towards her. 'I don't think she saw us.'

'She saw us all right. Or at least she saw me. And she cut me dead.'

'Surely not!' (She had, though, the cheeky upstart.)

Burning with impatience, Vin had to suit his pace to his mother's, and the crowd's shuffling movement. Even in the more open foyer, when they reached it, she held him back by leaning her weight on him. But Maggie had gone. The red velvet coat was nowhere to be seen.

He had tried to ring her at work, but she would not speak to him; had sent a letter to the hostel, but she sent it back with the few presents he had given her, done up in a neat parcel. Pride came to his rescue, anger at her unyielding attitude. He'd made the first advance; he'd tried to apologise. If she was not going to respond, then the devil take her. There were plenty of other girls.

But that was just the problem. There weren't plenty of girls like Maggie. She was unique. He had taken Jeanne out in a half-hearted manner, and she had taken him back to her bed at home, but he could scarcely rise to the occasion. Jeanne had not been pleased by his obvious lack of interest.

This was the first time he had seen Maggie since that unfortunate Mountain Trial. He had sold the Jaguar rather than get it repaired, and bought a supercharged Triumph. But he took no pleasure in the new car. Nothing was important to him anymore but the look of scorn in those wonderful eyes. He knew he had behaved badly. If she would just give him another chance . . .

That night he dreamed of her most vividly, and woke up to a wet sheet and an empty bed. Groaning, he embraced the pillow, murmuring 'Maggie! I love you.'

He looked forward to the Redex Round-Australia trial in which he had entered, an eleven thousand mile course almost non-stop. 'Unlucky in love, lucky at cars,' he said to himself. This was the sort of gruelling test he needed to stop himself from thinking.

The next day a letter came from her, which made him regret he would be going away.

Vin: (she wrote without preamble)

Of course I saw you with your mother last night, but do you know what it cost me to look through you like that? My legs trembled so at the sight of you that I could hardly climb the rest of the stairs. I was still trembling all over, an hour after I got home. I had been trying to tell myself I'd got over you, but obviously that isn't true.

Tomorrow I leave for two weeks' holiday! I'm going to the Island, where I have longed to go to lick my wounds. If you want to see me when I get back, send me a note to the Hostel. But I expect you have a new girl by now.

She signed it simply, 'Maggie.' No appeals, no reminders of past love, no protestations. She was leaving it up to him to make the next move.

Eleven

MAGGIE PINJARRA's third book, *Dingo and Dugong: Stories of Uncle Morgan*, which sold even better than the first two, was a result of her break with Vincent and her trip to the Island. Though she had appeared to reject him, she felt that it was really the other way round. He had not been serious in his proposal of marriage.

In her hurt she turned back to her own people – and realised what a wealth of material Grannie Nyora and Uncle Dingbat Morgan kept stored in their heads. It had never been written down, but was passed on from the old to the young over the generations. There were even some up-to-date stories in which spirit people, Bugeens and Doolagarls, were mixed up with modern things like rifles and motor cars.

Maggie, who had once felt shame at being seen in the main street of Rockhampton with her Auntie Maud Wandana (Billy Efate's mother) in her shapeless puce-coloured dress bulging over her great bulk, now identified strongly with the Aboriginal part of her family. Maud was very active in Aboriginal affairs. Maggie sought her out in her fibro house with its untidy garden and overgrown lawn on the outskirts of Emu Bay, to ask if she had any old stories. But she found Morgan the best source, perhaps because the men had traditionally been the song-makers and story tellers of the tribe.

Though she liked to forget about it now, Maggie had once tried to pass as Spanish or Portuguese; indeed, 'Pinjarra' was a corruption of Pinjaró, the name of the sailor Miguel Pinjaró who had deserted from a Portuguese whaler in the 1880s, and lived with Nyora as man and wife for thirty years.

Maggie's sister Marie had been living for years on the mainland, one of the few part-Aboriginal women who had a home right in the town among the houses of white people. Yet she was darker than Maggie, with the broad nose and heavy brows of her father's people. She was an active member of the Federal Council for the Advancement of Aborigines and Torres Strait Islanders. Her husband Billy had a good job on the Railways, but was often away travelling inland to Longreach and Mt Isa or north to Cairns. There was no colour-bar in the Railways. And those, like Billy, who were returned Servicemen always seemed to have an easier time in Queensland.

Maggie's Uncle Harold was accepted because of his singing voice. He had married Anna's sister Ellen, part-Islander like himself, and took his wife's surname of Brown. They had no family, so when Maggie finished Junior school they asked her to live with them in Townsville while she attended High School there. Aunt Ellen had encouraged her and helped her with her homework, so that Maggie did better than most girls of her background. She did a Commercial course with typing and shorthand, but knew that coloured girls were never employed as stenographers.

It was when she left school and was looking for a job in Rockhampton that she was tempted to deny her background. Filling out the application form, under 'Where born' she put 'Naturalised Australian, b. Portugal.' Nobody questioned it, and she got the job.

But Marie was most upset. 'What's the use denyin' it, you got Island and Aboriginal relatives all over the place. We have to stick together, girl, prove that we're good for somethin' more than just washing up and cleaning toilets an' that. At least we've got a branch of the FCAATI here, though the officers keep squabbling among themselves, gettin' nowhere.'

'I'll never do any good in Rocky,' said Maggie. 'They'll find out soon, and I'll be sacked. I'm going south, where I don't have *any* relatives.'

Marie glared at her. 'Why, what's the matter? You ashamed of your relatives? You ashamed of Billy and me?'

'Not of you and Billy, of course not. But the drunks I see sitting in the gutter outside the pubs, sleeping in the Botanic Gardens, begging for a handout. And some of the girls . . . You know them, everybody knows them. Someone told me they charge a shilling a time, behind the picture theatre, till they've got enough to go to the pictures.'

492

Marie looked depressed. She knew that much of it was true.

'Well, you know how it is. Those girls didn't have no education, it's the only way they know of earning money. Can't get jobs in town. Brought up in shacks, everybody sleeping together . . . If we can get a better deal, get kinder-gartens and pre-schools, proper education and housing, the next generation will be different, with a bit of pride of race. We'll have Aboriginal and Islander members of Parliament, and lawyers and ministers and everything. Not just drunks and no-hopers.'

'Bill isn't like that, or David.'

'No, but then the War saved Billy. He got his "dog collar" along with his Distinguished Service Medal, and he was allowed to get drunk with his mates at the RSL on Anzac Day. He could manage his own money, and have a bank account. Now, with his brother Dave, it was his boxing. If he could flatten a white feller in two rounds (and it never took him longer), he wasn't going to be scared to stand up to him socially, see?'

'And what about you?'

'Well, our Mum was a good many parts white, though our Dad was half Aborigine. We're real mixtures, you an' me an' Dan. I got the kinky hair from old Joseph Efate, you got the lighter skin, Dan looks real Abo. It's funny how it happens with mixed marriages. And then Billy looks Islander, yet his Mum, Auntie Maud, is pure Aboriginal.'

'Uncle Dave takes after her.'

'Yes, and he gets on all right in Melbourne. There's a big mob of "Koories" there, in Fitzroy. But Dave's kids are diff'runt again, more like Grandpa Tula.'

'And if I married white, would my kids be dark, some of them?'

'No, they'd probably be lighter than you. They might get the kinky hair, but. That seems to persist the longest. Tula was the one who took after his father, who went back to the islands and died there. None of the Efate family stayed in Maryborough. As for the Browns, Grandpa took off for the bush during the Depression, his mother died out West in Charleville, and Grandma Fiona drowned in the ferry disaster when the twin boys were lost.'

Maggie, remembering this conversation as she travelled north again on the rocking, narrow-gauge railway, reflected that she was lucky to have been born; what if Fiona had saved the two little boys instead of Anna and Ellen? She herself would not be here, would never have met Vin and fallen in love with him. Life! Who could fathom its complexities?

She wondered if Vin had got her letter yet.

The next move was up to him. Perhaps he wouldn't even answer it. But if he was sincere, he would insist that they get married and, as he said, to hell with his mother.

As for her own mother, Anna Pinjarra, Maggie remembered her only as someone slender and beautiful, who often wore a flower in her dark fuzzy hair, who smelt nice, and who died young of some mysterious disease of the blood.

When her first stories were published Maggie had not expected them to be taken up with such enthusiasm by the critics and the public, but this heady success had spurred her to write more. Now she wanted to write down the age-old legends of the coastal Aborigines, the Creation myths, the stories of giant animals and legendary journeys. But she had not counted on such riches as she uncovered once she got Morgan talking.

One story that fascinated her was about two sisters who, covered with salt from their long sea-journey, had travelled from an island far to the east. Steering their canoe by keeping the track of the Morning Star astern, they had reached this land and settled here. (Yet all the anthropologists said that the first people had come overland, by stepping-stones from Malaysia, or over dry land before the sea rose.)

Who knew how ancient this story might be? Generations of men had told and retold the story round their campfires, perhaps for many thousands of years. Books could be burnt, destroyed by insects, by flood, by mould, but the mind of man was indestructible. By the spoken word this story had survived, perhaps as a memory of a people who had come, like her Island forbears, from somewhere far out in the Pacific.

*   *   *

She found Marie much the same, though plumper than before and more ardently involved in the struggle for Aboriginal rights. Queensland, she said, was the most racist State in Australia, and had the most restrictive, paternalistic laws. The Aboriginal Reserves were run like prisons, and everything was run by 'the Department' – the Department of Aboriginal Affairs which controlled the lives of people on reserves from a thousand miles away in Brisbane. Aborigines were not allowed to drink, or to handle their own money.

'There's a taxi-driver in town,' said Marie, 'who charges our people four times the proper fare to take them anywhere. He gets them sly-grog, too, at a price – raw rotgut wine in flagons, plonk, terrible stuff.'

'And they say there's no discrimination!'

'Well, you know yourself how hard it is to get jobs up here, even for girls like you, with qualifications. In Townsville the Matron won't have them in the hospital as trainee nurses. They're discriminated against all their lives.

'It goes right back! A rope across the picture theatre for them to sit in front of, in the worst seats; a "black ward" at the hospital to have their babies in! And at school the teachers aren't really interested in them; if they show they're extra good at something like drawin' or paintin' that's just "natural ability". Nothin' clever about it.'

'I must go and see Auntie Maud,' said Maggie. 'How is she?'

'Pretty good. She's gettin' heavy on her feet, but, and her feet swell in the hot weather. We bought her an electric jug a while back, you know she always insists on cookin' on a wood stove.

'Well – ! She nearly had a fit. "Don't you leave me alone with that there jug!" she said. As if it might bite her, or blow up or something. She was dead scared of it at first. She's got used to it now, and really appreciates it. Of course Davey's in Melbourne now, but Billy goes out and chops some wood for her when he's home.'

'And Uncle Harold and Auntie Ellen are in America, are they?'

'Yair; he's mad to go there, I reckon. He was given some

sort of scholarship; but over there it's as bad as the North is here; if you're coloured, the only jobs are as janitors and housemaids and that, I believe. And he'll be treated just like a Negro.'

'Not by the people who matter, in the musical world.'

'Well, I wouldn't like to go there. What about you, anyway? You're a bit of a celebrity yourself, down South.'

'Oh yes. I get asked to posh parties, and to Library Week and so on. But there's still that basic something – you know – Us and Them?'

'I know, love. I've been accepted in this town for many years now. I'm even thinking of standin' as an alderman on the town Council, whaddaya know? Of course I won't have a hope; a woman *and* a darky.'

'It's not so bad in the South, I suppose because there are so few of us, and the white people don't feel they have to show they're on top.'

'It's white hypocrisy that's so immoral!' said Marie. 'They don't admit that Aboriginal child mortality is among the highest in the world: that there's leprosy in the Northern Territory, and a whole island of lepers at Fantôme, just off the coast at Townsville; that there's malnutrition and syphilis and people goin' blind from trachoma; a fifty per cent unemployment rate, and half our people living in shanties and dumps with no proper water supply. Underneath, they *hope* we'll die out; they *hope* the whole problem will solve itself, and there'll be a nice, clean, pure, white Australia! God save the bloody King!'

Maggie was a little startled at her sister's vehemence. She knew it was all true; she should be equally angry about it herself, but she had been too far removed from all these problems. Had she become a 'white Aborigine'? No, she was proud now of her Aboriginal and Pacific Island blood, and in getting her stories published she was, as she had told Vin, striking a blow against prejudice just as Harold was doing with his singing.

When she got back to South Australia, with bundles of notes waiting to be typed into stories, she found Vin's note waiting. By then he had left on the trial, so she worked long into the nights and listened to the radio reports of his pro-

496

gress: the broken windscreen, the nightmare drive to Carnarvon. He had added a postscript: 'I have been reading your stories, and I think I understand better now.'

She suddenly felt that everything was going to come right.

Though his relief driver argued and pleaded, for three days Vin had refused to give up the wheel. This was one of the worst sections, through the Kimberleys in the far North-west of the continent, and Vin would not trust anyone else to get them through it. Gaunt and red-eyed, staring into the cloud of red dust, which hid the competitor in front and the spine-jarring holes in the track (known as 'crabholes' but made by eddying rainwaters during the annual Wet, for they were at least two hundred miles from the coast), Vin drove with a grim concentration and so far without loss of points.

Quite suddenly, unconsciousness descended on him. It was only a few seconds' blackout, but in that time they were off the road and had 'gone exploring' over the lip of a steep embankment. The windscreen shattered.

Using levers and jacks, they managed to manhandle the light car between them back on to the road. Vin, shaken, gave up the driving seat.

The clear, icy cold of the inland night descended; the stars like chips of ice glittered in the blackness overhead, washed by the white luminosity of the Milky Way. Once more the Scorpion ruled the winter sky, a shining, beckoning curve beside that other, paler river of light. A wind like a sword cut their exposed faces. It had been thought they were out of the race, and when they drove into Wyndham on the far North-west coast there were cheers all round. The story of their endurance was sent off to the south by the newsmen waiting there.

This was only the beginning of their ordeal. The nearest replacement windscreen would be at Carnarvon, nearly a thousand miles to the south. They wrapped up their faces in scarves, and wearing plastic goggles against the wind, drove on.

By the time they left the West Australian city of Perth, breakdowns had thinned the field until only a dozen cars were left in the trial. Dust-filled carburettors, broken differentials and bent axles strewed the outback roads.

Crossing the Nullarbor Plain on the last leg of the trial, Vin began to have hallucinations. It was hot by day and cold by night in the treeless desert of limestone plain. The road was a nightmare of rough corrugations and potholes, filled with bulldust as fine as flour. Somewhere out of Madura, staring grimly ahead where the mirage painted an illusory lake over the dead-straight road, he thought he saw a bandicoot. It was sitting up, holding its paws in front of its face as though saying grace, or praying. Vin jammed on the brakes. They locked, the car skidded sideways into a deep drift, burying its nose as the dust rose in a wave, poured over the engine hood and flowed down again like water.

'What the hell are you doing? Did you go to sleep again?' cried his navigator.

'No – it was the bandicoot. I couldn't run it down.'

'What bandicoot, for Chrissake?'

'The one in the middle of the road. Where's it gone?' He pushed up his goggles. With his bloodshot eyes staring from a sweaty and grime-streaked face, he looked slightly mad.

'There's no bloody bandicoot. Here, you'd better let me take over while you have a sleep.'

'I tell you I was wide awake! It must have dived under a bush.'

His navigator looked round, then looked back at him pityingly. The level limestone plain, on which grew nothing but some stunted saltbush and a few white everlasting daisies stretched round them: scarcely enough shelter for a mouse. Behind them a whitish-grey cloud of dust appeared, growing larger each second.

'Hell! We don't want him to pass us, or we'll have to take his dust.'

They leaped from the car and began to shovel dust, taking it in turns to use the shovel or their bare hands. Vin flung himself into the driving seat just as the other car went past, showering them with small nodules of limestone and enveloping them in choking dust.

Vin swore. He started the engine and used low gear to accelerate fiercely, till he was just behind the other car, half-blinded by its dust. He tooted, but the car veered further to the centre of the road. He tried to get to the left, but it veered left.

'The bastard!' said Vin. 'He's trying to stop me getting through.'

He put two wheels off the track onto the rough stony verge. The tail swung wildly, clipped the other car with a vicious side-swipe, and then they were through on the wrong side. He had a glimpse through the dust of the other driver shaking his fist in rage.

'*Goodbye-ee, Don't cry-ee,*' sang Vin, putting his foot down and leaving him behind.

They made up time and had lost only a minute at the next control, out of Port Augusta. They were back on the tarmac and had only two hundred miles to go.

'We've got it made!' said Vin exultantly. He didn't care about the trophy, or the honour and glory of winning, or the five thousand pounds he stood to gain. He was proving something to himself, and to Maggie also. He had a feeling that winning her back was contingent on winning the trial.

It was night when the cars started arriving at the finish, a fenced-in paddock on the northern outskirts of the city where temporary quarters for the judges had been set up, and a canteen for weary drivers and waiting families and spectators.

As Vin was checking in, first of the cars to have completed the course, Franz Diamond came running up, wearing an official's arm-band and waving a betting card.

'You've done it, King Vincent!' he cried. 'Only three hours lost – no one will beat that. I had a tenner on you, just quietly: knew you'd walk it in. Congratulations.'

Vin and his co-driver smiled wearily at each other and shook hands. When they took off their goggles they looked like clowns, their faces painted in a mask of white dust with only the eye area a normal colour. Flash-bulbs popped, TV cameras and microphones were thrust into their faces. Enormous interest had followed the trial, the first to circle the continent. Its progress had been reported minutely each day, and there was a great welcoming crowd of enthusiasts.

When Vin had stiffly extracted his long legs from under the dash and was wiping dust from his face with the sleeve of his overalls, he felt a soft touch on his arm. From that touch a warm spot seemed to spread and travel up his veins to his heart. He turned, knowing she was there.

'Maggie!' he cried, and grabbed her in his arms, lifting her right off the ground. The spectators laughed and cheered, the cameras clicked.

'Is this your fiancée, Vincent?' asked a young reporter, pencil poised.

Vin looked at Maggie, one eyebrow raised comically. She smiled and nodded, a radiant smile showing all her very white teeth.

'Yes; you can say so,' said Vin. 'My fiancée, Miss Maggie Pinjarra – you know her, the author of *Little Brown Brother* and *The Dreaming*.'

They kissed again in front of the cameras, but it was as if they were alone in some new, miraculous country, innocent and happy as Adam and Eve before the Fall.

His mother said coldly, 'Of course, you are of age now and independent; there's nothing I can do about it, however much I disapprove. It will, of course, end in divorce. I hope you will have enough sense not to start a family.'

The morning and evening papers were spread on her bed, where she was taking morning tea. She still, Vin noticed, had the one coffee-biscuit with scalloped edges that he used to beg when he came to her bedroom early when he was little. He could still taste the soggy edges, melting in his mouth after they had been dipped in the hot tea. Like Proust and his madeleine.

'Have you thought seriously about what it will mean to marry this girl?' she went on.

'Of course I've thought seriously about it. Any amount of talking on your part will not alter the simple fact: I love her, and she's the only girl for me.'

'But Vincent – ' Her firm chin quivered, her heavy-lidded eyes grew moist. 'You might consider my feelings a little. You're all I have. And I'd hoped, in this big house, when you married we'd make an apartment for you and your wife and you could go on living here. But I can't say I want to share my home with a part-Kanaka, part-Aboriginal girl from the backblocks of Queensland. She's pretty, I suppose, but there are plenty of pretty girls. And her accent – ! Really. I can't understand you. I just can't understand you.'

'Because you don't want to understand! You're just prejudiced against Maggie, Mother.'

'And what if you two have children, they might be dark! To think that one of the Forbes family –'

'Mother! I am not a prize ram on a Forbes sheep station. I am not a breeding-sire who has to keep the strain pure for better wool-production! In fact, some of those early Forbes men probably had half-a-dozen coloured kids, but they didn't marry the mothers, so it was respectable. A black girl was all right for a bit of fornication on the side, but never for a wife, that would never do!'

'Vincent! What nonsense you talk!'

He strode angrily about the room.

'Anyway, I don't particularly want children. It would be impossible, trying to drag a couple of kids round with us to car meetings. I'm giving up Insurance; I'm going to become a professional driver.'

'I was so looking forward to a grandchild –'

'Well, don't look at me.'

' – but it would be better if you didn't start a family right away. You will get over this infatuation, and it will end in divorce, you mark my words. She's only after your money, you know, and the glamour of your car-racing. You could have married *anyone* –'

'Have you quite finished? It so happens that you couldn't be more wrong. Maggie is one of the few sincere girls I've met. She doesn't care two hoots about those things.'

'Oh, of course she's all sweetness now, until she has you safely hooked.' The innate vulgarity of the Forbes men, who had been too busy grabbing land and making money to develop the finer side of their natures, seemed to be concentrated in the person of their female descendant, who had never had to work for hers. Vin looked at his mother, quite alienated.

She went on: 'You'll find out soon enough. She'll be slovenly and dirty in the house, a fat blowsy old lubra by the time she's thirty-five. Don't say I didn't warn you. I don't say she's immoral but – '

'You've said just about enough!' Vin's face was white with suppressed anger. 'You trot out all these old prejudices, because you're jealous – yes, just plain jealous! You never liked Maggie, and you wouldn't have liked any girl I wanted to marry.'

'You're wrong, I hoped you might marry Jeanne Burgess.'

'Jeanne is just a high-class tramp. She'll turn it on for anyone who's in the news. A visiting Russian writer, an artist who's become fashionable, a new singing star, yes, and a driver who's had a big win. That's Jeanne for you.'

'I don't believe it.'

'Okay, don't believe it. But kindly don't talk of things you know nothing about.'

'Well, so long as you don't expect me to give you my blessing or come to the wedding,' she said, changing her ground. Her large nose, so like his own, turned pink. She brought a handkerchief out from under the pillow and dabbed at her eyes. 'I don't know what I've done to deserve such ingratitude – '

' "Do you want to bring my grey hairs in sorrow to the grave?" '

'What?'

'That's the next line isn't it? In the Wronged Mother act?'

'Really, Vincent! If your father were alive – '

'If Dad were alive he'd agree with me. You've always tried to run other people's lives for them. It's my belief he died from disappointment because I didn't go to see him when I got back from Melbourne. You kept me away from the hospital until it was too late. The Sister told me he had been asking for me.'

'That's nonsense.' But her eyes wavered from his.

'Well, you won't be running my life any longer. Maggie and I will find a place to live. We might go to Melbourne; it depends who I get for a sponsor. I'm leaving; I won't stay another night.'

He strode out, closing the door behind him with a finality which frightened her. She blew her nose, and took a gulp of cold tea. She would wait; time was on her side. He would get tired of this girl and come back home in the end.

She rang the bell.

'Take the tray please, Ethel. And see if there are any of Mr Vin's things in the ironing-basket. He will be leaving tonight. And get his wardrobe-trunk down from the top of the linen-press, will you?'

'Oh deyar!' Ethel's long jaw dropped in consternation. 'Have youse two been havin' a row about something? He's gone off without any breakfast.'

'My son is going to be married, Ethel. He'll be setting up house on his own.'

'Well now! Isn't that nice!'

'That, I am afraid, is a matter of opinion.'

Twelve

'IT ISN'T lunchtime yet, it's still morning,' said Maggie.

'Well, I say it is. Where's my watch? I must have left it in the bathroom.'

He rolled over and squinted at the daylight beyond the windows of the hotel bedroom. It was an old wooden hotel, with a balcony all round the first floor, decorated with white-painted iron lacework. 'I don't see how you can tell, you can't see the sun.'

'I just know,' said Maggie. 'The morning has a different feel. It's something . . . a feeling of promise, excitement, freshness. The afternoon is quieter.'

'You've just got sharper eyes, and can see faint shadows and measure their angles.'

'No, truly! I could tell with my eyes bandaged. You know that when I wake in the dark I always know what time it is. There's a midnight feeling and a pre-dawn feeling. Anyone could probably sense it if they didn't depend so much on clocks. I hate wearing a watch. Yet when my Mum was dying, they say, she insisted on being buried wearing an old rusted watch that hadn't gone for years.'

'Maybe you're seeing the Town Hall clock telepathically – if Yeppoon has such a thing.'

'I don't think I am,' said Maggie seriously. 'I believe in telepathy, though – animals have it, and young babies and a dog working sheep, or a child that plays up when it's mother is tense.'

'Well, I have distinct impression that it's lunch-time. I'm getting a telepathic message from my stomach.'

Maggie stretched her brown limbs luxuriously against the white sheets. 'But isn't it heavenly not to have to get up, ever?'

'What, never? We'd starve to death.'

Vin went to the bathroom and came back, picking up his watch. 'You're right, you know. It's only half past eleven. No chance of a meal in this pub before one.'

Maggie leaped out of bed. 'I know! There's that loaf of bread we brought in from the car, and the can of tuna. We can make sandwiches. Where's the tin-opener?'

When he saw how she was butchering the loaf with the ordinary knife they had brought, he took it out of her hand. 'Here, let me.' He cut four rounds of perfect straightness and exactly the same thickness. They sat on the bed, eating sandwiches and dropping crumbs. Maggie was supremely happy; she felt rounded and complete.

'Tomorrow we'll be home, on my island,' she said.

'You've wired your grandmother? She might get a shock if we just turn up, married.'

'She'd get a worse shock if we weren't. And I've let Marie know, too. She's staying at the island while Billy's away. There's only the one ferry each day, in the morning.'

'Couldn't we hire an outboard and go out today?' He prowled restlessly about the room. 'It's my idea of hell, doing nothing.'

'You haven't been exactly inactive since we've been married,' said Maggie, smiling. But she went cold all over. Was he bored with her company already?

He laughed. 'Yes, but there's a limit to the amount of indoor sport you can indulge in.'

'We could get a boat, but it would be expensive, and besides they're expecting us on the launch tomorrow. My brother's wife Ilona is the postmistress. So the whole island will know we're coming and be down to meet us. The mail's a bit erratic, but they will have got my wire. When the weather's rough the launch doesn't run. And when the tides are low, a horse and cart go out to the edge of the reef to meet it, because it can't get in to the jetty. Sometimes a mailbag gets dropped in the water.'

'I suppose I've got a thing about public transport, buses and trains and launches. I can't stand being jammed against other people. Just like I hated football at school: what they call "contact sports". Golf, now, I enjoy – but that's a game of skill, and each for himself.'

'You're a super-egotist.'

'Yes, but you love me.'

'I do; I can't think why.'

'Because I'm a dominant male, and you like being dominated.'

'I do not! I believe in equal rights. But I know I'm doubly disadvantaged. Women and Aborigines are both second-class citizens in this country.'

'Now don't get on your soap-box, Mrs Pankhurst.'

'I'm not! You beast!' They started a mock wrestling match, which he of course won, and which she wanted him to win. Then he put on some clothes and wandered out on to the wide balcony. She donned a dressing-gown and came to stand beside him. 'That's my island!' she said, pointing to one of several pale blue shapes against the sky, seeming to float on the turquoise sea.

'Let's get a boat anyway, and go exploring.'

'Would there be crocodiles in this river?' Vin looked about him with interest at the mangrove-shrouded banks of the tidal stream, the little jetty from which they had launched their hired boat. They had waited till dusk, when the tide would be at the full and the fish biting, according to Maggie the fisherman's daughter.

Their small dinghy with its outboard motor had no lights, but they carried a strong battery-powered torch. Mullet jumped all round the boat, slapping the still surface as they fell back. Vin wanted to drop in his line, but she told him he would be wasting his time; the mullet were not feeding, and anyway would not take a hook. As they chugged downstream the moon rose, just past the full. The sky was covered in a thin, formless veil of cloud. As it rose, the shrouded moon shed a diffused, ghostly light on the wide sandbars of the river mouth. They slipped smoothly out into the bay and anchored on a sandbank which was still exposed. Maggie baited the lines, using fresh prawns.

Vin cast over the stern into deep water. Almost at once the line went streaming out, the ratchet screaming. He reeled in slowly, giving the fish its head, then pumping it firmly back. At last a silver flash broke the water. He swung the flapping fish inboard, where it threw itself off the hook. As it flapped, it squeaked and groaned.

'I've never heard a fish groan before!' said Vin.

'It's a Grunter. They grunt and groan when you take them out of the water – it's rather horrible really.'

'I wish it would stop.'

'Kill it then,' said Maggie. 'You have a knife.'

'Ough! Blood! No thanks.'

'Then I will.' She took the sharp fish-knife and cut through the grunter's spine to let it bleed. Vin fastidiously drew back his feet.

'I don't think I want to catch any more. Let's take the boat further out – it's so calm.'

'Wait 'til I've caught another one. We'll have them for breakfast.'

When she had dispatched another fish, a sand whiting, Vin pulled the starting rope and they headed out from land. Maggie, seated in the bows, noticed vague pale shapes like drowned moons flowing back past the boat. Then the propeller hit something solid. The engine faltered, then recovered.

'I'm sure we're not hitting a sandbank,' said Vin, puzzled.

'It feels different, almost like going through jelly.'

'Jellyfish! Of course.'

They slowed down and examined the water. A thousand white shapes were coming to the surface, pulsing rhythmically, like pale parasols opening and closing. They went on, keeping the engine revving fast so that the check was only momentary as each lump of jelly was cut to pieces by the propeller. Vin had fished one out on the end of an oar, a heaving, squashy thing with fleshy tentacles. '*Not* a sea-wasp,' said Maggie. 'They only come this far south in the middle of summer.'

Now the mangrove-lined shore had receded to a low dark line and beyond lay the pale, misty, luminous expanse of the Pacific. The moon looked high and far away, like a small mother-of-pearl button fixed in the sky. It was impossible to judge distances: land and sea were formless.

'Don't go too far,' said Maggie nervously. 'It would be easy to lose your bearings on a night like this.'

'*What's that*?' Vin slowed the motor and peered intently ahead. 'That great dark shape – is it a dredge, perhaps?'

'I think it's a wreck. It has no lights.'

'It seems to be moving this way.' He fumbled with the torch and switched it on and off. 'They'd never see us in this light.'

They watched anxiously as the dark shape came nearer. Vin turned off the torch to rest the battery. Then Maggie laughed. 'I can see it now!' she cried. 'It's just driftwood – a dead tree. We must be nearly aground.'

At that moment they ran on a sandbank. Vin saw that the large shape in the distance had actually been a dead tree close by. Some trick of the light, and the lack of any point of reference, had made it appear so huge and menacing; and the movement had been their own.

They were in a maze of off-shore shallows. 'I'll have to get out and push, or we'll never get out of this.' He waded at the stern, pushing the boat, with the motor tilted up out of the way. The water was only a foot deep.

'Hop in, I'll row,' said Maggie. She switched on the torch and fitted the oars in the rowlocks. Its beam shone down into the water. '*Get in*!' she said. 'Get in the boat, quick!'

507

'Is it a c-crocodile?' asked Vin, his teeth chattering with excitement as he scrambled aboard.

'No, a sea-snake.' She flashed the torch ahead, and he saw a long pale shape, with narrow head and flattened tail, undulating just below the surface.

'Venomous?'

'Deadly. Don't get out of the boat again.'

'I won't!'

They rowed, and punted with the oars, for a long time before they were free. Maggie worried about the run-out at the mouth of the creek when the tide turned. But once over the sandbank where they had fished earlier, Vin opened the throttle and they sped back towards the bar. Thud, thud, thud went the jellyfish through the propeller. The air was suddenly chilly; the moon looked small and dull.

Maggie shivered.

'Are you cold, darling? Come back and sit by me.'

He wrapped a long arm round her. She felt its human comfort in the immensity of the night, this pale, limitless expanse. She, whose grandmother and unknown young uncles and father had all been drowned, felt a deep distrust of the open sea. Their little boat had seemed lost out there in the great flux of time and tide, the vast nebulous deeps of ocean and sky.

Awed and chastened, she clung to his hard, warm, living hand until they were safely back between the banks of the tidal creek.

'That expensive, that bed, I bet,' said Uncle Dingbat Morgan, stumping around on his pegleg and admiring the new bed. It had come over that day on the tourist launch, in sections, and he had been asked to help put it together: the two fancy ends of scrolled iron, painted white, with their knobs of polished brass; the iron frame and the four legs with castors. 'My word, that a pretty fine bed.'

'Well, I wanted to have it 'ere for Maggie and her feller when they comin' to stop. Then after, I kin have it me own self.'

Nyora had wanted such a bed for years, having become

used to sleeping in one like it when she was a young woman. She had been brought up on an Aboriginal Mission on Fraser Island, when the Department took her from her mother as a small child after her father was sent to the leper colony on Dayman Island. At the Mission, Nyora was taught to cook and keep house. Later she became cook on one of the coastal island resorts, just becoming popular.

A white man known as the Mad Artist lived there with his wife, painting for most of the year. In winter he made an extra income by letting huts to tourists, who dined each night on tropical fruit salads, and reef fish or lobster cooked by Nyora. Then the artist's wife, fed up with isolation and entertaining tourists, left him, and in time Nyora moved into the double bed with the brass knobs, and consoled the artist. But to her he was an old man. When the tourist launch brought a handsome young Portuguese sailor as deckhand one week, Nyora showed her interest.

The launch used to anchor each week in the lee of the island for the night, so that guests on board could do some fishing off the fringing reef first thing in the morning. As soon as the supper things had been cleared away and the bar closed for the night, Miguel the deckhand was over the side and rowing for the palm-fringed beach where Nyora awaited him, a purple orchid or a pale frangipani blossom in her dark hair.

One week when he failed to come ashore – they'd been out to the main reef that day, and Miguel had rowed the dinghy for miles while the tourists looked down through glass-bottomed boxes at the coral – she swam out in the dark, regardless of sharks and giant groper. She came down the steps to his little fo'castle cabin, glistening and dripping sea water like a dark brown mermaid.

Miguel rowed her back to shore later. Fortunately the artist was not a jealous type, and never asked where she had been. In fact he was tiring of Nyora and her youthful demands. Miguel was so impressed by her devotion in swimming out to him in the dark, that he asked her to marry him. He stayed on the tourist boat until the next cyclone season; the pay was good, though the hours were long. When he left he had enough money to buy his own boat, and he took Nyora with him. The only thing she regretted leaving was the brass-knobbed bedstead.

They sailed south, put in at Emu Bay, and ended up on Pandanus Island, more by accident than design. There they founded a family; relatives came from the mainland, and eventually the Pinjarras came to look on Pandanus as 'their' island. Miguel and his son Bert were both buried in the island cemetery, besides the youngest daughter, Violet.

Maggie's older brother, Dan and her Aunt Elsie both lived near Nyora.

Dan's pet bird, a Queensland Corella with a bare blue patch around its dark, knowing eye, rode on his shoulder wherever he went. The bird had a cage, but was never in it. He liked to perch on its roof to survey the world. On the rare nights when chicken was on the menu Dan would give him a drumstick to clean up. A supposedly vegetarian bird, he loved his chicken bone, and would wipe it lovingly on his feathers till his white breast was ruffled and greasy.

'Bloody bird's lost 'is tongue!' muttered Blue, the parrot, to himself. He had a rich and varied vocabulary and could swear in three languages, Portuguese, Batjala (an Aboriginal dialect), and English. He disdained such simple phrases as 'Pretty Polly'.

Being free to fly about the settlement, he was not always a welcome visitor, as he was fond of mischief. Chastised by Nyora for pulling all the pegs out of her washing and letting it fall in the sand, he went round the corner and nipped the tops off all her tomato plants. He then perched on the wire-netting by the front steps and said loudly in Dan's voice, 'Turn off that tap, you stupid bastards.'

Nyora threw a bucket of water over him and threatened to 'wring that bloody bird's neck' if he came near her. But Dan knew it was an empty threat. His grandmother accepted that where he went, Blue went also.

'Hand me that there bag,' said Uncle Morgan, reining in his big draught-horse which planted its large hoofs so confidently on the broken coral of Pandanus Island's fringing reef. He was up to his fetlocks in water, but quite unconcerned.

'Uncle, this is Vincent,' said Maggie as she scrambled up into the cart.

'How are ya, love?' The old man kissed her cheek and gave Vincent a straight look from under his heavy brows. He put out a dark hand. 'You Maggie's feller, eh? Pleased to meet ya.'

Vin, shaking his hand, felt suddenly shy. He was being looked over, assessed as a man, weighed in the balance by those shrewd old eyes. And to his horror he felt a twinge of revulsion. Those eyes were so very cloudy, bloodshot and unclear in the dark, pitted folds of skin. Would he feel like this about Maggie's beloved grandma?

'I hear you've got me in a book, girl,' said Uncle Morgan.

'Yes, I've brought you a copy. I hope you like it.'

The cart was loaded with mail and stores from the launch, then the old horse wheeled on his tracks and plodded back to the beach. Coconut palms, introduced by early voyagers, pisonia trees, and the native pandanus palms that gave the island its name, shaded the back of the beach, threw patterns on the smooth silver sand.

A few houses encircled the beach, some of them weekend shacks let to tourists. Maggie's grandmother lived in one of the old, unpainted wooden cottages facing the sea, shaded by palms and bowered in flowering frangipani creeper.

Nyora was waiting on the doorstep to greet them: a fat, dark brown woman with straggly grey hair, bare brown legs below a clean cotton dress, and feet thrust into old sand-shoes without laces. All this Vincent took in as they walked up a path edged with bleached coral boulders. Then Maggie began to run, and was folded against Nyora's capacious bosom.

When she spoke, Mrs Pinjarra's voice was soft and well-modulated, even if her grammar was astray. Vin kissed her cheek dutifully. Nyora stood back, holding him at arms' length to admire him, and he was reminded, ridiculously, of Mrs Burgess in her smart drawing-room.

'My word!' she said at last. 'Maggie's feller, you handsome! You sure you two's married proper?'

'Yes, Gran! In a church, I wrote to you about it.'

'Yes, well, I dunno that I ever set eyes on that letter.'

'I wrote to Marie, too. Where is Marie? And Dan, and everybody? I thought you'd all be down at the launch to meet us.' She was a bit hurt at her family's apparent lack of excitement at her return as a bride, even though it was only a few months since she'd been home.

'Marie thought it would be a bit much for Vin here, meetin' us all in a bunch. So we thought we'd let him get used to us slow, like. I can see youse are happy, anyways.'

'Very happy.'

'You be good to her, Vin! Whatever happen.'

'I will, don't worry.'

'We were going to bring you a bottle of champagne from the wedding breakfast, but it got drunk,' said Maggie.

'Ha! Champagne! Tea'll do me, thanks.'

She led them inside, where morning tea was ready in a big kitchen which was used as the living-room. Maggie unpacked a piece of wedding-cake for her.

Vin found that he got on well with Nyora. For a moment as her smoky eyes looked into his, he had felt an odd sensation. Could those eyes really see into the future, as Maggie claimed? And what had they seen to make her sound that almost warning note? Nyora had an ease of manner left from her days as a cook on a fashionable tourist island, and a remnant of her old flirtatious ways, so that as he caught her laughing glance he saw for a moment the slim, lovely, bright-eyed girl buried in this mountain of fat.

It was a clear, moonless night, warm and mild, with a faint breeze moving the palm fronds. They sat outside the house on the steps of the wooden porch or in canvas chairs on the sand, and talked in the light falling softly out the door from the lamp on the kitchen table.

Maggie was rapt in staring at the night sky away from the glare of street lights.

The moon was just rising out of the ocean and would soon flood the sky with pale light, dimming the stars. She looked up at the luminous curve of the Milky Way. The Scorpion, Maui's fish-hook, was dipping behind the central hills. No wonder there were poets and songmen among our people, she thought proudly. They had lived close to the earth, the mysterious stars, the shapes of shore and mountain; spirits talked to them from rocks and trees, and long-ago ancestors had formed with their magic the lineaments of the land. She was glad she had written down those stories before they were lost. Tonight Vincent was alien to her – other, different, *white*.

He sat talking with Nyora and Marie. He liked Maggie's sister, a strong, direct, no-nonsense person, more 'native' looking than he expected but with an air of proud self-reliance. Then Dan and Ilona came over, bringing some cold bottles of beer. Dan was the most like Nyora in features, or rather he was like his Uncle Morgan, but with a slender, well-formed body. Ilona was a straight-haired Maori from New Zealand, adding another mixture to the polyglot Pandanus Islanders.

Some friends arrived with a piano-accordion and a guitar. An impromptu concert began as the waning moon rose and flooded beach and bay with light. Some of the younger girls danced an Island dance; the men did a more vigorous one with much stamping of the feet.

Vin, helping to pour beer, handed a full glass to a big, quiet man who was the local carpenter.

'You're breaking the law, mate.'

'Eh? How do you mean?'

'Givin' al-co-hol to an Aboriginal,' he said, and downed the beer.

'What! You mean you can't drink on your own island, at a private party?'

'That's right. It's called protecting us for our own good. You see, we're primitive people, like, and we go mad with the grog. At least that's the theory.'

'But you could get an exemption?'

'I could, yair. We call it "the dog collar". It's insulting to have to carry a certificate to say you're fit to drink, so I won't get one. I can't go into a pub on the mainland, and me friends could go to gaol for givin' me a beer.'

'I saw several drunks in Rockhampton,' said Vin, 'and they were all European.'

'Maybe that's because we can't get the stuff.'

513

'Ha, ha!' said Marie. 'You know damn well anybody can get it, for a price.'

This man, Joe Berry, was more articulate than most.

'The North's no bloody good,' he said. 'You has to go south, like Maggie here, to get a good job. They don't want us except as railwaymen and labourers.'

'The Government says there's no discrimination –'

'Listen, mate, I've been fakin' discrim'nated against all me life. How many Abo kids you see swimming in the baths in Townsville? They has to take their chances with the sharks.'

'Sharks is kinder than people,' said Uncle Dingbat Morgan. 'They don't mind *who* they eat – white or brown all taste the same to them.' He thumped his wooden stump on the ground and laughed merrily.

'Yair, our people have bin treated rough, over the years,' said Dan, who had been rather silent. Perhaps he felt Joe was having a dig at him, as he had accepted the despised "dog collar", after proving that he could support himself by fishing. 'First they killed us off, now they're using our culture. The other day in Yeppoon, I see a didgeridoo made in Japan! And everybody's making bloody boomerangs.'

'Yes!' said Maggie. 'You'll see Aboriginal designs on ash-trays, and even printed on tea towels. I ask you! Some of those paintings might have sacred meanings, we shouldn't allow them to be exploited.'

'You're dead right, girl,' said Joe. 'Marie, why don't your mob do somethin' about it?'

'We got enough on our plate already, tryin' to do something for the young people.'

Vin listened to the talk without joining in, frightened of saying the wrong thing, acutely aware that he belonged to the race of 'killers' and 'exploiters'. Ever since he had arrived on Pandanus he had felt as if he were walking on pigeons' eggs.

That night he longed to make love to Maggie, to fortify his sense of possession, for she seemed suddenly strange. But he was inhibited by the nearness of her grandmother through the thin wall that separated her room from the sleepout where they lay, in the creaking brass-knobbed bed she had bought for them. He turned towards the wall so that he might not be

514

tempted, and Maggie lay staring out at the moon, withdrawn and silent.

Some time in the night they rolled together, and woke as usual in each other's arms.

'Was it wrong to bring you here, I wonder?' Maggie was looking at him seriously.

'It was right, and I'm glad I came. But promise you won't get as big as your grandmother.'

She giggled. 'I promise. I'll stay skinny like Dan. And Dan said to get up early, if we want Uncle Morgan to take us to the outer reef today.'

At dawn Maggie went with Dan to empty his fish-trap at low tide. It was an arrangement of stakes driven into the sand to lead the fish into one small wire-netted enclosure, which could be hoisted out of the water with a primitive winch at low tide.

Then what a desperate threshing, what a thunderous, mad effort to escape! She watched in awe as a giant pike, five feet long, with barracuda-like teeth, stood first on its tail and then on its head, while the smaller Queenfish darted round on their iridescent sides, shedding silvery scales. A small shark flung its jaws from side to side, slashing at smaller fish, long-toms and gar, that got in the way.

Dan killed the big fish with his gaff and threw the others into the well of his boat, where they would swim in salt water until delivered fresh to the coastal town.

They sailed straight into the rising sun, in Morgan's old motor launch with the wheezing engine. The weather was perfect, the sea like glass, and Maggie felt no nervousness as they headed out towards the Great Barrier of coral.

'Heigho, little fish, don't cry–y, don't cry!' sang Morgan, tapping in time with his wooden leg against the wall of the forecabin. He sat on the roof, steering with the horny toes of his one foot. This way he was high enough to see the dark patches which meant submerged coral.

Thirty miles further out, Maggie pointed ahead to where, on the horizon, appeared intermittent flashes of black and white: the great waves of the open ocean breaking on the

Barrier Reef. Morgan dropped anchor on a small island reef, surrounded by clear green water, and submerged at high tide.

Vin stared over the side of the dinghy which was pulled up for them to explore in. As they floated over the shallow pools he saw what he had often seen pictured: fairylike grottos where tiny fish like brilliant butterflies darted among flowering branches of lilac, blue, pink, green – all muted undersea colours.

A giant clam lay partly opened, its convoluted lips of peacock-coloured velvet pulsing slightly; dark-blue starfish and black brittle-stars, angel-fish waving their black-and-silver striped wings . . . he felt himself lost in a world before man, before there was any dry land. Then a streamlined electric-blue fish darting for shelter reminded him of his Maserati, and he was back in the surface world once more.

'Such clear water!' he said. 'It's as clear as air. Can't we get out of the boat?'

'Yairs, but you be careful, young feller. And wear your shoes.'

'The coral is sharp, and coral cuts turn septic,' said Maggie.

Hampered by his shoes, he clambered out and swam and walked a little, fascinated by the living colour below. When he dived, fish hung suspended to look into his eyes without apparent fear. He forgot there could be any danger in that silent, beautiful world.

He clambered back into the dinghy and they rowed to the launch, then up-anchored for a deep hole in the reef where Uncle Morgan handed out whole small herring for bait, and they dropped in their heavily-weighted lines. Vin's was soon snagged in the coral, but Morgan pulled up scarlet coral trout with blue dots on their skins, and Maggie a striped Maori with blue-lined lips. Then she gave a startled scream as Vin's line, which he had managed to free, broke the water.

'Don't touch 'im!' shouted Morgan. 'Cut the line! Cut the line!'

'What, and waste the hook? I'll get him off,' said Vin.

'*Don't*,' said Maggie quietly. 'It's a Stonefish. Have a good look at it, then we'll cut the line as Uncle Morgan says. You see those spines on its back? They're covered in a deadly poison. It's one of the Scorpion-fishes.'

Vin had heard of the Stonefish and the agonising death that could result from walking on one, when each spine became a hypodermic needle to inject poison deep into the flesh. The creature certainly looked evil. Its yellowish-lined mouth was gaping angrily, showing the whole bait-fish in its maw, the underslung jaw full of nasty teeth. The row of spines along its back were all erect, showing through the brown slime which camouflaged the creature when lying among coral rock on the bottom. Its body was covered with knobs and hollows like eroded rock, and its eyes were sunk in two deep caverns, like the sockets of a skull. It was Death personified.

'I'd like to kill it,' said Vin, full of hatred for the horrid thing. But Morgan quickly slashed through the line, and fish, hook and sinker dropped out of sight.

'He soon die with that lead in 'is stomach,' he said. 'More better you don't touch 'im. Me, I always wear a lining of tin in me sandshoe when I go into the fishtrap, ever since a mate of mine trod on one of them things. You know what he did? He put his foot in *boiling* water, he was that mad with the pain.'

Maggie shuddered, and Vin looked down soberly into the crystal water which housed such loveliness and such horrors. The water was the colour of Zircon the cat's eyes. He understood now why they had made him wear his shoes on the reef . . .

'*Vin, put on your shoes. Don't go outside in your socks.*' His mother's voice. Maggie would not have had to wear shoes as a child. He thought tenderly of that barefoot little girl, running on the silver sand. Why did he have to remember his mother now, at this time? He hadn't seen her before they left. She had sent no message, no wedding present, had behaved as if the wedding had not taken place.

She was an incredibly obstinate woman. Yet Vin felt guilty, and sorry for her in her stubborn loneliness, there in that big house with only the lugubrious Ethel for company, and Zircon the cat.

Uncle Morgan was unhooking a coral cod that must weigh all of five pounds. Then he wound in his line and began drawing up the anchor with his dark brown, capable hands.

He squinted at the sun, half down towards the horizon.

'Time we was goin',' he said. 'I like to get the reefs well behind me before dark.'

Before they left the island, Maggie insisted on Nyora reading Vin's fortune with the cards. Her dark face motionless, looking as seamed and lined as an old tree-root in the morning light, she set out the cards from a well-worn pack on the kitchen table. Maggie and Vin were silent as she studied the cards, her face impassive. She moved one or two, altered their positions.

'Will he become World Champion?' asked Maggie at last.

'Hush, girl! He will go far and fast, as I said years ago about the man you goin' to marry. I see travel . . . crowds o' people . . . flags. But – .' Abruptly her face closed in, she swept the cards together and gathered them into a pack. 'I see nothin' more.'

'But tell us, will we have children? How many?'

'I can't tell.' She shook her head, heaved herself up with two hands on the table, and turned to put the cards away. Maggie could not see her expression.

'All nonsense, eh Vin?' said Nyora, smiling at him. 'All nonsense I can see things.'

'It's not! She really can,' said Maggie. But she saw that her grandmother would not speak. Dan came to call them. He had a load of fish ready for market and would run them to the mainland in his cutter.

They picked up their car in Yeppoon, and turned southward. Speeding down the Bruce Highway towards Brisbane the second day, past green squares of sugar-cane plantations and crimson volcanic soil, they saw the amazing Glasshouse Mountains looking over the horizon; the road went right beside the largest. Two were like breasts, a young girl's and a woman's, one was like a giant phallus, and the nearest was the brooding, hunched, figure of a bearded man, his stone face turned towards the east.

'I'll bet your ancestors had some good myths about them,' said Vin, teasing her a little. 'That God-sized member, for instance – it could hardly have escaped their notice, the way they wove the landscape into their stories.'

'Yes,' said Maggie unsmiling. 'They're sure to have a legend about them, but I don't know it; except that the Old Man is called Tibrogargan.'

She would not admit to the feeling she had for those strange, dramatic, primeval shapes, which must have been regarded with awe by generations of Aborigines for thousands of years before the white man came; and which still stood there unchanged though the people had gone. His joking offended her. She stared silently out of the window away from him.

> South of the border,
> Down Mexico way!

carolled Vin as they crossed, after another three hours' driving, into New South Wales. The blue Pacific dipped and disappeared, swung into view again between two headlands. As they slowed, climbing a winding hillside, an orange Wanderer butterfly somehow became caught against the half-open quarter-window. It clung there desperately against the stream of wind. Maggie edged a finger under its threadlike legs and brought it into the shelter of the car. The fragile legs clung to her skin as if in panic.

'Poor thing!' She examined the orange and black patterning of its wings, its long black tongue curled like a clock-spring. This delicate creature, or at least its species, had existed as long as the mountains.

'Why is it, I wonder,' she mused aloud, 'that most people react to a spider with disgust, to a butterfly with pleasure? Why is a butterfly "beautiful" and a trapdoor spider "ugly"? Think how deadly the funnel-web spider looks! Surely creatures must grow appearances according to their natures . . . Crocodiles for instance, could never be mistaken for harmless lizards. And think of the shark's cold eye, and the gentle smile of the dolphin.'

'And what about the Stonefish?' Vin shuddered. 'I've never felt such loathing for anything. Horrible!'

'If I were classifying people as sharks or dolphins, I'd put Ace among the sharks. A cool, sleek killer.'

'Well, a lady-killer, anyway. And what about Giulio?'

'Definitely a porpoise. He's a sweetie-pie.'

The butterfly was climbing round her hand, opening and shutting its orange and black wings. 'I think our passenger wants to get off. Will you stop?'

'Just put it out the window.'

'At this speed? It would be killed. Slow down!'

He frowned, but slowed to about forty miles an hour. She put the butterfly near the open window. It sprang into the air, was sucked out by the draught and then swirled back against the glass, where it clung desperately in the slip-stream.

'Vin! Stop, stop!' But in that instant the butterfly lost its grip and was whirled away. 'Now you've probably killed it. Why couldn't you have stopped, for God's sake?'

'Because I want to get to Grafton before dark. The tail light's not working properly.'

The glib excuse tripped off his tongue so smoothly, yet she knew he had just invented it. The fact was that he hated to stop, or even slow down, once he had wound the car up to a satisfactory speed.

She shrank into her corner of the front seat, staring out the side window. Was Vin, too, one of the cold killers? Unwillingly she remembered the mother bandicoot.

Yes, she wanted four children. They had agreed not to start a family yet; it would obviously make travelling difficult, and they had only a small apartment in Sydney. It was not, Vin said, that they couldn't afford a baby, but he would have to get a new car if they were going to Europe, and they would enjoy children more later on.

At present Maggie's maternal instincts were in abeyance, or were satisfied by Vincent who was like a great child as he slept, nuzzling her breast. Yet sometimes she felt that all her unborn children, the babies she would one day have, were coiled up inside her like those tiny fronds of bracken fern: perfect, complete, waiting only to be called into life.

Thirteen

THE FIRST lesson Vin had to learn about motor racing was that it was very expensive. Though they lived frugally, in an old upstairs one-bedroom flat in Manly where he could go down for a swim every morning, they could only just live within their income on the annuity from his father's estate. Most of the money had gone to Rosetta.

Maggie had left the bank, but she took temporary secretarial jobs to keep her hand in. She also had a small income from her books which was precious to her because it made her feel independent. Though Vincent was naturally generous, she would hate to have to go to him and beg for money when she wanted a new dress. Her typewriter, she said, was her dowry.

The prize-money from big meetings was important now that Vin was a full-time professional. Free tyres and fuel came from endorsing certain brands, and he had other advertising commitments which brought in a sporadic income, but he did not have a regular sponsor. He had one good mechanic, Giulio Selmi, who was worth his weight in gold. The rest of the team were in it for the thrill of preparing a top car for a top driver. They asked only expenses to travel with the car and work on it, often for long hours, when necessary. Repairs and modifications (known as 'Demon Mods') were endless, for a racing car was never really 'finished'. Before each race the gear ratios were changed to suit the course, fine-tuning and compression altered for the altitude, tyres to suit the weather.

Vin transported with him a large tin trunk of replacement parts: crown wheel and pinions, gear cogwheels, brake shoes. One faulty valve could result in an expensive melted piston. The pistons were designed to 'run' at fairly low temperatures, thus avoiding a more expensive seize-up of the whole engine.

Vin was convinced that he had the skill, the ability, the tenacity to become a world-class driver. All he needed was luck, and the money to buy a world-class racer. Motor racing had become as necessary to him as a drug. It was more than the adulation of the crowd, the satisfaction of driving well, the thrill of danger. Call it obsession, courage, madness – he had heard it called all of these. But above all he had the fiercely competitive spirit, the bone-deep toughness and egotism which were needed in driving racing cars. As in mountain-climbing, the antagonist was not just a rival team or another driver, but the force of gravity itself.

Driving on bare concrete just a hair's breadth this side of loss of all control, you were like a man hanging on an ice-pick over a sheer precipice. It was a calculated risk. And as in mountaineering, a back-up team was essential: the pit crew.

Vin thought engineers a wonderful lot, though they did not like careless drivers who stripped gears and fouled-up spark plugs ('Careless drivers are soon car-less', as they were fond of saying). But they would put up with temperamental drivers and perfectionists like Vin who fussed before a race over every detail of preparation. All they could not bear was a driver who chickened-out, who lost a race because of over-caution. 'A driver has to have balls,' they said. And they could not deny that Vincent King had balls.

Engineers were necessary, but they cost money. So did melted pistons and broken camshafts, and the transport of the team to race meetings. He decided to gamble on the share market.

'I've an idea for getting some money, Mag,' he told her. 'You know there's been a new interest in goldmining shares lately – people have been wary of them since a few crook companies were floated in the West – and I've heard rumours about the new Tennant Creek field, and Wiluna in Western Australia. They're supposed to be as rich as the Golden Mile, yet investors are hanging back.

'You know my Great-grandpa Sam King made his fortune in the West out of gold. I'm going to sell my father's safe securities and buy shares in Australian Development NL.' (His father would be turning in his grave.) 'It's a gamble; we might lose the lot.'

'It's your money, darling, you do what you think best.'

*   *   *

As they sailed into the long, sheltered harbour of Wellington, New Zealand, Maggie looked at the beaches of black sand and thought of Pandanus Island's silver beaches, and of Ilona, Dan's wife, with her calm easy smile and long brown hair rippling below her waist. She hoped she might meet some Maoris, visit their homes, during her few days in New Zealand. Marie said that the Australian Aborigines could learn a lot from the Maoris, who had their own Members of Parliament and were more on an equal footing with the conquering white race.

But Wellington was an entirely English-seeming city, buffeted by strong winds, and she saw no sign of Maori culture and very few of the indigenous people. By the time they left she had not met one.

Vincent King was determined that nothing should go wrong for his race in New Zealand for points towards the Tasman Cup. Last night he had risked driving his team to mutiny with his requests: check and tighten the throttle linkages, check the ignition wires, plug gaps, rotor, distributor, hose clamps, ball joints, radiator hose: the shift linkage in the gearbox, the wheel bearings, steering column and anti-roll bar . . .

'Already we 'ave done all these theengs,' Guilio protested. 'Before the *macchina* leave Orstralia . . .'

'It won't hurt to check them again,' had said Vin, implacable. 'You don't know what sea-air might have done to the car, crossing the Tasman.'

At last, near midnight, he told them they'd better go and get some sleep. 'And thanks, chaps,' he added with his most winning smile. 'Now I know nothing can go wrong I'll sleep a lot better.' He put an arm round Giulio's shoulders.

'*Bene*. You would 'ave done better to go to sleep more early. *Buona notte*, Vincente – what ees left of it.' And Giulio had gone off grumbling. But he was not really upset.

They were racing at Levin, sixty miles from Wellington on the west coast. It was dry and hot, the grassy centre of the circuit burned brown and yellow towards the end of summer. Beer-booths and ice-cream stalls were doing a roaring trade. Tinny music from the amplifiers set round the track, and moving, restless, light-coloured crowds . . .

Vin sat on the starting-grid in his perfectly-prepared Maserati. Adrenalin pumped through his blood as he eased down helmet and visor; his team gave him a push-start, and the engine woke into life. The insistent stimulation of screaming motors, revving at the start of a race! It was joyful as a trumpet call. Sound, sound the trumpet, fill the fife . . . One crowded hour of glorious life was worth an age without a name.

Then the air exploded with a frantic clamour of accelerating motors, of squealing smoking rubber tyres. He was pressed back into the seat by gravity as the whole pack rocketed forward . . . into the long smooth straight, till the tachometer needle slanted towards the edge of the dial. He was no longer separate, but part of the car, or rather the car was an extension of himself. His was the power and the glory, and an exhilaration intensified by danger, though danger was not consciously in his mind. He raised his left arm as he passed the pits with a thumbs-up signal: all going well. The engine's clear resonant baritone kept its note without a falter.

Setting up the car for the next corner, he went through half-crabwise, in a controlled drift, following the exact line he'd worked out in practice.

He'd had a 'moment' during practice when dust flew, tyres howled as he slewed along on the verge of the track, on the very limits of control. He had fought the car back into line, but the experience had shaken him; he so rarely made a mistake.

Now, passing a slower car which had been placed ahead of him on the starting line (for that one mistake had caused him to get a place far back) he slip-streamed behind Ace in his red Alfa, letting him break the air-barrier of the 150-mile an hour wind. He was driving within inches of the back of the other car, trusting Ace, that veteran driver, not to do anything sudden or strange like braking in the middle of a straight. It seemed as if they were attached to some moving belt which conveyed them through space at the same speed exactly. Then, going wide on the next corner, he gunned the engine and got past. Now he was blazing the trail, with Ace following.

The Mazzer was tracking through the corners in fine style.

Vin could almost have relaxed at the wheel, except for that red car sitting on his tail like a bot-fly.

'Take it easy for the first two laps. You no wanta bend da macchina, onna new circuit.' Giulio's advice.

Damn Ace! The next bend was coming up . . . Suddenly, looking in his mirror, he saw that the red car was not there. Ace, winding up in an attempt to pass, had slid sideways off the track and was disappearing neatly among the straw bales . . .

Vin shut his mind to what might have happened after that. Past the pits – lap number three – All at once he found that the clutch was not taking hold with that solid, comforting feel, but floating down to the floor without resistance. Damn and blast! He nursed the car back to the pits without a gear change, and the mechanics went frantically to work. Ace came trundling round by a back way, unhurt and undamaged, and slid back among the circling field. The man had a charmed life.

'Corpo di Bacch! Bloody Barstid!' Giulio was mixing Tuscan and Australian oaths freely. The clutch plate, of all things! And they did not have a spare, even if there had been time to replace it. Vin was out of the race.

Maggie was secretly pleased to have him out of the car, standing beside her, making knowledgeable comments as the field went past, a bunch all together and four cars strung out in front. She could never tell who had lapped whom or which car was really first. When Vin was driving she watched his position only. She felt superstitiously that if she followed the blue car with her protective thoughts, it would come to no harm. Or rather Vincent would come to no harm. She didn't really care about the bloody car; sometimes she hated it.

It was a two day meeting, and the mechanics would work all night if it was possible to get the car in going order for tomorrow, but anyway he was out of the Tasman Cup. The visiting fast cars were crowd-pleasers and a big crowd was expected for the 15-lap Open Handicap.

Ace, in spite of having left the track, came in second behind a New Zealand home built Special which was the surprise of the day: 'The engine is an unromanced, virgin-pure, 287 Horsepower four-speed transmission job,' someone was telling Vincent.

Maggie went with him to congratulate Ace, who was unfolding his long length from his car, loosening the helmet from his blond hair. It had left a pink crease across his brow.

'I was barracking for you, once Vin was out of it,' she said.

'Thanks, love.' He bent to kiss her, still high on the excitement of the last two laps in which he had nearly caught the New Zealander. Something like an electric shock went through Maggie, as though she had touched one of those mysterious fish of deep waters, which stun with a high-voltage charge.

There was no doubt about it: Ace Diamond packed a tremendous charge. It travelled along her nerves to the tips of her fingers and the roots of her hair. She was very quiet as she and Vin drove back to their hotel in their hired car.

That night the local drivers turned on a superb party at a big, old farmhouse outside the town, though no one stayed very late because of the further races next day. Giulio arrived about nine o'clock, just when Vin was about to leave for the garage where they were working on the Maserati. Giulio's face was as long as its round, plump shape would allow.

'Ees no good, Vincente, amico. The clutch-plate they give us is useless. You cannot drive tomorrow!'

'God blast it! I bring the car thousands of miles across the sea, and I get to drive about three laps! It's bloody frustrating. I'm going to sell that rotten car.'

This was a threat he made whenever anything went wrong.

'I know how you feel, mate. Have a beer. Drown your sorrows.' Ace filled his glass, handed a full one to Giulio. 'Cheer up, Giulio baby. You did your best. Considering the rotten heap of junk you've got to work on. And the butcher who's driving it.'

He dodged a mock-blow from Vin, who was scowling and smiling at the same time. 'No, but seriously, Ace. Wouldn't you be mad? How would *you* feel?'

'As a matter of fact, I'm not all that keen on driving tomorrow. Met a little New Zealand chick who invited me into the country.' He winked at Giulio. 'Tell you what, King Vincent, you can drive the Alfa if you like.'

'What? You really mean it?'

'Sure I mean it. My mechanic's been over it, nothing bent

when I "went exploring" today. You can get Giulio to give it the once-over if you like.'

'I t'ink per'aps, yes.'

'OK, if you're sure you don't mind.'

'She'll be right. Tomorrow's just an exhibition.'

'Of course you know your car will be in good hands,' said Vin modestly.

With Giulio and Ace Diamond's mechanic, George, Vin now decided to go straight to the garage on the outskirts of the town where the Alfa was housed.

'You stay here, Maggie, and enjoy yourself. Give her a drink, Ace. I'll be back in about half an hour.'

Her mouth was open to protest, but Ace was putting a full beaker of red wine in her hand, while looking down at her with those eyes like chips of bright blue glass.

She drank the wine and began to feel a tingling all through her limbs, like an echo of the shock which had galvanised her that afternoon.

'You know, Franz,' she said, looking up at him, 'that was a very nice thing you did for Vin. There isn't any New Zealand girl, is there?'

'Not yet,' he grinned. 'But I'll soon find one. Give me time.'

'You gave up your car for your friend . . . He believed you, because he wanted to. I drink to: Ace, the Diamond with the heart of gold.'

She was standing before him, her head slightly tilted, her lips slightly open, when he bent his golden head and kissed her on the mouth.

'Don't ever – ever – do that again,' said Ace between his teeth.

'Do what?'

'Turn your face up at me like that! By God, if you were anyone else's wife but his – '

'What then?' Shaken though she had been, she was regaining her poise, enjoying his anger.

'It's just that I don't try to make it with my friends' girls. Does that surprise you? I do have a sort of code, you know: "Never do the dirty on a mate." '

'And what makes you think that I would co-operate? You are so used to girls falling flat before you – '

'Don't kid yourself, Maggie. I felt the vibrations. And I wasn't even trying.'

'You're a conceited beast.' She turned on her heel and left him, joining a group of wives who were discussing the biggest event of their lives, comparing notes on their experiences in labour. She was trembling. Had he been right? And where was Vin?

He soon returned, happy about the car, optimistic about tomorrow. 'Want to go, Mag? I know you're bored at these things. Wait while I have a drink, and then we'll go.'

Struck by something in her face, he examined her more closely. 'Your eyes are very bright tonight.'

'Vin, I love you. Let's go *now*.'

'All right. Just hold on a minute, I'll be back.'

He went over to the bar table, collected beer from a jug, and stopped to talk to Ace. When he had finished the beer he came over and took her elbow, but it was a long time before they made it to the door, getting involved with several groups on the way. Then they were out in the clear, warm summer night.

He handed her into the big sedan and got in. She sat as close to him as she could get. This was her own, her dearest Vincent. She ran a hand over his face, and he kissed her fingers.

They drove off. He changed gears expertly, and slipped a hand beneath her full skirt. 'I like that papery dress you're wearing. It's sort of like parchment, yet soft.'

She fell against his shoulder and kissed him, pressed her mouth to his ear. Melting with desire, she closed her thighs upon his hand. He quickly turned off into a side road, unmade, that went down to a river ford, and stopped beside the water.

'This is ridiculous,' he said, laughing a little as he started to undress her. 'When we have a perfectly good bed back at the hotel.'

'Oh please, please!' she moaned.

He lifted his mouth from hers for a moment to ask, 'Mag, is it all right? Is it safe?'

'Yes, yes, I'm wearing my "hat". Oh darling, darling, darling – '

For a moment there at the Car Club party she had desired Ace. She had responded to a fundamental biological attraction, nothing to do with love or even liking.

Now all that desire turned towards her husband; it was as if she had been separated from him for years, she could not get close enough to him, she wanted to annihilate herself, to be impaled, yes, even to the point of death. And the pang of pleasure that went through her was so sharp, so unendurably sweet, that she felt almost on the edge of dying.

Fourteen

THE DAY had dawned clear and beautiful. In Levin the pure smog-free skies were the pale translucent blue of a Morning Glory petal. The gardens of the suburban houses they passed on the way to the course were bright with flowers. Vin felt a surge of wellbeing. He was young, healthy, becoming famous, he had a lovely and warm-blooded wife, a different car to drive, in a new country.

Then, as he gunned the engine on the starting-grid, a little twinge of worry came from somewhere. *Those whom the Gods love die young*. He was too happy, too successful, too fortunate. The gods must have their envious eyes on him.

Forcing himself to think only of the present, he noted the crowd outside the Pit enclosure, the officials inside with their badges, the flag-marshals at the next corner, the starter with his flag at the ready. There was a good crowd even though the main races were yesterday, and half today's events were motor-cycle races. It gave him pleasure to know that he was one of the main drawcards. And no doubt, unacknowledged at the back of their minds, was the fearful hope of seeing him killed, or at least involved in a spectacular shunt.

They were off! Vin tried to navigate his way through a solid group of slower cars which had been ahead of him on handicap. They even had stock cars, ordinary sedans, in the race. It was a real butchers' picnic.

He was through the first bunch and hurtling down the second long straight on to a group of three cars still holding their original positions. He picked off one . . . two . . . and the third, just in time for a last-minute braking before the next corner. The crowd cheered. It had been nicely judged. He had gambled on the Alfa's brakes being as good as his own.

He settled down to a steady circling, the car running as if on rails. He was not going to over-extend himself. If the car didn't break down, if he didn't have to come in for a tyre-change, and if he could once get past the New Zealander Special, he had it made. He would nurse the car for the first dozen laps, and then go all out after the Mackintosh Special. It had been behind him on handicap, but had got ahead during the congestion at the start.

Levin was not much more than a country town in a remote corner of the Pacific. The meeting was casually run, spectators allowed to crowd on the corners, and yesterday, Ace said, he had actually seen a woman pushing a perambulator across the track in the middle of a race! Vin looked toward better things: the Monaco Grand Prix, round-the-houses high above the Mediterranean and then down again; himself in a 3-litre Ferrari V-12 developing 360 HP at 10,000 rpm – ah yes! Hairpins and right-angle bends, with a curving tunnel and then a drop below the wall into the sea. Up the hill and down again, about fifteen hundred gear changes to a race . . .

Or the Nurburgring among the pine-forests of Germany. The War had stopped motor sport, but it was picking up again in Europe. Winding round the Eidel Mountain – said to be a killer in the rain – fourteen miles of narrow, twisting road, fifteen laps meant 2,500 corners. Now *that* would be a challenge.

While part of his mind was day-dreaming thus, all his senses were alert to the instruments before him, the cars behind reflected in his mirror, the wheels tramping up and down in front. His eyes flicked continually from one to the other, keeping count of where he was, which corner was coming up, the exact speed at which to take it, the exact spot where he must brake if he was to get round.

Suddenly his grey eyes, narrowed behind their plastic visor – he had A-one vision at his last test – flew wide with horror. They stared at the front of the car, where the coil suspension was, and where the nut on the Panhard bar holding all together was quietly coming loose. He could see it. He could do nothing about it. He could not even brake suddenly without two cars cannoning into him from behind.

Oh God! A corner was coming up.

As the rear wheels began to take up their line to the right, he gently brought the wheel to dead centre – and suddenly it was gone, he had lost it. He had no control anymore. He snapped the wheel hard to the right, but it had no effect whatever. The car headed off the track, straight into a crowd of spectators.

His foot jammed on the brake; he felt the thud, the jolt, a whole series of thuds. Then there was the screaming. His eyes were wide open, staring in shock but seeing nothing, except a blur of running figures. He heard nothing but the screams, echoed by the scream of the ambulance siren, the wail of a police car. He sat motionless, gripping the wheel, his knuckles white. When someone, a track marshal, came to help him out, he had to prise Vin's fingers from the steering-wheel where they were locked.

The car had its nose buried in the earth, but was still right way up. He climbed out. He pointed a trembling arm at the bent front of the car. 'Panhard bar went. No steering.' And then he saw the blood. He took one step forward, and fainted.

'Maggie, it wasn't my fault! Tell them it wasn't my fault! The steering went.'

'Yes, yes, dear. They know. There'll have to be an inquest but it will clear you completely.'

She had to soothe him, over and over again, like a fractious child. He was lying in the hotel room with the blinds drawn, his mind half-sedated by the injection the doctor had given him.

'But there weren't any children, were there? Tell me there weren't any children.'

'No. You must stop worrying.' But there had been a little

girl, sitting on her father's shoulders to watch the pretty coloured cars, like wind-up toys, go flashing past. Then suddenly one of them had become huge, real, terrible, a red monster that knocked her father from beneath her, breaking both his legs, and threw her to the ground. She was in hospital with concussion.

'There was a man about fifty,' said Vin feverishly. 'He looked like my father. He was straight in front of me when I left the track.'

'Stop going over it, darling. It was not your fault! There was nothing you could have done. Ace is badly upset, he feels it was his fault, that the car wasn't prepared properly. And Giulio, too – though it wasn't his responsibility.'

'No; the responsibility was mine. I chose to drive, though my car was out of action. I shouldn't have been in the race at all. And just at the start, I had this feeling that I was going to be punished.' He rolled his head restlessly on the pillow. The doctor said he was in shock and must be kept quiet, but he went on rapidly: 'It wouldn't be so bad, somehow, if I was injured myself. But I got off Scot-free, and two people are dead.'

So far, thought Maggie. And seven injured.

She said, 'Vin! I'm going to get you a warm drink now, and then I'll leave you by yourself to rest. You must stop talking and let the injection work. You're suffering from shock, both physical and mental; you didn't get off Scot-free. Does your head ache?'

'Yes . . . No . . . A bit. What does it matter?' He glared at her with dilated pupils. 'Maggie, you've got to stick by me. There's just one good thing, they've got movie film of what happened. There was a cameraman on that corner, and it will prove I wasn't to blame. I wasn't going too fast, I wasn't trying to pass someone, I went into the corner correctly. The steering went. There was nothing I could do, nothing – '

'Yes, dear, you've been over all that with the police. There'll be no claims or court cases. The two – the men who died were covered by life insurance. The injured took a risk in attending a dangerous sport, just as you took a risk in driving.'

'I still would rather I had been killed.'

'Don't say that!'

After he had drunk the hot Milo she brought him, she took away one of the pillows and made him lie flat. She could not bear to look at his face. It looked . . . ravaged was the word. Or haunted.

Maggie returned to the sitting-room of their small suite and looked again at the front page of the morning paper, which she had folded small and hidden under some books. The Wellington Press was not friendly to the two Australian drivers, one of whom had imported the lethal car while the other had driven it. Neither of their cars had put up a performance to justify their coming anyway.

RACE CAR SLAMS INTO CROWD

The heading was brutally succinct. Then blurry photos of panicking people, mouths open, hands and arms raised to ward off disaster. As if flesh and bone could stop an eighty-mile-an-hour projectile of heavy metal.

> Pictured is some of the crowd at the corner where visiting Australian driver Vincent King's racing car left the track at Levin, mowing down a dozen spectators in its path. Two men died, and seven are in hospital with injuries, including a woman who is on the critically ill list. Names of the dead men have not been released until relatives are notified. The driver was treated for shock and abrasions, but was not seriously injured.

On an inside page was the story of the disaster, recounting the failure of King's car in the Tasman Cup race, and the subsequent taking over of his compatriot's Alfa-Romeo, a car he was not used to, in which he'd had only two practice runs, and which had apparently developed a fault in the steering halfway through the race.

Maggie skipped the description of the injured, the interviews with eye-witnesses. The article ended with a rhetorical question, 'Should this dangerous sport be banned, or at least controlled so that spectators are not allowed near the track?'

She tore the pages up small and flushed them down the lavatory. He was going to have to face the publicity, the coroner's inquest, the formal inquiry by FISA, the International Federation of motor sport. But she would shield him as long as she could. She peeped into the bedroom and saw that he was asleep at last.

Some time later she was dozing in an armchair – she was emotionally exhausted herself, and neither of them had slept much last night, even though Vin was sedated – when a groan and a muffled cry came from the bedroom. She sprang up and went to him, but he was still asleep. He flung himself on his side, his face buried in his arm. 'I'm sorry, Dad! I'm sorry!' he muttered.

Vin was so unwell for nearly six weeks after the crash that Maggie scarcely left his side. He had begun sleep-walking at night, as well as suffering from insomnia. He had no appetite, but Maggie tempted him with childish foods, things he had once told her his mother used to give him when he was sick: bread and hot milk with sugar, coddled egg in a cup with fresh breadcrumbs, an orange with a hole cut in the skin so that the contents could be scraped out with a teaspoon. They were all, Maggie noticed, able to be eaten with one hand, and a small spoon, like baby food: no mastery of the adult knife and fork was needed.

Vin had sold the Maserati in New Zealand for a good price, as it was the only car of its type in those parts. Ace would not let him pay for the damage to the Alfa. Vin announced his retirement from racing on his return to Australia. For a while poison-pen letters pursued him, and he scarcely left the house.

Then one day Maggie found him looking at a *Cars & Drivers* magazine in which a nearly new Ferrari was advertised.

'I know I said I'd given it up,' said Vin, 'but once the game has become your life, you can't give it up. You might as well be dead. I'm going to make an offer for this Ferrari here, and if I get it – . When I'm slowing down will be time enough to retire.'

'A Ferrari! But can we afford it?'

(She hadn't told him about the baby yet. She had suspected

her condition for some time, but had only just had it confirmed by her doctor. She had not wanted to worry Vin with the news in his depressed state, not being sure how he would take it. For herself, she was delighted.)

Vin smiled airily. 'Afford it? My dear girl, when I am World Champion we will live like millionaires. Only the best hotels for us, in the biggest cities in Europe. And besides – '

He sorted out the mail that had come with the magazine. There was an Annual Report from Australian Gold Development NL, and it was very promising.

'They've taken an option over Noble's Nob at Tennant Creek in the Northern Territory, and it's said to be very rich. The first exploratory shaft found ore averaging fifty to sixty ounces to the ton. That's phenomenal, though of course it might peter out. But at least we'll get some dividends from my gamble. They're going to purchase the mine and go all out for production.'

'So the shares will give us an income?'

'Yes; or we could sell them again and make a nice profit when the news of this report hits the share market.'

'Well then, you go ahead and buy the Ferrari, darling, if that will make you happy. I wouldn't want you not to go back to racing just because we're going to have a baby.'

'A baby!' He stared at her. 'When, for God's sake?'

'Not for a long time yet. About November.'

'But – but – ' He looked more bewildered than pleased. 'How did it happen? We've always taken precautions.'

'I think that night in the car, in New Zealand. I *was* wearing my diaphragm, but it must have slipped during the struggle in the front seat.' She stared at him uneasily, 'Oh Vin! Aren't you just a little bit pleased?'

'A baby! Hell, I don't know. I can't get used to the idea of being a father.' He smiled suddenly. 'Perhaps Mother will come round, and ask to see her grandson. Do you know what the family lawyer told me? She's decided to leave her money to a cats' home! To provide a home for Zircon after she dies, with his own private room. She's become quite dotty about that cat, apparently.'

But Maggie, remembering his mother, did not think she would 'come round'.

'I must get myself established with one of the *Écuries*. Must leave a name for my son,' he said, warming to the idea.

'Except that it might be a daughter.'

'Well, we'll have a son next time then. But for Christ's sake don't go and have twins.'

His reaction, not wildly enthusiastic, was much what she had expected, and at least he seemed more like his old self.

Fifteen

VINCENT KING was preparing for a race at the Calder Raceway with the new car tuned to perfection and already on the trailer, when a long-distance call came from Adelaide. Cousin Arthur King told him that Rosetta had had a slight stroke and was asking to see him.

Vin was both shocked at the news, and impatient. Why should this happen now, just when he was planning to make his comeback? His mother had refused to see him all this time, had not replied to his Christmas card, or written about the Levin disaster, of which she must have heard. Now that she was sick she wanted him. Well, she could wait another day. He was not going to give up the race. He heard himself saying, 'Sorry, Arthur, but I can't get away before tomorrow. I'll be there tomorrow night.'

He thrust the thought of his mother, and of his impending fatherhood, into the back of his mind for the duration of the race next day. It was the first time he had driven since Levin, nearly four months ago. Everyone would be watching to see if his nerve had gone. But he drove a perfect race, without a single mistake; cornered faster than any of the other cars, scored the fastest time of the day, and came in an easy winner. No, he was not ready to retire yet!

Late in the afternoon, tired but exhilarated, he relaxed completely while Maggie drove him to the airport. His mother was not seriously ill, and he would be able to give her the news of her coming grandchild. He had sent a wire and was met by the second cousin ('hoping he'll be left something by the old girl, I bet,' thought Vin) and his wife. Their faces were long and serious. Rosetta had suffered a second stroke, and it was thought she would never speak again.

Vin was overwhelmed by guilt. And yet, given the chance, he knew he would do the same thing again.

At first he thought his mother did not seem much changed. She was still a big, high-coloured woman, but as he bent over the bed to kiss her he saw that the side of her face away from him was drawn down: the corner of her mouth and her eye sagging strangely, giving her a sardonic look. He took her hand, and said brightly, 'I came as soon as I could, when I heard you were ill.'

She closed her eyes for a moment.

'Would you like me to get you anything? I couldn't find any flowers at the airport.' He was floundering. He hated sick-rooms. The eyes closed again, more emphatically.

'You're going to have a grandson,' he said. 'In about five months' time.'

Her brows lifted, her good eye opened wider.

'Would you like us to bring him to see you?'

At first he thought she had not heard. Then her eyes closed in rejection.

You obstinate old devil, he thought. We'll bring him, just the same. You'd like to see him, but not 'us,' not Maggie. Well, you'll just have to accept the mother of my child.

It was terribly hard keeping up a one-sided conversation, especially with that sardonic gaze bent upon him. Rosetta had had such a strong voice; it had been part of her forceful personality. It was a relief when he could get away and fly back to Sydney, after making arrangements for her to be nursed at home. He saw the doctor, who held out little hope for a recovery of 'normal functions'. The end would be a third and final stroke, but she might live for some years.

All thought of retiring forgotten, Vincent King went on to win the Australian Grand Prix in record time at Southport,

Queensland. Driving his new Ferrari, he also broke the lap record and cleaned up the field at Phillip Island. He now had enough silver cups to melt into an ingot.

The last race for the season was at the Mount Panorama circuit at Bathurst, west of Sydney. Once more Maggie polished brake drums and hovered on the outer edge of the male circle of camaraderie.

The men might have been talking a foreign language: 'Too much understeer . . . Tim says a lighter roll-bar would fix it . . . Now you don't have to get up in the middle of the night, Vin, to make sure the camshaft cover nuts are done up . . . We don't want any of your "Demon Mods" at the last moment, Giulio . . .'

Vin had asked them to change the gear ratio for the mountain circuit, and to set up the shock absorbers so the car wouldn't bottom on that bump before the Conrod corner. All flexible joints of the steering and suspension had been gone over with a fine-tooth comb; throttle linkages had been tightened, wheel-bearings checked.

'The forecast say rain, *piove alla matina*,' said Giulio. 'What-a you t'ink, Vin, we fit wet-weather treads?'

'No, they'll slow me up too much if it doesn't rain. You know they always get the forecasts back to front.'

'Okay.'

At last all was ready. The spare gears were packed into the battered tin trunk, everything was tidied away in the van and the car was polished of finger-marks. Vin drove Maggie back to the Canobolas Hotel, less noisy than the Railway Inn in Bathurst. He had a warm, relaxing bath, but he slept badly. Towards morning he dreamt of his father, a vivid but confused dream. Stanley King was shaking his head reprovingly: 'It's no use saying you're sorry.' – 'But what have I done?' asked Vin. – 'Your mother will never get over it, and now it's too late – too late – too late.'

Vin awoke sweating. He put an arm around Maggie, breathing peacefully at his side, and drifted off to sleep once more. He woke feeling he'd not had enough sleep, but forced himself to get up and look out the window. The sky was grey and threatening, the air felt warm, humid.

'Damn! Looks as if it might rain . . . P'raps I should have let

Giulio change the tyres, No, I'll risk it, it mightn't rain before tonight.'

'You will be careful today, darling?' said Maggie from the bed. 'Remember there'll be another mouth to feed soon.'

'I'm always careful,' said Vin, but he turned away and went to the bathroom. He didn't want to be reminded of the baby just now. Once *he* had been just such a promise of future life, six months in the womb, and what a blessing he had turned out to be! People longed for children, couldn't wait to perpetuate themselves, but how often did they turn out to be disappointments or worse? Vin felt that he had been nothing but a worry to his own father, a disappointment to his mother . . . He remembered his dream of last night, or half-remembered it: some kind of reproof or warning.

His spirits rose as always at the stimulating atmosphere of the circuit. The air had a breath of dampness; the clouds looked low enough to touch. The tinny blare of canned music, the spine-tingling note of engines screaming at the top of their bent – he absorbed it all like a drug as he shrugged on his overalls, pulled on the gold helmet and the gloves of battle.

He would not wear the woollen long johns today for fire protection; it got too hot in the cockpit of the car on a long race. He had no intention of crashing. He liked the mountain circuit with its sweeping bends, though it could be frightening at first, with its downhill straight and the terrifying corner which you came on blind, over a rise. At the end of Conrod Straight this downhill bend lay in wait, and the bumps in the surface meant that the car was often airborne as it reached the corner. You then had to brake the moment the wheels touched down, or you'd never get round.

Soon after his race began, it started to rain. On the next lap Giulio held up a signal that he should come in for a tyre change. He ignored it. Be damned to that! He was not going to lose his lead now.

Maggie, watching from the pits, was excited by the Roman Holiday atmosphere, but her spine was tense with anxiety. She felt, just because he was so dear to her and the father of her unborn child, that he was threatened. She would not dream of trying to make him give up racing, but the feeling of dread never left her entirely.

When it happened it was as if she had known, as if the scene had all been played out before. She did not see it; there was just this sudden break in the announcer's smooth patter, then his voice rising on a note of excitement, almost hysteria; the flag-marshalls slowing down the field, leaping out to wave their flags.

Up the hill, against the blue sky, a sullen column of black smoke rose and billowed in the air.

'. . . Yes, it's the Vincent King Ferrari, he has left the circuit and gone over the side into the trees. More fire extinguishers are needed, please.' His voice was drowned in the wail of the ambulance siren, the police car's note.

Maggie clutched Giulio's arm, her nails dug into the flesh below his rolled-up sleeve.

'Ees all-a-right, Signora. *Pian' piano*, ees nothing, *niente*. Vincente will be all-a-right.' He kept up his soothing patter while gently unclenching her fingers. Then he caught her as she swayed and fell. Someone brought water in a paper cup. Giulio set off at a run up the hill, towards the fire.

He struggled out of a nightmare in which he had picked up a Stonefish, and the burning pain of the deadly spines pierced his hands. Hateful creature! Looking into its cavernous eye-sockets, its sickly yellow mouth, he knew he was looking at Death.

'. . . Can you hear me, Vin?' It was Maggie, bending over the bed, her long dark hair falling in her eyes. He nodded. It was somehow too much effort to talk. The pain in his hands was real. He lifted them and saw they were swathed in bandages.

'Did I – crash? What happened? The car – '

'Burnt. There was only a shell left.'

He wasn't sure where they were. New Zealand? And all those people he had knocked down must be somewhere in this hospital. Burning. Burning burning burning. He remembered the flames, his overalls on fire. He had rolled on the grass, trying to beat out the flames with his hands. His throat felt burnt inside; he must have inhaled smoke and super-heated air.

'I – think,' said Vin, 'I would like – a beer.'

Someone moved towards the door. Ace. 'Right, I'll get you one, old chap. A Coopers?'

He was gone. Giulio moved into Vin's limited field of vision, from beyond the blur of bandages which surrounded his eyes like white blinkers. Was everyone here to take farewell of him, then?

'Vincente!' Giulio's lips trembled. He was too upset, apparently, to say more.

'Giulio! *Addio, amico mio. Moraturi, te salutamus.* Latin. It's –'

'Vin, hush darling. Don't try to talk.'

Little Mother Mag, treating him like a child. But she was crying. There were tears in her big brown eyes.

'Don't cry, Maggie. And – tell our son – from me –'

'We'll call him Forbes; Vincent is an unlucky name. But I think Joseph Forbes King –'

'M – Mother'll like – that.'

'She'll never know.'

'Promise me, Maggie. Promise – you'll take him – see her.'

She'd have promised him anything just then.

Ace Diamond came back with a bottle of beer, pulled off the top, and poured a glass for Vin. She held it for him while he sipped through a straw. Ace stood staring at his friend, absent-mindedly tearing the beer-bottle cap in half. He had enormously strong hands.

'Thanks . . . mate.' Vin swallowed with difficulty through his seared throat. His lungs hurt damnably. He gave a small sigh. 'Aah. That was good.'

His eyes closed, but not in sleep. They rolled up in his head so that only the whites showed below the lowered lids. His breath came in shallow gasps. 'It seems a pity – ' he whispered, and said no more.

'Vin! Oh Vin!' wailed Maggie. She reflected that a dying man did not make memorable statements or profound remarks about the hereafter. No. He said something simple and human, like 'I think I'd like a beer,' or 'It seems a pity.'

541

From the *Sydney Morning Herald*, August 9, 1949:

'It is one of the most dangerous, and most fascinating sports ever devised by man.' This was how Vince King once described motor racing, the sport to which he was dedicated and which has now claimed his life.

King's tragic death at Mt Panorama Circuit near Bathurst came just when he had fought back to the top after the serious accident in New Zealand earlier this year, which resulted in the death of three people, and which almost made King give up the sport – though he was exonerated from all blame. He was unquestionably the finest driver in Australia. His death has stunned Australians who only two months ago were hailing him as winner of the Australian Grand Prix, and the true champion that he was.

Vincent King tackled every race and every practice session with a great deal of seriousness, but out of the cockpit he could be an amusing companion and he was popular with his mechanics and pit crew.

He is survived by his wife and his widowed mother, Mrs Stanley King of Kensington, South Australia.

From the Melbourne *Sun*, August 10:

Did Vincent King, Australia's ace racing driver, die at Mt Panorama circuit because he was using inadequate tyres for the rain-wet surface?

The motor racing world ponders this question today as it mourns the slim, tall young driver who died of burns and shock twelve hours after his car left the track and hit a tree, bursting into flames. King had third-degree burns to most of his body, and possible internal injuries. It was estimated that the car was doing about 150 mph at the time. No other car was near him as King's Ferrari swerved off the track. Franz Diamond, fellow driver and friend of the dead man, said:

'So far as I can see, Vin's car went off in the straight, where it would appear that driver error could not come into it. The crash was unbelievable. There seems no reason for it, unless he went to sleep.'

Chief mechanic Giulio Selmi said he felt some mechanical defect must have developed, though the car had been most carefully prepared and he could not think what it could be. Track officials said the car was so badly damaged and gutted by fire that the cause of the accident would never be known.

It is believed that Vincent King's young widow is expecting their first child.

Sixteen

MAGGIE DID not attend the funeral. Instead of flowers, she had ordered a victor's wreath of laurel leaves, such as she had often seen placed round his shoulders. In the same hospital from which they had taken his body for burial, she lay in a bed with a raised foot, for she had started haemorrhaging the night before, and the doctor feared a miscarriage. He gave her an injection and told her to stay absolutely quiet.

Maggie did as she was bid. She was determined not to lose this baby, which was all she had left of Vin. She carried within her, in every cell of the growing foetus, some part of his body. *Joseph Forbes King*, she addressed her unborn son (for she knew it would be a boy), the world is a sad and dangerous place. Don't try to come into it too early, stay where you are safe a little longer.

> Baby, wait a little longer
> Till the little limbs are stronger,
> When his little limbs are stronger
> Baby too shall fly away.

A scrap from some book they'd had at the Mission school when she was learning to read. Her mind was a rag-bag of such scraps:

In the fell clutch of circumstance,
I have not winced nor cried aloud;
Beneath the bludgeonings of chance
My head is bloody but unbowed . . .

That was no comfort to her. Vin was dead, whether bludgeoned by Chance, or Fate, or half-unconscious choice. But he should not have died yet, not so young, not without seeing his son.

She knew that Giulio did not believe there was anything wrong with the car mechanically. She knew that Ace believed Vin had deliberately pulled the car out of line, in the middle of a straight where there were no spectators to be hurt, and no other drivers near; in some momentary aberration, some need to dare himself to do it, like a man playing Russian roulette. (Or a man burdened by unbearable guilt, who felt a need to punish himself?)

Maggie could not let herself believe this. She knew, better than anyone, of the melancholia he had fallen into after the New Zealand crash, the guilt-haunted nightmares, the dreams of punishment and atonement, the desperate self-justifications. It was an old guilt, going back perhaps to the time of his father's death. But to believe that he had *wanted* to die, that he had deliberately turned the wheel a fraction too far – no, she could not bear to think that. It would mean that he was willing to leave her and their future child, to condemn her to living alone. Perhaps he thought his mother would provide for the baby? Then she remembered the gold-mining shares. So he knew they would have something to live on.

She lay quiet, turning and turning the two-headed snake of silver on her wrist, where oxidation had made a grey mark. She had believed in the charm; she never took it off her wrist, and much good it had done! Well, perhaps it was a woman's charm for childbirth. She decided to keep on wearing it.

She would have liked to go and see Vin's grandmother, but Elaine, though she was seventy-five, had gone off on a sea voyage in a ship calling at several Indian ports on the way to England, where she was now staying with her Hamilton cousins.

Maggie had written to tell Marie and Nyora that she was a

widow, though Marie would probably have read about it in the paper. Now her sister wrote urging her to come to Rockhampton and have the baby at the local hospital, where she would be able to visit her, and there was no longer a 'black ward' for Aboriginal mothers.

'Things have improved a bit,' she wrote. 'Why not come and stay with me until the birth? You've always wanted to come home to lick your wounds, and later you could go out to the Island. I don't think you should stay alone in that empty flat. Billy has long leave coming up, and we're going for a trip, camping in the car. You and baby can have the house to yourselves for a couple of months.'

Maggie decided to accept Marie's invitation.

It would save rent, and besides she hated the flat with its memories. The full shock hit her when she returned, once past the danger of miscarriage, and began to pack Vin's clothes for the Salvation Army. His trophies – useless things, most of them – she took to a second-hand dealer, apart from a few important cups and medallions, which his son might like to have. But she felt too apathetic to pack her own things and leave for Queensland.

Sometimes she took the ferry from Manly and went across the Harbour to Circular Quay, just for the ride. She was never seasick, though the old South Steyne rolled in the Pacific swell coming past the Heads where the big liners passed out to the open sea.

She shrank from the well-meant sympathy of friends and acquaintances, wanting only to be alone, brooding over the past and her coming motherhood. There was a flood of sympathy cards and letters to be dealt with, many of them from people Vin had never known. And one postmarked Levin, containing a single line, unsigned: '*Now perhaps you know what it is like.*'

A bill from the undertaker, from the crematorium, from the florist, from the ambulance, from the doctor – oh God, would it never be done? And then a large, buff-coloured envelope arrived. She opened it.

'Notice of DEATH', it said in big, black, official type. Then she really believed it. It was like a blow against her heart. Vincent Forbes King, mother's maiden name Rosetta Forbes, father's name Stanley Macdonald King, wife née Agnes Pinjarra, was dead. A large red seal confirmed the fact.

Then there were the lawyers, and something called Probate, and the Will that left everything to her. She had to pay death duties on the gold shares. Everything else, except for a thousand dollars in Vin's bank account, had gone up in smoke with the Ferrari.

She packed up her things and left for Queensland to wait for the birth of Vincent's son.

It was a normal birth in every way, an easy birth as first babies go, but mother and child were both exhausted by it. Maggie caught a glimpse of two tiny, clenched fists and a face almost purple with rage as her son screamed his protest at being born. When she was able to take a good look at him next day, she began to laugh.

He was brought to her, still asleep, in a tight white bundle with a head protruding from it. She undid the bundle and examined this fascinating, new, living toy. His skin was dark yellow-brown, his eyebrows were marked as with the finest of brushes with Indian ink, and his little scalp, still frail with the fontanelle not yet closed, was covered with a film of tight, kinky red curls. Some gene persisting from great-great-grandfather Joseph Tula had reappeared in this scrap of humanity after skipping a generation.

Maggie laughed because she had promised Vincent to take him to see his grandmother. This would set Mrs King back on her heels! Then she wept, because his father would never see him.

She remembered that Vin's mother was possibly still bedridden from her stroke, perhaps was not even aware of her son's death. He had died for her years ago, anyway, when she altered her Will in favour of Zircon. Flowers had come from her, according to the florists' cards, but some friend or relation could have organised that. Flowers had come from nearly every State, from the Sporting Car Clubs and the Federation of Motor Sport.

Maggie wondered if, had Vin gone to see his mother that time before she had the second stroke, they might have been reconciled? Too late now. Well, good luck to Zircon! He would be the most pampered cat in the country when his mistress died.

BOOK FIVE

The Budding Leaf

1949–1969

Into this Universe, and *why* not knowing,
Nor *whence*, like Water willy-nilly flowing:
And out of it, as Wind along the Waste,
I know not *whither*, willy-nilly blowing.

Omar Khayyám, *The Rubáiyát*

One

On October 23, 1949, when Joseph Forbes King became a separate entity and drew his first breath, he was still linked cell by cell, generation by generation, to the beginnings of human life on earth. Though his father Vincent King was already dead, he lived on in every cell of his son's body. In terms of chance, Joe was very lucky to be alive. The chances of the sperm cell carrying his particular genes, fertilising the ripe egg which held his mother's heredity in its chromosomes, were about three million to one.

Maggie King had come back to coastal Queensland to have her baby. She wanted to be near her people, the Pinjarras and the Efates. They would never see one of their people, especially a relative, without a home while they had a roof over their own heads. Maggie knew she could stay indefinitely with her sister Marie, who had married her much older cousin Billy Efate, part-Aboriginal and part-Islander. He had come back a hero from the First World War, for which he had enlisted at the age of seventeen by lying about his age. He still kept the yellowed newspaper cuttings of 1919, the photograph in the local newspaper with the caption, 'Lance-Corporal Efate with his Distinguished Service Medal'. As a result of his career as a soldier he was accepted in the town, could drink with his white mates in the hotel bars and at the RSL Club.

He had a job on the Railways which took him away from home a lot, but being more than twenty years older than Marie he would be retiring soon, and Maggie planned then to move on to Townsville. There was, she hoped, less prejudice than in the old days about coloured girls working in offices. Meanwhile she stayed with Marie in Rockhampton, with visits to Pandanus Island in Keppel Bay where she was born.

Maggie had promised Vincent on his deathbed that she would take the baby to see old Mrs King. She dreaded the interview with Vin's mother, even if she was now helpless from her stroke; the older woman's dislike and disapproval had been so pronounced. But when Joe was six months old, she made the long flight to Adelaide and took a taxi out to the home in the suburbs where Mrs King still lived, looked after by a semi-trained nurse.

'Mrs King . . . Mrs King Junior has brought your grandson to see you,' said the nurse as Maggie waited. Rosetta King opened her eyes wide, the only part of her body that retained any movement, and turned them towards the door. She was still a big, imposing woman, even in her helpless state. She lay propped on pillows, motionless as a statue, so that she resembled a carving of some knight's lady on a mediaeval tomb, with her strong-boned face and aristocratic nose. The Siamese cat, Zircon, lay curled asleep at her feet.

As she came up to the bed, Maggie felt an emotion she had not expected: pity. All that pride and arrogance to be brought so low!

Rosetta King could neither speak nor write, but conveyed her wishes by opening and closing her eyes. Maggie touched the inert hand lying outside the coverlet.

'I called him Joseph,' she said. 'Joseph Forbes King. It was what Vin wanted. He said you would be pleased.'

Perhaps Mrs King was expecting to see somehow a replica of her son, with his neat, narrow head and straight brown hair and grey eyes; or perhaps even of her husband Stanley. But the only feature Joe seemed to have inherited from his father was a pair of slanting, flyaway eyebrows, so finely pencilled as yet as to be almost invisible.

Maggie presented the gurgling bundle of energy that was Vincent's son. Mrs King's eyes grew wide; she stared at the baby's curling cap of red hair, his bright black eyes, the delicately-brown face of her only grandson. Then she firmly closed her eyes and kept them closed.

She might have been asleep, or dead. Her iron-grey hair was set in corrugated waves; her face was set in a motionless mask, surprisingly smooth and unlined. The nurse spoke, touched her hand.

'Look, Mrs King – your grandson is just six months old, isn't he a bonnie babe? Look – he's smiling! Such a sunny-natured child!'

The heavy eyelids flickered, showing that she heard, but the eyes remained obstinately closed, the mouth set in its permanent twist which gave a sardonic expression to her face.

Maggie, who had set the baby down on the bed by his grandmother, picked him up again and turned away. The older woman's rejection was complete. Obviously she would not alter her Will in Joe's favour, if that was what Vin had hoped – even if she became physically capable of it. Maggie wondered, if Vin had outlived his mother, whether he might not have contested a Will that left everything to a cat?

As she carried Joe down the veranda steps, she told herself that she had expected no more of the meeting. She knew too well Rosetta King's implacable hostility, and lying brooding in bed she must have nursed it further. No doubt she blamed Maggie for her son's death, for the fact that Vin had not come to see her after the first stroke, even for the baby's red hair – though that was clearly from Vin's side of the family, from the Macdonalds. It was not the colour that would have upset Mrs King, but the tight frizzy curls of his great-great-grandfather Joseph Tula Efate, kidnapped from the Loyalty Islands and brought to Australia to work in the sugar plantations, eighty years ago.

The funny thing was that Vin's mother (if she was able to understand since her stroke) would believe that Joe was called after *her* father, Joseph Macdonald Forbes great-grandson of the pioneer Fergus Macdonald of Rothsay Station.

Maggie thought how strange it was that this little scrap of life, her son, had inherited something of all those adventurous ancestors, besides the Island warriors and headhunters, the tribal nomads and the nomad tribe of shearers and cane-cutters on her mother's side, the Browns, Efates and Pinjarras. It would be surprising if he grew up to live a settled, humdrum existence in the suburbs. And out west were all those rich Macdonald squatters, or graziers as they preferred to be called, who were his relatives too.

Not that she had any intention of appealing to them for financial help in bringing up her son. Equally she did not intend him to grow up in the closed world of Pandanus Island as she had done, surrounded by dark-skinned relatives and scared of white people as she had been as a child. There was enough income from Vin's investment in gold shares to make her ineligible for the widow's pension, even though his expensive racing car had been a total write-off, and she should be able to get a job with the secretarial experience she had gained in the South.

Before he was two, she took Joe for a long visit to dear wise old Grannie Nyora and Uncle Morgan and Aunt Elsie on Pandanus.

When Nyora first saw Joe she had laughed aloud.

'Ho, little carrot-top,' said Nyora, gathering him in her arms. 'I know where he get them curls, from his great-great-grandpappy Joseph Efate. You must of knowed when you named him, girl.'

'No, I chose his name before he was born.'

'So, what if he turn out to be a girl? And red! I dunno where he get that colour.'

'Vin's grandmother Elaine has red hair. Her great-grandfather was Scottish.'

'So was Anna's, too! Your Auntie Ellen never tell you that? He was, you know, mittonary, an' Joseph marry his daughter.'

'That's right! She's got an old clock he was supposed to have brought with him from Scotland.'

Maggie walked to the island graveyard with Joe, who refused to be carried but, leaning forward for balance on his two-year-old legs, sturdily climbed the gentle slope of the green headland to the place where Miguel, Nyora's husband, had the oldest grave. Beside him lay Violet, the little daughter who had died of measles, and Bert and Anna side by side.

'Your grandma and grandpa are under there,' she told Joe, as she sank down on the sandy soil among the tussocky wind-bent grasses. 'Albert and Anna, who both died young: my Mummy and Daddy.'

Joe staggered over the uneven soil and clasped an upright gravestone for balance. His little chubby dimpled hands traced the letters cut in the stone. For him words were still a mystery, sounds that issued from his mother's lips, only some of them with meaning: 'Good boy!' and 'No!' and 'Who's my

Joe?' and 'Mummy' . . . but 'Daddy' meant nothing. There was no one in his life who represented that sound.

He could not yet read the legend cut in the stone:

In Loving Memory of
ALBERT
husband of Anna, and
youngest son of
Miguel & Nyora Pinjarra.
Drowned at Sea
During the Cyclone of 1927.
Aged 28 years.

and of

ANNA,
Widow of the Above,
Died October 9, 1932,
Aged 27 years
— At Rest —

The grave of Miguel Pinjarra, Portuguese sailor, was older and the stone was worn by sea-winds, but his age when he died was still legible; he had lived as long as the two young people put together, or fifty-five years.

The baby boy was slapping the stone of his grandmother's grave approvingly, crooning to himself. The sun shone on his bright red curls, turning them to fiery gold. Yet he did not have the pale eyelashes and freckled skin that went so often with that colour hair. Maggie looked lovingly at his pale brown flawless skin and the bright black eyes which laughed at her as he turned his head over his shoulder. Behind and below him the sea made a backdrop of brilliant turquoise.

While the sea-breeze gently lifted her hair and the sun shone warmly on the back of her neck, Maggie had an odd feeling of timelessness. It was a moment of heightened consciousness such as she experienced at rare intervals, when the moment hung suspended, imbued with a strange significance. Then, almost with an audible click, the cogs and wheels engaged and time moved on once more.

In that moment she had seemed to see all the ancestors and progenitors of this one small boy, stretching in an endless chain into the past, one behind the other: their human links becoming smaller as they receded into the distance of space and time. A Scottish great-great-great-grandfather had given him his red hair; his Irish, Portuguese or Aboriginal and Island ancestors had provided some of the dominant genes which produced his bright black eyes; the fine slanting eyebrows had come through Elaine and Hamilton Forbes from a great-great-great-grandmother, had Maggie known it, called Betsy Hume, and his tight cap of curls from some unknown cannibal on the Loyalty Islands, who had begotten Tula Efate a hundred years ago.

And, most precious to her, he had his father's long bones and narrow feet and slanting brows: he was Vincent's son, even if old Mrs King was too obstinate to see it.

Frail bud on the ever-branching tree of life, he was the living link between past and future. And if he died without issue? Then this would be the end of the chain, the snapped-off twig . . . Since old Sam King had only one son that survived, and of William's four boys all but one had died young, Joe King was the last of his line.

Maggie picked Joe up and hugged him. He struggled impatiently to get back on the ground. There was another of those nice warm upright stones over there, just the right height for holding on to. Maggie laughed and let him go. Beyond the headland, the waves of the long, slow swell progressed towards the mainland, and time moved on once more.

Though her book, *Stories of Uncle Morgan* was still selling, Maggie had done no new writing since Vin died. It had been like a 'lost weekend' that lasted for two years. Now she felt the old creative urge start up again, rusty and creaking, tingling in her fingers; the island always made her want to write. The sharp sense of loss had become dulled. Was it possible that she would forget? Not the fact of her loss, which was ever-present, but *what* she had lost. Not reconciled, but simply unable to recall how it had been? That would be unbearable, a double loss. Fiercely she clung to her memories, taking them out and polishing them one by one.

And she had Joe as the living proof that it had not all been a dream. At first she had vivid dreams of Vincent, dreams in which he was never a ghostly figure, but in which, though she knew he was dead, his presence was a warm physical one. She had put Joe down for a sleep one day and had dozed off on top of the double bed. She opened her eyes some time later to find Vin standing beside the bed, smiling down at her. With a glad cry she sprang up and into his arms. He held her against him and kissed her gently, insistently, with his non-lips which had been so cruelly burned in the car fire, and then turned to ash at the crematorium.

When Maggie woke she felt his presence still, so clearly that she looked around, half expecting to see him somewhere in the room.

Gradually these dreams became less frequent, till she feared her physical memory of him would be lost in spite of photographs. Her favourite showed him sitting on his car, long-legged in blue overalls, a victor's wreath about his broad shoulders and a bottle of champagne foaming in one hand. Yet she had hated that car and the dedication that kept him from being entirely hers.

When the summer constellations came back, swinging up in the eastern sky some time after midnight, she caught her breath at the sight of Orion, the invincible Greek hero who had at last been brought low by the sting of a scorpion. That row of sparkling stars, the jewelled belt and sworded hip, reminded her of Vin. She remembered the night they had driven home from the beach that summer.

She gazed at his smiling face, fixed forever in the moment of triumph in the fadeless photograph. It was as strange to look on as the portrait of some sixteenth-century Pope, richly clad and rotund with good living, who long ago had crumbled into dust.

Two

It's a long way, to tickle Mary,
It's a long way, to go.
It's a long way to tickle Mary,
She's the fattest girl I know . . .

UNDER THE coconut palms on the beach at Rowe's Bay, a group of Aborigines was singing loudly, waving half-empty beer bottles in time to the tune of 'Tipperary'. They had hailed a taxi-driver in the centre of Townsville and ordered him to drive out to the Bay. It gave them a sense of power to buy the services of a 'gubba', a white man, and the use of his vehicle. The driver had promised to come back for them tomorrow morning, when they would have slept off today's bender. The driver always charged Aborigines twice the normal fare, knowing they would not argue. He also supplied them with the flagons of cheap wine they bought to make them drunk, with a mixture as well of rum and beer. Because it was illegal for them to buy alcohol, it cost them four times the proper amount.

In town, they knew they could always get drink from behind the Golden Horseshoe Cafe. They would order a shilling cup of tea, put down two pounds on the counter, then go round and through a door in the galvanised iron fence at the back. Waiting for them in a rubbish bin would be a sugar-bag holding a flagon of dark wine, or half a dozen bottles of beer, or a small flask of rum.

'Bad laws are made to be broken', and the law which said that Aborigines could not drink was broken all the time. The police chose not to notice, and those who supplied the alcohol were not prosecuted, but if they saw a dark-skinned man drinking, or the worse for liquor, he was taken to the lock-up. Depending on whether he went quietly or 'used offensive

558

language' and 'resisted arrest', he would spend the night, or a week in gaol. Since most of them used 'offensive language' in the form of four-letter words most of the time, they usually faced a second charge as well as a 'drunk and disorderly'.

The group under the palms had emptied their flagon and started on the beer. Someone threw the first empty beer bottle at the empty flagon, and it shattered with a magnificent crash. Some applauded, but one of the men protested: 'Eh, that flagon wort' a couple o' bob; what you bin smash-im for?'

'Ahr, two bob – that won't even buy a packet o' cigs.'

They had noticed a tall young man in tailored shorts, open-necked shirt and sandals standing under a fig-tree 'eyeing them off', as one of their number remarked. Immediately there was hostility in the group for the stranger. They were aware that to 'them', the white people, the 'Kooris' or dark people were objects of a rather distasteful curiosity. White tourists were taken out to Palm Island settlement, where many of these men had been born, to stare at 'the natives' in their regimented cottages while being warned 'not to talk to the inhabitants'. For the residents it was like living in a cage at the Zoo.

'What you lookin' at, mate?' asked one of the men. There was alcohol-induced belligerence in the question.

'Nothing . . . I was just wondering – '

'Ah! An ejjicated feller!' The well-modulated voice of the strange youth, not the usual Queensland drawl, and his neat clothes provoked further hostility.

'You writin' a paper for the 'Varsity, per'aps? On the drinkin' habits of the Australian Aborigine?'

There was a laugh at this, and a mutter which sounded like 'Get stuffed', and 'Piss off!'

'No, I was wondering if any of you know Maud Wandana or Billy and Marie Efate at Rocky? They're my aunties and uncle.'

Gaining confidence, the young man walked closer and they saw his black eyes and tight-curling hair, his light brown skin.

'Maud, she married an Islander, didn't she? What 'er name now?'

The speaker was handsome in a burly way, with dark moustache above his full lips.

'Efate, the same as my Uncle Billy, and Dave Efate the boxer. My Mum was a Pinjarra from Pandanus Island.'

'Oh, one o' that mob? But Billy died, I think, las' year.'

One of the older men, with a grey stubble on his chin, leant forward from the waist where he was squatting on the sand, peering at the newcomer with bloodshot dark eyes.

'What cate*gory* is he?' he kept asking.

'My name's Joe King, from Adelaide. Mum and I are on a holiday, she used to go to school in Townsville, but she was born on Pandanus. You know old Grannie Nyora?'

'Gord, she must be nigh on a hundred. She still goin' strong? 'Ere, avadrink mate,' the first man said, holding out a half-empty bottle.

Joe started looking for a glass, then caught himself and took a swig from the bottle before handing it back. 'Thanks.'

'What cate*gory* is he?'

> *Oh, he's the on'y one can tell to you,*
> *What the emu said to the kangaroo,*
> *In Townsville, cuttin' a rug –*

'What cate*gory* –'

'Shut up, Harry. He wants ter know what proportion of white blood you got,' he explained to Joe. 'You know, half, quarter, three-quarters.'

'Oh, my Dad was white, my Mum was three-quarters white, she was a bit of a mixture. Her mother was part Islander, and her Dad was Bert Pinjarra, old Nyora's son, and *she* was married to a European, a Portuguese. But the Portuguese've been sailing round the East for centuries, and he probably had some Singhalese or Indian blood as well. The other kids, except my mother Maggie, they were very dark.'

'Maggie Pinjarra! Not the writer; you her son?'

'I certainly am,' said Joe, grinning. He had felt nervous about meeting his mother's people in what was to him the Far North. Uncle Harold Brown and Aunt Ellen were in Melbourne, where he was now at the Conservatorium of Music.

Joe could scarcely remember Marie or Dan or Nyora, since Maggie had taken him back to Adelaide when he was little. They would be stopping to see them on the way back, when they broke their journey at Rockhampton.

In First Grade at Townsville, Joe had come home and asked her, 'What's a Kanaka, Mum?'

'Why? Who's been calling you that?' She knelt down and put her arms round him, looking anxiously into his face.

'They didn't. Only there's a song they was singin' in the playground, a bouncing song with a ball:

> Violets are blue,
> Roses are red,
> You're a Kanaka,
> You're dead.'

'It doesn't mean anything, it's just a rhyme like "Three Blind Mice".'

'But what's a Kanaka? I asked them at school, and they all started laughing at me.'

'It's – it's a name for Pacific Island people. Your great-great-grandpa was one. It meant an Islander man who worked in the sugar plantations in Queensland. My mother's people were Pacific Islanders, descended from Joseph Tula Efate of Lifu, in New Caledonia. You were named after him.'

'So I'm really a Kanaka?'

'Not "Kanaka". I don't like that word. You are a little bit Islander, a little bit Aboriginal on my Dadda's side. But he was half Portuguese. And your Daddy's people were white Australians, for five generations back.'

The next time he had come home from school in tears. The song they had sung at him was:

> God made little nigger boys
> He made them near a fence,
> He made them in a hurry
> And forgot to give them sense.

*　　*　　*

561

Maggie decided then to take him back to Adelaide for school. It held happy memories for her of the days when she first met Vincent, though she never went near the Aboriginal girls' hostel where she used to live. She dressed smartly, rented a house on the Fullarton tramline with a small garden where she could grow vegetables, and sent Joe to the Glen Osmond State School and later to the Unley Boys' High. For the same reasons that had sent her south to get a job when she first left school, she knew it would be easier for Joe than in Queensland. Though he looked 'different', he did not look Aboriginal, and in South Australia he could grow up with all the rights and advantages of a white citizen.

Now Joseph King was grown up, would be seventeen in a month or two, and he knew what 'nigger' meant. He squatted comfortably on his heels in his neat grey shorts as he talked to the men.

'Any of you tell when the Palm Island launch comes in?'

There was an uncomfortable silence. The men looked down at their hands; the older one who had asked Joe's 'category' spat on the ground.

'More better you ask someone else,' he muttered. 'We don't know nothin' about that place.'

' 'Cept it a good place to get out of!'

There was a laugh at this.

'But some of you must have been there in the launch?' Joe persisted.

The first man, who said his name was Bill Cotton, explained.

'No one's proud of bein' a Palm Islander,' he said. 'It's a Reserve, see, and it started off as a prison for blackfellers sent to gaol for a long term; and it's still run like a prison. There's more than a thousand of our people out there, tucked out o' sight, like, thirty miles away from the mainland. White people can't go there without a permit, and even if they get there they can't stay after dark. Our people can't leave without a permit signed by the Manager, and the on'y way to Townsville's in the Island launch. So he's got the whip-hand, see?'

'Yair. There was a big meetin' last year of the Aboriginal and Islanders Federal Council, with speakers from down south. And for that week the launch didn't run,' said a young man who hadn't spoken before.

'If you can hold down a job on the mainland, you're free to go "ashore" and come home once a month,' Bill said. 'But for a man with a family, it takes a lot of guts to leave altogether and battle for 'imself. Over there, he's got a house nearly rent-free, school for the kids, horspital and all. But if he leaves and takes out his citizenship papers, then he's on his own. It's a bit frightening at first. I s'spose we bin spoiled by too many handouts.'

'Speak for yourself, Bill,' said the younger man, who had long, curly dark hair and a rather fierce Malaysian cast of features. 'Me, I aint bin spoiled. I'm gonna take the effin' white man for every cent I can get. They took the whole of Queensland off of us, and pushed us off to a few shithouse places like Palm and Cherbourg and Yarrabah. Bloody concentration camps, that's all they are! And you know what else is out there?' He waved his hand towards the blue hump of Magnetic Island five miles away. 'A leper colony, that's what! On Fantôme Island. *Them* poor buggers never get ashore at all . . . And not a drop of drink's allowed on Palm, except for the bloody white staff's canteen.'

'But *you* could get a certificate of exemption, and drink in a pub in town if you wanted to?' asked Joe.

'Huh! The dorg-licence! No, thanks, I'd rather pay through the nose at the Greek's. Besides they wouldn't serve me in the effin' bar, you know that.'

'You never see a white man run in by the cops for bein' drunk,' said Bill. 'It's only us poor buggers they pick on.'

'I reckon,' said Joe, 'that the thing we've got to work for first, is citizenship rights for everybody. Most Australians want to see fair play, a fair go. There's going to be a referendum, where the whole population votes on the issue. Then after we've got that, Land Rights. Because then we'll have some power, we'll have the vote –'

'Land Rights, eh? Now you're talkin', young feller. Where did you get ejjicated? We need people like you, can talk to them Government bosses in Canberra. We'll never get nowhere with the Aborigines' Persecution Board in New South, or the Queensland Department of Aborigines and Torres Strait Islanders ... All they want is keep their cushy jobs, and keep the black in 'is place – which is down.'

He threw another empty bottle on the pile.

'Anyway, I want to get out to Palm Island and see conditions there for myself,' said Joe. 'I'll get Maggie to write an article for the *Sydney Morning Herald* or the *Canberra Times*; they'll take her stuff now that her name is known. And this leper island, too.'

'You'll never get to Fantôme,' said Bill. 'But you could get the tourist launch that goes round the islands and calls at Great Palm. I think it's Thursdays.'

'What do you blokes do for a crust? You all out of work?'

'No, I got a job as deck-'and on the Magnetic Island ferry, only this is me day off,' said Bill.

'An' I'm the yardman at the Reef Motel – gardenin' and odd jobs,' said the curly-haired Reuben.

A couple of the others were boners and offal-sweepers at the Ross River meatworks, 'taking a sickie'. Harry, with a gap-toothed grin, admitted he was on 'siddown money' from the Government.

'Last time the cops picked me up,' he said. 'They ask me, "You got any previous convictions, any old records?" "No," I ses, "but me sister's got plenty of old Bing Crosbys." Out at Woorabinda camp,' he added, 'when we was little, the local cops used to come in a car at night and shine a spotlight on yer. Just like they was spotlightin' for kangaroos. On'y they don't shoot us these days.'

'Why we get a taxi and come out 'ere,' said Reuben, 'is so the cops won't pick us up. You try drinkin' in the Gardens in town, they got to run you in – it's the Law. It's their job. But there's five or ten blackfellers for every white in the Townsville gaol, and that's not right. When you think how many more whites there are in town.'

A bottle of beer was passed round again. Joe didn't want another drink, but he recognised it, the drinking from one bottle, the communal defying of the Law, as a sort of mateship ritual. He took a swig, handed back the bottle, and rose to his feet.

'Well, thanks, fellers. I got to get back to my Mum. See you on the ferry, eh Bill? We're going over to Picnic Bay tomorrow.'

'Yair. See yer. I'm lookin' forward to meetin' the writer of them stories.'

Three

IT WAS many years since Maggie had caught the ferryboat which plied regularly between Magnetic Island and the Townsville Wharf. She was last there when Joe was a child, more than ten years ago. She bought a palm-leaf hat from a stall on the waterfront, elaborately woven from green pandanus fronds – a skill which had come across the Pacific from Hawaii. She jammed it on top of her long dark hair. She was wearing a brief halter-top and shorts of white towelling which showed off her long brown legs. She remembered how the other kids used to laugh at her skinny legs at school, so that she would sit miserably in the classroom at recess-time with her legs hidden under the desk.

She sat with Joe on the open foredeck, where they had their back to the glassed-in cabin where most of the passengers sat, entertained by a long-haired young man playing a guitar. Maggie leant against the canvas bag holding her towel and costume. She would not travel inside on the launch; her mother and aunt, who had survived the ferry disaster on Moreton Bay and had a vivid memory of how passengers were trapped inside when it turned over, had taught her always to travel outside.

The beach-bag reminded her of the day when, as a schoolgirl living with Auntie Ellen and Uncle Harold Brown, she had gone to the Kissing Point sea-baths where Aborigines didn't go, and dived defiantly into the jade-green water. She imagined she saw several white girls immediately climb out. After her swim she changed in a cubicle and left the baths, swinging her bathing-bag by its drawstring.

Feeling smart in her new orange-and-white sundress, her long wet hair satin-sleek against her head, fourteen-year-old Maggie followed the curve of the foreshore, the long sweep of yellow sand, back to the seafront park with its starved lawns and green exotic palms.

Townsville was in a low-rainfall belt, and there was rarely any rain in the dry warm winter months. The sky was cloudlessly blue, and against it flamed the cerise and crimson of flowering bougainvillea, tumbling down the cliff-face of Castle Hill like a coloured waterfall.

Maggie had felt a surge of well-being as she walked under the coconut-palms which leant above the sea. From behind a hibiscus shrub a large white bull-terrier confronted her. With flattened face and bulging eyes, its coat so short that it had a pink, naked look like a newly-shorn sheep, it was not an attractive animal. But Maggie, who usually got on well with dogs, held out her hand encouragingly. The dog's expression did not change; it uttered no sound, but quite suddenly it took her bare knee in its jaws.

This was unnerving. Maggie tried to pull away, and the dog growled in its throat.

'Let go! Lie down!' she shrieked. She swung the bag of wet bathers at its head. It let go for an instant to get a firmer grip, and she thrust the bag between its jaws. She saw its long white canine teeth and red-rimmed eyes.

A man who had been sitting on one of the seats facing the sea came to her rescue. He ran over and grabbed the dog by its collar, pulling it back on its haunches.

'The beast isn't mine,' he said apologetically, 'but I'll hold him while you get away. He does seem to have taken a dislike to you for some reason. Perhaps it was the beach-bag.'

The bull-terrier, barking and slavering, pulled against the collar till it nearly choked, but made no attempt to turn on the man who held it. Maggie uttered her thanks and ran, tears of fright streaming down her face.

At first Aunt Ellen could not get out of her what had

happened. But while she sniffed and sobbed, and Ellen bathed the grazes on her calf and knee with hydrogen peroxide, she calmed down enough to speak. 'Dogs always like me,' she gasped, 'but this one didn't. And it knew I was frightened. If that nice man hadn't pulled it off – '

'There, there. It hasn't bitten you, thank the Lord.'

'I think it took a dislike to the beach-bag. I was swinging it round.' But secretly Maggie feared there was another reason; the dog had sensed that she was 'different', just as the girls at the Baths had done. It was like that day in the playground when she came up to a group of white girls and one of them said, 'Oh–oh, looks like rain! Black clouds hanging around!'

And of course it would be a *white* dog . . .

Why, thought Maggie, remembering these experiences of her girlhood, why had she then chosen to come back here with Joe and perhaps expose him to the same sort of thing? She was glad she had decided to move to Adelaide and send him to school there. If only he did well and won a bursary, he could go to the University and perhaps become the first man of Aboriginal blood to get a degree . . .

They were staying in an on-site van at Rowe's Bay because it was cheaper than a motel. Maggie owned a small car, but Joe showed none of his father's interest in fast driving. She was relieved that he apparently had no yen for such an expensive and dangerous sport as motor racing, perhaps because he had never known his father. They had come all the way from Adelaide by train, but would fly back from Sydney. Maggie couldn't afford the air fare the whole way. It was Joe who had been keen to come on this trip to the Deep North, to the State of Queensland where he was born. He had already made some Aboriginal acquaintances, and this morning had introduced Maggie to Bill Cotton, the deck-hand – a little bleary-eyed from yesterday's drinking party.

Daydreaming as she sat on the deck, thinking of the time when she lived here, she saw the blue shape of Magnetic Island beginning to take on green and brown colours as they got nearer. She forgot to hang on to her new hat. A sudden cross-wind whirled it from her head and into the water, where it bobbed in the wake. The skipper in his glassed-in wheel-house above saw it go and immediately turned the small launch around in an arc, cutting his own wake. As they swept past, Bill scooped up the green hat with a boathook.

'Thank you!' cried Maggie, laughing, waving to the skipper.

'Here y'are – it's not very wet,' said Bill with a grin, handing it to her. He came and squatted beside Maggie and Joe on the foredeck. There were benches round the deck, mostly occupied by young people in swimming-things. 'Better leave it off for now, the skipper won't turn around a second time if yer lose it.'

'Of course not! I didn't expect him to this time. Thanks a lot, Bill.'

'Any time,' said Bill.

'Nice work with the boathook,' said Joe.

'Eh Joe, you didn't tell us your Mum was such a good sort. I never thought Maggie Pinjarra was young. I thought she'd be an old girl with grey hair in a hairnet, who'd bin collectin' stories for umpteen years.'

Maggie was quite pleased at being called 'young' at nearly forty, but felt embarrassed at the open admiration in his eyes. While bringing up Joe she had frozen off any man who showed an interest, determined to be faithful to Vin's memory and feeling that her son should come first while he was young and needed her. For years she had lived vicariously, through him. Now, in this heady tropical atmosphere, sailing over a sea as green as glass and warm as new milk, she felt life stirring in her veins. She was herself, Maggie King, not just the mother of Joseph.

Though she was only thirty-eight there were quite a few grey threads in her hair, which she covered with coloured rinses. Not just out of vanity, she told herself, but in order to keep her job as secretary to an Adelaide businessman – in the same Insurance office of which Vin's father had been manager. The fact that she was Mrs Vincent King still had some meaning in South Australia and had helped to get her the job.

Old Mrs King had died of a third and fatal stroke some time after Maggie's visit when Joe was a baby. Presumably Zircon was dead by now, and the money which had supported the pampered Siamese had gone to the cats' home where Mrs King had directed it.

The guitar-player on board had an offsider to collect 'donations'; he also (illegally) told fortunes. When he came out on deck with his collection box, Maggie put a small contribution in it. The man grasped her hand and began studying its lines.

'H'm, yes, interesting – you have a long lifeline, unbroken; that means good health and a ripe old age. Rather impulsive; artistic, that right? Could be an artist, a writer, an actress, no, with those long fingers you probably use your hands for something creative – a potter or a painter – No?' as Maggie laughed and shook her head.

'I use them for typing; I'm a secretary,' she said to deflate him.

Unruffled, he continued to study the lines on her palm.

'Could I hold your sunglasses for a moment?'

She handed them over. Still holding her hand in his left, he clasped the sunglasses in his right hand, closing his eyes. When he opened them, his face wore a look of horror. He handed back the sunglasses as though they burnt him, and thrust her hand away.

'What is it?' asked Maggie. 'What did you feel?'

The man was backing away from her. 'Something . . . I don't know.'

'You *must* know.' She was beginning to be annoyed.

'I don't know. Disaster . . . Death. Not for you, for other people. But you have bad vibes. You'd be a good person to keep away from.' And he disappeared down the three steps to the interior, after a quick look ahead as if to gauge how much further he would have to travel with her in the same boat.

Maggie was shaken. She looked at the back of Joe's curly head, where he stood right in the bows like a figurehead. Was it the future that man sensed, or the past? The ferry disaster where her grandmother and uncles were lost, her father tangled in his fishing-net, Vin burned to death in his racing car, her mother dying of cancer of the blood? Did she perhaps attract disaster, as an iron spire attracted lightning?

She told herself it was nonsense. Yet the man had been right in describing her attributes, and he certainly had not appeared to be acting. He had felt about her an aura of doom

. . . or was it the persecution of two dark races that he felt through her?

The ferry was slowing for Picnic Bay jetty. Bill threw a rope which someone caught and wound quickly round a bollard, holding it there while the passengers disembarked. The engine, idling, puttered quietly through its underwater exhaust while Bill stood by the gangway to help elderly passengers and attractive young girls across to the jetty.

'Let's go on to Arcadia, shall we?' said Maggie, suddenly remembering the beautiful little cove there for swimming, which was often rough from the south-easterly in the afternoons, but sheltered in the mornings.

They cast off again and skirted rocky reefs below rounded granite boulders which were whitened by the droppings of sea-eagles, their nests built in the spindly pines that seemed to grow straight out of the rock. Here the water was deep close inshore. The steep cliffs towered above, only a few yards from the boat. Tied up again at the next landing, the boat disgorged most of its passengers. Bill helped Maggie across the gap above the water and held her hand a fraction longer than necessary. Maggie was ridiculously pleased at this attention from a man so much younger than herself.

'I think he fancies you,' said Joe, as they walked round the curving causeway to Arcadia, bowered in exotic palms and flowering creepers.

'Rubbish!' said Maggie, but she was gay and talkative as they sat and sipped a drink under a thatched umbrella. They changed and walked across to Alma Bay, the narrow sandy cove in a cleft of rocks, where a shark mesh had been stretched between the granite headlands. They swam out and climbed on to a smooth, rounded, sun-warm boulder. And this at the end of winter!

Joe remarked to another young man stretched out on the next rock, that it was beaut to swim in a natural pool like this, safe from sharks yet open to the sea.

'Don't let it lull you into a false sense of security,' said the young man, a Queenslander by his accent and a Westerner on holiday by his slow drawl. 'The mesh got broken in the last cyclone, and they haven't got round to mending it. No sharks round here, but.'

He stood up and dived in, swimming leisurely back to the beach.

'I'm going to swim across to the rocks on the opposite side,' said Joe. 'Coming, Mum?'

'In a minute.' Maggie was filled with lazy wellbeing as the sun soaked into her back, while the clear salty drops dried on her arms where she rested her face. She watched with maternal pride as Joe streaked through the water in an easy crawl stroke. He had won several cups for swimming at school, which she had put with Vincent's motor-racing trophies.

Joe climbed out on the far side of the narrow cove and waved to her. Maggie looked down at the deliciously clear green water, the netted sunbeams wavering on the sandy bottom. It did look inviting. She began to cross with a slow, leisurely breast-stroke, enjoying the calm of the deep water. She was slightly more than halfway across when, taking a breath, she looked down and saw a large dark shape immediately beneath her.

All her blood seemed to congeal with shock. Then her heart began to pound, adrenalin pumped through her veins, and with threshing arms and legs she finished in a fast overarm. At any moment she expected to feel giant jaws close on her legs . . .

She reached the other side and clambered out, gasping.

'You trying to beat the Olympic record or something?' asked Joe.

'No . . . Oh, Joe! I saw a shark. Right below me. I saw it.'

She was panting for breath and trembling. Superstitiously she turned the silver snake bangle on her wrist, the double-headed snake that brought her luck.

'Oh, Mum! Go on! It was a pile of seaweed.'

'There's no seaweed round here. Besides, it was moving.'

'Perhaps a big stingray. Could have been.'

'Anyway, I'm going out around the rocks. Don't swim back across there! Please, Joe.'

'Oh, all right. But I'll bet you a million dollars it wasn't a shark.'

They walked across to the cafe at Arcadia for lunch. Joe ate two hamburgers, a milk shake and a cream bun. Maggie made this an excuse for saying they'd better not swim again. As they walked back around the lip of the cove they saw something, a dark shape, at the edge of the water. There were no other swimmers; they'd all gone off to lunch. They went down the steps to the beach. The wind was getting up, and small, choppy waves were breaking in the shallows. And there, half in and half out of the water, a huge turtle lay with his head bowed between his front flippers. There were tears running out of his ancient-looking eyes.

'Oh, poor thing, poor thing!' For half of his thick shell had been torn away, and there was a deep gash in the flesh of his back.

'A fast speedboat has hit him,' said Joe, 'or perhaps even the screw of a big ship. I wonder how far he's come like that?'

'Of course – that's what I must have seen in the water! He was coming ashore to die. Poor old thing!'

The turtle's head had dropped into the sand; his eyes were closed. Joe tried to lift his head, but it dropped down again, the sea washing over his beak and nostrils. 'I think he's dead,' he said.

There was nothing they could do; he was too heavy to lift, so they left him there.

They took the open-sided bus, Leaping Lena, to the far side of the island and swam and sunbathed at Horseshoe Bay, which was sheltered from the south-east wind. Small blue islands seemed to float on the horizon, out to the north and west: the Palm Group.

'I suppose they were all inhabited by our people, once,' said Joe. 'You know the Keppels and Pandanus were, for thousands of years, and Fraser Island had about three thousand Batjalas. Captain Cook saw them on his way up the coast in 1770. He mentioned "about fifty Indians" on one headland.'

Maggie was amused. 'Where have you been boning up on all this ancient history?'

'I got it from a book in the school library. And what's more, the Keppel Islanders had light curly hair with a lot of red in it. They reckoned it got curly because they were always swimming in the sea.' Joe towelled his tight red curls vigorously. 'So you see, in spite of mixtures, I might be a throw-back to a pure Keppel Island type.'

'I doubt it very much,' said Maggie. 'Genetically, Australian Aborigines don't "throw back". My mother had those frizzy curls, and Vin's grandmother was a red-head . . . I wonder if Elaine King is still alive? We might call and see her on our way back through Sydney.'

But Joe was not interested in elderly white relatives. He was fascinated at present with what seemed to him his unique inheritance of Aboriginal and Melanesian blood, disregarding all the other strands woven into his inheritance.

The last launch left for Townsville at five o'clock. They caught the bus back to Picnic Bay as the sheltered waters of Horseshoe Bay were beginning to take on the green and gold of evening, while the distant islands turned a deep lilac. Bill Cotton was interested when they told him about the turtle. 'That's good tucker,' he said.

Bill was attentive to Maggie on the way back. The guitarist and the fortune-teller were not aboard. Admonishing Maggie to hang on to her hat, Bill stood grasping a deck-stanchion, one bare brown foot resting on the seat that ran round inside the railing. He stood so that the flying spray from the starboard quarter was kept from Maggie by his sturdy frame, as she would not go inside out of the wind. He laughed when his ragged shorts and blue T-shirt were spattered by spray. She warmed to his spontaneous chivalry, his infectious grin.

As they tied up at the Ross River wharf, Joe jumped across the narrow space of green water without waiting for the gangplank. Maggie lingered for the crowd to go first and was one of the last ashore. Bill held her elbow and guided her across to the wharf.

'Eh, what about tonight?' he said in her ear.

'*What* about tonight?'

'I mean, what about comin' out with me? Take you for a spin in a taxi to the top of Castle Hill. There's a beaut view of the lights from up there.'

'You mean me and Joe?'

'No, no, I didn't mean Joe. Can't 'e go to the pictures?'

Maggie was a bit taken aback, but fearing to offend him she said, 'Look, I'm sorry, Bill . . . I'd love to, but we're going to Palm Island tomorrow, all day, and I'm a bit tired after swimming. I think I'll have an early night.'

'OK. Please yourself. P'raps another time.'

'Yes. Another time perhaps.' But she felt Bill had seen through her excuses, and she was ashamed. What was she scared of, why had she knocked him back?

Joe came across to them. 'Come on, Mum, I'm starving. Let's get back and have dinner.'

Four

ON THURSDAY they set off on a five-day cruise.

The Hayles tourist launch called at Dunk and Orpheus and other high, wooded islands before it made its way to Great Palm. Passengers slept and ate on board in rather cramped quarters. Maggie shared a cabin with two other women, while Joe bunked with an older man. One of Maggie's cabin-mates, a tall woman with a long, toothy face and an English accent, remarked that she was looking forward particularly to the visit to Palm Island. 'I believe it's a veritable Paradise,' she said.

Maggie looked cynical. 'That depends,' she said, 'on whether you have to live there all the time, or not.'

'But surely it's a most beautiful place.'

'The most beautiful place becomes a prison if you're not allowed to leave.' The woman looked mystified.

They reached the island early in the afternoon, following a delicious luncheon of fresh-caught reef fish and salad, with prawns in half an avocado as an entrée. Maggie had almost forgotten how superb Queensland seafood could be. There were lobsters and mud-crabs, barramundi and coral trout, small school prawns as sweet as nuts and big tiger-prawns with striped tails.

The island appeared like a wall of green. The hill that rose steeply behind the settlement was covered with rainforest and the small fanlike native palms which gave the place its name. Exotic coconut palms had been planted along the shore and about the white buildings, the impressive church built by an early Roman Catholic mission.

Most of the dark people who lived there had been introduced like the coconut palms. They had been born on the mainland or on other islands to north and south. They lived in neat cottages set in gardens behind paling fences, and there was besides a big conglomeration of institutional buildings: dormitories, kitchens, bakery, school, hospital, Domestic Science block and so on. One large building, they learned, was set aside for unmarried mothers.

Bill Cotton, born on Palm Island, had 'gone free' on the mainland. There were, he said, only about a hundred Palm Islanders, out of the 1,400 residents, who had 'made it' in the world outside. They were a mixed collection of full-blood and part-Aborigines and Islanders, all gathered in by the Government and brought to the Reserve to live; they were not given any alternative. The fringe-dwellers about places like Maryborough and Bundaberg and Townsville had become an embarrassment to the townspeople, so the police were brought in to round them up and transport them elsewhere. The only way ashore was in the Island launch which ran officially two or three times a week, staying overnight in Townsville.

Bill said that there was a facade of control by an Island Council of Aborigines, but they were 'lame ducks and tame Uncle Toms' appointed by the Manager himself.

Fifty years ago the Queensland Government had set aside the largest of the Palm Group 'for the sole use of the land's original inhabitants.' Fraser Island, which had been similarly set aside in 1900 – a seventy mile long sand island to the south – had been found too valuable to 'give away'. Yet the stated reason for making it an Aboriginal Reserve in the first place, as 'one great central permanent Aboriginal home for all South Queensland', was 'its entire worthlessness for white settlement'. Here twenty-six tribes, or their remnants, and fifty-six time-expired black prisoners were sent, without medicines, food, or shelter. Eventually it had been taken back for a Forestry Reserve for its valuable stands of cypress

575

pine, satinay and blackbutt. The people were moved to Cherbourg or Palm Island or Yarrabah.

Palm Island people now consisted of racial mixtures, displaced remnants, social misfits and descendants of criminals, which made them, said Bill, rather like the white people of Sydney. Orpheus Island nearby was a tourist resort, from which white people were brought on sight-seeing trips, and whisked away again before sunset.

Maggie found that the palm-leaf hat she had bought was woven here, but she was not allowed to buy one direct from the people, nor the painted coconuts and shell necklaces and woven pandanus mats which they also made. All were handled by 'the Department', with its headquarters and director a thousand miles away in Brisbane. The people were segregated almost like lepers from the tourists.

'I must ask you,' the cruise skipper said as they went ashore, 'to follow the rules, otherwise we won't be allowed to call here. They are: keep in a group; do not speak to the native people or give them money. You must not enter their homes, or buy handicrafts direct from them. There will be a guided tour where you can see the girls at work cooking and sewing and making handicrafts.

'These regulations, and the one against bringing any alcoholic liquor to the Island, were formulated – and I quote the Department of Aboriginal and Islander Affairs – "for the protection of Palm Islanders against exploitation." '

'Ha, ha!' said Joe King loudly.

He was given a look of irritation, both by the speaker and the other tourists, who realised that they were here on sufferance and had better comply.

The Assistant Manager, a youngish man in casual dress of shorts and shirt, came to greet the group of tourists and conduct them round. 'You keep him talking, Mum,' said Joe, 'while I get away and have a talk with some of the people. It's like Bill said, just like a prison.'

The ladies were exclaiming over the cute brown-eyed babies in the Maternity building (where the Sister in charge explained that every mother was 'given' a layette for the baby before she went home, though its cost came out of her Government maternity allowance). Maggie engaged the

Assistant Manager in conversation.

She explained who she was and that she was writing an article on Aboriginal affairs in Queensland for a southern newspaper. She saw that he immediately looked wary.

'Is it true, as I have heard,' asked Maggie, 'that the Island is "dry" and that the only alcohol allowed here officially is for the white staff?'

'Perfectly true. It's the policy all over Queensland that natives aren't allowed drink, except with a special permit. They're much better off without it.'

'But you know as well as I do that they can get it when they go to the mainland – taxi-drivers will get it for them, at a price. And then, just because it's prohibited, they drink too much.'

'Well, yes, we do have a problem with men going "ashore" sometimes. Very often they end up in gaol, and have to miss the launch back again.'

'And wouldn't it be better to have a wet canteen for the men on the island, so that they could get used to drinking in moderation? Even if it supplied only beer?'

'It's possible. That might come in time, but I don't think they're ready for it.'

As they moved on to the Domestic Science block, Maggie heard one of the white instructors showing off her star pupils' work: 'Yes, this girl bakes a beautiful cake, she makes our Christmas cakes every year . . . This one helps the baker. She makes excellent bread rolls.'

She the cat's mother, thought Maggie. The girls themselves said nothing, and neither of them appeared to have a name. She looked around and saw that Joe had disappeared.

'I suppose,' she remarked to the AM, 'that you have trouble with the men setting up whisky stills in the mountains, or brewing their own beer if they get a chance.'

'That's true, but it's "conduct prejudicial to good order and discipline on the settlement", and that carries a term of detention.'

'You have a magistrate calling?'

'No, they can be detained by the Manager. They can be confined to dormitories for a fortnight, or refused a pass to go to the mainland. You must have discipline.'

'But these are not children, Mr Smith! These are grown men.'

'Nevertheless they are not ready for independence, for running their own affairs, as yet.'

'Nor ever will be, while the Queensland Government keeps up this policy of paternalism. How are they ever to learn to drink, to manage money, to live without regulations, under this system? On Stradbroke Island, on Pandanus Island, at Hervey Bay, there are independent communities managing their own lives very well. *And* in Melbourne and Sydney.'

'Yes, but I think the more southern people find it easier to integrate. And then, in those communities you mention, you know yourself that there's a big admixture of Kanaka and Maori and even Indian and Phillipino – '

'My grandmother, Mr Smith, was pure Aboriginal, and she brought up a fine family on her own, after her husband died. And I have lived in the city for years.'

'But you, Mrs King, are a very exceptional woman, if I may say so. I have read your books and admired them.'

Maggie, who had been getting angry, accepted this tribute as a peace-offering. She saw Joe quietly joining the tail-end of the group, now taken in tow by the Matron of the hospital. She thanked Mr Smith and went over to join him. Mr Smith's parting words were, 'If you're writing anything for the paper, you'd better submit it first to the Director of the DOAIA in Brisbane.'

Like hell I will, thought Maggie.

She asked the Matron if there were any Aboriginal nurses.

'Oh, *no!*' said Matron, looking shocked. 'But we train the girls as wardsmaids.'

Joe now made his way to her side. She noticed some suppressed excitement about him. 'How did you get on?' she whispered.

'Shit! Have I got any material for you? It's like a bloody concentration camp, like a maximum-security prison.'

They walked apart from the group while Joe exploded, keeping his voice down with an effort.

'One family asked me in for a cup of tea. Quite a comfortable house; at least I only saw the kitchen. But they're planning to get away, to get a little place of their own in Townsville or down the coast at Bowen. They're sick of being regimented and supervised. They told me that two inspectors, a man and a woman, visit their house every Thursday to see that it's clean and well-kept. They don't wait to be invited in. One family that they said had dirty floors, they took the children away and put them in one of the island hostels. The sisters and brothers are separated, and they're separated from their parents. The illegitimate birth rate is enormous, because the young people are bored. There's nothing else to do. And "consorting with unmarried girls" is a crime which can lead to up to six months' confinement in the dormitory. So is refusing to work for rations, without a doctor's certificate to say you are sick. Smuggling a can of beer back on the launch means a fortnight's detention if you're caught. The Manager can have anyone arrested without trial for "conduct prejudicial to good order".'

'Yes, I know. I've just been talking to the Assistant Manager.'

'Well, I think the place stinks. And most of the people are too scared to do anything about it. They've been cowed, brow-beaten, kept down for about fifty years. By God it makes me mad.'

'Now Joe, keep your voice down. It's no good getting worked up about it.'

'Why shouldn't I get worked up? These are my people, and they're being oppressed by petty white officials. Honestly, the Queensland laws are like South Africa!'

'All right, I'll do an article about it. I'll try and get it published before the Referendum is held.'

'Good on you, Mum! We have to help them to fight; so many of the Old People won't stand up to officials; they've been pushed around all their lives, their children taken away from them and put in institutions; not even allowed to handle their own money – '

'I'd like to have seen them try to take Morgan and Elsie and Bert away from Grannie Nyora!'

As they caught up with the rest of the troop of tourists Maggie saw the Assistant Manager giving some sharp looks at Joe, trying to place his 'category', no doubt.

Suddenly there was a tremendous WHUMF! The ground shook, and from a rocky cleft in the green hillside towering above, a cloud of smoke and dust arose. People rushed out of their houses, chattering and pointing. Mr Smith started to run back towards his office. Shortly afterwards an official was seen to hurry along the jetty to the tourist launch, which blew its hooter to recall the passengers. When they got back no one seemed to know what had happened, but the skipper had been told to leave immediately.

'Joe! Do you know anything about this? Is it sabotage?' whispered Maggie. She wondered if he had somehow smuggled some explosives in with him. He often talked of violence, but so far had not been involved in any.

'No, but I can guess what's happened,' he replied with a grin. 'The whisky still has blown up. The men were telling me about it; it's in a cave up there. The officials will try to hush the whole thing up, but they know it goes on. Hope no one is injured.'

But he learned afterwards through his friend Bill Cotton that one man had been killed and another badly injured. The other two men had been at the opening of the cave and escaped injury, but both would certainly be sentenced to detention for 'conduct prejudicial . . . etc.'

As soon as they got back to the caravan, Maggie started on her article, which began:

'Feathery palms and green rainforest, mountains and water falls, sheltered beaches and coral reefs, and a winter climate that never falls below 70° by day – it sounds like a tourist's dream of paradise. Who then would want to leave Palm Island?'

Five

ON THE WAY back down the coast they broke the train journey at Rockhampton and stayed in the city with Marie. Maggie's sister was now a widow, Billy having enjoyed his retirement for only a few years before he died. Marie had become more militant in Aboriginal affairs and fell out with Maggie for her 'luke-warmness'.

'You've got a name now, girl!' she said. 'You should use it more to speak out for Land Rights, to criticise all the things that are wrong with the Queensland Act.'

'I *am* writing an article about conditions on Palm Island.'

'Well, that's something; that's a start.'

'What she wants to do is go to Canberra and kick up a stink there, make the Federal Government do something about it,' said Joe.

Marie thought that it was retirement that killed Billy Efate; after working all his life he couldn't get used to it. ' 'E always wanted to do somethin' special on weekends,' said Marie. 'Couldn't realise that 'is whole life was one long weekend. The doctor couldn't find anything really wrong with him, he just faded away.

'I think I might go out to Pandanus to live,' she added. 'Gran's goin' to have a fight there, a big tourist mob wants to turn it into a smart resort. I just hope she doesn't live to see that happen: it would break 'er heart.'

'They can't do that, can they?'

'They can't take the cottages away from our people, not after we've bin there so long. But they'll ruin the island with a lot of bloody trippers muckin' up the beaches with rubbish, an' then they'll start sayin' our places are an eyesore, they need painting, or they oughter be pulled down. I can just see it.'

Joe told her about the book by a Professor of Anthropology

who'd made a study of Aboriginal culture and language in coastal Queensland.

He had brought her for a present a copy of 'The Gurindji Blues,' his favourite record, a song by Ted Egan to drone-pipe and song-sticks, with an introduction by the Gurindji Land Rights leader, Vincent Lingiari. He was a tribal Aborigine whose English was slow and halting:

'Long time bifore white man come 'ere, all-about land belong to Gurindji, my people. Aboriginal man 'ere before the 'orse an' cattle come over this land, where I sittin' now. That the 'tory I got from my old father, and grandpa, that this land bilong to me. That what I bin keepin' on my mind. An' I still got it on my mind.'

Marie listened wide-eyed to the words of the song, while she felt the throb of the didgeridoo vibrating through her spine, and her scalp tingled to that ancient rhythm beaten out by the ironwood sticks:

> Poor bugger me, Gurindji,
> Long time work no wages we,
> Work for good old Lord Vestey,
> Little-bit flour, sugar and tea
> From Lord Vestey, to Gurindji.

> But poor bugger blackfeller, this countree,
> Gov'ment Law him talk 'long we
> Can't give-it land long blackfeller, see,
> Only spoil-im Gurindji . . .
> Oh poor bugger me, Gurindji.

> Poor bugger me, Gurindji,
> Gov'ment Boss him talk long we
> 'Buy-im own land, Gurindji,
> Buy-im back from Lord Vestey . . .'
> Oh poor we, Gurindji.

> Poor bugger blackfeller, Gurindji,
> S'pose we buy-im back country,
> What you reckon proper fee?
> Might be flour, sugar and tea

582

Marie listened intently till the last click of the song-sticks. 'What a beaut song!' she said when it was finished. 'It's got the real sound of the Old People in it, and the words are a little-bit, you know, satirical. Can I keep it, kid?'

''Course. I bought it for you.'

She put the phonograph needle back to the beginning again and listened to Lingiari's dignified, slow speech. Then the vibrating didgeridoo took up its compulsive rhythm, the ironwood sticks *tchonged* in time.

'He bought it with his own pocket-money, what's more,' said Maggie. 'It's a good song, but he's played it until I'm nearly mad, driven right up the wall.'

'I dunno what's wrong with you, Maggie. I could listen to it all day.'

'Same here,' said Joe. 'You know what the Gurindji did – they walked off Vestey's station at Wave Hill and set up camp at Wattie Creek. It must be the first time the Aborigines ever went on strike.'

'That makes them the same as white Australians, eh? They're always goin' on strike.'

'Yair, well the Gurindji took on one of the most powerful concerns in the world, run by some British Lords and beef barons. Vesteys were paying the Australian Government only fifty-five cents a square mile for their lease! And they held it to the year 2,000. So the Gurindji just took some fencing wire and cut some posts and run up a fence round the bit of land they wanted. They're still on that land, at Wattie Creek.'

'A pity they didn't "sit down" on more of the islands off the Queensland coast, the way Nyora and her family did on Pandanus,' said Marie. 'I've bin bonin' up on a bit of the local history too . . . What they did was kill off the Island people, and then round up all the mainland people, all the remains of the diff'runt tribes, and shunt them off to the islands out of the way. Lepers were put on little tiny islands with hardly any water, and left there to die.'

'This book I was telling you about,' said Joe. 'It says the

Chinese brought leprosy when they came to the Palmer goldfields in 1870.

'As for the islands, Magnetic was used as a prison for mainland Aborigines after the Island people had been "dispersed". Then the young men were all brought from Great Keppel to work on Ross's station near Rockhampton. They were half starved, so they broke into the store and stole some rations, and then ran away. The mounted police followed them right to the coast, where they were on Vosses' Point looking across at their island – of course they had no boat. When they saw the horsemen coming, they jumped into the sea and tried to swim the ten miles home, with bullets whipping round their ears. Only two made it.'

Marie drew a deep breath.

'How – how many men?' she asked.

'I dunno. But it was *all* the young men from the Island.'

'So, nowadays they don't shoot and poison us, but they're still takin' our land away. D'you know that Fraser Island was given to the blackfellers once, "To be made one great permanent Aboriginal home", accordin' to the Queensland Government? And of course Fraser belongs to the Forestry now. A "permanent Aboriginal home", they called it! It was never home, and it was never meant to be permanent. They hoped all the people would die before too long.'

'Yes, a chap called Bill Cotton was telling us about it, in Townsville.'

'And that's on'y some of it,' said Marie. 'But Maggie's not interested; she'd rather write about the old fairy-stories that Uncle Morgan tells her – '

'I am interested!' protested Maggie. 'I'm horrified. But I've no ability for writing factual, historical books. There are white men, educated men, beginning to write about the dark side of our history, much better equipped than me to do it.'

'And you're goin' back down south, away from the fight up 'ere.'

'Yes.' Maggie looked uncomfortable. 'I've got a good job there, and a nice house I rent, with a garden . . .'

'Huh, you're just a white Abo. You've got no guts, my girl.'

Maggie looked hurt but obstinate.

'Let's hope Joe sticks up for the dark people, even if he has got red hair.'

'The Keppel Islanders had red, curly hair,' said Joe eagerly, 'I was just telling Mum, I read it in this book – '

'Yair. It just so happens that Nyora's people came from Fraser Island, but. They was Batjalas, from further south.'

'Oh . . . yes. I forgot.' Joe looked crestfallen.

'Anyways, we're all mixtures. I got a bit of Scottish common sense from Great Grandma Emily, though I mightn't look it.'

Before catching the train for Brisbane and Sydney, Maggie and Joe went out to Pandanus Island in the daily launch to see Grannie Nyora, now getting very old. She was not quite sure of her birthdate but thought it was 1875, which would make her ninety-one. Joe would be seventeen next month.

Her mind was perfectly clear, but her legs had swollen and she moved about very slowly. Dan's wife Ilona came in each day to 'do' for her, to get her a warm mid-day meal, and to wash her hair for her once a week.

'Ah, I had pretty hair, once,' said Nyora, looking through her wet grey ringlets at Maggie. 'Dark brown and wavy and shiny – a bit like yours, girl.'

'Well, that's where I get it, I suppose.'

'Bert's hair was straight. But you don't get it from 'im, no. I'm sure o' that.'

The old woman bent such a peculiar look upon her that she wondered for a brief moment if Nyora really was getting senile? But no, she didn't believe it; those old dark eyes were still bright with intelligence.

'Remind me to tell you 'bout that, 'fore you go. This the las' time you see ol' Nyora.'

'I hope not, Grannie.'

'Yair. I been close-up finish. Had a good long life, eh?' she chuckled, while Ilona towelled her hair vigorously.

'Let me set it, Gran!' said Maggie. 'And put a hibiscus flower in it like you used to wear, you told me, when you were a girl.'

Nyora laughed. 'All right, girl. You play-about with it all you want.'

Ilona tipped out the rinsing-water under the pandanus

palm, now grown huge on bulbous stilt-like roots. She took the things inside and brought a brush and comb and bobby-pins out to where Nyora sat in a comfortable canvas chair.

'I'll go down and see if the launch has come in,' she said. Dan and Joe were out fishing. When she was gone, Nyora suddenly reached up and grasped one of Maggie's hands.

'Lissen, Maggie,' she said. 'While they's no one round, I gotta tell you somethin'. Somethin' affects Joe as well, but I not goin' tell 'im. He such a good kid, fond of the Old People; I wish 'e was my greatgrandson, I do. You gotta do what you t'ink best when he growed up to a man.'

Nyora released her hand, and Maggie went on mechanically pushing the grey hair into soft waves. What had she said? I *wish* Joe was my great-grandson – ?

'What are you trying to say, Gran? That Bert wasn't your son at all? Then whose was he?'

'No, that not it. Bert, 'e was mine and Miguel's all right. And Bert, 'e married your Mumma, Anna Brown. But Marie and Dan, they's on'y your half-sister an' brother.'

'Then who – who was my father? Joe's grandfather?'

'You know the gravestones up t' the cemetery? You see the date on Bert's grave? 'E was drowned in the '27 cyclone. But that wasn't in *December* that year; it was February.'

'But – but I wasn't born till 1928.'

'That right. And when is your birthday?'

'March the eleventh.'

'Exackly. So you must of bin a twelve month baby. On'y elephants take that long. We didn't get the stone till about a year after 'e died, so I got 'em to put just the year. And no one but me and Anna was any the wiser. She go down to Brisbane for two months while you born.'

Maggie's head whirled. She had not even been born on the island! Nyora was not her real grandmother!

She came round in front of Nyora, the wet comb still in her hand, and sank down in the sand in front of her chair. She took Nyora's dark wrinkled hand in hers.

'Gran, tell me! I must know. Does Marie or Dan know about this?'

'No. Marie was on the mainland, stayin' with Auntie Maud, and Dan was too young to work out dates. Morgan an' Elsie must've wondered, but they never said nothin'.'

'But *who* – ?'

'That just it, I dunno who, exackly. Anna went on this holiday down Caloundra way, and it seem she meet some Yankee feller off a yacht. After she came back she tell me she gonna have a baby. She not know 'is name, even.'

'Didn't even – know – his name! Oh, no!'

'She say – Anna tell me – he was a beaut feller, but they meet just this two mornin's on t' beach, then 'e has to sail away. She never see 'im again. He got fair hair, she say, and brown eyes.'

'Well! I'm – I'm flabbergasted! To think that my Mum . . . And that I'm not . . . and you're not my Gran, and I'm not – not even one little bit Aboriginal?'

'You still Anna's daughter. And you still my Maggie, what I helped to bring up. You still from Islander peoples.'

'Yes! Of course I am. I don't *feel* any different now you've told me. I'm like that magpie that Auntie Maud kept in the chook run when he was little, and he grew up trying to cluck like a hen. I'm not going to tell anyone.'

'Well, I dunno.' Nyora looked worried. 'Some'ow I not wantin' to die without tellin'. But you gotter think if you tell Joe or not. I worry 'bout 'im, Maggie.'

'Gran! What've you seen? Tell me! You knew Vin was going to get killed in his car, didn't you? What's going to happen to Joe, for God's sake?'

'Nothin' too bad – it's jus' – he headin' for trouble. I see p'leecemen – p'raps even gaol. He talkin' already about Freedom Rides, an' that. He gonna get mixed up with some wild mob, mebbe get hisself arrested.'

'Well, I don't think I can tell him. He identifies so strongly with the dark people, the Aborigines more than the Islanders. At least we're still Islanders, after all. But I feel a fraud – all my books came out under false pretences.'

'Nonsense, girl. You *feel* them stories, you write 'em down like no one else can write 'em. You doin' a great job.'

'Should I tell Marie?'

'I don't reckon, no. It don't affect her. 'Cept she might get upset, 'er mother gettin' off with a Yank! Plenty of girls done that in the last war. Specially in Queensland.'

Maggie smiled. 'That part of it doesn't worry me at all. She must have been terribly lonely after Dad – after Bert died. But it's a shock, all right!'

She went off for a long walk round the beach to compose herself before meeting Joe and the others. Perhaps this explained her lack of commitment to militancy, to the Aboriginal cause, which Marie found so exasperating. And yet, as she had told Nyora, she didn't *feel* any different. The Pandanus Islanders were her people, and always would be. She hoped the tourist development would come to nothing.

Back at Marie's for a couple of days before they returned home, Marie suggested they take the bus down to Emu Bay for the day to see old Auntie Maud Efate, Marie's Aboriginal mother-in-law. She was now in her eighties and did not get out much. Maggie made the excuse that she had to finish her article on Palm Island and wanted to go to the library in town to check something; so Joe and Marie went.

Maggie hurried into town, but not to the library. She went to the offices of the *Rockhampton Star*, on the banks of the Fitzroy River, and asked to see the files for 1927 and 1928.

With the heavy, bound files propped on a sloping desk, she began with the summer of '28. In January to April, the cyclone season, there was nothing; the only cyclone had hit far to the south, between Bundaberg and Fraser Island.

She was hoping that Nyora's memory might be faulty, after all. If her father had not died till 1928, she must be his daughter. But there was no news of lost fishermen or boats in the area. With a sinking heart she lifted the second file. 1927: December; November; October . . . nothing. Back to the beginning of the year; January: 'Cyclone crosses coast. Magnetic Island battered . . . degenerates to a rain depression.' February: 'Cyclone moving down the coast; huge seas at Mackay . . . Yeppoon . . . fishing boats feared lost. No communication with Keppel Islands . . .' And then a small item on the front page:

The body of Albert Pinjarra, fisherman, of Pandanus Island, was discovered yesterday during a
search by several boats after he failed to return
from a fishing trip undertaken in mountainous seas,
following the passage of the recent cyclone. His
boat was aground on a coral cay, not severely
damaged, but he had apparently fallen overboard
and become entangled in his own net . . .

The date was February, 1927.

Maggie clutched the wooden edges of the lectern, feeling
she might faint. She let the heavy file of bound newspapers fall
shut. So it was true. She was Anna's child, but not Bert's. She
was a by-blow, the result of a chance meeting between her
mother and some unknown American yachtsman. It occurred
to her only now that she could simply have got the Certificate
of Death from the Registrar, giving the date when her supposed father died. She had got a copy of her Birth Certificate
at the time of her marriage, and there was no doubt about
that. She had not been born until March of the following year.

Six

FROM A cheap hotel in lower Macleay Street, Sydney, they
could walk down to Wooloomooloo by steep steps cut in the
living rock, the ubiquitous Sydney sandstone. From there it
was a short way to the free entertainment of the Art Gallery in
the Domain, and to the Public Library on the corner of
Macquarie Street. Or they could take a ferry ride to Manly on
the old South Steyne steamer from Circular Quay.

One day they took a ferry to Rose Bay and walked round
South Head Road toward Vaucluse.

'I knew someone who lived here,' said Maggie to her son. 'Your great-grandmother, as a matter of fact, Mrs William King.'

'But this is a very posh suburb, isn't it?'

'It is now; anything with a Harbour view is a fabulous price. Besides, her mother was a Macdonald and her father was Hamilton Forbes – wealthy squatters on both sides.'

'Huh! I suppose they used to shoot the poor bloody blacks to make room for more sheep.'

'I believe she said one of her great-uncles was speared by them.'

'That just evens up the score a bit.'

'Wait a minute, it was down along here – · Number sixty-seven. The old lady must be dead by now. I met her before you were born, and she was over seventy then.'

They turned down a sloping road that led towards the Harbour along one of the many points of high, wooded land. Near the end of the street was a tangled garden with a thickset hedge and a wooden gate. Maggie stared at the old bungalow beyond. In the garden was a tall, thin woman with short iron-grey hair, picking roses.

Maggie had only meant to look, but she couldn't resist calling out, asking if Mrs Elaine King used to live here?

'She still does. Why?'

'I just wondered . . . She must be a very old lady by now.'

'Ninety-three next birthday.' The woman came closer and looked across the gate at Maggie, and then at Joe. 'Are you from India, by any chance?'

'No, no; I'm Maggie – Mrs Vincent King. And this is my son Joseph.'

'How d'you do? We never met, did we? I'm Anne King that was, now Greville. You must come in and see Mother.'

'Oh no, we won't trouble her. Is she bedridden?'

'Not at all. She gets up at seven every morning, dresses herself, and makes herself a cup of tea before I'm awake.' Anne was a bony, sallow-faced woman in her sixties, with no resemblance to her mother that Maggie could see except in her height. She opened the gate. 'So this is my great-nephew,' she said, shaking hands with Joe. 'I never met your father.

But I see you have Mother's red hair.'

'And the curls of my "Kanaka" ancestors, too,' said Joe defiantly.

Maggie's heart was beating uncomfortably. She would have dressed more carefully to meet Vin's relations if she had known when she set out. She was in white slacks and a knitted cotton top, and Joe was in shorts.

Anne let them in through the glass-panelled door she remembered, to the room with the sweeping view of the Harbour and the cluster of high-rise buildings that now marked the city centre. She declined a chair and stood looking at the view, while Joe examined with interest the tiger's skin on the floor, complete with white fangs and glaring yellow glass eyes. 'She may not remember me . . .' murmured Maggie.

Anne went to fetch her mother. 'Don't worry, her mind is clear as a bell,' she said.

Hearing a slow step in the passage, Maggie looked up, and there in the doorway stood Elaine King, tall and commanding as ever, in a long black dress that reached almost to her ankles. She wore an embroidered Kashmiri shawl about her shoulders, caught with a heavy silver brooch. Her grey hair, swept back in two loops into a small bun, held just a tinge of pink or orange, a ghost of its former colour.

'My dear!' She held out her thin hands, and Maggie took them in hers and kissed the withered cheek offered to her. Elaine patted the silver bracelet on Maggie's wrist. 'I see you haven't lost or broken it after all these years.'

'And I still have your wedding present, the stoneware bread crock you sent us.'

'Ah yes! Sad that your married life was so short . . . But happy?'

'Very happy.'

'It's such a long, long time since I was widowed. Sometimes I think that all the important things happened in the first half of my life. For the second half I have just existed. And I never met my great-grandson.'

'This is Joseph Forbes King. Joe, come and meet your great-grandmother.'

'Mother, you had better sit down first,' said Anne quietly.

'Yes, yes, I forget how old I am, till my legs start to tremble.'

She sank into a high-backed, tapestry covered chair. 'Now, my boy, come and give me a kiss.'

Joe stepped forward awkwardly and did as he was bid. Elaine held his hand and examined his face. 'Aye, you've got Fergus Macdonald's carroty hair, that I had when I was younger. Do you know, child, that my great-grandmother Kate Hamilton Forbes kissed me in Hobart when I was a child, nearly ninety years ago? So that I am a link between – how many generations? Six generations that bore the name of Forbes! All the same, I wish you'd called him William,' she said to Maggie. 'I never saw much of Joseph after he married and went to Queensland.'

'I didn't call him after that Joseph,' said Maggie.

'And I have lived through three wars! The Boer War, the First World War, and the Second World War. Thank goodness Vincent was too young for the last one,' said Elaine, 'and wasn't born for the first.' A look of pain crossed her face. 'What a waste, what a terrible waste of young men's lives! And now I suppose Joseph here will be just in time for the new one.'

Maggie went cold. 'You mean the Vietnam war? Surely it will be over before he's twenty!'

For they were conscripting young men to fight in Vietnam. The Prime Minister, Harold Holt, had just visited the United States and coined his catch-phrase, 'All the way with LBJ.' The National Service Act of 1964 called up Army trainees as soon as they turned twenty. But not *every* young man was summoned; some were exempt because of their occupations, while of the rest only those were called up whose birth-dates fell out of a barrel full of numbered marbles. What more suitable for a nation where, every year, all services stopped for five minutes all over the country while the Melbourne Cup was run? Fortunes were bet on the horse-race every November.

Maggie prayed that the war, in which the first conscript had been killed, would end soon. She had cut out of the daily paper a picture of a Vietnamese woman running screaming along a road, clutching the dead child whose blood stained the front of her blouse. What were we doing in Vietnam, anyway? No one seemed to know, but Prime Minister Holt talked about 'great and powerful friends,' and Lyndon Johnson was on a visit to Australia at his invitation.

'What do you think about the war, Joseph? What if you should be called up?'

'I wouldn't go. I'd be a conscientious objector. I've been taking part in anti-Vietnam marches in Adelaide. But at the moment I'm more interested in Aboriginal rights, Land Rights especially. And as for President Johnson coming here, look at the way the Americans have treated the Negroes! No wonder there's a Black Power movement in the States. We'll have to start something like that here. Especially in Queensland, the most racist State in Australia.

'And the Northern Territory's not much better, where they've got stockmen working for about a quarter of a white man's wage, and the women work in the homesteads for a bit of tea and sugar and the leftovers from the boss's table. That's why the Gurindji people walked out.'

'Yes, we read about that, Mother,' said Anne. 'They were on Vestey's big cattle station at Victoria Downs, and they asked for a bit of land of their own out of Vestey's huge lease – what was it, about 36,000 square miles of country?'

'Yes, that'd be right,' said Joe. 'And they've got a ninety-year lease. So the Gurindji ran up a fence round a bit of land at Wattie Creek. There was a sacred rock there, at Seal Gorge. I've got a recording of their leader, Vincent Lingiari, talking about it:

'Up come the manager, and he say, "Hey, you steal anurrer man's country." Oh yeah, that's all right, and I say, "No, well, what was before the Vestey born and I born? It was blackfeller country." And so it was, for thousands of years.'

'Yes, of course they've got right on their side,' said Elaine. 'After all, the British created a precedent when they gave India back to the Indians. But you won't catch them giving Australia back to the first Australians, not if they can help it.'

'They stole this country from my people. I suppose the first Forbes stole some of Tasmania, but the Tasmanians are all dead, so they can't ask for their land back!'

'You feel strongly about it, eh? What are you going to do about it?'

'Like I said, march, protest, attend meetings, go to Canberra if necessary and confront the Federal Government. It's no use trying to get anywhere with State Governments. Do you know, Great-Grandma, that there are leper colonies here in Australia? One in thirty Aborigines in the Territory has had leprosy at some time. And people up there are going blind from trachoma, and dying of tuberculosis.'

'No!' Elaine sat up very straight, clasping her hands tightly together in her lap. 'I didn't know that.'

'It's true,' said Maggie. 'The people in the North are living in dusty, squalid camps, with no proper water supply, and poor shelters of galvanised iron and hessian bags. In fact, even right here in New South Wales, if they choose to be independent, and not be herded into Reserves, then it's the shanty and the camp. Hygiene is impossible under those conditions. Children die of dysentery, old people of bronchitis, young people of TB, and there's leprosy and trachoma and VD . . . I hope you're not shocked.'

'I *am* shocked!' said Elaine, 'to think that I didn't know. I spent my life in India helping the lepers there, and the blind beggars, and all the time they were right here in my own country. I didn't know.'

'Because the Government hushes it up,' said Joe. 'They have Ministers for Aboriginal Affairs who never leave the cities. And in Queensland the Reserves are run like prison camps, and the laws are just like South Africa – '

'All right, Joe, you're not addressing a meeting,' said Maggie.

Elaine smiled. 'I see he can be eloquent and that he feels and can express his feelings about injustice. Perhaps he might be the first Member of Parliament of Aboriginal and Islander descent? Have you thought of University for him?'

'Yes, but I can't afford it. He's doing well this year at high school, but whether he'll get a bursary is another matter.'

'Where does he get this crusading spirit? It must be from you; I don't think Vincent ever showed much interest in social questions.'

'They say my mother's grandfather, Thomas Brown, was a bit of an activist and landed in gaol for his beliefs.'

'Well, I hope it won't come to that with Joe.'

'And my elder sister Marie is very active in the Federal Council for Advancement of Aboriginal and Torres Strait Islanders.'

'But they all squabble among themselves,' said Joe. 'They'll never beat the Government that way.'

Anne had brought out sherry and fruit-cake. Though Maggie protested that they hadn't meant to stay, it was very pleasant in that room with its big picture window. Hundreds of yachts criss-crossed the blue with their white sails, bobbing over the choppy waves like a lot of White Leghorns pecking up wheat. For it was Sunday, and half Sydney was out on the water.

'The only hope for us is for a Labour Government,' Joe was saying. 'The Libs are very hostile to Land Rights because of big business and vested interests. The Referendum will help, if there's a Yes vote. Under the present constitution, Aborigines and Islanders aren't even included when a census is taken. They might as well not exist.'

Anne and Maggie were quietly talking about gardening. Joe had his great-grandmother's complete attention. 'Yes, you should definitely stand for Parliament, my boy. But you must spend a few more years studying.'

Maggie put down her empty glass and said, 'Come, Joe. Get off your soapbox now. We have to catch the ferry back to the Quay.'

'We've been having an interesting conversation. I've learnt a lot,' said Elaine, 'about my own country.'

'I'll send you a copy of my last book – it's a collection of verse.' Maggie stood up to say goodbye. 'I'd have brought it along, but I had no idea we'd be seeing you.'

'I'm sorry we have lost touch. I suppose in these days of aeroplanes Adelaide is just next door, though it's a thousand miles away. You must call again when you're in Sydney.'

Maggie explained that on her salary flying was a bit too expensive, which was why Joe had just met his Queensland relatives for the first time since he was a small boy.

'And Rosetta cut Vincent out of her Will, did she? A pity

my poor Stan died first. Even so, he could have made a bit more provision for his only son, surely.'

'They were already estranged over Vin's car-racing, you see. I suppose he thought if he left most of his money to Rosetta it would stop Vin buying expensive racing cars, and that his mother would leave it to him eventually.'

'So she left it to a cats' home!'

Maggie shrugged. 'It doesn't matter. We manage all right; I've a small house I rent in Adelaide, and a good job, and a car of my own.'

'Write down your address; we'll send you a Christmas card, at least.'

Before they left Sydney, they were caught up in a protest rally that started in the Domain and spread to the streets through which President Johnson's cavalcade was to pass when he came from the airport. 'Look at all those little American flags!' said Joe scornfully, surveying the enthusiastic crowd that lined the route to cheer the first President of the USA ever to visit Australia while in office.

The protesters, mostly young, many of them students, chanted '*Ho! Ho! Ho Chi Minh*,' and as the escort of police motor-cycles and cars came nearer, with Premier Askin sitting beside the President in an open Rolls Royce, it changed to:

> *Hey, hey, LBJ!*
> *How many kids did you kill today?*

Maggie kept a firm hold of Joe's arm as he shouted and waved his fist. She felt the tension and excitement surging through him. A group of young men broke the police cordon and threw themselves down in the narrow street, blocking the way for the President's car. Askin leaned toward President Johnson with a fawning smile.

'Why don't you drive over the bastards?' he asked loudly.

Scuffles broke out between protesters and the wielders of the Stars and Stripes among the onlookers, and police moved in, using their batons. The protesters lying in the street were carried struggling to paddy-wagons, and the cavalcade moved on.

The marchers ran after the line of cars, waving their placards: MAKE LOVE NOT WAR and FREE SIMON TOWNSEND and END WAR IN VIETNAM NOW! A burly man carrying a small American flag grabbed one of the placards and smashed it down over the head of the man bearing it, and another fight broke out.

Young Simon Townsend had refused, as a conscientious objector, to accept his draft-card or to obey military orders. When he did not present himself for medical examination after the first order, he was gaoled for a week for non-compliance. Then he was taken to court and sentenced to an Army prison, where he was now living in solitary confinement.

Joe greatly admired his courage and said he would do the same. But he wondered uneasily what he would do if his name really came out of the barrel on his twentieth birthday. He suffered from claustrophobia to such an extent that he would climb hundreds of stairs rather than use a lift. Maggie had once shut him in the bathroom as a punishment, and he had gone berserk in that confined space.

Yet to fight in Vietnam would be against all his principles. He would have to refuse. He felt that it was a racist war, where white Americans were killing without compunction, burning with napalm, blasting with bombs, destroying the homes of 'gooks', 'slant-eyes' and 'slopes', little brown men to whom, consciously or unconsciously, they felt superior.

Prime Minister Holt had just committed another full battalion to the war. Yet Australian soldiers themselves did not seem to have their heart in the struggle. Stories were filtering back of the shooting of unarmed prisoners, of women being given the water-torture while Australian officers looked on. The troops were disaffected, and a new and hateful slang-word had crept into their vocabulary: 'fragging'. It described what happened when a hand-grenade was thrown into the tent of an unpopular officer while he slept.

By the end of the next year, Harold Holt would become disenchanted with Vietnam and refuse to commit any more troops or aircraft. Then, just before Christmas while he was holidaying at Portsea, he disappeared in mysterious circumstances – swept out by the undertow while swimming on a day when the seas were dangerous. But his body was never recovered, and there were dark rumours of sinister CIA involvement. Others thought he had become weary of the problems and deliberately took a risk, not caring much if he never made it back to shore. But at present, with beaming smile, he rode on a wave of euphoria while he welcomed his great and powerful friend to Canberra, the Federal capital.

Seven

WHEN THE September vacation was over, Maggie went back to work and Joe returned to school, a week late. Maggie still felt shattered by old Nyora's revelation. She had not told Joe. Perhaps when he was older he might be able to accept it, but not now. There seemed to be a need in his soul for something strong and ancient and Aboriginal that he could relate to. He had this sense of a beautiful and heroic past, now lost but part of him through his racial beginnings. Without it his life would lose half its meaning.

For Maggie, who was older and had been 'living white' for years, the shock was not so great, but it stopped her from writing. How could she go on letting herself be described as 'the Aboriginal authoress' – a phrase she disliked anyway. The best thing perhaps would be to stop using Aboriginal themes. She could travel out into the Pacific, find the island her great-grandfather Joseph came from, and write his story. It would be the story of an indentured labourer, a near-slave kidnapped and brought to Australia, and there becoming a citizen with a whole string of descendants growing up as Australians – David Efate's boys in Melbourne, May Tombua's, her own Joseph. It was a pity Harold and Ellen had not produced a son to carry on the name of Brown, since Fiona's twin boys were lost.

Maggie sent an early Christmas card to Elaine King in Sydney. Back came a note from Anne Greville to say that her mother had died the week before, shortly after her ninety-third birthday. It was difficult, she said, to believe that such a vital person was no more.

Maggie encouraged Joe to work hard, but he was often distracted by protest marches and the assertion of his Aboriginal identity. When the results came out in the New Year he had a credit in Economic History and had passed his leaving Honours exam, just scraping through in Intermediate mathematics, to qualify for a Degree course at University. To Maggie's disappointment his written English was his weakest subject, and he received only a 'Q', or qualified pass.

Joe thought he would like a job with the Federal Department of Aboriginal Affairs in Canberra, but he had no particular qualifications. Now if only, he said, he could get a Bachelor of Economics degree, he would have every chance.

'Why not law?' said Maggie. 'That's what your father did. You could appear for Aboriginal defendants in court.'

'No! Lawyers are crooks. And the judge would take one look at me and become even more biassed.'

'Judges are supposed to be impartial.'

'Ha! Don't give me that. You know what that word means, by the way: "Bi-assed". The same as "two-faced", only at the other end of the anatomy. Useful for sitting on fences.'

'Really, Joe!' She laughed.

For seventeen years Joe had been the only man in her life. But since coming back from Queensland she had been going out with an artist who lived in an old barn-loft in North Adelaide. She knew that he did not eat properly and drank too much, so she started taking him meals in the middle of the day. They consumed them from a table cluttered with art books, paint brushes in jars, and shallow plates full of dried colours which he used instead of a palette.

When he was sober Roy was a charming companion, urbane, witty, and cultivated: a tall, well-turned-out, even dandified figure when he dressed for a special occasion, with his neat Van Dyke beard and longish, straight fair hair going a little thin on top. But his hazel eyes were permanently bloodshot from the extravasation of blood from broken blood-vessels, the result of week-long alcoholic 'benders'. When drunk, Mr Hyde took over from Dr Jekyll. His tongue became waspish, his expression supercilious, his wit cruel rather than clever. In the last stages of inebriation he lost control of his limbs and would trip over something and lie giggling foolishly on the floor.

Once, going through some old sketches he had done on a world trip years ago, he was showing Maggie some water-colours of Edinburgh Castle, Chepstow, Tintern Abbey, Glastonbury ('all romantic ruins, like me,' said Roy with self-mockery), when he came across an early photograph taken in the studio he had in Sydney as a young man. It was, he said, on the top floor of a high-rise building; the sun came in through the north windows all day, and he had a view across the city to the Harbour and its winding wooded inlets and the huge iron bridge spanning its width.

'Portrait of the Artist as a Young Man,' he said, handing her the photograph.

Maggie stared at it, unable to speak. She wanted to cry. The face was a spiritual one, the eyes large and melancholy, the brow wide and thoughtful, with a youthful lock of hair falling across it, the mouth young, tender, with just a hint in its full curves of the self-indulgence that would be his undoing.

Now he was fifty, and his face was ruined. Alcoholism was slowly eroding his health and talent. Those early sketches, were done when he used to draw all the time in a fury of creativity: a tired passenger asleep on a railway station, a nun walking in her full habit against the wind, friends drinking at a party, arches in the Alhambra in Spain, some narrow steps in Salerno.

Looking from them to the sensitive, vulnerable face of that young man now spoiled by life and time, Maggie realised what a great potential had been lost. Was it the fatal weakness for drink that stopped him realising his potential as an artist, or the realisation that he would never be a great artist that turned him to drink? For a while she had hoped to rehabilitate him, even thought she might marry him, or at least bring him home to live with her and Joseph, feed him proper meals, with plenty of home-grown vegetables, and wean him from the cheap sherry and bottles of beer which were giving him an old man's paunch, a 'beer belly' which sat oddly on his tall, lean figure.

But then he got hopelessly drunk again, turned up at her house on a Sunday morning and fell off the kitchen chair she pushed him into while she made him black coffee.

'You're pissed, Roy,' said Joe with the uncompromising, judging stare of youth. 'Why don't you go home and sleep it off?'

She saw the contempt in his face. No, he would never accept Roy Gilham as a father-substitute.

She remembered the night she had met Roy at the house of some friends. When she arrived he was holding the floor, talking extravagantly and quoting poetry in a staunchless flow of eloquence. His young audience seemed to be spellbound. Maggie found that she was ignored, merely told to sit down and a drink thrust into her hand, while Roy continued in full spate.

She had not then seen any of his paintings, though she knew of his work. He had only recently arrived from Sydney, perhaps deciding, she thought cynically, to be a big frog in a smaller pond. For in Sydney the competition was fierce, and a few established names commanded most of the gallery sales and newspaper notices. In Adelaide the art world was more fluid, perhaps because of the influx of European artists after the war: Poles, Yugoslavs, Hungarians, Czechs, Austrians, even a few displaced Russians. The painters among them were out of all proportion to their numbers in the community.

As Roy and his disciples continued to ignore her, Maggie felt her nose distinctly put out of joint. She, as a published writer, had been something of a *guru* among the young poets and aspiring novelists. She drank her wine moodily. No one bothered to refill her glass.

Roy had a deep, well-modulated voice, an actor's voice, which he used effectively. Latin verses rolled off his tongue in chiming hexameters.

he proclaimed, while Maggie, who had no Latin, listened impatiently. Later she made a few sharp remarks, and challenged him on the accuracy of his quotation from Edward Thomas:

> Out of the wood of things that grow by night
> To be cut down by the sharp axe of light –

'That first line is wrong,' she said confidently.

'I assure you it's right.'

'I'll bet you anything!'

'Who's got a *Modern English Verse*? Or a collected Edward Thomas?'

But no one had. The argument was unresolved when Maggie got up and announced rather stiffly that she must go. Belatedly her young friends filled her glass and asked her to stay, but she insisted on leaving. Let this arrogant man have the floor to himself!

Roy got up – he was well over six feet – and striding across the room, lifted her shoulder high and carried her to the door, where he kissed her soundly and set her down. 'Don't you know I'm a fan of yours?' he said. 'I have all your books.'

True or not, Maggie accepted it as an olive-branch. She smiled for the first time at him, and as she went out to the car her heart fluttered like a girl's. Yes, she was actually looking forward to seeing him again.

In January a letter arrived from a lawyer with an address in George Street, Sydney. She had not prayed for help, but like an answer to prayer came the news that under the Will of Mrs Elaine Hamilton Forbes she was to receive a small legacy of $3,000, 'for the purpose of putting my great-grandson Joseph Forbes King through University.' Perhaps because she knew how Vincent as a young man had run through his grandfather Joseph Forbes' legacy, spending it all on fast cars and drinking parties, Elaine had not left anything directly to Joe.

'You'll have to work hard!' she admonished him. 'There's not enough money for you to spend more than three years on your course, so you must pass every end-of-year exam. If you get in at the University of Adelaide, you'll be able to save by living at home.'

But she saw that this was not at all what he wanted.

'No, I want to go to Sydney University. It's the oldest one, and besides they've got a terrific Students' Union there, and it's the headquarters for the students who've been going on Freedom Rides to Western towns. They're working for Land Rights, too, *and* rallying against the Vietnam War – '

'You'll be studying, not marching, I hope.'

By the time Probate was granted, and the money filtered through, Maggie hoped he would have changed his mind. But Joe insisted on applying to the University of Sydney. He had left it too late, for the first term began in March, and the Economics course was fully enrolled. There was no Economics Faculty at the University of New South Wales.

'What about Monash, in Victoria?'

'No, I'd rather go to the ANU in Canberra. It's only two hundred miles from Sydney; I could go up for weekends sometimes. And it might be easier to get from there into the DOAA.'

He was only just in time to enrol with a 'late application' in early February for which Maggie had to pay a late fee. The Australian National University was a very recent one, which specialised in post-graduate and research studies. It had been founded not much more than twenty years ago, but then Canberra itself was a new city. It was situated on what had been known in the last century as 'a sheepwalk', when old squatters like William Brodribb were getting their experience on the Monaro. Instead of just growing up like most cities, it had been deliberately planned to a magnificent design by the American architect Walter Burley Griffin. An artificial lake now made a central point for the city set on the sunbrowned plain in its ring of blue hills. In some ways it was still like a large country town, the only capital, it was said, where you could hear crows cawing overhead in the city centre.

Towards the end of summer, when Joe arrived for Orientation Week, the air was incredibly hot, dry and clear. The scent of thousands of eucalyptus trees (someone had suggested calling the new city 'Eucalypta') and the shade of exotic dark firs and green elms and birches refreshed the air.

More than two million trees had been planted. In fact, there were a lot more trees than people, and commercial activity (in the form of car yards, service stations and food stores) was firmly tucked out of sight among the greenery. All this, and the lack of any real night life, had earned for Canberra the title of 'the best-lighted cemetery in the Southern Hemisphere.'

It came alive only when Parliament was sitting in the long white building overlooking the lake. As soon as the House rose at the end of a session, the Members leapt on to private planes or commercial airliners and flew back to their native cities. Most of the permanent residents were civil servants, the Heads of Departments like Treasury and Defence and their proliferating staffs.

Even the University had a staid, middle-aged image, for the ANU was largely a research establishment, with a large School of Pacific Studies; but there were Faculties of Arts, Law, Economics and Science, and residential hostels for young students, in one of which Joe was able to get accommodation. Some students found it dull; there was nothing to do at night, apart from private parties, and public transport was almost non-existent.

But Joe liked the feel of Canberra. After the impersonal roar of traffic in Sydney, and Adelaide's bare, straight streets, he found it pleasant. There was sailing and swimming at the lake in summer. When the winter fogs came down they huddled round the inadequate radiators in the hostel, which could not combat the icy winds coming down from the snow-mountains to the south. But winter had its compensations, for the ANU students had built a ski-lodge in the Australian Alps at Guthega, and they would pile into cars and visit the snowfields at the weekend.

Joe and his girl Wendy had spent weekends together there. Wendy insisted on her independence and said she would sleep with someone else if she wanted to; though so far, she assured him, she hadn't wanted to. She didn't find sex so very pleasurable an activity anyway. ('It's my fault,' she told him. 'I guess I'm just basically frigid. Don't worry about it.')

The hostel was definitely segregated as far as the sexes were concerned. He said she would feel different in a really comfortable bed and with all the time in the world, instead of in a narrow bunk in the chalet with an alpenstock jammed under the door to keep out other students.

'We should get a place of our own next year,' he said.

'You mean, get married?'

'Not yet. Better wait till we're through study. But I do want to stay with you, Feathertop.' This was his pet name for her because of her soft, fluffy, wavy light brown hair.

At the hostel, nights were so cold that Joe would get warm under a long, hot shower – at least there was plenty of hot water – and then get into bed to study in a sweater and woollen socks. Maggie had brought him some warm pyjamas and a checked woollen rug for his bed. She took an extra week's holiday to come and see him settled in.

Eight

AFTER A Society of Arts exhibition opening in Kintore Avenue, Roy and Maggie were drinking beer in his studio barn, from Stein mugs he had brought back from Germany. A half-finished painting stood against the wall, a rich-coloured pattern of fruit and flowers. The only table was littered with art magazines, bunches of brushes standing in glass jars, and the old china plates he used for palettes, full of rainbow messes. A gentle breeze billowed the piece of Indonesian batik hung across the one big window. The old refrigerator in the corner shuddered to a stop. Presently it started up again, as though recalled to life.

'You mechanical thing, humming away there,' Roy addressed it. 'I suppose you'll still be stopping and starting when my heart has stopped forever. And they will say, "He was a man who used to notice such things".'

'Who was?'

'The late – Sir – Royston – Gilham. Late lamented Roy.'

'What things?' asked Maggie in a blurred voice. There had

been white wine at the opening, and because it was a warm night and she was thirsty, she had drunk too much on an empty stomach. Roy had asked her in to have an omelette on the way home and had brought out beer to celebrate his winning of the Society's annual prize. She would rather have had coffee. She pushed her empty plate aside and rested her elbows on the table. 'Notice what things?'

Roy said, ' "Shoes and ships and sealing-wax". And "the light in a blackbird's eye".'

'The light in a magpie's eye. Blackbirds're English.'

'Don't be so parochial. I was quoting Thomas Hardy. Or is it Robert Bridges? Anyhow, a Pom poet.'

'Why not Australian poet? Why not Maggie Pinjarra:

> The native thrush, like liquid light,
> Sings the clear sun above the height;
> The dollar-bird turns cartwheels; he
> Sounds like an ungreased axle-tree – '

'Just a catalogue. I'd rather read "What Bird is That?" And it's got pictures, too.'

'Oh dear!' She yawned hugely, showing her strong white teeth. 'I must go home. What about making us some coffee?'

'You don't have to go home. You can sleep here if you like.' He indicated the sagging double bed which was the only other furniture besides the hard kitchen chairs on which they sat, and a padded window seat. Roy lived and worked in one room, plus the tiny bathroom. The toilet was out in the yard.

Maggie looked at him. She had expected this proposal, but not tonight, and not in such casual fashion.

'You mean – in your bed?' she asked dimly.

She looked with some distaste at the tumbled, unmade bed, with its greyish sheets, old blankets and beautiful handwoven Greek bedspread. It was typical of Roy. He wouldn't think of tidying up the place, making the bed, putting flowers on the table, and leading up with subtle compliments to the subject of their becoming lovers. He would cover a scruffy bed with a bedspread which in his view made up for all its deficiencies.

Roy . . . Wasn't it Old French for King? Her own married name, Vin's name.

Roy refilled her glass.

'Oh! I don't want any more beer. I'd rather go to sleep.'

'Sleep! "Sleep that knits up the ravell'd sleeve of care; The death of each day's life, sore labour's balm . . ." '

And quoting Shakespeare hypnotically he drew her over to the bed. She paused only to slip out of her one-piece dress before sprawling on the bed, suddenly feeling tremendously happy. Beyond the open window, she was aware of a cricket chirr-chirring in the grass in a sleepy rhythm.

Maggie was cleaning out and defrosting Roy's refrigerator, a disgusting job which she always put off at home, till driven by the increasing squalor of her own fridge to do something about it. Roy had gone out to get some bread and milk for breakfast. (She had a common female phobia, of dying suddenly and having strangers go through her house, opening the door on a filthy fridge: 'Of course, she was one of *them*, can't expect them to have high standards of hygiene. But really, have you ever *seen* . . . ?'

In fact Maggie had been rigorously taught by her Aunt Ellen, whose own mother had been taught by her Scottish grandmother Emily Duguid, to keep her kitchen neat. She would never dig butter out of the butter-paper or leave dirty dishes in the sink. But refrigerators – ! They weren't invented in Emily's or Fiona's day, and they could have had no idea of what a dreadful chore it was to clean one . . .

Why, thought Maggie, as she scrubbed at hardened spills and wrestled with sliding trays which would not come out, why did whoever designed these things make them so hard to clean? She could imagine a designer sitting in an antiseptically clean office at the factory, drawing in all the grooved and moulded bits which would make the housewife's task more difficult. Such designers – men who had never done any housework in their lives – should be made to defrost and clean a dirty refrigerator every day for a month.

She pulled out the bottom crisper tray, revealing a withered gherkin like a small green turd. Some hardened scum might be spilled orange jelly. Great lumps of ice had cascaded out and the floor was awash with their melting. The crisper trays were lined with pieces of ancient lettuce which had turned to something like floating water weed, a mere green slime.

At last she had all the back walls and trays and ledges clean and shining – where she could reach them – and she turned the current on and began putting things back, after mopping the floor. 'Beastly thing!' she said to it, feeling like kicking the white box as it began a self-satisfied hum. She banged the door to with a vicious shove, and the flimsy plastic shelf at the bottom gave way. Bottles of wine and Coca-Cola – which Roy drank in a horrible mixture with sherry, believing that the coke would somehow neutralise the alcohol – crashed in a heap of broken glass and coloured froth.

Maggie swore for nearly a minute, scarcely repeating herself once. She had not known she had such a store of invective at her command, but it relieved her feelings a bit. Gingerly she cleared up the sharp bits of glass and mopped the floor a second time. In spite of the mess, only two bottles were broken.

'I say, you are a dear,' said Roy, coming back with the shopping, in the affected 'camp' accent he used sometimes. 'I can nevah cope with the horrid thing.'

'Shut up!' said Maggie furiously. 'And don't *ever* let it get in this state again.'

'Come and live here, then it wouldn't. "Come live with me and be my love, And we will all the pleasures prove – " '

'Let me go, I'm in a stinking mess.'

'All right, go and have a shower.'

She did so, but the shower alcove was black in the corners with mould and old soap, and its base was a rough grey cement that no amount of cascading hot water could make appear clean. No, she was not a Bohemian, she decided. She had woken wearing nothing but her silver snake bangle and had dressed before he woke, and gone outside to the smelly outhouse; where the door stuck, and for a few moments of panic she thought she was 'locked in the lavatory' like the old ladies in the song.

Now she wrapped herself in a Happy Coat she found hanging on a nail behind the shower room door.

'Roy!' she said sharply, coming back into the living room, 'There are flies sitting on the bread, and this butter's rancid, you should throw it out.'

'What's wrong with you today?' he asked good-humouredly. 'Is it the time of the month? You've got a nesting impulse going or something.'

'No, it's just that I can't stand *squalor*. Men can put up with squalor, not even notice it. Look at this breadboard, all over crumbs, and bits of parsley from when you made the omelette last night. And this frying-pan! When did you clean it last?'

'It cleans itself. You just wipe it out with a bit of paper while it's hot.'

'Erkh! And likewise, Yuk! You've left the eggshells on the table, and they weren't quite empty. Where's the dish-cloth?'

He handed her a dish-mop with a wire handle, a greyish cluster of cotton with nameless bits clinging to it. She held it at arms' length, went over and threw it out the window.

'Don't you have a Superwipe or a piece of cheesecloth or something? Or do I have to use the revolting sponge thing I used for the refrigerator?'

'Yes, since you've thrown out my favourite dish-mop. The cloths all have turpentine on them.'

Maggie's ill-humour, as she well knew, was not entirely due to Roy's poor housekeeping. She felt let down, for last night had not been a success. Long abuse of alcohol had affected Roy's performance. 'Your fire has melted my bar of iron,' he said. It was apt, and poetic, but it didn't make her feel any less frustrated. Besides she felt the phrase had been forged in the heat of other encounters; it had been used before.

She wiped down the table with a piece of paint-rag, and said brightly, 'Well, I must be going.'

'You look rather beaut in that short coat. Don't go yet.'

'No, I'm getting dressed.' She took up her clothes where she had left them at the shower-cubicle and got dressed again in that confined space. When she came back he looked depressed. He knew she was irritated with him. It had been so long since she had stayed with a man, and it had been no good. She kissed his cheek coolly, feeling its rough new stubble. He smelt of stale beer.

Alone once more, Roy poured sherry into a tumbler and topped it up with Coca-Cola: his first drink of the day.

Maggie had not been to Roy's studio for some time, had avoided even going to North Adelaide in case she might run into him. When she saw him again it was at a party, and Roy had been drinking heavily for two days. He held his arms wide and greeted her with a beaming smile, but when he essayed a kiss he nearly fell, and hung on to her for support.

'My fren' Maggie!' he said. 'You all know my fren' Maggie? The Ab . . . Aboriginal poetess. You all know Maggie's poems and stories. L'il Brown Bugger . . . Tales of Dreamtimesh . . . Dingo and Dingbats . . . Stories of Uncle Morgan and Uncle Remus an Uncle Tom and Uncle –'

'Shut up, Roy. You're drunk,' said Maggie, embarrassed for him and for herself.

'Tha's right; I'm drunk. But 'least I'm an artist. *You're* not even a poet's boo-bootlace. "Aborigin'l poetess" – ho yes – but if your stuff wasn't Aboriginal it woulden even be published. Not even – published. Hear? Let alone praished!'

'Roy!' Her face was stiff with hurt; she felt that if she tried to smile it would crack. She knew why he was hitting back at her, but it wasn't fair. And in front of all these people . . . not one of whom spoke up in her defence.

Roy tried to sit on a round padded cushion, but fell over backwards, spilling the contents of the glass he was holding. He lay with his legs in the air, giggling helplessly. Maggie left him there and went out to the kitchen to help with supper, feeling as if she had been stabbed in the back by a friend. What had hurt was that Roy confirmed her own secret fears, that her writing was not really anything unusual but had been taken up because of her supposed ancestry. She hated to be called 'the Aboriginal poetess', and he knew it. Even more so now that she knew it wasn't true anyway.

The next time she saw him he was sober and in his right mind, painting hard for a mixed exhibition at the Peel Street Gallery. He seemed to be blithely unaware or forgetful of his hurtful remarks. Maggie, who could never stay angry for long, soon forgave him and they became friends again. They continued to go to art shows together, and sometimes he came for a meal with her, offering to do the cooking. He could be so charming and amusing when sober that she forgave the things he said when he was drunk.

She came to depend on his companionship; she had no women friends, and she was quite alone for the first time since Joe was born. The house at first seemed unbearably empty. They celebrated the passing of the Referendum in May when ninety per cent of the white population voted that Aborigines were people, should be included in the next census, and should be given a great deal more support by the Commonwealth Government.

Roy sold a painting to the National Gallery of SA and was up in air for weeks. He was painting rich still-lifes with the texture of tapestries and the colours of stained glass, clear and glowing. But then Maggie dropped in to see him, toward the end of the year, and found him slumped on the window seat, staring with hooded eyes at the blank wall.

'What's up, Roy? I've brought a nice Polish salami and a bottle of olives. Do you have any fresh bread? I should have bought rolls.'

Roy remained motionless. 'It's all gone down the drain,' he said.

'What has?'

'My painting.' He waved an arm at a trio of half-finished canvases leaning against the wall. 'Can't finish anything.'

He got up and poured her a sherry. He half-filled a smeary tumbler for himself and topped it up with Coca-Cola.

'Didn't the doc. tell you to give that up?'

'Yes, but I have to do something. Can't just sit here staring at the bloody wall.'

Maggie cut bread on the crumb-covered board and jollied him into eating. Either the food or the sherry or perhaps even the sugar in the fizzy drink revived him. Soon he was talking in his old extravagant fashion. But she had glimpsed a depth of melancholy in those half-veiled eyes.

Joe did not want to come home for the Christmas vacation as there was a big Inter-Racial Seminar in Canberra early in

December, with delegates coming from all over Australia. Maggie was still working, but she went to Canberra for Christmas. She found Joe as thin as ever, but happy and enthusiastic about the seminar at which he had been asked to speak. But she feared he was not working as he should, cutting lectures and putting all his energies into protest and demonstration. Well, wasn't it to be expected? she asked herself. He had no academic background, no tradition of learning. Perhaps he would settle down next year.

Meanwhile she rejoiced in the inland city's clarity of air, the burning heat, the yellow grassy hills, the cloudless blue above, where black crows wavered with melancholy cries. The broad avenues, the vistas of distant buildings framed in white fountains, the level lake, even the floodlit blue flag with its white stars flying at night above Capital Hill, all gave her a feeling of exhilaration. If Canberra had failed as a city – lacking the true pulse of life that came from random growth – it succeeded as a spectacle. Burley Griffin's vision had at last materialised around the artificial lake that bore his name.

Stepping outside the Ainslie Hotel in the freshness of early evening, Maggie sniffed the scent of blue-gum leaves and watched a great full moon like a fabulous pearl rise above the floodlit dome of the War Memorial, glowing like an earthly moon. The moon climbed higher, no longer a gold-tinted pearl but a flat silver coin tossed on high. Heads or tails? It was all a gamble – life, death, inheritance, existence.

Canberra was still seething like an ant-heap when the Queen Ant has been killed. The Prime Minister, Harold Holt, had disappeared while swimming at Portsea and an intensive search was going on for his body. Prime Ministers had died in office before, but none in such mysterious and dramatic circumstances. There had been only two witnesses on the lonely beach; they had seen Holt trying to paddle shorewards while being swept backwards by the breakers. There had been a storm, and it was not the sort of day most people would choose for swimming. He was never seen again.

The President of the United States announced that he would fly to Australia for the funeral service, a funeral at which there was no coffin and no body.

Maggie bought a book for Roy in a Canberra bookshop, a

collected Edward Thomas. Rather smugly she marked the poem they had argued about, which began:

> Out of the wood of thoughts that grow by night
> To be cut down by the sharp axe of light,
> Out of the night, two cocks together crow,
> Cleaving the darkness like a silver blow –

The day after she got back home she learned that Roy was dead. He had been run over by a bus in the city while crossing North Terrace. Besides an acute sense of loss, Maggie felt somehow guilty, as if she could have prevented this accident if she hadn't been away.

She went to see Stanislaus, a Polish painter with an unpronounceable second name who had been his friend.

'He left a self-portrait, must have only just completed it,' said Stan. 'Ze paint was still not dry. I am looking after it; one of ze best szings he has done . . . Ze National Gallery should acquire it. You wish to see – ?'

'Yes,' said Maggie. 'Please.'

In a room where Stan's own swirling abstracts were hung or propped around the walls, there was a framed canvas hanging at eye level, catching the light from the window. Its colours were blue and yellow – the colours, Maggie realised, of Van Gogh's last paintings. Roy's eyes, dark, unfathomable, heavy-lidded, gazed out at her; the face held a sad, mocking smile. Behind his head on the painted wall was a Still Life, and a half-empty bottle of beer stood on the table by his elbow. Beside his shoulder the open, empty window – the batik hanging removed – showed the blackness of night, the nothingness beyond. Maggie felt a chill down her spine.

'And zis was written on a pad on the table. I removed it also, wiz ze painting.'

She read:

> Tomorrow and tomorrow and tomorrow
> Creeps in this petty pace from day to day,
> To the last syllable of recorded time,

And all our yesterdays have lighted fools
The way to dusty death . . . out, out, brief candle!

Maggie looked up, in tears. 'He wasn't drunk, then? He hadn't been drinking? It was deliberate.'

'Ze official verdict was death by misadventure. Ze bus driver, he was completely cleared. A witness has seen Roy run from behind a parked car, straight in front of ze bus.'

'Poor Roy! He was so alone.'

'We are all alone, my dear Maggie.'

'I knew he was depressed. But I was busy with my own affairs.'

'Zere is no reason to . . . blame yourzelf. Roy was unstable. Such an end was not unexpected.'

But Maggie went home in a black mood. To her, suicide was dreadful, unthinkable, not for religious reasons but because it meant a negation of life, and she was a life-affirmer.

Roy's death brought back the bad time after Vin died, when she had wondered and wondered if he had pulled the wheel just a little out of line on purpose, in some obscure suicidal impulse. She remembered the fortune-teller on the Magnetic Island ferry. Death and disaster!

Maggie fell into a nervous state which lasted for some months. She felt that Roy was haunting her, and it was an inimical ghost. Was he angry with the living because, now it was too late, he regretted being dead? This was fanciful, she knew. But the Old People had feared the ghosts of their own dead, binding their arms and legs with fishing lines so that they could not 'walk', wrapping them tightly in bark for tree-burial, or filling their graves with heavy stones and logs. And would never mention the name of the departed, in case it called him up, a vengeful ghost, a 'pekka', to harm the living.

Nine

DRESSED IN faded blue jeans and a bright red sweater, Joe was lying on the lawns at the ANU, staring up at the wide blue expanse of the inland sky. Wendy, beside him, was printing on cardboard with black texta-colour: MAKE LOVE NOT WAR. Joe and his red-headed friend Stuart were discussing starting a Black Power movement, arming themselves with petrol bombs against the police.

'Joe,' said Wendy mildly, 'I thought the whole idea was to keep the demos non-violent: linking arms, sitting down in the streets, getting arrested without resistance.'

'Bullshit!' said Joe. 'I don't go along with this non-violent stuff. Hell, the cops are *paid* to be violent!'

He'd had several brushes with the police during Freedom Rides to places like Moree and Collarenebri (where last century his great-grandfather had a girl called Gertie). For the first time he'd seen the Western plains where great flocks of sheep blocked the roads, flowing like water as the drovers parted them to let their vehicle pass. And somewhere out there, on a dry stage between rivers, his grandfather Chukka Brown had perished during the Depression years.

The other member of their group, Barry Bentham, sat with his eyes half-shut, taking no part in the conversation. Now he flung himself back on the grass, gazing at a khaki-coloured Air Force plane as it streaked from north to south. He said:

'Passive resistance won't save us from being conscripted for Vietnam –'

'Well, the Draft Resisters' Union is organising an anti-conscription march for the national conference next month,' said Wendy. 'That's why I'm doing the posters, for the big rally. There's going to be a really big demo. with a march to Parliament House. Students from all over will be here for the ANU Arts Festival – even Maoris from New Zealand.'

'Of course it's a racist war and that's partly why we're in it,' said Joe. 'Ever since Australians stopped shooting and

615

poisoning Aborigines, they've been lynching Chinese miners and hanging Kanakas.'

Barry sat up, his thin face tense, his eyes blazing. With one hand thumping his knee, he said, 'I don't care if they're Russian, German, Frenchman, Englishman, Australian or American,' he cried, 'they belong to the military caste. Throughout history they've been responsible for invasions – rape, looting, destruction, murder of civilians – the fire-bombing of Dresden, the concentration camps of the Boer War. And Hiroshima . . . . Now the Americans are napalming little brown men in Vietnam. Because they are a lot of racists!

'Look, the very language they use in Vietnam, the immoral jargon the Yanks come up with! "Gooks" are pulled out of their "hootches"; "slant-eyes" are "fragged" in underground shelters, then there's "waste them" and "body count", "fry", "search and destroy", and "anti-personnel". The last, in case you don't know, is a type of bomb that's loaded with sharp, lethal bits of steel, that you lob in a village "suspected of harbouring the VC". It wounds everyone within radius, including babies . . . Anyway, we're all agreed that we'll never go to this beastly war, even if we get our call-up papers?' He said it more as a statement than a question. 'We'll all refuse to do the Medical. It's a matter of principle. Complete non-cooperation.'

They all solemnly agreed. Wendy said she would refuse to roll a bandage, or knit a single sock. 'How some women can work in munition factories beats me,' she said.

'One sock wouldn't be much use to a soldier, anyhow,' said Stu, teasing her. She threw a book at him. Sometimes she was aware of a certain male exclusiveness in the group. 'The worst thing they've done in Vietnam,' she said, 'is using defoliant on the jungles and rice-paddies. A team of experts went over there and found suspicious birth-defects among the Vietnamese families exposed to the sprays. Millions of tons of the stuff. But of course it was all hushed up.'

'Harold Holt must have known about these things, or he ought to have known. But we're involved in Vietnam because the Liberals are cynically wooing American big business.'

' "Diggers for dollars," eh?'

616

'Of course. Canada has never had anything to do with this rotten war, nor Britain. But our Harold had to go to the States, grinning from ear to ear, and bow before "our great and powerful friends!"'

' "All the way with LBJ!" Yair, it's revolting all right. But Presidents are only temporary,' said Joe, thinking of the one with the same initials as himself who had been shot down like a dog in the street. 'I bet Johnson goes out at the next election. Well, I've got a lecture at eleven,' he said, picking up his books. 'Coming, Wendy?'

They wandered off, his arm in its red sleeve about her neck like a bright scarf.

When the story of the My Lai massacre came out soon after the University year began in 1968, Barry Bentham was almost mad with rage and disgust. He had been appalled by what he had read and seen in documentaries of the atom-bombing of Hiroshima and Nagasaki, but this had occurred before he was born. My Lai was a contemporary event: it had happened now, and a young man not much older than himself, Lieutenant Calley, had taken part in the cold-blooded shooting to death of more than a hundred civilians.

The news photographs documented the happening in relentless black and white. There was no need for colour to show the great dark stars of blood on white singlets, on women's shifts; or the chubby, defenceless curves of babies gunned down in their mothers' arms.

'You know, that's just how it was in Australia in the early days,' said Joe. 'Later, they used to find great heaps of Aboriginal skeletons where whole tribes were shot: men, women and children. If there'd been a newsreel cameraman around in Van Diemen's Land in the 1820s, for instance, the pictures they got would have been much like this except for the clothing. And later, on the mainland, at Myall Creek, and Rufus Creek, and Murdering Creek, and all the other great massacres. And there wasn't even a war on, officially. Only a war of extermination. I tell you a black man wasn't worth the lives of ten sheep, or half a dozen cattle. And if one white man was speared, fifty Aborigines would be shot.'

'Yes Joe, but this is happening *now*. Our contemporaries are committing these atrocities. And they expect us to take part in their filthy war! My God, did our fathers fight the Germans and the extermination camps, so that we could live to fight alongside such bloody murderers?'

They organised a ceremonial burning of Draft cards, and of the Prime Minister in effigy. Barry could not wait for his twentieth birthday, when he would make his stand for the cause.

Ten

AT THE launching of her last book Maggie had met the editor of an Adelaide evening paper: a big man with a slow deep voice and light, humorous blue eyes, who had a pipe stuck between his teeth most of the time, though when thinking over a problem or a reply to a question he would take it out and scratch reflectively behind his right ear with the stem. He had a luxuriant mane of silver hair.

He was complaining about the growing illiteracy among the young, 'or else I've just been unlucky,' he said. 'They send me girls who can't spell, who don't know the difference between a semi-colon and a comma, whose basic vocabulary is shockingly weak. I *did* have a good girl, who could write intelligently, but she went and got married and started a family.'

'One of the hazards of employing attractive girls,' said Maggie.

'Was she attractive? Yes, I suppose she was. She had become part of the office furniture for me, like a comfortable chair. It was a shock when she left.'

'Perhaps she was tired of being sat on.'

'Eh? Oh, ha! Yes I suppose I did rather take her for granted.'

'I've always thought it would be exciting to work in a newspaper office. Compared with Insurance, anyway. So if you need a mature, experienced secretary, not likely to get married – '

'Mrs King, would you really like the job? It's yours, just as soon as I can sack the half-witted schoolgirl I have at present.'

'Aren't you being rather impulsive? What about tests, references?'

'I *am* impulsive. But as for tests, I know you can write, and as for references, I take it you are holding down a job as a top secretary at the moment. Therefore – '

Maggie laughed. 'I'll have to give Sun Insurance at least a month's notice. I've been there for years.'

'Right. Let me know when you can start, and your desk will be ready for you. Sure you wouldn't rather have a place on the literary staff? I liked that article you did on Palm Island.'

'No, I don't think daily journalism is the best job for someone who wants to write. By the way, do you ever take your secretary with you when you travel interstate?'

He looked a little startled, and Maggie realised what he was thinking. She blushed. 'I happen to have a son at University in Canberra, you see. It would give me a chance to see him.'

'Oh! Of course. Yes, at least once a year, sometimes more.'

'I'm sure I shall like working for you, Mr Ryder. Thank you for offering me the job.'

His name was Rex! Another King . . . After a year she could not believe that there had ever been a time when he had not been part of her life. He was happily married; she was merely his secretary, yet she knew there was more between them than an ordinary employer-employee relationship. What she felt for him was certainly a kind of love, made up of admiration and shared crises and deep compatibility. What he felt for her was certainly a physical attraction, kept sternly in check; admiration for her as a writer and a woman and dependence on her as an efficient secretary.

Perhaps his wife shared a bed with him for eight hours out of the twenty-four, while Maggie shared a room with him for an equal time in every day except Sunday and Wednesday, when she had an afternoon off in place of Saturday. He always went to the races on Saturday afternoon, but came back in time to see the page proofs of the Sunday paper which they also produced. He was Editor-in-Chief of both newspapers,

,ut the *Evening Herald*, with its Managing Editor, was his; the weekend paper had its own Editor and its own staff, though produced in the same building by the same technicians.

In the big Editor's sanctum where the northern sun filtered through plane-trees made a leafy pattern on the carpet in summer, she had a small desk under the window. It was cluttered with typewriter, tape-recorder, dictaphone, telephone, memo pads, typing paper. His desk was a large polished expanse with two telephones, an intercom, 'In' and 'Out' baskets for letters, a blotting pad which she changed each day, a pile of copy-paper, and a variety of pens and pencils. He did not even own a blue pencil, but would make corrections in soft black lead with a 6B pencil.

She kept his desk clear of obstructions every noon when the Chief Sub. brought the page-proofs in for checking. Long galley-proofs, still damp, were brought by copy-boys and hung in festoons from springclips attached to the wall.

With his big, leonine head and distinguished-looking silver mane, he sat puffing his pipe as he read the page-proofs spread out on his desk. His hair was brushed decorously flat in the morning, but by midday when the paper 'went to bed', it was standing wildly on end from his habit of running his hand through it when concentrating. His curious light eyes, which she at first had thought were cold, could crinkle in an engaging smile. Sometimes he gave a short bark of laughter when the cartoon amused him.

Maggie sat in on the Editors' Conference each morning, taking notes, when the day's 'stories' were being discussed and a post-mortem was being held on yesterday's Page One. There was jubilation when they had scooped their deadly rival, the morning paper, and gloom when *The Register* had got in first. The Pictorial Editor, small and volatile, and the News Editor or Chief of Staff, tall and laconic, could never agree. The Editor-in-Chief and Mr Smith the Assistant Editor kept the peace between them.

Maggie had thought Mr Ryder rather a placid man, with his slow, deep voice and puffing pipe. Then one early afternoon, the finished first edition, folded so cleanly and smoothly, smelling sweetly of wood-pulp and printers' ink, was placed

620

on his desk as usual. He opened it, turned a couple of pages. Then he threw his pipe at the opposite wall.

'Bloody blazing hell!' he roared. He went rampaging out the door, waving the paper over his head like a battle-flag.

'Fitz!' he shouted, and 'Get me the Chief Sub-Editor!'

Maggie opened her paper, the Editor's private filing copy which it was her job to attach to his files. She turned two pages. On the leader page, the daily cartoon was printed upside down.

But this was only a minor disaster. What every newspaper proprietor feared, and what he exhorted his journalists to avoid at all costs, was an action for libel. Even a headline, which left out inverted commas or failed to add the word 'alleged,' could be actionable.

For almost the first time in her life Maggie had a woman friend, apart from her sister. This was the editor of the women's pages, known as the Social Editress. She was older than Maggie and inclined to criticise her, but Maggie grew used to her criticisms and did not mind them.

'Maggie, there's lipstick on your teeth!' she would hiss as they went up the stairs to snatch a half-hour lunchbreak in the canteen.

Until the paper was on the streets, no one could relax, but Penelope's were early pages, largely set up the day before, so she could finish before most of the others unless she had some special women's meeting or luncheon to cover.

'Do something about your hair, can't you, your ear's sticking through and it looks terrible,' she would cry or, if the hair was covered by a hat, 'Where on earth did you get that awful hat, at a jumble sale?'

She always criticised Maggie's dressing, yet her own left much to be desired. She liked comfortable tweed skirts and cardigans in winter, and linen skirts with cotton blouses in the summer, and she wore 'sensible' shoes, low-heeled brogues or sandals. She had never been known to wear a hat on her short-cropped fair hair. A cigarette smouldered in a long cigarette-holder between her lips, sending up curls of smoke which dyed her front hair a deeper tinge of yellow.

She would wander into the Editor's sanctum, sit on Maggie's desk, tell Rex a slightly blue joke and then with a snort of laughter amble out again.

'Good old Penelope. Best man on the staff,' said Rex Ryder with a twinkle.

'I know I'm plain; I've got used to the fact,' Penelope would say to Maggie, with a wry grin that showed her crooked teeth. 'There's no hope for *me* to look attractive, so I don't try. But you – you've got the face and figure, nice hair, complexion still pretty good, but you don't make enough of your assets. That dress – ' she tugged at the waist of Maggie's shift, which hung loose from shoulder to hemline. 'You might just as well wear a sack. What I say is, if you've got a waistline why not show it off?'

'But shirt-dresses are the latest thing, you know that.'

'Don't be a slave to fashion. Put a belt round the thing. You know why shifts and shirtdresses are fashionable? Because a couple of film stars and a Royal Mum happen to be pregnant this year! That's the real reason, so they can hide their shape in public.'

To please her, Maggie bought a fine plaited belt of gold leather ('Can I wear gold sandals if I go to school?' she had asked Marie all those years ago) and wore it to work next day. To her surprise it brought a comment from Rex Ryder.

'That looks better,' he said, pointing with the stem of his pipe.

'What? Oh, my dress!'

'Yes. Can't stand these shapeless sacks the girls are wearing now.'

'I'm glad you like it, Mr Ryder. It was Penelope's idea.'

Why was she so ridiculously pleased? After all these years as a secretary, was she falling in love with her boss? Besides, he'd silver hair! Well that was the age group she was in now, or nearly so. How the years had slipped away . . . She pulled the dress decorously over her knees while she took a letter.

But she admitted to a painful curiosity about his wife, until Stella Ryder came into the office one day. There was no comfort there for Maggie. She was a well-groomed blonde, attractive, a little plump, but only pleasantly so, with a calm, unlined face. *Self-satisfied*, thought Maggie, and then rebuked herself for being catty.

All the same, she was pleased that he did not take his wife with them when they flew to Melbourne for a conference. The newspaper chain which owned the *Evening Herald* had its HQ in Melbourne, and sitting-in at a meeting of the top executives Maggie realised that her boss was only an employee like herself. The newspaper's policy and finances were controlled from the Eastern States.

'You can pop up to Canberra and see your son if you like,' said Rex Ryder at the weekend. 'I shan't be needing you till Monday.'

She smiled gratefully and sent Joe a wire. It was a year since she had seen him. He had failed in two subjects the first year, but then First Year was always difficult, she told herself. He had to learn self-discipline and to work by himself.

He had borrowed an old Holden car from a fellow-student and met her at the airport. Maggie would have walked right past him, but the strange, scruffy young man said, 'Hullo, Mum!' and came up and gave her a kiss.

'Joe! It's lovely to see you. At least . . . What have you done to yourself?'

For the red curls which he used to keep trimmed in a tight cap had been allowed to grow into a wild halo, speading down to his shoulders and out in a wiry frizz which made his head disproportionately large on his thin body. A black skivvy made him look even thinner. A bright red bandeau was fitted round his forehead, and another round his right arm. He wore impenetrable dark glasses and a badge saying BLACK POWER. Maggie stared, trying to see her son in this caricature of an American Negro activist, complete with Afro hairstyle.

'For heaven's sake, take off those dark glasses, anyway. I can't recognise you, except for your voice,' she said irritably.

She stayed at the Civic, and took Joe to dinner at the Bistro, feeling they might not admit him to the hotel dining-room. He was too thin, she told him, taking pleasure in giving him a good meal and watching him eat. Without the dark glasses, with his fine, flyaway eyebrows and long dark eyes visible, she could at least recognise him. But his talk was all of violence, confrontation, destruction, brushes with 'the pigs' in anti-Vietnam marches, the iniquities of Aboriginal administration. 'Shooting between the eyes' was what he recommended for the Queensland Minister involved.

'Why the red bands?' Maggie had asked, and he said, 'They are for blood; they symbolise the blood of our people shed by the whites. And the black shirt is in mourning for them.'

'Yes, I can see the justice of that. But all this talk of shooting, and Black Power, and violence in the streets! Surely it is killing and violence that we're demonstrating against in the anti-Vietnam marches? And you're recommending it at home. Things like the Referendum are far more effective.' But, Joe pointed out, State Governments like Queensland could still pass their own repressive Acts. 'Do you think black people will now get equal pay for equal work, that their health standards will be the same as the whites', that there will be enough finance put up so that no Aboriginal child has to go without schooling, that there won't be discrimination in pubs in places like Moree and Townsville, even if the Law says the black man can drink alongside the white man? Not on your sweet life! All these beautiful polished phrases spouted in Parliament about "equality of opportunity" – it *sounds* all right, but it'll never get past the Administration, which is still stuck in the mud of last century.'

'At least,' said his mother, 'the Referendum has given the Commonwealth power to control Aboriginal affairs in the different States, and to override decisions by Governments like Queensland's.'

'Yes, but it won't do it. And anyway, Canberra's too far away. Canberra's 2,000 miles from Darwin, yet there aren't two officers in the Department there who've ever been to the Northern Territory or seen anything of Aboriginal life or problems. And look at Killoran in Brisbane – he directs all the Aboriginal affairs for the State, yet it's fifteen years since he's even been to Palm Island! I tell you, Mum, we've got to have revolution to get anything done!'

Maggie felt there was truth in what he said, but her whole mind and soul were against bloodshed and violence. Wasn't that why she attended anti-war rallies in Adelaide; and not just because her own son might be drawn into the Vietnam conflict? At the last rally there had been police cars everywhere, and Security men in plain clothes taking photographs of all who entered the hall. The Peace movement was being branded as Communist.

She knew the reason for her unease as she listened to Joe. She remembered old Nyora's prophecy that he was 'headin' for trouble'. And that man who had seen death and disaster in her palm . . .

'You got my letter telling you about Grannie Nyora?'

'Yes; sorry I haven't written, Mum, but you know how tied up I am. And she must have been awfully old. It wasn't a shock or anything.'

'No. In fact she said goodbye to me when we were on the island; she knew she hadn't long. At least she didn't see Pandanus turned into a tourist resort.'

'Are they still going ahead with that?'

'So Marie says. But Dan and Elsie and the others are going to fight the developers. They've got a lawyer in Rocky to take out an injunction against them.'

'I do wish I had time to go up there. I'd love to help in the fight.'

'Yes, you're just spoiling for a fight, aren't you?' said Maggie, smiling at him, but with a cold, heavy feeling at her heart. 'What you have to do is study harder in the next semester, and pass your end of year exams.'

She had put Elaine's bequest into a trust fund for him, but the way he was going there would not be enough to see him through his course. Selling her car would not help much; it was small and battered. If necessary she would sell the Northern Development gold shares, which were bringing in very little in dividends.

Back in Melbourne, she sat waiting for Rex Ryder in the lounge of the Oriental where they were booked in. Looking up from the vodka and tomato-juice she was sipping, she caught sight of his silver mane, his solid form away across the room. A shock of delight went through her, tingling to the tips of her fingers, sending a wave of colour to the roots of her hair. Confused, she kept her head down so that he would not see her until she had recovered her composure. That was it, then! Admit it! But she must not let him see her, blushing like a schoolgirl at the sight of him.

That night she dreamed vividly, as she often seemed to do

when travelling. She was in Rex's house (she had never been there, in reality) and stood at a bedroom door, looking in. There on a double bed Rex Ryder was making love to his wife; they lay on their sides so that her back was to Maggie, while he faced the door. He looked across and saw her but did not desist in his activities, holding his wife's body like a shield between him and Maggie.

He said no word, made no sign, yet looked straight at her over Stella's naked shoulder. Was she invisible, then? No, there was a message for her in his look: Leave us alone; see, I have someone else.

When she remembered this dream next day, Maggie was terribly shaken. It told her more about her own feelings and the way her subconscious thoughts had been running than was comfortable. Flying back to Adelaide she was constrained and shy with Rex, and she was relieved to get back to her own home.

Eleven

HAVING PROMISED to write more often, Joe sent his mother a cutting from the *Canberra Times*, (in which her article on Palm Island had appeared) and a letter describing the big meeting when five hundred people protesting on behalf of Aboriginal Land Rights marched the three miles from the ANU grounds to Parliament House. The meeting was quite orderly, and the police had behaved with restraint, though a few pine-cones had been thrown.

He also sent a copy of a letter he had written to the Editor, in reply to a correspondent. This man had suggested that part-Aborigines were now, since the Referendum, 'claiming to be Aborigines', in order to qualify for the new welfare and scholarship benefits, 'coming like termites back out of the white woodwork'.

'Sir –' Joe had written, 'I would like to enlighten your correspondent about the Aboriginal people of Australia, both fullblood and part-blood. What we want is good education, respect, pride in our ancestry, and more job opportunities. We don't want "sympathy" and handouts.

'If modern Australians would delve into our social past, they would be horrified at what they would find. The story is not a pretty one. All our lives Aborigines have lived as second-class citizens. I no longer wish for this situation; therefore I and approximately 200,000 others like me, claim our ancestry. We are Aboriginal Australians, and proud of it.

Joseph King.'

Oh dear! thought Maggie. He has burnt his bridges now. Not even a reference to his Islander forbears; he was emotionally tied to the Aboriginal people. She could never tell him now. And since Nyora was dead, not another living person but herself knew his true ancestry.

Wearing his red bandeau and giving the clenched-fist salute, Joe had addressed the crowd of protesters from the steps of Parliament House, until Commonwealth police came and hustled him down. He then leapt on the roof of a parked car and continued his harangue, while the crowd cheered.

'Must we native Old Australians rank as aliens in our own land?' he had cried passionately. 'We want brotherhood, not ostracism; proper homes, not the Reserve or the rubbish dump! We want equal pay with white workers and a decent education, and to be freed from mean and petty bureaucrats. The DOAA is set up not to protect the Aborigine and Islander, but to protect the rest of Australia from the embarrassment of the dark people. The Department is set up to *control* Aborigines living on missions and reserves, though allegedly for their 'protection and guidance'. Huh! Protection from what, and guidance to where?

'The policy of assimilation is an empty policy that has failed in all fields: health, education, wages, housing. The new word is "integration"; it is just as hollow. The greatest requirement today is for the return of Land Rights to the people: our land, which was taken from us. We demand – '

And here he was pulled forcibly down, as a policeman got into the car and began to drive it off. He fell heavily, all the breath knocked out of him for the moment. There were angry yells and a few punches were thrown, but the police, who had

627

been told to use restraint and not force a confrontation, made no arrests. Joe's friends helped him back to the hostel and put liniment on his bruises. But he was a hero. He scarcely felt them.

Joe's next adventure was more serious. There had been a scandalous occurrence at Woorabinda settlement, about eighty miles west of Rockhampton in Queensland. Aunt Marie wrote to Joe indignantly about it, for she knew the woman involved, who now lived in Townsville. She had been stopped while travelling to her brother's funeral and left on the side of the road. Her brother, who lived on the Woorabinda Reserve, had been taken to Fantôme Island where he was supposed to be cured of leprosy, but he died in Rockhampton on the way home. The DOAA office there had provided a hearse to take the body to Woorabinda for burial.

Marie's friend, a grandmother, had travelled all night from Townsville in the train. The officials told her she could travel in the front of the hearse with the Department driver and a young woman returning to Woorabinda from hospital.

They were about twenty miles from the settlement when a police car, driven by the local sergeant with the Manager of the settlement on board, intercepted them.

'All right! Pull over!' the policeman shouted. 'Now get out! Don't argue – all out, and take your port and all your things with you. What're you doing travelling in the hearse, anyway?'

'We was told – they said we could get a lift – '

'That's enough! Now you can burn all those things – infected cloth – and don't bring anything to the Mission, understand?'

'But I bought a new dress for the funeral! It's me only good dress.'

'You heard me!' said Sergeant O'Shea grimly. The driver, intimidated, got down and helped pile some dry wood and grass for a fire. Poor Grannie Rae wept as she saw her good things consumed by the flames – even her handbag. But she had hidden her little portable camera down the front of her dress.

'Will you give us a lift to the Settlement, then?' she asked through her tears.

'Certainly not!' said the Manager of the Reserve. 'We're not having leprosy germs in the car with us, eh Sergeant? You can stay here for now. I'll hold up the funeral till you get there.'

The other woman was too sick to protest. She just sat on the side of the road in the dust. 'I'll send a truck to pick you up, and you can travel on the tray,' said the Manager magnanimously.

The two women watched numbly as two hundred dollars' worth of new clothes and portmanteaux was consumed. Then the police car and the hearse drove off in a cloud of dust, abandoning them on the roadside in the heat. When Mrs Rae finally got to the Reserve, the funeral was over.

The whole community, usually browbeaten and apathetic, was made so angry when her story was told that they gathered in a threatening crowd outside the Manager's office, daring him to come out and face them. He stayed inside. Mrs Rae had taken a photograph of the charred remains of their goods, she told them. The Sergeant of Police telephoned for reinforcements from the two nearby towns, and at this show of force the people melted back to their homes. But Mrs Rae, said Marie, had informed the local Opposition Member, and given him the photographs. Questions would be asked in Parliament, both in Brisbane and Canberra.

Joe seethed with anger at this story. 'It's just typical!' he said to Wendy. 'Mean, bullying bureaucrats, pushing the people around, and they're too cowed to fight back. By God, I'd like to confront that Manager myself. In fact, I'm going to Queensland to organise a meeting of protest in Brisbane. Want to come?'

'I ought to be working, Joe; so should you. If you miss any more lectures and tutorials, your Prof. will hit the roof.'

'I don't care! This is more important.'

'All right, I'll come.'

'Good little Feathertop!'

Joe withdrew the whole of his next month's allowance and they travelled up to Sydney by hitch-hiking, and then splashed the money on a First-class sleeper in the overnight train to Brisbane; a return ticket.

Wendy relaxed in the rocking, swaying cradle of the bottom

bunk into which they were both jammed; the top bunk was still folded into the wall above their heads.

'Oh, why aren't you always like this?' he groaned. 'It's so marvellous when you open and accept me. Sometimes it's been like battering at a stone wall.'

'I know, I know. But I can't help it. Tonight, somehow – it's the movement of the train, the strangeness, I suppose – I feel free of all those hang-ups.'

'Would you like a joint? I've got some grass in my good old Drum Tobacco pouch.'

'No, really, I don't need it, Joe. Just you . . . You turn me on.'

But he knew it was not the train, it was his new status as a leader that excited her.

Pleasantly exhausted, they emerged at the South Brisbane Railway Station and took a taxi across the river. Joe bought a *Courier Mail*, and swore.

The Manager of the Reserve was recorded as saying that 'the incident' was closed. The people involved had clearly been 'illegal passengers in a Government vehicle'. The State Minister for Aboriginal Affairs said blandly that the complaints of the Woorabinda people were groundless, as the whole affair had been managed by the Department with 'due decorum'. It was unfortunate that the deceased's sister had missed the funeral, but the officers could not take the risk of infection being carried to the settlement.

A Brisbane doctor, asked to comment, said that these fears were exaggerated, that there had been no contact with the body, and even if there had, no danger was to be apprehended. It appeared that police and manager had 'over-reacted'.

'Over-reacted! Hell's bloody bells! Can you beat that slimy Ministerial statement, though! He's the one who keeps on referring to "Our Queensland Aborigines". It's time he learnt that we're not "his" pet Aborigines, but people; simply human beings.'

'I think it was the most inhuman thing I've ever heard of,' said Wendy, 'to stop that poor old thing going to her brother's funeral. And then make her burn all her things. I wouldn't have burnt them. I'd have refused.'

'Yes, and that's just the difference. You don't know what it's like to have been pauperised, and intimidated, and pushed around by police all your life. At least she saved her camera and got evidence of what happened.'

Joe said they would go to the FCAATI headquarters and organise a public meeting in King George Square. 'We'll have to get hold of Kath Walker,' he said. 'She'll know how to round up the people. She helps to edit their Newsletter.'

The result was 'the first violent Aboriginal demonstration in Queensland', as the *Courier* reported. Joe, who was a tall youth, seemed a foot taller as he strutted before Wendy. He 'had Killoran frightened', he boasted, for the Director of Aboriginal and Islander Affairs had refused to see more than five of the protesters in his office. 'Hiding behind a locked door! He's probably heard that I threatened him and the Minister with vengeance.'

Still euphoric, feeling like a prince who has come into his kingdom, Joe went to Parliament House in George Street the next day and asked to see the Minister for Aboriginal Affairs. To his mortification the Secretary did not recognise him. But the Minister received him somewhat nervously.

'I wonder could you step outside a moment,' Joe said politely, removing his dark glasses. 'There's something I'd like you to see.'

'Well, I'm a busy man . . . What is it?' asked the Minister fussily. But Joe's 'educated' voice disarmed him.

'It's something that, as Minister, I think you ought to see.'

As soon as they were out on the gravel drive in front of the steps, Joe said, 'I just want you to see stars!' He gave a swift uppercut to the man's nose, followed by a jab to the left eye.

'Now you'll know what it's like to be "little-bit black". You're going to have a beaut black eye by tomorrow. That's for Auntie Jean that was left on the side of the road and had her clothes burnt. "Due decorum", eh? You stinking, faking coward!' he roared. 'Backing up your paid bullies on the Reserves! You should be made to live as an Aborigine at Cherbourg or Woorabinda or Palm for just a month. Then you'd know what it was like!'

By now the orderly at the door had called the policeman on duty at the gates, and they held Joe, who did not struggle, till a

Black Maria arrived to cart him away.

The Minister was moaning and mopping his bleeding nose with a handkerchief. His eye had already swelled and closed. Joe stood indolently, staring at him. The sight of the blood excited him.

It was Wendy who got in touch with Maggie and asked her to raise as much as possible for bail, a lawyer's fees, and a possible fine. But Joe was remanded in custody to face a charge the following week of aggravated assault and abusive language against a Minister of the Crown. Maggie, who had read with a sinking heart about the incident in the afternoon's *Herald*, rang a sharebroker at once and arranged to sell her Northern Development gold shares. She would not touch Joe's trust fund, which was for his education. She asked Wendy to ring the newspaper office Collect as soon as she had any news.

'In here, you!' With an ungentle shove the warder pushed him into the cell. He stumbled on the threshold, cursing. Before he recovered himself, the door crashed shut.

He had been photographed, fingerprinted, searched; fortunately he had not been carrying the tobacco-pouch of marijuana, or that would have been another charge. He'd been taken straight before a Magistrate and remanded in custody until his case came up the following week. The Police opposed bail, stating that he was 'a trouble-maker from Interstate' and would skip over the border if allowed out. His Afro hair style, his black T-shirt were enough to condemn him.

Seven days of incarceration! He had tried to prepare himself mentally, but as his eyes took in the bare stone walls, the iron door, the high, barred window, he felt panic rising. The walls seemed to be closing in. His breath came in shorter and shorter gasps, he was starving for oxygen. Was this asthma?

Climbing on the shelf with its two grey blankets rolled at the bottom where he would sleep, he was able to reach the bars of the small window, and straining with all his strength he raised his chin to the level of his hands and looked out. The afternoon sun was shining, and up there was blue sky with wisps of silvery cloud. He took great gulps of fresh air. But his arms trembled with the strain. He let himself down again, into the stale, dank air and a smell which seemed to come from the toilet-bucket in the corner, though it was empty.

He began pacing up and down. Five steps; turn. Five steps back; turn. It made him giddy. He forced himself to sit on the bench, and to take slow, deep breaths. To calm his mind he tried to remember some of 'The Prisoner of Chillon':

> Since man first pent his fellow men
> Like beasts within an iron den . . .

Oh God, he could remember no more. His brain was reeling.

What about 'The Ballad of Reading Gaol'? Oscar Wilde had been inside for two years.

> I never saw a man who looked
> With such a wistful eye
> Upon that little tent of blue
> Which prisoners call the sky . . .

What came next? Something about silver clouds floating by . . . No good.

His throat closed up, so that he could not even swallow his own saliva. He clutched at his throat. In a moment he would start to bang on the door, scream to be let out. Then he heard a sound of echoing steps, a series of dull clangs coming closer . . . A section of the door slid back and a voice said, 'Tea, five-oh-nine.' An enamel mug and a tin plate with bread and cheese were slid on to the shelf where he was supposed to eat.

'Wait, wait!' he called to the human arm as it withdrew. 'How long do I have to stay in here? When do we get out of the cells?'

'Termorrer morning, 7 a.m.,' said the warder's voice. 'Lights go out at nine thirty.'

Somehow he got through the interminable first night. If only he'd smuggled in some sleeping pills! At Boggo Road there didn't seem to be any noise of traffic, or none that filtered into his cell. He might be shut in a cave somewhere in a desert in the centre of Australia. The grey blankets made his face itchy when he pulled them up to his chin. Ridiculously, what he longed for was a sheet, a sheet that he could pull over his head, and then he would sleep. When he did sleep, he woke with a start of terror, to almost total blackness. Where was he, where – ? Then he saw the tiny glimmer of the barred window. Once more he pulled himself up, and breathed the night air. The yard inside the prison walls was floodlit. That was the light he had seen. Something, a small rat or a giant cockroach, scuttled over the floor.

Without that little window I would go mad, he thought. But I'll get used to it. Only six more days!

But he didn't get used to it. If anything, it grew worse. He dreaded the inexorable progression of each day from morning to noon to early afternoon, to early evening when he would be shut up alone once more in his cell. He was like an animal kept in a dark box with just a tiny breathing hole in one end. For he was convinced, against all logic, that the gaol air was unbreathable and that it was only the small barred window that kept him alive.

They had taken away his black T-shirt with its 'Black is Beautiful' badge, his red armband and forehead bandeau. Dressed in the coarse prison grey, he felt as if his whole identity was dissolving in a grey anonymity. If only there was a mirror somewhere in which he could see his face, and reassure himself that he existed, Joseph Forbes King! He had always sought assurance from mirrors and glass shopfronts in the street that reflected his bush of hair and his slender figure. At least they hadn't cut his hair, yet. He held up his hands, but they meant nothing. They might have been the leaves and twigs of a tree.

And what if he didn't get out after seven days? What if they sentenced him to a year, two years? The lawyer assured him that he would get off with a bond, being a first offender. 'If you'd been armed, even with a pocket knife, there's no way I could have stopped you going to prison,' he said. 'Or even if you'd attacked the Minister inside Parliament House. But for God's sake don't shoot your mouth off to the judge about "Black Power" and "confrontation". Just shut up and let me do the talking, and answer questions as briefly as possible.'

Joe, much chastened by a few days in the cells, promised to do as he was told.

The case was over. He had been found guilty of assault and threatening language, but not of aggravated assault . . . Joseph stood meekly to receive his sentence.

'Joseph Forbes King . . . I order that you be released on a good behaviour bond of five hundred dollars . . . Bound over to keep the peace for two years . . .

'Lucky not to be gaoled, young man . . . Don't want your long-haired sort coming to Queensland, student agitators from the south. For your own good, keep out of Queensland in future.'

Joe bit his tongue . . . He wanted to shout at the stupid Beak: I was born in Queensland! Born and bred in bloody Queensland! My people owned part of it for thousands of years before your lot arrived.

But he didn't want to go back to gaol. He'd had enough. Maggie had sent the money, so he was free to leave. Good old Mum, he thought.

He was badly shaken by his short spell in gaol. He'd had a glimpse of the power of the Establishment, and what it could do to you if you broke its rules. Wendy took him straight to a friend's place in Holland Park where she was staying. In their room he curled up in her arms and sobbed like a child. He was really crying with relief that he had not been imprisoned. He scarcely thought about the good behaviour bond.

Twelve

WHEN JOE'S second-year results came out early in 1969, he was scarcely surprised to find he had failed in all but two subjects.

The Senior Lecturer had taken him to task on his return from Queensland the year before, and told him that he hadn't a hope of passing at the end of the year.

'As far as I can see you're just wasting your time, and ours,' he said. 'You'll have to do Second Year again, most probably. The only thing in your favour is that you're still young, since you won't be nineteen till October. But you've got your priorities all wrong. You could do more for your people by passing your exams and getting your degree, proving you can do it, than by marching and protesting and banging people on the nose!'

' "A sock on the jaw is often worth five files in the office", as Mr Chelston was fond of saying.'

'*The Letters of an Indian Judge*, eh? So you've been doing some reading outside your subject. Perhaps you should have done an Arts course.'

'I don't think so. I'm interested in *practical* sociology, not as a theory. And the economics of oppression –'

'Nevertheless, a term in gaol will put paid to your studies. And you'd better pull up your stocks next year, or you may not get another chance.' And with these ominous words he closed the interview.

Joe wandered downstairs and out into the spring sunshine. Groups of young people in jeans and sloppy-Joes, piles of books and notes under their arms, were talking on the lawns outside the Menzies library or drifting into the Refectory for coffee. It was a pleasant life at the ANU, and he was worried by the veiled threat in the Lecturer's last words. He did not want to be sent down. And what would Maggie say?

Maggie had a great deal to say when the results came out. Joe was at home for the long vacation, and she was enjoying having a man about the place to cut the lawn and put up shelves and replace plugs on electrical appliances – all things she was capable of doing herself, but she was not good at practical things and they exhausted her.

Since her letters at the time of his arrest, she had not said very much about his attack on the Queensland Minister. It worried her more than she could say. The good behaviour bond might keep him quiet for a while, but she feared that he would not rest until he had become a martyr. With a mother's fears and a writer's imagination, she saw Joe obtaining a gun, holding up the Federal Minister in Canberra, the gun going off perhaps by accident, the man falling in a pool of his own blood, Joe arrested, Joe in the condemned cell . . . She saw it all, in a series of vivid pictures, and was terrified.

It was not long since the last man had been hanged in Victoria, when Ronald Ryan went to the gallows protesting his innocence. There had been wild protests in the streets of Melbourne against capital punishment. What worse could befall a mother than to lose a son in this way? Mrs Ryan had begged to be allowed to have her son's body for burial. She had even petitioned the Premier of the State, but he refused to interfere with regulations. The body must be buried in quicklime in the prison grounds. 'How morbid can you get?' asked Premier Bolte with the supreme insensitivity of the hardened politician.

Joe was not aware of his mother's fears and imaginings, but he was startled at her anger over his results.

'I've had to sell my shares to raise money for your Court case and your bond,' she said 'and if you step over the line once I lose the bond. And this is how you repay me and your great-grandmother who made it possible for you to study! It's all this ridiculous Black Power business, violence and protest and anti-Vietnam marches – '

'You go in anti-war demos yourself.'

'Yes, but I'm not studying. This is your great chance, don't you see? You mustn't blow it. It makes me angry to see you behaving so idiotically.'

'I'm sorry, Mum, but you must admit the Queensland Minister was asking for it!'

'That doesn't excuse you for uttering threats and using physical violence against a man twice your age. A spell in gaol might be just what you need to straighten you out; give you time to think.'

'No, thanks! I *had* a spell in gaol, remember? Remanded in custody. I never want to go through that again.'

He told her about Wendy, and how she had looked after him when he came out. 'It nearly broke me, and I was only in seven days.'

Wendy was a country girl, he said. She had gone home to

637

the farm for the Long Vac. They were thinking of setting up house together next term, pooling their resources. He thought he would be more settled in a domestic situation. 'So any small contribution you could make would be welcome . . .'

'I don't think I'll be in a position to help for at least a year. Don't forget I have Income Tax to pay, and rent, and registration on my car – though I'll probably have to sell that to keep you there another year. For heaven's sake, try to keep out of trouble this year. Perhaps I should come and live in Canberra, and then you could save rent or Hostel fees.'

Joe grinned at her disarmingly. 'It's not quite the same thing as setting up house with a girl-friend, though, is it?'

'No, well –. Is she nice?'

'You'd love her.'

Maggie was relieved that he did not need her. The last thing she wanted was to give up her good job in Adelaide, and the painful joy of seeing Rex Ryder every day.

'Well, I'm not giving you a wedding present unless you get married properly.'

'We probably will, later on.'

Joe did not tell her that there was a chance he would be sacked if his work did not improve. Wendy had promised to make him study. His twentieth birthday was not till the end of the year, the 23rd of October, but he awaited the event with some trepidation. If he was sent down he would no longer have the status of a student, and if his date fell out of the barrel he would be drawn into the Draft. There would be no alternative between being sent off to Vietnam, with all the other young men whose birthdays were marked on the fatal marble, and going to prison. Before, it had been a matter of choice whether he wanted to force the issue by refusing his Medical. Now he might not have a choice.

Barry Bentham, to his own dismay, was one of the lucky ones. He was not to be conscripted. He felt cheated. He had waited eagerly for his twentieth birthday to arrive so that he could defy the authorities, but it was not to be.

Nixon had now replaced Johnson as President and had declared that he 'did not intend to be the first President of the United States to lose a war'. There did not seem to be any end to the conflict in sight, while bombing raids were carried further afield. To Barry's disgust, Nixon had ordered that Lieutenant Calley of the My Lai massacre should be given preferential treatment and seemed to condone his actions.

'He is guilty by any standards,' said Barry. 'According to the Charter of the International Military Tribunal at the Nuremberg Trials, the following acts are crimes under International Law: "Ill-treatment of civilian population . . . murder or ill-treatment of prisoners of war . . . wanton destruction of cities, towns, or villages . . . inhumane acts committed against any civilian population"; and so on. The Germans committed some frightful atrocities in the last War, but at least the German war criminals were brought to justice.'

'Calley was sentenced to a military prison.'

'Yes, with special privileges. And I bet Nixon lets him out. And what about all the villages that have been burned down, the napalming of children, the phosphorous bombs and antipersonnel bombs used against civilians? No one is being arrested over those. And yet My Lai was only one slightly worse incident than all the others.'

'Someone should arrest the president of the Dow Chemical Company,' said Joe. 'Did you read about the "new, improved Napalm-B with polystyrene"? Because they found that "the older formulations left much to be desired, particularly in adhesion". Yes, that was in a report of the *U.S. Chemical & Engineering News*. What it means, when you analyse those coolly clinical terms, is that the horrible stuff now clings to the skin and cannot be scraped off, so that the victim dies in agony. What sort of men can *invent* a thing like that? Use their human brains and ingenuity to produce "new, improved" horrors?'

'If they're clever enough to put a man on the moon, they're probably clever enough to destroy the world, let alone Vietnam.'

'Well, at least they haven't used their atom bomb there.'

'Give them time, give them time,' said Joe.

That week, after the monthly issue of National Service cards, there were riots in Canberra and Sydney and some windows of the US Embassy were broken. Eight draft cards were ceremoniously burnt on the steps of Parliament House.

The young offenders each received seven days' gaol for non-compliance with the National Service Act, which required them to present themselves for medical examination. The amended Act now provided for three years' gaol without option for those who refused to fight in Vietnam. Many of the protesters in the Draft Resisters' Union were not just conscientious objectors, opposed to war in general, but were objecting to conscription on principle, and to this war in particular.

They all went down to Sydney in the train for a big anti-Vietnam rally, festooning the carriages with slogans and rolls of toilet paper. They had a permit to march; as Joe wrote to his mother, it was perfectly legal. 'Yes, but you're missing lectures!' she said to herself fretfully.

By good fortune Joe was not arrested in Sydney, largely because Wendy hung on to his arm with all her weight – which had increased lately – and kept him out of the forefront of the fray.

'You've got to be careful, Joe!' she urged. 'If they catch you "disturbing the peace", even if it's just swearing at a copper, they can put you back in clink. Cool it, man, cool it! And you'd better let me carry the grass, or they could bust you for having that.'

'Yair, I know. Here you are, then. But you don't need to get so up-tight,' as he handed her the pouch marked "Drum Tobacco". 'I'd lose my bond, but it doesn't mean I'd go to gaol. It wasn't a suspended sentence.'

Joe wrote to say that he and Wendy were now sharing a flat, or rather part of a house, and would she like to come and stay? They could put a folding bed up for her in the living-room, which was large.

Maggie took her holidays during the August vacation and went to Canberra.

'You won't go and decide to live over there, will you?' asked Rex Ryder anxiously. 'It'll be bad enough doing without you for a fortnight. I've got spoilt; now no one else will do.'

Maggie glowed. 'No, Mr Ryder. I promise to come back. My son has a girl-friend there and doesn't need me.'

She had written that she would stay at Beauchamp House; she did not need a stretcher in their living-room. Joe and Wendy were sharing a house with two other couples, thus dividing the rent into six. They occupied the large living-room downstairs.

Wendy was relieved. 'What's the use of living with some-one,' she said to her girl-friend, 'if you have to have his mother to stay? I mean, you might as well be married.'

She was not very strong on housekeeping and rather dreaded Maggie's visit. She put the cat's box outside and cleaned the little bathroom which was also the laundry, with an early-model washing machine in one corner. Joe was meeting the plane and said he would go with his mother to her hotel, thus giving Wendy time to do the washing-up from yesterday which was still in the sink. They had meant to get up early and do it but had slept in. Only the cat jumping on the bed, wanting its breakfast, had woken them. Joe forgot about this when Maggie said at the airport that she'd like to take the taxi straight to their flat and meet Wendy. (She had some presents for the flat, and was more nervous than Wendy about the meeting; she wanted to get it over.)

When the taxi pulled up outside, Wendy said, 'Shit!' and began bundling clothes out of sight into the wardrobe. And all those dishes in the sink! Joe had said his mother was a bit fussy about kitchens, another reason she was glad Mrs King was not coming to stay. The kitchen was part of the big living room, and only a screen partly divided off the bedroom alcove.

Leaving only three mugs for morning coffee, Wendy grab-bed the dirty dishes and saucepans, piled them on a tray, and shoved them under the divan bed out of sight just as Joe knocked. She twitched the cottage weave bedspread down all round and went demurely to the door.

Joe, watching anxiously the two women in his life, saw that they liked each other. They talked while Wendy rinsed the mugs and put the percolator on the little portable stove. She hoped Maggie meant to take them out to dinner and didn't expect her to cook a meal.

'Is this your whole living area?' asked Maggie. 'It's a nice big room, and gets the morning sun.'

'We have the porch too, when the wind's not blowing from the southwest,' said Joe, indicating the terraced area outside the glass doors.

'Yes, it's better than a balcony. I like to be able to get my feet on the ground.'

She admired the bedspread and the "Doona", the light, down-filled quilt which kept out Canberra's chill. '*And* we have oil heating,' said Joe proudly. 'You won't find that in many Australian cities.'

'No, in Adelaide we just put up with the winter. Except for fireplaces, which leave your back cold.'

The coffee was ready, and the cat, a silky, smoky grey, woke and stretched its paws. It had been asleep under the table and Maggie had not seen it.

'What a pretty puss!' she said. 'Come here, pussy, pussy pussy!'

But the cat, aware of something that smelt like food under the bed, disappeared behind the screen and under the bedspread just as Maggie went to pick it up. She lifted the hanging side of the spread and looked for the cat.

'Here, pussy – !'

Wendy, one hand over her mouth, was making frantic signals to Joe, who looked back uncomprehendingly.

'Oh!' Maggie dropped the veil hastily over the pile of dirty plates and saucepans. She looked up at Wendy, whose face was pink, but who was trying not to laugh. 'Oh, dear! Do you always keep the washing-up under the bed?' And she started to laugh.

Maggie and Wendy sank side by side on the bed, laughing till the tears ran down their cheeks. Joe, mystified, began to pour the coffee. The cat bounded out and jumped on Wendy's lap.

'You devil, Tiger Tim. You did that on purpose!' Wendy gasped. The cat purred agreement. Joe looked under the bed, and then, in mock accusation, at Wendy. He said he would do the washing-up before he went to lectures. 'It's your fault!' she said. 'You came back too early!'

Maggie and Wendy were still laughing, getting on like a house on fire, taking it in turns to stroke the cat.

The visit was a success. She brought out her presents for the flat. 'How embarrassing!' said Wendy as Maggie handed her a pair of pretty floral tea-towels. They laughed again.

Joe put his arms round his two women, and kissed them both contentedly.

Thirteen

MAGGIE WENT back to Adelaide relieved in her mind about Joe. In spite of the wild hair and the black shirt, he was still her bright-eyed, affectionate son, hot-headed but surely not cruel, not a man likely to commit murder or even manslaughter. She felt that Wendy would be a steadying influence. Even more so if they had a baby, though how they'd be able to afford it . . . Grandma Maggie! She could not believe that she was old enough for the role, but it was certainly physically possible. Joe was nineteen and Wendy eighteen.

Penelope took her to task for worrying too much about her son, 'clucking like an old hen'. Let the young look after themselves, she said, they would soon enough be running the world and it was to be hoped they'd make a better fist of it than their predecessors.

'We've got ourselves into this mess in Vietnam,' she said, 'and it's like a quicksand. Once you've made the initial false step, it's not easy to get out. "*Sed pedem referre, hoc opus, hoc labor est*." '

What became known as 'the Collins case' was filling the court-report columns of the *Evening Herald* and its rival, the morning *Register*. Robert Collins, a full-blood Aborigine who had been born near Alice Springs, and who had never been to school, was arrested on South Australia's West Coast on suspicion of the rape and murder of a schoolgirl. Feelings ran high in the small town, and the man – he was only a youth of eighteen – was removed to Adelaide Gaol for his own safety.

643

The girl's body had been found in a cave, her head bashed in with a rock.

Collins had been working with a travelling circus as a general roustabout. At the initial inquiry evidence was given that he had been away from the tents and caravans for some hours. He admitted he had been drinking on the outskirts of the town but denied he had molested the girl. He was committed, however, for trial on a charge of murder.

As the sensational evidence unfolded, the story moved from the inside pages to the front page, with photographs of the eminent QC who had been brought from the Eastern States to defend the accused, at the behest of several champions of the Aborigines, churchmen among them.

The gist of the Police Prosecutor's case was that Collins should be convicted on circumstantial evidence. He admitted he had been in the area at the time of the murder, that he had been drinking and his memory of events was hazy, that he had seen the eleven-year-old girl but had not spoken to her or gone near her. All this was told in halting, ungrammatical English.

Then the police produced a signed, typewritten 'confession', which they said they had obtained after questioning the accused. He had been made to undress, and fresh scars had been noticed on his knees, which could have been made by the rocky floor of the cave.

Among the witnesses for the defence was an anthropologist who had grown up in Central Australia and could speak Collins' native dialect. He gave evidence that the illiterate man could not possibly have made the confession attributed to him. He could not even understand a lot of the expressions used. In short, he had been 'verballed', the confession read to him and then signed under duress.

When she had some free time, Maggie went and sat in the packed Supreme Court. She felt intimidated herself by the heavy polished cedar, the judge's rostrum, the tiers of seats, the Court orderlies, the barristers in their wigs and gowns. What must it be like for a simple bush boy like Robert Collins? His brow was set in wrinkles of worry and concentration as he strove to comprehend what was going on and whether they were going to hang him by the neck till he was dead. She saw the fear and bewilderment in his dark eyes.

Letters to the Editor were pouring in, both for and against –
some suggesting that Collins was being victimised because of
his colour. They could not be used now that the case was *sub
judice*, but Maggie read them all. Some were rabid with hate,
some reasoned appeals for impartiality.

The elderly judge presiding at the trial, however, showed
that his sympathies lay with the white majority whose racial
prejudices had been reinforced by the pictures of the young
man, showing a low, heavy brow, thick lips and smoky dark
eyes. The judge frequently interrupted Counsel for the Defence and disallowed his objections. The friction between
Judge and Queen's Counsel became obvious.

Perhaps because employing Maggie had given him an
interest in Aboriginal affairs, Rex Ryder took up the Collins
case as a sort of crusade: the unsophisticated black man,
intimidated by legal jargon and the trappings of the white
man's law, in danger of an uncomprehending death on the
gallows for a crime he denied having committed.

'This case is excellent for circulation!' he said to Maggie.
'The first edition is sold out the minute it hits the streets. I only
wish we could come out a bit later . . . Still, the Home and the
Final get a pretty good coverage.'

'A man's life is at stake,' said Maggie, 'and all you can think
of is that it sells more papers!'

'My dear Maggie, that's not true. I am impressed by the
sheer human interest of the case, and I hope to see Collins
acquitted. But you, naturally, feel an even greater sympathy
for someone in his position.'

She nearly told him then. She felt that she must tell him
sooner or later, to stop her feeling like a fraud. But what if he
just saw it as a 'story'? 'Well-known Writer Has No Aboriginal Blood! Maggie Pinjarra, known as the author of several
volumes of Aboriginal stories and legends, besides a book of
verse, today revealed that –'

No, perhaps she'd better not tell him. And what if it got
back to Joe?

* * *

It was shortly after his mother's visit that Wendy told Joe she was pregnant.

'I think it must have been the rocking of the Sydney train, or something,' she said. 'I'm sure I didn't forget to take the Pill. But anyway, there it is. I'm nearly three months gone.'

'Je–sus! Why didn't you *do* something about it?'

'I didn't know. I mean, I had some symptoms, but I couldn't believe it.'

'Neither can I.'

'Well, it's happened.'

He stared at her, 'as though,' she said afterwards, 'I had some strange disease.'

'You had something to do with it too, you know,' she said, rather nettled.

'That's the trouble. I don't want to reproduce myself. If it was just yours, and you really wanted to have it, I'd say right, go ahead. But I can't bear the thought of being responsible for another human being, another man being born into a world like this. What if it's a boy? What if he grows to be twenty years old just in time for the next war?'

Wendy looked miserable. 'It might be a girl, though.'

'It *might* be – and she'll have the same chances of being blown up in an atomic blast as a boy.'

They tacitly agreed to say no more about it for the time being, but the next day Joe handed Wendy part of a poem he had copied out, by Louis MacNeice; it was called 'Prayer Before Birth.' She read:

I am not yet born; console me.
I fear that the human race may with tall walls wall me,
with strong drugs dope me, with wise lies lure me,
on black rocks rack me, in blood-baths roll me . . .

I am not yet born; O fill me
With strength against those who would freeze my
humanity, would dragoon me into a lethal automaton,
would make me a cog in a machine . . . and against all those
    who would dissipate my entirety . . .
    like water held in the

       hands would spill me
    Let them not make me a stone and let them not spill me.
    Otherwise kill me.

Wendy read it through with a frozen face. Then she looked at
Joe and said, 'You will have to get some money for the
operation. I know a doctor who will do it, for a price.'

'Of course. I'll draw my next month's allowance, and
perhaps I could borrow a bit from Stu. We'll have to live very
frugally for a month and put off paying the rent.'

'But if you're called up at the end of the year, or go to
prison, I'll be all alone.' She began to cry. He put his arms
round her and stroked her soft hair.

'All the more reason not to have a baby to support. You
know it's the only sensible thing to do, Feathertop.'

'I suppose so,' she sighed. She didn't want the operation,
but she was used to giving in to Joe, letting him make the
decisions.

The next week a tiny foetus, three inches long and with its
toes and fingers already formed – though they lacked finger-
nails – lost its fragile hold on life and went down the Canberra
sewers. It, whether to have been boy or girl, carried with it the
inheritance of thousands of forbears, including sixty-two who
had either been born in or travelled to Australia.

Fourteen

IN HIS crucial last term, when he should have been revising
and preparing for his final exams – though he hadn't much
hope of passing in enough subjects to get his degree – Joe
became involved once more in an Aboriginal demonstration.
It arose over an Australian Broadcasting Commission film,
sponsored by the Royal Australian College of Oph-
thalmologists, about conditions in Northern Territory Abor-

iginal camps. After it had been shown once on television, officials of the Commonwealth Department of Health in Canberra tried to prevent its further showing because of its open reference to trachoma, or Sandy Blight, veneral disease and leprosy.

A Professor of Medicine had spoken in the film commentary about the impossibility of hygiene in dusty camps without proper water supply. He stated that one in twenty Aborigines contracted leprosy every year in one of the camps, while one in thirty had leprosy. The film had been made as a factual account of two years' work among victims of Sandy Blight, so called because one of the symptoms was an unbearable sensation of sand beneath the lids. There was a high incidence of blindness, and flies and dirty conditions helped the spread of the infection.

Joe, who knew that his great-grandmother Elaine had been cured of leprosy, but did not know that his great-great-grandfather on his father's side, Sam King, had once suffered from trachoma while prospecting in the Territory, took to the streets once more to demand that the film be shown.

Students and Aborigines picketed the Health Department and refused to allow anyone out or in to the building. Others gathered outside the ABC offices until it was announced that the film would be shown, and without any deletions. The students surged back to the Health Department, calling for the Director-General, Dr Gwynn.

He refused to see them, but when he came out in the late afternoon to drive home in his Commonwealth car, they surrounded him. He explained blandly that all his Department had asked of the ABC was that the 'inflated figures' for leprosy and VD should be amended or excised, as 'they only inflated the poor image that Aborigines already have in the community.'

There was a roar of protest at this.

'You bloody bureaucrat!' cried Joe, who was near the front. 'What sort of image do you think *you'd* have if you were forced to squat in the dust and heat in a dirty, fly-infested camp, with no running water and no proper latrines? Have you ever been to the Territory? Have you *seen* the conditions in the camps? "Amended figures" my arse! If the figures were ten times exaggerated, if there was only one with leprosy in every hundred and two with syphilis, that would still be a disgrace. But you don't want to admit the truth, you sanctimonious pig!'

At this stage one of the police standing by intervened, giving Joe a sharp push in the chest which sent him staggering backward into the crowd. The police made a pathway for the Director-General to his car. Joe, bouncing back again, gave the policeman who had pushed him a shove in the back. He was getting ready to kick him in the shins when he turned, when his arms were pinioned from behind and two policemen carried him struggling to a Black Maria while he shouted, 'Pigs! Pigs!'

Joe was back in the remand cells, waiting to be bailed out. He had been charged with offensive behaviour and resisting arrest. Wendy telephoned Maggie at once – the time in South Australia was half an hour behind, and it was only 4 p.m. there – to tell her Joe had been arrested again, in Canberra.

'Not again!' said Maggie despairingly. She thought for a moment, and said, 'I'll be over tomorrow night, before the weekend. He'll have to stay inside till I can raise the money and get there. I suppose he'll lose his bond. How much is bail fixed at?'

'Two hundred dollars. But we haven't anything like that much, since the abortion. It was rather expensive.'

'The abortion? What are you talking about? Do you mean that you – got rid of my grandchild?'

'Well, it was our decision, it was up to us. And Joe didn't want any children. He was afraid it would be a son and have to go to the next war.'

'And you, my dear? Wouldn't you like a son?'

'I –. I want what Joe wants,' said Wendy in a small voice.

'I see. I'll have a word with Joe when I see him.'

Maggie nursed her anger for a day and a night before she could get away. The Collins case was still on the front page, with altercations between the judge and the eminent QC enlivening proceedings. When Maggie explained to Rex Ryder the situation with her son, he let her go with his blessing.

'But try to get back by Monday morning,' he said. 'I need you here.'

This was music to Maggie's ears.

Rex had been working late, writing leaders on the Collins case. She had revelled in the chance to work back with him in the intimacy of the strangely quiet and empty building, with only the distant hum of cleaning staff's vacuum-cleaners sounding somewhere in the corridors.

Sometimes she dared to suggest a change in a word or a sentence here and there as she typed from his strong black pencil scrawl.

('I couldn't imagine a newspaperman who didn't use a typewriter,' she had said when she first joined his staff. 'Can't stand the rotten things,' said he.)

She loved even his handwriting, strung out in beautifully regular lines on the small sheets of copy-paper, the vigorous horizontal crossing of the t's, the impatient x's marking full stops.

'I promise to be back on Monday morning if it's humanly possible,' she said now. 'But I must get Joe released from custody first. He suffers badly from claustrophobia; he said he nearly went off his head after seven days in gaol.'

'Poor Collins will get life, if they don't hang him,' said Rex gloomily.

'You believe he's innocent, don't you?'

'I believe any man is innocent till he's proved guilty. And they haven't proved anything but that he was in the area. He's being tried on circumstantial evidence and prejudice. I don't believe in the cooked-up "confession". But I see no hope for him with this judge. And *you* know, none better, how colour prejudice affects judgment.'

Maggie decided that when she returned she would tell him the truth, that she was no more Aboriginal than he was, though she had been brought up among Aborigines from a tiny child.

She still planned a trip to New Caledonia and the Loyalty

Islands to trace her roots, and perhaps tell the story of great-grandfather Joseph Tula.

Before taking the bus to the airport, she drove her car round to several second-hand dealers, but the best cash offer she could get was $400. They all wanted to sell her another car. With the money in her purse she flew to Melbourne, and from there to Canberra. The pastures were still green with late spring; there was plenty of snow left on the Alps, though it must be melting by now. Their smooth, rounded slopes gleamed like clouds in the golden light of afternoon. Maggie gazed at the mountains and tried to calm her mind, to empty it of all thought. But it was no use. She kept rehearsing what she would say to Joe when he was released.

Seven hundred dollars he would have cost her this time, with the forfeited bond and the two hundred bail; even if he wasn't fined that much, she'd had to produce it. She was fed up with bailing him out and rescuing him from his own stupid actions. In two weeks he would reach his twentieth birthday, and it might all be taken out of her hands. She hoped he would not choose to go to gaol rather than do his National Service. Surely he could get some non-combatant job in the Army, as a stretcher-bearer or something, and not have to join against his will in the killing? She wanted him to stand up for his principles, but she knew how he would suffer in an Army prison.

She could only hope that his birth-date would not be among those to fall out of the fatal barrel.

Joe was released into his mother's custody; she had to enter into another bond of $250 and promise to keep him from street violence and abusive language. When they were alone at her cheap motel she turned on him.

'You deserve absolutely no further consideration from me,' she said coldly. 'I've done all I could; you've taken every penny I earned and now even my car is gone. And all for what? So you could pose in the streets as a kind of Che Guevara, a popular hero leading your people to freedom! Your people! What about all your white ancestors – Scots, Irish, Canadian, English, goodness knows what! Quite apart from the Islander heritage, which is different again.'

'You forgot Portuguese. And I can't help it if I identify

651

most strongly with my Aboriginal forefathers. I suppose it's got something to do with genes.' He was beginning to look sullen; he did not like her to throw up at him all she had done for him. That's what mothers were supposed to do, wasn't it? Women! Even Wendy had turned cold lately, seeming to blame him for not letting her bear his child.

'I didn't forget Portuguese. There's none that I know of in our ancestry.'

'What! But the graves on Pandanus Island? It's one of my earliest memories, holding on to a rough stone and feeling what must have been letters with my fingers . . . Miguel, and Bert – '

'Bert died before I was born. *Twelve months* before I was born! He was not my father, and Nyora was not your great-grandmother. So you see it's not "something to do with genes". I had no Aboriginal genes to pass on to you, that I know of.'

There was a stunned silence. Joe, who had been standing defensively by the window, groped for a chair and sat down.

'*Say that again*! I dare you to say that again.'

'You and I are of Islander, but not Aboriginal extraction. My father, in fact, was a visiting American that my mother met after Bert died.'

'A Yank! Not a bloody Yank! *Oh no!*' He bowed his curly head in his hands.

Maggie hadn't meant to say any of this and certainly hadn't realised that a connection with America, which was waging the war in Vietnam that he so bitterly opposed, would be especially unpalatable to Joe. She was frightened when she saw the glazed look of shock in his eyes.

'And what about you?' he cried. 'The Aboriginal writer! You fraud, oh you fraud, and you knew all the time! And Aunt Marie knew, I suppose – '

'Aunt Marie didn't know. *I* didn't know until just recently. It was old Nyora who told me, on our last visit. No one else knows. And now I wish I hadn't told you. But you carry the whole thing to such extremes! And that reminds me – why didn't you let Wendy have the baby? She – '

'What's she been saying to you? And it's our business anyway, not yours.'

'You forget that he – it – was my descendant too.'

'Oh, so that's it. You wanted to carry on the line; from great-great-grandpappy Joseph Tula to your whoring mother, down to your grandson, and generations unborn. "And Fiona begat Anna, and Anna begat Maggie, and Maggie begat Joseph", and Joseph isn't going to beget anyone.'

'Because you're selfish and spoilt. And my mother was not a whore.'

They glared at each other. It was the worst quarrel they'd ever had. For a moment she thought he was going to strike her. Then he pushed past her and flung out of the motel room and away. He did not return home; Wendy hadn't seen him, and Maggie left for Adelaide without seeing him again. She now wished her angry words unsaid, but it was too late. Remembering the look on his face, she felt that he would never forgive her. Yet he was blaming her for something which happened before she was born.

Fifteen

AFTER LEAVING the motel, Joe had not been back home, had not told Wendy of his mother's revelation. He could not face it yet. He pushed it to the back, or rather the side of his mind; it was there, but too painful to be looked at squarely and accepted. He had simply told Wendy he would not be at lectures, and had gone off walking in the bush to an old weekender hut he knew of. He took nothing but matches, candles, a sliced loaf of bread, and some cheese. There were enamel mugs and plates in the hut as he remembered, and a rainwater tank which caught fresh water from the roof. 'Better get used to living on bread and water,' he said to himself wryly. Stuart had already received his call-up, and according to their pact had burnt the card telling him to present himself for medical examination. He had been given seven days for non-compliance with the order and was now serving a three-year sentence in an Army prison outside Sydney.

Joe had received one letter from him, on heavily-ruled prison paper. Stu said he was going to appeal against the sentence, like Simon Townsend, who had finally been released – after several court cases – on the grounds of conscientious objection. (Townsend, kept in solitary confinement on a diet of bread and water, had created a precedent by winning his case, though he had by then served most of his sentence.)

Nearly three years shut away from the light and air!

Joe lit a fire in the old stone fireplace attached to the wooden hut and sat listening to the companionable flapping of the flame about a hollow root. His fateful twentieth birthday was due in a few days.

'I couldn't stand it!' thought Joe.

He could imagine it all too well, the confinement, the stench, the walls pressing in, the claustrophobia which was worse at night. And what if there was no window, just some fiendish modern air conditioning – no natural light, just a bare bulb burning night and day? Army prisons were presumably more recent, more up-to-date than the old State gaols. He could not bear it; he would go insane in three weeks, let alone three years. The two days last time while he had waited for Maggie to bail him out had been bad enough.

What was he to do? Where could he turn? He had no money and no passport, or he might have tried to leave the country. He might have gone and hidden on Pandanus Island with Dan and Uncle Morgan, but he was no longer one of them, they were not his people, and he couldn't ask them to take the risk of harbouring him. And he could not claim exemption as an Aborigine as he might have done once.

Not his people! There it was, the shattering fact that he had been avoiding. The Aborigines were not his people. The whole basis of his existence up to now had been swept away. He almost hated his mother for telling him; yet surely it was better to know than to go on living a lie. But would he have the courage to come out and say that it was all a mistake? After all the public statements he had made?

He had identified totally with his Aboriginal Australian ancestors, as he had thought them. Now he was adrift on a wide and shoreless sea. Wendy might have provided a sheet-anchor, but Wendy announced that as soon as his birthday was over she was going to live with Sylvie. And he had introduced them! It was ironic, all right. He wouldn't have felt so bad if Wendy had left him for another man, he told himself.

Sylvie was truly Aboriginal, or part-Aboriginal. It was evident that Wendy was attracted in some romantic way to what she regarded as 'primitive' types.

From his terrible dilemma he turned his mind back to that camping holiday with the two girls, the first day at Lake Nunga Nunga: 'The last happy day of my life,' thought Joe. It had turned disastrous in the end. But he had wanted to show off his bushmanship, his ability to live in the open like his nomad ancestors, to light fires and cook damper and provide food and shelter. Fortunately, he had given up the idea of building a bough and bark wurley or mia-mia and had taken a modern lightweight nylon tent, for it had rained seven inches in two days.

It was Sylvie, down from Brisbane where he had met her during the demonstrations over Woorabinda, who had suggested that he and Wendy should make their camping holiday a threesome.

'I can show you how to find native tucker, berries an' that, that you can eat – glassies, native cherry, midyim – and how to find "blackfeller's bread" and wild honey,' she said. 'My Dad remembered all the Old People taught 'im before I was born, an' he taught me.'

Joe had thought it a great idea, but Wendy objected at first. Then it occurred to her that if three was a crowd, at least it would stop Joe from importuning her at all hours of the day or night. From being rather indifferent to sex, she had become positively icelike since the abortion, finding it something to be endured, not enjoyed.

Stuart had let Joe have his old car as long as he paid the registration and insurance. They packed everything into it, water-tins and flour and butter and tea and sugar; no meat, for Joe said they would live off the land. They drove north along the Pacific coast and then west, which led them to a part of the

Northern Rivers which was semi-tropical, with bangalow palms and cabbage palms and blue waterlilies lighting the backwaters and billabongs.

Lake Nunga Nunga was in a huge shallow basin surrounded by an open forest of native pine and box trees. To get to it they had to drive over a rough dirt track, passing the last farm about thirty miles back.

The first day at Nunga Nunga was idyllic, with great piled clouds round the horizon and a clear blue zenith, reflected in the lake's calm waters in a paler, purer blue. Drifts of purple-blue waterlilies covered much of the surface with floating leaves and gold-stamened flower-cups. Dead, drowned trees turned to grey skeletons stood in the water, home to wood-ducks and whistling ducks and ibis.

The girls, not sure if there were fishermen about, swam not quite naked, each wearing the bottom half of a pair of brief bikinis. Joe was entranced as, treading water, he watched Sylvie in the shallows, bending above a delicate blue chalice, with a lily-bud stuck behind her ear, and her long dark hair trailing towards the water: vital, brown, sinuous, sensuous Sylvie!

Wendy's fair hair had seemed out of place in that mysterious basin, with low limestone hills at one end and at the other a high, dark dome of rock, rather menacing, and shaped like the head of a giant lizard.

Swimming in the deep, calm water, among the real and reflected flowers, Joe suddenly felt something grip his leg. He gave a yelp of fright: all those stories of Bunyips that haunted waterholes came back to him. But the something clawed up past his knee to his groin and gave a gentle squeeze there. Sylvie's laughing face broke the surface. She shook back her dark wet hair and looked at him provocatively: a water-lubra.

He grabbed her and kissed her and they sank under water still joined mouth to mouth, and came up gasping. Sylvie was thin, with small breasts and bony shoulders, the 'salt-cellar' showing deeply at her throat. But she radiated an air of intense vitality. Her lips were a dusky rose, and there was a flush of pink under her brown cheeks. Joe felt himself responding to her challenge. He began to wish they were alone, that he had not brought Wendy, who had been nearly impossible to live with lately, expecting a man to live like a monk most of the time while sharing a double bed with him. His immediate reaction to Sylvie told him how much he had been repressing his own instincts.

Joe made a creditable damper that night from self-raising flour and water, baking it to a light crustiness in the ashes. There was plenty of firewood, for many of the box and bloodwood trees seemed to have fallen and were quite dry. Just at sunset a flock of green-winged parrots crossed the lake, while a white egret stood in the shallows motionless as a bird carved from marble as it watched for fish.

Joe had not managed to catch any fish, though there should be yellow-belly and cod in the lake. But after sunset, when it was nearly dark, Sylvie landed two perch and an eel, which writhed and contorted on the hook like a snake.

'Good tucker this one,' she said in a parody of Pidgin English. Wendy shuddered and said *she* certainly didn't want to taste any.

After despatching the eel, Sylvie had showed Joe how to scald it in the big billy-can to remove the skin, then cut it into round steaks across the backbone, and boil it for ten minutes in salty water. 'Then tomorrow, we fry 'im. You'll say it's "proply good tucker" when you taste 'im.'

Wendy took another piece of damper and spread it with soft, salty butter. 'Why didn't you tell me you could cook, Joe?' she asked. 'This is much better than blotting-paper bread from the supermarket. And the fish is super.'

They had brought half a dozen cans of beer in a cold-box, and they lolled about the campfire after supper, talking and drinking and smoking a joint. Joe had been planning how he could pretend to catch another eel and get Sylvie away from the campfire. But as the limp, damp, hand-rolled marijuana cigarette passed from hand to hand, from mouth to mouth, he felt his mind expanding, his lips stretching in a helpless, happy smile. Everything was simple, beautiful, right, from the startled call of a waterbird to the magnificent stars flashing their cold blue steel overhead. There were flashes of lightning among the huge clouds that still stood around the horizon; above, the sky was intensely clear.

'I've heard of this place,' said Sylvie musingly. 'Nunga

Nunga! The "blackfellers" wouldn't camp here. They said that old goanna, who turned into a rock, he once drank all the water out of the lake till it was dry. And one day he going to spit it all out again, make an Old Man flood.'

When they had finished all the beer and a second joint, Joe murmured tranquilly, 'I'm stoned out of my mind,' and Wendy giggled. Sylvie suddenly leant over and undid the top of his jeans.

'Hey!' said Joe. 'Don't attack a defenceless man. It's two to one. Not fair.'

'That makes it all the better,' said Sylvie, kneeling by the fire and spreading their three sleeping-bags in a row on the ground. In one supple movement she slipped out of her halter-top and stretch-nylon shorts. 'We lie like three green beans, or if you like, three sausages in a pan,' she said. 'You here, Wendy. Now I'm curled behind you, and Joe behind me. I'll look after you, Wendy, you'll love it. Come on Joe, I hope you're not too stoned to play your part.'

'No, but I must just go and have a leak. A leak by the lake, ho, ho!' Everything seemed deliciously funny, unimportant.

Then he was lying on top of his sleeping-bag, the night air cool on his bare skin, and sinking himself in that delightful cleft or cavern where all day he had longed to be. At the same time Wendy felt a slender dark hand cup her breast, while another slid between her thighs.

Still entwined in their threesome, they fell into a gentle doze.

Towards midnight Joe opened his eyes and stared up at the enormous sky of stars. The fire had sunk down, and there was no moon. He gazed helplessly and rapturously upon them, wondering at the hugeness of space and the smallness of human beings. These mighty and mysterious objects, unimaginably far . . . these gorgeous constellations set thick with starry gems, these densely crowded globes of glowing light, systems beyond systems, clusters beyond clusters, and universes beyond universes, all wheeling and swaying, floating and circling round some distant, unknown centrepoint, in the pauseless measures of a perpetual dance of joy! It was a vision of pure harmony which he would keep to the end of his short life.

His eyes closed before the big black clouds began to move in from the west.

Suddenly it was raining. Not gentle, warm rain but great cold drops from a sky almost blacked over. Dragging their sleeping-bags they groped their way to the tent and crawled into them. Joe felt his heart thudding loudly in his chest. He was intensely aware of being alive and human in the formless blackness all around.

In the morning it was still raining heavily. They peered out at a changed world, grey and dank. The goanna's head lowered above the lake, the lilies had all closed their flower cups, and no bird sang. When Joe dragged himself out, in a waterproof jacket, to boil the billy for tea, he found that the lake edges had become a quagmire of sticky black mud. The lake had already risen six inches; it must be fed from underground springs as well as run-off. The water was now only a foot from the fireplace he had constructed so carefully, close to the water where the grass was green and there was no danger of starting a bushfire. There was still a coal glowing on the underside of a big log, and he fed this with small sticks and bark pulled from trees. The girls cheered when he appeared with mugs of tea, but Joe was gloomy. 'If this keeps up we'll never get the car out of here,' he said.

They decided to stay in the cramped tent till the rain stopped. Wendy had brought a pack of cards, so they went on playing all day. Bored and hungry, they gazed out in the afternoon at a slope gushing with springs and rivulets. A large brown snake, washed out of its hole, appeared beside the tent and wriggled away.

'Good tucker, that one?' asked Joe, trying to lighten the atmosphere.

Sylvie said, 'I'll fry that eel now, if you can build the fire up.'

But the fire was out. Not only out, but under water. The lake had risen over the fireplace and was now lapping at the tent-pegs. They opened a can of beans and ate them cold. When the rain eased a bit, Joe uprooted the tent and pitched it further up the slope, under some dark leaning trees.

Lying in their sleeping bags, surrounded by a sea of mud, they heard an ominous *Crash*! somewhere round the lake. Then another, nearer at hand.

'Trees falling!' said Sylvie, starting up. In the light of the battery-powered lamp the whites of her eyes shone, glistening, scared. 'That ol' goanna's got it in for us.'

Another *crash*! *whumph*! shook the ground.

'The rain has softened the soil,' said Joe, 'and the trees are falling. No wonder there was plenty of firewood.'

'I'm getting out of this!' said Wendy on a slightly hysterical note. 'I'm getting in the car. Fancy pitching the tent under the trees!'

'So'm I,' said Sylvie. They held towels and waterproofs over their heads and bolted for the car. Joe remained, feeling redundant. Why hadn't he felt in his bones that this was a sinister place? Sylvie had felt it. Now that Old Man, that goanna, was going to spew out all the water he had drunk from the lake in the past.

Another tree crashed, further round the lake shore. He lay tense, waiting for one to fall on the tent and crush him.

They had got away from the dreadful place in the end, wet, cold, hungry and coated in mud. Three times they had been bogged, but with one driving and two pushing they got out. Several times they had to build causeways of wood across creeks that had started to run into the lake. Wendy lost her shoes in almost bottomless mud and was in a thoroughly bad temper. Sylvie kept murmuring that it was a Spirit Place and they shouldn't have come here.

'Oh, shut up!' said Joe at last, goaded beyond endurance. 'It was just bad luck it rained, that's all. It was perfect the first day. That's all nonsense about the goanna.'

Sylvie turned her shoulder towards him and scarcely spoke to him on the long drive back to Sydney, where they left her and drove on to Canberra. They and the car had been coated in dried brown mud.

'All I want is a bath!' said Wendy, leaving him to unpack. 'I can't wait to get under that hot shower. What a bushman you turned out to be!'

*   *   *

He should have known then, thought Joe. He had tried to feel something about that lizard-shaped hill, that it really was a Dreamtime ancestor turned to stone. Sylvie said the Old People used to come there and get songs and stories that issued from the rock, but they would never camp there. But apart from his fear of falling trees, he had really felt nothing. Because he was not, and never had been, one of them.

He put another log on the hut fire. It was not cold; the weather was perfect, but he liked to watch the flames. An Aborigine would never have lit his campfire in a lake bed; he would have known by all the signs that the lake was unusually low, would have known, probably, that the rain was coming.

Anyway, he was still a Pacific Islander, though so far back that it seemed unreal to him. If he had a boat, now, he could sail out into the Pacific and disappear . . .

He returned home somewhat calmer in his mind.

Wendy silently handed him his Draft card.

Sixteen

WENDY WAS gone; he had quarrelled with his mother; he had lost his sense of belonging to the ancient race he had claimed as his own; he would be sure to fail to get his degree, and he was about to be sucked into the Draft. Yet he could not, would not, have anything to do with the war in Vietnam. What if he complied with the first order, and they found him medically unfit? But no, he was appallingly healthy. Barry came round and they ceremoniously burnt the card telling him to report.

On the other hand, he could not, would not, go back to gaol. What was he to do?

The answer came, clear and simple. He would end it all. Finish! Of course. He looked up a note he had taken from a book on suicide, a subject which had fascinated him for a while. The ancient Romans had made a cult of it, falling on their own swords; Brutus, Cato at Phillippi . . . Death before dishonour!

He had a scrapbook full of random notes; it was from this he had taken the MacNeice verses that he had handed to Wendy.

A child is born with two million million cells . . . An adult human body contains some sixty million. Every day it loses enough to fill a soup-plate. Skin flakes are exquisitely wrought crystalline polygons, whose surfaces form translucent pyramids. Love, hate, anger and worry all wear the body down . . .

Coulthard was an unfortunate explorer who lost his life by thirst, upon the western shores of Lake Torrens (a salt pan). His tin pannikin or pint pot was afterwards found with his name and the date of the last day he lived, scratched upon it. Many an unrecorded grave, many a high and noble mind, many a gallant victim to temerity and thirst, lies hidden in the wilds of Australia . . .

Famous Scorpios: Admiral Byrd; Madame Curie; Indira Gandhi; Robert Kennedy; Martin Luther; Pablo Picasso; Teddy Roosevelt; Pandit Nehru; Joseph Forbes King.

East Pakistan: Tens of thousand of people fled to higher ground when their homes were swept away in monsoon floods. Five thousand are believed to have drowned, and half a million houses are destroyed.

Ah! Here it was, the item he had been looking for:

Just as I would select my ship when I am about to go on a voyage, or my new house when I propose to take up residence, so I shall choose my death when I am ready to depart from this life. – Seneca.

He turned over several pages, references to big bauxite-mining companies taking over Aboriginal sacred sites, reports of anti-Vietnam rallies – how unimportant it all seemed, suddenly! He turned another page, and read:

Every existing being is born without reason, prolongs itself out of weakness, and dies by chance. – Jean Paul Sartre.

But he would not leave it to chance; he would take over the godlike power of deciding the how and when of his own death.

How – that was a problem. He had told Wendy to take Stu's car and look after it. He had no garage, and if left sitting in the street it would soon have tyres, battery, and every removable part stolen. There was always Lake Burley Griffin, certainly big enough and deep enough to drown most people. But he was too good a swimmer to go that way. He remembered his mother telling him about her Grandmother Fiona Brown, who swam around in choppy Moreton Bay for three hours, supporting her children, and eventually died of exhaustion. If it had been winter time and the lake full of freezing cold water it would be different. Hypothermia would soon set in, and he would die of the cold.

No. Sydney was the place: The Gap, the Harbour Bridge, any high building would do. Successful suicides happened there every day. Now that his mind was made up he felt calm, purposeful, almost as though he were planning a death for someone else. He had a week before they would come for him. Plenty of time to arrange his affairs. Should he write a note of farewell to Maggie, to Wendy? He thought not. His death would speak for him. Being still angry with Maggie, he could even contemplate with some satisfaction the agonies of self-reproach she must suffer. She, who had given him the precious gift of life, must realise that he had thrown the gift back in her face.

He even went to lectures in the last few days, took some notes which he would never use. All the stored knowledge and skills acquired in twenty years would soon be lost forever. How laboriously, for instance, he had learnt to stand upright without support, to walk balanced on two legs, to oppose the finger and thumb accurately in picking up objects, to move the tongue and lips in such a way as to form intelligible sounds, to read and write . . . He could no longer read; his mind would not settle. He played the radiogram endlessly, listening to Tchaikovsky's Sixth, the *Pathetique*, which ended on a low note of despair. And an Italian piece, *Silenzio*, based on the Last Post. *Dormi, tu ch'e si lontano . . . Dormi senza sogni . . .* Sleep without dreaming. That was all he asked. The long, quivering trumpet notes pierced him with unutterable melancholy. Like the howl of a dingo on the edge of the desert.

He made a packet of his records and some of his books and addressed it to Wendy. Then he walked out, leaving his spare clothes in the closet and his textbooks on the table, without bothering to lock the door.

Flying to Sydney on the early morning plane, he watched the metal wing beyond the window and thought, if only it would fall off, how simple it would be – all over in a minute, no forcing himself to the final jump. For he feared that his nerve would fail, that illogically he would fear the impact of the hard road, or the water hard as steel at a hundred and seventy feet below the bridge. Then he looked round at the other passengers, dozing or reading or chatting. No doubt they wanted to live.

But the plane landed safely and he took the Airways bus into the city terminal. By chance, lying on the seat where a tourist had left it, was a brochure on the beauties of the Blue Mountains. The Three Sisters . . . Katoomba . . . Govett's Leap . . . Wentworth Falls. Govett's Leap! It had a romantic sound. It must be steep, precipitous. And who was Govett, and did he leap to his death? An early bushranger, perhaps, pursued by the mounted police. It was an Australian tradition, after all:

> *Up jumped the swagman and dived into the billabong*
> *'You'll never catch me alive' said he . . .*

Freedom or death!

He had been given coffee and biscuits on the plane and did not want any lunch. This morning, eating a breakfast of Corn Crisps and milk, he had thought how ridiculous it was to be stoking this body for which he no longer had any use, with fuel to keep it going. But habit died hard, and he had to keep the strength to carry out his purpose. The hardest way to die, surely, requiring the utmost strength of will, would be to starve oneself to death.

Having no baggage to wait for, he walked out and got a cab from the rank, sitting in front with the driver in the companionable Sydney fashion. They talked about the cricket (Joe didn't even know there was a Shield match on, but he knew a few Sydney and Melbourne cricketers by name), and a little politics. He asked to driver to take him over the Harbour Bridge and back, and looking up past the electric railway at all those netting barriers put there to prevent the daring or suicidal from reaching the upper span, he was daunted. No, the Blue Mountains was the place. He liked the idea of Govett's Leap. To plunge into one of those blue ravines, into the rounded, feathery tops of the gum-trees far below. That was the place where he would choose to die.

He directed the cab to Central Station and looked up trains to the Blue Mountains. He remembered a visit he had made with Maggie when they were staying here three years ago. He'd heard of the marvellous blue light in the Mountain valleys, and it was true. Looking across the valley of the Three Sisters, tall pinnacles of sandstone left isolated by weathering, he had caught his breath at that ethereal colour which filled the valley like a mist. The colour was in the atmosphere; it draped the distances and the rocky clefts with mysterious light. There was a theory that it was caused by the diffusion of sunlight through drops of oil constantly being distilled and dispersed into the atmosphere by the innumerable leaves of a million eucalyptus trees.

He bought a ticket to Blackheath on the Mount Victoria line, the highest point of the range. There was a fast commuter service to the Mountains; people lived there and travelled up and down to Sydney to work.

They crossed the Nepean River, went through Penrith and began to climb. Cuttings through damp rocks, ferns and wild white heath growing in the cracks of the great square blocks of sandstone, seedling gums forcing the rocks apart with their sturdy roots . . .

Arrived at Blackheath railway station, Joe followed the sign which said 'Govett's Leap' along a road which led out of the town towards the thick scrub. Just then it occurred to him that though he had said to himself that his death would speak for him, if he disappeared without trace – if no one saw him jump – Maggie would not know what had happened to him, but would be left forever wondering and hoping. He would become just a 'missing person'.

The road ended in an open area with a car-park, with little picnic shelters of natural stone and wooden seats for tourists. It sloped towards a safety fence of stout iron mesh and bars set in concrete, edging a vast escarpment: the 'leap'. To the right a little waterfall tumbled into the valley far below. Directly beneath the lookout point the rock bulged out in a sloping ledge about sixty feet down; a fall to there would cause only injuries; he would have to get around that, go further down. No good while there were people about.

He turned back towards the shops and the Post Office, bought a postcard printed in rather lurid blue and green, and an envelope. He wrote right across the back:

Dear Mum,
    I shall not be returning from this place. This is the end of the road. I cannot face the alternatives, the Army or prison, and I've been drawn for the Draft. Sorry. This is just to say goodbye, in case I should never be found. Please tell Wendy.
                    Your son,
                    Joe.

After he had posted it, he thought, Well, I might have put 'Love'. He nearly turned back and bought another card. But what was the use? He already felt detached from life.

It was early afternoon and the blue colour was at its most intense. Joe gazed across the Grose Valley and down at the tops of the trees below him. How soft they looked from above! Gold-green and rounded as clouds, each with a nimbus of amber-coloured new leaves. Tourists wandered up, took colour-snapshots and admired the view. An old man sat on a wooden bench, gazing across the valley with rheumy eyes. Who would want to live to be old? thought Joe impatiently.

All the tourists from the last train had left. Joe wished the old man would go. At last he walked across and sat down beside him.

'G'day,' he said. 'Who was Govett, do you know?'

'G'day. Where you from, South Oss?'

'Sort of. My mother lives there.'

The ancient surveyed Joe's wild red curls and blue jeans and black T-shirt with some disfavour. 'You on holidays? Shouldn't you be at work, young feller?'

'I'm a student,' explained Joe. 'About Govett?'

'Govett? He was an early surveyor, who found this place in the 1830s. He never leapt over or anything.'

'Oh.' Joe was disappointed. It wasn't the scene of some romantic, spectacular death after all. 'No one would survive if they did go over there, though.'

'I dunno, it's surprising. One chap was supposed to have fallen over, and a party went down with a sack to pick up the pieces. They met him walking down the stream below the falls. There'd been some heavy snow, most unusual, and it broke his fall.'

'Hard to believe.'

'That's what they say, anyway. Any of the locals'll tell yer.'

'So no one was ever killed here?'

'I believe, years before there was a fence at the lookout – there's a story about a nursemaid out walking with a little boy. "Don't go near the edge, Mark," she says, and of course that's what the kid does. He slipped and went over before she could grab 'im. They say the girl never recovered, went off her head, remembering his scream as he fell. What worried her most, they reckon, was that his body was never found. Search parties went round into the valley, but whether the dingoes got 'im – '

'It's very thick bush down there.'

'Yes, well she figured he was so little, and, the trees breaking his fall, like, he might not have been killed outright. She couldn't bear to think of him all alone there, injured and scared; crying, and no one to hear him.'

Joe shivered. He got up and walked over to the railing,

looking down. The trees looked amazingly soft and thick. A last tourist leant over, snapped the view, and wandered off. The old man got up and waved. 'Be seeing yer!' He began slowly walking down the track to the kiosk.

Joe clasped the rail with whitened knuckles.

In Adelaide that morning, Maggie went out to the postbox in her dressing-gown, hoping for a letter from Joe. She had worked late the week before and had been told she needn't come in until ten. She had rung the flat in Canberra at the weekend and learnt from Wendy that he was away bushwalking somewhere, and that his Draft card had come. Joseph Forbes King, aged twenty, was one of the unlucky ones born on October 23rd. He had been born just before midnight, too. If only her labour had been delayed another hour – though she had longed for it to be over – Joe's birthdate would have been the 24th and might not have fallen out of the barrel.

There were no letters in the box. Turning to go back inside, holding up her long dressing-gown from the heavy dew, Maggie gave a gasp of distress. The strong gully-winds last night had battered the garden – one of the disadvantages of living in the foothills – and the little sapling she had planted, a native cypress, had been snapped off near the ground. She tried to prop it up, but the last thread of fibrous bark broke, the trunk oozed resinous sap. Just when it was established, and looking fine! She felt unreasonably distressed.

Joe sat in the train which descended rapidly from the mountains towards Sydney. Waking this morning on the bench in a stone shelter where he had slept, he had stretched his cold, cramped limbs with a sense of wonder that he was still alive. He stared at the paling sky. Far up, a wedgetail eagle circled, its feathers slightly gilded. Up there, the sun had risen.

He was reminded of an eagle they had seen once in a cage at a resort in South Australia. It was in a wire-netting enclosure about the size of a small fowl-run. The bird ignored this cramped space and clung to the wires at one end, glaring with yellow eyes at the unattainable sky beyond. It never moved or deigned to glance at passers-by. Joe had been made furiously angry by this sight, and wanted to stay the night so he could creep back at midnight and release the bird, but Maggie would not let him. He felt sure that the eagle would refuse to eat in such conditions and would soon be released by death.

It was still the only way out, for him. Nothing had changed. But he had failed in his first attempt; he had not jumped. He cursed the old man who had told him tales of people surviving that awesome drop. He could not bear to think, if he failed to kill himself, of lying injured somewhere below that green canopy, tormented by thirst and unable to move or to die. No. He would catch the first train in the morning back to Sydney, and somehow jump from the Harbour bridge. Other people had done it; it must be possible, and he would not survive a fall of a hundred and seventy feet to the water, even from the roadway level. Sixteen workmen had died that way just while the bridge was building.

The sun was coming in the north-eastern windows now. Joe got up and moved forward several seats, crossing over so that he sat in the warmth, for he was still chilled from his night in the open, even after a cup of tea at the railway waiting-room. His money was nearly gone.

As they clattered through stony cuttings, iron wheels flinging the spent miles back, he looked out at wisps of white steam rising from dew-damp rocks with the increasing warmth of the sun. The train had left Mt Victoria soon after 6 a.m. It seemed to be rocking a lot, with a jerky, uneasy motion.

'Statistics say you are safer in the air,' came into his mind from somewhere. 'Statistics say, statistics say,' the wheels took up the chant. Now they were down from the mountains and entering the western suburbs, the train still speeding on its way. It was approaching the Bold Street bridge at Granville which was carrying peak morning traffic to the city.

'Statistics say, statist – ' There was a sudden loud bang! somewhere ahead, then a frightening jerk. The worn leading wheels of the engine leapt from the rails on a slight curve just before the bridge, and the heavy engine struck the stanchions which supported the span. The first carriages turned over.

Just as the fourth carriage was passing beneath, the whole span collapsed on top of it.

Joseph Forbes King, together with most of the passengers in the carriage, was crushed under nearly two hundred tons of concrete and steel girders. It was as if a giant foot had descended from the sky and squashed them all like ants.

Beneath the great fallen slab, the roof of the carriage was only inches from the floor in places. Blood spurted out from between the cracks, the tiny space where seconds before had been living, breathing human beings. Clouds of dust and screams from the injured filled the air.

More than eighty people were dead, and another two hundred injured. One man, pinned beneath a slab of concrete, lost both legs but survived. If he had been sitting one seat further forward he would have died instantly. Some were able to talk to the rescuers, but died just as they were released. It was nine hours before rescue teams could cut through the twisted steel girders, and cranes could lift the concrete slab from the horror below. More than a week passed before blood-spattered personal papers could be sorted, and next-of-kin notified, if they did not know already, of their loss in that terrible disaster.

Seventeen

EMPTYING HER mailbox on the way inside, Maggie unsuspectingly cradled the postcard from Joe in one hand, her other hand burdened with a bag of groceries she had just picked up at the supermarket. She had got used to travelling to town by bus – it was only four miles – and even found it relaxing when she could get a seat and did not have to stand most of the way. It gave her a chance to read the morning paper on the way to work and the final edition of the evening paper on the way home. Everyone on the staff, according to the Editor, should read the papers 'from cover to cover' every day.

Penelope, who lived with her sister, said that Maggie should get a dog for company. But she actually enjoyed the quiet emptiness of the suburban house. When she turned the key in the lock and entered her own domain, she felt at peace.

Dumping the bag of groceries on the kitchen table, she tore open the envelope addressed in Joe's handwriting, with impatient fingers. Her eyes took in the words; her mind refused to comprehend them. Then she uttered a long, piercing wail and fell into a kitchen chair as though she had been poleaxed.

'Sorry'. That one laconic, inadequate word. No word of love, no explanation, nothing. 'This is just to say goodbye . . . Please tell Wendy.'

So when he wrote, he was alone. Where? Where from? The postcard said, 'Govett's Falls'. Feverishly she looked at the torn envelope. The Post Office stamp said 'Blackheath, N.S.W., 2 p.m.' That was in the Blue Mountains, somewhere toward Mt Victoria. What was he doing there? But of course it was obvious. 'I shall not be returning from this place. I cannot face the alternatives . . . ' He had gone there to take his life. Had he bought sleeping pills? A gun? 'In case I am never found.' Or would he cut his wrists in some secluded place in the bush? Or even leap over the Falls? Distraught, she rushed to the telephone. She had to do something, call for help. She rushed back to the envelope, searched feverishly for the date. Yesterday's date. It had come by Air Mail and arrived in this afternoon's delivery.

It was too late; he must be already gone by now. How was it possible; how could Joe have died and she not be aware, not feel some premonition? She had worried about him since Wendy told her on the phone about his Draft card arriving. She had been waiting daily for a letter. But she had never thought of this. They had parted in anger; she had called him selfish and spoilt, and she was never to see him again. O Joseph, my son, my son!

Blindly, shaking all over, she groped for the telephone and dialled the *Herald* office. The switchboard operator would be gone, but she knew the Editor's private number. If only he had not left! He'd stayed back while they got out a special late

671

edition on the Granville Bridge disaster. It had been in the early editions, but more news, terrible news, was coming through on the teleprinter from Sydney. Death toll mounting – hundred injured – appalling sights – rescue teams in danger from further collapse of the structure.

Clickclick, clickclick click. Mechanically, impersonally, the typewritten lines appeared, letter by letter, and were jerked into the cable room as the machine poked further out its white tongue of paper. Tales of bravery and of horror, of dreadful injuries and miraculous escapes, as it documented the disaster which was to shatter the lives and happiness of so many families in Sydney that day.

Maggie, in the midst of her own worries about her son, had spared a thought for the wives and mothers, husbands and sons whose nearest and dearest had left so casually on the morning train and would never return. But she was anxious to get home and see if there were any letters from Canberra, so she was glad when Rex Ryder said, an hour after they usually finished work, 'You'd better put on your bonnet and tippet and go home; I won't be needing you any more. You look worn out. I'll leave something on the dictaphone for you to type up in the morning.'

Maggie smiled wanly. 'I haven't been sleeping very well. It's Joe again – he's been called up for service in Vietnam!'

'Hell! I'm sorry, Maggie. That son is the worry of your life, isn't he? Well, just be thankful he wasn't travelling on the Western line in Sydney today.'

'At Granville?'

'Yes. It's one of the worst train disasters we've ever had. It's put the Collins case right off the front page. There's still stuff coming through, but it's in the *Register*'s time now.'

Maggie winced at the newspaperman's attitude to disaster. It was, above all, a 'story'. And it had happened in the *Herald*'s time.

'Well, I'll be going, then. I'll come in early tomorrow.'

Now, as she listened to the steady burr of the call-signal, seeming to echo in an empty building, she remembered his words. But Joe *had* been travelling on the Western Line, only yesterday. He had written from Blackheath. It was the 6.09 from Mount Victoria, further up the line, that had crashed. What if he had changed his mind and decided to come back on the morning train to Sydney?

'Oh no!' thought Maggie.

There was no answer; Rex had left. She sat numbly by the phone. Then she got up, stared at her red eyes in the mirror, and blew her swollen nose. She poured herself a stiff brandy and swallowed it neat. She dialled Penelope's home number. She strained her ears, waiting for Penelope's deep, reassuring voice to answer.

'Hello? Penelope Ross speaking.'

'Oh, Penny! Are you home?'

'Obviously.'

'I was w-wondering if you could possibly come over. Something's hap-happened, and I have to tell someone.'

'Are you crying? OK, I'll be right over. See you in about twenty minutes.'

She began to feel a little better now Penelope was coming. It was all some terrible mistake, and the phone would ring at any moment and it would be Joe to tell her he was all right. He might even be back at the flat. She remembered the last time she was staying there, she had said something to amuse him. Joe had rolled on the bed, kicking his legs and shaking his arms in delight; he laughed with his whole body, not just his eyes and mouth.

She dialled Canberra on long distance.

The call-tone went on and on, then suddenly a bright young voice said, 'Hello?'

'Is that Wendy? It's Maggie here.'

'No, Wendy's left the downstairs flat. There's no one here. I was just going past up the stairs, so I answered. The door was open.'

'Are you sure? Are her things gone?'

'Yes, she told us she was leaving.'

'Could you just see – just have a look if Joe's things are still there, his clothes and books and so on? It's his mother calling.'

'Right-oh. Hold on.'

The bright young voice came back. 'His things are in the wardrobe and the dresser. But we haven't seen anything of him for days. Wendy took the car.'

'So they split up?'

'Yes, I think so.'

'And you've no idea where he is?'

'No idea. Sorry.'

'That's all right. Thank you.'

Now a cold certainty began to take hold of her in place of her former speculations. His flat empty, his clothes left behind . . . She knew now that Joe was dead. Perhaps she did have a premonition, the morning when she found that young sapling snapped off in the gale.

Joe was the last of his line as it descended through her, the last link in the chain of life stretching back to the first Joseph and the first Browns and Kings and Macdonalds and Forbeses to set foot on Australian soil; the Duguids and O'Briens, Scottish missionaries and Irish immigrants that her Aunt Ellen had told her about; the many forefathers who had planted their seed so enthusiastically and founded their families in the new land.

He had left no seed. He would have no descendants. Finish!

She flung herself on her bed, curled up in a foetal position, defensive and small, and gave herself up to misery. Death and disaster! That was what the man on the ferry to Magnetic Island had seen. 'Not for you, but for other people.' She would live to a ripe old age, he said, but meanwhile everyone close to her would come to an unpleasant end.

The sound of Penelope's car pulling up outside made her get up sluggishly and go to the door. The brandy seemed to have anaesthetised her. She could scarcely feel her own limbs. The misery had receded to a dull ache behind her eyes. She had no tears left, it seemed.

'My dear girl, you look terrible!' Penelope greeted her. She had brought a cold cooked chicken which she put in the refrigerator. 'Have you a cold beer in here? Ah, yes! Now tell Aunt Penelope all about it.'

Maggie silently handed her the fateful postcard. Penelope read it through, then lit a cigarette in her long holder. 'When did you get this?'

'Just now, when I got home. It's dated yesterday, 2 p.m. If – if he was going to – he will have done it by now!'

'I think you need a drink.'

'I had a stiff brandy.'

'Then a beer chaser. No, sit there, I'll get it.' She took a bottle from the refrigerator and filled a large glass for Maggie and another for herself. 'Now get that into you.'

Maggie's hand shook, spilling some beer on the carpet, but she drank as she was bid. Penelope shook the straight fair hair back from her eyes.

'Now all you have to go on is this postcard? It might have been written on an impulse, might not mean that he would actually carry it out. The police would have been in touch with you, I should think.'

'Perhaps they are all busy at Granville.'

'Yes, that was a terrible thing. They're still digging bodies out.'

'You see, Joe has just received his call-up, and he said he'd refuse to go, but he has such a horror of going to gaol. And he can't count on exemption as a student, because he has no hope of passing his final exams, and they will kick him out of the University. He's bright enough, but he didn't work. And now his girl has left him, and we quarrelled when I was in Canberra, and now I'll never see him again. Never!'

The tears began to flow again in a scalding stream.

Penelope sat down beside her on the couch and patted her hand. 'There, there. We don't know anything for certain. And crying won't bring him back.'

'I know! I know!'

'Well, thank goodness I'm never likely to have any children. You know the matter with Joe, of course? Being an only child of a single parent. He had far too much of your attention all his life, and not enough discipline from a father. Why didn't you marry again?'

Maggie sighed. It all seemed far away now, her reasons foolish. 'I suppose I felt it would be disloyal to Vin. Silly, I know. And I thought I *ought* to give Joe all my attention. As you say, it was probably the worst thing for him. But he's only got into trouble since he went to live in Canberra, away from me.'

'Because you over-protected him when he was at home. So naturally he broke out when he got the chance.'

'There's something else I didn't tell you, Pen.'

'Well?'

'It's the thing that may have made him desperate enough . . . You see, I found out just recently, on my last trip back to Pandanus Island where I thought I'd been born, that I was born in Brisbane and my father had no Aboriginal blood. You can imagine the effect on Joe. I shouldn't have told him, but he was wasting his last year at Uni on all these protests, Land Rights and so on . . . You can tell Rex if you like. I've meant to tell him for some time.'

'Tell him yourself. Not that it would make any difference. He didn't employ you just as an exercise in race relations.'

'It made me feel such a fraud.'

'Not your fault. There's no point in making a great public announcement of it. Anyway, for those who find "colour" romantic, you're still a Pacific Islander.'

'Yes, I suppose so. But Penny, I've thought of something else. What if – even if he didn't really intend to take his own life, supposing he went back to Sydney this morning – if he caught the 6.09 a.m. from the Blue Mountains?'

'The one that hit the bridge? Oh. Oh dear!'

'Yes. It will be ages before they find out who was on board. Not like an aeroplane with a passenger list. I must go over there.'

'I wouldn't, old girl. I'd stay here, close to the telephone where they can contact you. Or Joe can find you, for that matter.'

'No, I must go. He could be injured, in hospital, dying. If I could just speak to him once more! Even if it was for the last t-time.'

'Now, don't start again. Have another beer, it will help you to sleep. And I've brought some knock-out pills the doctor gave me; they really work. Could you eat a piece of chicken?'

'I couldn't. I'm sorry.'

'I'll just make myself a sandwich.'

Penelope got up and knocked the long ash from the end of her cigarette. She went into the kitchen. 'Hullo, what's this?' she called. 'I'd better put these things away for you.'

It was the paper bag of groceries from the supermarket, from which spread a white, sticky pool which spread over the table and ran down to the floor. It was the carton of ice-cream Maggie had bought on her way home, completely melted.

Eighteen

THOUGH SHE had not expected to sleep, Penelope's 'knock-out pills', combined with another glass of brandy, had helped Maggie get through the night. She woke late, with a hang-over, and rushed into the office after swallowing a cup of strong black coffee, to ask Rex Ryder if she could have time off to go to Sydney. It was not a good time to ask for leave. Apart from the bridge disaster there was a crisis in the Collins case, with the eminent QC threatening to walk out and wash his hands of the case.

Rex's advice was the same as Penelope's. 'Better to wait here where Joe can contact you if he's still alive, or the police can find you if not. Your name will be at the University as his next of kin.' He persuaded her that she could not do any good in Sydney, where the injured had been taken to dozens of different hospitals, and many of the dead were unrecognis-able. It was only surmise that he had been on the train at all; he might just as well be on his way back to Canberra.

'No,' said Maggie. 'He would not be so cruel. He would know I had got the postcard by now. If he was not on that train, he is lying dead or injured somewhere in the Blue Mountains.' Her lips began to tremble. With an effort she stilled them and took the cover off her typewriter.

'If you want the day off, I'll understand.'

'No, I think I'd rather be working. I must try and stop thinking about it, or I'll go mad,' she said with a stifled sob. Rex, passing on the way to his own desk, gave her shoulder a sympathetic squeeze. She put up her hand, and grasped his

677

for a moment. Strength seemed to flow into her from those firm fingers.

Stories and pictures on the bridge disaster were still coming in next day, but were replaced on the front page by the Collins case. Mr Shaun, QC, had gathered up his gown and his papers and stalked out of the courtroom, announcing that he was getting nowhere with this judge.

The story was phoned through just in time for the home edition. Rex hastily drafted a poster to be rushed on to the streets in time to catch the collective eye of the home-going crowds.

SHAUN QUITS:
'I CANNOT
WORK WITH
THIS JUDGE!'

shouted the posters in the biggest, blackest type.

(A second QC was found to take on the defence of the Aboriginal Collins; but the jury, after a long retirement, found him guilty with a strong recommendation to mercy owing to his youth. He was sentenced to life imprisonment, which according to Aboriginal experts was equivalent to a death sentence; he would not survive incarceration in the city.)

It was while Rex was dictating a leading article for the following day's paper that Maggie told him what she had already told Penelope: that she was 'a complete fraud' as an Aboriginal writer, as she'd found on her last visit to Queensland, and it had stopped her writing.

'It doesn't matter in the least,' he said comfortably, puffing on his pipe. 'Mind you, it would make a good story, but of course my lips are sealed.'

'I'm just going to keep quiet about it,' she said, 'but you see it did matter, enormously, to my son Joe. I think – I'm afraid – it was my telling him that was the last straw. That and his call-up papers coming, and his girl leaving him; everything at once.'

'And you've still heard nothing definite from the police in Sydney? We're still getting lists, but of course they don't release the names of the dead till next of kin have been informed. You'd be the first to know. We have a full list of the injured, and he's not among them.'

'It's so terrible not – not knowing. I lie awake thinking, imagining, wondering. Surely they must have identified everyone by now?'

'Yes, you would think so . . . But . . . Oh God, Maggie, you have to face it. In places the carriage roof was only an inch from the floor. People . . . bodies would be, inextricably –'

'*Don't!*'

'I'm sorry, but you asked.'

'I can't bear to think about it.'

'No. I understand. But would suicide be easier to bear?'

'No! I don't know! You have never *brought forth* a son. It's not the same thing, being a father. If Joe is dead – and he must be dead – a part of me has died with him. I will never be the same again.'

When they had finished the article, Rex asked her to have dinner with him in town.

'I'm sorry, I don't feel like eating. I usually just boil or poach an egg when I get home.'

'You're not eating, and you're getting thinner every day. You must look after yourself.'

'Who for?' said Maggie bitterly. 'I have no one left. It doesn't matter if I live or die.'

'Maggie! It does matter. I care, for one.'

She smiled sadly. 'Thank you, Rex.' She had used his first name without even noticing it.

'Anyway, let me buy you a drink. Come up to The Black Bull before you go home.'

'Yes! I think I might turn into an alcoholic, though.'

He drove her home afterwards and kissed her lightly on the cheek. She did not invite him in. But the warmth she felt was not entirely from the Brandy Crusters she'd been drinking.

It was when she arrived home next day that she saw the police car parked outside her gate. Her heart seemed to stop beating; she held her breath all the way from the bus stop on the corner.

A lean young policeman unfolded himself from the front seat, and another got out of the other side door of the pale blue sedan. *They always hunt in pairs*, she thought irrelevantly.

'Mrs King? Mrs Agnes King?'

'Yes! What – '

'I'm afraid we have some rather distressing news for you. Could we go inside?'

'Yes, of course.' She fumbled for her key, dropped it on the ground. One of them handed it back to her. They followed her along the short gravel drive to the front door. Her hand trembled so that she could not unlock it. The younger constable took the key from her and opened the door.

In the living-room she put her handbag down on the table and turned to face them like an animal at bay.

'Mrs King, do you know the whereabouts of your son, Joseph Forbes King?' (He consulted a notebook.) 'He is believed to have been a passenger on the 6.09 train from Mount Victoria to Sydney on the morning of the eighth?'

'He – he – could have been. When I last heard from him he was at Blackheath. I've been asking the authorities in Sydney for news of him.'

'Mrs King, a number of the bodies have not been identified, but papers from the wreckage have been sorted and cleaned. Among them was your son's Students' Union card from the ANU, and an envelope with his name and address in Canberra. Police officers visited his lodgings in Canberra, and he had not been seen there since the day before the tragic accident in Sydney. So regretfully we have to inform you that he is presumed to be one of the victims.' The official voice suddenly became human. 'Here, sit down, madam. Can I get you something? A cup of tea? Do you have any brandy in the house?'

Maggie had not uttered a word or a cry. She sat as if turned to stone, staring in front of her. Now that it had happened, now that she knew the truth, she seemed unable to feel a thing. She began nervously bending the silver bangle open and shut, open and shut around her wrist. Much luck it had brought her, the stupid thing. With a dull sound the silver circlet cracked across, leaving the two heads of the snake lying separately in her palm.

'Madam – ?'

She turned her head slowly and looked at the young man in the neat uniform. Tall, like Joe, and not so very much older. Some mother's son . . .

'Is there anything we can get you?'

'Or someone – a friend or relative – we could call?'

'Penelope.' The word came through stiff lips. 'Miss Ross. Number's by phone.'

By the time she returned to work, she had not 'got over it'; she would never do that. But she had begun to feel a certain relief. After two weeks of uncertainty, it was a relief just to know. It was like watching the slow death of a loved one; when the agony was over, there was at first a feeling of release. And one thought buoyed her up. He had been on his way back. He must have given up the idea of suicide. It was an accident: all over in a moment, instant oblivion. Not suicide, thank God.

On her first morning, Rex Ryder who had been told the news by Penelope, took her two hands and drew her over to the padded cane chair which lent almost a drawing-room air to his carpeted study.

'Do you want to talk about it?' he asked.

'Not really, no. It's odd, but I feel rather at peace. Perhaps I'm just numb, it will wear off and the agony will start again. But for now – '

'Good, then I can burden you with my troubles. You haven't even seen a newspaper, I suppose? Don't know that we're being sued for twenty thousand for libel, contempt of court, and I don't know what else. All over that damned Collins case poster.'

'You mean the State Government is suing – ?'

'On behalf of its Supreme Court, yes. They want retractions, apologies – and my blood. Old Judge Lewis has it in for me, it seems.'

'For you personally?'

'And the paper. He has referred to it in private, I understand, as "that greasy yellow sausage-wrapper on North Terrace". Now, *that* is libellous. Our paper is not greasy. They want an abject apology from me, and either my immediate resignation or twenty thousand dollars!'

'But you *won't* resign, will you?'

'No! I've told Sir Lloyd – they summoned me to Melbourne, did you know? – that I'd not resign nor retract. What I put on that poster was substantially correct. Judge Lewis says they were not the words used by Mr Shaun, but my interpretation of them, therefore I had no right to enclose them in quotation marks. Twenty thousand for two quotation marks! It's a bit steep.'

'It's monstrous! And poor young Collins is in gaol?'

'On the judge's direction, the jury could hardly find otherwise than "Guilty". And now I'm to be tried too. Just because I went against the Establishment. You see, I'm not an Adelaide man, but an outsider. I might just as well be a leper.'

'Well, I'm sure your staff is behind you. What about our court reporter, John Jarvis?'

'He's backed me up. But it's no good. They want their pound of flesh.'

Maggie was intrigued by this turn of events; the whole of the Literary Department was buzzing with it. It helped to stop her from brooding.

But she was not prepared for the shock when she opened Rex Ryder's mail three mornings later. It included a formal letter from the Managing Director in Melbourne, Sir Lloyd Lintott, informing Mr Ryder that his services as Editor in Chief were no longer required. He had a fortnight's notice to quit. In other words, the sack.

He was down the corridor in the Subs.' Room when she opened it. After he came back, she waited till he had sat down and got his pipe well alight before, with trembling fingers, she laid the letter on his blotter on top of his pile of morning mail. Then she stood back, as though waiting for a time-bomb to explode.

He picked up the letter, and sat rigidly, reading.

'*Hell and damnation*!' His pipe hit the opposite wall, breaking the stem. 'The bastards! The rotten, stinking, crawling, lousy bastards! Maggie, have you read this? They've given me the sack! In a letter – didn't even tell me to my face!'

'Y-y-yes, Mr Ryder.'

'Thrown to the wolves! A sop to Cerberus! Thrown over board like a Jonah to save the ship. Making me a scapegoat!'

And mixing his metaphors wildly, he went on for some time. His grey mane stood out round his head like a nimbus. Then, kicking the pieces of broken pipe across the floor, he rampaged into the Assistant Editor's room next door, where through the wooden partition she could hear him loudly voicing the same sentiments.

'I should just walk straight out and let the paper go hang,' he said later. 'But I can't do it. I'll stick to my post for the next two weeks, while they get a new man from Melbourne to take my place. At least he'll have a good secretary who knows the ropes.'

'He won't, you know,' said Maggie quietly.

'Eh?'

'I will be sending in my resignation straight away. And I should think a lot of your staff will do the same, in protest.'

'My dear, I appreciate your loyalty. But they won't, of course. Most of them have wives and families to support, and journalists are always frightened of losing their jobs. If a paper folds, for instance, they're out on the street with no superannuation, nothing. And now I'll be unemployed myself. I'll never get another job in the Lintott chain.'

'But surely, there are other papers.'

'I don't know . . . I might leave the country. My wife wanted me to write the abject apology. They will print one, of course, as soon as I'm out. She says we can't afford the luxury of my "principles". And I've been losing a bit on the races lately – well, more than a bit.'

Leave the country! Maggie felt the desolation and depression which she had been keeping at bay sweep over her. She had no one, no one who cared whether she lived or died. Penny – well, she had her own life with her sister and her poker school and her other friends. Rex – she was just his secretary, and now he would not need one.

She went home in a black mood. To make things worse, someone rang from the house in Canberra and asked what she wanted done with Joe's things. 'I don't know. Burn them!' she shouted. 'Don't ever let me see them.'

*　　*　　*

Rex was moodily emptying his desk drawers, throwing things out, dropping papers he wanted into a cardboard box. It was late; he had put the paper to bed for the last time. There had been farewell speeches and a presentation, but only Fitz-william, the Chief Sub, who was near retirement age anyway, had followed Maggie's example and resigned. The paper would go on, and they needed their jobs. All the same, they felt he had been given a raw deal by the big bosses.

Maggie had also turned out her desk, collected her pens and erasers, and fitted the lid to the second typewriter, which was her own.

'I'm missing my car now I've sold it,' she sighed.

'I probably won't be able to afford one soon,' he said. 'Who was it said,

> When troubles come, they come not single spies,
> But in battalions?

'It was Shakespeare, you bet. Well, the latest thing is that my wife has left me. Yes. Stella informed me that she was not staying with an out-of-work journo who put his principles before his duty to his family. That means, to her. The kids are grown up and self-supporting, thank God. We had a nasty, cold, bitter row, and she brought up a lot of things, like my gambling, which she disapproved of. Even my hair! She says it's too long, "like an elderly hippie's". That hurt. Elderly!'

Maggie opened her mouth. She wanted to say, 'I love your hair', but she closed it again without speaking.

'So, I told her not to bother about leaving, I was going myself. Should have done it years ago. I realise now that I only stayed out of habit. Not even companionship any more. Just dull habit.'

'I'm sorry.' Maggie was looking down at her closed type-writer.

'And then I had realised for some time that your company, even for a few hours on a 'plane or in the office, meant more to me than a week of Sundays with her. God! How bored I was at home! No wonder I went to the races on Saturdays.'

Maggie had looked up at him with wide dark eyes, letting her feeling show. 'If – if you should need a secretary, I'd be willing to – to help out, I mean without pay.'

'My darling Maggie! I need a girl, a companion, and if she can type, all the better. Come on, I'll drive you home. Is this everything? I'll carry that machine.'

He stopped in the doorway and surveyed his former kingdom with a bitter look. 'Well, good riddance! I hope they've got the yes-man they deserve.'

On the way back to her house they stopped at an Italian restaurant. ('I bet you can't cook,' Rex had said teasingly, and Maggie said she could if there was anyone to cook for.)

'Well, we've both been felled by Fate, or whatever it is that controls our destinies,' said Rex when he had ordered the meal. 'So what do you say to us helping each other back on our feet? I was thinking about the Pacific, always meant to travel there. Might get a job on the *Fiji Times*, eh? You could travel as Mrs Ryder until I get a divorce, for the sake of the proprieties.'

'I would travel with you anywhere, dear Rex. You know that.' He took her hand and held it tightly. 'I was thinking about the Pacific, too. I want to go to the Loyalty Islands and trace my great-grandfather Joseph Tula's people. And my great-uncle George Tombua's. Perhaps I'll write a book about them.'

He said that sounded interesting, and he would like to do a book on the fatal impact of the European voyagers on the peoples of the Pacific: not just the blackbirders, but the first caravels of the Spanish and Portuguese, and later Cook and Bougainville, all bringing drink and disease to what had been Paradise. 'Perhaps we'll quarrel over the material, a case of Rex versus King.'

They discussed these plans animatedly while eating their tagliatelle. Then Maggie began to look stricken.

'What's wrong, darling?'

'Rex, you don't realise! I'm bad news. Everyone connected with me, everyone I love, is dogged by misfortune or comes to a violent end. I wouldn't want you – '

'Everyone you love, eh? And do I come into that category?'

'I think you know the answer to that. I've known for more than a year, but I hoped you hadn't noticed, or guessed. You must keep away from me. I might destroy you.'

685

'Maggie, my dearest! For an intelligent woman what nonsense you talk. Don't you think it's about time the luck changed? By the law of averages, you are due for some good things to happen. Perhaps this is the beginning of a new, happier life for both of us.'

She smiled uncertainly. 'Perhaps . . . But Rex, I don't think I want any more children. I don't want to be hurt like this again.'

'No, I understand. But we can go into that later. You may feel differently later on, when you've got over the shock . . . Maggie, let me stay at your place tonight? I don't want to go back to that house.'

'Oh yes, yes, yes! Please stay with me. And perhaps you can exorcise some of the ghosts that flit round my bed. Not just Vin, and Roy, and Joe. Sometimes I see a long line of ghostly women, my ancestors, stretching back into the past. How some of them must have suffered!'

'Well, you've had your quota of suffering. From now on I promise it will be different. I will look after you.'

The bottle of Chianti was empty. As they rose to go, she inverted her glass on the table-cloth.

'Turn down an empty glass.'

He took her arm, and together they walked out into the night.

BROWN SUGAR
by Nancy Cato

In *Forefathers*, Nancy Cato's award-winning saga of early Australia, one part of the complex, interwoven story was not told. *Brown Sugar*, set in Queensland in the 1860s, tells that story.

Angus Johnstone has built an empire and made a fortune on the backs of dirt-cheap Kanaka labour. Among the raw new lands, his daughter Helga dreams of artistic fame back in the old world, and his elder son James is haunted by the murder of his young wife.

While across the blue Pacific the blackbirding schooners ride the waves, laden down with their human cargo, skippered by captains who'd sail to Hell and back for the sake of a profit.

NEW ENGLISH LIBRARY

ALL THE RIVERS RUN
by Nancy Cato

Philadelphia Gordon is an artist, a riverboat skipper, a beautiful and independent woman. This epic novel, set against the panoramic countryside and winding rivers of Australia, is her story, as powerful and unforgettable as its heroine.

Orphaned by a shipwreck that cuts her off forever from her native England, thirteen-year-old Delie is living in Australia with her indolent Uncle Charles, severe Aunt Hester and wonderful, handsome cousin, Adam. Here, on the banks of her beloved Murray river, she is idyllically happy – and in love with Adam. But when Adam is drowned in a freak accident she is no longer welcome in her aunt's house and leaves to study painting, first in nearby Echuca, then in Melbourne. She soon attracts attention from the critics, and also from Brenton Edwards, the dashing captain of the paddle-steamer that bears her name, who changes her life with a proposal of marriage. Yet life on the river does not bring her complete happiness, for her husband begins to lose interest in her and she soon finds herself drawn to other men . . .

'Its precision of language, firmness of characterisation and richness of Australian setting invite comparison with *The Thornbirds*.'

Publishers Weekly

'A novel on the grand scale, with Australia as its background and a beautiful riverboat skipper as its wilful heroine.'

She

NEW ENGLISH LIBRARY

NORTH–WEST BY SOUTH
by Nancy Cato

This enthralling novel vividly reconstructs the story of Sir John Franklin, whose name has always been associated with the search for the North–West Passage.

Sir John Franklin arrived in 1836 as lieutenant-governor of Van Diemen's Land, as Tasmania was known in the early years of settlement. With his beautiful and intellectually emancipated wife, Jane, he did all he could to modify the harsh and inhuman policies regarding the convicts, and to prevent the slow elimination of the unfortunate Aborigines. Lady Franklin devoted herself to the collection of art treasures and indigenous plants for a small museum and botanical garden which she planned as part of her vision of a race of proud new Tasmanians, rich in culture and learning. She even adopted a little Aboriginal girl, Mathinna, bringing her into Government House and treating her like a daughter, anxious to show that kindness and education were essential for the Aborigines' survival.

Yet despite their sympathetic policies, the Franklins were hounded both by the reactionaries, and by humanitarian campaigners demanding drastic change. Soon after his recall to England, Sir John was to embark on the dangerous search for the North–West Passage. Tragically, he was never to return.

'Memorable . . . and powerfully told'
Australian Book Review

NEW ENGLISH LIBRARY

AND THE WILD BIRDS SING
by Lola Irish

Sydney in 1841: a rough tumult of a town. An upper-class few clung to their illusions of privilege while the streets teemed with brawling, chaotic life: the immigrant overflows of Britain's desperate slums, dispossessed Irish peasants, indentured servants and labourers, drunken seamen, political and religious refugees.

Into this sink-or-swim whirlpool of ambition, despair and hope, came Raunie, half Irish and half gipsy, just disembarked from the floating, fever-ridden squalor of the immigrant barque *May Queen*. Sixteen, pregnant and widowed, her wild flaunting beauty barely disguised by her filthy ragged clothes, she had nothing but the hard-won knowledge, wit and determination of a born survivor. But already she had sensed that in this harsh, half-lawless society there were possibilities as well as pitfalls, rewards as well as dangers.

'Enthralling . . . evocative, enjoyable and an absolute delight'

Publishing News

'A stirring saga, richly written'

Maisie Mosco, author of the
'Almonds and Raisins' trilogy

Post·A·Book

A Royal Mail service in association with the Book Marketing Council & The Booksellers Association.

Post-A-Book is a Post Office trademark.

Book Tokens

Give them the pleasure of choosing

Book Tokens can be bought and exchanged at most bookshops in Great Britain and Ireland.

NEL BESTSELLERS

NANCY CATO

☐ 04400 9	All The Rivers Run	£3.50
☐ 05362 8	Brown Sugar	£1.95
☐ 04932 9	North–West by South	£2.50

MAISIE MOSCO

☐ 05253 2	Almonds And Raisins	£2.50
☐ 05216 8	Scattered Seed	£2.50
☐ 05397 0	Children's Children	£2.50
☐ 05589 2	Between Two Worlds	£2.95
☐ 05784 4	A Sense Of Place	£2.95

HELEN VAN SLYKE

☐ 03351 1	The Best People	£2.50
☐ 03702 9	The Best Place To Be	£2.95
☐ 05032 7	The Heart Listens	£2.95
☐ 03055 5	The Mixed Blessing	£1.95
☐ 05241 9	The Rich And The Righteous	£2.25
☐ 05283 4	The Santa Ana Wind	£1.95

All these books are available at your local bookshop or newsagent, or can be ordered direct from the publisher. Just tick the titles you want and fill in the form below.

Prices and availability subject to change without notice.

Hodder & Stoughton Paperbacks, P.O. Box 11, Falmouth, Cornwall.

Please send cheque or postal order, and allow the following for postage and packing:

U.K. – 55p for one book, plus 22p for the second book, and 14p for each additional book ordered up to a £1.75 maximum.

B.F.P.O. and EIRE – 55p for the first book, plus 22p for the second book, and 14p per copy for the next 7 books, 8p per book thereafter.

OTHER OVERSEAS CUSTOMERS – £1.00 for the first book, plus 25p per copy for each additional book.

Name ....

Address ....

....